KT-119-397

HAWK QUEST

HAWK QUEST

Robert Lyndon

SPHERE

First published in Great Britain in 2012 by Sphere
Reprinted 2012

Copyright © 2012 Robert Lyndon

The moral right of the author has been asserted.

All ⟨   ⟩ in those
clear | **South Lanarkshire** | ʾmblance
| **Library Service** | ʾtal.

Nⓒ ⟨   ⟩ ed in a
retrieval | C70104451Y | ans, without
the prior p ⟨   ⟩ wise circulated
in any fo | **Askews & Holts** | ⟨   ⟩ ⟨ : is published
and | | ⟨   ⟩ on being
| H | £12.99 |

The onioɪ | 3435635 | ⟨   ⟩ logy by Kevin
Crossl | | ⟨   ⟩ rewer Ltd.

A CIP catalogue record for this book
is available from the British Library.

ISBN HB 978-1-84744-497-4
ISBN CF 978-1-84744-498-1

Typeset in Sabon by M Rules
Printed and bound in Great Britain by
Clays Ltd, St Ives plc

Papers used by Sphere are from well-managed forests
and other responsible sources.

MIX
Paper from
responsible sources
FSC® C104740

Sphere
An imprint of
Little, Brown Book Group
100 Victoria Embankment
London EC4Y 0DY

An Hachette UK Company
www.hachette.co.uk

www.littlebrown.co.uk

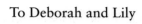

To Deborah and Lily

A NOTE ON LANGUAGES

In the eleventh century Danes, Norwegians, Swedes and Icelanders still spoke mutually intelligible languages related to English. With some effort, an Anglo-Saxon would have been able to understand a Scandinavian speaker.

A BRIEF CHRONOLOGY

1054	The Great Schism between the Latin and Greek Churches
1066	*September* King Harold of England defeats a Norwegian army at Stamford Bridge in Yorkshire
	October William of Normandy defeats Harold's army at Hastings in Sussex
	December William is crowned King of England
1069–70	After a revolt in northern England, William leads a punitive expedition into Northumbria and devastates the country between York and Durham
1071	*August* A Seljuk army under Alp Arslan – 'Valiant Lion' – routs the forces of the Byzantine Emperor at Manzikert, in what is now eastern Turkey. The victory opens up Anatolia to the Seljuks and leads ultimately to the First Crusade
1072	*June* King William invades Scotland
	November Alp Arslan is killed by a prisoner while on campaign in Persia

PRICES FOR GYRFALCONS IN MEDIEVAL ENGLAND

Domesday Book, compiled 1086–7, indicates that a gyrfalcon was worth £10, roughly equivalent to half the yearly income of a knight. The accounts of King Henry II record that in 1157 he paid more than £12 for four gyrfalcons that he sent as a gift to the Holy Roman Emperor Barbarossa. In 1162 it cost Henry £43 to send a ship to Norway to buy falcons. The same amount could have bought 250 cows, or 1200 sheep, or paid the wages of 50 agricultural workers for a year.

Northern Hunting Grounds

GREENLAND

ICELAND

Reykjavik · Skalholt

Westmann Is.

· Western Settlement

· Eastern Settlement

Horda

Shetland

Orkneys

North
Sea

· St Andrews

Dublin · York

· Norwic

London

Rouen

A. · Par
seine

Atlantic
Ocean

AQUITAINE

ARAGON

CASTILE · Zaragossa

N

0   200   400   600 miles

0   200   400   600   800   1000 kms

North Cape

Halogaland

Midaros

White Sea

L. Onega

L. Ladoga

R. Svir
Staraja Ladoga
R. Volkhov

Novgorod

R. Lovat

Polotsk

Smolensk
Gnezdovo

Bolghar

R. Volga

Baltic Sea

R. Dvina

Hamburg
SAXONY

RUS

Kiev
Vitichev

R. Dnieper

St Gregory Is.

Dnieper rapids

St Aitherios Is.

R. Danube

KRYM

Cherson

Black Sea

Caspian Sea

Venice

Rome

Varna

Constantinople

Sinop

Salerno

ANATOLIA

Tuz Gölü

Trebizond

Manzikert
(Site of Battle)

SICILY

Syracuse

Konya

Mediterranean Sea

Baghdad

Alexandria

Jerusalem

Red Sea

Hunger will devour one, storm wreck another.

The spear will slay one, and another will perish in battle ...

One will fall wingless from the high tree in the forest ...

One must walk alone in foreign places, tread unknown roads
among strangers ...

One will swing from the crooked gallows, hang in death ...

One at the mead-bench will be shorn of his life by the
sword's edge ...

To one, good fortune; to one a dole of suffering.

To one, joyful youth; to one, glory in combat, mastery in
war-play.

To one, skill at throwing or shooting; to one, luck at dice ...

One will amuse a gathering in the hall, gladden the drinkers
at the mead-bench ...

One will tame the wild bird, the proud hawk on his fist, until
the falcon grows gentle.

(From 'The Fortunes of Men' in the *Exeter Book*, England,
tenth century)

England, 1072

I

That morning a Norman cavalry patrol had captured a young Englishman foraging in the woods south of the River Tyne. After interrogating him, they decided he was an insurgent and hanged him on a high hill as a warning to the people in the valley below. The soldiers waited, hunched against the cold, until their victim's spasms stopped, and then they rode away. They were still in sight when the circling carrion birds flocked down and clustered on the corpse like vicious bats.

Towards evening a group of starving peasants crept up the hill and frightened off the birds. They cut down the corpse and laid it on the frozen ground. Eyes, tongue, nose and genitals were gone; its lipless mouth gaped in a silent scream. The men stood around it, billhooks in hand, exchanging neither looks nor words. At last one of them stepped forward, lifted up one of the dead man's arms, raised his blade and brought it down. The others joined in, hacking and sawing, while the crows and ravens skipped around them, squabbling for scraps.

The carrion birds erupted in raucous panic. The human scavengers looked up, frozen in acts of butchery, then rose with a gasp as a man came over the crest. He seemed to emerge from the earth, black against the raw February sky, a sword grasped in his hand. One of the scavengers shouted and the pack turned and ran. A woman dropped her booty, cried out and turned to retrieve it, but a companion grabbed her by the arm. She was still wailing, her face craned back, when he bundled her away.

The Frank watched them disappear, his breath smoking in the bitter air, then ran his sword back into its scabbard and dragged his skinny mule towards the gibbet. Even filthy and travel-worn, he was an intimidating figure – tall, with deep-set eyes and a jutting nose, unkempt hair coiling around a gaunt face, his cheekbones weathered to the colour of smoked eelskin.

His mule snorted as a crow trapped inside the corpse's ribcage thrashed free. He glanced at the mutilated body without much change of expression, then frowned. Ahead of him, pale in the twilight, lay the object that the woman had dropped. It seemed to be wrapped in cloth. He tethered the mule to the gibbet and walked over, stretched out one foot and turned the bundle over. He looked into the wizened face of a baby, only a few days old, its eyes tight-shut. His mouth pursed. The baby was alive.

He looked around. The carrion birds were beginning to settle again. There was nowhere to hide the baby. The birds would be swarming over it as soon as he left the summit. The merciful thing to do would be to end its suffering now, with one sword thrust. Even if its mother returned, the baby wouldn't survive the famine.

His eye fell on the gibbet. After a moment's indecision, he lifted the baby in his arms. At least it was well swaddled against the cold. He trudged back to his mule, opened a saddlepack and took out an empty sack. The baby gave a grizzling sound and its mouth moved in reflexive sucking gestures. He placed it in the sack, mounted his mule and tied the sack to the end of the hangman's rope, above the reach of wolves. It wouldn't keep the birds off for long, but he guessed that the mother would return once he'd left the hill.

He smiled a wintry smile. 'Hanged before you're a week old. If you live, you might make a reputation for yourself.'

The birds flared up again as another man shuffled onto the ridge. He stopped in his tracks when he saw the gibbet.

'Hurry up,' cried the Frank. 'It will be dark soon.'

Watching the youth approach, the Frank shook his head. The Sicilian was a walking scarecrow. Another night without food or shelter might finish him off, but the only place they would find bed and board would be among the men who'd hanged the wretched Englishman.

The Sicilian reeled to a standstill, eyes dark and dull in his bloodless face. He stared at the ruined corpse and made a sound of disgust.

'Who did that?'

'Starving peasants,' said the Frank, taking the mule's reins. 'They were still here when I arrived. It's lucky it wasn't you who was leading the way.'

The Sicilian's eyes skittered in all directions and settled on the sack. 'What's that?'

The Frank ignored the question. 'They won't have gone far. For all

I know, they're lying in wait for us.' He led the mule away. 'Stay close unless you want to end up in a cooking pot.'

Exhaustion rooted the Sicilian to the spot. 'I hate this country,' he muttered, so weary that he could only form thoughts by articulating them. 'Hate it!'

A faint mewing made him lurch back in fright. He could have sworn that it came from the sack. He looked for the Frank and was alarmed to see his outline already sinking below the horizon. The sack mewed again. Birds fell out of the stone-dead sky, black tatters landing all around him. One of them hopped onto the corpse's skull, cocked an eye at him and crammed its head into the yawning maw. 'Wait!' cried the Sicilian, wobbling over the grisly summit in pursuit of his master.

The Frank hurried into the dying light. The ground began to slope away and the outlines of distant hills came into view. Another few steps and he sank to his haunches, looking into a wide valley. Shadows flooded the river plain and he might not have spotted the castle if it hadn't been so new, its whitewashed timber keep still showing the wounds of the axe. It was tucked between the confluence of two tributaries, one flowing from the north, the other looping from the west. He traced the course of the river until it vanished into the darkness rising in the east. He rubbed his eyes and took another look at the castle. Norman without a doubt, laid out in a figure-of-eight, the keep perched on a motte within its own stockade, the hall and a scattering of smaller buildings occupying the lower enclosure. Not a bad position, he thought. Protected by rivers on two sides, each tributary spanned by an easily defended bridge.

His gaze lifted to another line of defence on the ridge a couple of miles behind the castle. In a lifetime of campaigning, he'd seen nothing like it – a wall punctuated by watchtowers marching straight across the landscape with no regard for natural obstacles. That must be the barrier the Romans had built to protect their northernmost frontier from the barbarians. And yes, against the darkness of oncoming night, the wintry hills beyond did have an end-of-the-world look.

A blur of smoke hung over the castle. He fancied he could see figures inching towards it from the surrounding fields. Not far downriver was a sizeable village, but the houses had a caved-in look and the outlying farmsteads were smudges of ash. Since crossing the Humber five days ago, the travellers hadn't passed a single occupied village. The harrying of the north, the dereliction was called – Norman revenge for an English and Danish uprising at York two winters ago. In the last of the light the Frank worked out that the way to the castle led through a wood.

The Sicilian flopped down beside him. 'Have you found it?'

The Frank pointed.

The Sicilian peered into the gloom. The spark of excitement faded and his face crumpled in disappointment. 'It's just a wooden tower.'

'What did you expect – a marble palace with gilded spires?' The Frank pushed himself upright. 'On your feet. It will be dark soon and there'll be no stars tonight.'

The Sicilian stayed on the ground. 'I don't think we should go down there.'

'What do you mean?'

'It's too dangerous. We can hand over the documents to the bishop in Durham.'

The Frank's jaw tightened. 'I've brought you safe across Europe, yet now, within sight of our destination, after all the hardships I've endured, you want us to turn *back*?'

The Sicilian twisted his knuckles. 'I never expected our journey to take so long. The Normans are practical in matters of succession. Our news may no longer be welcome.'

'Welcome or not, it will snow tonight. Durham's a day's walk behind us. The castle's our only shelter.'

All at once the carrion birds fell quiet. They rose in a flurry, circled once, then spiralled down towards the trees. When the ragged shapes had gone, there was a dragging silence.

'Here,' the Frank said, thrusting a hunk of bread at the Sicilian.

The youth stared at it. 'I thought all our food had gone.'

'A soldier always keeps a reserve. Go on. Take it.'

'But what about you?'

'I've already eaten my share.'

The Sicilian crammed the bread into his mouth. The Frank walked away so that he wouldn't have to endure the sounds of someone else eating. When he turned back, the youth was sobbing.

'What's the matter now?'

'I'm sorry, sir. I've been nothing but a burden and a trial.'

'Get on the mule,' the Frank ordered, cutting off the Sicilian's protests. 'It's not your comfort I'm worried about. I don't want to spend another night with a rock for a pillow.'

By the time they reached the wood, the trees had become invisible. The Frank took hold of the mule's tail and let it find its own way. He stumbled over roots, his feet splintering icy puddles. The snow that had been threatening all day began to fall, thin as dust at first. His face and hands grew numb.

He, too, loathed this country – the foul weather, the surly resignation of its natives, the edgy swagger of their conquerors. He wrapped his cape around his head and retreated into a sleepwalking dream. He was walking through orchards, a vineyard, a herb garden drowsy with bees. He entered a villa, crossed a cool tiled floor into a chamber where vine clippings glowed in the hearth. His wife rose smiling from her needlework. His children plunged towards him, screaming with delight at his miraculous return.

II

Their destinies had crossed last autumn on St Bernard's way across the Alps. The Frank, travelling under the name of Vallon, was on foot, having sold his horse and armour in Lyon. Soon after starting his descent into Italy, he passed a party of pilgrims and merchants glancing anxiously back at storm clouds massing in the south. A shaft of sunlight picked out a herdsman's summer settlement by a gorge far down the valley. It would be as far as he'd get that night.

He'd covered less than half the distance when the clouds snuffed out the sun. The temperature plummeted. A wind that started as a faraway sigh struck him with a blast of hail. Chin nuzzled into his chest, he struggled against the storm. The hail turned to snow, day turned to night. He lost the path, tripped over rocks, floundered through drifts.

He reached flatter ground and caught a whiff of smoke. He must be downwind of the settlement, the gorge to his left. He continued more slowly, probing with his sword until a mass denser than darkness blocked his way. A hut half-drifted over. He groped round the walls and found the door on the lee side. He kicked it open and stumbled into a chamber choked with smoke.

A figure leaped up on the far side of a fire. 'Please, don't harm us!'

Vallon made out a gangling youth with bolting eyes. In the gloom behind him another figure stirred in restless sleep. 'Calm yourself,' Vallon growled, sheathing his sword. He wedged the door shut, beat snow from his clothes and crouched by the flames.

'I crave your pardon,' the young man stammered. 'My nerves are stretched. This storm ...'

The figure in the corner muttered in a language Vallon didn't understand. The youth hurried back to him.

Vallon fed the fire with chips of dung and massaged the feeling back into his hands. He retired to the wall and gnawed a heel of bread. Draughts flustered a lamp in a niche above the pair in the corner. The man lying down wasn't sleeping. His chest wheezed like leaking bellows.

Vallon swigged some wine and winced. 'Your companion's sick.'

The young man's eyes were moist highlights. 'My master's dying.'

Vallon stopped chewing. 'It's not the plague, is it?'

'No, sir. I suspect a cancer of the chest. My master's been ailing ever since we left Rome. This morning he was too weak to seat his mule. Our party had to leave us behind. My master insisted we go on, but then the storm caught us and our groom ran away.'

Vallon spat out the sour wine and wandered over. No doubt of it, the old man would be rid of his cares before dawn. But what a life was written on that face – skin stretched sheer over flared cheekbones, the nose of a fastidious eagle, one dark, hooded eye, the other a puckered scar. And his garments glossed an exotic tale – silk robe fastened with ivory toggles, pantaloons tucked into kidskin boots, a cape of sable that must have cost more than the ring winking on his bony hand.

The dark eye found him. Thin wide lips parted. 'You've come.'

Vallon's neck prickled. The old man must imagine that the spectre of death had arrived to usher him through the last gate. 'You're mistaken. I'm just a traveller sheltering from the storm.'

The dying man absorbed this without contradiction. 'A pilgrim walking to Jerusalem.'

'I'm travelling to Constantinople to join the imperial guard. If I pass through Rome, I might light a candle at St Peter's.'

'A soldier of fortune,' the old man said. 'Good, good.' He muttered something in Greek that made the youth glance sharply at Vallon. Struggling for breath, the old man groped beneath his cape, drew out a soft leather binder and pressed it into his attendant's hand. The youth seemed reluctant to take it. The old man clawed at his arm and spoke with urgency. Again the youth glanced at Vallon before answering. Whatever response he made – some vow or pledge – it seemed to satisfy the dying man. His hand fell away. His eye closed.

'He's going,' the youth murmured.

The old man's eye flicked open and fixed on Vallon. He whispered – a rustle like crumpled parchment relaxing. Then his stare travelled up to some region beyond sight. When Vallon looked down, the eye was already veiled.

Silence gathered like a mist.

'What did he say?'

'I'm not sure,' the youth sobbed. 'Something about the mystery of the rivers.'

Vallon crossed himself. 'Who was he?'

The youth snuffled. 'Cosmas of Byzantium, also called Mono-phalmos, the "One-Eyed".'

'A priest?'

'Philosopher, geographer and diplomat. The greatest explorer of our age. He's sailed up the Nile to the pyramid at Giza, explored the palace at Petra, read manuscripts from Pergamum given by Mark Antony to Queen Cleopatra. He's seen lapis lazuli mines in Persia, uni-corn hunts in Arabia, clove and pepper plantations in India.'

'You're a Greek, too.'

'Yes, sir. From Syracuse in Sicily.'

Fatigue quenched Vallon's curiosity. The fire was nearly out. He lay down on the dirt floor and wrapped his cloak about him. Sleep wouldn't come. The Sicilian was intoning a mass, the dirge merging with the droning wind.

Vallon hoisted himself on one elbow. 'That's enough. Your master's at rest. Now let me take mine.'

'I swore to keep him safe. And within a month, he's dead.'

Vallon pulled his cloak over his head. 'He *is* safe. Now go to sleep.'

He skated in and out of nasty dreams. Surfacing from one hag-ridden doze, he saw the Sicilian crouched over the Greek, sliding the ring from his master's hand. He'd already removed the fine fur cloak. Vallon sat up.

Their eyes met. The Sicilian carried the cape across and arranged it over Vallon's shoulders. Vallon said nothing. The Sicilian went back to his corner and stretched out with a groan. Vallon placed his sword upright on the ground and rested his chin on the pommel. He stared ahead, blinking like an owl, each blink a memory, each blink slower than the last until his eyes stayed closed and he fell asleep to the roar of the storm.

He woke to the dripping of water and mysterious muffled thuds. Daylight filtered through chinks in the walls. A mouse scurried from his side, where the Sicilian had laid white bread, cheese, some figs and a leather flask. Vallon took the meal to the door and stepped into scorching sunshine. Streams of meltwater braided the cliffs. Footprints ploughed a blue furrow towards animal pens. A slab of snow flopped from an overhang. Vallon squinted up at the pass, half-wondering if the party had reached the summit refuge. During his halt there, a monk had shown him an ice chamber stacked with the corpses of travellers withered in the postures in which they'd been dug from the snow. Vallon tilted the flask and swallowed tart red wine. A glow spread through him. When he'd eaten, he cleaned his teeth with a twig and rinsed out his mouth.

Only a spear's throw from the hut, the gorge plunged into shadows. He went to the brink, loosened his breeches and pissed, aware that if his path last night had strayed by an arm's span, he would now be a mash of blood and bones too deep in the earth even for vultures to find.

Back inside the hut he lit the lamp with flint and steel and gathered his possessions. The Greek lay like an effigy, hands folded on his chest.

'I wish we'd had time to talk,' Vallon heard himself say. 'There are things you might be able to explain.' A bitter taste filled his mouth and there was a deadness at his core.

A raven croaked overhead. Vallon bowed and blew out the lamp.

'Maybe we'll meet again, when death has laid his consoling hand on *my* heart.'

He padded towards the door and pulled it open to find the Sicilian waiting with a trim bay pony and a fine grey mule. Vallon almost smiled at the contrast between the youth's mournful expression and the gaiety of his costume. He wore a wool cloak trimmed with blue satin, pointed shoes of laughable impracticality, and a soft round hat sporting a jaunty cockade. It wasn't just fright that made his eyes bulge; nature had given him an expression of permanent startlement. He had a nose like a quill and the lips of a girl.

'I thought you'd gone.'

'What! Leave my master before committing him to rest?'

A proper burial was impossible in that stony ground. They laid him in a scrape overlooking the south and heaped rocks over him. The Sicilian planted a makeshift cross on the cairn. After praying, he gazed around at the peaks and glaciers.

'He insisted on being buried where he died, but how bitter that a man who's witnessed the glories of civilisation should lie in such a savage spot.'

A vulture trailed its hunger across the slopes. The clanking of cow bells floated up from distant pastures.

Vallon rose from his knees. 'He chose his grave well. He has the whole world at his feet now.' He mounted the mule and turned it downhill. 'My thanks for the food.'

'Wait!'

Deep drifts blocked Vallon's path. It was like wading through icy gruel. But the foothills shimmered in hazy heat. By noon he would be riding over soft green turf. This evening he would dine on hot meat and blue-red wine.

'Sir, I beg you.'

'You have an uphill path. You'd better start now if you want to cross the pass by nightfall.'

The Sicilian caught up, panting. 'Aren't you curious to know what adventure set us on this path?'

'On a lonely road, it's not wise to confide in strangers.'

'I was with my master for only three weeks. But his journey began two months earlier, at Manzikert.'

That checked Vallon. He'd first heard of Manzikert in an inn near the Rhône. Since then he'd been bumping into the story at every wayside halt, the tale growing wilder with each telling. Most accounts agreed that in late summer a Muslim army had defeated the Emperor of Byzantium at a place called Manzikert, on the eastern marches of Anatolia. Some travellers said that the Emperor Romanus had been taken captive. Others that he was dead or deposed, that the pilgrim route to Jerusalem was closed, that the Muslims were camped outside the walls of Constantinople. Most alarming of all, these invaders weren't Arabs, but a race of Turkoman nomads who had swarmed out of the east like locusts only a generation ago. Seljuks, they called themselves – half-man, half-horse, drinkers of blood.

'Your master travelled with the Emperor's army?'

'As an adviser on the Turks' customs. He survived the slaughter and helped negotiate ransom terms for the Byzantine lords and their allies. When that was done, he returned to Constantinople, took a ship to Italy and crossed to the monastery at Monte Cassino. One of his oldest friends is a monk there – Constantine of Africa.' The Sicilian's eyes bulged expectantly.

Vallon shook his head.

'The most brilliant physician in Christendom. Before entering the monastery, he taught at the Salerno medical school. Where,' the Sicilian declared, grinning with pride, 'I'm a student. When Cosmas explained the purpose of his journey, Constantine selected me to be his secretary and travelling companion.'

Vallon must have raised his eyebrows.

'Sir, I'm a promising physician. I'm well schooled in the classics and can speak Arabic. My French is adequate, you'll agree. I also know geometry and algebra, and can expound the astronomical theories of Ptolemy, Hipparchus and Alhazen. In short, Constantine considered that I was qualified to minister to my master's physical needs, and wouldn't affront his intellect.'

'It must,' Vallon said, 'be an extremely important mission.'

The Sicilian slid out a packet wrapped in linen.

Vallon removed a silk binder seeded with pearls and embroidered with gold. Inside were two manuscripts, one written in Roman letters, the other in an unfamiliar script, both stamped with a seal resembling a bow and arrow.

'I've neglected my letters,' he admitted.

'The Persian document is a guarantee of safe passage through Seljuk territory. The Latin text is a ransom demand addressed to Count Olbec, a Norman magnate whose eldest son, Sir Walter, was taken prisoner at Manzikert. We're – we were – on our way to deliver it.'

'I'm disappointed. I thought you must be searching for the Holy Grail.'

'What?'

'Why would an old and ailing philosopher take such pains to secure the freedom of a Norman mercenary?'

'Oh, I see. Yes, sir, you're right.' The Sicilian seemed flustered. 'Cosmas had never visited the lands beyond the Alps. He planned to call on scholars in Paris and London. All his life he searched for knowledge at its source, however distant that might be.'

Vallon massaged his forehead. The Sicilian was giving him a headache. 'Why burden me with information I don't want?'

The Sicilian cast his eyes down. 'After contemplating my predicament, I've concluded that I lack the constitution to complete the assignment on my own.'

'You should have consulted me earlier. I could have spared you a sleepless night.'

'I'm aware that I lack your martial skills and courage.'

Vallon frowned. 'You don't imagine that I'll take on the mission?'

'Oh, I have no intention of turning back. I'll serve you as loyally as I would have served Cosmas.'

Anger rose in Vallon's face. 'You insolent pup. Your master's hardly cold in the ground and already you're fawning around for another.'

The Sicilian's cheeks burned. 'You said you were a soldier for hire.' He fumbled inside his tunic. 'I'll pay for your service. There.'

Vallon hefted the leather purse, loosened the drawstring and dribbled silver coins into his palm.

'Dirhams from Afghanistan,' the Sicilian said. 'But silver is silver no matter whose head it wears. Is it enough?'

'The money will run through your fingers like sand. There'll be bribes to pay, armed escorts to hire.'

'Not if I ride under your protection.'

Vallon made allowance for the Sicilian's youth. 'Suppose I agree. In a month or two I'd be back at this spot no better off than you see me now.' He lobbed the purse across and continued on his way.

The Sicilian caught up with him. 'A lord as grand as Olbec will reward you well for bringing him news of his heir's deliverance.'

Vallon scratched his ribs. The hut had been crawling with vermin. 'Never heard of him.'

'With respect, that means little. Norman adventurers rise to glory from nothing. In my own short life they've conquered England and half of Italy. Here's the seal of Olbec's house.'

Vallon glanced at a medallion stamped with the image of an equestrian knight. 'Your master wore another ring.'

After a moment's hesitation the Sicilian withdrew it on a cord from inside his tunic. 'I don't know what kind of jewel it is, only that it's as old as Babylon.'

The colours of the gemstone slithered according to how Vallon angled it to the light. Without thinking, he slipped the ring on.

'Cosmas used it to predict the weather,' the Sicilian said. 'Now the jewel appears blue, but yesterday, well before the storm, it turned as black as midnight.'

Vallon tried to remove the ring.

'Keep it,' the Sicilian said. 'It will be an advantage to know under what conditions you'll engage the enemy.'

'I don't need magic to tell me how to plan a battle.'

But as hard as he tried, Vallon couldn't twist the ring off. He had an image of the Greek's cunning stare. 'Before your master died, he passed you something. What was it?'

'Oh, that. Only a copy of Constantine's guide for travellers, the *Viaticum peregrinantis*. I have it here,' the Sicilian said, patting his saddlebag. 'In a casket containing healing herbs and medicines.'

'What else?'

The Sicilian produced a filigreed brass disc similar to one Vallon had lifted from a Moorish captain he'd killed in Castile.

'It's an astrolabe,' the Sicilian explained. 'An Arab star guide.'

Next he showed Vallon an ivory plaque with a conical pin at its centre and a border of geometric carvings. Onto the pin he placed a small iron model of a fish.

'Master Cosmas obtained it from a Cathay merchant on the Silk Road. The Chinese call it a south-pointing mysterious fish. Observe.'

Holding the device at arm's length, he moved it in a semicircle, first one way, then the other. He wheeled his pony and repeated the demonstration.

'You see, wherever I position myself, the fish remains constant, pointing to the south. But every direction has its opposite. And the opposite of south is north – the way my path lies.'

'And mine leads south, so let's agree the double pointer is a guide for each of us.'

The Sicilian clung like a burr. 'You said you were riding to the wars. There are wars in the north, too. Ride with me and you'll ride in comfort.'

'If I wanted comfort, I'd have cut your throat and taken your silver.'

'I wouldn't speak so frankly if I wasn't certain of your character.'

'I've stolen your master's mule.'

'A gift. I can't handle two mounts. Besides, a knight shouldn't travel on foot.'

'Who said I was a knight?'

'Your speech and noble bearing. That splendid sword you carry.'

It was like being pestered by flies. Vallon reined in. 'I'll tell you the difference between north and south. First, I prefer to do my fighting in the sun, not slogging in the mud. Second, I can't return to France. I'm an outlaw. Any man who takes me will receive the same bounty as if he'd delivered a wolf's head. I don't mind dying in combat, but I've no wish to meet my end hanging in a village square while some pork butcher pulls out my entrails and holds them up for my inspection.'

The Sicilian bit his downy lip.

'You're right about one thing,' said Vallon. 'You're too tender for the task. I'll let you follow me as far as Aosta. Take the ransom note to the Benedictines. For a few of those coins, they'll post it from abbey to abbey. It will reach Normandy long before you could deliver it.'

The Sicilian looked back at the pass. 'My master said a journey uncompleted is like a story half-told.'

'Don't be ridiculous. A journey's a tiresome passage between one place and another.'

The Sicilian's eyes swam. 'No. I must go on.'

Vallon heaved a sigh. 'Payment for my advice,' he said, holding up the finger banded by the ring he couldn't take off. 'Sell that pretty pony and buy a nag. Exchange your gay costume for pilgrim drab. Shave your head, carry a staff and mumble prayers. Join an escorted company and only sleep in hospices. Don't blab about ransoms or wave coins and alchemists' toys about.' He flicked the mule's reins. 'We're done.'

He thought he'd ridden clear when the Sicilian's dismal postscript lodged.

'The Count's lands aren't in Normandy. He fought with Duke William in the English campaign. His fief's in England. Far to the north.'

Vallon laughed.

'I know I won't reach it on my own.'

'Then we part in agreement.'

'That's why I was so heartened when Master Cosmas promised you would be my guide and protector.'

Vallon whirled.

'With his dying breath, he said fortune had appointed you to lead the way.'

'Appointed? He was sick in his wits!' Vallon wrenched off the cape. 'I won't wear a dead man's mantle.' He made another futile attempt to remove the ring. 'Don't say another word. Don't follow me another step. If you do ...' He slapped the mule's neck, squeezed its flanks.

It wouldn't budge. It rolled its eyes and laid its ears back.

Vallon booted its ribs.

The beast reared. In the moment it took him to regain control, Vallon heard a muted fracture. From the nearest summit to the west a cornice fell like a severed wing and exploded into fragments that skipped and bounded into the valley. The slope began to crawl, accelerating, until the whole snowfield was sliding. The mass surged across the valley floor and smashed against the opposite side in a cloud of frozen surf.

When Vallon's ears stopped ringing, the first thing he heard was a noise like pebbles clicking together. A black-and-red bird flirted on a rock, cocking its tail and fluttering its wings. Vallon knew that if the Sicilian hadn't delayed him, he would have been right in the path of the avalanche.

Twice in the last twenty-four hours, fate had steered him away from what he deserved. There had to be a reason. His shoulders slumped.

'Show me that pagan contraption again.'

He played with the compass, but couldn't outwit its mechanism.

Magic or trickery, it didn't matter. Whatever direction he took, in the end he would find what he was looking for, or it would find him.

'If I employ you as my servant, you'll learn to curb your tongue.'

The Sicilian hung the cloak about Vallon. 'Gladly. But with your permission, when the road is lonely and the night long, I'll entertain you with tales from the ancients. Or, since you're a military man, perhaps we could discuss strategy. Recently, I've been reading Polybius's account of Hannibal's campaigns.'

Vallon gave him a look.

'And if you should fall ill, I'll restore you to health by the grace of God. In fact, I've already diagnosed your condition.'

'Oh, yes?'

'The melancholy cast of your features, your restless sleep – those are the symptoms of lovesickness. Tell me I'm right. Tell me that you lost your lady to another and mean to win her back by feats of arms.'

Vallon bared his teeth. 'Can you make a hanged and quartered man skip?'

The Sicilian's expression turned solemn. 'Only God can perform miracles.'

'Then start praying we aren't caught in France.'

Vallon steered the mule around, not sure which of them was the dumber weathercock. The gem on his finger mirrored the flawless sky. The prospect of retracing his steps freighted his feelings with lead.

'You'd better tell me your name.'

If the Sicilian had worn a tail, it would have been wagging. 'My lord, I'm called Hero.'

III

Hero found himself at a standstill in the middle of black nowhere. They were still in the trees and the faint rustling he could hear was snow sifting through bare branches. A dog driven mad by loneliness barked a long way off. Movement close by made his eyes stiffen in their sockets.

'Is that you, sir?'

'Who else?'

'Why have we stopped?'

'I can smell smoke. We must be near a settlement.'

Hero populated the night with Norman patrols, Danish pirates, English cannibals . . . 'Let's rest here until daylight.'

'By morning you'll be as stiff as a fish.'

Tears pricked Hero's eyes. 'Yes, sir.'

'So stay awake. And stop your teeth clattering.'

Jaws clamped together, Hero continued downhill in blind zigzags. Eventually he sensed from a loosening of the night that the trees were thinning. He smelled turned earth and the sour reek of a burned-out hamlet. The going became easier. After the lurching descent, it was like floating on darkness. The hiss of fast-flowing water grew louder until it smothered all other sounds.

'The castle's upstream,' Vallon murmured, steering Hero that way. After a while, they stopped again.

'We're at the bridge.'

They felt their way across the wooden boards. The castle must be directly above them, blotted out by darkness and snow.

'Stay here,' said Vallon, and disappeared.

The river wouldn't settle on an even note. Each splash and gurgle strung Hero's nerves tighter. The snow had fattened into flakes. A thread of ice-water trickled down his spine. He sagged over the mule's neck and groaned. This was punishment for pride, he decided, recalling how he'd ridden out from Salerno convinced that he was destined to witness a thousand wonders to impress his fellow scholars when he returned home.

Home. Longing clogged his throat. He saw the white house above the busy harbour. He hovered above it like a ghost, looking in at his careworn mother and his five sisters. The Five Furies he used to call them, but what he would give to be back in their company. There they were, chattering like starlings and applying make-up until Theodora, the youngest and least cruel, said, peering into the polished brass mirror, 'I wonder where our dear Hero is.'

He gulped on his heartsickness.

'Not so loud,' Vallon hissed at his side. 'We're within bowshot of the walls and there are watchmen above the gate.'

'What will we do?'

'Tell me what Sir Walter looks like. Come on.'

Hero gathered his wits. 'Master Cosmas said that he was handsome and had an engaging wit.'

'You mentioned a younger brother.'

'Richard, a weakling.'

Vallon brooded for a while. 'Well, we accomplish nothing by standing here.' He stepped forward a pace and cupped his hands around his mouth. 'Peace! Two travellers carrying urgent news for Count Olbec.'

Shouts of alarm overhead and the hiss of an arrow flying wild. A horn blared and a bell began to clang. When it stopped, Hero heard the distant counterpoint of cushioned hoofbeats.

He wrenched the mule around. 'Mount up. We still have time to reach the trees.'

Vallon dragged him to earth. 'They'll follow our trail. Stand close and hide your fear. Normans despise weakness.'

More shouts. The gate grated open and cavalry bearing torches crashed out.

Hero crossed himself. Vallon gripped his arm.

'Leave the talking to me. One wrong answer and we could end up twisting in the wind like that poor soul on the hill.'

I won't flinch, Hero vowed. I'll face death as bravely as noble Archimedes.

The squadron descended on them like a machine welded by flames, the torches roaring in the wind of their passing. The horses' armoured heads swung like hammers; the concussion of hooves shivered Hero's chest. They were going to ride over him. Pound him into a smear of gristle.

He whimpered and covered his eyes.

The charge stopped so close that he could feel the horses' snorting breath on his face. When the anticipated blow didn't fall, he peered between his fingers to find himself walled in by a picket of swords with flames dancing along their blades.

A face thrust forward, hot eyes glinting each side of beaked iron.

'Take his sword.'

One of the soldiers vaulted from his horse and advanced on Vallon. Hero held his breath. He knew that the sword was sacred. Each night, no matter how hard the day's journey had been, Vallon carefully polished it with oil and Tripoli powder. Surely he wouldn't surrender it without resistance.

Vallon didn't even glance round as the soldier drew the weapon and handed it over. The leader held the watered steel blade to the light. 'Where did you obtain a sword of this quality?'

'From a Moor outside the walls of Zaragoza.'

'Stole it, I warrant.'

'After a fashion. I had to kill him before he consented to part with it.'

The beaked face craned forward again.

'There's a curfew. You know the penalty for breaking it.'

'My business with Count Olbec is too important to brook delay. I'd be obliged if you'd take me to your lord.'

The Norman braced one foot against Vallon's shoulder. 'My father's drunk. I'm Drogo, his son. You can state your business to me.'

Hero's stomach churned. Drogo? Master Cosmas hadn't mentioned any Drogo.

Vallon patted his chest. 'I've been burdened with it since last summer. It will keep for one more night.'

Drogo straightened his leg, shoving Vallon back. 'You'll tell me now or I'll string the pair of you up by the balls.'

Hero's testicles leaped. It wasn't an empty threat. In York, three days ago, he'd seen a howling man separated from the parts that should have given him most pleasure.

'Your brother's alive!' he squeaked.

Drogo waved down the murmur of astonishment. 'The rogue's lying and I'll flay anyone who repeats the falsehood.' His tongue flickered. 'There may be more of them. Fulk, Drax, Roussel – stay with me. The rest of you, cross the river and spread out. They're probably hiding in the woods. Don't return until you've found them.'

He waited until the riders had been absorbed by the snow, then spurred in a circle around the travellers.

'My brother's dead. He died fighting under the Emperor's banner at Manzikert.'

Hero filched a look at Vallon.

'A false report,' said the Frank. 'I visited Sir Walter two weeks after the battle. He's in good health. He took a blow to the head in the fighting, but suffered no lasting injury.'

'I don't believe you.'

'Do you think I'd waste half a year carrying a lie to this dismal frontier?'

Drogo angled his sword under Vallon's chin. 'Give me proof.'

'Before the proper audience.'

Drogo drew back his sword. 'I'll send you to the rightful audience.'

'Inside the saddlepack,' Hero blurted. 'Ransom terms.'

The soldiers ransacked their goods. One of them found the seal ring and passed it to Drogo.

'Where did you steal this?'

'Your brother gave it to me.'

'Liar. You cut it from his dead hand.'

A soldier held up the documents. Drogo crammed them under his surcoat. He hooked the astrolabe on the tip of his sword. 'Devil's baubles,' he said, flicking it away.

A soldier tried to wrench the ring off Vallon's hand. When it wouldn't budge, he drew his knife.

'Wait,' Drogo said, and hunched forward. 'What do they call you? What's your profession?'

'Vallon, a Frank who fought with Norman mercenaries in Anatolia. And this is my servant, Hero, a Greek from Sicily.'

'How did you save your skin, Frank?'

'I was on a reconnaissance to the north when the Seljuks attacked. No one knew they were so close. After the disaster, word reached us that they wanted men to negotiate ransoms for the prisoners. I went out of Christian duty.'

Drogo snorted. 'Describe my brother.'

'Fair, well made. His quick wit has made him a favourite at the Emir's court.'

Drogo breathed in through his nose. Far away and lonely came the faint note of a bugle. Drogo twisted in his saddle as if alerted by another sound, but Hero knew there was no other sound – only the creaking of leather and the sputtering of torches and the thumping of his heart. Snow was collecting between the links of Drogo's mail and Hero knew what he was thinking. They were hidden from mortal sight. This circle in the night was the place where they would die.

'Take them across the river and kill them. I'll stay here with the horses. When the others return, tell them you cut down the foreigners as they tried to escape.'

Two of the soldiers prodded Vallon forward at swordpoint. The one called Drax grasped Hero by his neck and began hustling him over the bridge.

'And fetch me that ring,' Drogo bellowed.

Why hadn't Vallon heeded his warning? Hero agonised as he stumbled after his master. It had been an act of suicide to go barging into the castle at night.

He was halfway across the bridge when a wordless shout ahead of him made Drax stop and tighten his grip. All Hero could see were the torches carried by Vallon's escort swinging in the snow-filled night. One of them fell and fizzled out. Hero heard a succession of cryptic thumps and exclamations, the clash of metal, a cry of pain and then a faint splash. A moment later the other torch died, leaving everything on the far bank a mystery.

Drax shook Hero. 'Move and you're dead.' He released his hold and raised his sword and torch, making futile fanning movements to clear his vision. 'Fulk? Roussel?'

Someone moaned.

'Fulk, is that you? For Christ's sake, answer.'

'*I think my wrist's broken.*'

'Where's Roussel?'

'*The Frank has my sword across his throat.*'

'Oh, shit!'

'What's going on?' Drogo shouted.

Drax turned his head. Hero heard him swallow. 'The Frank must have broken free and seized Fulk's sword.'

Vallon's voice carried from the void. 'Drogo, I have your men at my mercy. Release my servant.'

'Do nothing without my order,' Drogo roared. The bridge began to tremble, a seismic forewarning of his rage. Hero shrank aside as he swept past. When he reached the other side, he stood in his stirrups and held his torch high. By its puny light Hero saw Vallon armed with a sword, holding Roussel in a necklock, Fulk doubled over, nursing one hand under his shoulder.

'It wasn't my fault,' he groaned. 'Roussel slipped and barged into me. The Frank took advantage of the—'

'Silence! I'll deal with you poltroon idiots later.' Drogo spurred his horse towards Vallon. 'As for you ...'

22

Vallon retreated, using Roussel as a shield. 'We have no quarrel.'

'No quarrel?' The gulf between this statement and the enormity of Drogo's wrath rendered him speechless. When Drogo found his voice, it came from a different register, guttural, as if thickened by blood. 'I'll make you repeat those words when I'm standing with my foot on your neck.'

Vallon shoved his hostage away and took guard. Encumbered by torch, sword and shield, Drogo had to guide his horse with his knees. He circled one way, then the other, the snow falling so thickly that Hero could only make out fitful shapes.

'You'd better dismount,' Vallon said. 'You can't fight with your hands full.'

Drogo acknowledged his handicap. 'Drax, get up here with your light.'

Drax cursed and dragged Hero forward. Drogo backed up to him and leaned to hand him his torch.

'Sir, I can guard the prisoner or hold the torches, but I can't do both.'

Drogo kicked out. 'God's veins, am I entirely surrounded by cretins? Cut his throat.'

Drax eyed Hero, shaking his head, then brought his sword up.

'Stay your hand,' Vallon said. 'Here come more lights.'

Hero risked a backward look. A glow approaching through the snow resolved itself into several bobbing torches.

'Let them come,' Drogo snarled. 'There's no need for concealment now. Assault on a Norman is a capital crime. The more witnesses the better.'

'Including your mother?' Vallon said.

'My mother? What about my mother?'

Vallon relaxed his stance. 'I think she's about to join us.'

Five riders filed past Hero. Four were soldiers, the last a small shape muffled from head to toe. Drogo swore under his breath.

'What's the cause of the alarm?' the woman demanded. 'Who is that man? What's happening here?'

Drogo rode towards her. 'My lady, you shouldn't be out in such foul weather. You'll catch a flux.'

'Answer my question.'

'They're thieves. Foreign fly-by-nights with stolen relics.'

'Ransom terms for your son,' Vallon said.

'A forgery. As soon as I challenged him for proof, he made a bolt for it. He injured Fulk and robbed him of his sword. Look there if you don't believe me.'

'Show me the documents.'

'My lady, false hopes will only aggravate old wounds. I have too much respect for your grief to allow scum to—'

'I'll nurse my sorrows. You will attend your father. Now give me the documents.'

Drogo slapped the packet into her hand.

'If any harm comes to these strangers, you'll answer to the Count.' She drifted back into the snow. 'Don't keep him waiting. You know what he's like when he's taken drink.'

Drogo rammed his sword into its scabbard and rode back towards Vallon. He looked down on the Frank, breathing heavily, then swung a mailed arm into his face with a force that sent Vallon sprawling.

'Don't imagine it's over between us.'

Vallon picked himself up. He spat blood, wiped his mouth and gave a wolfish grin. 'I see where you get your temper from.'

Drogo regarded him with naked hatred. 'Lady Margaret's no blood relative of mine.' He raked his spurs down his horse's flanks. 'And nor is Walter.'

IV

Stumbling across the bailey at swordpoint, Hero glimpsed men dishevelled by sleep peering from the doorway of the great hall. Then his escort prodded him through another gate and up the castle mound to a stairway at the base of the keep. Beasts lowed behind its wooden walls. So this is where my journey of discovery ends, he thought. At a glorified cowshed.

A knee shunted him up the steps. He climbed blind through the snow. Hands shoved him into a chamber. The door slammed behind him. He gasped for breath and wiped snow from his eyes. At the far end of the room, vaguely lit by tapers stuck into wall sconces, a group of figures waited in front of a tapestry screen. At their centre a burly man with a round, cropped head leaned his weight on a stick and pushed up from his seat. Hero winced. A hideous scar running from temple to jaw bisected the man's face into two misaligned halves – the mouth askew, one eye fixed in a bolting stare, the other narrowed in a drowsy squint.

Lady Margaret sat beside him fidgeting with Sir Walter's seal ring, her mouth compressed into a determined little bud that belied her girlish figure. A priest with pouchy cheeks shuffled attendance, one hand clutching the documents, the other fiddling with a crucifix. Behind them stood another man, his face blotched by shadow.

Drogo strode past, pulling off his helmet to reveal a meaty face wealed by the imprint of cold metal. His eyes, glittering under pale lashes, projected fury but also bafflement, as if events had a habit of slipping out of his control. Even when he stopped before his father, he couldn't stay still, tapping his feet, slapping his sword hilt. He was an engine lacking a brake.

'My lord, I intended bringing you these men as soon as I'd finished questioning them.'

Olbec waved him down, his lop-sided stare fixed on Vallon. 'You say Sir Walter lives.' The two sides of his mouth moved slightly out of phase.

'He's alive, well-fed, warmly clothed, comfortably housed.' Vallon stroked his cloak, which by now resembled rat more than sable. 'Given the choice, I'd change places with him this moment.'

Margaret clapped her hands. 'Bring food. Prepare their quarters.'

Hero collapsed onto a bench shoved behind his knees. Olbec lowered himself onto his seat with a pained grunt, one leg sticking straight out. Vallon and Drogo remained standing. Hero saw that the face of the man in the background wasn't masked by a trick of light, but by a dark blemish. This must be Richard, the weakling son.

Servants brought tepid broth and coarse bread. Hero wolfed it down. When he'd scoured his bowl, Vallon was still sipping from his. Olbec fumed at the delay and shot forward as soon as Vallon laid the vessel aside.

'Now then. A full account.'

Vallon rinsed his hands in a fingerbowl. 'Not until your son returns our property and apologises for his churlishness.'

Drogo sprang at Vallon.

'Stop!'

Olbec's out-thrust head resembled a disfigured tortoise. 'You crept into my domain by night. This border is infested with Scottish brigands and English rebels. You should thank God Drogo didn't cut you down on the spot.'

'And so should you. If he had, Sir Walter would be dead by autumn.'

'You'll have your possessions,' Margaret cried, pulling her husband back. 'Where's my son held?'

'When I left him, he was lodged at a civilised establishment a week's ride east of Constantinople.'

'Civilised?' Olbec spluttered. 'The Turks aren't members of Adam's race. They'll roast their own babies rather than go without a meal. When they wreck a city, they rebuild its walls with the skulls of its defenders.'

'Stories they spread to demoralise their enemies. It's true that the common soldiers have no more use for civilisation than a wolf has for a sheep pen. But their masters have won an empire and know that to hold it they must rule rather than ravage. For that reason they employ Persian and Arab administrators.' Vallon nodded towards the priest. 'One of them set down the terms for your son's release.'

Olbec swung round. 'You dumb dog. How much longer do you need?'

The priest groaned. 'If only the scribe had been a more learned man.'

'It's as I said,' Drogo snapped. 'The documents are forgeries.'

Vallon plucked the manuscript from the priest and gave it to Hero. 'No frills.'

Hero rose. His hands trembled. He opened his mouth and emitted a pathetic squeak. He cleared his throat and tried again.

'"Greetings noble lord, and the mercy of God be with you. Know that Suleyman ibn Kutalmish, Defender of Islam, Strong Hand of the Commander of the Faithful, Emir of Rum, Marquis of the Horizons, Victorious Captain in the Army of the Valiant Lion, Right Hand of—"'

Olbec hammered his stick on the floor. Spittle flew. 'I don't want to hear this heathen bullshit. Get to the meat.'

'My lord, the Emir pledges to release Sir Walter in exchange for the

26

following indemnities: "Item. One thousand gold nomismata or their equal by weight."'

'What in hell's name are nomismata?'

'Byzantine coins, my lord. Seventy-two nomismata make one Roman pound, which is the equivalent of twelve English troy ounces, making a total of sixty-nine pounds.'

Olbec gripped his knees.

'"Item. Ten pounds of finest Baltic amber. Item. Six bolts of . . ."' Hero's voice trailed away. Olbec's face had knotted in the fixity of a man straining to shift a turd the size and shape of a brick.

Drogo sniggered. 'It seems that Walter hasn't lost his talent for exaggeration.'

The scar down Olbec's face thickened into a livid rope. 'Sixty-nine pounds of gold! My estate isn't worth a twentieth that much. God knows, King William himself would struggle to raise such a sum.'

'And,' Drogo pointed out, 'His Majesty won't drain the exchequer to ransom a knight who fought for heretics while the King's loyal vassals were advancing William's cause in England.'

Margaret darted a vicious glance at him. 'You want Walter dead.'

'He shames our name. By God, if I'd been at that battle, I'd have cut my throat rather than let myself be taken by barbarians who suck from their horses' teats.'

'My son's as good as dead,' Margaret wailed.

'There's an alternative,' said Hero.

They leaned forward again.

Hero was beginning to enjoy being the centre of attention. 'Outside warfare, the Emir's chief delights are hawking and hunting. He prides himself on possessing the finest falcons in Islam. He'll set aside the previous demands in exchange for two matched casts of gyrfalcons, each one as white as a virgin's breasts or the first snows of winter.'

Lady Margaret broke the imaginative silence. 'What's a gyrfalcon?'

'The largest, rarest and most noble of hawks. They're variable in plumage, ranging from charcoal-black to purest white. The palest and therefore the most valuable live at the world's northernmost end, in Hyperborea, on the islands of Iceland and Greenland. The Portuguese call them *letrados* because their markings resemble the letters of a manuscript. To the Byzantines, they are known as—'

Vallon kicked him. 'What my servant means is that four white falcons will secure your son's liberty.'

Olbec brightened cautiously. 'Four falcons doesn't sound too steep. How much do they cost?'

'The finest specimens fetch as much as two good war-horses.'

Olbec winced. 'Well, that's a price worth paying for my lady's happiness.'

'The price will be much higher than that,' Drogo said. He menaced Hero with a smile. 'Tell us, Greek, how we lay our hands on four gyrfalcons as white as virgins' breasts that live at the world's end?'

'Sir, some fly south to escape the winter and are trapped on a plain in Norway. The Norwegian king reserves them as gifts for his fellow monarchs.'

'Then I'll petition William to request a royal gift.' Olbec rubbed his hands. 'That's settled.'

Margaret, staring at Hero, plucked at her husband's sleeve. 'I see a "but" in his eyes.'

Olbec saw it too. His smile died. 'What's the problem? Are we at war with Norway?'

Vallon stepped in. 'The falcons aren't trapped until October. That will be too late. The Emir has a wager with a rival lord to settle who possesses the finest hawk. They've agreed a trial this autumn.'

'And if they don't reach him in time?'

'I imagine your son will be sold as a slave. Since the Emir is well disposed towards him, he'll probably let him keep his balls.'

Margaret swooned. Olbec caught her. She squirmed to face him. 'We must send our own expedition to these islands.'

'I don't even know where they are.'

'Iceland is a week's voyage from north Britain,' Hero said. 'Greenland lies another week's passage to the north-west.'

'They must trade with civilised lands,' Margaret insisted.

'Yes, my lady. Each summer a merchant fleet leaves Norway for Iceland, returning before the autumn storms. Gyrfalcons are usually included in the cargo.'

'There's the solution,' Margaret cried.

'And how will the falcons be carried to Anatolia?' Drogo demanded.

Margaret pointed at Vallon. 'The same route this man travelled.'

'It's taken him half a year to bring us a piece of parchment. Imagine how much longer it will take to transport falcons overland to Anatolia.'

'There's an alternative route,' Hero said. 'Your blood-ancestors, the Norsemen, discovered it. It's called the Road to the Greeks.'

Olbec waved his hand. 'Go on.'

'From Norway the falcons would be shipped up the Baltic Sea to Novgorod, a northern trade centre in the Land of the Rus. Then, by a series of portages, they would be transported south to Kiev. At the Russian capital they would be consigned to one of the merchant fleets that voyage down the Dnieper to the Black Sea. Having reached the coast, they would be taken by ship to Constantinople.' Hero saw that he'd lost his audience. 'From there,' he said on a dying note, 'they would complete the journey into Anatolia.'

Nobody spoke. Hero sensed their imaginations spreading out like ripples beyond the horizons of their understanding. Iceland. Greenland. Rus. The Black Sea. Mysterious city-states with outlandish names scattered to the four corners of the world. Even Drogo had been stunned into silence.

'The voyage can be completed in three months,' Hero added. 'So I'm told.'

Lady Margaret pointed at Vallon. 'Do you know this route?'

'Only at second-hand. In Castile I heard an account of its perils from an ancient Viking who'd made the journey fifty years earlier. He set out from Novgorod with more than forty companions, all battle-hardened warriors. They were transporting a cargo of slaves. Within days they found themselves caught up in wars between rival Russian princes. They lost a ship and its crew before they reached the capital. South of Kiev the river plunges into a series of cataracts. The old Viking told me their names. He called one the Gulper, another the Echoer, a third the Insatiable. The torrents claimed the lives of another six men. Once the Vikings reached calm water, they found themselves in territory overrun by savage nomads. Day after day they fought running battles with horse archers. Of the forty Vikings who left Novgorod, eleven reached the Black Sea. And none of their cargo survived.' Vallon shrugged. 'Fortune was no friend of that Viking. A few months later Moorish pirates captured him.'

'That was fifty years ago,' Margaret said in a small voice. 'Perhaps conditions have improved.'

'It's not only the dangers,' Olbec groaned. 'Think of the cost.'

'We can borrow from the moneylenders in York.'

'We burned York two winters ago,' Drogo pointed out.

'Lincoln, then, or London. Paris, Milan, if necessary. I don't care!' Margaret squeezed her temples.

'My lady, a loan would be secured against our property, movable and immovable,' said Olbec. 'We could forfeit our estate.'

Margaret rounded on the Count. 'And I could lose my son. I implore you, rescue him. If you don't, I'll return to Normandy and enter a nunnery.' She clutched her throat. 'No, I'll swallow poison. I couldn't live knowing that my family had done nothing to save my first-born.'

Olbec knuckled his eyes. 'Even if we could raise the finance, who would man the expedition? Who would lead it? I'm too broken-down to make such a journey and Drogo's services are pledged to William for the Scottish campaign.'

Margaret had no answer to that.

Vallon caught Hero's eye. 'It's clear that you won't settle this matter tonight,' he told Olbec. 'Our part's done. By your leave, we'll take our rest.'

Drogo blocked him. 'I'm not done with you.'

'Let them retire,' Olbec ordered.

'He's a mercenary. He didn't journey here out of love for Walter.'

'You're right,' Vallon said. 'Your brother swore that my labours would be handsomely rewarded. He boasted of his rich inheritance.' Vallon's gaze wandered over the stark wooden walls. 'If I'd known the truth, I'd have left him to rot.'

Olbec struggled to his feet. 'You deserve a reward, but you've heard how things stand. Listen, I know a good fighting man when I see one. Ride with us on the Scottish campaign. Prizes will be won in the north, and I swear that a generous share of the spoils will go to you.'

Vallon inclined his head. 'You flatter me, but this climate makes my sword arm stiff and slow. I'll follow the wind as soon as it turns south.'

Olbec subsided in grumpy resignation. 'Then all I can give you is my thanks and a safe conduct.'

Vallon bowed.

Drogo barged against him. 'I'll escort you myself.'

*

'Don't blame you for turning down the old man,' said the man-at-arms who guided them out. 'You think Northumbria is bad, but Scotland – what a shithole. The natives eat the same food as their horses and live in hovels I wouldn't put a pig—'

'Drogo and Walter are stepbrothers,' Vallon cut in.

The man-at-arms chuckled. 'Sounds like Sir Walter forgot to tell you.'

'Yes,' said Vallon with fake resentment. 'He claimed he was the sole heir.'

'Right, it's like this. Drogo's the eldest son of the Count's first wife, a farm girl from the next village. She died giving birth to Richard. Reckon she took one look at his face and lost the will to live. Lady Margaret had been married, too. Widowed at fourteen, when she was still carrying Walter. Much classier breed. Her family holds land near Evreux. But here's the strange thing. Walter and Drogo were born on the same day. Sort of twins.'

'And rivals.'

'Been fighting since they began to crawl. Would have killed one another by now if Lady Margaret hadn't persuaded Walter to go abroad.' The man-at-arms laughed. 'So golden boy's alive. Doesn't surprise me. Could talk his way out of hell, that one. But you don't need me to tell you how smooth-tongued he can be. Here we are,' he said, pushing open a shed door with a mock flourish. 'The guest suite.'

Clean rushes carpeted the floor. A basin of water steamed on a brazier. Clothes had been laid out on two sleeping platforms.

The man-at-arms lounged against the door. 'You didn't say where you were from.'

'Aquitaine,' Vallon said, steering him out. 'Nowhere you would have heard of.'

Hero collapsed on to his bed. There wasn't a bone or muscle in his body that didn't cry out for relief. Through sticky eyes he watched Vallon strip off and wash himself. Where his clothes had protected him from the weather, his body was as white as a peeled stick. Hero had a vision of the warriors carved in stone on the walls of Salerno cathedral.

Vallon shook him awake. 'Did you foul yourself when the Normans charged?'

31

Hero's response was slurred. 'No, sir.'

'Even so, you're filthy. Wash yourself. You'll feel better for it.'

Hero hobbled over to the brazier.

Vallon yawned. 'Drogo's going to be a problem.'

Hero shuddered. 'He's a wild beast.'

Vallon laughed. 'Born with wasps in his hair and a wolf at his throat. Still, put yourself in his skin. We've brought him the worst news imaginable.'

Hero turned. Vallon lay on his back, his sword by his side.

'Sir, considering that he has us at his mercy, you seem remarkably unconcerned.'

Vallon didn't answer for a moment. 'Lady Margaret's a determined lady, wouldn't you say?'

'Yes, sir. How did you know she was in the party that came to our rescue?'

'Because I wrote giving warning of our arrival.'

Stung that Vallon hadn't told him, Hero risked a criticism. 'You took too great a risk, sir. You should have waited in Durham until she sent for us.'

'I wasn't sure how much influence Drogo wielded. Suppose we'd waited and Drogo had turned up to escort us. He would have returned to the castle with sad news – an ambush on a lonely road, the foreigners slain . . . ' Vallon waved a hand.

Hero toppled back on to his bed. He was so tired that at first he missed the significance of what Vallon had said. He jerked upright. 'You knew about Drogo, too?'

'I made enquiries about the family in London. I'm not so foolhardy as to rush into the unknown.'

Hero crossed his arms over his chest. His mouth set in a resentful line.

Vallon's head rolled to face him. 'I didn't want to burden you with more fears than you already carry.'

'Thank you for your consideration,' Hero said in a tight voice.

Vallon smiled. 'If it's any consolation, you've acquitted yourself better than I expected. To tell the truth, I never thought you'd get as far as the Channel.'

Hero's lip trembled at this double-sided compliment. 'Then you're not angry with me.'

'Angry for what?'

'For leading you on this vile and unprofitable enterprise.'

'You didn't lead me anywhere,' Vallon said. He reached for the lamp and nipped out the flame. 'If anyone's to blame, it's that one-eyed magus we buried in the Alps.'

V

Wayland drew back the wattle shutter and watched the foreigners walking towards the hall. Since their arrival, the snow had fallen without pause for two days. Now the sky was ablaze with stars and the strangers cast shadows as black as ink.

A bell rasped. On Wayland's gloved left hand, tethered by leash and jesses, sat a goshawk with its eyelids stitched together. He'd trapped her four days ago in a net baited with a dove. She was a passager, still in her juvenile plumage, her buff chest streaked with umber barbs. After jessing her and seeling her eyes, Wayland had left her undisturbed until he judged from the sharpness of her breastbone that she was keen enough to be handled. Since he had picked her up yesterday evening she hadn't left his fist. She wouldn't sleep until she ate. Until she ate, he wouldn't get any sleep.

When the strangers disappeared into the hall, Wayland closed the shutter and turned. The arena for this battle of wills was a mews of riven oak lit by a single lamp. Behind a canvas drape at the opposite end, two peregrines – falcon and tiercel – dozed like small idols on a beam perch. Wayland began to pace the earth floor, four steps forward, four steps back. A brindled hound lying by his pallet tracked his movements with sleepy eyes. The dog was enormous, heavier than most full-grown men. Part mastiff, part greyhound, part wolf, its bloodline went back to the Celtic warhounds prized by Britain's Roman invaders.

As he patrolled, Wayland drew a fillet of pigeon breast across the goshawk's feet. She ignored it. She couldn't see and had no sense of smell. The food was merely an irritant. Wayland stroked her back and shoulders with a quill. She didn't react to that, either. Pinching her

33

long middle toe provoked a feeble hiss – nothing like the outraged gasps that had greeted the lightest touch when he caught her. He knew she was ready to eat. Some hawks fed the first night, most refused for a day or two, but only once had Wayland found a hawk that would rather starve than submit. That had been a goshawk, too – a haggard so old that its eyes had darkened to the colour of pigeon's blood. It had spent a day and a night thrashing upside down from his glove before he cut its jesses and cast it back into the wild.

Wayland was less focused on his task than he should have been. The garrison was buzzing with stories about the strangers. A mysterious Frankish veteran of far-off wars had broken Fulk's wrist and held a sword against Roussel's throat. And got away with it! His servant – his catamite said some – was an astrologer who spoke every known tongue and carried medicines blessed by the Pope. Wayland was desperate to get a closer look at them, but he couldn't leave the hut until he'd manned the hawk. Deciding to force the pace, he pulled the hawk's right leg down with thumb and forefinger, applying pressure until she snaked her head at his hand. Her beak closed on pigeon breast instead. She wrenched off a wedge, imagining she'd got her enemy, and flicked it away. But the taste lingered. She salivated and shifted into a more balanced stance. Wayland held his breath as she inflated her feathers, swelling as if building up to a violent sneeze. She roused with a furious rattle, flicked her tail, tightened her talons and bent her head.

The dog's eyes opened. It lifted its craggy head, listening, then sprang up in one unconsidered movement. The commotion made the hawk bate so violently that the draught of her wings blew out the lamp. In the blackout Wayland couldn't control her twisting and flapping. He opened the shutter and by the wash of starlight managed to scoop her back on to his fist and untwist her jesses. Mouth agape, chest heaving, she squatted on his glove like a spastic chicken. Wayland knew that the setback meant the loss of another night's sleep, but he couldn't set her down now. If he did, all the advances he'd made would be reversed, and he'd have to go through the whole tedious process from scratch. The dog, oblivious to his reproachful growl, threatened the door, its muzzle rucked back from canines the size of small tusks.

A fist banged. 'You're wanted in the hall. Quick!'

Wayland half-opened the door. Raul the German stood there, panting with urgency. Wayland pointed to the hawk, then at its perch.

'Bring it with you.'

Wayland reached for the muzzle hanging from a peg. The dog was supposed to wear it whenever it left the hut.

Raul yanked his arm. 'No time for that.'

Wayland followed him into the rigid night. His feet slithered in icy ruts. Constellations frozen in their orbits outlined the keep. The dog padded beside him, its shoulders on a level with his hips. The hawk, stupefied by the rush of sensations, crouched on his fist.

Raul glanced back excitedly. 'They're talking about an expedition to Norway. If they're after falcons, they'll need a falconer.' He stopped. 'This could be our chance.'

To escape, he meant. To go home. Raul was from the Saxony coast, the main breadwinner in a sprawling family who'd lost their farm in a North Sea flood. He'd gone abroad to seek his fortune and, after various misadventures on land and sea, had taken service with the Normans as a crossbowman. A bearded, barrel-chested stump of a man with a weakness for drink, women and sentimental songs, his discipline away from the battlefield was atrocious. Ten years older than Wayland, he'd attached himself to the tall English youth, although they had little in common beyond the fact that both were outsiders.

Wayland shifted him aside. When he reached the hall, the dog lay down by the entrance without being told. He went in.

'Hey,' Raul called. 'If they're looking for volunteers, put in a word for me.'

Most of the men in the high-beamed chamber were asleep. A few fuddled faces looked up from ale cups and dice games. Drogo's voice carried through the screen separating the communal quarters from the Count's receiving chamber.

'Watch it,' one of the soldiers said. 'They've been arguing for hours. The old man's pissed.'

Wayland parted the drapes. Olbec and Margaret were seated in X-frame armchairs placed on a dais. Drogo paced in front of them, his face like a scalded pig, punching the palm of one hand to drive home some point or other. The strangers had their backs to Wayland, the Frank slouched yet alert, the Sicilian braced in nervous concentration. Wayland spotted Richard sitting alone in a corner.

'I admit it,' Drogo said. 'I don't know a lot about falcons. Hawking's too namby-pamby for my taste. Where's the risk, where's the danger? But I know one thing. Hawks are prey to endless ailments. They die from the smallest slight. Tie a healthy falcon down in the evening and next morning you return to find a bundle of feathers. Buy a dozen gyrfalcons in Norway and you'd be lucky if a single bird survived the journey.'

Margaret jabbed Olbec. 'Don't listen to him. His opinion's warped by malice.'

Drogo spread his arms in frustration. 'For once, my lady, set aside your prejudices and consider the practicalities. What will you feed the hawks on during the journey?'

Spots of red highlighted Margaret's cheeks. 'Pigeons, seagulls, sheep, fish!'

Wayland had forgotten about the goshawk. Its emphatic rouse attracted everyone's attention. Faces turned as the hawk took a tentative bite. The taste of flesh dissolved its fear. It began a ravenous assault on the pigeon, tearing off large chunks, gasping and wheezing to force them down.

Wayland had lived close to nature and judged everything by the degree of danger it posed. The Frank's gaze, at once piercing and indifferent, showed him to be very dangerous indeed. The Sicilian was no threat at all. His bulging eyes made Wayland think of a startled hare.

'The falconer,' Olbec announced.

'I expected an older man,' Vallon said.

Olbec had perked up. 'Well built, though, and he has a cunning way with animals. That goshawk, for example. Trapped only a few days ago and already feeding as freely as a pet dove. I swear the boy can bewitch animals.' The Count slurped his ale. 'If anyone can bring the gyrfalcons safe to their destination, it's him.'

'Does he know what a gyrfalcon is?' Hero asked.

Drogo uttered a contemptuous laugh. 'Even if he did, he can't answer. He's as mute as a stone.'

'It's true that he can't speak,' Olbec said. 'Elves or divers stole his tongue when he lived wild in the forest. Walter caught him when he was hunting upriver. The hounds ran him to earth outside a cave. He was clad in skins and feathers, looked more like an animal than a Christian man.'

Hero's eyes widened. 'How long had he been living in the wilderness?'

'God knows. Probably since birth.'

'Suckled by wolves,' Hero breathed. 'Do you call him Romulus?'

'Romulus? We call him Wayland because that was the name carved on a cross he wore around his neck. A Danish name, but the writing was in English. He had a dog with him. Ferocious brute, big as a bull-calf. Still got it. First-rate hunting hound. That beast's dumb, too.'

Drogo turned on Hero. 'Because he'd cut its voice strings so that it wouldn't betray him when he was poaching our deer. If it had been me who'd caught him, he'd have lost more than his tongue.'

'Why did Walter show charity?' Hero asked, addressing Olbec.

'Ah,' Olbec said, relishing the tale. 'Walter said it was like a scene from a fable. When he rode up, he expected to find a wolf at bay. But no, the hounds were seated in a circle around the boy. He'd charmed them.'

'And that dog of his had torn out the throat of the lead hound. He should have been thrown to the pack.' Drogo's head whipped round. 'You see? No matter how much you feed a wolf, it keeps staring back at the forest. By God, show me that face again and I'll have you flogged.'

Wayland lowered his eyes. His heart pounded.

'Look at me,' Hero said. 'Wayland, look at me.'

'Do as you're told,' Olbec ordered.

Wayland slowly raised his head.

Hero frowned. 'He can understand speech.'

Olbec belched. 'There'd be no point wasting house space on him if he was deaf as well as dumb.'

'Yes, but if he once had the gift of words, they would have been English or Danish. Yet he understands French, which he must have learned in your household.'

'Where else?'

'What I'm saying is that even though he can't speak, he possesses the faculty for language.'

'Who cares,' Margaret snapped. 'Tell him what he has to do.'

Olbec held out his cup for a refill. 'Listen closely, young Wayland. Sir Walter, your master, is held prisoner by barbarians in a foreign land. You must repay his kindness by helping to secure his release. His jailer demands four falcons in return for his freedom. These falcons are larger, paler and more beautiful than any that you have seen. They dwell far to the north in a country of ice and fire, and their nature has been forged accordingly. Each year, a few of these paragons find their way to Norway. This summer you will join an expedition to that land, select the finest specimens, and care for them on their journey south.'

'You'll be responsible for their survival.' Margaret added. 'If they die, my son's life is forfeit, and you'll suffer the consequence.'

'Don't frighten the boy,' Olbec said, patting her arm. He beckoned Wayland closer. 'Imagine falcons so noble that only kings and emperors have title to them. White ones, as big as eagles. You'll voyage further than most knights travel in a lifetime. On your return journey, you might even make a pilgrimage to Jerusalem.' Olbec's eyes swam. 'By God, I wish I was going with you.'

Most of this had passed over Wayland's head. He tried to imagine a white falcon as big as an eagle and produced a mental picture of a swan with a hooked beak and wings like the angels his mother had described.

Drogo clapped in mock applause. 'What an excellent choice: a dumb falconer for a dumb enterprise. Now all we need is a crew to match. Oh yes, and a leader. I know,' he said, pointing at the figure in the shadows, 'why don't we send Richard?'

'I'd go. Anything to get away from here.'

'We'll commission an agent,' said Margaret. 'A merchant adventurer experienced in the northern trade.'

'You'll lose control the moment he sets sail. The chances are you'd never see him or our money again.'

'Drogo's right.'

It took Wayland a moment to work out that it was the Frank who'd spoken.

Vallon stood. 'If breath were wind, by now you could have blown a fleet to Norway. But no ship leaves harbour without a captain. What kind of man are you looking for? He would have to be a man you trusted through and through. A man brave enough to cut through the known hazards and resourceful enough to navigate around perils as yet unseen. He would have to be a man who, if he couldn't find a path, would make his own. You might find a man who has one of these qualities. You won't find a man who has them all.'

Wayland sensed crosscurrents swirling about the chamber. Drogo cocked his head in puzzlement.

'For a moment I thought you were proposing to take up the challenge.'

'God forbid. I lack both the qualities and the incentive.'

Margaret slapped the arm of her chair. 'He's a stranger. His words carry no weight.'

But Vallon's intervention had tilted the balance. Olbec rapped his stick on the floor. 'I'd hazard my fortune if I was sure that it would secure Walter's release, but it seems to me that we'd lose the one without gaining the other. No, my lady, I've reached my decision. I'll send an ambassador to Anatolia and frankly state my position, offering a ransom more in keeping with our station. What do you think, Vallon? You know the Emir; you say he holds Walter in affection. Surely he's open to reason.'

'He's a rational man. I'm sure he'd consider your offer carefully.'

Margaret shot out of her chair, her arms rigid by her side. Her eyes raked around the room. 'Since none of you will help, I'll make my own arrangements.' Gathering up her skirts, she ran out of the chamber.

Drogo clasped Olbec's hand. 'Well said, Father. Too many times you've let your lady's passions cloud your judgement.'

Olbec looked up at him with curdled eyes. 'Not so clouded that I can't divine your motives.'

The screen parted and a soldier rushed in.

'What's wrong?' Drogo demanded.

'Guilbert went outside for a piss. Didn't see the dog in the snow. Next moment he's flat on his back with that hellhound at his throat.'

Drogo turned on Wayland. 'I warned you.'

Wayland stuck two fingers in his mouth and whistled. Nailed feet hammered on the floor and moments later the dog loped through the curtain like a creature out of myth or nightmare, its eyes sulphurous yellow, its steely hackles rimed with frost. When it saw Drogo's threatening stance, its muzzle wrinkled in black corrugations. Wayland hissed. The dog made straight for him, lay down at his feet and began licking its paws.

Olbec held up his cup for another refill. 'I'm not wrong, am I? The boy can enchant the beasts.'

*

39

Raul was waiting when Wayland left the hall. 'Are they going to send an expedition?' he demanded, trotting alongside. 'Are you going on it? Is there a place for me?'

Wayland waved him away. There were too many things to think about. When Raul persisted, the dog rounded on him, grating its teeth in warning. Wayland went into his hut and Raul kicked the door behind him. 'I thought we were friends.'

Wayland tied the goshawk to her perch and lay back on his pallet. He watched the hawk in the smoky light. She'd eaten most of the pigeon and her crop bulged. She stropped her beak on the perch, lifted one foot, extended her middle toe and delicately scratched her throat. The movement agitated the bell on one of her tail feathers. She twisted her head about to settle the contents of her crop. Her feathers relaxed and she drew one clenched foot up under a downy apron. She was asleep. Tomorrow he'd cut one stitch from each eyelid. In a week she would be feeding outdoors in daylight. Another three weeks and she would be flying free. He'd won.

Strange, Wayland thought, how quickly hunger and exhaustion mastered fear and hatred. He was neither jessed nor seeled, rarely went hungry, and could come and go as he pleased. Neither necessity nor affection bound him to the castle, yet at the end of each day, some weakness on his part made him turn his steps back towards the people he loathed. He fingered the cross at his neck. He would escape when spring came, he vowed. He would leave at the same time as the strangers, taking his own path. He blew out the lamp. Turning on his side, he grasped the dog's ruff and wrapped it round his hand, unaware that he used to do the same with his mother's hair.

The dog was his only tangible link with the past, a place he tried to block off. Sometimes, though, it erupted in dreams that woke him in a sweat of horror. And sometimes, like now, it rose up like a picture emerging from a dark pool.

His mother had sent him and his younger sister to gather mushrooms in the forest. He'd been fourteen, his sister ten, the dog just a clumsy overgrown pup. Three years had passed since King Harold's defeat, but Wayland had seen his first Normans only in the last month. From a safe distance he'd watched the soldiers in their ringed armour supervising the construction of their castle on the Tyne.

The farm where he lived lay ten miles upriver, a few acres of clearing in a remnant of ancient wildwood cut by a deep ravine. There were seven in the family. His mother was English, his father a Danish freeman, the son of a Viking who'd sailed for England in the bodyguard of the great Cnut. Grandfather was still alive, a bedridden giant who called on the Norse gods and wore a Hammer of Thor amulet. Wayland had an older brother and sister, Thorkell and Hilda. His little sister was called Edith. At his mother's insistence, all the children had been baptised, the girls taking English names, the boys Danish.

It was a good autumn for mushrooms. As Wayland picked, he could hear the rhythmic blows of his father's axe, a sound as familiar as his heartbeat. When the basket was full, Edith said she wanted to look for a bear. Wayland knew there were no bears left in the forest. Grandfather had killed the last one himself and had one of its teeth to prove it. Wayland wasn't convinced that the claim was true, but he liked the story and he often asked the old man to tell it. Grandpa told him other stories when his mother wasn't around – thrilling, pagan tales about treacherous gods and monsters and the battle at the end of the world.

He found fresh deer slots and began following them to the river, the pup ranging ahead. They could hear water sliding down the ravine. The pup sat and tilted its head on one side, listening with such comic intensity that Edith laughed. The sound of the axe had stopped. Wayland thought he heard a cry. He waited for it to come again, but it didn't. The dog whimpered.

Wayland sat his sister down under a tree and told her not to wander away or wolves would eat her up.

'I'm not afraid of wolves. They only cross the river in winter.'

'Trolls, then. Trolls live in the Pot.'

The Pot was the deepest pool in the ravine, a cauldron of black water walled in by dripping cliffs and overhung by trees that gripped the earth with roots like gnarled fingers. Edith looked towards it through the mossy gloom. She brushed at her cross. 'Can the dog stay with me?'

'You know he won't leave my side. I'll tell you what. While I'm gone, you can think of a name for him.'

'I've already chosen one. It's—'

'Tell me when I get back,' Wayland said, breaking into a run.

The pup thought it was a game and bounded ahead before crouching to spring up in mock ambush. Wayland began to feel a bit foolish. His mother would scold him for leaving Edith alone in the darkening wood.

As he approached the clearing he heard voices and the clinking of harness. He threw himself down, grabbed the pup by the scruff and wormed through the forest litter until he reached the treeline.

There was too much horror to take in at one glance. Two Norman soldiers held Hilda and his mother outside the house. Another pair had pinned his father face down over the chopping block. Thorkell lay on his back, his face a bloody mask. Then Wayland saw the mounted man at the far end of the clearing. He spurred his horse and charged, slashed down and half severed his father's arm. Whooping, the rider galloped to the other end of the clearing, turned and pounded back. This time Wayland saw his father's head roll off the stump and blood squirt from his neck.

His mother and sister were screaming. They were still screaming when the men dragged them into the house. Their screams grew muffled and then stopped. After a while the man who'd murdered his father came out, his face splattered with blood. He took a pitcher of water and poured it over his head. When he mounted his horse, he reeled in the saddle as if drunk. One by one the other men came out, tying up their breeches. Wayland prayed that his mother and sister would come out. After a while smoke coiled from the door. The killers didn't leave. Flames began to lick up the thatch. The blaze grew and the Normans laughed and held out their hands to it. Even where Wayland lay he could feel the singeing gusts. The Normans left. One of them carried a deer carcass slung over his horse. Another was draped with live chickens. The others drove two cows, a horse and oxen before them.

Wayland ran towards the blaze. The heat frizzled his hair and blistered his face before it beat him back. He stood screaming as the roof dropped into the house and a ball of fire rolled into the sky. He watched the walls collapse and then he sank to the ground, his mind numbed by all he had seen.

He became aware of the dog pushing its head against his legs. His face and hands were scalded and peeling. He registered that it was dusk and remembered his sister. He tried to run, but his legs wouldn't obey him. He reeled and tripped, staggered into trees.

The basket of mushrooms was still under the tree, but Edith was gone. He listened. There were only the sounds of the wood settling to rest. He called, softly at first, then louder. An owl shrieked. He found Edith's trail wandering towards the gorge. The trees were thickest in this part of the wood, spreading twilight even on the sunniest days. The dog was too young and shocked to help. It sidled against him, getting under his feet, while he searched and called until it was too dark to see. He slid down with his back against a tree. A wind sprang up and rain began to spit. For a time he continued to call, his voice growing hoarse. Then he sat still, his eyes vacant, the dog pressed shivering against him as he relived one nightmare while anticipating the next.

In the dripping grey dawn he tracked his sister through a graveyard of windfallen giants along the edge of the ravine. Her trail stopped at a hole by the base of an old ash. For a moment he thought she might have fallen into an animal den. But when he peered down through the tangle of roots he saw water far below. Edith's body floated into view, face down, turning in the current, her long blonde hair fanned about her. He climbed down and pulled her out, kissed her white face and held her tight against him. When he let go, he felt something wither and twist inside him. He removed her crucifix, threw back his head and howled at the gods or monsters that had inflicted such hideous cruelties.

From that day on he never spoke a word.

VI

It snowed again and then froze. For a week winter held the country in a deadlock. It froze so hard that shelves of ice formed on the riverbanks and trees split at night with sharp cracks. Inside the great hall the garrison huddled around the hearth like corpses in a prehistoric burial chamber. Fresh food grew short. Men's teeth wobbled in their gums. Every day Wayland and his dog went out to check traps and snares, traipsing through the ice-encased woods like figures in a woodcut. Sometimes Raul accompanied them, his crossbow slung over his back, a knife tucked into loops at the front of his fox fur hat.

A week before Lent the wind shifted in the night and the garrison woke to find winter in retreat. Plates of ice spun down the river. By evening it had spilled over its banks and carried away one of the bridges. Next morning Hero saw an uprooted tree surging down the torrent, a hare clinging to one end of the trunk, a fox facing it at the other end.

Three days later Hero entered the hut to find Vallon lying just as he'd left him, brooding over their confinement.

Hero cleared his throat. 'The waters are starting to subside. In a day or two conditions will be good enough for travel.'

Vallon grunted.

Hero tried again. 'Olbec's announced a hunt for the day after tomorrow.'

'It isn't the hunting season.'

'We need the meat. There'll be a feast in the evening. Drogo wanted you to take the field with him.'

Vallon snorted. 'We know what quarry he's after.'

'Have no fear. Lady Margaret insisted that you accompany her party.'

Vallon's eyes turned. 'Will the Count be with her?'

Hero shook his head. 'His wounds make it too painful to ride. He'll stay behind and organise the festivities.'

Vallon stared off pensively for a moment, then swung his legs to the floor. 'Tell the lady I'd be honoured to attend her.'

Before cock's crow Wayland, with two huntsmen and a forester, left the castle to quest for a stag with at least ten tines on his antlers. The huntsmen were accompanied by lymers – big, heavyset hounds with drooping jowls and doleful expressions. Their function was to locate the stag and track it in silence to its covert. The hunt breakfast was in full swing when one of the huntsmen returned to report that they'd harboured a hart of twelve in a wood beyond the Roman wall. Gravely he uncapped his horn and rolled fumets on to the table. Drogo and his comrades passed the deer droppings about, sniffed them, rolled them between their fingers, and agreed that they belonged to no rascal but a warrantable beast.

Hero watched the hunting party sally out. Ahead went the huntsmen, leading hounds leashed in couples. Drogo led the field and behind them rode the ladies, Margaret wrapped in furs and silks, Vallon at her side on a borrowed palfrey. His hair had been trimmed and fell in auburn waves to his shoulders. His bearing made Hero's heart swell with pride. He waved and received a dignified acknowledgement. Last came the priest, borne along on an ox-drawn butcher's cart, gripping the front rail like a mariner facing an oncoming storm.

The horses cantered away over the turf, throwing up green divots. Clouds sailed across a gentian sky. Snow still lay rotting in the shadows, but banks of primroses had flowered and from every thicket birds sang with pent-up energy. In the fields around the castle peasants followed the age-old rhythm of the plough. Hero closed his eyes, relishing the sun on his face, the smell of turned earth. Spring had arrived. The knot of dread in his guts relaxed. He felt an intense sense of well-being.

When the tableau had passed from sight, he returned to the guesthouse and laid out parchment and gall ink on the rough table. He dipped his quill and raised it like a wand, but the magic he expected to conjure wasn't forthcoming. He knuckled his brow. He scratched his head. He sighed. Transferring thoughts onto parchment was no easy task. So many words to choose from, so many ways of arranging them. He sucked the end of his quill, trying to decide what rhetorical style was most appropriate for his subject.

The flame of creativity dwindled and died. He puffed out his cheeks, crossed his hands behind his head and stared at the roof. The day that had only a short while ago seemed full of promise now stretched into limbo. A bee droned through the door, bumbled around the room and flew back out. Hero looked vacantly through the sunlit doorway. After a while he became aware of the silence. He stood up, tiptoed to the entrance and peered in all directions. The bailey was empty except for two guards sunning themselves outside the gatehouse. He went back inside, lifted his medicine casket from beside his bed and carried it to the table. The lid was carved with floral designs. He raised it, placed one hand under it and pressed one of the carved flowers. The false bottom swung down and out slid the leather folder that Master Cosmas had pressed on him in his dying moments. He opened it. Inside were six manuscript pages. It was a letter – part of a letter – written in poor Greek on stained and creased sheets made, so Cosmas had told him, from pulverised hemp.

Hero's heart had begun to beat fast.

Our Majesty John, by the grace of God and the might of our Lord Jesus, greets his brother ruler, the emperor of the Romans, wishing you health, prosperity and continued enjoyment of divine favour.

Our Excellency has been informed that reports of our greatness have reached you. If you wish to know the vastness of our power, then believe that our Majesty exceeds in might and riches all the kings of the earth. Only if you can count the stars of the heavens and the sands of the desert will you be able to measure the vastness of our realm. Our Magnificence rules the Three Indias and our lands extend from Greater India, where the body of our beloved St Thomas the Apostle rests – he who brought the gospel of Jesus to our realm – to Far India across the sea.

Hero turned the pages, skipping dozens of paragraphs describing in mind-boggling detail the wonders and amazements of this ruler's territories.

As a devout Christian, the writer went on, *it grieves us to hear that a great schism has opened between the Church in Rome and the Church in Constantinople. Surely it is Satan's work that enmity and strife have broken out in Christendom at a time when she has never been more threatened. Noble brother, I beseech you to make peace with the father in Rome and set aside your differences so that you stand united against our common foes, the Arabs and Turks. Be assured you will not face them alone. Know that we are under vow to visit the sepulchre of our Lord Jesus with a great army, as befits the glory of our Majesty, to subdue and destroy the enemies of Christ, and to exalt his blessed name.*

In token of our Christian friendship, I send you not gold or jewels – notwithstanding we possess treasures unequalled under heaven. Instead I send you riches for the soul, the true account of Jesus's life and teachings, written by he who knew him best, he who alone possesses the hidden wisdom imparted by our Lord Saviour during ...

A shadow slipped through the door. Hero looked up to register Richard's presence. There was no time to hide the letter. Covering it with his blank sheet of parchment, he began to scrawl the first thing that came into his head.

Another wonder that Master Cosmas told me. In the year I was born a great fire appeared in the southern sky and burned so bright that it was no hardship to read outside at midnight. For ten years the light shone, gradually waning, and when it was gone that part of the heavens where it had blazed was filled with many stars that had not shone before.

Richard had sidled up and was leaning over in a way that Hero found intensely irritating. 'What are you writing?' the Norman asked from behind his hand.

'An account of our journey. If you don't mind, I require peace to pen my recollections.'

'When your narrative reaches these parts, you should include a description of the wall built by Hadrian. Not far from here stand shrines and castles unchanged since Rome's legions occupied them.'

'That might be worth a visit,' Hero conceded. 'Perhaps I'll go tomorrow.'

'Not on your own. It's too dangerous.'

Hero smiled condescendingly. 'You're speaking to a man who's crossed the Alps.'

'A month before you arrived, three scouts rode north and never returned. The Scots probably ate them.'

Hero went back to his manuscript, but found he'd lost the thread.

'I'll arrange an escort if you teach me the mystery of writing.'

'It takes years of study.'

'I would be a diligent student. I'd like to cultivate at least one talent.'

Hero put down his pen. 'Show me your face. Come on. Don't be shy.'

Richard lowered his hand, revealing a plum-coloured birthmark that stained one cheek from mouth to ear. His features were pale and pinched, but his eyes, Hero decided, held a spark of intelligence.

'I've seen worse disfigurements.'

'Is it a bargain?'

Hero gave a resigned sigh. 'We begin with alpha-beta, the letters that form the bricks of language. First is alpha, from the Hebrew hieroglyph of an ox's head, signifying "leader".'

The light dimmed. A burly figure blocked the doorway. Richard jumped up, knocking over the inkpot.

'Now look what you've done. Your hands are as clumsy as your wits.'

'Get out,' Olbec ordered, cuffing Richard as he scuttled past. 'God, how could I have fathered such a maggot? Can't handle a sword or lance. Can't stay on a horse. Should have been drowned at birth.' Olbec's attention turned to Hero, who was frantically blotting the page. 'Forget about that,' he growled.

'He's ruined my only sheet.'

'I might be able to help there,' Olbec said. He straddled the bench and examined Hero like a peasant sizing up livestock. 'A doctor, eh?'

'Not yet licensed. I still have to complete my practical study, and then I intend to do a year's anatomy course.'

'How old are you?'

'Nineteen this summer.'

'Dear Lord, what I'd give to be nineteen again. Everything to look forward to – battles to fight, lands to win, women to bed.'

'I'm not sure that my vocation leads me on such an heroic course. If you'd care to tell me what ails you. I understand that your wounds trouble you.'

Olbec glanced at the doorway.

'Nothing you tell me will pass beyond these walls,' said Hero. 'My oath to Hippocrates binds me to confidentiality.'

Olbec prodded the Sicilian's chest. 'Forget Hippo-what's-his-name. You'll keep your trap shut because I'll cut your heart out if you repeat one word.' He went to the entrance, peered about, then pulled the door shut. 'What opinion have you formed of my wife?'

'A chaste and pious lady of impeccable morals,' Hero said in a rush.

Olbec digested this character reference. 'All those things, of course, but speaking man to man, I must tell you that my lady knows how to give and receive earthly pleasures.'

'Piety and passion in perfect balance. You're blessed, my lord.'

'Not as much as I'd like to be. Margaret hasn't spoken to me since the night I refused her plea for an expedition to Norway. Women wield silence as soldiers use a lance.'

'I sympathise, sir. My sisters made my—'

'Younger than me, of course. No problem there until I picked up this wound at Senlac. We were blade to blade with Harold's shield wall. One of his house carls – big as a bear – swung at me with his axe. An inch closer and he'd have split me from crown to chops.' Olbec massaged his groin. 'A miracle he didn't relieve me of my manhood.'

Spare me his intimate wounds, Hero prayed.

Olbec drummed on the table. 'I'll be plain. My wife wants another child. She's young enough and – well, she fears for the succession.'

'But you have three sons.'

'Walter's a hostage, Richard's a milksop, and Drogo has too much red choler for his own good.' Olbec hesitated. 'Last Christmas a Scottish witch came begging at the castle gate. In return for a sop she told my lady's fortune. The ungrateful hag prophesied that only one of Lady Margaret's menfolk would be alive to celebrate Christ's next birthday. Superstitious rubbish, of course, but you know what women are like. Or you soon will,' he added on a glum note. 'Anyway, the problem is ... the problem is ...'

'You fail to rise to the occasion,' Hero prompted.

A squall crossed Olbec's face. Then he laughed. 'You might look like a frightened frog, but you're not stupid.'

'I recommend rest and sweet wine. I've heard that mead's a good aphrodisiac.'

'Drink it by the bucketful. Tastes like sweetened horse piss and has about the same effect.'

'Perhaps if you drank less.'

'Arabs,' Olbec said, taking a veer. 'You have them in Sicily. I've heard they're a virile race.'

'As are you Normans.'

'Except the Arabs use potions.'

'Their pharmaceutical skills are more advanced than ours,' Hero admitted. 'They have many potions. There's one efficacious compound that they apply to their feet.'

'Feet? Who's talking about feet? It's not my feet that let me down.'

'No, sir. You refer to your *membranus lignae*. Your staff of manhood.'

'If you mean my prick, we're speaking a common language.'

'Indeed.'

'Right. Here's the deal. Prepare a potion that will make me delight my lady and I'll give you enough parchment to write the gospels.'

'But I don't have the necessary ingredients.'

'I've told the quartermaster to give you everything you need.'

Hero could imagine what manner of things lay mouldering in the castle's apothecary. Newts, nail parings, withered sheep's foetuses ...

'Well, what do you say?'

Hero nodded dumbly.

'Good,' Olbec said, pushing himself up.

When Hero examined the contents of his pharmacopoeia, he found plenty of medicines to soothe the senses, but nothing to inflame them. He clasped his head and groaned.

The quartermaster was a surly tyrant, the remote but undisputed ruler of the kitchen annexe, his presence signalled by snarls and obscenities and the frequent yelps of his unfortunate scullions. He eyed Hero over the counter with outright hostility.

'What's this about? What's the boss after?'

Hero made his first demand modest. 'Honey.'

With ill grace, the quartermaster produced a pot and banged it down.

'Also, some pepper and ginger.'

The quartermaster recoiled like a mother accosted by a baby-snatcher. 'You're not having my pepper. Do you know how much it costs?'

'Without pepper, I can't formulate the physic to treat your lord's condition.'

The quartermaster crossed his arms. 'What condition?'

'That's a private matter between patient and physician.'

'Private be buggered. The whole world knows what's wrong with the old man.'

Hero glanced behind him before replying. 'You mean the pain and stiffness in his thighs?'

'Ha! It's not stiffness that plagues him. The opposite more like. Man that age, wife with appetites.' The quartermaster tapped his nose.

'Then give me the pepper I need to restore harmony to the marriage.'

'Not a chance.'

'Very well,' Hero said in a tremulous voice. 'I'll report your lack of cooperation.' He made to leave.

'Oi, pop-eye. Come back. This is what you want.'

Hero sniffed at a small linen bag. 'What is it?'

'My secret, but I guarantee it'll put iron into the limpest of tools.' The quartermaster folded his arms again. 'Would the young scholar be requiring anything else?'

'Only some leeches. Oh, and a mortar and pestle.'

'Sweet Jesus,' the quartermaster sighed, and lumbered back into his sanctum. He returned and slammed them on the counter. 'Now fuck off.'

At the wall the company divided, the hunters cantering north towards a block of woodland, Lady Margaret's party dismounting under a Roman milecastle overlooking the North Tyne. Vallon gave Margaret his arm. Together they walked through an arched gateway into a hushed courtyard carpeted with turf. In the far corner a flight of broken steps climbed to a wall-walk. Opposite the gate, accessed from the walkway, was a square tower. Stairs climbed the interior to the roof, where servants had spread cushions. Vallon crossed to the parapet and gazed down on the ruins of a Roman fort similar to those he'd seen in southern France and Spain. From the wood came bugle notes and the cries of the huntsmen encouraging the lymers: *Ho moy, ho moy! Cy va, cy va! Tut, tut, tut!*

A page came puffing backwards up the steps, lugging a wicker basket. The women nibbled honeyed angelica and sipped posset and chatted about the weather and their children and the frightfulness of life on the frontier. Vallon joined in the small talk until his face ached from forced smiling. He was beginning to think that this was indeed just a picnic when Margaret clapped her hands.

'I know you're all curious about our handsome French captain. He's been our guest for three weeks and we still know hardly anything about him. The captain's uncomfortable in the presence of so many ladies. I think we'll get nothing out of him unless I quiz him alone.'

She shooed her giggling entourage downstairs. The priest was last to leave and Vallon could see from the sweat greasing his brow that his anxiety went deeper than concern about leaving a stranger alone with his lord's wife.

The women's voices faded. Margaret turned her rouged and smiling face. 'I mean it, I won't rest until I've sucked you dry.'

'My history would be a great disappointment to you.'

'Men don't know what excites a woman's interest. It's not descriptions of dreary battles that titillate us. It's the subtle personal details.'

'You'll find me most unsubtle.'

'Then let's start at the beginning. Are you married? Do you have family?'

'No wife or family. No estate or property. I earn my living by the sword alone. As you must have gathered, it's not a good living.'

'It's a handsome weapon, though. The inlay on the hilt is exquisite, and I positively *covet* the jewel on the pommel.'

'It's Moorish, forged in Toledo from steel, not iron. It's harder than a Norman blade.'

Her eyes widened. 'Harder than a Norman sword. Can I feel it?'

'Madam.'

'No, let me draw it out for myself.'

Using both hands, she slid the blade from its scabbard. The effort brought colour to her cheeks. 'How bright it gleams. When did you last use it?'

'Against the Moors in Spain.'

'That long ago. A blade as fine as this should be drawn more often.' She breathed on it, looking up at him from under her plucked brows, and rubbed the steel with the cuff of her gown. 'Let me feel the tip. Oh, how keen it is. Look how it's pricked me.'

Vallon held out his hand. 'Your husband wouldn't be pleased to learn that you'd taken harm from my sword.'

'I promise I won't tell him, no matter how deep you thrust.'

The faint baying of the hounds rose to a demented yodelling.

'The hounds have found,' Vallon said, taking back the sword. 'You don't want to miss the chase.' He went and stood at the parapet and watched the wood. Some of the hunters had taken up positions around it.

'Some would call your manner intimidating.'

'I'm sorry my society disappoints you.'

'No, I admire a man who suggests strength rather than flaunts it. Besides, I suspect you aren't as unfeeling as you pretend.'

'The stag,' Vallon said.

It emerged from the forest and plunged down a ribbon of snow, the hounds pouring after it. Drogo headed the field, lashing his horse.

Margaret traced a line down the back of Vallon's hand. 'I'm sure that given time, I could bring you to bay.'

He trapped her hand. 'A beast at bay is dangerous.'

She brushed against him. 'Risk adds to the pleasure.'

52

Vallon stepped away. 'You forget I'm your lord's guest.'

She pouted. 'Perhaps there's another reason for your coldness. I've seen the way the Greek youth follows you with his great mooning eyes.'

Vallon looked into her face. 'Why don't you tell me your real purpose.'

For a moment it seemed that she would continue her pretence. Or perhaps her flirtation was genuine. But then she turned and crossed her arms as if the air had grown chilly. 'I own land in Normandy. I'm prepared to use it as security against a loan to finance an expedition to the north.'

Vallon made no response. The stag was keeping to the valley rim. So far, the hounds hadn't closed the gap.

'I want you to command it.'

'No.'

'Think of it as a trading expedition. You can use any surplus to buy furs, ivory and slaves. Any profit you make is yours. For my part, all I want is my son safe at home.'

'It's not worth the gamble.'

'It's a more rewarding proposition than the one that brought you here in rags.'

'I'm not talking about *my* chances. As soon as your money's in my hands, what's to stop me stealing it?'

'Your word. I'd trust that from a man who travelled so far on Walter's behalf.'

'I've never met Sir Walter. I was never in Anatolia and first heard the name Manzikert weeks after the battle. Your son's welfare is of no interest to me.'

Margaret's lips whitened. 'You mean he's dead?' She clenched her hands.

He caught her wrists. 'The documents are genuine. Your son survived the battle. As far as I know, he's still alive.'

She sagged against him, her voice muffled by his chest. 'Why did you come here? What game are you playing?'

'No game. Let's just say that I was caught up in one of fate's eddies. I won't be sucked into that pool again.'

She pulled back. 'I would still trust you. If you planned to cheat me, you wouldn't have admitted your lie.'

'Mother love is blind.'

Margaret stamped her foot. 'If I repeat what you've told me, Drogo will kill you on the spot.'

'He plans to kill me anyway.'

The stag reached a high hedge and broke right, towards the mile-castle. By the time it realised its error and leaped the obstacle, it was close enough for Vallon to see its backward staring eye. The hounds poured over the hedge in a hysterical wave. They were going to catch it, Vallon thought.

'I can help you escape.'

Vallon turned.

'Strong drink will flow tonight,' she said. 'By midnight almost everyone will be unconscious. If you leave when the matins bell chimes, you'll find the gate open.'

Vallon put Margaret's larger scheme out of his mind. There would be time enough to consider it once they got clear – if they got clear. 'That will give us only a few hours' start. Drogo will catch us before we reach the next valley.'

'Take the falconer. He knows every inch of this country.'

Vallon focused on practicalities. 'Horses?'

'I can't arrange that without exciting suspicion. Besides, speed won't save you. Guile and good fortune are your only weapons, and you obviously have guile.'

Vallon was thinking fast now. 'We'll need provisions. It will be days before we can risk going near habitation.'

Margaret pointed at the basket. 'Food and blankets.' She reached into her cuff and produced a purse. 'Enough silver to get you to Norwich.'

'Is that where the deeds are to be handed over?'

'The moneylender's called Aaron. The king brought him to England from Rouen, not far from my estate. My family's done business with him before. I've prepared letters to send to him. They'll be in his hands by the time you arrive.'

Vallon watched the hunt. The stag was tiring and the hounds were closing on it. Riders converged from different directions.

'Richard will be going with you.'

'No! My servant's enough of a handicap as it is.'

'Richard's not such a fool as he looks. He helped me hatch this scheme. He acts as my attorney. He'll present the deeds and seal the contract. Besides, his presence will give you safe conduct. If you're challenged by Norman patrols, Richard will show them documents vouching that you're carrying out a commission on my behalf.'

'Does the Count know?'

'He suspects. Don't worry, I know how to soothe his anger.'

'Not Drogo's, though.'

'He won't harm me in his father's house.'

The stag entered the ruined fort. Confused by the maze of walls and trenches, it headed one way then the other. It scaled a section of tumbled rampart, saw a vertical drop on the other side, and ran along the wall until it reached a dead end. Cornered, it turned to face the oncoming pack and lowered its antlers. The nearest riders raised their horns to blow the mote and recheat, signalling that the stag had been bayed. Drogo rode up and leaped off his horse. The hounds closed on the stag and swirled around it.

'If you knew Walter, you would gladly do as I ask,' said Margaret. 'I know he lied to you – I mean, I know he lied – but you must understand his motives. He's not like Drogo. He has charm and grace. Even the Count favours him over his natural son.'

One of the huntsmen darted behind the stag to cut its hamstring. Drogo advanced through the heaving mass of hounds, his sword drawn. Vallon saw the hart stagger and go down. The hunters blew the death, and the refrain was taken up all along the valley.

Margaret dangled the purse. Vallon pushed it aside.

'I'll give you my decision this evening.'

The hunters returned under a bloodshot sky, the priest sharing the trundling cart with the butchered stag and the carcass of a boar the party had killed in the afternoon. In the hall, servants piled the hearth so high that the flames threatened the roof. The men were already drunk when a procession of skivvies carried out the stag and placed it over the coals on a spit turned by cranked treadles.

Seizing his moment, Hero gave Olbec the potion. 'Apply it shortly before you retire. You say that your wife wishes to conceive. What position do you usually assume?'

'On top. What do the Arabs do?'

'They have many positions,' Hero said, relying on information picked up from whispers between his sisters. 'One of them, particularly recommended for couples wishing to conceive ... No, it's disrespectful to talk of carnal matters when your lady sits only a few feet away.'

Olbec seized his sleeve. 'No, go on.'

'From behind, the lady on her knees, head between her arms.'

'Like a ram, eh? Grr! Makes my blood rise to think of it.'

After the venison had been ceremonially carved and served, Olbec rose, declaring that his wife's expedition had fatigued her but that the merriment should continue after they had retired. In two days the Lent fast would begin, so eat, drink, make merry. The company stood and banged their drinking vessels. Olbec weaved in Hero's direction and slapped down a thick ream of manuscripts. 'Here you are. Got them from the priest.'

'You've taken the physic?'

'The whole bottle. I can feel it working already.'

'I made it extra strength. I hope it didn't produce too fierce a sensation.'

Olbec belched. 'Burned a bit as it went down.'

'Down?'

The old goat winked. 'I'm not taking any chances. I drank it.'

Hero riffled through the manuscripts. They were beautiful, each page illuminated with gilt and paintings in miniature. His face fell. 'I can't deface holy script.'

Olbec jabbed the wad of parchment. 'Nothing sacred about this lot. It's just a collection of worthless English chronicles and a few rhymes and riddles. I got a clerk in Durham to translate some. Here's one I remember. It goes like this:

I'm a strange creature, for I satisfy women,
a service to the neighbours! No one suffers
at my hands except for my slayer.
I grow very tall, erect in a bed,
I'm hairy underneath. From time to time
a beautiful girl, the brave daughter
of some churl dares to hold me,
grips my russet skin, robs me of my head
and puts me in the pantry. At once that girl
with plaited hair who has confined me
remembers our meeting. Her eye moistens.

Olbec winked. 'What's the answer?'

Hero blushed.

Olbec pinched his cheek. 'You've got a dirty mind, young monk.' He swayed towards the door, where his wife waited with a fixed smile. 'It's an onion,' he bawled.

Hero tried to spot Richard among the revellers. He was ashamed of his outburst over the spilt ink. He also kept one eye on the door, half-expecting the Count to come crashing through in impotent fury. The orgy of feasting had ended and now the soldiers were playing some kind of drinking game that involved daubing their faces with soot, standing on benches stacked on the tables, and chanting an obscene ditty which Drogo orchestrated with his sword. In another part of the hall, Raul arm-wrestled two Normans simultaneously while a third soldier poured mead into his upraised mouth. A table collapsed and a brawl broke out. Hero had lost count of the ale cups he'd drunk. He was reaching for another when a hand closed over the vessel.

He smiled woozily up at Vallon.

'Time to sober up. We're leaving tonight. Put your eyes back in their sockets. Go to our quarters and pack. When you've done that, wait for me in the falconer's hut.'

'But I can't. Tomorrow I'm going to the Roman wall with Richard.'

Vallon leaned forward. 'I'll make it plain. Do as I say or stay here and go down into a cold grave.'

As soon as Hero tottered into the cold damp air, nausea swept over him. He clutched his knees and vomited. When he'd finished retching he heard a laugh. Drogo straddled the doorway, bare-chested and sweating, a cup dangling in one hand, his sword loose in the other.

'Off to beddy-byes, you Greek poof. Master will be along soon to tuck you up.'

He reeled inside and pulled the door shut, leaving Hero in the dark. Deeper than dark. Thick mist had risen from the river, making a mystery of everything around him. He tried to gather his bearings. The guesthouse was set against the stockade to the left of the hall. He groped through the fog, hands outstretched like a ghost.

He was almost sober by the time he found the guest quarters. Hands fumbling, he bundled everything into a blanket and embarked on another blind journey to Wayland's hut. He collided with a building and felt his way along the walls until he found the door.

'Wayland, are you there? It's Hero. Master Vallon sent me.'

No answer. Opening the door a crack, he saw two tremulous lights. He shrank back. He had the wrong building. This was the chapel, and there was a man praying before the altar. An instant later he realised that the kneeling man was Vallon.

He waited for his master to finish. It seemed to him that Vallon was making a confession. He caught the occasional words – 'penance' and 'blood of the innocent', and then quite clearly he heard Vallon say, 'I'm a lost soul. What does it matter where my journey takes me or whether I reach the end?'

The bleak utterance chilled Hero. He must have moved. Vallon stopped. 'Who's there?'

'Only me, sir.'

Vallon stood and walked towards him. 'How long have you been listening? What did you hear?'

'Nothing, sir. I took a wrong turning in the dark. I have the baggage. Where are we going?'

'Away. I always light a candle before leaving on a campaign.' Vallon gestured towards the altar. 'I've lit one for you, too.'

Campaign? What campaign?

Vallon steered him to Wayland's hut. The interior was rank with animal smells. A lamp lit Richard's anxious face. Another person floated out of the shadows, a ring gleaming in one ear, his hair in a sidelock.

'What's that tosspot doing here?' Vallon demanded.

Raul was pie-eyed. He swayed forward. 'At your service, Captain. You'd have found me in more soldier-like condition if Wayland had told me about your flight earlier.'

Vallon stepped towards Wayland. 'Who else knows?'

Wayland gave a quick shake of his head.

Vallon shook Raul by the shoulders. 'Tell me why I should take you. Speak up.'

Raul fumbled for his crossbow, turning like a dog searching for its tail. 'Captain, I can put a bolt through a man's eye at a hundred paces. I've served in three armies around the Baltic and I know how to deal with rascally Norwegian merchants.' He screwed up his eyes and held up a finger, his face contorted by some gastric turmoil. 'And I'm strong as a bear.' He gave a flabby wave that covered Hero and Richard. 'How far do you think you'll get with these two sissys to nurse?' Blinking, he pawed at Hero's arm. 'No disrespect.'

Vallon pushed him away in disgust and addressed Wayland. 'It's blacker than Hades out there. Are you sure you can lead us to the Roman tower?'

Wayland nodded and held up a coil of rope knotted at intervals. He'd muzzled his dog and fitted it with a spiked collar.

The bell began to chime a solemn end to the day's frivolities. 'That's the signal,' Vallon said. 'There's no time to lose. The mist is on our side for now, but it will slow our escape and it will soon disappear when the sun rises. We move as fast as we can.'

Wayland picked up two draped cages and slung them over his shoulders. He unmuzzled his dog, reached for his bow and stepped through the door, the rope trailing behind him. The fugitives took hold of it, each grasping a knot, and went out into the soggy night.

A few diehards were still whooping it up at the hall, but the rest of the world had gone to sleep. The runaways shuffled forward like felons or penitents. They hadn't gone far when Hero shunted into the man in front and the man behind barked his heel. Hero heard muted voices from above. They must be under the gatehouse.

'Is it open?' he heard Vallon whisper.

Hero didn't hear the reply, but soon the rope tightened in his hands and he found himself moving again. He didn't know he was at the gate until he was through and someone slid the bar to behind them.

'Stay together,' Vallon whispered. 'If anyone gets separated, no one's going back for them.'

VII

Wayland led the way up a wooded hillside with the runaways blundering behind him. Condensation pattered through the branches and splashed on their heads with maddening unpredictability. After a long, fractious climb they cleared the mist and saw the milecastle ahead of them. By the time they reached it, a seam of cold yellow light was cracking open on the eastern horizon. Wayland looked back over a sea of cloud broken by dark reefs and islands. Away to the west, snow-covered hills glimmered under the fading stars. Not a breath of wind.

Richard sobbed on the grass as if his heart would burst. Raul went into the tower to collect the supplies.

'Look,' Hero wheezed, pointing at a tiny silhouette on a summit miles to the south. 'There's the gibbet we passed on our journey here.'

Vallon straightened up, panting. 'At the pace you travel, we'll all be food for crows before noon. Which way now?'

Wayland pointed west, along the wall. Its course was visible for miles, rising and falling through the mist like the backbone of a sea monster.

'Let's go,' Vallon said, leading off. The other runaways jerked into motion. Vallon glanced back. 'What are you waiting for?'

Wayland gestured at the cages.

'He wants to release the hawks,' Raul said.

'I don't give a rat's arse what he wants.'

'Captain, Wayland does things his own way.'

'Not any more. And that goes for you, too.'

'Understood, sir, but we need Wayland more than he needs us. Best leave him be.' Raul emitted a rasping belch, shouldered the basket and lurched off like a demonic pedlar. After a moment's angry indecision, Vallon followed him.

Wayland was in no hurry. He waited until the sun rose and the cloud ocean flushed pink before opening the cage containing the goshawk. It gave him a glare, bobbed its head and rowed away into the mist. By evening it would be as wild as the day he'd caught it. He released the peregrines. He hadn't flown them since Sir Walter's depar-ture more than a year ago. They spent their days blocked out in the weathering yard, fanning their wings and tracking their wild kin cir-cling down the wind. The falcon flew heavily and landed on the tower, but the tiercel winnowed into the sky as if he'd been waiting for this moment and knew exactly what course to follow. Up and up he went, a dark flickering star that Wayland watched as if it carried his hopes and dreams. He didn't blink until the sky closed over it.

The fugitives had reached the next milecastle. Vallon turned and gestured, then dropped his arm and led the ragtag caravan away.

When they had walked out of his life, Wayland passed through the castle gate. In the long shadows the mounds and hollows in the courtyard resembled graves. His gaze wandered over the empty parapets. He smacked his palms together and the clap bounced back from the walls like an echo through time. He scratched the dog's head. *It's just you and me now.*

He frowned and went back through the gate. The faint tolling of a bell told him that the escape had been discovered. He sat down, imagining the scene at the castle – the soldiers with thumping headaches and addled eyes cursing as they tried to disentangle armour and harness with hands that seemed to have sprouted five thumbs. Their horses would be sore from yesterday's hunt, but the Normans would use dogs to track the runaways. They wouldn't get far. Already the mist was lifting.

Wayland shouldered his pack and set off downhill on a course that would bring him to the South Tyne miles upstream. He had no qualms about abandoning the fugitives. Vallon and Hero meant nothing to him, and Richard was a Norman and therefore a sworn enemy. He bore Raul no ill will, nor was he bound to him by friendship. He had no friends. He didn't need friends. He was like the goshawk, a shadow in the forest, gone in the first glimpse.

In any case, there was nothing he could do to save them. He'd only agreed to Vallon's request because it suited his own purposes. Their flight would distract the Normans while he made good his own escape. By nightfall, when they were lying hacked in pieces, he'd be safe in a forest hideaway.

As if some force was acting against his limbs, he found his steps slowing until he came to a stop. The dog watched him, ears pricked. Wayland looked back at the wall, then down into the valley. He leaned and spat. The dog, anticipating his next move, sprang away downhill. Wayland whistled and turned back towards the wall. I'm not doing it for the strangers, he told himself. I'm doing it for the look on Drogo's face when he realises who's outwitted him.

By the time he caught up with the fugitives it was broad daylight and only a few ribbons of mist clung to the slopes. The country on all sides was dreary common, open and almost treeless.

'We have to get off the wall,' Vallon gasped.

Wayland lay down and put his ear to the antique paving.

'How far are they behind us?'

Wayland pointed at a milecastle and held up two fingers.

He scourged them on, amazed at how slowly other people moved. They were nearly at the next castle when he stopped and put a finger to his lips. Soon they all heard it – the distant belling of hounds. Hero and Richard stumbled on, throwing terrified glances behind them. They came over a rise and a flock of sheep stampeded across a part-walled enclosure below. The sheep stopped in a bunch, all looking back, the ewes stamping their feet. Two mean-looking dogs streaked over the turf. A boy and a girl emerged from behind a cairn and stared up at the fugitives.

'That's all we need,' Hero groaned.

The children ran at the sheep, waving sticks and crying out. The dogs turned and chivvied the flock through a gap and down into a gulley.

Wayland stripped Raul and Hero of their cloaks. Richard cringed away. 'Give it to him,' Vallon said, pulling off his cape.

Wayland pushed him to the edge of the wall and pointed at the gulley.

'He wants us to follow the sheep. Quick, before the soldiers come in sight.'

Wayland grabbed Raul and mimed the route they must take. *South to the river then west to the first ford. On the other side follow the river until you reach a stream flowing in from the south. Go up the valley until the stream divides. Wait for me there.*

Raul slapped Wayland's shoulder to show that he understood, took hold of Richard and plunged off the wall. Wayland didn't wait to see how they got on. He tied some of the runaways' clothes to his girdle, the rest to the dog's collar, then took from his pack a bag containing a concoction of musk and castor. He smeared the foul-smelling grease on his feet. The hue and cry drew closer.

The next section of wall ran as straight as a rule. Wayland dropped into the great ditch on the south side and broke into an easy lope, matching the dog stride for stride. A milecastle slid by. The next one stuck up like a rotten molar. Wayland scaled the broken turret and lay facing the way he had come. His breathing eased. On a stone beside him a bored or homesick legionnaire had scratched a prayer or obscenity or declaration of love. A lark sang its heart out so high in the blue that Wayland couldn't spot it – singing at heaven's gate, his mother would have said.

When Wayland looked down, he saw riders stitched into the landscape on each side of the wall. One, two, three. They disappeared into a dip and others took their place. When all were clear, Wayland had counted thirteen, plus four hounds.

The hounds checked at the spot where the fugitives had left the wall. One of them ran down into the sheep pasture. The others didn't follow. Their baying intensified. A rider rode after the wayward hound and whipped it back into line. The pack drew on.

Wayland slithered down from the tower. Ahead the way divided, a broad track descending through gentler terrain to the south, the wall switchbacking along a scarp with a steep drop on the north face. A moor dotted by loughs sloped up to a forest of ancient pines. He'd been in the forest years ago with his father and they had stood at this same spot.

'See the trees in front,' his father had said. 'Those are the champions, frozen in their advance by a thunderbolt thrown by Odin.'

'Our mother says Odin and all the other gods don't exist,' he'd said. 'She says there's only one God and his son is Jesus Christ, the light of the world.'

His father had scuffed Wayland's hair. 'Jesus has yet to shine his light into all parts. But don't tell your mother I said so or she'll deny me all comforts for a month.'

Wayland checked the knots securing the cast-offs. He followed the wall, his breathing growing harsher with the ascent. When he reached the first crag, he scrambled down where a horse couldn't follow and hared off north, trying to keep below the contours. The land grew wilder, rough pasture and cottongrass giving way to heather and springy mosses. Drab little birds started up at his feet.

He reached the treeline and looked back. The frieze of riders was climbing the scarp, and from the way they rode their mounts he knew they hadn't spotted his breakout. He jogged into the forest.

This was where the real effort had to be made, distance gained until the hunters had been lured so far from their quarry that they would need another day to recover from the deception. Wayland broke into a run and his mind closed down. All he was conscious of was his feet flying over the ground, the trees sliding back, the sun flickering between their high black crowns. He emerged from the forest on to an empty moor and ran on. Cresting a ridge, he saw in the distance two men astride shaggy ponies who stood in their stirrups to better make him out. When he went over the next horizon they were still watching, wondering perhaps if the running man and his giant dog were flesh and blood or apparitions from a mythical past.

On he went, running, trotting or walking as the going dictated, until he came to the rim of a wide basin thinly wooded with birches. At the bottom a burn swollen by meltwater tumbled down steps before dividing around a boulder and plunging into a clough. He untied the cast-offs and stowed them in his backpack. While he waited for his breathing to slow, he studied the waterfall, calculating the distance from the bank to the boulder and from there to the far side. Thirty feet at least. The current dashed at the rock, sometimes washing over it. He couldn't cross in two separate moves. All or nothing.

He swallowed two deep breaths and hurtled down the slope. By the time he came to the burn he couldn't have stopped if he'd wanted to. He took off too short, sprang off the rock, and hung for an age before crashing on to the other bank with a force that jarred him to his eyeballs. The dog thumped into the heather beside him. Wayland gave a breathless laugh and ruffled its mane. He drank from the peaty stream and planned his next move. Not far above them lay a whinstone slab half buried in rank heather. They sank down against it and shared meat and bread.

The day was warm and still, the clouds anchored to the ground by their shadows. Budding leaves hazed the birches in luminous green. A moor owl quartered the opposite slope. The bugling of the hounds woke Wayland from a doze. He watched them work down the scent line and recognised them by their markings – Marte and Marteau, Ostine and Lose. Marteau ran lame, skipping along on three legs, the fourth loosely tucked up.

Riders notched the skyline. They remained on the ridge for some time, searching for movement. By now they must be wondering how such pedestrian quarry could outpace them for so long. They started their descent and from the way the horses sidestepped, Wayland knew they were pretty used up. He smeared peat on his face and drew sacking over his hair. He selected his heaviest arrow and stuck it in the ground by his bow.

The hounds rushed up to the waterfall and jostled on the brink. They tested the current and found it too strong. Their voices died. They cast upstream and down, each time returning to the fall.

The riders pulled up. Their horses were blowing hard. Some soldiers dismounted. The rest slumped over their horses' necks. Their sweat-streaked faces were still besooted and the smudges around their bloodshot eyes gave them the look of plague victims. Some wore no armour. Drax had pulled on his mail over his nightshirt. Drogo's mount was lathered and its head splashed with pink froth. Man or beast, he used both the same.

The huntsman scratched his head. 'The hounds say they crossed here.'

Drogo slid off his horse. 'Don't be an imbecile. The current would have swept them over the fall.'

'One of them crossed.'

Drogo jerked. 'Wayland?'

The huntsman nodded. 'I saw him course a deer once and he leaped a chasm I wouldn't have set a horse at.'

'Then where are the rest of them?' Drogo surveyed all around. 'It's a ruse. They must have backtracked. They can't be far.'

'They're not here. The scent's fresh. They're on foot. We should have caught up with them long ago. Wayland's leading us a dance.'

Drogo clubbed the huntsman to the ground. 'Where did we lose them?'

The man felt his jaw. 'I don't know,' he mumbled.

Drogo kicked him. 'Tell me, damn you.'

'Back at the wall where the hounds checked and Ostine began following a different line. I thought that sheep had led her astray because the others went on stronger than before. Since then they've run steadfast.'

Drogo stared back in a frenzy of disbelief. 'By now they could be across the Tyne. They could be in the next county.'

Wayland notched arrow to bowstring.

Drogo's eyes switched. 'Who's got the freshest horse? Guilbert, ride for home and send parties in all directions. Raise the alarm in Durham. Send word to York. I'll follow you direct.' He caught hold of his horse and dragged himself up. He stared across the river, his eyes burning like coals. 'The bastard can't be far away. He's probably watching us.'

'We'll pin him another day,' Roussel said.

Drogo's gaze skewered him. 'None of this would be necessary if you and Drax had dealt with the Frank. Well, now the two of you can make amends. Take the huntsman and four others.' Drogo gathered his reins. 'Nothing less than the falconer's head on a spike will make me forgive you.'

Wayland stood, drew, aimed and loosed. The arrow skewed off Drogo's mailed shoulder. His horse reared and the other riders milled, grasping for their weapons.

Wayland bellied away through the heather. Aimless bolts hissed overhead. When he was out of range, he stood up. Drogo sat clutching his shoulder, though the arrow hadn't penetrated. The riders had closed up in combat formation, shield to shield. Wayland brandished his bow. He threw back his head and spread his arms in a wordless display of triumph.

In slanting afternoon sunshine, he sat at the edge of the wildwood and watched his hunters far below picking their way across the South Tyne. The huntsman carried lame Marteau over his saddle, and the other hounds quested in silence. When all seven riders had crossed, Wayland rose and massaged his aching calves. Since dawn he'd covered more than twenty miles. He yoked his bow across his shoulders and went into the trees, up through the childhood smells of violets and wood anemones. The dog remembered the forest and stuck close to heel, its tail drooping. Wayland entered the home clearing with the weary tread of a mourner. Ash and hazel had colonised the cultivated strips and the place where the house had stood was a riot of nettles.

Behind the house a byre had collapsed into a tangle of poles choked by ivy and brambles. He pushed between them. They weren't stout enough to stop a charging horse, but the weeds grew dense enough to screen him from sight. He'd passed several spots where he could have ambushed the Normans without much risk to himself, but he wanted them to know why he'd led them here. Roussel and Drax had been members of the gang that had murdered his family; he wanted to see recognition flare before he killed them.

While he waited, he picked burrs from between the dog's pads. He took six ash arrows from his quiver and planted them to hand. The sun sank into the trees. Blue dusk suffused the air. Rooks cawed on their nests. It was very peaceful.

A jay squawked in the wood and the rooks lifted from their nests. A wren scolded at the edge of the clearing. Wayland heard the ragged panting of the hounds and drew his knife. The greenery trembled and Ostine appeared in front of him. She stopped and threw back her head, but before she could utter a sound the dog smashed into her, bowling her over. The other hounds broke cover. When they saw the dog they whimpered and squirmed in submission. Wayland crouched in front of them and cradled their muzzles. He looked into their eyes and smiled. *Make a sound, and I'll cut your throats.* They lay down and began licking their sore limbs.

Two riders came out of the trees. They stopped and surveyed the clearing, then one of them gestured and the other five emerged. All were armoured, wearing helmets. Two of them held loaded crossbows. Wayland's mouth grew dry. He wiped his palms and raised his bow.

The encircling forest made the soldiers edgy. They advanced stirrup to stirrup, peering over their shields. Wayland bent his bow, sighting on Roussel's chest. *That's far enough.* They kept coming. They were only twenty yards in front of him when they halted. Swarms of midges clouded around them. The horses tossed their heads; their flanks twitched.

Roussel dragged his forearm across his cheeks. 'I'm being eaten alive.'

Drax's head patrolled from side to side. Wayland watched his eyes. Shoot the moment he realises where he is. Shoot and then run.

'Roussel.'

'What?' Roussel demanded, scratching his wrist on the edge of his shield.

'I know this place. We both do.'

Roussel stopped scratching.

'Don't you remember? There was a cottage over there. You can still make out the fields.'

Roussel pulled back on his reins. 'Jesus, you're right.'

'It must be a coincidence. We left no one alive.'

'Don't be so sure. Walter captured the falconer not far from here.

He must have grown up in these woods.' Roussel looked around the clearing. 'You know what I think?'

'What?'

'He could have lost us any time it pleased him. We're not hunting him; he's hunting us.'

Drax gave a nervous laugh. 'One against seven. Are you serious?'

'The odds might not be as good as that. The Frank must have fled south. We've been chasing the falconer in a circle. He could be leading us into an ambush.'

'What do you want to do?'

'I say we get out of here.'

'Drogo will crucify us.'

'We tell him we tracked the falconer until nightfall and found ourselves in a forest, with no food or shelter. What were we supposed to do?' Roussel turned to the huntsman. 'Call off the hounds.'

Relief was what Wayland felt. Standing only a few yards from seven armoured horse soldiers, he'd felt his resolve leaking away. At best he would have been able to release only one arrow, and he wasn't confident that it would have hit the mark. The effort of holding his heavy bow at full draw was making his aim waver. He slackened off and let his breath go.

If only the huntsman had used his horn. Instead he took a bone whistle from around his neck and blew a thin note barely audible to the human ear. One of the hounds whimpered.

Roussel lifted his sword. 'Straight ahead!'

Wayland drew and let fly. The arrow skewered Roussel's mailed wrist, punched through his iron helmet and sliced through bone and brain. Wayland's last sight of him was him leaning back, his hand pinned to his backthrown head as if scandalised.

'Charge!'

Wayland turned and ran, clawing through the poles. He'd expected the Normans to scatter, but he'd underestimated their discipline, their confidence in their armour and horsepower.

'There he goes!'

He was in the forest, breaking for the ravine, when he realised 4his second mistake. In the years since he'd left the wildwood, the familiar trails had become overgrown. Branches snagged him, thickets thwarted him. While he struggled to make distance, the horses battered their way through, gaining with every stride. They were so close that he didn't have time to fit another arrow.

'I see him. Spread out. Don't let him get around our flanks.'

A fallen tree blocked Wayland's path. The trunk was too high to hurdle, too long to run around. He vaulted up, and as he gathered himself to spring down the other side, a blow between his shoulders knocked him over.

'Got him! Hit him fair and square!'

Wayland sprawled winded on the far side. He knew he'd been hard hit. The fact that he felt no pain meant nothing. He'd seen deer shot through the heart run a hundred yards before their legs folded. He spat dirt from his mouth and staggered on, his breath sawing in his throat. The ground fell steeply towards the edge of the ravine and he had to brake his descent by grabbing at trees. A dead birch snapped off in his hand. Arms flailing, he careered down the slope. The mouth of the ravine rushed up towards him. He threw himself on his side and tobogganed feet first through the mulch. His right knee hit a stump with a sickening wrench. He clawed his hands into the earth and managed to halt only a few feet from the drop. He turned and saw four Normans on foot slip-sliding down the slope. When he stood, the pain in his knee made his leg buckle. He abandoned his plan to climb down into the gorge and lie up until nightfall.

He limped right, downstream, towards the Pot. The cliffs upstream of the pool leaned close together and for as long as he could remember the gap had been bridged by a fallen ash. He remembered his mother's fright when she'd found him and Edith playing dare in the middle of the bridge. That had been years ago. By now the tree might have rotted and collapsed. Out of the corner of his eye he saw two of the mounted Normans keeping pace with him on the crest of the slope.

The tree was still there, carpeted with mosses and bracketed with fungi. Wayland looked back to see how much time he had left. Even wounded and lame, he'd outpaced the dismounted soldiers. He felt his back. The bolt had penetrated his pack. His hand came away sticky with blood. The wound must be fatal, but it seemed important that he use his remaining strength to drag himself out of his hunters' reach. It was the instinct of a mortally wounded animal.

The shouts of the soldiers grew louder. The horsemen above were guiding them. One of them stopped and took aim with his crossbow. Wayland watched him as if trapped in a dream. The bolt leaped from the track. He dived headlong and heard it fizz past and splinter on the other side of the gorge. He hauled himself onto the trunk. The spongy wood came away in handfuls. Fifty feet below, the river spouted into the black waters of the Pot where he'd recovered his sister's body.

Ignoring the pain in his leg, he crossed the tree at a delicate run. As he jumped off, another bolt tugged at his sleeve. On this side of the gorge the forest understorey was choked with holly and hazel. He threw himself into cover and dragged himself up the slope until he reached the base of an alder. He sprawled against it, sobbing with exhaustion and pain. He felt sick and light-headed and guessed that he'd lost so much blood that he would soon pass out. The dog nuzzled him and then began to lick at his back. Wayland was so shocked that he smacked it across the jaws. It retreated and lay down with its head couched on its legs, watching him with unblinking reproach.

Wayland could read the dog's mind. Tentatively, he felt for the pack. Strange. He expected it to be pinned to his back, but it moved freely. He reached over his shoulder, took hold of the crossbow bolt and pulled. The pack lifted. Understanding struck. He threw back his head and laughed. Unnerved by the strange sound, the dog moved away and curled up at a distance.

Wayland struggled out of the pack. The lower part was sopping with blood. He could smell its sickly odour. He unlaced the pack, dug his hand into it and scooped out a handful of bloody porridge. The gore came from the boar they had killed yesterday. He'd poured it into a bladder, intending to use it for pudding. He held out the mess to the dog. Unsure of his mood, it stayed where it was.

Time had gone awry. He had no idea how long he'd been sitting at the base of the alder. For all he knew, the Normans had crossed the bridge and were creeping up on him. He scrambled forward. They were still on the other side, four of them crouched on guard behind trees, the huntsman kneeling on the ground.

'. . . bleeding like a stuck pig. He's not going far.'

Drax touched the huntsman's hand, examined his fingers, then bent and wiped them on the leaf litter. He stared across the gorge.

'It's nearly night,' one of the soldiers said. 'And the dog will be with him. He'll have crawled off to die in a hole. Leave it until morning.'

Drax looked up at the trees steepling into the darkening sky. 'Roussel was my comrade. The least I can do is recover his murderer's corpse. Rufus, come with me. The rest of you, cover us.'

Drax climbed onto the bridge and began to shuffle across, holding out his sword and shield for balance. Wayland watched him. He waited until he'd reached the middle before sighting. It was an awkward shot, a steep downward angle, the target hard to make out in the gloom. He didn't see where his first arrow went. Drax heard it and stopped, teetering for balance. Wayland shot again and clicked his tongue in annoyance as the arrow dived into the tree behind Drax's feet.

'Get back!'

Rufus managed to scurry to safety. Drax turned, manoeuvring like an old man. Wayland shifted to a better vantage but he didn't have to draw again. Drax's feet slipped. His legs shot out from under him. He dropped his weapons and managed to hook his arms over the trunk. His legs flailed as he tried to drag himself up, but the rotten wood provided no purchase. He clung for a moment by sheer terrified willpower, then dropped howling into the gorge.

The soldiers didn't make a sound. Like defeated phantoms, they backed into the trees behind their upraised shields. With a drawn-out groan, Wayland lay down on his back. He spread his limbs and lay unmoving while the sky turned to black and stars blinked through the tree canopy. He grew cold, but still he didn't move. Bats flitted overhead. Beside him the dog gobbled the mess of blood and meal. Images of the day's events broke into his consciousness like bubbles. Ever since the day he'd seen his family massacred, he'd fantasised about taking his revenge. He'd imagined the triumph he would feel. Well, now the moment had come, and he didn't feel a thing.

He crossed the river upstream and sent the dog scouting ahead. It returned and told him that the soldiers had left. In the dark it took him a long time to find his family's graves. He knelt beside the weed-covered mounds and lit five candles. The flames conjured up spirits. They hovered around him, his mother anxious and disapproving, his grandfather exultant, Edith still lost and scared.

He couldn't bring them back. Killing a hundred Normans wouldn't bring them back. Memory was the only bridge between the living and the dead. He'd returned to guard that link, but now he was back he knew that the woods wouldn't provide a sanctuary for long. The world that had seemed so vast when he was a child was growing smaller each year. The Normans had caught him once; sooner or later they would catch him again. To survive, he would have to move on, across the fells to the west, into unknown territory.

Loneliness overwhelmed him. For the first time in years he yearned for human company. He thought of the fugitives. If they had followed his directions, they would be camped a few miles upriver. Using his bow as a crutch, he levered himself upright and stood with bowed head.

Beloved parents and grandfather, dear brother and sisters, forgive me. I have to go away. I don't know where my path will take me, but I don't think it will lead back here. I won't forget you. Wherever I go, I'll cherish the thought of you.

He limped away. At the edge of the clearing he stopped for one last look. The candles burned tiny in the dark. Once they had flickered out, nothing would remain to tell a stranger that a family had lived here. Tears spangled his vision. He turned away and went on.

VIII

Hero and Richard sat side by side under a shared blanket. The fire had dwindled to a single tongue of flame. Raul lay snoring on the other side of it. Vallon was keeping watch somewhere in the trees on the crag above.

Hero was trying to teach Richard how to calculate latitude by measuring the angular elevation of the Pole Star with his astrolabe. Richard had difficulty locating the correct star. 'Not that one,' said Hero. 'Further right. Between the Great Bear and Cassiopeia – the constellation shaped like the letter W.'

'I think I've got it,' said Richard. 'I expected it to be brighter.'

'Now suspend the astrolabe as steadily as you can and line up the sighting bar.'

Richard pivoted the bar and squinted up it.

'Let me see,' Hero said, taking the astrolabe from him. He read off the star's apparent position from the scale on the rim of the instrument. 'Hmm, more than ten degrees out.'

'What's a degree?'

'It's an arc equal to the 360th part of the Earth's circumference.'

Richard thought about it. 'You're saying that the Earth is round?'

'Of course. That's why the horizon curves when you view the sea from a height.'

'I've only seen the sea once, when we crossed from Normandy. I was sick the whole passage.' Richard frowned. 'If the earth is round, we must live on top of it. Otherwise we'd fall off.'

'Wasps walk round apples without falling off.'

'They have more legs than we do. They can walk upside down on a ceiling.'

'There must be some force that keeps us grounded,' Hero conceded. 'Perhaps it's the same force that makes the needle of my compass point south and north.'

Richard sighed in drowsy admiration. 'How much you know. Tell me more.'

Hero watched the stars sliding around Polaris. Raul gave a rasping snore that tailed off into vigorous lip smacking. 'It's time you told *me* something. Why have you come with us?'

'I had to leave. At the castle, I had no say in my future.'

'That's not what I meant. Vallon isn't interested in your future. This must have something to do with the ransom.'

'Hasn't he told you?'

'There hasn't been time to talk. I didn't even know we were leaving until last night.'

'Keep it down,' Raul growled.

Richard moved closer. 'Lady Margaret has persuaded Vallon to lead an expedition to Norway. First we have to raise the finance. We're travelling south to a Jewish moneylender. I'm not allowed to tell you where. Vallon says that the fewer people know, the safer for all of us.'

Even though it was the answer he'd been expecting, Hero was shocked. 'Vallon's not going to Norway. Why would he risk his life to save a man he's never met – a man whose brother tried to kill us?'

'Vallon can use some of the money to trade and make a profit on the venture.'

'That shows how little you know him. He's a soldier, not a merchant. It's just a trick to escape. Once he has your mother's money, that's the last you'll see of him. You should have talked to me before running away.'

'But he swore an oath.'

'Who wouldn't if it meant saving his skin? Look at Walter and his lies. Everyone lies when it suits his purpose. I should know.'

'You?'

'From the beginning, our journey hasn't been what it seems.'

'What do you mean?'

Hero couldn't stop himself now. 'Ask yourself why Master Cosmas agreed to win Walter's freedom.'

'You told me that he wanted to visit Britain before he died.'

'Walter possesses something that Cosmas wanted – something he offered on condition that Cosmas obtain his release.'

'What is it?'

'Suppose I told you that at the eastern end of the world lies a realm greater than any built since the reign of the Caesars.'

'China? I've heard you speak of it.'

'Not China. This is a Christian realm.' Hero patted his pack. 'I have a letter written by the ruler of that country. It's addressed to the Byzantine Emperor.'

'What does it say?'

'The ruler offers to lead an army against the Turks and Arabs. That's not all. As a token of his allegiance, he sent a gift with the letter – something that will stand the world on its head.'

Someone or something not far away gave a heavy sigh. Hero and Richard clutched each other. Raul had heard the noise, too. He crawled to the fire, blew life into an ember and lit a taper shielded inside a horn. Holding the torch aloft, he crept forward. Hero followed him, then stopped with a gasp, the dog's snarl printed on his retina.

'Tell Vallon,' Raul said.

Hero scrambled up the hillside. 'Sir? Sir?'

'Over here. You two talk loud enough to wake the dead. And what the hell were you doing waving a torch?'

'It's Wayland. He's back.'

*

Raul took Vallon to one side and muttered in his ear. Vallon looked down into Wayland's sullen blinks, then turned to Hero and Richard. 'Wait by the fire.'

'Something's wrong,' Hero whispered. 'I've never seen him look so grave.'

Richard glanced at the dark figures. 'Go on with your story. You were telling me about a gift.'

Hero was regretting his indiscretion. 'No, my tongue ran away with me. I gave my word to Cosmas that I wouldn't repeat the secret to anyone.'

'Not even Vallon?'

'No, not even him.'

'But—'

'Ssh!' Vallon was returning towards the fire. 'You must forget about the letter.' Vallon was only feet away. 'Swear it, or forfeit my friendship.'

'Very well. I swear.'

Vallon stared into the embers and spoke in a colourless voice. 'I'd hoped that we'd be safe once we'd put ourselves beyond Drogo's reach. We hadn't committed any crime, and with Richard to vouch for us, we had every chance of reaching our destination. Not any more. Wayland has killed two of the count's men – Roussel and Drax.'

Raul spat into the fire.

'I'm not shedding tears for them either. But there's no crime more serious than the murder of a Norman. From now on every sword will be raised against us. Richard, your name and title are no longer any protection. If we're caught, you'll swing alongside us. You'd better leave us at the next town. Tell the Count we took you against your will.'

Richard stirred one foot miserably.

'Wayland killed the Normans only a few miles from here,' Vallon said. 'The others probably rode straight back to the castle. Drogo won't wait until morning before coming after us. He could be here by daybreak.'

Raul loosened his breeches and pissed on the fire. 'We'd better get started then.'

Vallon began to gather his belongings.

'Is Wayland coming with us?' Hero asked.

'He can come or go as he pleases. The damage is done.'

*

75

Wayland guided them south-west, across the grain of the country. They crossed a barren common by starlight and dropped into a wooded valley as the first faint wash of dawn spread in the east. They began their next ascent with sunlight fanning through the gaps behind them. They climbed a steep moor dotted with wind-racked junipers. The sun grew warm on their backs. Around them curlews cried their liquid song and grouse burst cackling out of the heather. Vallon didn't call the first halt until mid-morning. Everyone was struggling, Wayland included. After they'd eaten, Vallon told him to stay behind and watch for pursuit. The Frank led the others on. At noon they were still climbing, one false summit leading to another.

Vallon reached the top first. Against the sky an old grey druid leaned into the wind with his cloak blowing out behind him. When Vallon approached, he saw that the figure was an ancient runestone covered by a mat of shaggy lichens. He sat against it, pulled off his boots and looked at his blistered heels. He put his boots back on and waited for the others to straggle up. Hero and Richard could hardly put one foot in front of the other.

At last Wayland appeared, hobbling with the help of a stave.

'Any sign of them?'

Wayland shook his head and went past and stopped on the western skyline. Vallon struggled up and joined him. Beneath their feet the land spilled into a broad vale chequered with fields and veined by tracks. Wisps of smoke rose from dozens of hamlets. On the other side, snow-capped mountains cradled lakes in crooked folds. Figures like mites crept along a road that followed the valley north-west towards a plain bounded by a shining firth.

Vallon studied Wayland. The falconer was a good-looking youth, tall and straight, with yellow hair and a disconcertingly clear blue gaze. Vallon's anger at his wanton behaviour was tempered by curiosity and grudging admiration. It took courage to kill two Norman cavalrymen. More than that, it took grim intent.

Wayland became aware of Vallon's scrutiny and turned to face it. Not many people could look Vallon straight in the eye. The Frank faced towards the south. They were on the spine of the country – a range of bald fells wearing rags of snow and curving away on each side like the hull of an upturned boat. 'See this ring,' he said. 'This morning the stone was as blue as your eyes. Now it's clouding over. The weather will turn soon.'

Wayland studied the ring, then glanced at the sky. He nodded as if he didn't need gadgets to predict the weather.

They followed the felltops south and bivouacked among the ghostly grey spoilheaps of a lead mine abandoned in Roman times. Richard fell asleep at supper with his spoon half raised to his lips and had to be put to bed like a child. Next day they continued south through a needling drizzle and didn't encounter a living soul. They camped under a ledge in a stony gill and chewed their food woodenly, hardly exchanging a word.

Dawn broke like blood percolating through dirty water. All morning showers scudded in from the north-west. The fugitives were already cold and wet when they turned to see a curtain of black cloud closing down on them. It cast the mountains to the west into darkness and spread over the vale like a contagion.

There was no shelter on the fell. The storm knocked them sideways. Pellets of rain lashed them. The rain thickened into sleet and then wet snow that clogged their eyes and balled on their feet. Hero came struggling up to Vallon, shielding his face in the crook of his elbow. The wind blew the words away.

Vallon cupped a hand to his ear. 'I can't hear you.'

'I said, Richard's in a dreadful plight.'

'It's only a squall,' Vallon shouted. 'It will soon pass.'

'He can't endure much longer. Come, see for yourself.'

Richard looked like he'd been poleaxed, his eyes rolled up in his skull and his face deathly grey. He rambled in a slurred voice and lashed out when Vallon caught hold of him.

'Raul, Wayland, take his arms.'

They went where the wind buffeted them, skittering in the blasts, their cloaks streaming out in front. They reached a sheepfold and collapsed in the lee and crouched around Richard with their hands tucked up into their armpits. The snow streaked past with hypnotic intensity.

The wind slackened and the snow stopped. The fugitives looked at each other and saw that they'd grown old, with white hair and brows. The darkness began to lift and the pale disc of the sun blinked through the streaming overcast. In the watery light, Vallon saw that they'd been driven to the eastern side of the fell and were looking down a steep dale.

'Do you know this country?' he asked Wayland.

The falconer turned a circle and shook his head.

Hero was chafing Richard's hands. 'He can't spend the night up here. All our bedding is drenched.'

'I knew he was the weakest link,' said Vallon. 'But I didn't think he'd break so soon.'

The last black tendrils of stormcloud floated east. The wind dropped to nothing and sunlight bathed the hills. The snow began to melt before their eyes, leaving icy filigrees in the shadows. Far down the dale Vallon spotted a solitary farmstead in a bright green triangle of cultivation. He shaded his eyes and studied it.

'I can see a man working a field.'

Wayland held up two fingers.

'Two men, then, and no other habitation for miles. We'll risk it.'

They followed a rushing burn, keeping out of sight of the house. When they were close, Vallon climbed the gulley and peered over the edge. The farmstead was a windowless cottage of unmortared whinstone, the joints plugged with turves, the roof thatched with blackened ling. Fumes drifted out of the central smokehole. Attached to the cottage was a byre. Downhill of the house a man guided an ox-drawn plough through the thin soil. In an adjoining field another man was repairing a stone wall near a hobbled horse. Scrawny chickens pecked around the homestead.

'Wait here,' Vallon said.

He rose and began to walk towards the house. He'd gone only a few yards when a little girl herding two slat-ribbed cows appeared round a bend in the stream. She cried out and fled downriver, whacking the cows on their bony rumps. The chickens flew squawking onto the roof ridge. The men sprinted for the house.

Vallon signalled for the others to show themselves. The peasants rushed out armed with swords. Vallon kept his own sword sheathed and walked forward until they raised their weapons. They were youths, possibly twins. Vallon pointed back at the fugitives, then tilted his head and laid it on his hands, miming sleep. The youths flapped their arms at him. When he didn't leave, they advanced with swords hoisted, looking to each other for courage. Vallon stood his ground. He held out a silver penny.

They frowned at each other. One of them shook his head, but the other said something and reached out to take the coin at full stretch. They moved back a pace. From the reverent way they handled the coin, passing it between them as if it were a charm, Vallon guessed that money played little part in their economy.

The two men stepped apart and beckoned Vallon to pass between them. He signalled for the others to wait. The youths closed up behind him.

He ducked through the doorway into a room dark except for the dim glow of a peat hearth. A woman stood pressed against the far wall with her arms crossed over her breast. Around the walls were four stone sleeping ledges, like burial niches. A slate table with stumps for stools completed the furnishings.

The men began to question him. The only word he could understand was 'Normans'.

'Not Norman,' he said. 'Normans ...' He made a throat-cutting gesture.

He went out and waved the fugitives forward. They laid Richard in one of the bed niches and covered him with blankets. They hung their own sodden bedding on the smoke-blackened beams above the fire, then they crouched around the flame, holding out their hands in worship. The little girl came in and watched the strangers in mute fascination. Vallon donated what remained of their provisions to the woman – some beans and wheat flour, a venison shank, half a pot of honey and a nugget of salt. The woman slapped her daughter's hand away and bore the scraps off as though they were treasure.

Ulf and Hakon, her sons were called, descendants of Viking invaders from Ireland. The swords they carried were the same arms their ancestors had waded ashore with, but now the blades were blunter than the ploughshares with which they scratched a living. Ulf told them that the Normans rarely came this far west. The last time they'd seen any was two years ago, when King William led his army through the Pennines after wasting Northumbria. The nearest strongholds were at York and Durham, more than a day's ride to the east.

The room began to fill with peat smoke. Vallon went outside and sat on a rock and watched the hills turn velvety black under a golden sky. Hero came out and sat beside him.

'Richard says you've agreed to lead an expedition to Norway.'

'I'll explain my intentions tomorrow, when we've rested and are seated at table.' Vallon saw Hero bite his lip. He changed the subject and made his tone light. 'Tell me what you think of our travelling companions.'

'Richard's more intelligent than I took him for. In fact he's surprisingly quick-witted.'

Vallon nodded. 'Determined, too. He told me that he'd rather take his chances with us than return to the castle. What about the falconer?'

Hero grew more animated. 'He's a rare creature. The defiant way he looks at you – like a hawk.'

'He could do with some manning. I've never met a more impudent peasant.'

'Perhaps he's of gentler birth than that. Give him a bath and a proper suit of clothes and he'd cut a fine figure in any company. No, wait. He can read – which is more than anyone else in the Count's household can do. The other morning he picked up one of the pages Olbec gave me and I saw his lips form words. If only he could speak, what a fascinating tale he could tell.'

'He doesn't need the gift of speech while he has you to romance his life.'

Hero reddened. 'I think he's a highborn Englishman whose land was stolen by the Normans. Sir, don't scoff. History has many accounts of noblemen who were robbed of their inheritance and abandoned in the wild. Besides Romulus and Remus, there were Amphion and Zethus, sons of Zeus and Antiope, who were exposed in the mountains by their wicked uncle. And then there's Poseidon's son, Hippothous, raised by wild mares in Eleusis. Not to mention Jason and Achilles, both reared on Mount Pelion by the Centaur Chiron. In fact, when I see Wayland run, I'm reminded of Homer's epithet for Achilles: *podarkes* – "the swift of foot".'

Vallon laughed. 'Enough. You've spent so long with your head in books that you can't separate fact from fantasy.' He gave Hero's knee an affectionate cuff. 'I'm going to miss you.'

'Miss me?'

At that moment Raul poked his head out of the door and shouted that supper was ready. The first star had appeared in the east. Vallon rose and stretched. 'Well, it will take more than a scrub and a haircut to civilise our crossbowman.'

'He's as rough as a boar, but his heart is kind.'

'Gallows-bait. I've had a hundred men like Raul under my command and I've hanged a good few of them. For a penny a day and the prospect of plunder, he'd follow a fool to hell. Somewhere in a lonely corner of this world, there's an unmarked grave waiting for Raul. Let's eat.'

The others were already seated at table when they went in. Ulf bowed his head over the food and muttered a grace. The simple ceremony caught Vallon off guard. A lump filled his throat. He swallowed it. A man easily moved to tears cries only for himself.

Richard had recovered sufficiently to sit at table and sip a bowl of broth. The others ate a gruel of oats and beans containing nameless bits of gristle. For bread there was a gritty loaf of barley mixed with ground pulses.

The girl watched the strangers in breathless silence.

Hero picked at his portion. 'What is this?' he whispered. 'Do you think it might be pig's ear?'

Raul laughed. 'It's pig's something.'

Hero put down his bowl.

'I'll have it if you don't want it.'

'It's food taken from other men's mouths,' said Vallon. 'Show some respect.'

After supper Ulf guided them to the byre. Vallon fell unconscious to the ruminations of cattle and the soft clucking of poultry. At some incalculable hour, he was woken by one of the brothers whispering in the doorway. He heard Wayland step over the sleeping figures and go out with his bow, the dog padding at his heels. Vallon shrugged and went back to sleep.

He spent the morning keeping watch, while Raul helped Hakon repair the stone wall. Hero stayed indoors giving Richard a writing lesson. Wayland and Ulf returned in the late morning with a brace of blackcock they'd shot at their lekking ground and a brown hare the dog had coursed and killed. They swung them on to the polished slate and everyone gathered round to admire the still life.

That night they dined on civet of game spiced with juniper and wild thyme. The brothers brought out a barrel of ale and the mood turned festive. The girl sat on Raul's knee and watched him make a coin vanish from his hand and reappear behind his ear. No matter how many times he performed the trick, she wanted to see it again.

'We should be observing the Lent fast,' Richard said.

Raul drained his cup and banged it down. 'I've done enough penance these last few days to purge my soul for a lifetime.'

Vallon rapped on the table. All eyes turned to him. Raul set the girl down.

'There's not much to say. We've left ourselves so open to the mercy of events that I can't predict what tomorrow will bring, let alone next week. Our first goal is to reach a moneylender. I won't tell you where he conducts his business in case any of you are captured. If we negotiate that hurdle, I intend leading a voyage to Norway in search of gyrfalcons. The falcons will be carried through Rus to Anatolia. We might make a profit on the enterprise. If we do, each of you will receive a share. Don't get too excited, Raul. If there's one thing I'm sure of, it's that not everyone who begins the journey will end it. That's all you need to know for now.'

Hero sunk his head. Wayland stared ahead as though thinking about something else. Raul grinned and raised his cup. 'Fortune or a grave!'

'A grave is the most likely outcome. Riders will be carrying our descriptions to every garrison in the north.' Vallon's eyes panned around the company. 'Let's face it, we're not difficult to recognise. Ulf has offered to guide us tomorrow. In a day or two we'll reach more populated country. If necessary, we'll travel at night. Once we reach the lowlands and have to follow highways, we'll split up. Wayland and Raul will scout ahead and search for refuges where we can eat and sleep. Richard and Hero will travel with me. We'll meet up each evening.'

In the dead of night Vallon was still awake, his mind as restless as the mice rustling in the straw around him. Hero couldn't sleep either. A blood-curdling shriek brought him upright with a gasp. A ghostly white shape wafted off the beam above and flitted through a slit in the gable. Hero crossed himself.

'Only an owl,' Vallon said.

'A bird of ill omen.'

'You'd better tell me what's gnawing you.'

'Sir, do you really intend to command an expedition to Norway?'

'I thought that was it.'

'Forgive me, sir. It's just that, after all we've been through, to undertake a new and even more dangerous journey seems perverse.'

'Not as perverse as all that. When our paths first crossed, I was on my way to Constantinople. That's still my destination. The falcons will lead me there by a different route.'

'But Rus is so dangerous. Cosmas told me that it's descended into anarchy. Then there are the nomads on the southern steppe. Do you know what they did to a Russian prince who fell into their hands?'

'Killed him – slowly, I imagine.'

'And then turned his skull into a drinking cup.'

'Hero, I'm still subject to arrest in France. I'd rather face a few savages than risk a third crossing of my homeland.'

'There's no need to return through France.'

Vallon had an inkling of what was coming. 'Oh?'

'You don't owe anything to Olbec's family. Quite the reverse. We travelled all that way on Walter's behalf, and how did they reward us? Not only did Drogo try to kill us, but Olbec was ready to see us depart without a penny.'

'You're saying that I should steal the money intended for the expedition.'

'It would be no more than just payment for the services you've rendered.'

'So you think I should leave Walter to rot.'

'Your very words, sir, when you discovered that he'd lied about his family's wealth.'

'I'd have lied if I'd been in his position.'

'With respect, I don't believe you would.'

Vallon rounded on him. 'You know nothing about life's harsh turns. You don't know what it's like to be a prisoner. You don't know how it feels to see the weeks turning into months, not knowing if you'll ever see home again.'

'You, sir? A prisoner.'

Vallon fell back. 'Fortunes of war. Now go to sleep. It will be light soon and we've got a long day ahead.'

Hero settled in the straw. Vallon knew what was troubling him. They'd been travelling for nearly half a year, yet the real journey had hardly begun.

'You must miss home.'

'Not as much as I miss the medical school. What about you, sir? Tonight is the first time I've heard you speak about home.'

'I don't have a home. I'm an outlaw.'

'Yes, I know. But before that.'

'There's no before.'

Vallon stared through the darkness, remembering a sad song about an exiled knight turning for one last look at home and seeing open doors and gates without locks, windows without faces, the hall stripped of cloaks and mantles, the mews and stables empty, the horses gone, the falcons flown away.

He sighed. There was no going back. No matter how far he travelled, the road would always be leading him away.

'Sir, you sound heavy of heart.'

'Indigestion. I supped too well.'

Time passed. Vallon may even have dozed. 'Do you remember your master's last words?'

'About you being sent to show me the way?'

Vallon lifted himself on to one elbow. 'Did he really say that?'

'He said it, sir.'

Vallon subsided again. 'It wasn't that. It was what he said before – something about the mystery of the rivers.'

'Rivers with no known beginnings or endings. There was a river in Asia that he'd always wanted to follow – a river that leads into a fabulous land. Actually, sir, I've been meaning to confess something that—'

But Vallon was lost in his own thoughts. 'I've been thinking about it. There's no mystery about rivers. They're born in the mountains, issuing from a spring as a baby emerges from the womb. They begin life boisterous, dashing about with ceaseless energy but no purpose. Gradually they become deeper and steadier. They grow broad and stately and proud. Next they turn sluggish and become confused, sometimes wandering off into backwaters. Finally, they lose their strength and merge into the sea.'

IX

Four days later the hills petered out. From the last outlier, Vallon, Hero and Richard stood looking south over a great forest still clad in its winter coat. Strands of smoke rose in places from the canopy.

'That must be Sherwood,' said Vallon. 'Raul says it's one of the last refuges of the English resistance.'

'Then we can relax our guard,' Hero said.

'On the contrary. From now on, we must be especially vigilant. Everyone we have dealings with, observe them closely. Look behind the smile. Trust no one.'

They descended a rutted track glinting with puddles. The forest closed around them – huge and ancient oaks with knuckled roots and fissured trunks spreading into vaulted crowns. The trees stood widely spaced and the ground beneath them was nearly bare. The fugitives stared down the empty avenues leading away in all directions. No one spoke.

The sun was sinking like flames in a smoky forge when they came to a millrace and followed it into a woodland village clumped around a green. It had rained on and off since morning and carts had churned the road to slurry. The travellers' feet sucked in the mud. Some of the cottages had corn dolls tied to their doors. Vallon passed a tavern with a weathered sign depicting a man grinning out from branches and vines. Looking closer, Vallon saw that the greenery was sprouting from the man's eyes, nose and mouth.

A cheerful hubbub came from the tavern. Hero and Richard eyed its lamplit windows with longing.

'Not safe,' Vallon said, and trudged on. A flock of geese mantled their wings and hissed at him. He'd reached the next house when he heard a familiar voice muffled by laughter and jeers. Frowning, he retraced his steps and stooped through the tavern door.

The room was crowded, but no one saw him enter. Everybody's attention was craned on some drama taking place in a space around the hearth. Peering over their shoulders, Vallon saw Raul squatting on his haunches, one hand laid on the floor, a lad of about ten balancing on it. Raul's face contused. Veins knotted on his temples. Slowly the boy came off the floor until he was level with Raul's bent knees, suspended on a perfectly straight arm. Again, the veins on Raul's temple bulged. He sprang to full height, at the same time swinging his arm up until the boy was poised above his head. The lad lost his balance and fell. Raul caught him, lowered him to the ground and tousled his hair.

Vallon pushed through the applause and catcalls. 'What the hell are you playing at?'

The crowd turned as if pulled by a string. When they saw the set of Vallon's mouth, the sword hilt jutting at his side, they edged away and returned to their ale-benches. Raul gave a tipsy salute.

'Captain, I was providing some harmless entertainment in return for the hospitality shown by these good souls.'

Vallon registered Wayland seated in a booth, the dog lying muzzled at his feet like some monstrous trophy.

'I told you to keep away from public places.'

'We can't hide from everyone we meet. Now we're in tamer parts, it's safer to blend in.'

'You call that blending in?'

The boy who'd featured in Raul's stunt presented him with a cup of ale. Raul raised it to a man leaning against the counter separating the drinking hall from the landlord's quarters. The man raised his own cup. Vallon appraised him. Lean and wiry, dressed in a filthy green jerkin and leggings, ears sticking out through a tangle of rat-tails under a leather skullcap.

'Who's that?'

'His name's Leofric. We met him on the road. He's a charcoal burner.'

'What did you tell him about us?'

Raul tugged his earring. 'I told him we were a party of travelling showmen.'

'A *what?*'

'Travelling entertainers who perform at fairs and festivals. I said that we'd done poor business in the provinces and were heading back to London for the Easter holiday.'

'I suppose that was your strongman act?'

Raul grinned. 'Not bad, eh?' He pointed at Wayland. 'And that's Wolfboy and his performing dog. Does whatever Wolfboy tells it to do.'

'Wayland's dumb.'

'That's what makes it such a great act.'

Hero smothered a laugh. 'What's my role?'

'Storyteller,' said Raul. 'Captain, you're the Swordmaster, a champion of France who fought in Castile with El Cid. You take on all comers, three at a time – a penny if they beat you.' Raul stifled a hiccup. ''Course, you don't use real swords.'

Vallon shook his head at this nonsense and crossed to Wayland's booth. He slid his sword under the table and subsided on to a bench. As soon as the weight was off his feet, he wondered how he would get up again.

'Since we're here, you might as well fetch us some ale.'

Raul came back balancing three cups. 'The landlord asks if we want supper.' He raised his eyebrows. 'Nice dish of salt cod?'

The landlord stood behind the counter, smiling broadly, sharpening a knife on a steel. The boy sat on the board, swinging his legs.

'Very well,' Vallon said. 'But we leave as soon as we've eaten.'

'Can't we stay the night?' Richard said.

'No. We've already attracted too much attention.'

Richard looked like he would cry. 'Sir, it's been three days since we slept under a roof.'

Raul patted his hand. 'Don't you fret. I've already found us beds. Leofric's invited us to sleep at his cottage. It's deep in the woods, Captain, well off the beaten track.'

Vallon studied the charcoal burner again. He was standing with his back to the room, sharing a joke with the landlord. He reached across the counter and cut a slice off a flitch of bacon with what looked like a flensing knife.

Vallon was tempted to accept. His joints ached from the damp that seeped into them at night.

'Thank your friend and tell him we'll be making our own arrangements.'

'Like what? Another ditch?'

Hero's expression turned mutinous. 'We can't go on living like animals. Lower than animals. Even the birds and beasts have their nests.'

Richard gave a flimsy cough of agreement.

Vallon looked at them over the rim of his cup. 'We don't accept invitations from strangers.'

Muttering under his breath, Raul went off to break the news to the charcoal burner. Vallon watched them. The man looked put out by the snub, but no more than was to be expected. He didn't protest too much; he didn't try to persuade. He touched his cup to Raul's and shook hands when they parted. When the landlord came over with a platter of cod, Vallon dismissed the matter from his mind. He ate a few mouthfuls, then put his dish aside. He felt feverish. It had begun to rain again. For a while he listened to the water dripping off the eaves. The stuffy atmosphere made him sleepy. His head began to droop.

He woke from an ugly dream to find that the room had grown quiet. His fever was worse. The light hurt his eyes. Across the table, Hero and Richard lay fast asleep, heads cradled on their forearms. Raul sat in a bleary doze with his chin propped on his hand.

It had stopped raining. The tavern was nearly empty. Three locals sat talking quietly on an ale-bench beside the dying fire. When he looked at them, two averted their eyes. The other was old and sightless.

Vallon pulled Raul's hand from under his chin. The German surfaced with a splutter.

'How long have I been asleep?'

Raul bored a knuckle into his forehead. 'Don't know, but you had a fair old snooze. I reckoned you needed the rest.' He threw his arms around Hero and Richard, and dropped his voice. 'Didn't want to wake these two, either.'

When Vallon stood, pain as piercing as a hot wire shot down one leg. He screwed his eyes shut and held on to the table. Raul reached out in concern. 'Are you all right, Captain? You don't look too good.'

'The charcoal burner. When did he leave?'

Raul pulled at his beard. 'Couldn't say.'

'What did he say when you told him we wouldn't be lodging with him?'

'Acted very decent, considering. Wished me a good night and said he'd look out for us on the road tomorrow.'

Vallon straightened with a shuddering breath. 'We've been set up.'

'Captain, you haven't even spoken to the man. You don't know the first thing about him.'

Vallon leaned over, hands braced on the table. 'Why would a penniless charcoal burner offer to put up five strangers?'

'I told him we'd pay.'

'You boasted that I had a purse stuffed with silver.'

'What's wrong with you, Captain? All I said was that he wouldn't go out of pocket.'

'Oh, yes,' said Vallon, 'he was going to make us pay.' He lurched round. The landlord's smile seemed to have been pasted on to his face. It reminded Vallon of the grinning grotesque on the tavern sign. The boy was still on the counter, still swinging his legs.

'Ask him to give us lodgings for the night.'

'Captain, I thought—'

'Do as I say.'

The innkeeper greeted Raul's request with an apologetic refusal.

'There's no room. He says there's an inn at the next village.'

'Tell him the night's dark and we're weary. We'll pay to sleep in his stable.'

The request seemed to exhaust the landlord's good humour. Raul pulled a face. 'He says that if we're so desperate for a bed, why did we turn down Leofric's offer?'

The boy on the counter had stopped swinging his legs. It was probably the fever, but Vallon had the impression that the boy's beetle-black eyes were bright with malice.

The landlord began clearing up, making an ostentatious clatter. The remaining drinkers had left. Vallon shook Hero and Richard. 'Wake up. It's time we were going.' He looked around. 'Where's Wayland?

'He doesn't like being cooped up,' said Raul. 'He must have gone outside for some fresh air.'

A crescent moon cast enough light for Wayland to keep the charcoal burner in sight. The man walked briskly down the middle of the track, singing under his breath. Wayland and the dog kept to the grassy verge. He'd been outside when the charcoal burner left the tavern, followed by the boy. The two had stood close, talking more like conspirators than friends taking their leave, and they'd parted without goodnights. There'd been no time for Wayland to take his suspicions to Vallon. By the time the boy went back inside, the charcoal burner was nearly out of sight, heading down one of the rides that radiated out from the village.

It was beginning to look like Wayland's instincts had played him false. The charcoal burner gave every impression of a man intent on getting home. If he looks back, Wayland decided, I'll know I'm right. Any man walking through a dark wood with dirty work on his mind would glance over his shoulder from time to time.

But the charcoal burner had eyes only for the road ahead. Wayland reckoned off one mile passed, then another. He'd been on the move since dawn and he contemplated with sinking heart the slog back to the village. Not a thing stirred in the trees. The only sounds were his own faint footfalls and the occasional click of his bow against his belt. The deeper he walked into the forest, the more conscious he became of his own presence. It was strange. He was stalking a man, yet Wayland felt it was he who was the centre of attention. Watching the bobbing figure in the moonlight, he had the unpleasant notion that the charcoal burner knew he was there, that he was luring him on. Another nasty fancy insinuated itself. He had the feeling that if he caught up with him and turned him round, it wouldn't be the charcoal burner's face he saw beneath the cap.

The man stopped. Wayland froze. At this distance he was just a shadow among shadows, a shape that no night-time traveller would turn back to investigate.

The charcoal burner walked backwards in a circle, as if he'd missed his turning and was trying to establish his whereabouts. He looked all about. He walked to one side of the ride, then began to cross to the other.

Cloud veiled the moon. When the crescent reappeared, the charcoal burner was gone. Wayland had last seen him near a stag-headed oak of enormous girth.

Wayland waited to make sure the charcoal burner didn't return. The dog watched him, trembling. He nodded and it crossed the road like a wraith.

His gaze roamed about as he tried to work out the significance of the place. He couldn't see any track leading off the ride. The only thing out of the ordinary was the old oak. His eyes kept returning to it, and the more he looked at it, the more it seemed to be looking back at *him*. Wayland's shoulders hunched in an involuntary shiver. It wasn't just his imagination. The oak had a face – two empty sockets above a gaping mouth. He fingered the cross at his neck.

The dog's soundless return made him start. It led him across the ride and began to skirt round the oak, looking at it sidelong, like a fox eyeing a scarecrow.

Wait.

When Wayland saw the oak up close, he smiled at the tricks moonlight could play. Age and decay had hollowed out a cave at its base, and the two eyes were only the scars left by long-fallen branches. He saw something dangling from the top of the hollow. Thinking it might have been left there by the charcoal burner, he reached out and then snatched back his hand. It was a dead cat on a cord, its mouth frozen in a mummified snarl. He glanced over his shoulder before looking back at the hollow. The darkness inside was deep enough to hide a man. Wayland went cold all over at the thought that someone – some *thing* – was waiting with baleful concentration for him to come within reach.

He backed away and almost tripped over the dog. It took his sleeve in its mouth and tugged him away.

They went into the trees. The massive boles encircled them. There was little undergrowth – just a few hazel coppices and the occasional gleam of holly. Wayland struck a trail of sorts that descended a gentle slope. The dog's relaxed gait told him that the charcoal burner was a long way ahead. He broke into a lope.

They must have covered more than a mile when the dog clamped itself to the ground. Wayland squatted beside it. He smelled woodsmoke and pig shit. As he crept forward, it occurred to him that the charcoal burner would have a dog. Too late to worry about that. The trees thinned and he made out the shape of a hut in a clearing. Pale smoke drifted from its roof and a splinter of light showed at a shuttered window. Pigs grunted on the other side of the clearing. He heard low voices, then the sound of a door closing.

He ran light-footed towards the house and sidled up to the window. What he expected to see – what he hoped to see – was the charcoal burner at home with his family, yawning by the hearth, pulling his boots off. Wayland put his eye to the chink and his throat dried. Swaying tallow lamps lit a room full of men with long matted hair and beards, dressed in crudely stitched hides and the greenish jerkins that

Wayland took to be the uniform of a company bound to some malign purpose. He knew what they were; Ulf had warned him about them. Men of the woods. Former resistance fighters turned bandits and cut-throats.

A man scabbed with dirt moved aside and Wayland saw the charcoal burner standing before a dark-haired man sitting with his back to the window. He was clean-shaven and looked almost civilised in that wild company. Around his collar hung a necklace of dried fungi – some rustic charm or remedy.

'Travelling entertainers, Ash. That's what the German said. And maybe they are. Anyway, they're foreigners – all but one, a dumb English youth. Wolfboy, the German called him. He's got a dog, a monster, looks like it's bred more for the bear pit than the theatre. You wouldn't want to run into that hound on a dark night.'

Ash made a curt gesture.

'Shame to kill it,' the charcoal burner said. 'I wouldn't mind having that dog myself.'

Ash wasn't interested in the dog. 'Who else is in the party?'

'A couple of young boobies and a Frenchie – a Frank, not a Norman. Tough, mean-looking fellow, knows how to handle himself. The German said he fought in Spain. He challenges people to cross swords with him.'

'I don't like the sound of this crew,' said a bystander. 'A night ambush is always chancy. It only takes one of them to get away and—'

'Shut up,' Ash said. He turned back to the charcoal burner. 'Why didn't you bring them here?'

The charcoal burner showed graveyard teeth. 'I was going to. It was all set up. I'd got the German well-bladdered, your boy was about to bring you the news, then Frenchie turned up and told the German they'd be going on down the road.'

Ash leaned back on his stool. 'You must have given yourself away.'

'On my life. I did everything just like I always do. Ask your uncle.'

Ash scratched his knee. 'What goods are they carrying?'

'I'm not promising you the moon. To tell the truth, they look like they've spent the last week dossing on a dunghill, but – and you'd hate yourself for missing the chance – the Frenchie carries a jewelled sword that must be worth its weight in silver. He wears a fine ring, too, and paid for his meal in coin.'

Ash fingered his necklace. 'If they've got money, why have they been sleeping rough?'

The charcoal burner dropped to his haunches. 'That's what *I* was wondering. What if they're on the run? There might be a bounty on them.'

Ash didn't answer. No one disturbed his thoughts. At last he sniffed, wiped a finger under his nose, reached for his sword and laid it across his lap.

'How soon do we expect them?'

'They're probably leaving the tavern about now. I told your uncle to keep them happy until I was well clear.'

'They might camp in the woods. Finding them won't be easy.'

'Edric's going to follow them. If they sleep out, so much the better. We can fall on them at first light.'

Ash's cheeks lifted in a smile. 'Edric's a good lad.'

'He's his father's boy.'

Wayland realised they were talking about the youngster Raul had lifted one-handed above his head.

Ash stood, crossed to the opposite wall and unhooked a rusty mail vest cut down from a Norman hauberk. He raised his arms and shrugged it on and turned around and showed his face. It was expressionless, his eyes as flat as coins. Wayland raised his hand to his throat and gave a slow swallow. The charm around Ash's neck was a string of withered human ears.

Ash looked straight at him, walked towards the window and flung out his hands. Wayland threw himself to one side and pressed back against the wall behind the half-opened shutter. He drew his knife.

'A quarter moon,' Ash said, inches from his ear. 'Wear your hoods and mantles. Muffle your blades.' He pulled the shutters close.

Heart in mouth, Wayland returned to the peephole to see the outlaws grabbing swords, bows, billhooks, spears, an axe. They pulled on shapeless hoods and mantles covered with twigs and leaves. In the rancid light they looked like members of some infernal sect.

'We'll wait for them at the goblin oak,' said Ash. 'Leofric, you and Siward go back down the road as far as the next turning. Let them pass, then fall in behind. Keep well into the trees.'

'What about Edric?'

'Bring him with you. The boy can watch. It will be a good lesson.'

'Maybe they can put on their show before we kill them. Edric would like that.'

Ash breathed in through his nose. The man who'd spoken looked away. 'Sorry, Master Ash.'

'Take one alive for questioning. Kill all the others. Make sure the Frenchie dies in the first volley. Don't give him a chance to use his sword. We'll hide the bodies well away from the road. The swine will deal with them in the morning.'

Someone laughed. 'Your hogs eat better than we do.'

Before Wayland could flesh out this image, the outlaws began to make for the door. He raced to the edge of the clearing and dropped behind a tree. Nine cowled shapes came out of the hut. They filed past him at spitting distance, breath steaming through the slits in their hoods.

The pigs in their enclosure squealed with excitement. They knew what the outlaws' departure betokened. It was as though a feeding bell had been rung.

Wayland's first impulse was to run and warn Vallon. But what if the fugitives had left the road and the boy was already on his way to Ash? Even with the dog's help, it might take all night to find the fugitives' camp. He thought of torching the cottage, but the outlaws would be a mile away before the building was ablaze and might not see the fire.

He couldn't wait any longer. The outlaws were already out of sight. Wayland was about to follow when he thought of something else. He sprinted back to the hut, kicked open the door and plunged inside. On the wall hung one of the hoods and capes the outlaws wore as camouflage. He struggled into the cape and pulled the mask over his head.

When he caught up with the outlaws, they were strung out over fifty yards of trail. He looked for the moon and saw it floating tiny and remote above the trees. Vallon must have stopped for the night by now. Wayland reached a decision. He would shadow the outlaws as far as the oak, then tail the charcoal burner and his partner down the ride. Once he'd dealt with them, he'd lie up and wait for the boy. He'd choose a spot far enough away from the oak to give the travellers plenty of warning if they were still on the road.

About halfway to the ride, the outlaws stopped and bunched. After a whispered exchange, two shapes detached themselves and disappeared into the trees to the right. When Wayland realised that Leofric and Siward were taking a short cut, he teetered with indecision. If he followed them, he might miss the boy returning to the oak. If he stayed with the main party and the fugitives were still on the road, he'd lose the chance to warn them before the two bandits met up with the boy.

Wayland struck out after the scouts.

They were woodsmen on their home ground and moved with assurance, ill-defined shapes flitting through moonlight and shadow. Wayland followed at a stealthy jog. The moon drifted behind a skein of cloud. Darkness stole across the forest floor, hiding Wayland's quarry. Worried that he might blunder into them, he slowed to a walk. He could feel the bandits getting away from him.

Here.

The dog turned and Wayland laid his hand on its neck.

They went on at speed, Wayland trusting to the dog's nose.

Without warning, the dog sank down. It turned a grave eye, telling him that the outlaws had halted and were close. The moon played hide and seek in the clouds. Wayland could make out the ride to his left. Ahead was a glade dotted with clumps of undergrowth. One of the shapes separated into two. A figure ghosted towards the ride, checked that it was empty, then ran into the trees on the other side.

It would be easier to deal with the outlaws singly, but how? Even if he could disarm them without shedding blood, it would take too long. The boy might have already passed by and reached the rendezvous. He had to get back as soon as possible.

He patted the dog's shoulder and pointed across the ride. *Kill him.*

It stood, took a few steps, then looked back.

He pulled up his mask. *Kill him.*

The dog loped off without a sound.

The moon showed itself again, casting faint shadows. Wayland could see the remaining bandit half hidden behind a tree. He would have to skirt around until he had a clear target. He began his stalk, soundless as a cat's shadow, until the man's back was in view. Wayland didn't know if it was Leofric or Siward and didn't care. Given the chance, either man would kill him as casually as he would swat a fly. Wayland summoned up an image of Ash, those dead black eyes. He thought of the fugitives and imagined what the gang would do to the one they captured. He braced back, leaning away from the curve of the bow. At full draw, the arrow was pointing halfway to the moon. He brought it down in a smooth arc, watching the iron leaf at its tip, poised to release the moment the point passed down the man's spine.

His target jumped aside. Wayland blinked. The bandit was leaning out from the tree, like a runner tensed for the off. He'd heard the stifled commotion on the other side of the ride. Before Wayland could sight again, the bandit pushed off from the tree and went zigzagging into the dark.

Wayland emptied his lungs in a sigh of frustration. Now he would have to stalk the man again. This time it would be more difficult. The bandit would be nervous.

A long-eared owl gave a cooing moan – 'oo-oo-oo'. If Wayland hadn't been such an excellent mimic himself, he would have sworn that the call was genuine. The bandit expected an answer. But Wayland knew that his accomplice was dead, gaping up through the branches with his blood leaking from his throat.

The outlaw repeated the call.

If he didn't get a response this time, he'd know that something was wrong. Wayland cupped his hands around his mouth and echoed the owl's plaintive cry.

No answer. The bandit must be wondering why his partner had crossed back over the ride. Or perhaps he'd given the wrong call.

He hooted again. Still no response. The silence pressed in on him. His heart beat against his ribs.

Somewhere a twig snapped underfoot. Wayland tensed, all his senses out on stalks.

Ahead of him, a piece of forest began to move, creeping away from him. He stepped from cover and walked towards it, making no attempt at concealment.

The bandit whirled, his arrow pointing at Wayland's chest. He fluttered a hand across his eyes.

'Siward?'

Wayland raised a hand and kept walking.

The charcoal burner ran at him. 'What are you doing? What was that noise?'

Wayland put a finger to his lips.

'They'll be here any moment,' the charcoal burner whispered. 'Why have you come back?'

Wayland was so close that he could see the man's eyes through the slots in his hood. He stabbed his finger and the charcoal burner turned.

'What?'

Wayland stepped in close and swung his knife back, elbow locked.

The charcoal burner tensed and put a hand to his ear. 'Something's coming.'

From afar came a faint but forceful scuffling, heading their way. The sound grew louder – a helter-skelter gallop, a relentless . . . what? The charcoal burner stepped back, colliding with Wayland.

Out of the trees came the dog, racing in a wide curve, its paws scrabbling for purchase. It saw the two men and skidded to a stop. Slowly it turned its head and there it stood, faintly luminous in the shadows, vapour pluming from its jaws.

'Oh my God!' the charcoal burner breathed. His bow twanged and Wayland heard the arrow go skittering across the leaf litter.

'Shoot!' cried the charcoal burner, fumbling for another arrow.

The dog was already into its charge, a grey-black blur. The charcoal burner dropped his bow and grabbed for his knife. He managed to throw up one arm before the dog flattened him.

Wayland ran forward. The dog had the man's shoulder in its jaws and was shaking him like a terrier shakes a rat. The knife flew out of his grip. Wayland seized the dog's mane and tried to wrestle the beast off.

No!

He hauled it away bucking and lunging on its hind legs.

Leave him!

The dog looked at him with blood-crazed eyes.

Leave him.

The dog stalked off in a stiff-legged circle. The charcoal burner scuttled backwards on his elbows. Wayland followed and stood over him, holding his knife. The charcoal burner looked up at the falconer, his hood twisted and the fabric over his mouth sucking in and out. Wayland leaned down and pulled the man's hood off. He took off his own hood. The charcoal burner's eyes rolled up into his skull and his head flopped back.

Wayland trussed him hand and foot and tied him to a tree. He slashed the man's hood into strips and gagged and blindfolded him.

Then he went in search of the boy.

Vallon's eyes tracked from side to side, probing the forest margins. All lay quiet as the grave. Raul carried his crossbow loaded, occasionally turning and walking backwards to check the ride behind.

'How far have we come?' asked Vallon.

'Two miles at least. It must be nearly midnight.' Raul nudged his chin in the direction of Hero and Richard. 'Those two are ready to drop.'

'Not yet.'

'Captain, if you're worried there's an ambush ahead, why are you leading us into it?'

'Wayland knows this is the road we're taking.'

'We might not see him until morning. You know what he's like. He might have gone hunting. Or more likely, he's tucked up in a cosy roost.'

'If he is, I'll kill him.'

They walked on into the oppressive silence.

'I was in a wood like this once,' said Raul. 'It was in Normandy, the dead of winter, just before Yuletide. I had a week's leave and my wages and I was going to spend them in Rouen. I'd set out in good time, but it snowed in the afternoon and I took a wrong fork. A dreary day it was, sky as dark as doom, not a house or a soul to be seen. I came to a forest and followed a track through it. No other travellers had trodden that path all day. When night fell I was still in the wood, only a sprinkling of stars to keep me straight. Walking through that winter wood, I felt like I was the only being in the world, so I took out my whistle and played a tune to keep myself company. Then I stopped whistling because I had the feeling that I had more company than I cared for.

'It was the trees. It was as if they were turning round to look at me as I passed. I watched them out of the corner of my eye and I swear I saw them bunching up on me. That was bad enough, but then . . .

'Something touched my back. I shot into the air and jumped round. "Who's there?" I called, but no one answered. Nothing but trees and snow. Right, I told myself, pay no heed to the bogles and bugbears.

98

Easier said than done, Captain. As I went on, the flesh on my back was crawling, itching for another touch. Well, it didn't come, but something else did. I heard it creeping up on me – *scritch-scratch, scritch-scratch*. Froze the blood in my veins, stopped me in my tracks. Whatever was after me stopped, too. This time I didn't dare turn round, because I knew that whatever was behind me had wings and horns and eyes as big as trenchers. I walked on, my knees knocking, and that thing came walking after me. Every time I stopped, it stopped, and every time I went on, it kept coming after me.

'It came closer – *scritch-scratch, scritch-scratch*. I began to walk faster, then faster still, but it just kept its own sweet pace a few feet behind me. Captain, I've fought in many a battle and I swear I never run from the enemy, but that thing at my heels scared me more than any mortal man with sword or lance. My nerve cracked, I don't mind admitting it, and I broke into a flat-out run. But fast as I ran, there was no getting away from it. I could hear it catching up, getting closer, hissing with rage and breathing down my neck.

'Just when I thought it would sink its claws into me, I saw a flame in the trees ahead. A woodcutter's camp. I ran for it as if Old Nick himself was after me, which for all I knew he was, and threw myself down by the fire gibbering like a loony. The old woodcutter, bless his soul, he looked down at me, and then he looked behind me and a very peculiar expression came over his face.

'"What is it?"' I cried.

'Slowly he put out his bony hand and pointed. I scrambled round. And then I saw it.'

'Saw what?' Vallon said, keeping his eyes on the trees.

Raul halted, wheezing with laughter. 'A length of rope that had worked loose from my pack and was dragging behind me.'

Vallon didn't laugh, didn't break step. 'Raul, you're a drunken blowhard.'

'Wait. I ain't finished.'

Vallon grabbed him. 'I heard a cry.'

Raul's eyes patrolled. 'Probably a fox.'

Vallon turned. 'Wayland's not coming. We'll find a path through the forest.'

'Without Wayland, we'll go round in circles. Let's make camp and move on at first light.'

Vallon felt a spurt of fury. 'What does the wretch think he's doing? If this was a regular company, I'd have him hanged for desertion.'

Raul took his arm. 'Come on, Captain, I'll find us a place to rest.'

'Sir,' Hero said, pointing down the ride.

Vallon made out a flicker of movement. He drew his sword. 'Everybody into the trees.'

They ran for cover. Raul went down on one knee and took aim. Vallon watched the advancing shape take on human outline. 'It's Wayland,' he said. 'Wayland and his dog.'

Raul slapped him on the shoulder. 'I don't deny it, Captain. I feel happier with him back. If anyone thinks they can spring a surprise on us, they'd have to get up a lot earlier than Wayland.'

'There's someone with him,' said Hero.

'It's the boy from the tavern,' said Vallon. He looked the other way. 'Stay hidden.'

Wayland swayed to a standstill in front of them. He'd roped the boy to the dog's collar. Looped over his shoulder was some kind of ragged and leafy garment.

'Raul, find out what's happening.'

Vallon scanned the road while the German questioned Wayland.

When Raul rejoined him, he was as solemn as an owl. 'You were right, Captain. There are seven cut-throats waiting up ahead by an old oak. There were two others, but Wayland dealt with them.'

'Killed them?'

'The dog killed one. He tied the other up.'

'He should have killed him.'

'I know, but there's a tender streak in the lad.'

'What's the boy's part in this?'

'He was tracking us in case we slept in the forest. His father's the leader. The outlaws start them young in these parts.'

'What are we going to do?' Hero whispered.

'Wayland knows where they're lurking,' Raul told him. 'We'll be long gone by the time they discover we've taken a different path.'

Vallon looked at the falconer. 'Can you guide us around the ambush?'

Wayland looked uncertainly at Hero and Richard.

'They ain't up to it,' said Raul. 'They're dead for lack of sleep.'

'They'll be dead all right. We have to get out of the forest before daylight.'

Wayland pointed at the boy, then at the dog, then made a sweeping gesture down the ride. He pointed at the fugitives and made the same gesture.

Vallon frowned. 'I think he's saying we should go on down the track, using the boy as a hostage.'

Wayland pointed at himself, then across the ride, and moved his hand in a half circle, indicating that he would make his way back until he was behind the outlaws' position.

Vallon looked at the boy. 'Find out his father's name.'

At Raul's approach, the boy backed to the end of his tether, breathing in and out through his nose. Raul wrapped one hand around the boy's collar and hoisted him off the ground. 'Give us your father's name, you little shit.'

The boy uttered a choked syllable.

'What was that? Ash, did you say?'

The boy jerked his head up and down. Raul dropped him. 'Sounded like Ash.'

Wayland nodded.

Vallon's eyes patrolled the dark avenue. 'Imagine how many travellers have met their deaths along this road.' He turned to Raul. 'I think we should put back into Ash's life some of the terror he's dealt out.'

To the waiting outlaws it must have seemed like a cavalcade from fairyland, the boy lolling astride the giant dog, Vallon's sword glinting across his shoulder, the other fugitives in close attendance.

The procession halted a bowshot short of the oak.

'Ash?' Raul shouted. 'Ash? Your eyes don't deceive you. That's your son on the dog, and it will rip the life from him just as cruelly as it tore out Siward's throat. Leofric's dead, too. Wolfboy killed him. Do you want to know where Wolfboy is? He's closer than you think. He's watching you. He's cloaked and hooded in your own uniform. Look at your neighbour. Look close. Are you sure he's the man you take him for? Are you sure it's a man at all? Wolfboy can change form. Listen.'

Stark silence, and then a sound that made the hairs on Vallon's neck

101

stand up. The dog that everyone thought was mute lifted its head and joined in. The mournful howling of hunting wolves rose up until it enveloped the forest, and then it fell away, leaving a tingling hush.

'The show's over,' Raul cried. 'Don't follow us if you want to see your boy again. Do as I say and you'll find him unharmed at the next village.'

The procession moved on. A mile beyond the ambush site, the trees gave way to open common. Raul puffed out his cheeks. 'Captain, that was the longest walk of my life. My back felt as wide as a barn.'

Vallon frowned at him. 'How did you know I fought alongside Rodrigo Diaz?'

'The Cid? I didn't. It was just showman's patter.' He missed a step. 'Wasn't it?'

'Go on with the others.'

Raul's footsteps faded. The road behind stretched away like a ribbon of blackened silver. Up ahead, a dog began to yap. Vallon touched his brow with the back of his hand. He felt as if he'd walked through a bad dream.

X

On a mild overcast afternoon at the beginning of April, the runagates gathered by a busy crossroads on the Ermine Way, a few miles south of Stamford. In the surrounding fields, peasants were sowing and harrowing, the same scene repeated all the way to the flat horizons, as though the peasants themselves were a crop.

The company lounged back on their elbows, legs outstretched, heels propped on toes, watching the passing traffic. Nobody bothered them. After three weeks sleeping rough, they looked a thoroughly villainous crew. So did many of the other itinerants on that highway. Carters, drovers, vagabonds and refugees criss-crossed the junction, where a makeshift bazaar of stalls and booths offered refreshments, charms and horoscopes. A squadron of Norman cavalry rode by looking neither left nor right and went highstepping south, towards London. Raul farted.

'What are we waiting for?' asked Hero.

Vallon stood and squinted north to the highway's vanishing point where a small but important outline had appeared against the milky sky. It advanced slowly, slower than a man walks, gradually shaping itself into a wagon train of four great carts, each drawn by six oxen and piled so high with bales and kegs that they resembled lurching siege engines. Whips snaked and cracked. Two thuggish outriders flanked the convoy and crop-eared mastiffs stalked between the wheels. A feral-looking boy darted from wagon to wagon, greasing the axles with lard. The driver of the leading vehicle was whippet-thin with a face like a shrivelled wineskin. Beside him sat the train captain, an immensely fat merchant with dewlaps spilling over his fur muff.

Vallon walked into the road with Raul and held up a hand. The teamster drove back the mastiffs with whiplashes of stinging precision. Vallon leaned on the drawbar while Raul translated. When Hero saw the merchant turn his piggy eyes towards him, he had a premonition of ill fate.

Money changed hands. Vallon walked back, took Hero's elbow and led him aside.

'Are we going to London?'

'You are. This is where we part company.'

Hero felt hot and cold at the same time. 'How have I offended you?'

'You haven't. The truth is, we're stepping deeper into danger, and you're not cut out for it.'

'I'm tougher than Richard.'

'Richard has no choice but to flee these shores. You have better things to do with your life.'

'But I vowed to serve you.'

'I release you from that vow,' Vallon said. He kissed Hero on both cheeks and stood back. 'Don't think I won't miss your company. Evenings around the hearth won't be the same without your stories and speculations.'

It was happening too fast for Hero to muster an argument. The teamster rolled his whip. Vallon raised his arm. 'The fare's been paid. The merchant's a rogue, but he won't harm you. I told him I'd be joining you in London.' He pressed money into Hero's hand. 'I'm sorry I can't spare more. I know you'll reach home, though. Apply yourself to your studies. Write to me in Byzantium. Astonish me with news of your achievements. God speed you and keep you.' He squeezed Hero's shoulder and turned away.

One by one, the others came up to make their farewells. Richard sobbed openly. Raul grasped him in a bear hug. Wayland regarded him with cool blue eyes, looked like he might shake his hand, then nodded and turned.

The wagon train trundled into motion. Hero watched his companions walk away down the highway, travelling east. Vallon didn't look back. Didn't turn his head once.

Hero wept. All his life the men he loved had disappointed him. His father had dandled all five of his sisters and died three months before the birth of his only son. Cosmas, the man who could have taught him everything, had been with him for less than a month. And now Vallon, the captain whom he'd vowed to follow until death, had discarded him without a backward glance.

He really was all alone. His companions had crossed the horizon in one direction; the wagon train had disappeared in the other. Only the serfs remained, stooped and wretched in the clotted light. Hero dragged himself up and shuffled towards London.

Around the campfire that night, Vallon told the remaining fugitives that the first leg of their journey was nearly over: in two days they would reach Norwich.

'Tomorrow we'll hire three mules and buy new clothes. Next day we'll enter Norwich separately. Richard, you'll ride ahead and find lodgings and make contact with the moneylender. Wayland will escort you as far as the city walls. Go in by yourself. It will be safer. Use a false name and say that you're travelling on family business.'

'One of the soldiers might recognise me. If news of our crimes has reached Norwich ...'

'If the worst happens, tell them the truth about the ransom and the moneylender. Remember you're Olbec's son. You don't take shit from common soldiers. Wayland, if Richard runs into trouble, wait for us outside the west gate. Raul and I will join you by sunset. We'll be travelling as military engineer and engineer's assistant.'

'All the gates will be watched,' Raul said. 'The guards will ask for papers.'

'Lady Margaret gave me documents carrying the royal seal. No soldier would dare open them.' Vallon laced his hands behind his head. 'Well,' he said through a yawn, 'the night after next we'll eat like lords and sleep under goose down.'

His assurances fell into a queasy silence. Everyone knew that Norwich was one of the most formidable Norman strongholds in England. Three hundred soldiers manned its castle, and they would be alert. Less than a year ago the garrison had helped capture the Isle of Ely, the last redoubt of English resistance, only a day's ride to the south. The rebel leader called Hereward had escaped the encirclement and was still at large, rebuilding his forces, it was rumoured.

Richard and Wayland left for Norwich at cockcrow. Vallon and Raul followed at noon, riding across the levels under a huge blue sky. Vallon wore his hair cropped short, Norman style, and was clothed in clerical grey. Miles before they reached Norwich, they could see the castle dominating the skyline.

They halted at a drinking trough well short of the west gate and mingled with other travellers watering their animals. Wooden walls surrounded the city and a guard tower bridged the gate. Curfew was approaching and the road was busy.

'No sign of Wayland,' Vallon said. 'Let's hope the Normans haven't arrested him.'

Raul spat. 'They'd have more chance of catching the wind.'

Vallon led his mule back to the road. They eased into the stream of travellers. The sergeant of the guard, a hard-bitten veteran, watched them approach.

'That one's trouble,' said Raul.

The sergeant crooked a finger. 'You two. Move to one side. Get down.'

Vallon stayed mounted. The sergeant strutted up to him. 'Didn't you hear me?'

'I heard,' Vallon said in a clipped voice, 'and I've a good mind to repay your insolence with the flat of my sword. I'm Ralph of Dijon, military engineer, travelling on the King's commission. As for my business, that's not for you to know.'

'Papers.'

The sergeant returned them after examining the seal. He hailed a soldier who was rubbing down a horse outside the tower. 'Hey, Fitz, escort these two to the castle.'

'That won't be necessary,' said Vallon. 'I want to take a look at the city's outer fortifications while there's still light.'

The sergeant's jaw jutted. 'The castellan doesn't like visitors dropping in unannounced. I'll send Fitz to let him know you're on your way.'

'No, you won't. My job is to inspect the King's defences any way I see fit. This is a surprise inspection. That's why the castellan isn't expecting me.' He flicked the documents. 'Understood?'

The sergeant stiffened to attention. 'Sir.'

They could hear him muttering obscenities as they rode through the gate. 'He won't forget you in a hurry,' Raul said.

'I know. Let's hope he doesn't enquire about us at the castle.'

Raul stood on tiptoe. 'There's Wayland.'

The falconer turned his back on them and went up the thoroughfare, dodging through a crowd of vendors and shoppers. Vallon and Raul followed, pestered by a swarm of touts and beggars, the lame and the blind hopping and tapping in their wake. From every doorway children observed them with sharp urban eyes. Months had passed since Vallon had been in a city. He breathed in the pungent mixture of woodsmoke, sawn timber, meat, tallow, bread, livestock and shit. They turned a corner by a church with a round stone tower and left the stink and hubbub behind. Two turnings later they were in a narrow lane deserted except for a rooting hog. Wayland stopped at an iron-reinforced gate in a high wall and jangled a bell.

Richard opened the gate and led them into a courtyard paved with moss-grown cobbles. On three sides stood an ancient house with a timbered gallery, once level but now undulating and sprouting weeds. Doves cooed on the tiled roof. A well of silence filled the court.

'You said you wanted somewhere quiet.'

'It's perfect.'

Richard beamed. 'It belonged to an English merchant. I rented it from his widow, two months' rent in advance. She thinks you're a French wine importer. I took a room for Wayland and Raul at the White Hart, by the cornmarket.'

'Did you find the moneylender?'

'It wasn't difficult. His house is right under the castle walls.'

'Has he received the letters?'

'Days ago. He'll see us tomorrow, after sunset.'

'Why so late?'

'It's the Sabbath.'

'How did he react when you gave him our names? Did he seem nervous?'

'I didn't meet him. I wasn't invited into the house. I spoke to someone through a grille.'

Bells were striking compline when Vallon and Richard set off for their appointment with Aaron. In the dusk-shrouded streets, shopkeepers were boarding up their premises and citizens hurried homewards. The castle keep loomed bone-white against the bruised sky.

'I wish Hero was with us,' said Richard. 'He deserves to see our business brought to a successful conclusion.'

'Success isn't guaranteed. Drogo must have guessed our intention. There aren't many moneylenders in England. He could have got to them first.'

'He doesn't have any power over the Jews. They're not even Norman subjects. The King brought them from Rouen as his personal chattels.'

The street opened into a wide plaza surrounding the castle – a massive structure built on a huge artificial mound. In the middle of the open space stood a scaffold and several whipping posts. The heads of executed malefactors sprouted from poles planted above the castle gate. Aaron the Jew's house lay within sight of the gateway, on the corner of a street leading down to the haymarket. It was a substantial two-storey stone hall, the ground floor blind, the windows on the first floor barred and shuttered. Steps led up to an arched door braced with iron straps. Vallon lifted the heavy knocker.

A grilled flap opened and a grave-looking eye regarded them through the lattice. Several bolts were struck before the door swung open. A young man with delicate features ushered them inside. Instead of the usual aisled hall, a corridor led down one side of the house past a series of rooms. Vallon had a sense of life lived behind closed doors. He thought he heard muted female voices. The last doorway stood open. The youth bade them enter. The room was neither large nor extravagantly furnished, yet the glint of silver, the thick Moorish carpet and the scent of beeswax gave the chamber an air of restrained opulence. Aaron, dressed in a silk gown and turban, stood at a polished table that held a bowl containing a pot-pourri of rose petals. Behind him a fire burned in a wall-hearth. By the shuttered glass window a pair of goldfinches twittered in a cage.

'Please,' he said. 'Be seated.'

'I believe you've received letters from my mother,' Richard said.

Aaron smoothed a roll of parchment and let it flick back. 'Lady Margaret wishes to pledge lands in Normandy as security for a loan.'

Richard reached under his cape. 'Here are the deeds. I understand that the estate is valued at more than three hundred pounds.'

Aaron angled the documents to the candlelight. 'On paper, yes, but I'll have to ask my agent to make an independent valuation.'

'How long will that take?'

'Hard to say. Not more than six weeks.'

'Six weeks!'

'It depends on conditions at sea. The last time I crossed to Normandy, I had to wait eight days for a favourable wind.'

Richard shot Vallon an appalled glance. 'The ransom deadline looms close. My brother's life hangs in the balance.'

Aaron's dark eyes remained calm. 'The property may have deteriorated. I have to make sure that it isn't entailed. There may be other legal encumbrances.'

Vallon touched Richard's wrist. 'I'm the man who carried the ransom terms to Lady Margaret,' he said. 'There are complications that Richard is embarrassed to speak about. Sir Walter has a step-brother of the same age. There's a long history of rivalry. Until I arrived, he had every reason to believe that his brother was dead, leaving him the undisputed heir.'

'I see.'

'He's already put obstacles in our path. Given enough time, he could sabotage our venture entirely.'

Aaron composed his hands on the table. 'This isn't the first ransom I've dealt with. You aren't the first to find yourselves embroiled in a family dispute. I'm sorry, but it makes no difference. If all goes well, we should be able to seal the contract in three weeks.' He looked past his guests, brows arching. 'Yes, Moise?'

His son murmured something in Ladino – the hybrid Spanish-Hebrew tongue used by the Sephardim of Iberia.

'Excuse me,' Aaron said, and crossed to the door.

'We can't wait three weeks,' Richard whispered.

'We might not be around that long,' Vallon said, watching the pair at the door. The interruption was clearly unexpected. Aaron looked startled, concerned, then resigned, but when he returned, his expression had settled into courteous inscrutability.

'A young man has called at the house – a Greek who speaks excellent Arabic. He claims to be your servant.'

Vallon had been so sure that the visitor was Drogo or one of his agents that it took a moment to sink in. 'Hero's no longer my servant. I dismissed him three days ago. No, "dismissed" is too harsh. I released him so that he could return to his studies.'

Aaron frowned politely. 'What does he study?'

'Medicine. But there's no branch of philosophy that doesn't excite his curiosity.'

'Do you want me to send him away?'

'By your leave, it would be better if he joined us.'

Aaron nodded at Moise. In a little while Hero tottered through the doorway. He looked wasted, his eyes as dark and vacant as a moth's. Richard gasped with concern and ran to him. When Hero saw Vallon he began to blubber. Vallon only just managed to stop the Sicilian from falling at his feet and kissing his hands.

'Sit down,' Aaron said, guiding Hero to a stool. 'You're exhausted. You're ill. Which is ironic. Your master says that you're a student of medicine.'

Hero nodded and snuffled.

'Which school do you attend?'

'The university at Salerno.'

Aaron's face lit up. 'The finest in the Christian world. Have you ever met Constantine the African?'

'He was one of my teachers. It's because of Constantine that I'm here.'

Aaron's brows rose halfway to his turban. He laid his arm around Hero's shoulders. 'You'd better explain. Moise, bring some soup for the boy. Wine and biscuits for our other guests.'

While Hero recounted how Constantine had recruited him, Vallon and Richard sipped wine from rare beakers of Damascus glass. When Hero had finished, Aaron softly pounded the table. 'Your master's right: go back to school and complete your education. It's a ludicrous undertaking. Four gyrfalcons to be carried from Norway to Anatolia by way of Rus, the expedition to be led by men who are neither traders nor navigators. I wouldn't consider the proposition for a moment.'

'We run the risk,' Vallon pointed out. 'Whatever happens to us, you won't be out of pocket.'

Aaron ignored the Frank's bad manners. He warmed his hands before the fire. 'What's the minimum amount you need?'

'Not less than a hundred pounds.'

'Including the cost of trade goods?'

'I'm not a merchant. I hadn't thought of it as a trading venture.'

'Pardon me, but if I'm to advance the money, I want to know that it's working. There's no sense sailing all that way in an empty ship. I imagine Norway lacks many commodities.'

Hero nodded. 'They have no wine and little corn.'

'And presumably they have some resources that would find a market in the south.'

'Woollens, salted and smoked fish, eider down.'

Aaron spread his hands. 'You see. You must be businesslike. The falcons are perishable goods. At least protect yourselves against their possible loss.'

Vallon's eyes narrowed. 'Are you saying you'll give us the money?'

Aaron permitted himself a smile. 'I'll advance you one hundred and twenty pounds. The term of the loan is for one calendar year. Interest will be charged at twopence in the pound, compounded weekly. That's more than fifty per cent in the year. Yes, I know what you're thinking. Usurer. But the King takes more than half. Besides, I don't expect you to redeem the pledge.'

Vallon couldn't stop his eyes drifting towards the lower floor. Aaron interpreted the look.

'I don't keep money here. Come back the day after tomorrow, at noon.'

Vallon rose. 'Can you help us charter a ship?'

'I know several merchants who trade with Flanders and Normandy. I'll make enquiries, but my guess is that none of them would make a crossing to Norway.'

Vallon wasn't sure how to express his gratitude, or whether he should express it at all. Eventually he held out a hand.

Aaron held on to it. 'Your face is familiar. Did you campaign in Castile?'

Vallon looked him in the eye. 'Yes.'

Aaron released his hand. 'Moise will show you out.'

As Vallon and Richard made for the door, father and son held a whispered conference.

'One moment.'

Vallon turned.

'My son reminds me that last summer a man called applying for a loan. What was his name? Never mind. He was a Norwegian, one of the few survivors of the invasion defeated by the English at Stamford Bridge. He escaped in a ship which was blown on to the shores of East Anglia. He wanted money to repair the ship. He offered to repay me in fish, and when I told him I wasn't a fishmonger, he tried to sell me an orphan English girl. Even if he'd had collateral, I would have refused him. He was a repulsive wretch, careless with the truth and a little touched in the wits.'

'I think we can do better than that.'

'I only mention him for these reasons,' Aaron said. He counted them off on his hand. 'He has a ship; he needs money to repair it; he wishes to return to his homeland.' Aaron held up another finger. 'And, as I said, he's crazy. I wish I could recall his name. It will come to me the moment you leave.'

'Where will we find him?'

Aaron conferred with Moise. 'A town called Lynn. It's a day's ride north, on the Wash.'

On the steps outside the entrance, Vallon watched soldiers moving in the glow of braziers by the castle gates.

'Come here,' Aaron said to Hero. 'You know that Jews in England are forbidden to follow any trade other than moneylending.'

'Yes, sir.'

'I'm a wealthy man. I can travel anywhere in the kingdom without paying tolls. In a court of law my word is worth the testimony of twelve native-born Englishmen. I have many personal blessings – my family, my religion, my books, my garden. Yet the truth is, I'm confined to a cage.'

'We ought to be going,' Vallon said, eyeing the soldiers.

'I didn't choose to be a moneylender,' Aaron continued. 'My ambition was to follow the law, but ...' With a little roll of the hand, he dismissed the tidal waves of history. 'You must be a scholar of great promise to have been singled out by Constantine Africanus. Don't waste your talents out of misguided devotion to a ...' Aaron looked at Vallon. '*Condottiere*.'

'There'll be time for my studies when I return.'

'Ha! The optimism of youth, the bliss of ignorance. There's never enough time.'

Aaron closed the door. Bolts were shot, chains rattled. The key turned in the lock.

Hero eyed Vallon. 'Don't be angry, sir.'

'Why did you come back?'

'I couldn't forget how Cosmas had said an unfinished journey was like a story without an ending. How could I leave without knowing how this one ends?'

Vallon shook his head. 'Not all travellers reach their destination, not all journeys end happily.'

'There's another reason – something that's been plaguing my conscience.'

Two of the soldiers had begun walking towards them across the plaza. 'Tell me later.'

They were at the foot of the steps when the judas hole opened. 'Snorri,' Aaron called. 'That's the Norwegian's name.'

'Leave us,' Vallon said. He waited until Richard had gone, then sat down on a stool by the open window. Hero remained standing in the middle of the room, clasping his medicine casket. A single candle burned on the table. The only other light came from the moon rising in the east.

'Well?'

Hero spoke in a barely audible voice. 'When you asked me why Cosmas had gone to such pains to rescue Walter, I told you that he'd acted out of pity and a desire to visit England. I wasn't speaking the whole truth.'

Vallon remembered his doubts about the old man's motives. He rested a foot on the window ledge. 'I've had a trying day and I'm in no mood to question or catechise. If you have a confession to make, get on with it.'

'It's true that Cosmas went to the Sultan's camp after the disaster at Manzikert. It's true that he helped negotiate ransom terms for some of the more noble prisoners, including the Emperor Romanus. While he was involved in these negotiations, he received a message from Sir Walter. It was a strange message and one that greatly excited his curiosity. Walter claimed to have in his possession documents sent by the ruler of a distant Christian realm. One of the documents was a letter addressed to the Byzantine Emperor, offering to forge an alliance against the Turks and Saracens.'

'How did Walter come by the letter?'

'While raiding into Armenia, he sacked a Muslim town. The governor gave him the documents in exchange for his life. He himself had obtained them after his troops intercepted a caravan travelling from the east. Cosmas knew how important an alliance could be. He believed that the defeat at Manzikert would lead to a Holy War. He went to the camp where Walter was being held. The Norman showed him the documents and offered them in exchange for his release. Cosmas persuaded Walter to give him the first few pages of the letter, in which the ruler offers an alliance and describes the glories of his far-off realm. The rest of the letter – explaining how an embassy can reach his land – together with the other document, Walter wouldn't part with. He said that he'd hand them over once Cosmas had bought his freedom.'

'For a king's ransom.'

'That was the first setback. The Emir couldn't understand why Cosmas would want to free a low-ranking mercenary, so out of mischief or suspicion he set his demands impossibly high.'

'Go on.'

'Cosmas intended to raise the ransom from the patriarch in Constantinople. But before he reached the capital, he discovered that the newly returned Emperor had been deposed by his nephew.'

'The traitor who provoked the rout at Manzikert.'

'Yes, sir. Cosmas knew that as one of Romanus's advisors, his own life was in jeopardy. He fled to Italy.' Hero's voice faltered.

'Sit down,' Vallon said. He waited until Hero was seated, cradling the chest on his knees. 'We've reached Italy. What then?'

'He visited his old friend Constantine. It was at this point that I was recruited, but I swear I had no knowledge of the documents. All they told me was that we would be travelling to England on a matter of great importance. By the time we left Rome, Cosmas was already showing signs of his fatal illness. I urged him to turn back, but he wouldn't abandon the journey. The quest had become an obsession.'

'When did he take you into his confidence?'

'Not until the night you found us in the storm. He passed the letter to me before he died.'

'You still have it?'

'Yes, sir. It's hidden in my medicine chest.' Hero made a move to open it.

'Later. What's the name of this ruler?'

'He doesn't boast a regal title. Out of Christian humility, he calls himself Prester or priest – Prester John.'

Vallon frowned. 'I've heard the Moors speak of him.'

'As have I. Cosmas heard rumours of him as far east as Samarkand, as far south as Egypt. Some say that he's descended from one of Alexander the Great's generals. Others claim that his line goes back to Gaspar, one of the Magi who visited the baby Jesus in Bethlehem.'

'Where does his realm lie?'

'Somewhere in the three Indias. When Cosmas made an expedition into Greater India, he discovered several Christian communities founded by the apostle Thomas, the patron saint of Prester John's realm. Cosmas believes that the seat of his empire is to be found in India the Far, a land that travellers of old call Ethiopia.'

Vallon nodded without really taking it in. For him, India was a place receding into myth and mist.

'Describe it.'

Hero ran his hands over the lid of the chest. 'Prester John says that it lies next to the original Eden. It's divided into seventy-two provinces, each with its own king, some of whom are pagan but all tributary to the supreme ruler. Twelve archbishops and twenty bishops administer to the spiritual welfare of the ruler's subjects. A river called Physon flows into his realm from Eden. Along this river is a clear fountain with miraculous properties. Anyone who drinks of its waters will be restored to youth and vigour.'

Vallon suppressed a smile. 'Cosmas was mortally ill. Did he hope to bathe in the fountain of eternal youth?'

'I don't know about that, but he told me that if he'd obtained the documents, he would have sold them to finance a voyage to Prester John's court.'

'More than one document, you say.'

'Yes, sir. The other is a gospel whose existence has been long suspected, but not confirmed until now – the Gospel of St Thomas.'

Vallon levitated from his stool. 'The Gospel of St Thomas.'

'Including the Secret Sayings of Jesus, recorded in his lifetime.'

Vallon scratched his head. 'Does the world need another gospel?'

'Cosmas told me that this one is of inestimable importance. Scholars believe that the four Biblical gospels were written by followers of the apostles, long after their deaths. But the St Thomas gospel was written in his own lifetime, dictated in his own words. Imagine – a first-hand account of Jesus's life by one of his closest disciples. Let me read you the opening verses.'

Hero opened the secret drawer and extracted a sheet of parchment. 'The gospel's written in old Greek. Walter allowed Cosmas to read some of it and transcribe the first page. This is how it begins: *Herein is set down the Gospel of Judas Thomas called Didymus, in which I shall show you what no eye has seen, tell you what no ear has heard, give you what no hand has touched, and open up the secret places of the human heart.*'

The words resonated in Vallon's head. His skin prickled. 'You said that Cosmas intended to sell the documents.'

'Not merely for personal gain. In the year of my birth, Rome and Constantinople broke off relations in a dispute over which is the head and mother of the Churches. Cosmas hoped that Prester John's offer of an alliance against the enemies of Christendom might help mend the schism. Cosmas also had other calculations. In his lifetime he's seen political power slip from Constantinople to Rome. Although Byzantium is the richer empire, her territories are small and isolated, while Rome's ecclesiastical jurisdiction extends throughout Europe. He believed that if Constantinople possessed the Gospel of St Thomas, it would strengthen the patriarch's hand in his dealings with the pope.'

Church politics meant nothing to Vallon. For him it was enough that he believed in God, prayed more or less daily, and wasn't surprised or disappointed when his prayers went unanswered.

'Why didn't you tell me?'

'Cosmas swore me to secrecy. He knew nothing about you except that you were a mercenary. He thought you might steal the letter and sell it in Rome. In his last few days he wasn't in his proper state of mind.'

'Did he expect you to continue the quest on your own?'

Hero hung his head. 'At first I was honoured to be given the task. That excitement didn't last long. Once I'd considered what the mission would involve, I knew it was beyond me. I wanted to tell you, but with every passing day it became more difficult to confess my deception. I feared your anger. I thought you'd punish me by driving me away.'

'What were you going to do with the information?'

'Hold it close until we'd completed our journey to England. I hoped that Olbec would reward us for bringing him news of his son. I didn't know that Walter had exaggerated his family's wealth or concealed Drogo's existence. My intention once we'd parted company was to return to Italy and hand the letter over to the patriarch in Sicily.'

'All without a word to me.'

Hero averted his face. 'Punish me as you see fit. If you cast me away again, it would be no more than I deserve.'

Vallon leaned forward. 'Hero, I guarded you safe throughout our long journey. For your sake I risked my life, endured cold, hunger and exhaustion.' He stabbed a finger. 'By all rights, in all honour, I should kill you.'

Hero's eyes bolted. 'Yes, sir. My treachery is unforgivable.'

Vallon stared at him. 'What a fool you are.' He kicked the stool over. 'What a fool am I!' He paced around the room. 'In any other circumstances I would have known that Cosmas wouldn't be travelling to England without some secret motive. The reason I didn't was that my mind was clouded by grief.' Vallon stopped, face darkening, and pointed a trembling finger. 'You simpered and flattered.' Vallon pitched his voice high. '"Oh, sir, you are strong and I am weak. Please help me."' Vallon whirled and braced his hands each side of the window.

Hero began to sob. 'I know you were troubled in mind and are troubled still.'

Vallon's vision cleared. He looked out into the garden. A carpet of

116

mist had lapped up from the river and ducks quacked in the murk. He drew a shaky breath and straightened up. 'What are the documents worth?'

'Whatever price you ask. Enough gold to keep you comfortable for life. A duke's title and estate. But first you have to get your hands on them, and I think that will be impossible.'

'Why?'

'It's as Aaron said. A voyage to Norway and then a journey through Rus and across the Black Sea. Sir, even an army couldn't complete such an epic undertaking.'

Vallon turned. 'A group of determined individuals can travel further and faster than any army. Cosmas proved that. You told me that he journeyed to the ends of the world and didn't even carry arms.'

'Yes, sir. But Cosmas was exceptional.'

'Does Walter know what the documents are worth?'

'He knows they're valuable, but doesn't understand wherein their value lies. He can't read and his circumstances make it impossible for him to make a translation.'

Vallon stared into the night, a vast enterprise beginning to take shape in his mind. 'Go to bed.'

'Sir?'

'Go to bed. I need to think.'

'Are you done with me, or is this merely a suspension of punishment?'

'I won't punish you. Your conscience may have saved our lives. If you hadn't shown up at Aaron's house, we'd be kicking our heels for the next month.'

'Does that mean I can stay?'

'Perhaps that *is* your punishment. I gave you a chance to quit the enterprise; there won't be another. You're tied to my destiny now.'

'As you will it.'

'Nothing can be set in motion until we have the money. Until then, I don't want you to stray beyond the house. Tell no one about the documents.'

A long pause. 'I almost confided in Richard. It was a burden too great to bear.'

'Now you share it with me. Keep it that way.'

Hero's feet dragged as he left the room.

Vallon put up a hand. 'On second thoughts, you might as well make yourself of service.'

'Whatever you command.'

'Get all the rest you can. The day after tomorrow, go to Lynn and find the Norwegian. Take Raul and Wayland. It will probably be a wasted journey, but it will keep the three of you out of mischief.'

When Hero had gone, Vallon stood at the window gazing at the moon. He shivered. It wasn't the dank river air that brought him out in goosebumps. He'd embarked on the journey as an act of penance, but now he had a nobler purpose – one ordained by heaven. Appointed to show the way, Cosmas had said, that dark all-seeing eye fixed on him. Vallon dropped to his knees and raised his hands in prayer.

'Dear Lord, thank you for giving me this task. I'll pursue it with all my might, and if I succeed, then by Your grace and if it pleases You, redeem me of my grievous sins.'

Moonlight sharpened his profile, etched deep shadows on his face. It was late. He closed the shutters, lay down on his bed and for the first time in months slept like a baby.

XI

The expedition to track down Snorri started in a muddle. When Hero arrived at the inn by dawn's first light, Raul couldn't be found. Wayland had last seen him reeling into the night with a jug of mead clutched in one hand and a nervous-looking whore in the other. On the road from Norwich, Hero's mule cast a shoe and it was midday before a smith sent them on their way again. Trying to make up for lost time, they took directions from a peasant and ended up back at the crossroads they'd started from. Nightfall caught them miles short of Lynn, forcing them to take shelter in a rat-infested barn, where they discovered that neither of them had brought any food. Wayland stalked out in disgust and spent the rest of the night under a wrecked cart.

Tempers were still frayed when they reached Lynn, a fledgling port straddling a lagoon where the Great Ouse flowed into the Wash. Here they faced another problem. Hero couldn't speak English and Wayland couldn't speak at all. Eventually, Hero went into the settlement to make such enquiries as he could, leaving Wayland by a ferry upstream.

The day was calm and warm. Wayland sat hugging his knees, watching wildfowl rise and fall over distant mud flats. This was his first close view of the sea and it was nothing like the tempestuous ocean his grandfather's tales had painted on his imagination. Yet something about the brilliant monotony entranced him. His mind dissolved into it, transporting him across horizons to a land where dwelt white falcons as big as eagles.

Hero flung himself down. 'I knew this was a fool's errand.' He rolled over and doled out biscuits. 'Snorri was here on Tuesday, selling fish at the market. But you can forget about the ship. None of the locals has seen it. They say he's a crackbrain.' Hero waved across the river. 'He lives up the coast, a day's journey there and back. We'd need a guide to find our way through the marshes, but we can't risk anyone finding out what we're up to.'

Wayland could see where this was leading.

Hero sat up. 'If it was up to me, I'd say the hell with it. By now Vallon will have the money. He can take his pick of ships. If we go chasing around in the marshes, we won't get back to Norwich until tomorrow.' He paused. 'What do *you* think?'

Wayland stood and set off towards the ferry.

'Are you sure you don't want me to come with you?'

Wayland waved his hand. *No.*

Hero hurried after him and held out a purse. 'You'd better take this. In case there is a ship. To show that we're serious.'

Paths made with bundles of withies ran through the marsh, diverting Wayland to peat cuttings or salt pans or little islands whose residents – all strangely alike in feature – shook their fists and hurled clods until he retreated. Other trails followed some logic lost on Wayland, ending in reed-choked culs-de-sac or petering out in sludgy wallows. He set his own course, jumping fleets and ditches, until he reached a mere too deep to wade and too boggy to bypass. Balked, he headed for the coast and followed the shoreline, negotiating saltings where the tides had hollowed out holes big enough to swallow a horse and cart. The terrain was too flat to offer a view of the way ahead and several times he detoured on to peninsulas that dead-ended in mud flats or sandspits.

It was well past noon when he reached the mouth of a deep, sluggish creek. He wiped sweat from his eyes. Upriver, reed beds stretched across the horizon. In their shade stood a squalid dwelling thrown together from driftwood and hides. He slaked his thirst with rainwater from a barrel next to the hovel and then looked about. The rustling of the reeds sounded like scandalised whispering.

He walked out on to a sand bar and faced the salty breeze. Sunlight on the water dazzled like broken glass. Something hissed overhead and he looked up to see a flock of waders flare round and bunch together like smoke sucked back to its source. A falcon threw up from its stoop, glanced over its shoulder and flicked over in another dive. Again the flock jinked and closed up with a soft whoosh of wings. The falcon jabbed and probed for an opening, the waders twisting and turning, one moment black against the sky, the next almost invisible in the sea glare.

The falcon spread its wings and sailed down to a bleached horn of driftwood where it preened and roused before flying away low across the sea.

When Wayland turned there was a girl standing on the grass, her long blonde hair backlit by the sun. His insides cartwheeled. He shielded his eyes and saw the dog galloping towards her.

'No!'

The dog stopped, astonished. It looked back, tail wagging uncertainly. Wayland ran up and caught hold of it. His heart pounded. The girl watched him with eyes as pale as water.

'Why are you looking at me like that?' she said.

Wayland passed a hand over his eyes. 'Nothing. I thought you were ... It doesn't matter.'

'That's the biggest dog I've ever seen. Can I stroke him?'

'I wouldn't if I were you. He isn't safe with strangers.'

The dog broke free and reared up, planting its front paws on her shoulders, knocking her backwards. She laughed and pushed it off. It flopped on its side and wriggled like a puppy. She knelt and tickled its chest. She looked up, brushing a strand of hair from her face. Something broke inside Wayland.

'He likes me.'

'You remind him of somebody.'

'What's he called?'

'He doesn't have a name. I never got round to choosing one.'

'That's silly. All dogs have names. Like people. Mine's Syth. What's yours?'

'Wayland.'

'You talk funny. Where do you live?'

'Nowhere. I came from Northumbria.'

'Is that a long way?'

'Yes.'

'Lynn's as far as I know. Except for heaven. Are you looking for Snorri?'

'That depends. Does he have a ship?'

'No, only a little punt.'

Apart from her colouring and wide, luminous eyes, the girl didn't really resemble his sister. She was so thin that he'd taken her for a starveling child, but she couldn't have been much younger than him. Her threadbare tunic hung torn at the collar, exposing most of one pale and grubby breast.

She crossed her arms and gripped her bony white shoulders. 'You keep staring at me. It's rude.'

'I'm sorry.'

'I forgive you.'

'What?'

'I forgive you.'

Sadness overwhelmed him. 'I have to go,' he said. 'What's the shortest way back to Lynn?'

She didn't answer.

'Never mind. I'll find my own path.' He scuffed the ground with his toe. 'Well, then.'

'I've never seen the ship. He's hidden it in the fen.'

Wayland looked at the swaying reeds. 'Do you know when he'll be back?'

'Soon. He's fishing. He's been gone since dawn.'

'What's he like?'

'He's disgusting.'

Wayland sank down. The girl sank down, too. They watched each other. Wayland broke a biscuit in half. 'What did you say your name was?'

'Syth. I told you. You should pay more attention.'

He hid a smile. That really did sound like his sister.

She clutched the biscuit in both hands and devoured it like an animal, darting glances up at him. She was so skinny that he fancied he could see her bones through her skin. He handed her his own share. 'I already ate,' he said, and went and studied the sea.

'Here he comes.'

Out of the marsh came a man poling one-handed, the pole steadied between his ribs and the stump of his other arm. Some further disfigurement on his forehead – a brand burned into the bone. An ugly specimen, features squeezed together, no chin to speak of, a wispy beard crusted with food and snot.

He stepped ashore, tied up the punt and lifted out a plaited rush pot. Ignoring Wayland, he reached inside and dangled an enormous eel in front of the girl. Writhing black and bronze coils half-filled the pot.

'Look at 'em beauties. Fattened 'em on a corpse I found drownded in the fosse. Picked him white in a night, they did. I'll sell these 'uns at Norwich. Normans like eels. Won't tell 'em how they got so meaty.' His accent was a weird mixture of Norse and some local dialect that sounded like feet slurping in mud.

Wayland stepped in front of him. 'I hear you're master of a ship.'

'Lots of furriners lose their way in the marshes,' said Snorri, raising his voice. 'Ain't I right, me dear?'

'We want to charter it.'

Snorri pointed at his punt. 'Titty thing like that? Buy yer own. I need thissun for me fishing.'

'I'm talking about the knarr you sailed from Norway in.'

Snorri cackled. He turned in a circle, arms spread wide. 'You see any knarr?'

'The one you've hidden in the marshes.'

Snorri scowled at the girl. 'Go look iffen ye want. Search all year. Don't blame me iffen ye come to harm. Fens and fitties ain't no place for folk what ain't bred and born to 'em.'

'We'll pay you.'

Snorri looked straight at Wayland for the first time. 'Git on. Ye ain't got nowt but the breeks to cover yer arse.'

Wayland opened the purse and flashed silver. Snorri's tongue darted over his lips. Wayland pulled the pursestring tight.

'Show me that 'un again.'

Wayland put the purse away.

Snorri leered. 'Sell ye the girl iffen ye fancy. Pretty little mother. Make ye a good wife.'

Wayland glanced at her. 'She isn't yours to sell.'

'Ain't no one else's. Kin all dead. If t'weren't for me kindness, she'd be graveyard mould too. Don't ye fret. She's a virgin far as I know. Protecting me investment. But that don't mean she can't do things to make a fella's eyes bulge.' He pumped his stump up and down. 'She's me right-hand girl iffen ye get me meaning.'

The girl clutched her torn tunic and fled.

'Her'll be back,' Snorri said. 'Nowheres else to go.'

Wayland fought back the urge to strangle him. The dog's teeth chattered with rage. 'I'm not interested in the girl.'

'Iffen ye want a ship so bad, why don't ye charter one in Norwich or Lowestoft?'

'Come on,' Wayland said to the dog.

'Where ye want to go, anyhow?'

Wayland gave a loose wave.

Feet padded behind him. Snorri pawed at his elbow. 'Let me taste that silver.'

Wayland held up a coin. Snorri snatched it, licked it, bit it, closing his eyes like a gourmet savouring a delicacy. Wayland plucked the coin from his hand.

'Satisfied?'

'German. Ye can't get enough of that.'

'Have you got a ship or not?'

'Come with me, young master, and we'll see what Snorri's got.'

He stepped into the punt and held out a hand. Wayland ignored it and climbed in. Snorri pushed off.

'Folk say me wits is twizzled, but that don't bother me. Fact is, I judge a man's sense by how rum he thinks I be. Ye can't bamboozle Snorri Snorrason. In the fens, Snorri be king. Any harm comes to me, ye'll never git out on yer ownsome.'

Wayland saw his hand brush a knife ground to a sliver.

Snorri cackled. 'I makes ye nervous, don't I? I makes ye twitchy.'

'Look at the dog. Go on, look at it.'

Snorri looked. His grin curdled.

'It's the dog that's nervous. Like you said, you'll never get back on your ownsome.'

Snorri left the main river channel and navigated an amphibious maze. Some of the waterways were as broad as fields, some no wider than the punt. Wayland and the dog sat upright in the bow, marvelling at the wealth of wildlife. Huge black rafts of coot scooted across the meres like panicked monks. Ducks banked in tight echelons. Skeins of geese scrolled overhead. Birds of shapes and patterns Wayland had never seen before stalked and muttered in the reed beds.

Snorri bared a broken yellow smile. 'Lost already, ain't ye?'

Wayland looked about him. Channels and inlets led away in all directions. The sun gave few clues to direction. One minute it was in his eyes, the next athwart him. Looking behind, he couldn't have said which passage they'd just taken.

'Took me five years to find me way to and fro. And that's only because I was apprentice to a man whose folk have lived in these marshes since Noah's flood set 'em down hereways. He had six webbed toes on each foot and that's no lie. Taught me all he knew.' Snorri tapped his temple. 'All in here. Ain't no signs or waymarks. Place changes from year to year, storm to storm.'

'They say you fought at Stamford Bridge.'

Snorri didn't answer and after a while Wayland stopped waiting for an answer.

'Two hundred ships crossed from Norway and when the fighting was done, no more than thirty sailed for home. I lost me arm on the retreat, and the two were with me were wounded worse than me, one of them holding his guts in his lap. They were dead that same day, the sail gone. Even if I'd got both me hands, a man can't row to Norway. I drifted for three days and on the fourth day a wind crashed me on this coast. That's where me master found me.'

'Was he the one who firebranded you?'

Snorri clapped his hand to his forehead. 'That's a lie. That was done in battle.'

Mumbling, he poled on. They came out of an alley into a mere, startling a heron into clumsy flight. Snorri stopped poling. The punt glided until it nudged the bank. The ripples died.

Cautiously, Wayland stepped on to the spongy shore. Snorri pulled the punt out of the water and led the way towards a thicket of reeds. He stopped in front of them.

'I don't see any ship,' Wayland said.

'Ye ain't supposed to.'

Wayland looked all about.

'She's right afront of ye,' Snorri said. He grabbed the reeds with both hands and pulled. A six-foot gap opened up and Wayland found himself looking at a section of clinkered hull.

'There she be. *Shearwater*. Me sea-steerer, me wave-rider.'

'It's a wreck.'

Snorri was outraged. 'She's not even seven years old.' He rapped on the hull. 'Hear that? Oak heartwood, not a trace of worm. See that,' he said, pointing to the stempost. 'That come out of a ship that sailed to Norway in a fleet led by Cnut. Carved from a single tree. What d'ye think of that?'

'My grandfather fought with Cnut.'

Snorri regarded him. 'Thought ye might have a drop of Viking blood.' He stroked the rivets that joined the strakes. 'Forged by me uncle, the cunningest smith in Hordaland. And looky here,' he said, leaning over the gunwale and pointing to the lashings that tied the strakes to the frame below the waterline. 'That ain't no cheap spruce root. That be whalebristle.'

Wayland swung himself up onto the deck. The ship was much bigger than he'd expected. 'It's holed.'

'Course she's holed. If she wasn't hurt, I'd be back in Hordaland, drinking in the ale hall with me comrades.'

The ship lay canted over in a silted-up channel. Wayland looked back at the mere. 'You'll never get it out. The water's too shallow.'

'No shallower than the day I brung her here. She draws less than two feet without ballast. Asides, ye're looking the wrong way.' Snorri pointed his nub in the opposite direction to the mere. 'The river's only a titty bit yonder.'

'How many men needed to row?'

'Oh me, oh my, the man knows nowt about shipcraft. She's a sailing ship, ye numpty. In a fair wind I could sail her to Norway on me own-some.'

'And if the wind isn't fair?'

'Four at a pinch, six would be better. Wouldn't quarrel with eight.'

'Is it repairable?'

Snorri stroked the hull with pride. 'A boat as well crafted as thissun can take a lot of harm before she loses seaworthiness. Like a living thing, almost mends herself.'

'How long to repair it?'

'Hold ye hard. Ye're jumping ahead of yerself.'

'Just tell me what needs doing.'

Snorri twisted his scraggy beard. 'First there's the oak for the new strakes. Not any old oak, but oak standing two hundred year and rooted in clay, riven when green and tied with rivets shaped to clinch and tempered so they give in heavy seas. A boat's like a horse. Ye want them yielding no matter how hard ye ride. Needs a new sail of close-wove wool or linen. Ye can buy good flax from Suffolk, but Norfolk wool is stronger. The caulking needs seeing to, and then there's—'

'How much?'

Snorri sucked through the gaps in his teeth. 'Materials and labour, ye're looking at sixteen pounds.'

'Quiet.'

Snorri cringed. 'Course, depends where ye voyage. If it's a sea cross-ing, there ain't no good cutting corners. Ye'd regret those pennies when the waves start coming up over yer eyes. But if ye were just coasting, maybe ye could make do with pine boards and—'

'I said shut up.'

The dog's ears were pricked.

'Only a bull of the bog,' Snorri said. 'Lots of marsh fowl make calls like humankind. I tell ye, there's places even Snorri Snorrason don't like to be abroad after dark, when the corpse candles light and the lantern men go walking.'

'Take me back.'

After a while Snorri heard the cries, too. 'Ye didn't say ye'd brung more furriners.'

Three men were waiting by Snorri's shack – Hero, Richard and a stocky, bearded stranger they must have recruited as a guide.

Hero's expression was doom-struck. 'We're finished,' he said. 'Vallon's been taken. Raul, too.'

XII

Richard spoke in a stunned staccato. 'Noon yesterday we went to collect the money. Aaron was anxious, didn't want to admit us. Enquiries were being made about us. The transaction was off. Vallon forced himself into the house, showed his sword, told Aaron that he'd take him down to hell if he didn't produce the money. As soon as we got it, we returned to the house. Raul was waiting. He warned us that soldiers were combing the city street by street. Vallon was burying the money in a midden behind the house when they turned up. They broke down the gate. Raul held them up. The soldiers gave him a terrible beating. They would have killed him if I hadn't told them I was Count Olbec's son. They were the same ones who questioned Vallon and Raul at the west gate. The sergeant said they were arresting them on murder warrants sworn by Drogo. They demanded to know your whereabouts. I told them we hadn't seen you since the day we left the castle and that Hero had parted company with us days ago.'

'They don't know about the moneylender,' Hero added. 'Richard merely told them that he was carrying out business for Lady Margaret.'

'I showed them her letters, but it made no difference. There's a reward at stake. The sergeant's going to hold them until Drogo arrives.'

'He's in Lincoln,' Hero said. 'Messengers won't reach him until tomorrow, but when they do, he'll ride flat out for Norwich. We've got less than two days to rescue them.'

Richard wrung his hands. 'We'll never get them out. They're guarded night and day.'

'They're not in the castle,' Hero said. 'They're in the tower over the west gate. The soldiers intend keeping the reward for themselves.'

'It doesn't make any difference,' Richard said. 'They're locked in a cell on the top floor. They've put Raul in chains. The guards took me up to see them.'

Hero sat down. There was a long silence. 'If we recovered the money, we could try bribing them.'

Richard shook his head. 'Drogo would slaughter them if they let Vallon go.'

'What about creating a diversion – a hullabaloo that would bring the soldiers out of the tower?'

'Like what?'

'I don't know. A fire.'

'Don't be ridiculous.'

'All right. Forget it.'

Hero put his fists on his knees and laid his forehead on them. Another silence.

'Hero?'

'I'm thinking.'

At last he raised his head. 'You say they don't know about the inn.'

'It won't take them long to find out – not with the way Raul's been carrying on.'

Hero stood and walked off, punching the palm of one hand. 'Describe the tower.'

'The gateway passes under it. On one side is a stable, on the other a guardroom with stairs to the tower.'

'How many floors?'

'Three above the gate, I think. Yes, three.'

'How many soldiers?'

'Eight – four on gate duty, four with the prisoners.'

'And you're sure they didn't follow you?'

'I'm certain. I told them I was going to ride to Lincoln to settle matters with Drogo. I rode until it got too dark to see the road.' Richard began to tremble.

'How often do the guards change?'

'I don't know. Back home it's every four hours.'

'What's the Normans' favourite food?'

Richard looked askance. 'What's that got to do with anything?'

Wayland dusted off the seat of his breeches and went over to Snorri's hut. He pulled back the greasy hide that served as a door and went inside.

'We have to get back to Norwich,' Hero said.

Richard's eyes were haggard. 'I can't ride another foot. I haven't slept a wink.'

'Not you. You stay here.'

Wayland emerged from the hut carrying a rush creel. He set it down before Hero and took off the lid.

Hero squirmed back. 'What are those for?'

'You said you wanted food,' Wayland told him.

Hero stared at Wayland, glanced at Richard, looked back at Wayland. Dumbstruck. 'You spoke. How ...? What ...?'

Wayland looked down the coast. Syth was gone. He smiled. 'An angel came to me.'

Riding by night they approached the walls of Norwich while it was still dark. They dozed shivering on their mules until the city began to take shape against the morning sky. Low clouds wept a thin drizzle. They waited until the west gate opened and traffic began to flow before moving closer. Hero studied the tower. A square building roofed with thatch, its timber walls pierced by loopholes. Sheep grazed in front of it, but after curfew the ground would be empty. Hero raised his eyes to the sky, praying that the dreary weather would last another night.

He turned to Wayland. 'I'll go into the tower as soon as the guards change after dark. It might be a while before I get the chance to signal.'

They retreated to a nearby copse. Wayland hobbled the mules and left the dog to guard them. Then he and Hero skirted the city on foot and approached the north gate. Costermongers cried their wares at the entrance. Two guards manned the gate, chatting up a pair of English girls.

Wayland looked at Hero. 'Ready?'

Hero gave a convulsive yawn. 'Now or never.'

At first it seemed like they would stroll through unnoticed. Then one of the giggling girls pointed at random and the guard she was flirting with followed her throwaway gesture and noticed Hero. Their eyes met.

'Keep walking,' Wayland said.

'They're going to stop me. I know it.'

'Give me the eels. Stay three or four paces behind me.'

Wayland strode ahead, whistling a jaunty air. The soldier didn't even look at him. He stepped away from the girls and was about to stop Hero when Wayland tripped and sprawled, sending the creel flying. Half the eels shot out and the others began to slither for freedom. A crone selling charms shrieked and clambered onto her stool. A retailer of palm crosses waved one in each hand. The girls screamed and threw themselves into the arms of the soldiers. A mule laden with clay pots shied against a barrow heaped with Easter buns.

Wayland scurried through the wreckage. 'My precious eels! Help me, good citizens. That's a week's work escaping.'

A boy made of mud and sores darted from nowhere, grabbed one of the eels and raced off with it lashing under his arm. Other urchins dashed forward and began scooping up the buns. The guards didn't hinder Wayland, but they didn't help him. They were falling about laughing, punching each other in mirth. By the time Wayland had gathered up the last eel, Hero was inside the city.

They met up at the White Hart.

'Your dish will be ready by evening,' Wayland said. 'Give the dame a penny for her trouble.'

'Run through what you have to do.'

Wayland sighed. They'd gone over the plan a dozen times. 'I sneak into the house and recover the chest. I buy a heavy axe and a stout hemp rope.'

'At least thirty yards.'

'I leave by the same gate ...' Wayland paused. 'The guards might wonder why I came in with eels and left with cordage.'

'No, they won't. You're a fisherman who traded his catch for tackle.'

'Unless they look in the chest.'

'Buy a net to wrap up the silver.'

'I return to my position outside the west gate. Then I wait. For how long?'

'If we're not with you by sunrise, assume the worst.'

Wayland looked at him. Hero tried to smile. 'Aren't you going to wish me luck?'

Awkwardly, Wayland extended his hand.

*

130

Hero sat in his room at the inn, unpicking the hem of his tunic. He coiled a long length of twine around the hem and loosely sewed it up again. Maddening, fiddly work, but when he'd finished it was still only early afternoon. He lay on his bed unable to rest. He kept getting up and sneaking to the door, imagining he'd heard footfalls on the stair. It was almost a relief when the church bells rang vespers. He left the inn, went through the dusky streets towards the west gate and spied on the sentries until one of them beat a gong to announce the curfew. A few latecomers hurried in, the last of them speeded on his way by the sergeant's boot, and then the guards pulled the double doors shut and barred them with a balk of timber. They went inside the guard-room and not long afterwards the next watch came out.

Hero returned to the inn and collected the supper basket and a leather wine bottle. By the time he returned to the tower it was dark and the streets nearly empty. Torches guttered each side of the gate-way. One of the sentries lounged against the guardhouse entrance, sucking a toothpick. The other three sat inside around a brazier, play-ing dice.

Hero took a couple of deep breaths and hurried up. 'Is this where Vallon the Frank's held?'

The guard took the toothpick out of his mouth. 'Who's asking?'

'I'm Hero, his servant. Why are you holding him?'

The guard turned to his confederates. 'Fetch the sergeant.'

In a little while the sergeant came hurrying down the stairs, pulling on his tunic. His complexion was livid, one side of his jaw bruised and swollen. 'Where have you been hiding?'

'I've been away on my master's business. I only got back this evening. As soon as I heard he'd been arrested, I came straight here.'

'What business?'

'That's confidential.'

The sergeant grabbed him by the throat. 'What business?'

'For the Lady Margaret. More than that I'm not permitted to say.'

'Go easy, Sarge,' one of the soldiers said.

The sergeant let go. Hero massaged his windpipe. 'What charge are you holding my master on?'

The sergeant bellied up to him. 'Don't play the fucking innocent with me. Murder, warranted by a justice in Durham.'

'Murder? That's ridiculous. Who's been murdered?'

One of the soldiers shifted uneasily. 'I dunno, Sarge. He doesn't act like a man with a price on his head. And those papers from Olbec's wife looked genuine. I've served with Drogo. Good man to have beside you in a ruck, but a nasty temper, always picking fights. This might be just a family squabble.'

'Makes no fucking difference. The Frank impersonated an official of the king. Acted high and mighty, weaselled his way past me with false documents. *Me!* I'm not having that.' He kicked Hero's basket. 'What's that?'

'Supper for my master.' With shaking fingers, Hero unwrapped the linen cloth covering the basket and looped the cloth through his belt.

The sergeant sniffed the stew. 'That's too good for those scumbags.' He took out the wine bottle.

'It's for the German. He gets in a queer temper if he goes too long without drink.'

The sergeant crooked his face up. 'See this? The German did that. Nearly broke my jaw. *He's* going to the whipping post. I'll swing the lash myself. I'll cut him to shreds. I'll lay his fucking spine open.'

Hero could hardly speak for fear. 'He was only doing his job. If he's committed an offence, we'll pay the fine. There's no need to take your grievance to law.'

A smile spread across the sergeant's face. 'Lads, one way or the other we'll come out a few bob ahead.'

One of the soldiers dipped a finger into the stew and licked it. 'Mmm. Matelot of eels with prunes, like my mum used to make.'

The sergeant smacked his hand. 'You'll get your share when you come off duty.' He nodded at one of the other guards. 'Search him.'

After a rough examination, the guard stepped back and shook his head.

'Take him up.'

Two soldiers frogmarched Hero up the stairs. As he climbed the tower, he tried to memorise the layout. The first floor was a storeroom and armoury. By the time he reached the sleeping quarters on the second floor, he couldn't hear any sounds from below. When the sergeant opened the door to the top floor, the first thing Hero saw was Vallon's sword and Raul's crossbow propped against the wall behind a table occupied by the off-duty guards. Vallon was seated on a pallet behind closely spaced posts that divided the room from floor to rafter.

Raul sat slumped in a corner of the cell like a malevolent doll, shackled hand and foot and tethered by a chain to a ring in the wall. His eyes had closed into puffy slits and his bloated mouth stretched in a clown's smile.

Vallon jumped up and grabbed the bars. 'About time. Have you arranged our release?'

'Listen to him,' the sergeant said. He walked up to the bars. 'The only release you'll get will come at the end of a rope, but not before I've skewered you from arsehole to eyeball. Just one more night and then Drogo will be here with testimony to hang you. In the meantime, why don't you watch us enjoy the supper your servant's brought.'

Vallon kicked the bars and swung away.

The sergeant fiddled with a heavy wooden bolt secured by a crude tumbler lock. He opened the door and shoved Hero into the cell.

Vallon took his arm. 'How did they catch you?'

'They didn't. I gave myself up.'

Vallon winced. 'That's taking loyalty too far.'

'No, sir. I came to get you out.'

'How?'

'The food's drugged.'

They watched the soldiers lay the table. The sergeant ladled stew and poured wine. He raised his cup to the prisoners. 'Sure you don't want any? It's delicious.'

'Whew. This wine packs a punch.'

'It's the German's favourite brew,' said Hero. 'It might be too strong for Norman heads.'

One of the soldiers scowled. 'I can outdrink any poxy German.'

'I've seen him empty two bottles in one sitting.'

Vallon nudged Hero with his foot, warning him not to over-egg it. 'What's in it?' he whispered.

'Opium, henbane and mandragora. It's a drowsy syrup used by the surgeons at Salerno.'

'How long does it take to work?'

'I don't know. Constantine prescribed it for the pain in Cosmas' chest – one spoonful to help him sleep.'

'How much did you put in the wine?'

'About half a pint.'

By the time the soldiers had finished the meal, they'd grown very mellow. One of them yawned. 'I'm for my pit,' he said, and lurched out of the door.

'Me, too,' another said. He rose and had to steady himself against the table. He eyed the door as if taking aim, launched off and found himself heading in the wrong direction. 'Whoops.' He corrected his course and tacked towards the door. 'Whoops.'

When they'd gone, the sergeant fumbled for a chequers board. 'Best of five for a farthing.'

Halfway through the second game, his opponent gave a breathy laugh and rubbed his eyes. 'Blimey, the wine creeps up on you. I can see two boards.' He sat blinking slowly, his head alternately drooping and jerking upright, slowly and inexorably sagging to the table.

The sergeant's breathing grew harsh. With great effort he turned his head, some belated conjecture dawning. He swore and made an attempt to rise, the movement sweeping platters off the table. He almost made it to his feet before his legs buckled and he collapsed, banging his head on the bench and sprawling in a slack-limbed heap.

'Christ almighty,' Vallon said in a faint voice. 'Now what?'

'Which wall faces away from the city?'

'This one.'

Hero crossed to a loophole, pulling the cloth out of his belt. He put his arm through the slit and waved.

'I don't know how much time we've got,' Vallon said. 'The duty guards sometimes come up.'

Hero put his finger to his lip, his mouth strained in concentration. A vixen yipped.

'That's Wayland. He's waiting below with a rope.'

Vallon frowned at the loophole.

'Not that way,' Hero said, and jabbed a thumb towards the roof.

Vallon smiled. He squatted. 'On my shoulders.'

He straightened to full height and Hero wrapped his arms around one of the collar beams. Another boost from Vallon and he was lying across the beam. He swung his legs over and groped to his feet. Holding on to a rafter, he shuffled to his right and began wrenching out the spars threaded into the thatch.

Vallon jumped for the beam but couldn't reach it. Raul had braced himself against the wall, trying to wrench out the ring anchoring his chain. Vallon lent his strength. There was a creaking and groaning and the ring tore loose. Raul made a stirrup with his manacled hands and hoisted Vallon up to the beam. He and Hero ripped the battens out and tore at the thatch, straw cascading over their heads until Hero, spitting and blinking, saw the sky.

'Keep going,' Vallon told him.

They continued demolishing the thatch until they'd cleared a space between rafters and roof joists.

'Move aside,' Vallon said.

He bent and sprang, hooking his elbows over adjacent rafters. He dangled, grunting with effort, then hauled himself up through the gap. He lay on the thatch, one hand hooked around a rafter, the other stretched down.

'Give me your hand.'

He grasped Hero's wrist and dragged him up. Hero thrashed until he managed to locate a joist and braced his feet against it. Vallon manoeuvred alongside him and they sat looking out from the city. The sky was beginning to clear. Moonlight rimmed the top of a cloudbank. From somewhere on the ground came a snatch of voices and a gust of laughter.

Hero ripped open the seam of his tunic and pulled out the twine. He tied a lead plug to one end and paid out the cord. He was beginning to worry that he'd miscalculated the length when he felt it go slack. A moment later he felt three quick tugs.

'Wayland's got it.'

'Give it to me.'

Vallon hauled in the line. A rope came snaking up over the roof. Vallon gathered it in coils. It went tight and there was a dragging clunk from below.

'Careful,' said Hero. 'There's an axe tied to it.'

Vallon drew it up as if it were a cargo of eggs. The rope went taut and wouldn't move. Vallon slackened off, then pulled again. 'It's snagged under the eaves.' He jiggled and teased, but couldn't free the axe from the overhang. His face gleamed with sweat. 'Hold this,' he said, handing Hero the section of rope tied to the axe. Carrying the free end, he went back down the hole and lashed it around the crossbeam, leaving a length hanging to the floor.

Once more he heaved himself up on to the roof. He rested until he'd regained his wind, then walked backwards down the fixed rope.

When he reached the eaves, he leaned over at full stretch, feeling for the axe.

'Give it some slack.'

Hero eased off.

'Pull.'

Hero yanked and the axe came slithering up. Vallon hauled himself up the fixed rope, untied the axe and dropped it to Raul before climbing down himself. Everything was taking longer than Hero had expected.

'Lie on your side and put your arms out,' Vallon panted. He raised the axe and brought it down, severing the chain between Raul's hands and feet. 'Now your feet,' he said, and brought the axe down again.

From his perch on the roof, Hero could see part way into the soldier's quarters. One of the sergeant's legs was in sight. He thought he saw it move. As he opened his mouth, Vallon shifted position, blocking his view.

'Spread your hands,' Vallon told Raul. 'Don't move.'

The axe descended and Raul sprang up. Vallon wiped his forehead with his arm.

'Sir?'

Vallon looked up. 'What's the matter?'

'The sergeant. I can't see him.'

Vallon whirled and froze. Raul seemed to run in two directions at once, then scrambled for the dangling rope.

'No time!' Vallon shouted. 'Break down the door.'

Raul attacked the bolt with blows that shivered the tower.

'Hurry!'

The bolt splintered and Raul kicked the door open. He and Vallon charged through it shoulder to shoulder and grabbed their weapons.

'What about me?' Hero cried.

'Climb down. Don't wait for us. When you reach the ground, run.'

Hero heard their feet clattering on the steps, dying away. He peered in terror down the steep pitch of the roof. He knew he didn't have the strength to climb down unaided. From the belly of the building came a muffled shout. There was a long interval of silence, then the sound of someone running from the tower, followed by a furious clanking, both noises fading away up the street. A shutter opened somewhere and a voice called out. Hero dithered, losing time, until he realised that he had no choice but to take the stairs. He slid down to the beam, burning his hands, and dropped to the floor. The guard who'd fallen asleep playing chequers still lay slumped over the table. Hero tiptoed to the door and looked down into the soldiers' sleeping quarters. The stairs were empty and two of the guards lay in drugged abandon on their pallets. Hero crept down step by step, one hand brushing the wall. When he reached the next floor, he listened as hard as he could, then went through the door. Halfway down the next flight the sergeant lay spread-eagled with his head cleft from crown to neck. At the bottom another soldier slumped half decapitated against the door-jamb. Blood everywhere – sprayed up the walls, pooled on the floor. Hero's feet slipped in it. Behind the door sat another soldier, holding his stomach. He was still alive. When he saw Hero, his lips moved.

'Help me.'

'I'm sorry,' Hero whimpered. 'I'm sorry.'

The guardhouse was empty, the brazier still burning, the dice lying as they had fallen. One of the soldiers sprawled face down outside the entrance. Hero found Vallon struggling to lift the beam barring the gates. He swung round, his face freckled with blood. 'Take the other end.'

'Where's Raul?'

'One of the soldiers got away. Raul went after him.'

Between them they lifted the beam. Vallon barged the doors open. There was a jangling up the street and he spun and raised his sword. Raul staggered towards them clutching his side, still wearing manacles and dragging the severed chain. 'Lost him,' he gasped.

Shouts carried from the city centre.

'Let's go,' Vallon said, then checked. 'Did you bring the mules?'

'They're with Wayland.'

'How many?'

'Two.'

'Not enough. We won't get clear on foot.' Vallon made for the stable at a dead run. 'Raul, give me a hand. Hero, watch the street.'

Hero was dimly aware of shutters opening and householders crying out in alarm. He kept seeing the pleading stare of the dying soldier on the stair. Someone touched his arm. Wayland had materialised out of the dark. He gestured with his chin at the guard lying near the entrance.

'There are more inside. It's a charnel house.' Hero's stomach heaved.

Vallon and Raul ran two saddled horses out of the stable. Lights were beginning to spark on the castle ramparts. A bugle blew.

'They're coming,' Vallon said. He helped Hero on to one of the mules, then mounted his horse. 'Ride like the devil.'

They galloped clear of the town, Vallon dragging Hero's mule by its reins. They reached a river and forded it, the water cold to their knees. On the other side Vallon pulled up. The city cast a shadow in the night, three columns of lights crawling out from its base.

'It isn't just Drogo now,' said Vallon. 'The Normans won't leave a rock unturned until they've caught us. They'll be watching all the ports. We'll have to turn west, lie up in a forest.'

'We found the ship.'

'You found it! Where?'

'Wayland will tell you.'

'It's damaged,' the falconer muttered.

Vallon's jaw dropped. 'He spoke. Am I dreaming? Is this a night of miracles?' He grasped Wayland's arm. 'Damaged, you say. How badly? How long to make it seaworthy?'

'I don't know. Days, Snorri said.'

'We don't have days,' Raul said. 'Drogo will find out about the ship from the moneylender.'

Vallon thought about it. 'Aaron won't admit to knowing about the ship, and even Drogo will think twice about harming one of the King's money-spinners.' He turned back to Wayland. 'Where's the ship berthed?'

'It's not in a harbour. It's hidden in the marshes.'

One of the torchlit columns was bobbing in their direction. 'Better get moving,' Raul said.

'Ride on,' Vallon said. He heeled his horse alongside Hero. The moon emerged from the clouds, lighting one side of his blood-spattered face. He spread his arms in an embrace, but Hero beat them away.

'We had to kill the soldiers,' Vallon told him. 'If we hadn't, all three of us would be dead. We wouldn't have suffered clean deaths. Before they hanged us they would have broken us on the rack. They would have wound ropes around our temples until our eyes sprang from their sockets and our brains leaked from our ears.'

'This isn't why I came back,' Hero shouted.

'And that's why I sent you away.'

Tears and snot ran down Hero's face. 'I was going to be a doctor. I was going to save lives.'

Vallon shook him. 'You have. You saved mine. You saved Raul's. You saved yourself.' He wrenched at his reins. 'Now shut up and ride.'

XIII

Sunset was gilding the reed tops as Snorri ferried the last of the fugitives to the island. Euphoria had given way to gloom. It seemed to Vallon that they'd reached a dead end rather than a sanctuary. All their hopes rested on a crippled ship and a man of barely human form. Even if the ship was salvageable, Vallon couldn't see how they could float it out of the marsh. And if they did manage to reach the sea, they still had to find a crew. Wherever Vallon looked, he saw problems. No shelter except for a rotting lean-to. No wood for fuel, no fresh water except what little they'd brought with them. And, having left the horses and mules hobbled behind Snorri's shack, they had only the punt for transport.

While Raul and Richard stripped the ship of its camouflage, Snorri scuttled about showing off its features.

The knarr was a sturdy workhorse, fifty feet from stem to stern and more than thirteen across the beam. Amidships was a hold with space for fifteen tons of cargo and two small half-decks at each end that could be used for shelter and cooking in foul weather. Stored upside down across the hold was the ship's boat, about fifteen feet long. Thirteen overlapping strakes made up each side of *Shearwater*'s hull. In the topmost strake below the gunwale were eight oar ports – two on each side of the fore and aft decks. Snorri showed Vallon the side-rudder he'd removed from its fittings on the starboard quarter. He showed him the pine mast he'd set aside on trestles. Most of the damage was confined to the starboard hull, where timbers had been stove in over a length of about twelve feet. To row the knarr to its resting place, Snorri had lowered its draught by offloading tons of stone ballast at the mouth of the creek.

139

All this Snorri explained in a mixture of mangled English and mutilated French.

'Where did you learn your French?' Vallon asked.

Snorri rubbed thumb and forefinger together. 'In Norwich market. Normans be me best customers.'

Vallon and Raul's eyes met.

Richard and Wayland drifted away as the light began to fail. Vallon made another inspection and stood back, chin in hand. The ship was sounder than he'd first thought.

Snorri fawned in front of him. 'What d'ye think, cap'n?'

'Where will you find the timber and other materials?'

'Norwich, cap'n. Ain't nowhere nearer for what we need.'

'How long to make it seaworthy?'

'Three weeks iffen ye want her nice and shipshape.'

'You've got five days.'

Vallon didn't wait for Snorri's response. He paced off the distance between the ship and the river. Ninety yards. He looked back along the mud-filled channel.

'It will take us a month to dig it out.'

'I been ponderin' that meself. I knows a few sturdy fellas who'd be happy to work for a good day rate.'

'Will they keep their mouths shut?'

'Oh yes, cap'n. Marsh folk be tight as clams.'

'We need a couple of boats to get about. And I want the horses brought here.'

'You leave it to Snorri, cap'n.' He bared his atrocious teeth. 'We ain't discussed fees and other particulars.'

Vallon studied the ship again. 'Let's cost the repairs.'

When he joined the rest of the company, a bloated spring moon was floating free of the marsh. Geese passed in relays across its face, crying like hounds. Snorri hovered at the fringe of the firelight, rubbing his hands.

'Well, gentlemens, mebbes it's time ye told Snorri what haven ye're bound for.'

'Sit down,' said Vallon.

Snorri lowered himself to the ground, grinning cautiously.

'The Normans are hunting us,' Vallon said.

'I knew ye were wrong'uns the moment I set eyes on that Wayland. I ain't got no more affection for Normans than what you have, but it ain't what ye're running from that pesters me. It's where ye're going.'

'Iceland. A trading expedition. We're after falcons.'

Snorri's grin remained intact. The others stopped eating and looked at each other. Snorri jumped up. 'I ain't going to Iceland.'

Vallon patted the bullion chest. 'We'll pay you well.' He scooped up a handful of coins and poured them back. 'A fee or a share of the profits. Your choice.'

Snorri's tongue flickered. 'What goods are ye trading?'

'Whatever finds a ready market. You'd know more about that than me.'

'Ye can't go wrong with timber. There ain't no forests in Iceland.'

'Apart from falcons, what goods do they have in exchange?'

'Woollens and down, whalemeat and cod. And they ship walrus ivory and white bearskins from the Greenland settlements.'

'Snorri, it sounds to me like this voyage could set you up for life.'

Snorri's lips rolled back. 'What's my share?'

'One-fifth.'

'One-fifth,' Snorri repeated. 'One-fifth.' He dropped to his haunches. 'Where ye taking 'em?'

Vallon accepted a shank of smoke-blackened mutton from Raul. 'We'll be trading as we go. Timber to Iceland, ivory to Rus.'

'Rus!'

Vallon wrenched at the tough meat. 'Further than that. The falcons are bound for Anatolia.'

'Where's that?'

'East of Constantinople.'

Snorri bobbed back up. 'East of Miklagard! That ain't a possibility.'

Vallon shrugged. 'That's our problem. Carry us as far as Norway and your job's done.'

Snorri looked cornered. 'I got to sleep on it.'

Vallon stood and put an arm around his shoulders. 'I need your answer tonight. Tomorrow, I want you to go to Norwich and buy the materials. Why don't you take a stroll and mull things over?'

Snorri backed into the dark. They could hear him conducting a debate with himself.

'I thought we were sailing for Norway,' Richard said.

'Change of plan. It's April now. The trading fleet from Iceland won't reach Norway until late summer. There's no certainty that it will be carrying gyrfalcons, let alone white ones. Even if it did, we'd have to pay a fortune for them. We have the whole summer ahead of us. We can sail to Iceland at our leisure. Wayland can harvest the falcons at their nests or trap the choicest specimens. They won't cost us a penny.'

Wayland nodded.

'Another consideration. Drogo knows what purpose is driving us. Our crimes are serious enough to have been brought to the King's notice. England must have diplomatic relations with Norway. I don't want to spend the next four months worrying about being arrested. In Iceland we'll be beyond the Normans' reach.'

'Makes sense,' Raul said.

'I don't want to sail anywhere with Snorri,' Richard said. 'He has habits so foul it makes me sick just to think of them.'

'Hush,' said Wayland. 'Here he comes.'

Snorri planted himself in front of Vallon. 'Cap'n, I been thinkin' about it all ways round and I ain't voyaging to Iceland. Six years I been cast away, every day dreaming of home. I'll tell ye what I'll do. I'll take ye to the Orkney Isles for twenty pounds. Those are Norwegian islands, cap'n, lying a titty bit off Scotland's north coast. Ye can charter an Iceland-bound ship there.'

'How many days' sailing?'

'Depends on the wind. A week at least, and the same again afore ye reach the Iceland shore.'

'Twenty pounds for a week's passage? You're already getting twelve to repair the ship. I'll pay you another five.'

'No, no. She's my ship and I set the fare.'

'You'll not find any other passengers for that broken-down old scow.'

'Aye, and ye'll not find another ship. Ye're in no position to bargain.'

'I'm not bargaining. Your ship is our only way out and I won't let your money-grubbing stand in our way.'

'Knock him on the head and drop him in the bog,' said Raul.

'Hold ye hard. I didn't say I ain't open to negotiation. What do ye say to fifteen pound?'

Vallon didn't answer.

'Twelve?'

'Seven, and I'll throw in the crew's wages. That's my last word.'

Snorri's face writhed. ''Tis a hard bargain ye drive. How many of ye be sailors?'

Only Raul raised a hand.

'Is that all? There ain't no deep-water sailors hereabouts.'

'You're the ship's master. Finding a crew's your job.'

'Mebbe I could take on a few men up Humberside. It's the getting yonder that vexes me.'

'We'll manage. Wayland's strong and clever with his hands. I'm not too proud to dirty mine. We'll find tasks for Richard and Hero.'

Snorri shuffled his feet. He rubbed his palms. 'Well, gentlemens, seeing as it's an early start, I think I'll lay me head down.' He went off to his shelter.

'There's a bounty on us,' Richard said. 'Do you trust him?'

'No, but I think his treachery will take longer in the hatching. Raul, go with him as far as the coast and stand lookout. You and Wayland will take turns keeping watch.'

With the onset of night, it had grown chilly. A keen easterly rattled the reeds. Raul placed another piece of driftwood on the fire. The company watched the flames flatten and twist in the wind. Hero gave a shiver that had nothing to do with the cold.

'Someone walk over your grave?'

'I was thinking about the voyage. Days and days out of sight of land.'

Raul gnawed on a bone. 'It ain't too bad once you get over the puking.'

Vallon stirred the fire with a stick. Sparks flew down the wind. 'Where did you do your sailing?'

'On a Baltic slaver.'

'Did you ever land in Rus?'

'We raided the coast a few times. It's a heathen race dwells on that shore. Skin you alive if they get a chance.'

Richard straightened up in indignation. 'Heathens or not, slaving's an unholy occupation.'

Raul looked up from under half-lidded eyes. 'Maybe, but it pays well.' He waved the bone in Vallon's direction. 'Speaking of which, you ain't said what wages we're drawing.'

'We'll have to husband the money if we're going to charter another ship and buy trade goods.' Vallon saw Raul's face cloud. 'Whatever profit we make, you and Wayland will receive a tenth.'

Raul choked on his food. 'You're saying you'll give me and Wayland a tenth.'

'Each. Since you're sharing the risks, you deserve a fair share of the rewards.'

Raul pulled an astonished face at Wayland.

'How come you gave it up?' the falconer asked him.

'Gave what up?'

'Slaving.'

Raul tossed the bone into the fire. 'I was shipwrecked. That's how come.'

Snorri left at dawn, saying he'd be back within three days. Vallon and Hero began cutting withies and rushes for lean-to's, while Wayland started scything the reeds along the channel. Mid-morning, four fen men rowed to the island towing two boats loaded with water kegs and firewood. The men climbed out carrying spades, billhooks and mattocks. They grinned shyly, not quite meeting anyone's eye, and seemed undismayed by the backbreaking task Vallon set them.

At noon Wayland took one of the spare boats and set off through the marsh to relieve Raul. He found the German whittling a knife handle in the marram grass by the creek.

Wayland shared out bread and cheese. Raul peeled an onion and ate it as if it were an apple. The first swallows were back, cutting tangents across the water. A column of cormorants straggled north against a cloudbank massed on the horizon. The wind blew fresh from the east but the clouds never came any nearer.

'Iceland,' Raul said. 'Long way to go for a few falcons.'

'White ones that only kings and emperors are allowed to fly.'

'I'll believe it when I see one.'

Raul raised his crossbow and took casual aim at a seal basking in the shallows. Wayland put a hand on the bow. Raul lowered the weapon. 'If you make it to Miklagard, what will you do with your share?'

Wayland shrugged. Wealth meant nothing to him. In the forest his family had lived as well as any lord. Everything they needed could be had for free or obtained by barter.

'You could do worse than join the Varangians, like Vallon.'

'Varangians?'

'Imperial guard. Used to be all Vikings, but since the Normans invaded, a lot of Englishmen have taken service with them. Not just common folk. There's thanes and even an earl or two. Once you've served your time, the emperor gives you a decent holding of land.'

'Is that what you intend to do?'

'Not me. I've done enough warring. I've got it all worked out. I'm going to open a tavern, take a wife – maybe a slave girl from Rus. I'll buy my family out of bondage and set them up with land and herring boats.'

'How many close kin do you have?'

'Father died in the flood that took our farm. Mother lived only a few months longer. When I left home, I had three younger brothers and three older sisters. That was eight years ago, so I suppose a few will have gone to their graves. I can't wait to see their faces when I show up. What a feast I'll throw.'

Wayland had heard Raul's fantasies before and knew he'd piss them away.

'You ain't never told me about your own family.'

'Some other time,' Wayland said. He looked down the empty curve of coastline. He could make out the sails of two fishing boats heading in for Lynn.

'There's just one thing bothers me,' Raul said.

'What's that?'

'The captain. It would be a week's work to know what he's thinking, but I can tell you he ain't on this frolic for the profits. If he was, he wouldn't be so generous to the likes of you and me. Most commanders I served under, you were lucky to see any silver except what you got by plunder.'

'So what's your complaint?'

'If I'm going to follow a man God knows where, I like to know why he's going there.'

A flock of waders alighted at the waterline. They ran forward in little spurts, their legs flickering like the spokes of a wheel.

'You must have noticed how Vallon don't sleep easy,' Raul said. 'Tossing and turning like a goblin was riding on his shoulders.'

'I don't sleep easy thinking about what the Normans would do to us.'

'That's another thing. Vallon's an outlaw twice over – in France as well as England. I heard Hero telling Richard about it.'

'What was his crime?'

'Don't know, but it must have been grievous to drive him this far from home.'

The waders sprang into the air with piping cries. Wayland watched them fly off.

Raul stood and shouldered his crossbow. 'All I'm saying is, the goblin that's riding Vallon is steering all of us.'

Wayland made his way down the strand. A V-shaped ripple heading for shore caught his attention. An otter landed, shook its fur into spikes and sat up, clasping a fish. Wayland approached to within twenty feet before it saw him and dived back. He picked up the fish – an ugly, lop-sided creature that reminded him of Snorri. The otter surfaced and watched him, only its black eyes and whiskery muzzle showing. Wayland lobbed the fish but the otter was gone before it hit the water.

He'd started back up the shore when another movement caught his eye. A harrier glided over the reeds, its cat-like face fixed on the ground. Suddenly it swerved as if startled out of a dream. Two snipe flushed from close to the same spot and jinked upwards with grating cries. The dog hadn't noticed anything amiss. Wayland walked up the beach, ordered the dog to drop and stepped inside the fen.

He placed his feet with care, making no sound louder than the reeds chafing in the breeze. He went deeper into the marsh and worked round in a semicircle until he saw Syth. She was crouching with her back towards him, clutching a bunch of reed stems, leaning out as far as she dared, one leg stretched for balance. A wide ditch lay between them. He stepped knee-deep into it and was halfway across when some sound or sense made her tense and turn. Her hand flew to her mouth and she sprang away with startling quickness. He floundered out of the ditch and raced after her. She darted into thicker growth. She knew the marsh better than he did. She was getting away. He put on a spurt and lunged and grabbed her tunic just as she dodged. It tore away in his hand and she sprawled half naked into the mud.

He jumped back as if scorched and threw the rag at her. She pulled it up to her throat. They watched each other, gasping.

'Why are you spying on us?'

Her eyes darted from side to side.

'Have you told anyone we're here?'

Syth shook her head – a single movement, like a tic. Her huge eyes were ringed with violet and her bones moved under her skin like shadows.

'When did you last eat?'

Her head sagged and she began to shake with husky sobs. Looking down at the delicate architecture of her spine, Wayland felt clumsy and at a loss. He experienced another sensation, too – the beginnings of arousal. The dog came splashing through the reeds. It made straight for Syth and began licking her tears. She flung her arms around its neck and buried her face in its fur.

'Wait here,' said Wayland. 'I'll bring you some food.'

Vallon was supervising the dredging of the channel when Wayland reached the island. He broke off with a frown. Wayland went to the larder and collected loaves, biscuits, mutton, cheese – whatever he could lay his hands on.

Vallon walked over. 'What are you playing at? You're supposed to be keeping watch.'

'The dog will tell me if anyone comes.'

Wayland began walking back to the boat.

'Stop there.'

Wayland stopped. He looked down at his feet, then turned to face Vallon.

'I need some money.'

The others had left off working. Raul came over.

'I'll deal with this,' Vallon told him. He waited for Raul to leave. 'What do you want money for? There's nothing to spend it on.'

'I need it, that's all.'

Vallon seemed to study something vaguely interesting behind Wayland. 'If you've made up your mind to leave us, I won't stop you. But you're not decamping until the rest of us have sailed.'

'I'm not deserting. I just ... I just ...' For the first time in Vallon's presence, Wayland's composure deserted him.

'How much?'

'Whatever's owing to me.'

Vallon regarded him gravely, then went to his treasury. He returned, but didn't hand over the money immediately. 'I've had all sorts under my command – thieves, murderers, rapists, the scum of the earth.'

'I'm none of those things.'

'I'd understand you better if you were. Here,' he said, handing over some coins. 'It's more than you're entitled to. Don't leave your post again without good reason.'

Wayland took a few steps, then stopped and turned. 'Sir?' It was the first time he'd addressed Vallon by title.

'Yes.'

'Have you ever seen a gyrfalcon – a white one?'

'No.'

'But they do exist?'

'I believe they do. Stay with us and you'll see wonders undreamed of.'

Wayland found Syth shivering where he'd left her, the dog's head in her lap. She paid no attention to the food. She looked at him red-eyed. 'I only did those things to Snorri because I was starving. I never let him put it into me.'

Wayland closed his eyes. He thrust the money at her. 'Go away.'

'Go where?'

'Away. It's dangerous here.'

'Why? What have you done?'

'We've killed Normans. You mustn't tell anyone you've seen us.'

She got to her feet. Her mouth trembled. 'Let me stay. I'll cook and sew for you. I'll be worth my keep.'

'Go away,' he cried, making shooing motions. 'Don't come here again.'

She backed away, clutching the torn tunic. He raised his hand in a parody of threat. She turned and ran down the shore, elbows out, heels flying, getting smaller and smaller until her outline was lost in the grain of the distance.

When Wayland moved off, the dog didn't follow. It lay stretched out with its head on its elbows, ears drooping.

'Don't say another word,' Wayland told it.

XIV

Days of toil and waiting. On the third evening, Raul stayed on the coast until dark, but Snorri didn't appear. Nor did he show up the next day. That night, passed in a limbo of uncertainty, was the low point of their time on the island. Wayland was glad when next day's lookout duty took him away to the coast. The wind had swung west and strengthened, pouring through the reeds and blowing rainclouds across the Wash. The clouds thickened and the shining band marking the horizon dwindled until sea and sky merged into drab grey.

The dog twitched awake and sat staring across the river. Wayland called it into cover and fitted an arrow. After a little while Snorri emerged on the opposite bank and peered about. He wore new clothes and he'd trimmed his hair and beard. When he thought the coast was clear, he went back into the reeds and came out leading two heavily laden mules.

Wayland stepped forward. 'We thought you'd given us up.'

'Mercy!' cried Snorri, clapping his hand to his chest. 'You put the heart across me jumping out like that.'

Wayland poled across. 'What took you so long?'

'I been on the go from dawn to dark, ordering this, checking that. Four days it took for the timber to be milled and the ironwork forged. There wasn't enough wool in all Norwich for the sail. I had to send to Yarmouth for extra ells.' Snorri slapped a bulging pannier. 'This here ain't even a tenth of the load. Had to hire two carts to carry it all.' He gestured towards the hinterland. 'They're back yonder.'

'Are the Normans still looking for us?'

Snorri cackled. 'Put it this way. I'd be ten pounds to the good if I'd given ye in.'

'Why didn't you?'

'Don't ye be looking at me like that, Master Wayland. Snorri's word is as good as a bond.'

Using all the men, mules and boats, it took the rest of the day to transport everything to the camp. Vallon and Snorri went over the goods item by item – timber, sailcloth, cordage, rivets, plates, nails, rawhide, skins, pitch, tallow, charcoal, linseed oil, turpentine, lard, horsehair,

149

glue, adzes, awls, augers, an anvil, bellows, tongs, hammers, planes, saws, kettles, cauldrons, kegs, needles, thread, sacks . . .

Vallon discussed the programme of works with Snorri. 'Who's going to fit the new timbers?'

''Tis fixed. There'll be a carpenter here tomorrow.'

'That still leaves us short-handed. It's a shame to waste Raul and Wayland on lookout duty.'

Snorri glanced at the fenmen. 'I'll have a word.'

Next morning the four dredgers arrived accompanied by two more fenmen. The carpenter was a tall, loose-limbed fellow with a face as placid as a saint's. The lookout was small, bow-legged, with quick, deep-set eyes. 'He's a fowler,' said Snorri. 'Knows the marshes as well as what I do. Ain't nobody can sneak past that 'un.'

Snorri and the carpenter set to work with adzes, trimming the planks to match the existing strakes. They were of graduated thickness, two inches at the waterline, slimming to half that at the gunwale. Raul looked on, wincing, until Snorri thrust his adze at him. 'Ye have a go iffen ye think ye can do better.'

Raul hefted the adze. 'Out of my way, you ugly heathen.' He placed his feet each side of a plank, made a few practise swings, and then began paring off shavings almost as cleanly as if he were using a smoothing plane.

'Ye've done that afore.'

Raul spat. 'I've done most things before. And some of them twice. And three times a night with your sister.'

To bend the planks to fit the curve of the crossbeams, each one had to be steamed in a wooden chamber until it was pliant. Hero's job was to keep a fire glowing under the kettle that supplied the steam. When the planks had been sawn to fit between the existing strakes, the carpenters bevelled the ends to form scarf joints. Once they fitted flush, they clinched the joints with rivets and plates heated over charcoal to cherry red and proofed in a mixture of smoking tar, linseed oil and turpentine. Richard tended the cauldron used to simmer the mixture and was also given the job of slathering the waterproofing over the timbers.

Wayland stitched together the homespun panels for the sail. Each panel measured about six feet by five, and thirty of them went into a complete sail. It wasn't long before his fingertips were blistered from pulling the needle through the fabric.

At twilight Vallon took stock of the day's progress. Only one strake had been repaired. Hero had let the fire he was tending go out, while Richard had ignited the proofing compound not once, but twice. Wayland had stitched four panels together and his fingers were on fire.

'Ye can't expect everything to go sweet the first day,' said Snorri. 'The marsh folk will bring some seamstresses tomorrow.'

Three of them turned up – two middle-aged dames and a wall-eyed girl with the figure of a fertility goddess. As she worked, the girl kept glancing at Wayland and stretching provocatively.

Raul came by and noticed the girl's brazen gestures. He grinned. 'You want me to cover while you two get acquainted?'

Wayland reddened.

'You ain't never bedded a girl, have you?'

Wayland kept his head down and went on stitching.

'Ain't seen you drunk, neither. Or heard you curse. Proper monk you are.'

'There's worse things to be.'

Raul crouched down. 'I'll tell you what's wrong with monks. All their days on earth they shun the tavern and the whorehouse, and then, never having lived, they die for an eternity of the same. Where's the attraction in that?'

'Raul,' Vallon shouted. 'Get back to work.'

Raul winked. 'Live for today – that's my motto. Because tomorrow Death may tweak you by the ear and say, "Come on, laddie. Time to be going."'

That day they fitted two more strakes and stitched ten panels together. Another three days and they'd repaired the hull. The rudder was ready to be lashed in place, the sail was nearly complete and the fenmen had dredged the channel.

After work they ate around a driftwood fire that spat flames the colours of the rainbow. Raul spun dubious yarns about scrapes in foreign parts. Snorri recounted the saga of his late commander, Harald Hardrada, the 'thunderbolt of the north' who, exiled from Norway, had fought first for the Russians then for the Byzantines before returning to Norway and seizing the crown, and who had died with an arrow in his gizzard on the field at Stamford Bridge.

When Snorri had finished, there was a mellow silence. The fire crackled and the mottled moon rode high.

'Hero,' Vallon said, 'why don't you tell us the story of Prester John and his fabulous realm?'

Everyone looked up expectantly.

'You're mocking me,' Hero muttered.

'Go on,' Richard urged. 'Please tell us.'

Hero shrugged and spoke in a throwaway voice. 'Prester John is the ruler and high priest of an empire that lies next to the garden where Adam was born. More than seventy kings pay tribute to him. When he goes to war he rides an elephant and carries a gold cross twenty feet high. Among his subjects is a queen who commands a hundred thousand women who fight as bravely as men. These warriors are called Amazons, from their custom of cutting off their left breasts to make it easier to draw the bow. Once a year they permit men of a neighbouring country to visit them and satisfy their lascivious desires. If any man outstays the allotted time, he's put to death.'

Hero looked up to see everyone open-mouthed.

'The treasures,' Vallon said. 'Don't forget the treasures.'

Hero smiled. 'Prester John lives in a palace with an ebony roof and crystal windows. Above the gables are golden apples inset with carbuncles, so that the gold shines by day and the carbuncles by night. He dines on a table made of emeralds set on ivory columns, and he sleeps on a bed of sapphire. The precious stones come from the bed of a river that flows for only three days in seven. The jewels are so large and abundant that even the common people eat off platters carved from topaz and chrysolite. Prester John welcomes all strangers and pilgrims and loads them with treasure before they leave.'

Raul lay back and drummed his heels.

'There's only one problem,' said Vallon. 'No one knows the way to this potentate's kingdom.'

Raul rolled upright and punched Wayland's knee. 'What say you and me go looking for it?'

Wayland shook his head and smiled into the fire. Though he kept in the background and rarely spoke, he didn't feel left out. With the passing of the days, a new feeling had developed inside him – a sense of fellowship.

*

Next morning he was rubbing tallow into the sailcloth to make it wind-tight when the dog cocked its ears and made for the water's edge. Wayland followed, turning his head to pick up any unusual sound. In a little while the fowler poled into sight.

Wayland knew they'd been found. 'Soldiers?'

'Aye. Eight of them. They come by boat from Lynn.'

The others hurried up and Wayland explained the situation.

'We'd better take a look,' said Vallon. 'Wayland, go with the fowler. Raul, bring your crossbow.'

The fowler led them close to the coast and lifted his hand. Wayland heard faint voices. He signalled to Vallon and Raul. The three of them climbed out and waded through the reeds, working around the voices until they were near the edge of the marsh. Vallon and Raul moved too clumsily. Wayland made them stay back while he crept forward.

He parted the reeds. The ship lay anchored off the mouth of the creek. Three soldiers remained aboard with the crew. Four clustered by Snorri's shack. The fifth stood facing the marsh, taking bearings while a stocky, bearded man pointed with the air of someone giving directions.

Wayland made his way back. 'They know we're here. Their guide's the man who brought Hero and Richard.'

Vallon pinched the bridge of his nose. 'The ship's only a rumour. Wayland found it – what? – nine, ten days ago. Nobody's seen us here since then. They can't be certain that we're in the marsh.'

Raul sniffed and spat. 'With respect, Captain, your arse is sucking wind. There'll be an army up here tomorrow.'

Vallon dipped a hand into the water. 'When's high tide?'

'Not long before midnight,' said Wayland.

'We won't make the ship ready by then. We'll have to try for the following rise. Wayland, stay and keep watch. Report back at dusk.'

'They might send a messenger back by land and wait overnight,' Raul said. 'If they do that, we'll have to fight our way out.'

Vallon raked a hand through his hair. He glanced at the ring, then showed the gem to Wayland and Raul. The future was shadowy.

Well before nightfall the soldiers returned to the ship and rowed away from the shore. When the oars were just a dark pulse, the crew hoisted sail and the ship nosed south. Wayland hurried back to the island.

153

A scene of frantic activity greeted him. They'd floated *Shearwater*. Without ballast, she sat on the water rather than in it, listing at an alarming angle. Snorri and the carpenter were fitting the rudder. They'd hoisted the mast on board and lashed it down ready for raising, its top leaning up from the rear of the hold. Raul and one of the fenmen were hitching mules to ropes attached to the stempost. The rest were lugging cargo aboard.

'They've gone,' Wayland shouted.

Vallon gave a wild laugh. 'A full moon and a spring tide. Tonight's the night.'

'Do you need me here?'

'No. Warn us if they come.'

Wayland returned to the coast. The sky faded to black. The night was very still and a long time passing. He sat listening to the sea breathing in and out. His eyes closed and his sister appeared before him in a dream. When he opened his eyes she was still there, pale as death in the darkness on the other side of the river.

'Syth?'

The vision faded. Wayland crossed himself. No mortal being, but a marsh sprite or will o' the wisp.

Fog rolled in during the small hours. When daylight came he could see no further than an arrow's flight across the stagnant sea. Occasionally the murk thinned and a mournful gleam indicated the direction of the sun, then another veil drifted over and everything sank back into dismal half light. Sounds carried a long way. Wayland heard cries of frustration upriver. He checked the state of the tide. A knot began to tighten in his guts.

He jumped up when he heard a boat approaching. Raul appeared out of the clammy overcast, his beard and hair matted with mud. He gave Wayland a rancid grin.

'Ain't you the lucky one? While you've been twiddling your dick, we've been slaving up to our arses in mud.'

'Can't you get the ship out?'

Raul spat. 'Floated her clear by midnight, rowed fifty yards downriver and grounded. Managed to work her free and then got stuck again. Snorri said we were drawing too much water, so Vallon had all of us get out and haul her off.'

'Have the marshmen gone?'

'All but the carpenter and the fowler, and they only volunteered at the point of the captain's sword.'

'How far have you got?'

'I'd say we ain't even halfway.' Raul wiped a dewdrop from his nose. 'What's the tide doing?'

'Coming up to full.'

Raul peered down the coast. 'They won't come by ship in this fog. And they can't cross the marsh at high water. I reckon we still got time.'

Someone upriver gave a drawn-out cry.

'That's Vallon. You'd better get back.'

Raul climbed into his boat. 'Wayland?'

'What?'

Raul raised a clenched fist. 'Fortune or a grave.'

Wayland watched the water level creeping up. A shoal of mullet drifted into the creek and marked time on slowly fanning fins. The water rose in jerks and shivers. It reached the high tide mark and went on rising. Wayland felt the lunar force dragging at his own blood.

The tide twitched and stopped. Flotsam circled in the slack current.

Wayland paced, slapping his thighs, willing the ship to appear. 'Come on.'

The tide turned. The flotsam began drifting out to sea. Water sucked and gurgled as the marsh began to drain. Wayland breathed an ebbing sigh of his own. The Normans would have thrown a cordon around the marsh. The fugitives would have to go their separate ways. Wayland knew that he could escape, but after that . . . Disappointment pierced him.

He wandered down to the end of the sand bar. The saltings he'd crossed dry-shod on his first journey lay submerged, eelgrass waving under the surface like the scalps of a drowned multitude. Waterfowl babbled and squawked in the mist. The dog began to tremble. Wayland crouched beside it and laid a hand on its neck.

'They're on their way,' he said, and stuck two fingers in his mouth and blew a piercing whistle.

Very faint and far away he heard a cry. He ran to the river and peered upstream. The fog lay so heavy on the water that he couldn't even see the other side. He cupped his hands to his mouth. 'Ho!'

No answer. Perhaps the ship had grounded again and they needed his help. He plunged into the reeds, following the river bank. He must have struggled quarter of a mile before he heard an uncoordinated splashing. The sound came closer. A shape gathered and *Shearwater* loomed through the mist.

Vallon leaned out from the bow. 'How close are they?'

'Close.'

The ship glided level. Raul and the carpenter stood on the foredeck, fending off the bank with oars. Snorri manned the rudder, but the knarr was showing too much freeboard to be steered and spun in its own length as the tide carried it downriver. The ship's boat tied to its stern drifted in its orbit like a wayward satellite.

'You'll have to jump,' Raul called.

Wayland kept pace with the knarr, waiting for it to come within distance. Its sides were above the level of the bank and he had only a few feet of run-up. Grunting, he took his chance, got one foot on to the gunwale, and would have toppled back if Raul hadn't seized his tunic. The dog sprang aboard unaided.

'Take an oar,' Vallon ordered. 'Try to keep us in mid-channel.'

The ebb swept them downriver, Vallon calling out hazards. 'That's more like it. Hero, Richard, don't just sit there. Lend a hand.'

The reed walls began to fall back as the river widened.

'Nearly there.'

They passed Snorri's shack and stared down the shore. It was empty.

The tide carried them out into the sea. 'Ship oars,' Vallon cried. He ran to the stern and put a hand to his ear.

'What's keeping them?' Raul panted.

'They might have lost their way,' said Vallon. 'The tide's still high and some of the ditches are deep enough to drown a horse.' He turned to Snorri. 'Prepare to raise the mast.'

Snorri pointed back towards the river. 'We can't.'

'What's the problem?'

'It's the ballast,' said Raul. 'Without ballast, the mast would capsize us.'

'How much do we need?'

'A ship this size ... ten tons at least.'

'Can we use sand? Dig it from one of the offshore bars?'

Snorri wailed. The shoals were more mud than sand. To carry it back to the ship would mean wading waist-deep. On the falling tide the ship might end up stranded.

'Let's sort out the ballast later,' said Raul, casting nervous glances down the coast.

'Later will be too late,' Vallon said. 'The Normans will come by sea as well as land. Drogo will commandeer every ship he can lay hands on.' He turned to Snorri. 'How many can he muster?'

'A dozen at least.'

'You hear that? The fog won't hide us for long. We have to make the ship ready for sailing.'

The realisation that after all their labours Drogo still had the upper hand silenced everybody. Vallon clenched both hands on his head and walked to the stern. Everyone watched him.

Vallon lowered his hands. 'We have to go back.'

Raul opened his mouth to speak, then thought better of it.

They rowed standing up, walking two steps forward, two steps back. *Shearwater* rode so high that the oars clipped the surface and the rudder couldn't bite. The ship veered like a leaf in an eddy.

'The ship's boat,' said Vallon. 'We'll tow her in.'

Into the boat they clambered – Vallon, Wayland, Raul and the carpenter. Vallon raised his oar. 'On the count of three ... heave. Again. Heave. Once more. She's coming. Now, deep and steady. That's it. Keep to the channel or we risk grounding. Raul, no need to crick your neck. The Normans will let you know when they're here.'

Wayland rowed until his shoulders burned in their sockets and the sweat ran down his chest. They nuzzled into the mouth of the creek.

'Not far now. Put your backs into it.'

They made land and hauled the ship to the bank. The Normans were still out of sight or sound. 'Set your dog on guard,' Vallon told Wayland. He led the way to the ballast at a shambling run. Snorri had off-loaded the stones on to a ledge of turf above the high tide mark. Over the years, grass and weeds had grown over the pile. Vallon clawed with both hands and unearthed a stone as smooth as an egg and bigger than a man's head.

'Fetch spades,' he told Snorri. 'Hero and Richard, dig them out. 'You,' he said to the carpenter, 'get aboard and pass them down to Snorri. The rest of us will carry.' He clapped his hands. 'Go to it.'

Wayland hoisted a stone and set off at a clumsy trot. Back he came for the next one. After his fifth run, he stopped counting. Everyone had settled into a brutish rythm. Back and forth they toiled, wearing a greasy furrow in the turf, blundering into each other like beasts. Raul improvised a sledge from a plank and sacking and dragged five or six stones at a time. Crossing paths with Wayland, he grinned like a troll. 'Ain't this hell for breakfast?'

Wayland slowed to a trudge. Ahead of him Vallon skidded on the mud, dropped his burden with a gasp and clutched his ribs. Wayland started towards him, but Vallon, features drawn with pain, shook his head.

As the pile grew smaller and *Shearwater* settled closer to her water-line, Wayland allowed himself the possibility that the task might be completed and there dawned the realisation that a thing that seemed impossible could be achieved by cooperation harnessed to a strong will.

There must have been more than a ton of ballast remaining when the dog came loping up the shore and took up position beside him, its jaws rucked and its mane a-quiver. Everyone stopped. Wayland set down his load. From down the coast came a faint roar, like surf crashing on a distant beach. It came again – the sound of thousands of wildfowl panicked into simultaneous flight.

'That's it,' Vallon shouted. 'Everyone aboard.'

Before Wayland reached the ship, another flock of birds roared into the sky and billowed overhead, making a tremendous clamour and passing so close that he could see their wings slicing through the murk. Some of the birds plunged into the shallows around him.

'Captain!' Raul shouted.

Wayland saw the fowler and carpenter running for the reeds. Snorri was preparing to cast off. 'Leave them,' Vallon ordered.

They poled and thrashed away from the shore.

'Keep going. We're not out of danger yet.'

But they had nothing left to give and they set down their oars and collapsed groaning on the boards.

Raul caught his breath. 'Here they come.'

Through the hammering of his heart, Wayland heard the sound of riders forging through water.

Vallon grabbed the sternpost. 'God's blood! Somebody on the shore. Looks like a girl.'

Wayland came up off the deck. Syth was standing at the water's edge with her hands clasped as if in prayer.

Vallon whipped round. 'Row, damn you.'

Wayland advanced like a sleepwalker.

Vallon raised his hand. 'Get back to your place.'

Wayland leaped on to the gunwale and threw himself into the sea. The cold squeezed the breath out of him. He floundered and went under. His feet kicked bottom and he found himself in water up to his neck. The dog appeared at his side. He wrapped its mane round his hand and half-swam, half-waded towards the shore. Syth hadn't moved.

'Walk towards me.'

Syth took a few timid steps. 'I can't swim.'

As he staggered the last few feet, the first riders came spewing out of the fog like warriors from a nether world. They rode in ones and twos and random groups, men and horses slathered with mud. One of the horses went into a ditch or hole and cartwheeled with a tremendous splash.

Wayland dithered. The leading soldiers were already galloping up the sand bar and he knew he didn't have time to reach the marsh with Syth.

'Wayland!'

Raul was standing in the stern, whirling a rope. Vallon was beside him, making frantic beckoning gestures. Wayland grabbed Syth and dragged her into the sea.

The bed sloped gently and he was only thigh deep when he heard furious splashing and glanced back to see four or five cavalrymen plunging after him. He ploughed on, grunting with effort, the soldiers getting closer. He drew his knife and was about to turn at bay when the bottom shelved and he sank.

He surfaced spluttering, saw the nearest rider aim a lance and kicked away into the deeper water. He'd dropped his knife but still had hold of Syth. He guided her hand towards the dog's collar. 'Hang on to it.'

The riders had worked out that Wayland had fallen into a tidal channel. They detoured right, feeling their way along its margin, moving faster than Wayland. Step by step the nearest rider drew level with him, the water up to his mount's chest. He already had his sword drawn and he transferred it to his left hand and shifted his weight on to his left stirrup and leaned over and raised the sword. He looked colossal. Without purchase or footing there was nothing Wayland could do to evade the stroke and he knew he was going to die. Everything slowed down. The soldier had his sword poised and was leaning out to make certain of his strike. Wayland could see the measured determination in his eyes. He held the position for an age and then he leaned even further and dropped his sword and toppled into the sea in front of Wayland. He surfaced, gargling, blood welling in the back of his mouth. Then the weight of his armour pulled him under and he didn't rise again. His horse had lost its footing and thrashed wildly. Its panic infected the other horses. One of them reared and spun, throwing its rider.

Wayland looked for Syth. She was ahead of him, still hanging on to the dog. He thrashed after them and grasped the dog's tail. The dog grunted and turned its head, the whites of its eyes showing. The burden was too much for it.

'Go!'

Wayland tried to follow but his legs were cramping up and he began to founder. The world became more water than sky, the ship poised high above him.

'Wayland!'

Vallon launched a rope. Wayland didn't see where it fell. Raul was taking aim with a crossbow and Wayland realised what had killed the soldier.

'Wayland!'

Vallon had retrieved the rope and was whirling it again. Wayland knew there wouldn't be another chance and he watched the line snake out and splash down ahead of him. With the last of his strength, he lunged for it. He made a turn around his wrist and Vallon began dragging him forward.

'Wait!'

The line slackened. Wayland called to the dog. It turned and paddled towards him, towing Syth's dead weight. He fumbled one hand under the dog's collar and grasped Syth with the other. Her eyes were closed. The line bit into his wrist as Vallon began to tow them in. There was a grey interval and then the dark wall of the hull rode up above Wayland and hands reached down.

Raul hauled him up and over. He flopped on all fours and retched until it felt like he'd turned himself inside out. Raul was rubbing him with a piece of sailcloth, cursing all the while.

'Syth,' he mumbled, and struggled into a kneeling position. She was lying face down a few feet away with Hero astride her, pumping her chest. Wayland looked around in a daze. He reached for the gunwale and tried to pull himself up.

'Keep down,' Raul cried. 'We're still in range.'

'Where's the dog?'

'We couldn't get hold of it.'

It was treading water astern, falling back. In a little while it would be beyond rescue. Wayland groaned and dragged himself forward hand over hand. He leaned over, but he couldn't get anywhere near the dog.

Raul pulled him back. 'It's no use. We have to leave it.'

Wayland shoved him away. 'Where's the rope? Get me a rope.'

'You crazy bastard,' Raul shouted. He pinned Wayland with both arms. 'Captain, lend a hand. He's planning to go over the side again.'

Vallon swore and ran towards them at a crouch. 'Haven't you put us in enough peril? I'm not risking our lives for a dog.' He pointed at the shore, his features distorted by anger. 'Look at that.'

Wayland registered a line of soldiers crouched along the shoreline, loosing bolts at the ship. 'Let go,' he croaked. 'I'm not leaving the dog.'

Raul gripped harder, then suddenly released him and slapped the deck. 'Shit!' He looked at Vallon. 'I'll go. Keep a tight hold because I swim even worse than Wayland.'

He hung from the stern and dropped. When he surfaced, his face was knotted up as if a stake had been pushed up his rectum. He kicked off like a maimed frog. Wayland called to the dog, imploring it to swim towards him. Raul thrashed up to it and managed to loop the rope through the collar. Vallon and Wayland hauled them alongside and hoisted Raul aboard. It took all three of them to manhandle the dog over the side. It kicked and bucked and pitched on the deck half strangled. It stood straddle-legged, head hanging, like a dying calf, then it vomited seawater. It stood looking at its own puke, shook itself, then walked unsteadily towards Wayland, gave him a feeble lick and collapsed.

Wayland seized Raul's arm. 'I won't forget this.'

Raul fought for breath. 'Nor will I!'

Wayland crawled over to Syth. Hero and Richard had covered her with blankets and were chafing her limbs.

'Is she dead?'

Hero threw him a shocked glance 'No. I think she'll be all right if we can keep her warm.'

Wayland uncovered her face. It was mottled and waxy and the sight of it brought back old horrors. He shook her. 'Syth, don't die.'

Her eyelids fluttered, her lips moved.

'I'll get a sleeping bag,' Hero said.

Wayland pressed his cold body against her. Shivers convulsed him. The dog flopped down beside them. He noticed crossbow bolts sticking out of the ship's timbers and became aware of the motion of the ship pecking in the small waves. There was a voice in his head that wouldn't go away – a familiar voice intoning what sounded like a curse or malediction.

He raised his head. On the ship, nobody moved and apart from the voice in his head, everything was smothered in an eerie silence. Vallon stood in the bow, staring out to sea. Hero had doubled over like a stringless puppet. Richard looked stunned. Raul met Wayland's eye and spat with eloquence.

Wayland groped for the gunwale and pulled himself upright at the second attempt. The Normans moved like shadows on the fading shore. He shook his head and screwed a finger into his ear.

It was Drogo's disembodied voice that wouldn't go away.

'*You're all bound for hell. Your leader isn't called Vallon. His name is Guy de Crion. He killed his own wife and murdered the Duke of Aquitaine's nephew. Do you hear me? You're all bound for hell.*'

To the North

XV

Shearwater drifted fog-bound on the tidal swill. Someone was screeching. It was Snorri. He was capering around the edge of the hold, stamping his feet and shaking his fist. 'Christ,' Vallon groaned. He made his way aft, stumbling as if the ship were rolling in a swell.

'What the devil's wrong with you?'

''Tis the girl, cap'n. We have to get her off.'

'Calm down. We'll put her ashore at the first opportunity.'

'No, no. She's jinxed. There'll be no getting away while she's on board.'

Vallon glanced into the hold. The girl sat cocooned in a sleeping sack with Wayland on one side, the dog on the other. It would be a brave man who tried to come between them.

'What do you expect me to do? Throw her overboard?'

Snorri grasped Vallon's sleeve. 'She can paddle back on me punt.'

'Send her back to the Normans? Are you mad?'

'Cap'n, I swear we're doomed if we don't get rid of her.'

'We're doomed if you don't get this ship under way.' With great effort, Vallon made his tone conciliatory. 'You're the sailing master. We're relying on you.' He gave Snorri's shoulder a squeeze and lowered his voice. 'Have no fear. I'll deal with the girl.'

Snorri regarded him with watery hope. 'Ye promise? She's a cunning little mother.'

Vallon turned his head. 'Wayland, on deck.'

Wayland climbed up and made to walk past. Vallon checked him. 'The rest of you, over here. We're going to get the ship under sail.'

Raul looked up dully. 'There ain't no wind.'

'I know that, you blockhead. We need to be ready when it comes.'

Raul manhandled himself upright. Hero and Richard clambered to their feet like wounded insects.

'You think you have no strength left,' Vallon told them. 'But I guarantee you won't feel weary when the Normans grapple with us.' He stepped back. 'Master Snorri, set the mast if you please.'

Snorri gave a high-pitched giggle. 'There ain't enough hands.'

'What! How many do you need?'

'Six to pull her upright, four to hold her steady, two to lever her into the old woman. Never saw it done with less than eight and that was in harbour with the hands pulling on shore.'

Vallon stared at the mast – a pine trunk forty feet long with a base as thick as a man's waist. It had taken a dozen men to lift it aboard and slide its lower end into the hold. Now they had to raise it through seventy degrees with half that number – including a man with only one arm and two youths as feeble as noviciates after a week's fast.

'Raul has the strength of three. We'll lift it somehow.'

'Cap'n, if she slips, she'll smash my ship and then where will we be?'

Hero stepped forward. 'We could keep the mast centred by lashing two rails lengthways across the hold.' He pointed at the yard and its spare stowed along the port side. 'Those look long enough.'

'At last, someone who uses his head.' Vallon turned to the rest of the crew. 'Well, what are you waiting for?'

Raul twiddled his hat in his hands. 'Captain, not being funny, but none of us have sat down to food since yesterday.'

'All right. Change into dry clothes and snatch a meal.'

Vallon was as stupefied by toil as the rest of them. He plopped down onto a thwart, palping the torn muscles in his side. His palms were blistered and split, his fingers swollen and the tips corpse-white. When he kicked off his wet breeches, he saw that the skin on his inner thighs had been rubbed raw. He sponged himself with clean water. Clothed afresh, he felt a little better.

'Sir, take this,' Richard said, offering him bread and mutton and a cup of ale.

He ate only a few mouthfuls before impatience got the better of him. 'Drogo will be halfway to Lynn by now. Let's get to work.'

'See the old woman,' Snorri said, pointing at a coffin-size block of oak spanning the four centre frames. 'The socket in the middle takes the mast foot. The block on top of her, we call that 'un the mast fish. She closes round the mast front and sides. Takes the strain when the ship's under sail. Knock a wedge into the groove at the back and that mast ain't goin' nowheres.'

'Got that?' said Vallon.

166

First they inched the mast forward to align its foot with the socket in the keelson. Even that dull task showed Vallon what weight and forces they were dealing with. Snorri adjusted the mast fish and greased the foot to ease entry. 'Need a man down here to guide her in.'

Vallon glanced around. 'Wayland, that'll be your job.'

Raul nudged the falconer. 'I saw a man lose his mitts doing that.'

'Damn your flapping tongue.'

Snorri placed a silver coin in the socket.

'What's that for?' asked Wayland.

'To pay the ferryman if I'm drownded.'

Raul sneaked a glance at Vallon and flipped down a coin of his own.

They lashed the yards each side of the mast, using thwarts at each end of the hold as anchor points. At Hero's suggestion, they tied a crosspiece between the yards to prevent the mast from being pulled too far forward.

Snorri uncoiled the anchor line one-handed. 'Need a man with knotcraft to tie this to the mast head.'

Raul shinned up the sloping mast and tied the line about five feet below the top. 'You sure that's fast?' Snorri called.

'Make a noose for your head and we'll see.'

Snorri walked forward paying out the line. 'Now we rig the gin.'

This was a stout pole fifteen feet long with a forked top. Snorri passed the free end of the line over the fork, then Wayland and Raul lifted it vertical and dropped its base into a socket forward of the hold. The line from the mast now slanted up over the fork, then down to the hands mustered on the foredeck. Snorri stood to one side and coordinated their efforts. 'Take up slack.'

Vallon pulled in line.

'Tighter. The line's sappy. Brace.'

Vallon pulled until he could feel the inertia of the mast.

'All together now – heave!'

Vallon threw himself back on his heels. The hemp thrummed and water flew off it, but the mast didn't budge.

Snorri, half a-squat, exhorted them. 'Pull will ye. Pull can't ye. Make it a long pull. Make it a strong pull. What d'ye call that? I've seen kiddies haul harder. Pull for your lives, damn ye. Break yer backs. Pop yer lungs!'

This time they raised the mast a few inches, but the weight was too much to bear and it sagged back.

They stood blowing like horses, shaking their hands.

'We need more leverage,' Vallon gasped. His eye fell on one of the oars. He stumbled forward.

'Don't ye go breaking that,' Snorri cried. 'There's timber in the hold.'

Vallon found an eight-foot balk of oak and took up position behind the mast, holding the beam like a harpoon. Once more the crew wrapped their hands around the line and hauled away. The mast rose a few inches – enough for him to slip the beam into the gap. Reaching as high as he could, he hung all his weight from the lever. The veins in his neck stood out. A string of snot dangled from his nose.

'Now she comes,' Snorri cried.

With a resentful creaking, the mast shifted a few degrees towards the upright. The beam slipped and Vallon tripped, but when he looked up, the mast was still suspended. 'Keep it there,' he panted, and staggered back to join the rest of the crew.

The lever had made the critical difference. Slowly the mast swung upright, the work becoming easier with every degree gained. Snorri regulated progress. 'Just a little ways more. Titty bit further. Whoa!'

At close to plumb, the mast felt almost weightless. Snorri gathered the free end of the line from each man in turn and lashed it around the stem. 'Now we fit the foot.'

With some barging and levering from Raul and Wayland, the mast seemed to find its own way into the keelson, sinking home with a judder.

Snorri and Raul lashed the mast fish tight around the base. When they'd driven in the wedge, Snorri straightened, examined the mast from all angles, and then looked at Vallon. 'Job's a good 'un.'

The crew sank down groaning.

'Time for sitting about later,' said Vallon. 'We still have to rig her.'

In fact only Snorri and Raul had the know-how. After helping to hoist the yard and watching the skein of shrouds and stays begin to take shape, Vallon went into the bow to check the tide. The fog still held them in stale suspension. Dew dropped like rain from the cordage. The clothes he'd put on dry a short time ago bristled with moisture.

He sensed someone behind him. Hero, with eyes cast down, offered him a cup of ale. Vallon drained it and wiped his mouth. 'What time do you make it?'

'I've lost track. I don't even know which way we're facing. Thank God Drogo's as blind as us.'

'I'm not so sure. Listen to the racket the birds are making out to sea. I suspect the fog's only lying along the coast and the Normans are waiting for us to stick our noses out.'

'Then let's pray that the fog lasts till nightfall.'

Vallon was struck by a memory. 'Do animals have the power of thought?'

Hero blinked at such an odd question. 'Aristotle states that man is the only rational animal. Why do you ask?'

Vallon stared into the fog. 'I shared quarters once with a rat that showed human cunning. Every evening, after I'd put my platter down, that rat would come for the crumbs. Always at the same time, from the same hole, following the same path. To hide itself, the rat crept along with a scrap of cloth on its back. Wouldn't you say that showed it had the power of reasoning?'

Hero pondered. 'Because the rat couldn't see you, it assumed that you couldn't see it. In fact, its cleverness was a form of stupidity, because you could have killed it any time.' He shifted his stance. 'Sir, the quarters you refer to – was that the prison you mentioned?'

Vallon nodded. 'I'll tell you about it later.'

Snorri gave a shout. Vallon swung round and clapped a hand to his face. The breeze had died almost immediately, but its caress lingered on his cheek. 'Was that a favourable wind?'

'Aye, south-westerly.'

'Are we ready to sail?'

Snorri glowered at Raul. 'There's a heap of fettling to do, but we'll limp along.'

Everyone waited with faces uplifted. Vallon opened and closed his hands on his thighs. He caught Raul looking at him and forced himself to stay still.

Another breath puckered the sea. The sail gave a flaccid flap before sagging.

'I wish it was dark,' said Hero.

'Psst!'

Wayland was jabbing ahead at a point off larboard.

Vallon crossed towards him as softly as foot could fall and craned forward. All he could hear was the distant lamentation of gulls, but he didn't doubt Wayland's warning. The youth had ears like a fox. At last the faint rhythm of men rowing was borne on to his senses. One moment the boat sounded so close that he could hear voices, the next it had faded away.

He glanced round. Raul was spanning his crossbow. Vallon put his head close to Wayland's. 'Where are they?'

Wayland pointed.

Vallon squinted in concentration. He heard the splash of a fluffed oar and saw a flicker of foam. A ship floated into smudged focus not more than a hundred yards away. It was heading shoreward with its sail furled and its crew bent over their oars. There was a moment when they passed so close that any of them glancing to their right would have spotted *Shearwater*. But no one looked and a few moments later the ship ghosted away.

'Get your bow,' he told Wayland. 'There'll be more of them.'

'Here comes the wind,' Raul said, facing astern.

Shearwater dipped. The sail filled and the mast groaned. Wayland was fitting a bowstring. The old one must have slackened in the sodden atmosphere. *Shearwater* got under way, trailing a gurgling wake. The fog drifted past like slow rain. Gaps opened in the murk and Vallon's eyes darted in expectation of more Norman ships. Ahead of them the fog thinned and brightened to a rosy pink. A slant of late evening sunlight threw *Shearwater*'s shadow on to the screen, and then, as though a door had swung open, they were in the clear.

It was sunset, the sea molten between gleaming black mudflats.

'Hell fire!'

In the channel dead ahead, not more than quarter of a mile off, a fishing boat freighted to the gunwales with Normans lay idle in the small waves. Some of the soldiers lounged at their oars. Others were raising the sail. A soldier spotted *Shearwater* and shouted.

'There are more coming out of Lynn,' Wayland called.

Vallon saw sails breaking the horizon miles to the south. 'Forget them for now.'

Their predicament looked hopeless. The Normans were directly downwind, blocking the middle of the channel, mudflats on both sides. No room to outflank them. Even if they could have got to leeward, in this light breeze the Normans could row faster than *Shearwater* could sail. She was bearing down on the boat at no more than walking speed. Soon they'd be within crossbow range. Vallon cupped a hand to his mouth. 'Snorri, hold your course. You hear me? Straight ahead.'

Raul sucked air through his teeth. 'Captain, they outnumber us five to one.'

'I know it. Thirty men in a boat half the size of ours. Look how they're getting in each other's way. And they won't be feeling too lively after rowing from Lynn.'

The soldiers were tripping over each other as they scrambled to get underway. Their movements rocked the boat so violently that they threatened to swamp it. Some of them had taken up oars and were flailing the water. Others were struggling into their hauberks. The boat nosed about uncertainly.

'They'll have smartened up by the time we reach them,' said Raul.

Vallon shielded his eyes. 'I don't see any archers.'

'No, they're infantry. Swords and lances.'

Shearwater heeled as the bow came round.

'What the . . .!' Vallon charged aft. 'I told you to hold your course.'

'I can get round,' Snorri cried, leaning against the tiller.

'They'll catch us before we've gone a furlong.' Vallon wrenched the tiller from him. 'Ram them.'

'I ain't wrecking my ship.'

'It's twice the size of that cockleshell. We'll crack it like a nut.'

Whang went Raul's crossbow. Vallon raised his sword. 'Do . . . as . . . I . . . say.'

Snorri shook his fist. 'Ye'll pay fer any damage.'

Vallon ran back to the bow. Raul pulled a face to show that he'd missed.

Features began to form on the faces of the enemy. An officer had set half the soldiers to rowing. In the bow, half a dozen spearmen jostled to make space for each other. The rest of the force lined the sides, banging their swords against their kite-shaped shields and chanting '*Dex aie, Dex aie.*'

Wayland in one fluent movement bent his bow and loosed. Vallon watched the arrow arc up, lost it as it descended, then heard a cry that showed it had hit its mark.

'Fluky devil,' said Raul, still reloading his weapon. Wayland had already strung another arrow and was aiming again.

The vessels were less than a hundred yards apart and the Normans had realised that *Shearwater* was on a collision course. The superiority in numbers that had seemed irresistible from afar didn't look so overwhelming as they contemplated a ship four times their weight bearing down on them. Their war cries petered out. Some of the men in the bow jerked their heads from side to side, searching for avenues of escape.

'Starboard stop!' the officer shouted.

'Too late,' Vallon murmured as the boat began to swing to port. The strange silence that preceded battle descended. Strange because it magnified ordinary sounds – the crying of gulls, water burbling under the bow, the rustling of the sail.

'After the spears, prepare for boarders.'

Raul snuggled his crossbow tiller into his shoulder and triggered a bolt that spun one of the soldiers on his axis.

The change of course and the lethal darts had thrown the spearmen into disorder and only four of them launched their lances. Neither their aim nor footing was sure, and the three men on *Shearwater*'s foredeck easily avoided the missiles.

'Brace yourselves,' Vallon said.

Shearwater's stem collided with the boat, stoving in its hull just behind the bow and shearing off a few oars. Men tumbled. Stays parted with brittle pops and the mast lolled. Of the half dozen Normans who'd been prepared to board, only two made it, the others either knocked over or falling short. Wayland shot one of the boarders in mid-jump. Raul charged the other, lifted him as if he weighed no more than straw and pitched him overboard.

'Behind you!'

Vallon whirled to see another soldier milling on to the deck, his helmet spilling off. Before Vallon could reach him, he was on his feet again. 'To me!' he called, and took one step forward and then stopped, spitted by a spear launched by his own side. Vallon caught him as he pitched forward, the two locked together for a moment like lovers.

'Brave lad,' Vallon said, and shoved the corpse away.

The collision hadn't checked *Shearwater*'s momentum. Vallon glimpsed a gallery of howling faces sliding past. Another spear just missed him. One soldier in a fit of fury hurled his sword end over end.

Then the boat was behind them, already awash, its company crying out in terror of drowning.

'Anyone hurt?' Vallon called. 'Hero? Richard?'

They climbed out of the hold, knuckling their mouths when they saw the two corpses. Vallon glanced round. 'Raul, put those men over the side.'

He went to the stern and rested both hands on the post. The fishing boat had rolled on its side and the Normans were clinging to the hull. The breeze had blown away the fog and he could see the ship that had passed them heading back out to sea.

Hero was watching him in horror when he turned. Vallon ran his sword into its scabbard. 'I sent you away because I wanted to spare you such sights.' He stepped past and then stopped. 'If there's a providence that looks after rats, why shouldn't it bestow a kindly glance on us?'

The sun's lidded eye slid below the land. The ship in their wake had halted to pick up the survivors of the wreck. Snorri came bustling out the hold. 'I told ye yer madness would wreck us. We've sprung planks. We're shipping water. We're like to founder.'

Vallon waved tiredly at Raul. 'Take a look.'

Raul spat with deliberation. 'I reckon I died without anyone telling me and now I'm working my way through hell.'

'Hell wouldn't have you.'

Raul grinned as if Vallon had paid him a compliment.

Shearwater sailed on with Vallon manning the rudder. He kept watch on the ships to the south. There were five of them, sailing parallel with *Shearwater*, making no attempt to close. They were racing to block the mouth of the Wash, where sandbanks constricted the exit. If they reached it first and formed a blockade, *Shearwater* would have to slip between vessels stationed no more than half a mile apart. Colour drained from the sky and the night came down. The enemy ships receded from sight as the sea darkened and stars began to prick the sky. The darkness wouldn't last long. Soon the moon, only one day off full, would rise and light the seascape as bright as day.

Vallon looked up at Wayland, balanced on the yard thirty feet above deck. 'Can you still see them?'

'Yes. They're holding the same course.'

Snorri and Raul emerged from the hold. 'Just a little leak,' said Raul. 'We plugged it. The girl's keeping an eye on it.'

Snorri took the tiller. They sailed on. A subterranean glow spread up from the east and the moon rose huge and tremulous, gold at first, paling to a marbled eggshell. The Norman ships appeared again like pale lanterns.

'Will we beat them to the entrance?' Vallon asked Snorri.

'It'll be ticklish close.'

'You said that *Shearwater* can outsail any English mudskipper.'

'Aye, but they've got a clear passage up the Lynn channel, while we got to steer round the Mare's Tail.'

'A sandbank?'

'Girt big island more like. Three miles long and curves south.'

'Forcing us towards the Norman fleet.'

Snorri tittered, as he did when stressed. 'Aye. Right into their path.'

Wayland stayed aloft with instructions to keep an eye out for shoals. Raul reloaded his crossbow, standing with both feet on the arms and then, after inflating his chest, pulling up the string in one vein-popping effort. He claimed that it had a three hundred-pound draw and could shoot a bolt clear through two armoured soldiers. Vallon didn't doubt it. In an idle moment, he'd tried to span the weapon and found that he could barely deflect the cord. Since their journey began, Raul had kept up a running debate with Wayland about who had the more deadly weapon, Raul insisting that the cross-bow was more accurate and powerful, Wayland – when he could be bothered to reply – pointing out that he could loose six arrows for every dart that Raul shot.

'Sandbank ahead,' Wayland called.

It broached the sea like the back of a half-submerged whale. Snorri steered the ship a few points to starboard, while Raul used a tacking boom fitted to the sail's forward leech to keep it exposed to the full draw of the wind. *Shearwater*'s speed hardly lessened, but now they were angling towards the enemy. The Norman ships were pulling ahead. Vallon could see the headlands on each side of the Wash's mouth and knew that the two leading ships would reach it first. Even if *Shearwater* evaded their initial attack, the manoeuvres would allow the other vessels to join the action. The nearest of them wasn't more than a mile to starboard and *Shearwater* still hadn't reached the end of the Mare's Tail.

Vallon tapped his foot without being aware of it. They still hadn't cleared the sandbank and all but one of the Norman ships were showing their sterns. The laggard was square on to *Shearwater*, so close that Vallon could see figures moving along its side.

'The leading ships are reefing sail,' Raul shouted. 'They're going to lie in wait.'

Vallon watched the slow convergence. The two leading Norman ships were separating and the others were moving to fill the gap. Vallon joined Snorri. 'Any ideas?'

'We ain't goin' to smash through. Those ships are as big as *Shearwater*.'

'Clear water ahead,' Wayland cried.

'We got one trick we can play,' Snorri said. 'Soon as we get round the Mare's Tail, tack hard to port and run for a channel that'll bring us out at the northern tip of the Wash. The Normans can't turn into the wind. They'll have to go round the far side of the bar.'

Shearwater slid out from the end of the sandbank. Vallon saw that Snorri's proposed course would shave the edge of the bay.

'We got to decide quick,' said Snorri.

'Do it.'

Snorri called out to Raul and leaned on the rudder. In the uncertain light the Normans didn't spot the change of course, or perhaps they thought it was a feint. By the time they reacted and began to track across the bay, *Shearwater* was heading north, across the wind.

The two leading Norman ships still had the advantage of sea room. As the coast drew closer, Vallon began to think that Snorri's gambit had forced them into a corner. Ahead was a channel between coastal mudflats and a narrow bar of sand. One of the Norman ships was shadowing them less than half a mile downwind, while its partner took a more seaward route. Like dogs coursing a rabbit. They were nearly at the entrance of the channel. Once inside they would be committed. If the Norman ship reached the other end first, interception was certain.

Shearwater took the inshore passage. The Norman ship with a lead of perhaps two hundred yards kept to the other side of the bar. Vallon could hear its commander shouting instructions. On *Shearwater* there was silence. Wayland kept lowering his bow and brushing his sleeve across his mouth.

'I think we're gaining on them,' said Hero.

Anxious minutes went by before Vallon dared to believe that he was right. They pulled level, the two ships sailing up different sides of the sandbank like shadows of each other. The Normans crowded the side, roaring a challenge.

'Definitely gaining,' Hero said.

The soldiers saw it, too, and their cries turned to wails of frustration. Out to sea they'd enjoyed the better of the wind, but in the lee of the coast, *Shearwater* was the more efficient vessel.

Yard by yard *Shearwater* increased her lead. When she slid out from the channel she was a bowshot ahead of her pursuer, only two bowshots from the shore. So close that Vallon could see a light in a coastal settlement.

Snorri cavorted. 'They won't catch us now.'

Vallon went aft, touching each man's arm in passing. 'Well done,' he murmured. 'Well done.'

Raul punched the air. 'Fate spares the undoomed warrior.'

They headed into open sea. Vallon watched until the sails behind them were very small before turning.

'Everyone stand down. Fill your bellies and get some rest.' As Wayland walked past, Vallon reached out and caught him by the sleeve. 'Not you.'

Wayland stood before him mute and defiant. His actions had been unforgivable. Vallon had hanged men for lesser offences. He had to make an example. God knows, discipline was lax enough as it was. If he let Wayland's insubordination go unpunished, every man would take it as licence to do as he pleased. All this Vallon knew, and at the same time he recognised that he couldn't afford to lose the falconer. He and the rest of the rabble were all Vallon had. The constraints on what punishment he could mete out made him even angrier.

'You endangered all our lives by going back for the girl. If we weren't so short-handed, I'd have left you to be killed.'

'I thank you for your mercy. We both thank you.'

'Never mind that. The girl can't stay. A pet has no place on this ship.'

Wayland sucked in his cheeks and stared past him.

'We'll put her ashore when we next make land.'

'She doesn't have anywhere to go. Her family's dead.'

Vallon thumped the gunwale. 'We're not a refuge for orphans. The girl goes.'

Wayland swallowed and lifted his gaze.

'If you care about her, you must see that it's for her own good. Think of the risks if she stays.'

'She's not afraid of the voyage. Her father was a fisherman.'

'I'm not talking about the perils of the sea. A woman on a ship full of men is a recipe for disaster. You know how Raul behaves when he's taken a skinful.'

'Raul wouldn't dare touch her.'

'You see. You're already contemplating the challenge.' Vallon sank back. 'We'll be taking on more hands and I'm not in a position to pick and choose. Doubtless we'll end up with some men of base character. I've seen the madness that infects soldiers when a woman is set loose in their company. God knows, I've buried enough of them.'

'The dog will kill anyone who lays a finger on her.'

'Is that supposed to reassure me?'

Wayland lapsed back into silence.

Vallon leaned back. 'Then there's Snorri.'

Wayland met his eyes. 'What about him?'

'Don't pretend there isn't bad blood between him and the girl. I care nothing for his superstitions, but we rely on his cooperation.'

Wayland gave a contemptuous smile. 'He'll betray us with or without the girl.'

Vallon's eyes narrowed. 'Explain yourself.'

'His wits have grown soft. He talks to himself without knowing it. He plans to rob us.'

Vallon shifted on his seat. 'Well, I'll deal with that problem in due course.' His voice hardened. 'It changes nothing. The girl goes.'

Wayland looked at his feet. 'I'm sorry.'

Vallon softened his tone. 'I'm sure your motives were kind, and by good fortune your rashness didn't result in our ruin. We'll set the girl down adequately provided for. The money will come from your share of the profits. That will be your punishment and you must agree that it's milder than you deserve.'

Wayland lifted his eyes. 'I meant, I'm sorry I can't remain in your service.'

'Don't tell me you intend to go with her.'

'You said I could leave once you'd set sail.'

Vallon gestured in the direction of the coast. 'The girl's stolen your wits. That isn't your native country. You won't find anything there except poverty and death. You're an outlaw with a price on your head. Someone will turn you in. Even if you get away from the coast, you have no land and no one to protect you. At best you'll end up a bondman guiding a plough. Is that what you want?'

Wayland's eyes flashed. 'I'll find a forest where we'll live as well as any lord and lady.'

'Rubbish. When you ran wild, you ran alone. Think what it will mean to saddle yourself with a girl. You're only – what? – seventeen? Too young to tie yourself down.'

Wayland didn't answer. Vallon had been speaking in a heightened whisper, aware that Snorri was straining to overhear. He beckoned Wayland closer. 'Our relationship has been thorny. You haven't shown me the respect that's due. No, don't interrupt. I speak from experience, not vanity. Every enterprise must have a leader. From the outset you've only submitted to my authority when it suited you. I would have let you go your own way long ago if I hadn't seen in you some admirable qualities. You're brave, resourceful, sharp-witted. Learn to submit to your superiors and you could have a bright future.'

Wayland kept his face down.

'I thought you wanted to trap gyrfalcons.'

Wayland raised his head. 'I do. That's why I joined you.'

'Then don't throw the opportunity away. Only once in a lifetime can a man follow a dream.'

Wayland's voice choked. 'I can't abandon her. I made a pledge.'

'Of marriage?'

'Not that.'

'What then?'

The dog came pattering down the deck. Wayland cuffed it and it lay down with its eyes fixed on Vallon's face. He crossed his arms.

'So that's your final word. If the girl goes, you go too.'

Wayland composed himself. 'Yes.'

Vallon gave a slow expiring sigh and looked across the moon's silvery track. The land was out of sight. All horizons were empty. He rubbed his forehead.

'Bring her to me.'

'You won't frighten her?'

'Just fetch her.'

When Wayland had gone, Vallon contemplated how low his stock had fallen. Only two years ago he'd commanded armies. With a wave of an arm he'd brought squadrons sweeping into action. He'd ridden into towns at the head of his troops and seen the shuttered dread of citizens who knew he wielded the power of life or death. He'd doomed deserters and cowards to the rope without a moment's thought. Now he was reduced to negotiating with a peasant over his sweetheart.

Syth moved so softly that he didn't hear her approach until her shadow fell over him. Taller than he'd expected, slim as a reed, with eyes like a cat's, something fey in her aspect. He almost reached out and touched her to see if she was real.

'So you're the dove who's lured my haggard away.'

She darted a glance at Wayland.

'What's her name?'

'Syth.'

Vallon stared out to sea. 'The Normans know we haven't quit these shores for good. They'll be hunting us up and down the coast. We daren't put ashore for several days – long enough for you to come to your senses. In the meantime, the girl must crop her hair and wear men's clothes. She sleeps alone and you'll keep a chaste distance at all times. While she's with us, she might as well earn her keep. Can she cook and sew? Does she have any other talents?'

Wayland translated Vallon's conditions. The girl's hands went to her hair.

'She won't be any trouble,' Wayland said.

Vallon waved a hand in dismissal. 'Go and get something to eat.'

Wayland hesitated. 'What about you, sir?'

Vallon pulled his cloak about him. 'Just get out of my sight.'

XVI

Hero picked his way towards the bow. He'd checked on Vallon several times during the night, covering him with fleeces and blankets as the wind freshened. Now he stood before the shapeless heap and cleared his throat. When that didn't wake the Frank, he reached out and gave a tentative prod.

Vallon reared up.

'Don't be alarmed, sir. It's only me. I've brought you some pottage. Eat it while it's warm.'

Vallon groaned and felt his ribs. 'I feel as if I've been broken on the wheel.' He supped from the bowl, his eyes switching back and forth. 'What time is it?'

'Not long before dawn. We've been running east all night.'

Vallon grunted and resumed eating. 'This is better than the slops Raul serves up.'

'The girl made it. She seems to have made a complete recovery. She's a strange thing.'

Vallon's spoon stopped halfway to his mouth. He shrugged and continued eating. 'Has everyone found a place to sleep?'

'We're still feeling our way. We'll organise things better by daylight.'

Vallon handed back his bowl and leaned against the stempost with his face to the stars.

Hero turned the bowl in his hands. 'Do you think Drogo will leave us in peace now?'

Vallon gave a jagged laugh. 'We're a bone in his gullet. He won't rest until he's spat it out.' Vallon squinted at Hero. 'You heard his denunciation of me.'

'I paid no attention to his slanders.'

'He spoke the bald truth.' Vallon shifted to make space. 'Sit down. A long road stretches ahead and you may as well know what sort of man is taking you down it.'

Hero was trembling. Vallon pulled a blanket over him. For a time they just sat there, the ship rocking through the waves, Snorri half-asleep at the rudder, the rest of the company pitched in heaps on the deck.

'I won't weary you with a long history,' said Vallon. 'My family were minor nobles holding a small grant of land from Guillaume, Duke of Aquitaine and Count of Poitiers. I was a page at his court and fought my first battle under his banner at the age of seventeen. I acquitted myself well and rose in rank. My promotion to captain before I was twenty caused resentment among some knights of nobler birth. I began my campaigning in Spain nine years ago, when I was twenty-one.'

Hero must have betrayed surprise.

'You thought I was older,' said Vallon. 'You'll soon discover what stamped these lines on my face. Back to the Spanish expedition. The pope had called for a crusade against the Moors. Guillaume was one of several Frankish nobles who answered the summons. After joining our Spanish allies, the army besieged the town of Barbastro in the Muslim kingdom of Lerida. They took the town after forty days and massacred or enslaved its inhabitants. I took no part in the blood-shed – only because I'd been sent to guard against a counter-attack from Zaragoza. The ruler of that state was the King of Lerida's brother, Emir al-Muqtadir. Remember that name.

'At Barbastro the crusade ended. Those who'd taken part in the assault went home laden with booty and slaves. I returned no richer than when I'd left Aquitaine. The following year I married a girl I'd known since childhood. She was five years younger than me. It was an advantageous match, bringing with it a useful dowry.'

'Was she beautiful?'

Vallon drew back to see Hero's face. 'Yes, she was.' He seemed to lose his thread. 'Anyway, although my first journey into Spain hadn't enriched me, I'd seen enough to know that the country offered oppor-tunities for a poor knight. The Moorish empire had fragmented into a score of warring states. I sought leave from Guillaume to return to Spain as a knight for hire. At his suggestion, I took service with King Ferdinand of Castile and Leon. My first action under Ferdinand was a punitive expedition against al-Muqtadir of Zaragoza. The Emir had retaken Barbastro and killed the Frankish and Spanish garrison. Until

181

then he'd been a Castilian tributary; in fact Ferdinand and al-Muqtadir had fought as allies against Castile's rivals. Emboldened by his success at Barbastro, the Emir broke off relations with Castile. Our expedition against him was inconclusive, and within a year Ferdinand was dead. His empire was divided between his three sons. I transferred my allegiance to the eldest, Sancho II of Castile.

'Two years later we laid Zaragoza under siege for a second time. This campaign was successful and al-Muqtadir sued for peace, paying a large ransom and swearing tribute to Sancho. The alliance was important because by this time Castile was fighting a war on three fronts – against Aragon to the east, and against Leon and Galicia to the west and north.

'For the next three years I fought against Sancho's enemies. After each campaigning season, I returned home to Aquitaine. My marriage was happy and bore three children. The youngest was still unborn when I made my final journey into Spain. With me was a nephew of the duke, a youth called Roland. Guillaume had put him under my wing to learn the arts of war. I knew the youth. His estate lay a day's ride from mine and he was a frequent visitor. Roland was nineteen, uncommonly handsome, a fine singer and dancer, every inch the courtly noble. In short, nature had bestowed on him all the talents that I lack.'

Vallon looked around. 'He was also treacherous and cowardly. It took me a while to learn his true character. To my face he was charming and respectful; behind my back he sneered at my modest birth and resented serving under me. The action that caused my ruin was trivial. Sancho had received intelligence that Emir al-Muqtadir planned to break the treaty with Castile. I was ordered to lead a small reconnaissance squadron to the Zaragoza border. There were only twelve of us, including Roland and two of his companions. Our task was to seek for signs that the Emir was planning an invasion. On no account were we to mount a provocation.

'You can probably guess what happened. Towards the end of a tedious day during which we saw nothing but a few shepherds, we rounded a corner and surprised two Moorish scouts. They galloped off down a dry riverbed. Before I could stop him, Roland and his companions sped off in pursuit. I shouted at them to stop. I warned them it was a trap. They paid no attention.

'We chased after them, but we were too late. Less than a mile down the gully Roland had run into a troop of Moorish cavalry. They'd already killed his companions and Roland was on his knees, begging for mercy. The enemy was too strong for us. The Moors killed every member of the patrol except for me and Roland. Him they saved because he was the nephew of a duke and would bring a good ransom. I was spared only because one of the Moorish officers recognised me.

'We were taken to Aljaferia, the Emir's summer palace in Zaragoza. Al-Muqtadir knew me by reputation – knew that I'd been part of the army that had massacred his brother's subjects in Barbastro, knew me again from my part in the two invasions of Zaragoza. There was no reason for him to show me mercy except the possibility of ransom. The terms were too high for me to meet, and I knew that Sancho wouldn't look kindly on a soldier of fortune – that's all I was – who'd jeopardised an important treaty at a critical juncture in his wars against his brothers. Roland assured me that his uncle and my lord, the Duke of Aquitaine, would pay both ransoms. He composed the letter himself and it was duly despatched. For the next month we shared comfortable quarters in the palace. Then one morning, Roland was summoned to the Emir's throne-room. He returned in a distraught state. His ransom had been received, but for some inexplicable reason mine had been delayed. He swore that he'd arrange my release or return to share my fate.'

Vallon continued in a monotone. 'A month passed, two months. One morning at dawn, four months into my incarceration, guards came for me. With no word of explanation, they bound me and bundled me into a cart. We left the city travelling south and by noon we'd reached my new prison. The place was called Cadrete – a harsh fortress on top of a rocky hill. When we passed through the gate, my escort blinded me with a hood. As they marched me to my cell, I tried to construct a picture of my surroundings. First they led me deep into the castle on a level stone floor. I walked ninety steps before we halted at a door secured by a lock and three bolts. On the other side we descended a flight of twelve stone steps. We halted again and I heard lamps being lit and a hatch open in the floor. Guards lowered a ladder through the hatch. They guided me onto the ladder and ordered me to descend. I counted twenty-eight rungs before I reached the bottom. My guards removed my hood. Then they climbed the ladder, pulled it up after them and closed the trap, leaving me in absolute darkness.' Vallon paused. 'Do you know what an oubliette is?'

Hero shivered. 'A pit where prisoners are consigned to oblivion.'

'It was shaped like a beehive with a trapdoor in the roof twenty feet above the floor. No other opening, and my jailer always kept the hatch shut except at my daily mealtime. In the floor was a small hole dropping into a pit that served as a latrine and a graveyard. The skeletons of former prisoners lay scattered in this tomb, as I saw that evening when my jailer came to serve me my rations. This duty consisted of lowering a pail containing food and a lamp. As soon as I'd eaten, the jailer pulled the pail and light up again, condemning me to darkness until the next day. I used to draw out my meals just to savour the luxury of that little orange flame. Once I refused to send the lamp back up and for punishment the guard left me for days with neither food nor light. How many days I can't say. Except for the routine of my daily meal, I had no means of measuring time.'

'This is where you befriended the rat,' said Hero.

'I used to talk to him. He was a creature of such regular habits that if he was late appearing, I grew anxious. I'd worry that he'd died and I'd be left with no company but my own.'

'Oh, sir!'

Vallon stared at a place beyond anybody's sight but his own. 'I managed to prise a flake of stone from the wall and used it to scratch a calendar. Weeks lengthened into months. My hair hung down my back and my fingernails grew into talons. Lice plagued me.'

Hero shuddered. 'I would have gone mad. I couldn't have borne such suffering.'

'I came close to killing myself several times. I wondered then and wonder now how many of the bodies lying in the pit had taken their own lives.' Vallon paused and then spoke in a firmer tone. 'Since it was clear that no help would come from Aquitaine, I implored the Emir to ask for King Sancho's intervention in consideration of the services I'd rendered him and his father. About seven months into my confinement, a servant of the Emir brought Sancho's answer. The king no longer loved me or considered me under his protection. He'd received evidence that I was the one who'd invaded the Emir's lands. Roland had poisoned his mind.'

'What a viper! But why would they take his word above yours?'

'Birth. Roland was the nephew of a duke. His claims would always carry more weight than those of a middle-ranking commander from modest stock. Perhaps Roland had convinced himself that his version of events was accurate. I've learned that a man who wants to deceive others must first deceive himself. I still don't know the truth. I had no time to seek it out after I escaped.'

'But you did escape. Thank God for that!'

Vallon kneaded his ribs. 'Another month went by and then my regular guard was replaced. My new jailer was an older man with a weakness for wine. He performed his duties sloppily, bringing my daily ration any time it suited him. After one visit, he left the trapdoor open, and from that day on he never bothered to close it. Why take the trouble? It was as far out of my reach as heaven. That lapse gave me hope. The chamber above had a window that admitted enough light to take the edge off the darkness. I already knew that the chamber had a flight of steps leading up to a locked door. My jailer often left this door open while he served me my dole. During these intervals I sometimes heard sacks and barrels being shifted and loaded onto carts. It was clear that the outer chamber was a storeroom or warehouse leading into the castle yard.

'How to reach it, though? The ladder was the only means and my jailers had lowered it only once since putting me into the pit. I decided to put my jailer's negligence to the test. When he brought my next meal, I feigned sickness. He merely jeered and left. The next day I pretended to be unconscious or dead. He was a slipshod guardian, but not so lax as to descend the ladder on his own. He summoned two soldiers to guard the trapdoor while he climbed down to examine me. After nearly a year confined in that pit, I was so wasted that my jailer easily persuaded himself that I would soon join the bones in the tomb below. In fact, I worried that he'd make an end of me there and tip me down himself. Eventually he climbed out.

'From the corner of my eye I watched him leave. He hauled up the ladder. I was sure that with the other soldiers watching, he'd shut the trap. He didn't. He left the end of the ladder sticking out over the hatch before shoving it aside with one foot. I knew that its end was no more than a foot or two from the edge of the trap.

'I'd better explain how the ladder was constructed. It was about twenty-five feet long with a central shaft six or seven inches square, augered to take the rungs. As soon as I heard the bolts shoot home on the outer door, I set to work cutting my blankets into strips with my rock. It took me until well after noon to knot together a rope long enough to reach beyond the trapdoor. At one end of the rope I made a pocket to take the rock.'

'You planned to snag the ladder and pull it down,' said Hero.

'Not quite. The ladder was heavy and the trap too small to tip it through. The best I could hope for was to drag the ladder across the hatch and use it as a beam. Well, I tried a hundred times. Most of my throws missed the hatch completely, and several times the weighted end fell back and struck me. Remember that I was weak and I was standing in the dark aiming at a target not more than two feet square. On the few occasions when the stone did hit the ladder, it bounced off. Only once did it catch, but it sprang loose when I applied pressure. My neck and back ached from my efforts. I was almost glad when darkness put an end to them. I sank down against the wall in a wretched state. I hadn't eaten for two days and I was quaking with cold. Summer or winter, my cell was always as chilly as the grave. I woke all night with the conviction that it would be my last and by degrees a sort of peace fell on me. The end was near and I almost welcomed it. In this mood of resignation I woke to see morning beginning to take shape in the trapdoor.'

Vallon shrugged. 'I don't even remember making my last throw. Only that when I pulled on the rope, it held fast. I yanked to free it and put a swift end to false hope. It held. I hung my weight on it. The ladder slid and then stopped. It had jammed against the trapdoor. When the rope didn't give and wouldn't give, I retreated to the wall of my cell and sat looking up at the line. Now that my chance had come, I didn't dare take it.

'The morning was well advanced when I forced myself to grip the rope. With my first attempt, I barely dragged myself off the ground before dropping back. I tried again, failed again. I grew angry with myself. Every moment I wasted was a moment nearer to the time when my jailer appeared. I told myself that I'd never get another chance – that if I didn't escape now, I would be dead within days. Seizing the rope again, I managed to climb two or three feet before my strength went. I hung there, supporting my weight on a knot in the

186

rope until I'd recovered sufficiently to go on. In this way, inch by inch and foot by foot, I made my way up to the hatch.'

Hero clapped his hands.

'I crawled out into the upper chamber. It was lit by one narrow window high in the wall. I climbed the stairs to the door. It was locked and bolted. I put my ear to it and heard nothing. I waited on the top step and was nearly asleep when the key turned. I hid to one side of the steps. My jailer drew the bolts and stepped through.'

'You killed him.'

'It was quick – quicker than the death he would have suffered at the Emir's hand. I took his sword and knife, dropped him into my cell and closed the trap. Then I went out and locked the door behind me.

'I was in a warehouse stacked with wine, corn and oil. At the far end a wicket stood ajar in a pair of heavy doors. I hadn't seen the sun for almost a year and the light burned my eyes. When my blindness passed, I found myself looking across a busy courtyard. It was a cloudless morning. I thought it was early September; in fact it was almost October.

'Two peasants leading mules came towards the doors. Parked behind the entrance was a cart laden with wine barrels. I rapped on the staves and discovered they were empty. I just had time to climb into one and pull the lid down before the carters entered.

'They were in no hurry to get started. Eventually I heard them putting the mules in the traces. Before they'd finished, a soldier came in. "Is Yasin with the Frank?" he asked, referring to my jailer. I didn't hear an answer, but there must have been some response because the soldier said: "That's odd. I saw him come this way after morning prayers." Then I heard him walking away up the warehouse. His footsteps faded away and there was a terrible silence that I was sure would be broken by a shout of alarm. Instead I heard his footsteps returning briskly. "When he shows up, tell him the captain of the guard wants to see him."

'The response was sweet. "We're just off," one of the carters said. "We'd have left by now if our escort had shown up." I had to endure another wait before this man arrived. He was mounted. The carters climbed up and drove out into the court. They stopped at the castle gate and a sentry asked where they were going.

'"Fetching wine from Penaflor," the escort said. I knew the place. It's a village about ten miles north of Zaragoza.

'The cart moved off and descended the road from the castle. When we were well clear, I raised the lid of the cask just enough to see out. There was no chance of me making a dash for it. The road was busy and I was so feeble that the escort would have ridden me down before I'd got a few yards. We passed through Zaragoza and continued north. By now I was sure that the Moors had discovered my escape. The guards would soon work out how I'd left the castle and riders would be lashing their horses in pursuit. Every mile we plodded increased the chances of capture, but although the road was quiet, I was so stiff from my confinement that I didn't dare risk breaking out.

'Finally we stopped. I heard the carters call out and climb down. A little later a child brought fodder and water for the mules. Then everything went quiet. I lifted the lid. It was late afternoon and the first thing I saw was a hill terraced with vines. I looked the other way and saw a farmhouse with the escort's horse tethered outside. Two children playing in the dust. A woman called and the children ran into the house. I struggled out of the barrel. My legs had fallen asleep and I rolled off the cart like a log. I dragged myself into the vineyard. When I could stand without my legs giving way, I made my way up the hill-side.'

Hero saw Vallon's head sink. He seemed to have fallen asleep. Hero reached out and touched his arm. Vallon raised his head. He looked old.

'There's not much left to tell. I calculated north by the sun and travelled by night. I didn't see any sign of pursuit. I had no shoes and the ground cut my feet. I was starving. I raided a hencoop and stole some eggs. Even when I crossed into Aragon and ran into a Spanish patrol, I wasn't safe. Aragon was at war with Castile, so I pretended that my wits were unstrung. I was in such a verminous and degraded state that the soldiers wanted no part of me and sent me on my way with a crust and a few coins. Somehow I crossed the Pyrenees.'

Hero looked quickly at Vallon and just as quickly looked away. 'You found your way home.'

Vallon stroked his mouth as if a web were being spun across it. 'Every step of the way I'd dreamed of my return. The grapes would be ripening, the bees stirring among the lavender. I'd push open the gate and walk up the path and enter the door and hear from the hall within the voices of my wife and children. I'd step into their presence and my wife would look up from her needlework, the glow of the fire on her face. At first she wouldn't recognise me, then alarm would change to dawning hope and she would stand up and straighten her dress and take a step towards me as if confronted by a ghost.'

Vallon laughed low in his throat. 'I reached my home at dead of night with a storm approaching. Lightning shaped the walls out of the darkness. I approached the villa like a thief. The doors and windows were barred and shuttered, everyone asleep. I forced open a window and climbed in. The storm was drawing closer. I went into the entrance hall. A flash of lightning showed me a sword lying on a coffer. It was *my* sword, surrendered by me to the Emir of Zaragoza. I picked it up and climbed the stairs to my lady's chamber.

'I opened it. By now the storm was overhead. A barb of lightning revealed my wife lying against a man. The clouds burst and raindrops as big as grapes splashed on the roof. I opened the shutters and breathed in the dusty smell of rain falling on parched ground. I knew I'd never see my home again.'

Vallon's features were set in a rigid smile.

'I stood waiting. Wind came with the rain and rattled the shutters. Roland twitched awake. Thunder crashed and the room filled with blue light. Roland started up. "Who's there?" he cried.'

Hero fingered his throat.

'I didn't answer. My wife woke and clung to her lover. I waited for the next stroke of lightning and that was the last thing they saw. I didn't prolong their suffering. I ended their lives with two strokes.'

Hero was silent for a while. 'What about your children?'

'I was going to kill them, too.' Vallon rounded on Hero. 'Honour gone, prospects gone, everything gone. What would you have done?'

Hero swung his head.

'I went to their nursery. The storm had woken them and their old nurse was comforting them, cradling the son who hadn't been born when I left for Spain. Even my eldest didn't recognise me and shrieked in terror. Their nurse had been my nurse and it was she who realised that this bloodstained ghoul was her master. She clutched the children to her and begged for mercy. She swore that my wife had thought I was dead. Roland had told her that I'd been wounded in action and had died in prison. He'd helped commit my remains to the ground. I think he probably bribed the Emir to kill me, but the old fox must have decided to bury me alive in case I might serve some future purpose. The nurse told me that Roland began to visit my wife to console her in her grief. Their friendship deepened and ... Well, who cares about that? I left my children unharmed, took horse and armour, and rode away. I travelled east, intending to cross into Italy. Three weeks later I met you and your one-eyed master.'

Hero picked at his knees. 'If you'd known that Roland had deceived your wife, would you have spared her?'

'No. Of course not.'

'Didn't you love her?'

'What's that got to do with it?'

Hero saw that the night was lifting. 'What was her name?'

Vallon shook his head. 'It doesn't matter.'

XVII

Wayland woke cold and queasy in a dull grey dawn. He lay listening to the wind moaning in the shrouds, someone throwing up. Draped in his blanket, he felt for the side and stood blinking at the endless whitecaps. Not a sail to be seen or any sight of land. They were still sailing north-east, pitching through lumpy waves and scudding rain. The stink of tallow and tar and vomit made his gorge rise. Sweat broke out on his brow. Gripping the gunwale with both hands, he puked over the side. When he was done, he leaned on the gunwale and turned his head to see who the other victim might be. It was Vallon, propped in exactly the same wretched condition.

A day of retching misery lay in store for everyone except Snorri and Syth. She'd been sailing since she could walk and darted about as blithely as a lark. Despite his own seasickness, Vallon didn't spare himself or allow the others to shirk. Joints had shrunk during the ship's lay-up and Wayland had to take his turn bailing out the hold and hammering tarred wool into the leaking seams. He shifted ballast to adjust the trim and helped brace the rigging. On Vallon's orders, Raul and

Snorri drilled everyone in the basics of seamanship. Wayland learned the rudiments of reefing and lowering the sail, how to use the tacking boom to keep the sail drawing when heading close to the wind.

He was still seasick in the evening and went to his rest without supper, dossing down amidships in his wet clothes. But for the warmth of the dog at his side, he wouldn't have slept a wink. He woke in a seizure of shivering under a field of stars. The wind had turned, bringing sharp clear air from the east. The dog was gone. He sat up and whistled softly.

'He's down here with me.'

Wayland went to the edge of the hold. Syth had been given the aft half-deck for her sleeping quarters. Her eyes shone pale in the starlight.

She giggled. 'He wanted somewhere warm.'

'That's all right. He can stay.'

'You're shivering. Why don't you come down, too? I want to talk to you.'

Wayland glanced behind him. 'No. I'll be sick.'

Syth yawned. 'Poor Wayland. Goodnight then.'

The night lay long before him. What was he going to do about Syth? The problem tugged like a hook in his gut. Of course she couldn't accompany them on such a dangerous voyage, but where did that leave him? The last thing he wanted was to be stuck on an unfamiliar shore with a girl he hardly knew. He cringed when he recalled his ridiculous ultimatum to Vallon. That stuff about making a pledge. He hadn't made any pledge. He'd been thinking of his sister – and Syth wasn't his sister.

He watched the stars turn in their course and knew that he'd have to leave her behind. When he'd threatened to quit the expedition, he'd been speaking in French. Syth couldn't have understood, so it wasn't like he'd be breaking his word. She must realise that there was no place for her on the ship. It would be cruel to keep her here. He'd risked his life saving her from the Normans. She couldn't expect more of him than that. The more he thought about it, the more he agreed with Vallon. Set the girl down at the earliest opportunity.

With this decision firmly lodged, Wayland rolled up in his blanket and turned on his side.

Waking into the new day, he felt like a man reborn. Vallon had let him lie late and the sun was level with the yardarm and shone warm on his face. His nausea was gone and his head clear. He sat up. Spray burst in rainbows over the bow. Water chattered along the hull. He watched the deck flex as *Shearwater* swooped over the swell. As Snorri had said, the ship was almost like a living thing. He rose and stood against the oak stempost that his grandfather might have touched. A school of dolphins rode escort, corkscrewing across the bow in chains of bubbles, two of them riding the pressure wave.

Feet padded on the deck. He turned and his grin died. Syth came dashing up with a bowl of porridge. She performed all her errands at a barefoot and almost soundless run. She'd hacked her hair short, which only emphasised her girlish features. The men's clothes she wore wouldn't have fooled anybody.

Wayland took the bowl. Syth bobbed her head, encouraging him to eat. He steeled himself.

'We'll be landing in the next day or two.'

Her lips were parted. Her wide eyes searched him. She looked like a child whose only wish is to please.

'You'll be going ashore.'

'With you?'

'No, of course not. I'm travelling to Iceland.'

Panic filled her eyes. She retreated a few paces. The dog was with her and it stared at Wayland.

'We'll give you money. You don't have to go back to the fen. You could go to Norwich.'

'I don't want to go to Norwich. I want to stay with you.'

'You can't. We'll be voyaging for months. Imagine being cooped up on a ship full of strange men.'

Syth looked back down the deck. 'I don't mind.'

'Well, I do.'

Her lips quivered. 'I thought you liked me. Why else did you rescue me?'

'Because the Normans would have killed you. That doesn't mean I have to take care of you for ever. It's not just me. Everyone wants you off the ship. You get in the way. You're a nuisance.'

'How?'

Wayland struck off at a tangent. 'The way you sing without knowing that you're singing. It drives me mad.'

'Raul likes it. He told me it reminds him of home.'

'And the way you laugh over things that aren't funny.'

'Like what?'

'Like yesterday, when Vallon was practising lowering the yard and it swung round and knocked him flat.'

'That *was* funny.'

'No, it wasn't. He'd just finished spewing his guts out. You don't laugh at the captain.'

Syth cast a look at her bare feet. She wiggled her toes. 'I'm sorry. I won't laugh or sing again.'

Wayland swallowed. 'It makes no difference. You're leaving.'

Syth's face puckered, then she whirled and fled with the dog at her heels. Everyone had stopped work to watch. Vallon ordered them back to their duties. Wayland turned and clutched the stempost, a painful pressure in his chest.

'Back to crusts and water,' Vallon said, lobbing the remains of a cold and meagre supper over the side. Syth had taken to the hold with the dog and hadn't been seen since her showdown with Wayland.

Vallon looked over the company. Everyone was assembled except for Snorri, who ate alone by the rudder. 'Tomorrow we'll try to grab a couple of extra hands. Snorri reckons we'll sight land before daybreak. If this wind keeps up, we should reach the coast somewhere near the Humber estuary.'

'Drogo will be expecting us,' said Raul. 'He'll have posted lookouts all along the coast.'

Vallon nodded. 'He knows we daren't risk putting into a port. He must calculate that we'll try to take on crew from a fishing village, so he'll post guards in the larger ones and send flying pickets to keep watch on the others. Our best chance is to pick up a couple of men from an inland settlement not too far from the coast. Snorri knows several likely villages south of the Humber. We'll creep in before it gets light.' Vallon looked at Wayland and Raul. 'Think you two can manage on your own?'

Raul teased a scrap of gristle from between his teeth. 'Snatch them, you said.'

'I don't imagine you'll find volunteers.'

*

Shearwater rolled in the dying swell a mile from the coast. Seagulls floated in and out of the darkness overhead. England had shrunk to a black sliver under the starry sky. A void in the coastline marked the Humber estuary. Wayland could make out the end of a spit curving from its northern shore.

'The village is about a mile inland,' Snorri murmured. 'The peasants will be in their fields before sunrise.'

Vallon turned. 'Ready?'

Wayland nodded, his throat tight.

'Don't take any chances. We can always try again another day. We'll stand out to sea for as long as we can. If you're not back by nightfall, I'll assume you've been captured.'

Wayland and Raul exchanged glances and picked up their weapons.

Snorri pawed Wayland's arm. 'Don't forget the girl.'

Wayland glanced aft. Syth had emerged from the hold and was standing on the stern deck with the dog.

Vallon felt for his purse. 'You'd better give her this.'

Wayland stared at the coins.

'You told me you'd settled the matter,' said Vallon.

'I did. I mean, I thought I had.'

Syth stood nibbling her knuckles. The dog sat beside her, upright and alert.

'Then what are you waiting for?'

'She doesn't want to go.'

'What she wants doesn't matter. You've decided and that's all there is to it.'

'I was thinking—'

'It's too late for thinking. We don't have all day. Fetch her.'

Wayland swung his head away. Vallon's jaw tightened. 'Raul, put the girl in the boat.'

Raul glanced at Wayland. 'Captain—'

'Raul,' Vallon said very quietly. 'Get the girl.'

With another look at Wayland, Raul began to walk towards Syth. Before he'd taken three steps, the dog was on its feet, a thunderous growl shaking its frame. Raul stopped. 'I ain't risking it, Captain. Only Wayland can get near the dog when it's in that mood.'

Vallon mouthed a profanity, drew his sword and marched down the deck. The dog sprang forward with saliva strung between its jaws.

194

'Don't!' Wayland shouted.

Vallon looked back, his face dark with rage. 'Fetch the girl or I will.'

'It's no good. I can't leave her. I was going to, but I can't.'

'Jesus wept. If you cared for her, you'd be the first to set her ashore.'

'I know. I can't explain.'

Vallon walked towards him, breathing heavily. 'So we're back where we started. If the girl leaves, we say goodbye to you.'

'I don't want to leave.'

Vallon's breathing steadied. His features settled into calm. He glanced at the paling stars and put his sword back into its scabbard. 'It will soon be light. You'd better go.'

Wayland took a step towards him. 'Does that mean—'

'Go!'

Snorri sprang at Vallon. 'But ye promised!'

Vallon thrust him aside. Raul grabbed Wayland.

They pelted for the ship's boat. As Raul cast off, the dog launched out from the ship and crashed into the boat. They began to pull for the shore. Looking back, Wayland saw Syth run to the bow and give him a dazzling smile and an ecstatic little wave.

They grated on to a shingle beach and dragged the boat above a tide-mark of matted kelp. After three days at sea, Wayland's legs wobbled disconcertingly. He could just see the knarr's outline. He ordered the dog to watch over the boat and they set off inland. Grey light filmed the grass. Their feet left black prints in the dew. By the time they reached the village common, hedgerow birds were chorusing.

A placid river bounded the fields. The village itself was tucked behind a line of elms. Nestling rooks made an appalling racket in the trees. Wayland sat against a willow. Raul carved a loaf and held out a wedge.

Wayland shook his head.

Raul didn't take his eyes off him.

'You needn't bother,' Wayland told him. 'Anything you say, Vallon's already said it.'

Raul began to chew. 'I've known you since Walter dragged you out of the forest, and I never saw you do one sappy thing until that girl appeared. Never saw you so much as glance at a maid. Now look at you. Off your food. Can't sleep. You're smitten bad, my friend.'

Wayland eyed the trees turning from black to green. A rooster crowed. 'I feel terrible.'

'Only one cure. Dump her before it's too late. You'll soon get over it. She's pretty enough, I grant you, but there's always another girl in the next town. A youth as handsome as you won't even have to pay for your pleasure.'

Wayland plucked at a clump of grass.

'It ain't like she'll perish of want.'

'I know. I'd made up my mind, but when it came to it, I didn't have the heart.'

Raul stopped chewing and seemed to study Wayland in a new light. He tapped him on the wrist with his crust. 'She's bewitched you.'

Wayland was prepared to believe anything. 'Do you think so?'

'Know it. Only a witch could have made you jump into the sea in front of a Norman army. She's put a spell on the dog, too. Look at the way it follows her like a lamb. And her eyes – weird.'

Wayland threw the grass stems away. The sun had risen behind them. A delicate rack of clouds was taking shape in the heavens. A cuckoo called sleepily from a distant covert.

Raul leaned back and crossed his hands over his belly. 'I knew a man who fell in love with a witch. Most beautiful creature he'd ever seen – fair like your Syth, but with a bit more flesh on her. Anyway, this gorgeous creature took the man to her bed and granted him every delight he could wish for. At last his pleasure was done and he lay back with his love in his arms. You know what happened then?'

'What?'

Raul sat upright. 'Right before his eyes, her face began to slide off her skull and her flesh fell away from her ribs. Instead of holding a beauty to his bosom, he was clutching a corpse full of worms and maggots.'

Wayland stared at him in horror.

Raul brushed crumbs from his mouth. 'Yonder comes one.'

Wayland tore his gaze away. A pale and ragged urchin wandered in their direction, gazing around as if the world were full of wonders. He went into a strip of sprouting rye and clapped his hands. A few buntings flew into the nearest hedgerow. After several more desultory claps, the boy peeped furtively around before shifting a couple of boundary stones on his family's strip. Then he wandered over to the hedge and began to work his way along it, peering into the branches for nests.

Raul stood impatiently. 'Where are the rest of the sluggards?'

A bell began to chime.

Raul slapped his knee. 'Fools that we are! It's Sunday. Everyone's in church.' He gave a wicked chuckle. 'So much the better.'

They marched up a lane lined by cruck houses with garden plots in front and enclosures at the back. Milch cows eyed them dreamily, hanks of lush spring grass clamped in their jaws. Blossom-time had arrived and the apple trees and quinces were smothered in white and pink sprays. Children fetching water or fodder fled squealing from the raiders, stopping at a safe distance to watch them through splayed fingers. They fell in behind, the bolder youngsters throwing out their chests and swinging their limbs in parody of Raul's gait. By the time Wayland and Raul reached the church, they had a sizeable following.

Through a screen of dark yews, Wayland saw a stone nave and a square tower with triangular arcades and pointed windows. Sheep grazed in the graveyard. The raiders leaned their weapons outside the heavy oak door.

'Don't you think we should wait until mass is over?' Wayland said.

'Leave it to me. Remember, we're dealing with shit-shovellers who've never travelled further than the local market. No point puzzling their pates with talk of Iceland and the Road to the Greeks.'

Clawing off his cap, Raul stepped through the door. Wayland ducked in after him, sketching the sign of the cross. Sunbeams splaying through the windows lit a congregation divided each side of the aisle, some lounging against the pillars, a few standing upright, most squatting on the rush-covered floor. Many appeared to be asleep. Two rustics at the back observed the strangers' entrance and nudged their neighbours, the warning rippling out until the whole congregation stood upright and staring. Raul put a finger to his lips. Only the priest at the altar remained unaware of their presence. Eyes closed, head tilted back, he continued reciting the mass in a barely audible murmur. Wayland's gaze lifted towards the shadowed vault. His eyes drifted to a wall painting of the Last Judgement showing Christ on his throne, the righteous winged as angels to his right, the sinners naked and

197

fearful on his left, below them the damned being pitched into the cauldron and everlasting fire. He thought of his family in their unmarked graves.

The droning stopped. The priest advanced to the door of the rood screen and contemplated his flock with irritation. 'On his last visit,' he said, 'your temporal lord summoned me with a complaint about this parish. He's sorely vexed by the sin of sloth into which many of you have fallen.'

Raul nudged Wayland. 'Damned if he ain't going to start preachifying. Keep an eye out.' The German stomped up the aisle.

The priest started back in alarm. 'Who are you?'

'Step aside. I'll deliver your sermon and save time as well as souls.' Raul turned.

'Sloth,' he said, letting the word fill the nave. 'Sloth is the enemy of enterprise and the leech of profit. Me and my comrade are delegated by our captain to recruit two or three fellows to join us on a voyage of enterprise. We're looking for men of strength and resolution, preferably stalwarts who've seen battle and have crewed on a ship. We chose this parish because we heard it bred right brave men.'

Watching from the door, Wayland shook his head. With his outlandish sidelock, matted beard and rancid jerkin, Raul looked like the flotsam of some defeated barbarian horde. Close to, he smelled like a polecat.

Raul jingled coins. 'A halfpenny for each day you serve, including rest days and holy days. Plus,' he said, holding up a finger as if in benediction, 'full keep. You won't have to spend a penny of your wages on bed and board.' He did his disappearing trick with a coin. 'And even that ain't all. Any gain we make by trade is divvied up. Fair shares for all. Ain't that right, Wayland?'

The congregation turned and gawped.

'You'll be well paid and well treated.'

'Hear that? The word of an Englishman.' Raul gave a toothy smile. 'Obviously, we ain't taking just anyone. We're picky. But for two or three who ain't afraid of honest toil, here's the chance to raise yourselves up.'

The congregation exchanged nods and conjectures. Wayland began to think that Raul might pull it off.

'How far are you sailing?' someone asked.

'Like as not you'll be home to help with the harvest. Not that you'll have to toil in the fields again – not with your swags of silver.'

'How far?'

'North.'

'Where north?'

Raul glared at the questioner. 'Orkney.'

The worshippers stuck out their bottom lips and shrugged. 'Is that on the other side of the river?' one asked.

''Course it is, ye numpty,' someone snorted. 'There ain't no Orkney this side of Humber.'

'It's north of the Humber,' Raul conceded. 'Not far.'

A swallow dived through the door, just missing Wayland's head, and swooped up to its nest in the roof beams.

Raul trickled silver from palm to palm. 'A halfpenny a day and all found.'

They thought about it like a convocation of philosophers. Not a man came forward.

'Are you so content with your lives?' Raul demanded. 'Does your landlord treat you that well?'

'He treats us like willows,' came a cry from the back. 'He thinks the more he crops us, the better we'll sprout.'

Laughter was followed by other complaints. 'He fines us when we marry. He fines us when we die.'

'He forbids us to grind our corn at home and charges us to use his own mill.'

'Where we have to wait three days for flour made from last year's mouldy gleanings.'

Raul spread his arms in evangelical fervour. 'Brethren, here's the chance to throw off your yokes. Here's the cure to your earthly miseries.' He stepped up to one of the dissenters, a well-set man of about thirty. 'You have a bold tongue. I like the cut of you. You've seen action if I ain't mistook.'

'I fought with the English king's fyrd at Stamford.'

'I knew it. You're just the sort of stout-limbed fellow we're looking for.'

The man shook his head. 'I'm married with three bairns and an ailing mother.'

'Ah, but think how richly you'll be able to provide for them when you return.'

'I can't. I'm tied to my fields.'

'No man's tied. Come on, shake the mud off your feet.'

'Leave him be,' Wayland said.

Raul scowled at him and confronted another serf. 'How about you?'

The man rubbed his knees and spoke inaudibly. Raul cocked a hand to his ear. 'What's that?'

Wayland turned. 'He says, "Who'll look after his bees?"'

Raul yanked his sidelock. 'Sweet Jesus. It's like plucking feathers off a toad.'

He went from man to man, receiving the same mumbled negatives. He craned back in amazement. 'What! None of you. Your Viking fore-fathers must be kicking in the cold earth. All right. Dream your dreams of mangels. Count your haystacks. Spend the rest of your days staring up an ox's arse while you squelch through the mud with your toes sticking out of your shoes and the clothes raggedy on your back and your kids perishing at home from hunger.'

'I'll come.'

Raul swung round. 'Show yourself.'

Out of the congregation limped a tall and bony labourer with knees and elbows staring from threadbare homespun, big hands dangling from knobbly wrists.

Raul eyed him dubiously. 'Who might you be?'

'Garrick, a widower and poor freeman. Death has separated me from my kin and I'll soon join them if I stay here, for my fields are too few to furnish a living.'

Raul stalked around the peasant, sizing him up. 'You're lame. Was that done on the battlefield?'

Someone laughed. 'He fell out of a tree when he was a boy. Bad luck and trouble have followed Garrick all his days.'

Raul shoved him aside. 'Sorry, we want able-bodied men.'

'Let me see him,' Wayland called.

'Vallon won't thank us for signing up a scarecrow.'

'Bring him here.'

Raul marched Garrick to the door. Hunger and toil were stamped on every feature, but a wry light gleamed in his hollow grey eyes. Something in Wayland warmed to him.

'Are you ill?'

'If hunger's a sickness, then I'm mortally ill.'

Wayland smiled. 'Show me your hands.'

Garrick spread blackened and calloused mitts as big as shovels.

'The journey will be hard.'

'Staying here will be harder. I ate the last of my harvest before Lent.'

'He'll do,' said Wayland. 'Find one more and then we'll be off.'

Raul glared into the body of the church. 'The angel Gabriel couldn't sweet talk that lot through the pearly gates. I'll just take whoever I fancy.'

'I don't want to separate men from their families,' Wayland said.

'You heard Vallon. Grab them, he said. We can't dicker about waiting for these clodhoppers to make up their minds.'

The boys in the churchyard yelled and began jumping up and down, pointing at a rider and two men on foot hastening across the fields.

Wayland took a few steps down the path. 'Who are they?' he asked Garrick.

'Daegmund the bailiff and his bullies, Aiken and Brant. The bane of our lives and the goad of our days.'

Wayland shaded his eyes. The bailiff was lashing his mule roughshod over the peasants' crops. He jounced in the saddle, his pudding bowl haircut flopping up and down. Two footsoldiers in shabby leather armour trotted behind him.

'We'd better not wait on their coming,' Garrick said.

Wayland took up his bow and reached for an arrow. 'Will they fight?'

'Not Daegmund. The boldest thing about him is his collar, for it grips the throat of a thief daily. He uses his bullies for the rough stuff.'

'Local men?'

'No. Daegmund doesn't trust men of the manor. He has too many sly dealings to hide. He hired those ruffians in Grimsby.'

The worshippers had left the church to spectate. The bailiff hauled up his mule beyond the graveyard. Pudgy and glandular, he cut an unvalorous figure for all that he wielded a sword and staff. His guards came panting up and stationed themselves on each side, scraping clods off their shoes and trying to disguise how winded they were. They carried old and abused single-edged Saxon swords. Their quilted leather gambesons leaked stuffing. Daegmund passed a hand across his eyes.

'What's this I spy? What's this? Trespassers on my lord's manor. Armed nuisances. Disturbers of the King's peace. State your business.'

Raul spat carefully. 'We're recruiting men for a trading expedition.'

The bailiff's eyes bulged. 'These serfs are my lord's possessions. Every man and his chattels exist at his will and disposition.'

'He won't miss a brace.'

The bailiff brandished his staff. 'Arrest those rogues. Bind them. Each man who assists will have their week-work remitted for a month.'

Raul pushed out his cheek with his tongue. 'Generous soul, ain't he?'

The bailiff pointed a quivering finger. 'I've raised the hue. Soldiers are on their way. You'll hang.'

'If they catch us, they'll do a lot worse than hang us.'

One of the guards felt for the bailiff's knee. Daegmund leaned down with a hand cocked over his ear and what he heard made him straighten with a start, his face as red as a cockscomb.

'Those men are felons and murderers. They're members of a gang that broke out of Norwich after slaughtering their guards. That's the measure of their wickedness.'

'That's right,' Raul shouted, silencing the buzz. 'I stopped counting how many Normans we killed after the first twenty.'

The bailiff's eyes shimmied. 'There's ten shillings on each of their heads.'

Raul advanced a step. 'You're a lying sack of shit. The price was more than a pound a fortnight ago, and that was before we sank a Norman ship. We must be worth at least double now.'

'A share of the reward to every man who helps turn them in.' Daegmund kicked out at one of his bodyguards. 'Lead the way. Seize them.'

As Brant and Aiken advanced into the graveyard, Raul levelled his crossbow at the bailiff. 'Keep them coming. You'll be the first to die.'

Daegmund waved his men back as if he were trying to put out flames. Wayland studied his minders. Both of middling height, red-cheeked, built like small dray horses.

'What about taking those two?'

Raul sniffed. 'Could do worse, I suppose.'

Wayland checked the mood of the congregation. It wasn't wise to underestimate peasants. He began to walk forward.

'Help!' yelped the bailiff, yanking his mule around.

One of the guards waggled his sword. Wayland stopped.

'Which one of you is Brant?'

'Don't ye tell him,' said the one on the right.

Wayland smiled at the one on the left. 'You're Brant.'

Brant gave a sly nod. He looked a bit simple.

'We're bound for the north on a merchant venture. Hiring crew who'll work hard for a good wage. You and your partner look like likely lads.'

'What's he saying?' cried the bailiff from a safe distance.

'How much does that tub of guts pay you?'

'Don't answer,' Aiken said. 'You'll only get us into trouble.'

'You're already in trouble.'

'Four shillings each quarter day,' said Brant. 'And we're still waiting for last quarter's wages.'

'Take service with us and we'll pay you double and all found, plus a share of the profits. Show them, Raul.'

At sight of the silver, Brant slid his tongue along his teeth and looked sidelong at his partner.

'Words are cheap,' Aiken told him. 'Once they've got you on their ship, fancy promises don't mean shit. They'll work you like a mule and kick you like a cur.'

'How do you think your master will treat you when we leave with Garrick?'

The bailiff had spurred closer. 'Stand firm. Do your duty and I'll forgive any trespasses you've done me this day.'

Wayland nudged his chin. 'Who do you believe? Him or me?'

'He's right,' Brant told Aiken. 'Unless we stop them, we're finished here.'

Aiken looked away, jaw jutting.

'Our ship's waiting,' Wayland said.

Brant reached for Aiken's arm. Excitement lit his face. 'Let's join them and make our fortunes.'

Aiken glowered at the ground and swung his head from side to side.

Brant laughed. 'Then I'll go alone.' He scanned the scenery around as though committing it to memory, took two quick breaths and stepped to Wayland's side. Turning, he looked back across an invisible line. 'I'll come back rich,' he said. 'You'll see.'

Aiken raised his head. 'Half the Norman army is hunting those pirates. You'll be dead before next Sunday.'

Daegmund was shaking his fist and looking set to have a fit.

'We're done here,' Wayland told Raul.

They began to back away. The parishioners watched with solemn expressions. They'd reached the graveyard wall when the bailiff spurred his mule around Aiken and rained sickening blows on his head.

XVIII

Heeling against a light easterly, *Shearwater* headed north about ten miles out from the coast. It was late afternoon. Shifting columns of yellow light fanned through the clouds. Hero compared the direction of the wind-vane on the ship's stern with their actual course. He looked at the thin black line to westward.

'Your move,' said Richard.

Hero turned his attention back to the *shatranj* game. He advanced one of his pawns. 'We'll be lucky to reach Scotland without having to land again.'

Vallon had decided to stay at sea until they were out of Norman territory. Drogo would have posted news of their crimes to every coastal garrison. All likely landing sites would be under watch and fishing crews would have been alerted to report any sighting or rumour of their passage.

Richard looked up blankly.

'We can't sail closer to the wind than about forty degrees,' Hero explained. He made an angle with his hands. 'We're not far off that now. If this wind shifts any further to the east, we'll be driven on to the coast.'

'It's only another three days to Scotland,' Richard said. He moved one of his knights and sat back. 'Your move.'

Hero had scratched an eight-by-eight grid on a plank and collected pebbles of different shapes and colours for the pieces. This was only Richard's third game, but he was a quick learner. He'd lost the first two, but somehow had managed to gain a two-pawn advantage in this one. Hero decided that he'd better concentrate. He examined the position, then advanced a *rukh* to threaten Richard's general.

While Richard plotted his next move, Hero studied the new crew members. 'Will the new men fit in, do you think?'

Richard glanced behind him. Garrick was leaning back against the gunwale, his lame leg propped up behind him, talking with Syth. She was describing something with her hands in a way that made him laugh and sketch his own version in the air.

'Old Garrick's a decent chap,' said Richard.

Hero smiled. 'What an appetite he has. At the rate he eats, we'll run out of food before we reach Scotland.'

Richard's hand hovered over the board. 'I'm not so keen on Brant. He's a lout.'

Hero didn't take to Brant either. Right now he was sniggering with Snorri on the stern deck.

'So long as he pulls his weight.'

'He leers at Syth.'

'Really?'

'I saw him ogling her at supper last night.'

'I hope Vallon didn't notice.'

'Of course he did. Vallon notices everything.'

Richard moved one of his elephants diagonally two squares, capturing another pawn. Hero forgot Brant in his effort to save the game. After much indecision, he moved a knight. Without hesitation, Richard slid a *rukh* up the board.

'Check.'

Hero muttered to himself. He reached for his king, withdrew his hand, reached out again.

'It won't do you any good,' Richard said.

'He's right,' said Vallon, squatting down beside them. 'If he moves his knight thus, and then his elephant so, he has you in checkmate.'

'Are you sure?'

'Quite sure.'

Hero knocked over his king and rocked back in disgust. 'It's these crude pieces. I can't tell one from another. I only improvised them to teach Richard the rules. I won't play again until Raul has carved us a proper set.'

Vallon gave him a reproving look, then took both of them by their shoulders. 'I have a favour to ask. Now that our venture is under way, it's time we put our affairs on a businesslike footing. We need a treasurer to manage our finances.'

'I don't mind keeping the accounts,' Hero said.

Vallon squeezed his shoulder. 'I was wondering if Richard might take on the task. You said that he's quick with numbers.'

Hero responded to the prompt. 'Oh, he is. He even understands the concept of zero.'

A pained smile crossed Vallon's face. On their journey through France, Hero had tried long and hard to convince him of the magical properties of zero. Vallon failed to see the value of a number that wasn't a number, a signifier meaning nothing.

'All I want is a tally of our transactions. How much we spend, earn and owe, tabulated on a daily basis. Richard, do you think that's within your grasp?'

Richard flushed with pleasure. 'I'll do my best.' Until now, Vallon hadn't acknowledged that he possessed any talents.

'Excellent,' said Vallon. He stood. 'One more thing. We're outnumbered by English speakers. We won't hear another French voice for months. If we're going to trade with the Norsemen, we'd better learn their tongue. Wayland has agreed to teach us.'

'Wayland?'

'No one else can. It will keep his mind off the girl.'

Hero exchanged looks with Richard. Since the scene on the morning the raiding party went ashore, there had been an unofficial moratorium on the subject of Syth.

'Are you reconciled to her presence?' Hero asked.

'I can't fault her willingness. She cooks well, keeps things trim and adds a bit of cheer.' Vallon shrugged. 'We'll see.'

Hero's attention must have drifted towards Brant.

Vallon intercepted his look. 'I intend paying him off as soon as we get to Scotland. He won't interfere with Syth while she has the dog to protect her. Even I tread warily around that brute.'

*

Two days later Brant was dead, fulfilling Aiken's prophecy with time to spare.

He was lucky not to have been killed a day earlier, just north of the Tyne river. The sun had sunk below the horizon, leaving the coastline contoured in crimson. Hero and the other students were seated around Wayland on the foredeck, having an English lesson. Syth was cooking supper below. A vicious snarling down in the hold shattered the peace. Wayland sprinted aft and the others ran after him. When Hero got there, Brant stood backed into a corner, swinging a bailing bucket in a flimsy effort to ward off the dog. Wayland must have given an order because the dog turned its head and leaped up on to the forward half-deck. Only then did Hero see Syth, crouched by the brazier.

Vallon seized Wayland as he made to jump down. He spoke into his ear, gripping so tightly that both men quaked. Whatever he said was enough to make Wayland back off and walk away, shooting murderous looks over his shoulder.

Vallon pretended to be surprised to find the rest of the crew spectating. 'Haven't you got anything better to do?'

Snorri crowed as Vallon climbed into the hold. 'I told ye the little mother would stir up trouble.'

When Vallon returned to continue his lesson, he acted as if nothing had happened.

'So where were we?'

Next day a spitting easterly threatened to pin them to the coast. Only determined rowing kept them off the shore. On their seaward side, surf broke around a swarm of islets and reefs. To the west, a massive ruin commanded the coast.

'That's Bamburgh,' Richard said. 'It used to be the stronghold of the Northumbrian kings. My father told me the Normans plan to rebuild it.'

'Anyone see if it's manned?' Vallon asked.

Hero's eyes were too sticky with brine to see clearly.

'There's scaffolding on one of the walls,' Wayland said.

'Well, if anyone's there, they've seen us. Keep rowing.'

Even with six oars manned, they struggled to make headway. They'd spotted the castle not long after midday and it was still in sight behind them by late afternoon.

Raul pointed. 'Ship to starboard!'

A fishing boat carrying four men bore down on them out of the mizzle and cut across their stern almost within hailing distance. Vallon and some of the others raised their hands. The crew of the other vessel stared hard and none of them lifted a finger in greeting.

'Don't like the look of that,' Raul said.

With the wind filling its sail, the boat rapidly made shore and disappeared into the mouth of a lagoon. *Shearwater* crept on. Directly ahead, an indeterminate smear hardened into a low headland poking a mile out to sea.

'We ain't going to get round that,' said Raul.

Vallon dug in with his oar. 'Keep at it. We'll try to row into the lee before dark.'

On they struggled, their progress slowing the closer they came to the headland.

'We're caught in a tidal rip,' Raul shouted. 'It's carrying us backwards.'

Vallon couldn't work it out. Under the cliffs towards the point of the headland, the sea was as flat as pewter. Close inshore, the sea was combed into ragged lines of foam cutting across the waves. He pointed at the headland. 'I think it might be an island.'

'Doesn't matter,' Raul shouted. 'We ain't going to reach it on this tide.'

Vallon growled with frustration. 'Drop anchor. We'll wait for the tide to turn.'

The anchor dragged through the sandy bottom and then held, tethering *Shearwater* close to a long and lonely beach backed by high dunes. Vallon issued orders. 'Raul, Brant, row Wayland ashore.' He turned to the falconer. 'Make your way up the beach and see what's ahead.'

'Can we go ashore, too?' Hero asked. After four days at sea he yearned to feel solid ground underfoot.

Vallon glanced back towards the inlet where the fishing boat had disappeared. 'We're not safe here. Keep watch from the dunes. Don't wander off.'

Hero stepped on to a strand that had been swept clear of all human traces except for the weathered ribs of a ship half buried in the sand. He and Richard scrambled up a steep dune capped with marram grass.

A miniature desert spread inland. Some of the dunes were aligned to the prevailing wind, others arranged as chaotically as the waves chopping at *Shearwater*. Looking back, Hero saw the anchored knarr straining against the current. Wayland and his dog were tiny outlines running up the beach. The sun was a pale blister in the overcast. Hero shivered.

He was run down. All of them were. Never really warm, never really dry, never a full night's sleep. They'd eaten all the fresh food and their diet was a monotony of stale bread, salted herrings and porridge. Even the drinking water had run so short that Vallon had imposed rationing. Hero had noticed that cuts and scratches were slow to heal.

Beside him, Richard echoed his dejection with a sigh.

'Don't lose heart,' Hero said. 'We'll soon be in Scottish waters.'

'So much time and effort, and we're only back where we started from. If I had a good horse, I could be home by daybreak tomorrow.' Richard's mouth twisted. 'Imagine the reception I'd receive.'

Hero realised just how much Richard had sacrificed. 'Do you regret your decision to come with us?'

Richard's face grew still. 'No. I could have borne my father's contempt and Drogo's blows if Margaret had shown me any affection. Even the hardiest plant shrivels in barren soil.' He traced a pattern in the sand. 'The only thing I regret is the blood that's been spilled. I never imagined that Drogo would pursue his grudge so violently.' Richard swept away his tracing.

'There's no stain on your hands.'

'That's not how my family will see it. I'll never be able to return to England. Perhaps I could come to Italy with you. I was wondering about taking Holy Orders. Do you think I might be accepted?'

Hero smiled. 'I'm sure that any monastery would be delighted to receive you.'

'If I practise my writing, perhaps they would let me work in the scriptorium.'

'Writing all day can be drudgery. It will make your sight grow dim and your back crooked.'

'But think how much I'll learn.'

'Richard, if we complete this journey, you'll have learned more than any book scholar.'

'Hey! Are you two deaf?'

Raul stood on the beach, hands on hips. Wayland was jogging back towards the ship. The tide had begun to go out and *Shearwater* rode more easily at anchor.

Raul came puffing up the dune. 'Vallon wants us back on board.' He reached the crest and swept his eyes about. 'Where's Brant?'

Hero frowned. 'How would I know?'

'I thought he was with you.'

'We haven't seen him since we landed.'

Raul thumped his forehead with his hand. 'Shit!'

'He's probably just stretching his legs,' Hero said. 'Do you want us to take a look?'

Raul glared around. 'Make it quick. If he ain't shown up by the time Wayland gets here, we're leaving.'

Hero and Richard clambered over the dunes, clawing up the steep windward faces and scampering down the lee slopes. The sandhills formed a maze as convoluted as the ruins of a city. Each time Hero reached a crest, he called Brant's name in a voice that fell muffled into the labyrinth.

'Look,' Richard said, pointing at a scattering of bones in the next hollow.

Hero prodded a human skull with his foot. The chalky cranium had been smashed in. Judging by the number of other bones scattered about, a massacre had been committed here. 'They look very old,' he said. 'I wonder if the victims were from the ship we saw on the beach.'

Richard looked behind him. 'Perhaps we should go back.'

'Let's climb one more ridge.'

From the top they scanned the waste. Grasses flickered in the wind. The sand crawled around their feet. Gulls hung stacked in the sky for as high as the eye could see. The glaucous shapes drifted slowly backwards on the wind, uttering woeful cries.

'We're wasting time,' Hero said. 'Brant's deserted.'

'Wait. I thought I heard a voice.'

'Only the gulls.'

'No. Listen.'

Hero raised his head. 'You're imagining it.'

'There it comes again. Listen.'

'It's nothing. Let's go.'

But as Hero turned into the wind he caught the tail-end of

movement over to his left. He picked it up again and thought it was an animal scuttling along a dune. It stopped and he saw that it was Brant, only his head showing. Arms flailing with effort, Brant gained the crest and threw a desperate glance behind him before flinging himself into the next hollow. Hero knew that he was fleeing for his life, yet his own reactions were strangely sluggish. It was as if he were spectating an event in some parallel world. When Brant appeared again, he was close enough for Hero to see the terror on his face. He must have noticed them because he seemed to shake his head in despair before floundering down into the next gully.

He was still hidden when the warhorses came rearing up out of the sand-sea behind him, swinging their heads like mallets, their hooves smashing breaches in the crest.

'Run!'

Arms windmilling, they raced down the face. The Normans rode in different directions, weaving across each other, the horses galloping haywire though the warren of gullies.

Sliding down the next scarp, Richard tore his shoe and stumbled on with one sole flapping. They reached another summit and risked a backward glance. By some quirk of timing, all the Normans were hidden in the depressions. Then suddenly, like marionettes jerked on a string, up they rose, whipping their horses, bracing back in their saddles for the next crashing descent. Richard's breaths came in wheezing gasps. Hero was so winded that he scrabbled up the last slope on all fours.

Raul and Wayland were waiting by the boat. Hero gave a feeble shout and they looked up, idly curious for an instant before springing into action. Hero launched into space, lost his footing and somersaulted down to the beach. Head spinning, he looked up at Wayland and found enough breath to speak.

'Normans. Chasing Brant.'

Wayland lugged them down the beach. Raul was pushing the boat into the surf.

Wayland dragged them through the waves. Raul seized them one in each hand and plucked them aboard. They grabbed oars. Hero squirmed round to see Brant stagger on to the last dune. He covered his face with his hands at the awful sight of the boat rowing away. A spear flew past him and he plunged off the crest.

'We can't just leave him,' Hero cried.

'He left us,' Raul panted, not breaking rhythm.

Brant fell down the dune as if part of him were broken. When he gained his feet, he seemed disoriented, limping away up the beach before turning towards the boat. His right leg had an arrow in the thigh and dragged behind him. He was halfway down the strand when the first Normans rode on to the sand ridge. They saw that he couldn't escape and halted while the rest of the force gathered. Upwards of twenty crested the skyline by the time Brant staggered to the water's edge. He spread his arms, his mouth gaping in a howl of outrage.

Some of the Normans dismounted and left their horses and descended on foot. Others led their mounts sideways down the face, while the bolder cavaliers kicked with their spurs, their steeds sliding down the dune on their hindquarters. One soldier drew a bow and aimed at Brant, but an officer shouted and the archer slackened off.

Raul grabbed his crossbow. 'Stop rowing!'

'He's a dead man,' said Wayland. 'Don't waste your bolts.'

Raul backhanded him across the chest. 'Stop rowing.'

He knelt, resting one elbow on the thwart to steady his aim.

Brant turned to face his hunters and held up his hands in a gesture so abject that Hero groaned for pity.

'Everyone keep still,' Raul ordered.

The boat slopped up and down. Raul muttered something and froze into greater concentration. Hero heard a small explosion as the pent-up energy of the bolt was released. Brant arched back, hands fluttering, took a couple of steps sideways and pitched into the shallows.

Raul picked up his oar. 'I had to kill him. He'd have told them our course and destination.'

Two soldiers ran into the sea to recover the body. The rest gathered around their commander. Hero could see him giving directions. The force split, half a dozen men riding back up on to the dunes, the rest galloping hard up the beach.

'What are they up to?'

'I don't know,' said Raul, 'but they ain't given up on us.'

*

212

On board *Shearwater*, Wayland reported that the island was cut off from the mainland by a shallow bay riddled with banks and bars.

'Is there a way out?' Vallon asked.

'There's a narrow channel at the other end.'

'That's probably where the cavalry are making for,' said Raul.

'Any shipping in the bay?'

Wayland shook his head.

'What about the island? Is it inhabited?'

'I saw only ruins.'

Vallon studied the dunes. Against the gloomy evening sky, the Norman soldiers waited in menacing silhouette. The detachment that had galloped north was out of sight. The tidal current had eased and the wind had fallen. 'We'll take a look at the bay,' he said.

They rowed parallel with the beach, the soldiers on the dunes reining in their horses to keep pace with them. The fugitives reached the point at the end of the beach. The bay was draining to mud, veined by dozens of channels gleaming in the gathering dark. 'We won't cross it without stranding,' said Vallon. He studied the island and pointed at its rocky southern point less than a mile away. 'Make for the shelter of the cliffs.'

Night caught up with them before they reached the lee. They felt their way in and dropped anchor when they heard the sound of waves sucking among rocks. Hero tried to conjecture some form in the darkness. Seals moaned out on the flats. Surf boomed on the cliffs around the headland.

'Do you want me to go ashore and explore?' Wayland asked Vallon.

'Wait a while.'

Just then a light appeared high above them.

'The Normans must have crossed on to the island,' Raul muttered.

'They wouldn't wave a lantern. Everybody stay quiet.'

Hero watched the lantern bobbing down the black face of night. The light reached sea level and stopped. A voice called.

'Anyone catch that?'

'Sounded like English,' said Wayland. 'English and then another language.'

'Don't you go answering,' Raul hissed. 'They could be wreckers.'

The voice called again and the lantern swung like a censer.

'He's speaking Latin,' said Hero. '*Pax vobiscum*. Peace be with you. *Venite in ripam. Nolite timere*. Come ashore. Don't be afraid.'

Raul spat. 'Not likely. Wreckers try all sorts of tricks to lure sailors into their clutches.'

Vallon snorted. 'How many wreckers do you know who speak Latin? Maybe there's a monastery on the island. Hero, ask him who he is.'

Hero made a trumpet with his hands. '*Quis es tu?*'

Laughter in the dark. 'Brother Cuthbert, *erimetes sum.*'

'He says he's a hermit monk.'

'Ask him if there are any Normans on the island.'

Hero turned to Wayland. 'You ask. I think English is his native tongue.'

Wayland called out. An answer came from the night. 'He says there aren't any Normans. The island's been deserted for many years. He's the only man left on it.'

Vallon tapped his mouth. 'Hero, go ashore with Raul and question the hermit. Find out if the Normans can reach the island. Learn as much as you can about the coast.'

'Can I go, too?' said Richard.

'I suppose so. But don't take all night. Tell the hermit to snuff out his lamp. The Normans will be able to see it from the mainland.'

Raul rowed towards the light. Hero gathered himself in the bow and sprang on to a boulder slippery with sea wrack.

'*Salvete amici,*' called the hermit. 'Are you monks? Have my brothers sent you?'

His head was cowled and the glow from his lantern threw his face into shadow.

'Put the light out,' Raul growled.

'But the night is dark and you don't know the path.'

Raul whisked the lamp away and extinguished the flame. 'I ain't following you up any path. What is this place?'

The hermit gave a bronchial laugh. 'You must have travelled from far away. This is the holy island of Lindisfarne, the place where Christianity first reached England.'

'Deserted, you said.'

Another phlegmy laugh. 'Nobody has lived on Lindisfarne since Vikings destroyed the monastery two centuries ago.'

'Can anyone sail to it across the bay?'

'Not on an ebbing tide and the night so dark.'

'That's all we need to know,' said Raul. 'Let's go back.'

'Not just yet,' said Hero. 'I'd like to hear the history of the place.'

'Me, too,' said Richard.

'Well, I'm staying right here,' said Raul. 'If you hear me yell, don't stop to wonder why.'

Hero could just about descry the hermit's shape. 'Sir, please take us to your shelter. *Duc nos in cellam tuam, domine, quaeso.*'

Brother Cuthbert led them up a gully, guiding them around invisible hazards. It was so dark that Richard had to cling to Hero's sleeve. They negotiated pillars of rock and then Cuthbert stopped.

'Here we are. *Intrate.* Come in, come in.'

Hero worked out that the hermit's retreat was a cave with a patch of sailcloth for a weather-shield. When he put his head inside, the stench made him gag. Like rats rotting under a sack.

Richard clapped a hand to his mouth. 'Urgh!'

'Ssh. Think of the purity of his soul.'

Dying coals reddened fitfully on the ground. Hero and Richard sat on one side of the fire, Cuthbert on the other.

'You're the first visitors I've received since Easter,' Cuthbert said across the gulf. 'Which one of you speaks such polished Latin? Have you come to Lindisfarne on pilgrimage?'

'We're pilgrims of a sort. We're voyaging to the far north.'

'Carrying the word of Christ?'

'No, we're on a trading mission.'

Hero spoke in Latin and had to translate for Richard's benefit. The young Norman was uneasy.

'Ask him to light the lamp.'

Cuthbert met the request with an apology. 'I have little fuel to spare. There is light in this place, though – a light bright enough to illuminate the darkest of nights.'

'Tell us about your island,' Hero said.

Cuthbert related how, in the seventh century, St Aidan had brought Christianity to Northumbria and founded the monastery on Lindisfarne. In that same year, Cuthbert's sainted namesake was born. After ten years of missionary work, Cuthbert retreated to a hermitage on Inner Farne – one of the sea-swept islands they'd sailed past earlier. Asked by pope and king to become the second bishop, Cuthbert reluctantly agreed, but after two years he retired to his hermitage to die. Eleven years later, at the ceremony of Cuthbert's Elevation, the monks opened his coffin to find his body complete and uncorrupt. News of the miracle brought pilgrims flocking to the shrine. Then Vikings sacked the monastery and the surviving brothers took St Cuthbert's body to the mainland and enshrined it in their monastery at Durham.

Several times during his narrative, Cuthbert broke off, coughing. His breathing had a stertorous quality that Hero found as disturbing as the stink.

'You're ill,' he said. 'You should be in a hospital.'

'If there's a cure for me, I'll find it here by the divine power that preserved Cuthbert's flesh after death.'

'What's he saying?' Richard whispered.

Hero had stopped translating. A chill settled on his body. 'If the saint's relics can cure all ills, you should be in Durham where his body lies.'

Cuthbert gave another choking cough and swallowed a bolus of mucus. 'My community expelled me.'

Hero fingered his throat. He'd heard that racked coughing before. 'Light your lamp. We brought some gifts for you. They include oil.'

Cuthbert blew life into the coals and kindled a twist of straw. The flames singed his hands as he set the taper to the wick, but he didn't flinch. Shadows crept up the walls. Cuthbert set down the lamp and squatted with his cowled head downcast. Hero picked up the light.

'Show us your face.'

'I'd rather spare you the sight.'

'I won't be shocked. I know what ails you.'

Cuthbert slowly raised his head. Hero drew a sharp intake of breath. The hermit's eyes looked out from behind a carapace of scales and nodules. Half his nose had rotted away, corrupted by an infection he couldn't even feel.

'A leper!' Richard shouted, jumping up. 'We've been sitting with a leper.' He backed out of the cave so violently that he tore the windbreak from its mounts.

Cuthbert's anguished eyes stared out at Hero. 'Aren't you frightened?'

'I was a student of medicine. I've visited leper hospitals.'

'To cure them.'

'There is no cure.'

Cuthbert stared past him. 'Yes, there is. I've witnessed many miracles on Lindisfarne.'

'How long have you been here?'

'This is my second year. The local fishermen leave food for me and I sometimes take eggs from the seabirds. Last winter was hard, but now that summer is approaching, pilgrims will be returning to the island. Sometimes a dozen or more cross the causeway in a single day.'

'Causeway?'

'I forget. You don't know the island. The causeway is a path exposed at low tide.'

'You said nobody could reach the island by night.'

'I said no one would sail here in the dark.'

Hero looked over his shoulder at the entrance. 'The tide must be almost at its lowest now.'

'But who would make such a crossing?'

'Excuse me, I have to go.' Hero stood. 'We're fugitives from the Normans. They'll be here soon. For your own sake, you mustn't tell them you've seen us.' He remembered the bundle and held it out. 'This is for you. It's not much. Some bread and fish. A blanket. I'm sorry, I have to go.'

Cuthbert's blessings followed Hero as he stumbled down the gully. On the shoreline he blundered into Raul and Richard. The German laughed.

'That'll teach you to follow strange voices in the night.'

'He spat his vile humours over me,' Richard cried.

'Both of you shut up!'

In silence they rowed to the ship. Hero told Vallon about the causeway and nothing else. Cuthbert had descended with his lamp to the shore again. Vallon looked away from it into the dark sky.

'The wind's easing all the time. Raise the anchor.'

The crew strained over the oars, heading around the point. Cuthbert followed them along the shore as if to light their way. They had almost reached the tip of Lindisfarne when out from the mainland crept a column of flares, processing over the face of the sea like communicants bound for midnight mass.

'Forgive my outburst,' Richard said, brushing Hero's shoulder. 'I was shocked.'

Hero reached up and for a moment their fingers locked. 'Of course I forgive you.' He gave a long groan. 'What an awful day it's been.'

Cuthbert's voice carried faintly across the water.

'What's he saying?' Richard asked.

Hero choked back tears. '*Benedicti sitis peregrini.* Bless you, pilgrims.'

XIX

They scraped north for two more days and late on the second afternoon they nosed into the mouth of a wide firth, rounding a great plug of basalt almost hidden behind a blizzard of seabirds. *Shearwater* sailed through the birds' fishing grounds. Boobies sheared the sky in their thousands, folding back their wings and plummeting like darts into the waves. Emerging from the storm, the company found themselves in a busy sea-lane. Edinburgh was only a short run down the southern shore of the firth. Vallon told Snorri to hold a northward course.

'Ain't we putting in at the capital?' Raul asked. 'We won't find a better place to take on trade goods.'

'The Normans will have an embassy there. If they find out we've landed, they'll demand our arrest. With invasion threatening, the Scots won't refuse them.'

'Handing us over to the Normans ain't going to stop them invading.'

'I know, but the Scots will want to avoid any provocation,' said Vallon. 'Giving us up would be a sop that costs nothing.'

Raul wasn't happy and vented his discontent to Wayland. 'We ain't going to make our fortunes by ducking every hazard.'

Although Wayland refused to be drawn, his own attitude to the voyage was beginning to sour. All they had left for food was bread and enough water for two cups daily. Conversation had dried up and Syth no longer sang as she worked. His skin itched and burned with saltwater sores.

By midnight they'd passed the firth's northern point. On they sailed, steering by the light of a pared down moon. Early next morning, under a pastel sky, the weary crew rowed into the bishopric of St Andrews and tied up inside a breakwater.

Wayland had expected something grander and Raul was disgusted, complaining that the town didn't even have a proper harbour. On a promontory north of the city, masons were at work on a church tower; otherwise, the only buildings more than one storey high were a few shingled houses on the waterfront. The rest of the settlement was a muddle of shaggy hovels.

Vallon and Raul rowed ashore with Snorri to find lodgings and sound out the prospects for trade. Wayland mooched on deck, watching the comings and goings on the quay. The port was used by traders from across northern Europe, and *Shearwater*'s arrival attracted little attention. Among the groups of Scots dressed in plaid were swaggering Norsemen wearing baggy breeches gathered at the knee.

It was afternoon before the shore party returned. They'd met with a representative of the civic governor who'd arranged accommodation for them in a house reserved for merchants. Vallon told the company that the governor had invited him to dine on the morrow, and that the outlook for trade was limited. At this season of the year there was little grain to be had. They might find some malt, and there was a sawmill five miles out of town where they could buy timber. Raul and Wayland would go there the day after tomorrow, when they'd rested.

The company transferred ashore, leaving Snorri and Garrick on board. Worn out by their voyage, the crew retired to bed early. Vallon had a room to himself at the top of the house. The others paired up according to ties of friendship or habit. Syth and the dog were segregated in the kitchen, a place overrun by rats that scrabbled in the straw and fought over the greasy cook pots. On the morning Wayland left for the sawmill, he found her curled asleep in the passage. Light from the door fell on her face. He studied it more closely than he'd dared do when she was awake, pulled her blanket over her shoulders, and joined Raul in the morning sunshine.

The sawmill was in a forest clearing that sloped down to a shallow loch. Raul knew his timber and proved a shrewd bargainer, rejecting the trees that the mill owner tried to fob off on him. This one had been felled too hard and had the shakes. That one was too knotty. Another was marred by a vein of soft brown pith. 'It's foxy,' said Raul, and stared disgustedly at the surrounding pines. 'Truth is, compared with Baltic wainscot, none of this wood's fit for anything but burning.'

When Raul had made his selection, Wayland helped lever the squared trunks on to a sledge. Bullocks dragged the load to a wagon waiting on the road. With time on his hands, he found a log of straight-grained ash and cleft it with a handaxe to make arrows. A boy approached and offered to sell him a creel of trout caught in the lochan that morning. They weighed three or four to a pound and Wayland wrapped them in moss and cooked them in embers for the midday meal. He and Raul ate them with bannocks by the waterside, then they just sat with their thoughts. A breeze swished through the treetops. Fish dimpled the surface of the loch. Across the water a lime-washed steading stood seated on its reflection. A man was chopping wood outside it, the sound of each blow not carrying until he'd raised the axe for the next stroke. Blue hills footed in shadow far to the west.

Raul nodded towards the cottage. 'Think you and Syth would be happy there?'

'Hm?'

'You'll be planning to settle down. Raise a family.'

Wayland was shocked. 'It never crossed my mind.'

Raul gave his leftovers to the dog. 'I wasn't much older than you when I left home. Never stopped travelling since, never been to the same place twice. You get weary after a while.'

'You'll be able to settle with your share of the profits.'

'Aye, I'll find a resting place sooner or later.' Raul stood up, clasped both hands above his head and stretched. 'Ah, well. Mustn't weaken.'

Wayland took a last look at the hills and followed him back to work.

They hiked into town under a benign sunset and picked their way down alleys that were little more than open drains. Ahead of them a lean sow and her litter of striped piglets slurped at a trickle of effluent. She raised her head and flared her snout. Wayland stopped and put his hand across Raul's chest.

'It's only a piggy-wiggy,' said Raul.

A moment later both of them were quick-stepping backwards before the sow's grunting charge. They took a turn at random and went down the next lane.

'What a shit-hole,' Raul said when they reached the next muddy crossroads. He looked around him like a man planning an escape. 'Where do you reckon a fellow might find a drink in this dump?'

'Forget it. Vallon told us to return in good time.'

'Just a cup to wash the sawdust from our throats.'

'Not me.'

A man came out of a house and went off down the street. Raul ran after him, calling. Turning, he trotted backwards. 'Sure you won't come?'

Wayland shook his head and returned to the lodgings.

That evening Syth paused by his seat when she served him supper. He looked up. Their eyes met and held. She moved on and Wayland glanced around, certain that the others must have sensed the current that had passed between them.

Vallon returned very late from his appointment with the governor. The meeting had been cordial. The governor knew that the Normans were mustering on the border, and he was grateful for the intelligence that Vallon was able to provide about Norman tactics.

'Will the Scots fight?' Hero asked.

'The governor doubts it. They're too busy fighting each other.'

Vallon gave reassuring news about the state of affairs in the earldom of Orkney. After generations of blood feuding, the title had passed to two brothers called Thorfinnson. They'd been captured at Stamford Bridge, but had been well treated and harboured no animosity against the English or foreigners in general.

When he'd finished, Vallon looked around the company. 'Where's Raul?'

Wayland kept his eyes down.

'I asked a question.'

'We parted in the town at sunset.'

Vallon's expression darkened but he said nothing more.

In the small hours Wayland was woken by drunken shouts. He raised himself on to his elbows. He heard a thud, followed by slurred oaths. Cursing, he got up and felt his way down to the street. Raul lay on his back outside the door. His drinking companions lurched away down the waterfront, their discordant song fading into the night. Wayland dragged Raul inside and propped him against the wall.

'Ish'at you, Wayland? Why don't you come and have a little drink with Raul?'

'Vallon will skin you.'

Raul squinted up. 'Fuck him.'

Wayland left him there and went back to bed. Next morning he woke him by hurling a bucket of water into his face. Raul lunged at the falconer, spluttering. Wayland stood his ground.

'Vallon's waiting for you on board.'

Raul tottered to the ship. Vallon stood on deck, his face stony, the rest of the company arraigned to hear his verdict. Raul, still besotted, brought himself to attention, chest out, head up, glazed and blood-veined eyes staring into space. Swaying slightly.

Vallon stepped up to him. 'I'd flog you if your hide wasn't thicker than your wits.'

'Yes, Captain.'

'Shut up. Now I know why you've served in half the armies of Europe. You're a disgrace. Shut up and listen because I won't tell you again. One more lapse and I'll discharge you without a penny. You can find your own way home.' Vallon stepped back. 'That's a solemn oath. Understood?'

'Yes, Captain.'

'You can sweat off your hangover at the sawmill. Now get out of my sight.'

As Raul weaved away, Vallon took Wayland's arm. 'Look out for him. Make sure he's back by sunset.'

Out at the timberyard, Raul seized the top handle of the pit saw and set to like a man possessed, sawing away until the woodman in the pit cried mercy and another replaced him. Raul bared his gap-toothed grin at Wayland. 'Work hard, live hard. You're a long time dead.'

The day had started warm and grew increasingly oppressive. The air stilled and the trees fell motionless to the tips of their branches. The loch settled into a sheet as flat as tin and not a single fish rose to kiss its surface. Southwards, the sky dulled and took on a coppery tinge.

Raul came over, wiping his brow on his sleeve. 'We'd better knock off. If it storms like it's fixing to storm, the road will be a mire by dark.'

Lightning quaked over the southern horizon as they lashed down the load. Thunder rolled, spooking the bullocks. Their driver had to goad them to keep them headed down the track. Wayland and Raul rode on top of the wagon, estimating their progress against the stain creeping across the sky. By the time the town came in sight, everything had taken on the spectral tones of a world in eclipse.

They'd reached the outskirts when a bolt of lightning blinded Wayland and a crash of thunder jangled his senses. The skies opened, the deluge falling plumb and the downpour so heavy that it obliterated the ground under a carpet of spray. The bullocks went mad and bucked off the road, dragging the cart into a field already turning into a lake. The waggoner jumped off to disentangle the traces. Wayland slid down to give a hand. The lightning was almost continuous, every-thing searing white between blinks of darkness.

The bullocks had made a cat's cradle of their harness. Raul appeared at Wayland's side and cut the beasts loose with half a dozen slashes of his knife. Off they careered, bucking into the storm with the waggoner in hopeless pursuit.

Raul laughed like a madman. 'I know the place for us,' he shouted, and ran sloshing through the flooded alleys.

Wayland caught up with him outside a hall hung with a taverner's sign. 'Don't you ever learn?'

Raul held up both palms as a pledge of good behaviour. Runoff from the thatch cascaded onto their heads. Water swilled around their ankles. 'We'll leave as soon as the rain stops. My oath.'

He dived through the door. Another barb sparked to earth with an ear-splitting crackle. Wayland dashed water from his eyes and crossed the step into a dark and tranquil dive. An elderly dogsbody seated by the door rose and took their weapons, down to the knife in Raul's hat. 'Rules of the house,' the German said. 'Some rough customers cross this threshold.' Wayland followed him closely, looking out for possi-ble trouble. The devil's chapels – that's what his mother called ale houses. This den was large and reeked with peat smoke from a huge central hearth. By the light of tallow candles, Wayland made out a sur-prisingly large number of drinkers.

They called out greetings and grinned as Raul bellied up to the counter. The taverner was already setting up drinks with an expression of resignation. 'I'll say one thing for the Scots,' Raul said. 'They brew a good ale.'

They took their drinks to a bench by the fire. Wayland heeled off his shoes and stretched out his feet. His leggings began to steam. He felt pleasantly tired. The dog stretched out to toast its flanks.

'That fire burns all year round,' said Raul. 'Ain't gone out for a hundred years.'

'I suppose this is where you got sozzled last night.'

Raul looked about to refresh his memory. He raised his cup to a group playing dice over by the wall. 'See that Pictish galoot with the red hair? Goes by the name of Malcolm.'

Wayland saw a wild-looking individual who responded to Raul's gesture by placing a protective hand over his drinking vessel. His companions laughed and slapped the table.

'I wouldn't want to cross that one,' said Wayland.

'I did just that. Him and me had a fearful stramash. He insulted me dreadful, called me a son of a whore, dog breath, pig's pizzle. On and on, scarcely drawing breath and never repeating himself. Oh, he's a fine bletherskate. Not that I understood his words exactly, but I got his meaning. Especially at the end when he hiked up his skirt and waggled his filthy hairy arse at me.'

Wayland goggled. 'What did you do to upset him?'

'A bet, and one that I won. You'd have been proud of me.'

Wayland blinked. 'It's a miracle we didn't find you on a midden with your throat cut.'

'I'd taken just enough ale to give my tongue wings. Every insult and slight that he dealt, I topped it. I won't give you my speech word by word because I've forgotten it, but you'd have admired the way I capped my performance.'

'How?'

'I walked over, undid my breeks and pissed into his ale cup.'

'Oh lord,' Wayland groaned. He stole a look at Malcolm and his cronies. 'What did he do? What did his friends do?'

'Bought me drinks. Clapped me on the back and said I was a champion slanderer.' Raul spluttered with laughter. 'See your face,' he said, his head sinking to the table. He cocked his eyes up like an evil toad. 'Don't you see? It was a game. Insulting people is a sport around here. Flyting, they call it.' Raul drained his ale and pointed at Wayland's cup. 'Same again?'

'No,' Wayland said faintly. He jumped up with his hands clenched by his side. 'Absolutely not.'

'It's still pissing down.'

'We're out of here.'

But as Wayland turned to go, the door wrenched open to a peal of thunder and three laughing gallants entered, shaking rain from their cloaks. The doorman bowed and scraped before them, making no attempt to relieve them of their swords. Customers on all sides hoisted their cups with cries of welcome. The arrivals were men of consequence. Their leader, tall and swarthily handsome, wore his long black hair dressed in oiled ringlets. Down his back hung a cape of indigo wool hemmed with gilt brocade and fastened at the neck with a clasp, beautifully worked, depicting serpents eating their tails. Gold ringed his fingers and silver bangles as big as quoits dangled on his wrists. His sword hilt was of carved ivory wrapped with silver wire, its pommel fashioned into the shape of a beaked monster. His arrival was a signal for celebration. Conversations grew livelier and a fiddler who played for drinks took up his rebeck and began to saw away.

'A Scottish chieftain?' Wayland whispered.

'Irish swells. Don't rush away just yet. Let's find out what brings them to this burgh.'

On his progress to the bar, the dashing leader noticed Wayland's dog and drew his companions' attention to it. When the taverner had served them, they leaned with their backs against the counter, reviewing the clientele as if it were a troupe recruited for their entertainment. The leader drank from his silver-mounted beaker and looked Wayland and Raul over with insolent intensity. He wiped suds from his lip and flashed square white teeth. 'Lachlan's the name,' he said. 'And these bucks are my associates, O'Neil and Regan. You'll be the traders from England.'

'Aye,' Raul said. 'We're nearly done in this port. There's precious little worth buying.'

Lachlan strolled over. 'I'm a merchant myself. Headed for London.'

'Oh yes?' Raul said. 'What goods do you trade in?'

'Slaves. Mainly slaves.'

Raul made a stealthy survey of the drinkers. 'You sell Scottish slaves to the English?'

Lachlan parked himself at the end of their bench and smiled. 'The very opposite. I sell English slaves to the Scots and Norwegians, but I save the best for the mart in Dublin.' He clicked his fingers. 'Taverner, two cups of corn ale for my English friends.'

'Thank you,' Wayland said. 'We were just leaving.' His dog heaved up and shook itself.

Lachlan waved in its direction. 'That's a fine hound you've got.'

Wayland dipped his head in acknowledgement.

Lachlan sauntered towards the dog. It looked to Wayland for instruction and stood still, its eyes following Lachlan as he circled it, assessing its points and passing on his appraisal to his companions.

'There's wolf in that hound. And Irish, too, if I'm not mistaken. Where did you come by it?'

'My father bred it in Northumberland.'

'What do you call him?'

'He doesn't have a name.'

Lachlan spluttered into his ale. 'You must value your dog very low if he's not worth a name.'

Raul stepped in. 'Wayland couldn't name the dog because he lost his tongue, and when he found it again, it had learned to do his bidding without a word being spoken.'

'You're jesting.'

'Cross my heart. It's uncanny.'

Lachlan regarded Wayland. 'Do you pit it?'

'What?'

Lachlan enunciated as if addressing a half-wit. 'Does it fight other dogs for wagers?'

'No.'

'Nor with bears or bulls or other beasts?'

'No, it doesn't fight.'

The news saddened Lachlan. 'That's a good dog going to waste,' he told O'Neil and Regan. He turned back to Wayland. 'How much will you take for it?'

'It's not for sale.'

Lachlan clucked his tongue. 'Everything's for sale, lad. You'll find that out when you're better acquainted with life.'

'I don't want to sell it.'

'I won't even haggle. Name your price.'

Wayland swallowed and shook his head.

'You're called "Wayland" if I heard a'right.'

'Yes, sir.' Wayland hated that craven 'sir', but there was something about the rich Irish slaver that made him feel like a bumpkin.

'Well, Wayland, you'll find that when Lachlan takes a fancy to something, he won't be shaken loose.' He opened a silver-mesh purse and laid pennies on the table coin by coin until Wayland stopped counting and looked away as if he were being shown something obscene. Lachlan sprinkled another few coins for good measure. 'No man can say I'm a stinter. That's as much as I'd pay for a slave.'

Wayland stood mute and miserable.

'Go on, lad, pick it up.'

'You'd be wasting your money. The dog won't go with you.'

Lachlan's voice was soothing. 'I don't want it for a pet. I won't gentle it. Just give me care of it for a week and I swear it will know me for its master. By god, there's not a dog whelped that I can't man.' He raised his beaker. 'Am I right, boys?'

The dog clacked its teeth and made for Wayland.

Lachlan laughed. 'I fancy he'd like to sink his chops into me.' He struck his thigh. 'Damn, it's a crime to have such a game beast and not make sport with it.'

'Come on,' Wayland told Raul. 'Vallon will be wondering what's keeping us.'

'Is Vallon your master?'

Wayland kept going and was halfway to the door when Lachlan said his name again. Wayland stopped.

Lachlan's hand fell on his shoulder. He spoke into Wayland's ear. 'I've bought virgins from their mothers who fell to their knees and kissed my hand in gratitude. You can't argue with silver. If I were to go to your master Vallon, I guarantee that by midnight you and your dog would be my legal property.'

Wayland could see the gold gleaming on Lachlan's fingers. 'I told you. The dog's not for sale.'

Lachlan flicked Wayland's scalp. 'Away with you then, and take your nameless cur with you. I was being over-generous. The glim flattered it. Now it stands in clearer light, I can see it's too long-boned to make a fighting dog.'

They would have left unscathed if Raul hadn't tried to get in the last word. 'That dog's no cur.'

Lachlan had already turned away and seemed to have dismissed the matter. 'What else do you call a dog that's too gutless to fight?'

'It doesn't fight because it doesn't need to.'

'Shut up,' Wayland hissed.

Lachlan appealed to his friends. 'A pair of riddlers. A dog that does what it's told without being told and doesn't fight because it doesn't have to.'

Raul's face was flushed. 'The dog kills whatever stands in its way. It doesn't fight them. It just kills them.'

Wayland groaned.

Lachlan caressed his jaw. 'Does that go for dogs?'

Raul shrugged. 'I ain't seen one yet that would stand up to it.'

Lachlan grinned. 'Fetch Dormarth,' he said, and Regan hurried out. 'Do you know that name?' he asked Wayland. 'In Ireland's old religion, Dormarth is the hound that guards the gate of hell.'

Lachlan picked up a coin and let it drop back on to the pile. 'My offer still stands. Your dog won't be worth a penny dead.'

Wayland's breath shuddered in his throat. 'Nor yours.'

Lachlan cocked a brow. 'If you fancy it that highly, you'll want to wager on the outcome.'

'I don't have any money to gamble.'

Lachlan laughed. 'Hazard your own person. A lad as comely as you would fetch a pot of silver in Dublin town.' He reached out to pat Wayland's face.

Raul pushed between them. 'What odds are you offering?'

'Three to one suit you?'

'Done.'

Raul shook out the few coins left over from his debauches. Lachlan eyed them with contempt. He made a showman's gesture to the rest of the room. 'Step up and place your bets.'

A few tipplers impressed by the size of Wayland's dog chanced a penny on it, but Lachlan's reputation as a connoisseur of fighting dogs was generally known, and he had to double the odds before people began to unbelt their purses.

'Why are you so miffed?' Raul muttered to Wayland. 'We ain't going to wriggle out of it, so we might as well make some money.'

Wayland shoved him away. 'I've had it with you.'

News of the contest had spread and citizens were flooding into the alehouse. Lachlan told the taverner to broach a keg at his own expense and the atmosphere in the hall grew rowdy. A pair of prostitutes linked at the elbow circled the crowd like overblown roses. Over by the door the taverner was charging a farthing admission, his assistant laying pennies on a block and chopping them in quarters with a cleaver. Lachlan presided over the festivities, glad-handing the new arrivals and encouraging them to bet. Wayland laid a soothing hand on his dog. Both of them hated crushes. More and more people pressed in, until only the space cleared for the fight was empty and even the rafters had been occupied. The table holding the stakes was heaped with coins minted in every country in Europe and principalities far beyond.

Lachlan came over to Wayland. 'Leash your dog. Do you know how to scratch?'

'The dog has never felt a leash and doesn't care for rules.'

'Fair play. We'll let them scrap until only one of them's left standing.'

'*Wayland!*'

The cry had come from the entrance. The taverner and his assistant were trying to force the door shut against a mob of latecomers. Wayland glimpsed Syth's face bobbing up and down behind the scrum.

'Get Vallon!'

Lachlan heard the exchange and took a step forward, but Syth had already gone and the taverner was shoving the door shut.

The room quietened in anticipation. Wayland's dog panted in distress. 'Let's have some air in here,' said Lachlan. His order was relayed through the crowd until shutters were opened and a sluggish draught flowed through the hall. Thunder trundled away in the distance.

Wayland heard strangulated grunts and the sound of scrabbling feet.

'Unbar the door,' Regan shouted from outside. 'I can hardly hold him.'

Lachlan smiled at Wayland. 'Open up,' he called. 'Make way. Watch yourselves. This one bites.'

Wayland and his dog exchanged looks. The door barged open and the crowd in front of it shrank away on each side. Down the aisle charged a pale block of bone and muscle, towing Regan on his heels.

Everyone cringed from such unbridled ferocity. As Lachlan turned to view the arena, Wayland's dog disappeared into the startled spectators.

Amid the buzz of disappointment, Dormarth tore loose and went rampaging round the pit, whimpering as he sucked up the smell of his vanished opponent. Wayland had never countenanced such a hideous brute. It was smaller than a mastiff in height, yet it carried on its squat limbs and bull neck a skull as large as the head of his own giant hound. With its high-set slitted eyes, ears cropped to the bone, and huge teeth curving up from underslung bottom jaw, it reminded him of some monster fished up from depths where sunlight never reached. Ropes of scar tissue braided its muzzle and from its rump twirled a rat-like tail that seemed to have been added as an obscene joke. Dormarth picked up the scent of his dog on him and lunged against his waist with unhinged jaws. Wayland could determine the minds of dogs as well as other men could fathom their fellows, but there was nothing to plumb in this beast's brain except an insane lust to kill its own kind.

Lachlan gave Dormarth a kick that would have crippled gentler breeds and walked up to Wayland. 'Did you order your dog to turn tail?'

'I told you it doesn't fight.'

'Call it back.'

'I will not.'

'Your dog wins by forfeit,' Raul said, with a reproachful look at Wayland.

Lachlan stood with legs akimbo, his hand on his sword. 'We agreed on a contest and you defaulted. I never overlook a broken contract.'

'I agreed nothing.'

Blood rose in a tide up Lachlan's face. He appealed to the crowd. 'What say you? You paid to see a fight. Say aye if you want your money's worth.'

The mob bayed and pounded tables.

'Give him your sword,' Lachlan told Regan. Wayland took it. He had no choice. Raul had realised where things were heading and his face was drawn in the rictus of a man contemplating a disaster of his own making. Lachlan wandered to the other side of the circle and began swishing his sword as if trying to unstick it from his hand. Wayland heard the engorged breathing of the spectators. A breath of night air wafted through the open windows. He whistled.

As Lachlan sank into a combat stance, the spectators against one wall shuddered. Two standing at the front toppled like skittles and the dog hurtled past them into the arena. Before anyone had registered its return, it smashed into Dormarth, bowling him over like a keg. Dormarth rolled into the fire and sizzled in the coals before springing up in a stench of singed hair. While he was still unsighted, Wayland's dog seized him by a front haunch and swung him against the table holding the stake money. Silver sprayed across the room. Dormarth arched as if double-jointed and buried his teeth in the dog's left shoulder. He clung like a horrible parasite as Wayland's dog whirled. Both dogs let go simultaneously and went for each other's muzzles, their teeth meeting with a clash. The dog reared on its hind legs, forcing Dormarth up, and they went steepling around the arena in a stiff-legged gavotte until the dog imposed its greater height and weight and forced Dormarth over. Dormarth released his hold and lunged for the dog's throat, but the dog was quicker and knew no rules. It barged Dormarth's head away, followed up with the full weight of its body and clamped its jaws across Dormarth's spine. It lifted him like a sack and swung him to the ground with a 'whumph' that drew sickened groans from the spectators. Again and again the dog smashed its opponent to the floor, Lachlan dancing from foot to foot around the battle.

'Call your dog off!'

Even when Wayland had dragged it away, Dormarth wouldn't give up. Spine broken, innards ruptured, he dragged himself on his front legs, his useless rear trailing the contents of bowel and bladder.

'Don't just stand there!' Lachlan shouted. 'Kill him.'

Regan lifted his sword in both hands and Dormarth swallowed the blade as if it were a reward. The crowd moaned with ecstatic revulsion.

The dog sat before Wayland, its lungs whooping and blood splashing from its torn muzzle. But for those sounds, you could have parcelled out the silence.

'By God, I never saw anything like it.'

Someone swung down from a roof beam to claim his winnings. Lachlan wafted his sword as if to ward off a catastrophe he hadn't yet got the measure of.

A rap sounded on the door. It came again, louder.

Lachlan's cheek muscles knotted and unknotted. He waved a hand. 'See who's there.'

Bolts were hammered open. The mob by the door gave way and Vallon and Garrick entered with drawn swords. Raul snatched Regan's sword from Wayland.

'We heard there was a riot,' Vallon said. 'Are my men acting rowdy? Have they disturbed the peace?'

Lachlan looked at the remains of Dormarth. He looked at Wayland. He looked at Wayland's bloodied dog. He looked at Raul hefting Regan's sword. In the end he didn't know where to fasten his gaze.

Raul began picking coins from the straw. 'Captain, there was a wager on who had the best fighting dog.'

Someone hauled Dormarth's mutilated corpse past Vallon. 'An evening's harmless sport,' he said. 'Good. Well, I'm sorry to drag my company away, but it looks like the entertainment is over.'

Lachlan took a step towards him. Vallon raised his chin. 'Yes?'

Lachlan put on a brave face. 'You'll be Wayland's master. Stay and share a cup before parting.'

Vallon spurned the handshake. 'We have a long day ahead of us. I'll bid you goodnight.'

Outside, he grabbed Wayland and Raul by their thrapples and hoisted them on tiptoe.

'It wasn't our fault,' Raul wheezed. 'The Irishman was determined to see a fight.'

Vallon glared at Wayland for corroboration.

'It's true. The man wanted revenge because I wouldn't sell him my dog.'

Vallon growled, then dropped them and strode off towards the harbour. Raul rubbed his throat and grinned at Wayland.

'Ain't you glad I fixed things the way I did?'

Wayland punched him so hard that he trotted several steps backwards before falling flat in the mud. He lay dabbing his pulpy nose.

'God's teeth, there wasn't no cause for that.'

Wayland stood over him. 'I could kill you.'

Raul wrenched himself out of the quagmire with a great sucking sound and fished around for his hat. He pulled it on, mud and all, and blinked at Wayland.

232

'You're the only man I'd take that from,' he said, and went sploshing down the street.

Someone laughed softly. Syth was standing on the other side of the lane. He managed a wan smile and she came towards him. They looked at each other without speaking and then walked side by side to the harbour, their glances never quite coinciding. She put her hand around his waist. By chance, her hand slipped under the hem of his tunic and she rubbed her fingers quickly up and down his back, and then withdrew her hand as if she hoped he hadn't noticed. Wayland stopped, rooted by the sensation of her warm hand on his bare skin. He reached for her but she dodged aside.

'Oh,' she cried. 'The dog's hurt.'

The dog licked her once, its attention fixed on the empty street behind them. The storm growled far to the north. She looked up at Wayland.

'It's not right that he doesn't have a name.'

'You choose one.'

'Really?'

'Really.'

XX

Lachlan's ship had left harbour by the time the company was up. They went on with their business. Vallon hired a pilot to steer them to Orkney, overriding Snorri's furious protests. It was the governor who'd insisted that they engage a navigator familiar with the treacherous currents around the islands. David was the pilot's name – a dark and melancholy Pict who spoke English and Norse, having plied his trade at every port between Lowestoft and the Faroes. The governor also gave them introductions to local traders. By the third day following the dogfight, the hold was half full with their purchases. As well as timber, *Shearwater* was carrying malt, salt, a ton of pig iron and dozens of clay cooking vessels.

That evening the governor's French-speaking secretary called at the lodgings and asked for a private audience. Vallon took him up to his room and closed the door. The emissary refused the offer of refreshments and remained standing.

'This afternoon,' he said, 'information arrived from the king's seat in Edinburgh concerning a gang of outlaws who, having wreaked havoc in England, fled by ship to Scotland. Since the King wishes to maintain cordial relations with his neighbour, he's sent orders to his governors that they detain all arrivals from the south. If there's any suspicion that they match the description of the felons, they're to be transported to the capital for interrogation, pending their despatch into Norman custody.'

Vallon crossed to the casement and looked down at the empty quayside. 'What do they look like?'

'Their leader is a Frankish mercenary who commands a crew drawn from several countries. There's even a Norman traitor with them. And a savage dog of uncommon size.'

Vallon turned. 'Not easily overlooked.'

'No. It so happens that the governor was called away on business before the letters arrived and therefore wasn't able to give the matter his immediate attention. He won't be back until morning when, of course, he'll attend to the King's commands with all the urgency that they deserve.'

Vallon clicked his tongue. 'What a pity I won't be able to say farewell to his Excellency and thank him for all his kindness. You see, we've concluded our dealings here and will be sailing tonight. Only our personal effects have to be loaded.'

The secretary nodded and went to the door. He paused with one hand on the latch. 'The weather is set fair from the south. Two days' sailing should carry you beyond the King's writ. If I were you, I wouldn't land before then.'

They exchanged bows and the secretary left. Vallon waited at the window until his footsteps died away on the cobbles, then hurried to the top of the stairs. 'Raul! Wayland! All of you! Look lively! We're sailing tonight!'

When the governor's men-at-arms marched down the quay early next morning, they found the hostel deserted and *Shearwater*'s berth empty. Fingers fanned against the rising sun, the commander of the militia could just make out a fleck of sail bearing north.

Back at sea, the company spent the day re-establishing routines. A week ashore had restored their vigour and put them in good heart for the journey ahead. They were handy at their duties now, willing team members who were also confident enough to act on their own initiative. Watching Garrick lash the end of a shroud around a cleat, Vallon found it hard to believe that less than a month ago he'd never set foot on a ship. All in all, Vallon was content. April had given way to the lingering twilights of May. *Shearwater* was covering eighty miles a day. By this time tomorrow they'd be beyond Drogo's reach.

Only one cloud darkened the outlook. Everyone was aware of it, but no one drew attention to it until the next evening, when Hero and Richard approached Vallon as he stood at the bow in an ocean reverie. They were nervous, neither wanting to be the first to speak. Richard held a bundle of documents. Vallon invited them to sit.

'I see you've spent the day bringing our accounts up to date. How do they stand?'

'After all our expenses, we're left with little more than sixty pounds. I can itemise the outgoings if you want.'

'No need,' said Vallon. Sixty pounds was less than he'd expected. 'How much do you think our cargo will fetch in Iceland?'

'I'm sure we'll make a profit in kind.'

'That's the problem,' Hero said. 'The Icelanders don't deal in specie. We won't be able to sell for silver until we reach Norway or Rus. Before then, we might have emptied our exchequer. We'll have to hire a ship for the crossing to Iceland, and then charter another vessel to take us south. Raul thinks we'll be lucky to find a captain willing to take us on either voyage for less than thirty pounds. There's our money gone on transport alone.'

Syth was cooking on the stern deck and savoury smells reached Vallon. 'I know you wouldn't have brought the problem to me if you hadn't thought of a solution.'

Hero glanced at Richard. 'We were sure you'd anticipated it yourself when you took on David.'

Vallon pretended not to understand. 'I hired David to pilot us only as far as Orkney.'

Another look passed between the youths. 'He'd be willing to stay until we reach the Faroes,' Hero said. 'With David navigating, we can give Orkney a miss.'

Vallon dropped his pretence. 'You're suggesting we steal Snorri's ship.'

Richard's birthmark coloured. 'Unless we hang on to *Shearwater*, we'll run out of money before completing our journey.'

'Where does that leave Snorri?'

Hero moved closer. 'Put him ashore with what's due to him. Pay him compensation if you wish. Twenty pounds would give him a comfortable start back in Norway.'

Vallon looked out to sea. They'd rounded the cape marking the northernmost point of the Scottish king's dominion, and now they were beginning the long western passage towards Sutherland and Caithness. 'Our next landing will be in Norwegian territory. Drop Snorri among his own kind and he'd swear a suit against us for theft. Since Iceland is tied to Norway by blood and trade, he'd be able to pursue his case against us even there.'

Hero and Richard didn't answer.

'You think I should kill him.'

Richard ducked his head and blinked as if he had something in his eye. Hero spoke in an urgent whisper. 'Wayland and Raul are sure that Snorri intends to double-cross us. When we were in harbour, Raul saw him talking to a Norwegian crew who sailed to Orkney a few days before we left. Raul says that the way the men looked him over made him feel like a goose ready for plucking.'

Vallon conned the ship. Snorri was at the tiller. Raul stood behind him whipping a rope's end, one eye on the conference at the bow.

'If we were to murder him, the crime would poison our enterprise. How would your consciences bear it? And David wouldn't serve with men who'd killed the ship's master.'

'I don't want anyone's death on my conscience,' said Richard. 'We just thought you should hear our concerns.'

'I share them and I think I have the remedy. It will be expensive, though. Wipe the guilty look off your faces and tell Snorri I want a word.'

Watching the Norwegian come forward, Vallon wondered if he had any inkling that his life hung in the balance. His manner had grown more confident, less ingratiating since they'd left St Andrews.

Vallon assumed a pleasant aspect and made small talk about the fine weather and sailing prospects, before getting down to business. 'Do you still intend to end our partnership once we reach Orkney?'

'Aye, my heart is set on returning home.'

'Suppose I increased my original offer – one-third of everything we gain by trade. Generous terms by any measure.'

'I can take on cargo of me own in Orkney. It's the beginning of the sailing season. Ye'll have no trouble finding a fresh charter in Kirkwall. I'll find ye one meself.'

'How much will it cost?'

'Twenty pound.'

'And another twenty to Norway.'

'Aye. Thereabouts.'

Vallon mused on the sums. 'I'll tell you what. I'll give you forty pounds to buy *Shearwater* outright. That's in addition to the sum we already owe you. It will almost empty our chest of silver, but it will give us freedom of action. With fifty pounds in ready money, you'll be able to buy a ship as good as *Shearwater* with silver to spare.'

Snorri had begun shaking his head before Vallon had finished. 'I ain't selling *Shearwater* fer any price.'

Vallon made his final throw. 'All right. You won't have to part with her. Agree to join us on the voyage and you'll get the forty pounds – *plus* one-third of the profits, *plus* your ship back once we reach Rus. If that seems too good to be true, I'm happy to have the contract notarised in a court of your choosing. What do you say?'

Watching Snorri make his calculations, Vallon thought he'd hooked him. He wondered if he'd been too generous.

Snorri sneered. 'Ye're desperate, ain't ye? Not so high and mighty now.' He stamped his foot. 'I say no to yer offer. Mebbe I'd've looked more kindly on it if ye hadn't used me so ill, shown me more respect, kept yer word about the girl.'

'Perhaps there's another reason.' Vallon raised up. 'When we first met, I suspected that you planned to betray us. I hoped that time would sweeten your intentions, but it begins to look as if my fears were justified.'

The brand on Snorri's forehead turned livid. He shook his good arm at Vallon. 'I know what ye're hatching. Ye mean to rob me of me ship. Well, ye won't get away with it. I've sent messages to Orkney. If *Shearwater* arrives without me, ye'll be arrested for piracy and manslaughter. However far ye run, the law will catch ye.'

'It won't be me who breaks our agreement,' said Vallon. 'Once you've brought us safe to Orkney and helped find us another ship, your obligation is discharged and I'll pay you your due.'

'Ye'd better.' Snorri shuffled his feet, aware that Vallon hadn't finished.

Vallon stared past him. 'But if I come by proof that you don't intend keeping your side of the bargain . . . ' He smiled – the expression conveying the very opposite of a smile.

Another concern – at least for Wayland and Syth – was the dog. Its injuries were worse than had first appeared. On the third day it refused food and lay stretched on its side, breathing fast. Next morning its head was badly swollen, its eyes half shut and oozing matter. Hero prescribed a liquid diet and poultices of warm seawater. Vallon had little affection for the beast and privately wished it good riddance. Syth was distraught and spent all her free time nursing it, applying brine-soaked cloths to its head. When it showed no improvement, she dissolved a block of salt in boiling water. She let the solution cool just enough to be able to dip a hand in it, then Wayland held the dog down while she wrapped the hot cloth around the dog's muzzle. The dog thrashed so violently that it dragged both minders along the deck. When the poultice cooled, Syth renewed it. She must have applied the cloth a dozen times before one of the puncture wounds in its muzzle burst and erupted a gout of pus together with one of Dormarth's broken canines. Syth ran around showing off the tooth on the stained bandage as if it were a piece of the true cross.

A little later the dog rose as unsteadily as a newborn foal and licked at a bowl of bran moistened with broth. When they beached on the Caithness coast next evening, it was fully recovered and galloped splashing along the surf-line, putting wave after wave of gulls to flight. Syth ran behind it with her arms outstretched and Wayland jogged along wearing an embarrassed grin.

They tucked up overnight in the mouth of a river called Berriedale. David said that if the wind stayed in their favour, they would reach Wick next day and be in Orkney two days later. Vallon decided not to stop at Wick and ordered the crew to fill the water barrels. Waking early, he saw Wayland walking into camp with a deer slung over his shoulders. He'd risen before dawn and shot the buck in a wood upstream. The company gorged on venison and lingered late in the haven, wandering up the riverbank and bathing in amber-coloured pools under the leaning oaks. It was as if they knew that this was the last time they'd set foot on British shores.

Noon had passed before they struck out again, coasting under rugged cliffs where wild doves burst forth on clapping wings and veered overhead before diving back to their crags. Sooty birds no bigger than swallows flitted in *Shearwater*'s wake, pattering their feet across the surface as if too feeble to stay aloft.

'Mother Carey's chickens,' said Raul. He saw that the phrase meant nothing to Vallon. 'Mother Carey's the queen of the sea. Sits on the bottom combing her long green hair with the rib bones of drowned mariners.' Raul nodded towards the pilot who stood in the bow gazing at the headlands stepping away to the north. 'David had three sons and the sea took them all every one. Two in a storm, the other in a fishing accident. Never found but one body and the crabs had done nothing to improve his appearance.'

Vallon didn't answer. Raul steered him around so that Snorri couldn't see their faces. 'Captain, we got to act soon. Just slip me the nod. I'll do it tonight. No one will see. In the morning Snorri will be gone and by nightfall everyone will have forgotten him.'

'I'm not going to discount a man's life on nothing more than suspicion.'

'Captain, you know it's stronger than that.'

'We have to take on supplies in Orkney and we'll be arrested if we land without Snorri. Do nothing without my orders.' Vallon pushed past Raul to show that the discussion was ended.

Two days later, with the sun spearing through clouds, they launched across the strait between the mainland and the Orkney Isles. The sea kicked up into peaks. Random bits of the archipelago showed over the waves for a moment then sank from sight as *Shearwater* dipped into the next trough. David had timed the crossing to avoid the tides that poured through the passage. Even so, *Shearwater* lurched and skidded in the cross-currents and overfalls. They skirted a whirlpool that David said was whipped up by a sea-witch grinding salt for the world's oceans on a giant quern. A long island slid by to the east. Drab moorland broken by green pastures dotted with the occasional turf house. Stunted trees bent by the wind. Two boys bareback on a horse raced them to the ness at the end of the island and sat waving until they were gone from sight.

Shearwater sailed between headlands into a wide sea basin ringed by more islands. The largest filled the northern horizon. 'Horse Island,' Raul said. 'Kirkwall lies on the other side. David says it'll take us the rest of the day to work our way around.'

Vallon was dazed by the glare off the waves, the constant joggling. 'I'm going to snatch some sleep.'

He curled up like a dog and drifted off to the cries of gulls. He woke muzzy-headed to find *Shearwater* threading a channel between two islands. A school of porpoises drilled through the waves. David and Raul stood at the bow, bright coronas forming behind them each time *Shearwater* took a crest. Vallon drank from a dipper and made his way forward.

Raul nodded at the island to port. 'Nearly there. We've come round Horse Island. Kirkwall's tucked down a bay the other end of this channel. Remember, Captain, once we land, Snorri will be the one calling the shots.'

'We won't enter harbour. Ask David to find an anchorage close to the port – an uninhabited island would be ideal.'

Vallon kept an eye on Snorri while Raul quizzed David.

Raul came back. 'There's a scrap of land a couple of miles north of the harbour. They used to put thieves and witches on it. Nothing there now except sheep.'

Vallon went to break the news to Snorri. 'David knows an island where we can anchor overnight. I'm not putting into Kirkwall until I know what sort of reception we can expect. You can go ashore if you wish.'

'Ye must think I'm a saphead. Soon as I step off, ye'll make a run for it.'

'Snorri, if I wanted to steal your ship, I wouldn't have waited until we were under the eyes of your countrymen. Besides, David's leaving us. We'd never find our way to Iceland without a pilot.'

A figure appeared atop a cliff on Horse Island. Vallon saw him turn and signal inland.

'Thieves Holm,' Raul called.

It was only a few acres of rough grass rising a few feet above high tide. As they neared it, the town of Kirkwall came into view at the head of a bay to the south. Vallon saw a church and a scattering of farms, a few ships moored in the harbour. Raul and Wayland began lowering the sail. Seals dragged themselves into the sea and a flock of feral sheep that had been feeding on seaweed stotted away. David dropped anchor and the company rowed ashore. Vallon stepped on to land to find that his feet wouldn't work properly, groping at air instead of finding ground. He flopped down. The rest of the company gathered around him, leaving only Snorri on board.

Vallon watched him watching them. 'Raul, I want David to go ashore with Snorri and follow him. See who he meets and whether he tries to find us a ship.' Vallon felt inside his tunic and produced a purse. 'That's twice the fee we agreed.'

'Sailboat heading out from Kirkwall,' said Wayland.

Vallon watched it draw nearer. 'Nine men on board. Too many to be fishermen.'

'David reckons it's the harbourmaster,' Raul said.

'Everyone back to the ship.'

'What if they try to seize us?' said Raul.

'I think they'd have come in a bigger vessel. Have your weapons ready, but don't show them unless I give the word.'

The boat crabbed across a back-eddy. All of its occupants were armed. In the bow stood an iron-jawed man with side-whiskers. David hailed him and he gaped in recognition.

'He's called Sweyn,' said Raul. 'Likes to throw his weight about.'

The harbourmaster was shouting questions. 'Tell him to keep off,' Vallon said.

David called out. The boat kept coming.

Vallon drew his sword. 'I mean it. No one boards without my permission. Raul, show them your crossbow.'

Confronted by the show of arms, the Norwegians sheered off and hung in the current. The harbourmaster shook his fist and shouted. David looked at Vallon in alarm.

'It ain't a good idea to mortify the harbourmaster,' Raul said.

'We aren't in his harbour and I'll decide who sets foot on this ship. Tell him to land on the island and we'll let him and two of his men come aboard. Tell him that I'm a mad foreigner and I don't trust strangers. If he doesn't agree, we'll up anchor and be off.'

Snorri wailed on hearing this ultimatum and added his voice to

David's, telling the harbourmaster that he was the owner of the ship and had kin on Orkney and that he could vouch for the peaceful intentions of the company. Exchanges went back and forth until the harbourmaster gave up the wrangle and ordered his crew to put him and two bodyguards ashore. Wayland and Garrick picked them up in the ship's boat.

Sweyn stepped aboard glaring at Vallon as though he'd like to grind him into the earth. While Raul described their mission, he cast his eyes around the ship and its company, examined the contents of the hold. Before Raul had finished, he made for the side, gesturing for *Shearwater*'s crew to follow.

'He's ordering us into harbour,' said Raul.

'I'm not going anywhere. David and Snorri are the only ones who are leaving.'

Another flurry of arguments before the harbourmaster gave up. He clicked his fingers under Vallon's nose.

'We still have to pay harbour dues,' said Raul. 'Best pay up.'

Vallon put on a show of anger before parting with the money. Sweyn tucked it away and climbed into the boat with David. Snorri hesitated.

'We can't go anywhere without a pilot,' Vallon reminded him.

Snorri left and the sailboat pulled away. It was evening, the islands black under the westering sun.

Raul put down his crossbow and rolled his shoulders. 'We ain't made any friends here. Better keep a sharp lookout.'

Thick cloud sagged low in the morning sky. Fitful gusts from the west made *Shearwater* hunt around her mooring. A few fishing boats began working in the shelter of Kirkwall bay. The morning wore on and the wind grew stronger.

'What if David don't come back?' Raul said.

'We'll sail without him. We'll pick up another pilot in the Faroes or wait for a convoy from Norway.'

'Captain, them Faroes ain't more than fly specks in an ocean of sea.'

'David must have given you sailing directions.'

'Oh, aye. Island-hop up to the Shetlands, then sail north-west keeping the ship's stem a handspan to the left of the pole star. Next day look out for a current of pale water and the day after that head towards a cloud castle, keeping your eyes peeled for weed drifting south ... Captain, learning the signs is a life's work. Even with experienced skippers, not half the ships that leave for Iceland make it. Most turn back. The rest are never heard of again.'

'Boat heading our way,' Wayland called.

David was aboard with two men. They ignored Vallon's waves to come alongside and ran up to the island.

'The harbourmaster's forbidden David to board in case we make a run for it,' said Raul. 'Sweyn says we have to be in harbour before dark or he'll impound *Shearwater*.'

'To hell with the harbourmaster. Let's find out what Snorri's been up to.'

They rowed to the island and questioned David at length. Raul turned to Vallon with a glow of self-vindication. 'I told you Snorri was in up to the hubs. First thing he did was go to an ale house. David was too canny to go in himself. Instead, he paid a man to skulk and it was money well spent. First of all Snorri made enquiries about his kinsmen from Hordaland. Someone went to fetch them and after a while two brothers turned up and the three went into a huddle. Then another man came in and they went on with their palaver.'

'Any idea what they talked about?'

'They took good care no one could hear. After a time they left and rode away to the brothers' farm. There wasn't more the spy could do, so he went back and told David what he'd seen. Now the thing is, none of the men Snorri met owns a ship 'cept for maybe a little fishing boat. And David spent this morning down at the harbour, checking if anyone had been asking about ships for charter. Snorri never showed his ugly face the whole while. I told you he was a bald-faced liar.'

'Here he comes,' said Wayland.

A fishing boat approached, crewed by four men. Vallon and his men returned to *Shearwater*.

'Three of them are the ones that were with Snorri. Captain, we can raise the sail and be out of here before they come alongside.'

Vallon's jaw worked. 'Not yet. I warned Snorri what would happen if he broke our agreement.'

Snorri hove up with a grin. His escort also wore expressions of such good cheer that Raul spat in disbelief. 'Look at them. Don't tell me they ain't rogues.'

Vallon leaned out. 'Snorri, tell your friends to stay in the boat.'

Snorri climbed aboard still grinning. 'I found ye a ship like I said I would. A right good 'un.'

Vallon nodded towards the Norwegians. 'Owned by those men?'

Snorri looked at them. 'No, but they put me on to it.'

'In Kirkwall?'

'No. She's in a bay a titty bit down the coast.'

So Snorri's treachery wasn't cut and dried. 'Bring the ship up here so that we can inspect it.'

'Against this wind? Cap'n, we'd best shift before it gets any stronger.'

'We have to discuss it,' said Vallon. He drew Raul and Wayland to one side.

'He's lying,' said Raul. 'Why waste any more time on him?'

Wayland nodded agreement.

Vallon stretched his mouth and clacked his teeth. 'That leaves us with no choice but to take *Shearwater*. Raul, persuade David to pilot us to the Faroes. He can name his fee within reason.'

'I already tried. He don't want any part in piracy and he ain't going against the harbourmaster's orders. He's got his livelihood to consider.'

'Then we'll do without him.'

'It's awful bad timing, Captain. There's filthy weather brewing.'

The sea was already showing its teeth. 'It can't be helped.'

'What do you plan to do with Snorri?'

'Get rid of him.'

'About time.'

Vallon went up to him. 'How much does your friend want for his ship?'

'Negotiable, I'd say.'

'We'll take a look at it. I'm not taking your friends on board. They can either row back to Kirkwall or accept a tow.'

The Norwegians tied a line to *Shearwater*'s stern. The crew raised anchor, brought the ship about and hoisted sail. *Shearwater* gathered way. David remained on the island and didn't raise his hand in response to Vallon's wave.

Snorri had taken the tiller.

'Why did you let his cronies tag along?' Raul asked.

'You'll see,' said Vallon. He watched the shore to starboard. They passed a small bay. He turned and shouted into the wind. 'How much further?'

'Around the next headland.'

Sure enough, when they cleared the cape, Vallon saw a ship moored at the end of the bay.

Snorri began to bring the ship round. 'I told ye I'd find ye a charter.'

'Cut the tow,' Vallon told Raul. 'Wayland, prepare to take the helm.'

Raul ran to the stern and slashed the line tethering the boat. Its crew cried out and Snorri ran from the tiller and clawed at him. 'What are ye doing?' He turned blasted eyes on Vallon. 'What are ye doing?'

Vallon stepped forward and shoved a packet of silver down his tunic. 'That's payment in full.' He pushed Snorri towards the stern. 'Jump while your friends are close enough to save you.'

'Jump from me own ship?'

The boat's crew were fitting oars.

'You'll drown if you wait any longer.'

Snorri patted the silver. 'Ye said ye'd pay me forty pounds for me ship. There ain't one-quarter of that here.'

'Forty pounds of silver would drag you to the bottom. Raul, throw him overboard.'

'Wait! I'll take ye to Iceland like ye want.' Snorri's voice rose to a scream as Raul clinched him in a bear-hug and lifted him kicking to the stem. 'Curse ye! Curse ye all!' He was still cursing when Raul pitched him into the sea.

He disappeared and Vallon thought he'd gone. Then his face bobbed up. The boat rowed towards him. *Shearwater* was running fast downwind and Vallon didn't see if it reached him in time.

Raul glared at Vallon. 'You might as well have hanged him. Stretching his neck in front of the harbourmaster wouldn't get us into any more trouble than what you've just done. Throwing him off his ship in front of witnesses ... Why didn't ye let me cut his throat on the quiet?'

'Remember who you're speaking to,' Vallon snapped. The islands were merging into a darkening haze. The wind hummed in the shrouds and whisked foam from the grey-green waves. 'I'm appointing you sailing master. Prepare the ship for the storm.'

XXI

The wind was blowing half a gale, shredding the wavetops into ribbons. Raul ordered the crew to tie down everything that wasn't fixed. Hero and Richard were given the job of packing the clay vessels in straw. Garrick and Wayland struggled to secure the timber. The logs had been stacked in a wooden cradle fixed to the beams, but Raul was worried that they would shift in heavy seas and ordered them to be lashed tight.

Down in the hold was a horrible place to be. Hero could hear seams straining and the mast groaning in its socket. Each time a wave whacked the hull, he expected to see the planking give way and the ocean flood in. As *Shearwater* left the lee of the Orkneys and met the Atlantic rollers, the pitching settled into a longer rhythm of stomach-churning swoops. The mast head no longer jerked and twitched, but swung in wild rotations.

Hero finished his task and climbed on deck. They were racing tight-reefed before the wind, the swell running so high that down in the troughs he could see only the crests directly fore and aft. They looked almost as tall as *Shearwater*'s mast. He made his way to the helm, flailing for balance and then fetching up against the side at a skittering run. The wind droned so loud in the rigging that he had to shout.

'I can't see land. I thought we were meant to use the islands as stepping stones.'

'Wind's backing south,' yelled Raul. 'I don't know how far east the Orkneys go. Can't risk being driven on to a lee shore.'

Shearwater slid into another trough, burying herself to within a foot of the gunwale. Spray flew the length of the ship. Hero clung to a shroud. 'The waves will swallow us.'

Raul slapped the tiller. 'No, they won't. Look how smoothly the old lady rides – like a cow on skates. Ain't nothing to do except sit it out. Tie yourself to a line just in case.'

Hero huddled next to Richard on the stern thwart. Garrick tied ropes around their waists and made the ends fast through an oar port. The wind yowled in the shrouds. Fear squatted like a dog in Hero's chest. A wave pitched him onto the deck. He hooked his hands around the back of the thwart, shifting his hold as the ship rose and fell. Each time the deck lifted, his stomach dropped away into his feet; each time it sank, his stomach climbed into his throat. Richard hunched over beside him, strings of yellow bile dangling from his chin. With the coming of night, Hero couldn't see the waves before they struck and had to anticipate when to brace. His hands seized into claws. A wave catching them broadside staggered the ship and convulsed him with water so cold that he couldn't breathe. Richard clutched him.

'We're going to die!'

'I don't care!'

A hand groped at his shoulder. 'Richard?' cried Vallon.

'It's Hero. Richard's beside me.'

'Good lads. How are you bearing up?'

'Awful.'

'That's the spirit.'

With a clap on the back, Vallon was gone. Hero couldn't imagine how he'd get through the night. Nothing but din and blackness, the screaming wind and swooping waves. Eventually the sheer brutality of the elements battered him into a stunned trance, dulling terror and shutting down his mind.

He raised his stinging eyes for the thousandth time to see the first grey signs of day. Grinning crests leered out of the dark and Richard's face showed as something more definite than a blur.

Black cloud patches still raced past, but the pall was thinning. The sun rose and shot livid rays through the wrack. Hero worked his neck from side to side, trying to loosen sinews stretched as taut as hawsers. He fumbled at his safety line with fingers as useless as sticks. He stood, fell back again, and then propped himself shivering against the gunwale and looked out across the white-maned rollers. Raul was still at the helm, working the tiller to keep *Shearwater* at right angles to the swell. Every so often he looked behind him to read the oncoming sea. Hero was about to struggle forward when Raul made another inspection and gaped.

Hero turned. What he saw was so unexpected that at first he thought exhaustion had warped his sense of perception. The horizon loomed above him like a green-black wall, only the wall was moving and his heart stopped as he realised that it was a rogue wave sweeping soundlessly up on them, foam beginning to cream along its crest and slide down its face. The wind dropped to nothing and there was an ear-popping silence. *Shearwater* was in the lee of the wave, shut off from the storm. Hero flung himself down and gripped the thwart just before the wave struck. It caught *Shearwater* by the stern and swung her up and up until Hero, staring terror-stricken down the ship's length, was certain it would pitch stern over stem. For a moment that seemed to last for ever the ship hung weightless on the peak, then the crest surged past and Hero toppled backwards as *Shearwater* slid into the following trough. Raul was screaming something and Hero grabbed the thwart, aware that another roller was about to hit. It smashed over the stern and boiled across the deck, scraping him off the thwart and tumbling him over the side. His lifeline brought him up with a shock and he took water into his lungs.

He was underwater, rolling through a green chaos of bubbles, unable to tell up from down. He popped to the surface and for a moment saw Wayland and Garrick leaning out to grab his lifeline. Another wave swept him back under and dragged him deep. The sea roared in his ears and then he felt the rope yank tight around his waist and he came flailing into the light. Wayland dragged him to the side and Garrick hauled him gasping and choking on to the deck.

Wayland's anxious face stared at him. 'Are you hurt?'

Hero couldn't speak. His lungs felt like they'd been scoured with sand.

Wayland took him under his armpits and hoisted him into a sitting position. The stern thwart was empty. He saw the frayed end of a safety line trailing on the deck.

'Richard!'

'He's alive,' said Wayland. 'The wave tossed him into the hold. Everyone's safe, but we've been swamped. We have to bail out before another wave hits.'

Hero managed to nod through another fit of coughing. Wayland lifted him to his feet. He saw Richard standing dumbfounded in the hold, water sloshing up to his thighs. Garrick was supporting him, fending off barrels of salt that had broken loose and were surging up and down the hold. *Shearwater* had lost a foot of buoyancy and rode as ponderously as a log. Vallon threw a bucket at Hero.

'You and Richard stay on deck.'

Hero stared at the flooded hold. Bailing would be as effective as taking a spoon to a lake.

'We ain't going to sink,' Raul shouted. 'The timber will keep us afloat even if we fill to the gunwales. Now get bailing before we ship another wave.'

Wayland had already thrown himself into the task, scooping water as fast as he could and swinging the bucket up to Syth. Garrick and Vallon joined him. Up on deck Hero laboured away mechanically. The wind was falling and the clouds were breaking.

All morning they toiled and the water level was only a couple of inches lower than when they'd started. There came a time when Hero tried to raise his bucket and couldn't.

'That's enough for now,' said Vallon.

They ate cold rations in their soaking clothes and then resumed their toil. The wind had slackened to a light southerly, and though the swell still ran high, the danger of swamping was receding. Raul even raised a scrap of sail to give better steerage.

It was late evening before they'd emptied the hold. Hero crawled out weeping from the pain in his hands. The air had fallen still. A fiery reef stretched along the horizon. Slowly the whole sky turned red, staining the sea crimson and flooding the faces of the company. Then the light died and the clouds cooled down through green to black. Venus glowed in the west, Mars twinkled red and green. The Pole Star appeared. They were alone on the ocean.

Hero's teeth chattered. 'Where do you think we are?' he asked Raul.

Raul's beard was grey with salt. 'Must have cleared the Shetlands by now. The Faroes should be about two days to the north-west.'

Hero looked at the rollers sweeping past. 'We might already be too far north. I think we should set a course due west.'

Raul seemed to juggle directions in his hands. 'You sure about that?'

'No.'

'West it is,' said Raul. He leaned against the tiller and *Shearwater* turned, trailing a phosphorescent wake.

Hero slept right through the next day in his exhaustion. He woke to a lulling motion, the sail rippling above him. The sun had gone down, its resting place marked by a golden plume of cloud fading to pink.

Far out on the still waters, the glossy black flukes of a whale arched out of the sea and slapped down in a soundless fountain of spray.

Hero looked to the helm. 'Any sign of land?'

Raul shook his head. 'Nothing.'

The night was so calm and clear that the celestial sphere was mirrored on the sea's surface. The day following was equally brilliant, yet under an empty blue sky that would have revealed land fifty miles off, they saw nothing but herds of grampuses and a solitary fulmar that Raul said was a wanderer of the deep ocean and no harbinger of land.

Two more days slid by and they knew that they must have missed the Faroes. They sailed on, at first keeping west and then, losing confidence, heading north. Raul organised the company into watches, dividing his time at the helm with Garrick and Wayland. In the late afternoon on the sixth day, Hero was standing watch alone in the bow. *Shearwater* lay becalmed, the waves flopping round-shouldered against her hull. Everyone else was asleep. Garrick hung over the tiller, steering through a dream. Vallon rested on his back with one hand over his eyes. Raul slumped against the bulwark with his legs straight out and his mouth open. Wayland and Syth lay back to back with the dog couched beside them.

Staring into the immensity of sea and sky, Hero had the sensation of floating in a dimension between time and eternity. The sea looked strange, the horizon having retreated to an immense distance and taken on a dished appearance. What if they'd travelled out of the known world into a realm where the laws of nature no longer applied? Master Cosmas had told him that under the pivot of the Pole Star, beyond the north winds, lay the land of the Hyperboreans, a place sweeter and more blessed than anyone could imagine.

Then he saw land. A high plateau cleft by ice-filled valleys with wind-scoured ridges, vertical headlands stepping away to the east.

'Land! Land ahead.'

As though released from a spell, the company woke and rubbed their eyes and crowded forward.

'No doubt about it,' said Raul.

'How long to reach it?' Vallon asked.

'Hard to say. A day's sailing with a fresh breeze.'

The company marvelled at their destination, pointing at mountains and ice-caps and fjords. The sun dipped towards the horizon and the sky began to separate into washes of rose and lapis. The island rippled and floated.

Vallon rubbed his eyes. 'What's happening?'

'It's fading away,' said Wayland.

Hero gaped in disbelief as his island melted into air.

Richard sighed. 'It was just a phantom. A fairy island.'

'But it must be real. You all saw it.'

'The ocean plays tricks,' said Raul. 'It shows you what you want to see.'

Hero was close to tears. 'Then why can't I see it now?'

Next day *Shearwater* drifted aimless under a mist-sheeted sun. Hero was playing a lacklustre game of *shatranj* with Richard when Raul raised a cry. 'We've got a visitor.'

Everyone raised their eyes towards a small bird perched on the yardarm.

Hero stood. 'Where did it come from?'

'Just appeared,' said Raul. 'Wayland noticed the dog staring up at it like the fox in the fable.'

The bird had a smoky grey back, a black eye mask and a white rump. 'I've seen birds like that in Sicily,' Hero said. 'They must fly north in the summer.'

'Keep your eyes on it,' said Vallon. 'Mark which direction it takes.'

The lonely migrant was in no hurry to depart. It preened, fanned its tail and warbled to itself. Hero was only half watching when it uttered a sharp *chacking* note and darted off.

'Watch which way it goes.'

It was just a speck when Hero saw it merge into a wispy grey flock flying low across the sea.

'Raul, steer the same course.'

'There ain't nothing to give me a bearing.'

Hero backed away. 'Keep pointing along the path the birds took. Don't let the ship drift.'

He hurried to his pack and took from his chest the mysterious direction finder. With great care he set it down on a thwart. The fish-shaped needle wandered around the horizon before settling in a lolling arc. Hero looked up to find the rest of the company still holding out their hands in the self-conscious attitude of amateur actors. 'North,' he cried. 'The birds flew due north.'

'Follow them,' said Vallon.

Raul looked at the compass with scepticism. 'You trust that thing?'

'I've tested it and it's as true a guide as the Pole Star.'

But there was no wind that day to put his claim to the proof. *Shearwater* drifted around the compass needle like a small lost planet. With the coming of dark, they were still no wiser, although the sighting of a clump of seaweed gave them hope that land might be near. Hero crouched over the compass by lamplight until a breeze from the east blew away the cloud and revealed the Pole Star almost exactly where the diviner had predicted.

He waited up all night until a thread of pale yellow appeared on the eastern horizon. The sun rose and he saw to the north a long low bank of cloud.

'Could be land,' said Vallon.

'Pray that it is,' Raul said. 'We're precious low on food.'

They sailed nearer. Gulls appeared, trailing in their wake.

'Ice,' Raul said, pointing at a chilly gleam high up in the cloud vapours. 'David said there's an ice mountain on Iceland's southern coast. If we're where I think we are, we have to sail west. We should come to some islands before the day's over.'

They skirted the shrouded coast. Wayland climbed to the yard to look for their next landmark, and in the late afternoon he called out that he could see islands ahead. One by one they appeared out of the drizzle – some like squat fortresses, another like a sleeping green whale, one of them an ugly pile of wrinkled slag with smoke wafting from its flanks.

In a fine misting rain, they made for the largest island, sailing under massive cliffs with clouds snagged on the ledges like tufts of cotton. Surf burst in caves and grottoes. They rounded a tall headland domed with grass and found a haven enfolded between tumbling hills. Once inside, the entrance seemed to close behind them. The sea surge faded to a distant echo, almost drowned out by the cries of birds nesting on the cliffs ringing the harbour. Sea parrots whirred in front of the ship and seals hoisted themselves high in the water to watch the intruders. The faint bleating of sheep floated down from the heights. Raul ran up towards the end of the cove and let go the anchor. The company jumped into the shallows and waded on to a beach of silky black sand. Hero staggered up it with his arms open and buried his face in the sweet turf.

In the morning they woke to find their camp ringed by a delegation of crouching savages who eyed the argonauts as if undecided whether to worship them or eat them. Raul initiated negotiations. The isles were called the Westmans after Irish slaves who'd fled here from their Norwegian master two centuries ago. The present inhabitants – fewer than eighty souls – eked out their fishing and fowling by trading with the occasional passing ship and plundering wrecks. In return for a dozen nails and a block of salt, Raul obtained a side of mutton and a string of sea parrots culled at their nests that morning.

The company rested in the haven for two days, sleeping, eating or just staring across the bay. The place had a monastic calm and in months and years to come, when Hero was heavy of heart, memories of that cove would come stealing back to ease his troubled mind. It was not a place where he would choose to live, but he sometimes thought that it was a place where, in the fullness of time, he would be content to die.

They left with detailed sailing directions. Two days brought them to Iceland's south-west peninsula. From here they tacked north-east along an uninhabited coastline of ash and lava. The sun was bleeding into the sea behind them when Wayland called out that he could see the settlement of Smoking Bay.

Richard grabbed Hero by both shoulders and shook him hard enough to rattle his teeth.

'We're here!'

Gliding towards the harbour, Hero kept revising his expectations downwards. He hadn't expected a city, or even a fair-sized town, but he had anticipated more than a sprinkling of houses – not even a vil-lage – backed by a few farmsteads. Only the sight of two knarrs tied alongside a stone jetty convinced him that Reykjavik had any con-nection with the civilised world.

As they crossed the bar, Richard told him that it was the twenty-first or twenty-second of May. More than thirty days had rolled round since their flight from England.

Iceland and Greenland

XXII

Beacons must have been lit to announce their coming. How else to explain the crowd gathered on the jetty to watch their arrival? Others were still trickling in by foot and on horse, some fresh from their fields and carrying hoes or mattocks. A man with a plaited beard and rings in his ears directed *Shearwater* to a mooring.

'You do the talking,' Vallon told Wayland.

The harbourmaster waved a staff to hold back the crowd. 'Where are you from?' he shouted.

'England.'

'What are you carrying?'

'Mixed goods.'

The harbourmaster sprang on board and looked the company over. 'Are you the master?' he asked Vallon.

'He doesn't speak your language well,' said Wayland. 'He's a Frank.'

The harbourmaster was delighted. 'I've never seen a Frenchman before. I thought they were smaller than that.'

'We've got a German and a Sicilian, too.'

'What's a Sicilian?'

Wayland presented Hero. The harbourmaster studied him with blatant curiosity. 'He's not a monk, is he?'

'No. A student of medicine.'

'Good. We've got enough foreign monks on Iceland. A pair arrived from Norway a week ago. Germans sent by the mother church to save our souls from perdition.'

Raul spat. 'Damn. Beaten by a pair of crows.'

Several Icelanders had sneaked on to the ship to examine the cargo. The harbourmaster chased them off and looked into the hold. 'You won't have any trouble shifting that timber. What are you after in exchange?'

'We'll decide when we've seen what's on offer. First we need to find lodgings.'

The harbourmaster pointed out a pair of bothies set back from the

257

harbour. 'That's all we've got for outlanders. Most foreign traders stay with kin or business partners.'

'They're no good,' said Wayland. 'We'll be here all summer. We need somewhere large enough to house us in comfort and store our goods.'

The harbourmaster faced Vallon with an air of mild expectation. It became apparent that an inducement was required. Richard slipped the man a couple of coins.

'I'll see what I can do.'

'Where are those ships from?' Wayland asked, pointing at the pair down the jetty.

'I'd say they're from betwixt and between. They're Norway ships that should have gone home last autumn, but they sailed too late and were taken aback by westerlies. Couldn't get round the Reykjanes peninsula. Been here all winter. Be careful how you talk to the crews. They're on short tethers.'

The harbourmaster left the ship and talked to a youth on horseback. The youth rode away. The crowd had begun to disperse. The company put the ship in order before eating. Afterwards, Wayland went ashore, but there was little to see and he soon returned to the ship and settled down to sleep.

It was still luminous night when the dog nuzzled him awake. Three men leading two spare mounts came riding along the jetty, their sturdy little horses stepping out at a curious running walk. The harbourmaster trotted alongside the leading rider, holding on to his stirrup.

'Wake up,' Wayland called. 'We've got company.'

The delegation reined in beside *Shearwater* and dismounted. The harbourmaster gestured towards the rider he'd been escorting. 'This man has a large house for rent.'

Wayland glanced at Vallon. 'Invite him aboard.'

The visitors climbed to the deck. Their leader was a dignified old gentleman with eyes like blue buttons and a neat fringe of white beard. He searched all their faces before offering Vallon his hand.

'He's a chieftain,' Wayland said. 'His name's Ottar Thordarson. He owns a hall that we might find suitable. It's about ten miles from the coast.'

Ottar was eyeing the contents of the hold with polite avidity.

'What does he want in return?'

'He's interested in buying our timber.'

Vallon looked into Ottar's candid blue eyes. 'He's welcome to take a closer look.'

The visitors walked around the hold, discussing the timber. Finally, Ottar stopped, passed one hand across his mouth and nodded.

'He says he'll take the lot,' Wayland said.

Vallon laughed. 'We'll negotiate once we've seen the house.'

'We can visit it today. That's why he brought spare horses.'

'You and I will go,' said Vallon. 'Raul, you're in charge of the ship.'

The sun was on the rise when they set off inland. The fields soon fell behind and they followed a rough road beaten out on a plain of lava. Wayland had never seen such an inhospitable landscape. Ottar took pride in pointing out its diabolic features – underground furnaces, mountains that melted and flowed like rivers, springs hot enough to boil a cow.

'Do falcons live here?' Wayland asked. 'White ones?'

'Yes, there are falcons,' said Ottar. He pointed east towards a range of peaks floating in the clear air. 'Two days' ride. Three days' ride.'

Wayland fell back alongside Vallon. 'He says there are falcons.'

Vallon smiled. 'Good.' He patted Wayland's arm. 'Good.'

They rode on and came to a district so cauterised that not a blade of grass or patch of lichen had taken hold. Steam wafted up from the ground and the stink of brimstone caught in the back of Wayland's throat. Off to their left stood a smoking black mountain resembling the remains of a gargantuan bonfire. They breasted a bare horizon and sat looking down into a broad river valley partly inundated by lava. Near the river stood a large farmstead isolated between lobes of slag. The road took a diversion close to the house and then went wriggling away to the east.

'What happened here?' Vallon asked.

'This is Ottar's hall,' Wayland said. 'His family built it in the first set-tlement. They've farmed here for two hundred years. This used to be one of the most fertile valleys in Iceland, but last spring Ottar woke in the night and saw flames spewing from that mountain. By morning molten rock had begun to flow into the valley. For three months streams of lava crept across the fields, and by winter Ottar had to abandon the hall. He's building a new one on the other side of his estate. He was going to salvage the beams from the old house, but he'd prefer to let the hall die in its own time and stand as a monument to his ancestors. That's why he wants our timber.'

Vallon looked at Ottar. He looked at the hall. 'Tell him he has first refusal.'

They descended towards the house, the horses treading with care on the lava. The hall resembled a giant upturned ship entirely carpeted with turf. An old woman came out of a ramshackle outbuilding and limped weeping across a tiny meadow grazed by a solitary cow. She showered kisses on Ottar's hand and he jumped down and kissed her cheeks and held her by her shoulders and spoke in soothing and affectionate tones.

'Her name's Gisla,' Wayland told Vallon. 'She was nurse to Ottar's children. Her own kin lie buried in a cemetery that was covered by the lava, and she didn't want to leave them. She'll cook and clean for us. Ottar says she talks a lot. She's lonely.'

Vallon slid off his horse and studied the house. Its turf eaves were so low that the structure looked like it had grown out of the ground. Wildflowers grew on its roof. Ottar opened the door and led them into the shadowy interior. A bird like the one that had landed on the ship fluttered from beam to beam before escaping into the light. Wayland felt that he'd been in the hall before. It was a replica of the home his grandfather had told him about. Here was the main chamber arranged around the long pit hearth where the menfolk gathered to eat and talk, and there were the retainers' bunks against each wall. Down that end was the booth where the householders retired for privacy, and above it was a gallery for their daughters. Wayland ran his hand over figures carved on the timber supports.

'Ottar's four sons and four daughters grew up here. It was a happy place.'

'Excuse us one moment,' said Vallon.

They went to the door. Through the aperture Wayland could see blue sky dotted with a few shavings of cloud. A rider passed in slow silhouette along the road.

'What do you think?' said Vallon.

'I think we should take it.'

'So do I. It will be good to have a place we can call home for a while.'

*

As part of the agreement, Ottar supplied four horses and arranged for guards to keep an eye on *Shearwater*. Within two days the company had set up residence in Ottarshall.

Vallon took the householder's booth and the men slept in the ground-floor bunks. Syth had the sleeping platform above, from where she pelted Raul with bits of clinker when his snoring became unbearable.

Two days later Wayland, Raul and a guide called Ingolf rode away into the interior to search for gyrfalcon eyries. They followed the serpentine twists of a river through a grassy flood plain. Wayland lost count of the crossings they made before they left the valley and struck up through a forest of dwarf birches that barely reached their stirrups. Over the next ridge they traversed a barren moor with their heads bent against squalls of sleet. The wind dropped and snow fell fine as dust from a clear sky. That night they watched the sun sink smoking beneath the watershed they'd crossed at dawn. Four seasons in a single day. Next day they picked their way on foot across bogs, jumping from cushions of green and yellow moss. On the other side they rode up a gorge guarded by pillars shaped like men. Ingolf said they were giants turned to stone after being caught by the sun as they journeyed between their subterranean haunts.

They crossed a flat summit dotted with tarns, each tarn tenanted by a pair of courting phalaropes that gyrated round each other like leaves caught in gusts of wind. They camped by the shorelines of lakes and lay wakeful in the long twilight listening to loons calling with cries of such desolation that Wayland's nape crawled. They negotiated frozen torrents of black slag, their horses shying from fissures where lobes of molten rock pulsed like a beating heart or a foetus hatching in its underground womb. They watched geysers spouting and cauldrons of mud spitting like thick porridge.

Whenever possible they slept at farms. Over bowls of skyr, they would ask about gyrfalcons and the men would lead them out and shield their eyes and point to far-off cliffs trimmed with snow and say that the falcons had nests there. At last they passed beyond settled parts, wandering over moraines and fields of clinker under the dome of an ice cap. A dozen times on that journey, Wayland stopped and found a place out of the wind and watched the crags above until his eyes ached.

Twelve days later they rode back to Ottarshall so sore and tired that they had to be helped down from their horses. Raul's face was blistered, his eyelids raw as wounds. When Syth placed a bowl in Wayland's hands, he cupped it on his lap like an invalid and went on staring straight ahead.

'We saw only three falcons,' he said at last. 'All of them were alone. We found half a dozen nests and every one was deserted. I found several places where the falcons pluck their prey, but there were few signs of fresh kills.' He scratched his brow. 'The falcons feed mainly on snow grouse and this year there are very few. The farmers told us that the falcons only breed when the grouse are common.'

'You explored only a small region,' Vallon said. 'You'll find your falcons elsewhere.'

Wayland began to spoon food into his mouth. 'Ingolf says they're plentiful in the north-west fjords. It's a week's journey.'

'You have plenty of time. We don't have to leave until the beginning of August.'

Wayland waved his spoon. 'There's another disappointment. All the falcons I saw were grey.'

'Maybe there aren't white gyrfalcons.'

'Yes, there are. But not on Iceland.'

'You're going to love this,' said Raul. The German sat leaning back with his legs shoved out and his eyes shut.

'The palest falcons live in Greenland,' Wayland said. 'Ingolf used to deal with a Norwegian merchant who imported them from an agent in the Western Settlement. They were caught by trappers in the northern hunting grounds.'

Vallon scraped back his stool. 'You're not going to Greenland.'

'Wait. Falcons aren't the only precious commodity in Greenland. 'There are also walrus skins and ivory, the horns of sea unicorns, the pelts of white bears.'

Hero broke the silence that followed. 'Those sound more profitable than the goods available here. Apart from horses, the Icelanders have only woollens and fish. They're not going to fetch high prices in Norway or Rus.'

Vallon walked up and down. 'How will you get there?'

'On *Shearwater*, of course.'

Vallon shook his head. 'I'm not risking the ship. If you really think a voyage to Greenland is worthwhile, you'll have to make the passage on another vessel.'

Wayland yawned. 'We'll need our own ship to carry us to the hunting grounds. They lie a long way north of the settlements.'

Vallon glanced at Raul. 'What do you say?'

He shrugged. 'We came here to trade, and *Shearwater*'s lying idle. Why not?'

'What will you do for crew? You'll need a pilot.'

'Finding hands won't be a problem,' said Wayland. 'There are good profits to be made in the Greenland trade.'

Vallon noticed Syth staring at Wayland with her hands clasped at her waist. 'All right. Make enquiries. But remember that we have to leave Iceland before the autumn storms set in.'

Wayland's enquiries soon bore fruit. An embassage from the bishop in Skalholt made the long day's ride west and presented themselves at the hall with a request. The bishop had heard that the outlanders were planning a voyage to Greenland. It so happened that a week before their own arrival, two monks from the archdiocese of Hamburg-Bremen had landed on Iceland. The German archbishop had sent them to check that apostasy hadn't taken root among his most remote parishioners. Over a meal prepared by Gisla and Syth, the ambassador explained that Iceland's bishop found the attentions of these two holy fathers vexing. He was from Viking stock. In fact his own father had been a terrible pagan who had died unshriven, and his methods of nurturing the new faith didn't sit square with the prescriptions laid down by the established church. In short, he wished to get the two monks off his back and had suggested that they pursue their missionary work in Greenland.

'We'll need a crew and pilot,' Wayland said.

'That's easily arranged,' said the ambassador.

Within three days a skilled complement had been mustered, and two days later *Shearwater* was ready to leave. Wayland was packing for the voyage when Vallon came by.

'Do you want to take the girl?'

Wayland looked past him. Syth stood forlorn in the doorway.

'You'll need someone to cook for you,' said Vallon. 'The old woman will look after our needs.'

Wayland shrugged as if he didn't care one way or the other. 'I suppose she might be useful.'

'You'll be doing us a favour,' Vallon said. 'She'd only pine away in your absence.'

XXIII

In the middle of an early June night as bright as day, Wayland left Iceland with Raul and Syth. Their pilot was a morose fellow called Gunnar, a martyr to disabling headaches. Also on board were the two monks. Father Saxo was fat with a head as bald as peeled garlic and took a relaxed view of human frailty. Father Hilbert was thin, with ears like a bat and an implacable belief in man's innate wickedness. Neither had been out of Germany before, but they knew exactly what to expect of the Greenlanders.

'They daren't leave their houses in the wintertime,' Father Saxo told Raul. 'If they do, they're burned by a cold so extreme that when they wipe their noses, the whole nose pulls off.'

Father Hilbert nodded. 'And the nose having broken off, they throw it away.'

'I'd better be careful how I piss then,' said Raul.

The monks exchanged looks. Saxo leaned forward. 'When did you last attend mass?'

'Not long after Easter,' Raul said with a straight face.

'Did you confess your sins?'

Raul winked at Wayland. 'I was in too much of a hurry.'

Hilbert pinned him with an earnest gaze. 'Do you wish to make confession now?'

Raul looked out across the placid ocean. 'How long have you got, Father?'

The passage went smoothly. Six days out of Reykjavik, Wayland saw his first icebergs – emaciated wrecks, all ribs and hollows. They rounded Cape Farewell on Greenland's southern tip and in a diffused light drifted north with huge mountains to starboard. They didn't land at the Eastern Settlement. To reach it they would have had to sail thirty miles up an ice-strewn fjord. Instead, they tacked and rowed only as far as the first farmstead. Here the monks took their leave. With them went the pilot, who declared that he was too ill to go any further, and two of the Icelandic crewmen. Replacing them wasn't difficult. Ships were rare in Greenland and half a dozen settlers begged to accompany the foreigners on the searoad north. After two nights ashore, the company sailed on and reached the Western Settlement at night on the third day.

It lay at the head of a long fjord – just a few sod houses with hay-fields under a black-and-white backdrop of mountains. *Shearwater* landed at a farm in a bay on the north shore and the Greenlanders and remaining Icelanders disembarked to complete their journeys on foot. Wayland, Raul and Syth stood in the twilight silence, wondering why people would choose to settle in such a barren outpost.

They'd just sat down to breakfast next morning when a man stuck his grinning face above the gunwale.

'Well met, far-farers.'

The dog advanced on him. The stranger whistled in admiration. 'What a monster,' he said, chucking it under the jaw. 'The wolf Fenrir who devoured Odin couldn't have been bigger. If he fathers a litter during your stay, I'll pay a good price for a dog pup. I'll call him Skoll after the wolf who chases the sun.' Up he breezed – a powerfully built man followed by a sturdy boy. He gave Syth a formal bow. 'Good morning, lovely daughter.' Wayland and Raul had risen uncertainly. He shook each by the hand. 'Orm the Greedy,' he said. 'This is my son, Glum. I hear you're looking for a guide to take you to the northern hunting grounds. You're in luck. I've trapped and hunted there most summers for thirty years.' He sniffed appreciatively. 'Hot wheaten scones with fresh butter. Don't let them grow cold on my account.'

Wayland sank back on his seat. 'Would you care to share our meal?'

'By all means,' said Orm. He plonked himself down on a thwart, helped himself to a scone and trowelled butter on it.

Wayland studied the Greenlander. His main impression was of grizzled red hair. A great shock of it on the man's head, long ragged moustaches, bushy eyebrows that grew straight up, giving him an air of perpetual astonishment. Bright blue eyes nestled in wrinkles. His son was cast in the same stocky mould but was as hangdog as his father was outgoing. On his right temple was an indentation the size and shape of an egg.

'You're after falcons,' Orm said. 'I know where to find them.'

'White ones?'

'Pale as the winter moon.' Orm arched his incredible eyebrows at Syth. 'Can you spare a little more butter, lovely maid?'

Raul eyed him suspiciously. 'What kind of arrangement are you proposing?'

Orm crammed another scone under his moustache. 'A fair one. You need a guide and a crew. I need a ship.'

'How many crew?'

'Four friends as well as my son. We'll be netting auks, killing whales and walrus, trapping foxes. We'll be away six weeks.'

'It seems to me that you have the better part of the deal.'

Orm jabbed with his knife. 'The falcons are hard to find and harder to reach. How many are you after?'

The ransom stipulated four, but Wayland had always counted on taking more to make up for losses on the journey south. 'Eight should be enough.'

'That's a lot of gaping beaks to feed. Don't worry. I'll make sure they never go hungry. Do you have the stomach for heights?'

Wayland hesitated. 'I once climbed a hundred-foot beech in a gale to free a hawk tangled by her jesses.'

'It's not trees you'll be climbing. The falcons nest on crags in the clouds. I've been birding on cliffs since I could walk. Glum, too. That reminds me. I hear you have iron.'

Raul narrowed his eyes. 'Suppose we have?'

'You'll need ice axes. I can get them forged by tomorrow evening and we can be off on the dawn tide. What do you say?'

Wayland looked at Raul. He looked at Glum standing with his face downcast. 'He's rather young, isn't he?'

'A boy can stand where a man will fall. Glum's as agile as a goat.'

'What happened to his head?'

'A stone hit him when he was collecting auks' eggs. He was only seven. Don't worry, his wits are still the right way out. He's always been tight-tongued.'

'Syth will be coming with us,' said Wayland.

Orm hesitated only for a fraction. 'Excellent. I haven't tasted scones as good as these since my mother died.'

'Have the last one.'

'Are you sure?'

Wayland stood. 'You'll supply all the necessary equipment.'

'Everything.'

Wayland stuck out his hand. 'It's a deal.'

Orm sealed the contract with a crushing grip. Back on the jetty he paused. 'Do you have beer?'

'We drank it,' said Raul. 'We've still got barley and malt.'

'Then we have everything we need. A hunter must have ale to toast his triumphs and console him in his failures.'

Off he went, whistling. Raul and Wayland pulled faces at each other.

All next day Orm and his friends loaded *Shearwater* with hunting paraphernalia. They had long horsehair ropes, scaling ladders, traps and nets of various kinds, harpoons, fishing lines and hooks, barrels of salt and fermented whey, tents. They stowed a skiff in the hold and lashed a whaler on deck alongside *Shearwater*'s boat. Since they wouldn't find wood in the north, they carried fuel bricks made from straw and dried cow dung. The Greenlanders were in holiday mood, singing and joking as they worked.

A dozen or so of their relatives turned out to bless the enterprise and watch them set sail. They felt their way north in thick fog, borne along past icebergs wreathed in silence. Three days later the fog released them into a realm of permanent daylight and air so clear that they could sometimes see their next destination more than a day before they reached it. Icebergs as big as cathedrals drifted by in ponds of turquoise meltwater, the cold blue light of thousand-year-old winters entombed at their cores. They passed one of the glaciers that calved these monsters and watched cliffs of ice collapse thunderously into the sea, raising waves that sent *Shearwater* pitching wildly. The next day they sailed into an upwelling current the colour of hyacinths on which every kind of native creature that swam or flew had converged. An ominous cloud out to sea turned into a flock of auks a mile wide that whirred past in a sooty squall. Wherever Wayland looked, he could see whales breaching or sounding. The loud reports of their flukes smacking the water kept him awake almost as much as the sun shining at midnight.

That same sunlit night orcas switchbacked ahead of the ship, their backs glowing like polished manganese. One of them launched out of the ocean and pirouetted on its tail before crashing back. They disappeared and the sea settled into a silky calm. Syth was standing next to Wayland in the bow and he watched her stroke a strand of sun-bleached hair from her eyes. He noticed how her eyes took on the colours of the sea – amethyst, violet, cobalt. She had filled out and grown from girl to young woman. He gathered himself to speak, not knowing what he was going to say except that it would be irrevocable.

She noticed his attention and put her hands on her hips and gave a mock pout. 'What?'

'Nothing,' he said, meaning 'everything'. 'I'm glad your hair's grown. It makes you look ... pretty.' He winced at the lame compliment.

She looked down, suddenly as shy as he was. 'The day we met you said I reminded you of someone. You never said who.'

Wayland didn't stop to think. 'My sister.'

Syth's smile tightened. 'Oh.'

'Only at first sight.'

Orm released Wayland from his torment by thumping him between the shoulderblades. 'Not far now.'

Syth turned eagerly, a girl again. 'Will we see snow bears?'

Orm laughed. 'I doubt it, lovely daughter. In all my trips I've only seen three. They live further north.' His brows waggled. 'So much the better. They're bigger than bulls and so strong that they can flip a seal clean over their shoulders. You won't even see them coming. Do you know why?'

Syth gave a quick shake of her head.

'They spend all their lives on snow and they're white all over – except for their black noses. So when they stalk prey, they cover their noses with their paws ... ' Orm suited action to word, '... and creep up, closer and closer ... ' Orm lurched in a crude pantomime of bear strategy, '... until they have you in their grasp and then – Grrr! No, be thankful you won't see any bears.'

268

Syth giggled. 'I don't believe you. About bears covering their noses, I mean.'

'Why do you think my eyebrows stand on end? It's because of all the amazing things I've seen in the northland. Up here it's like living in a daylight dream.'

A pleasant silence fell. *Shearwater*'s sail flapped and filled. The sun was dipping to the lowest point on its endless circle.

'Where does Greenland end?' Wayland asked.

'In mist and ice, the evening of the world and its dawn, the abode of the dead and the realm of the first gods.'

Wayland nodded towards the west. 'Do you know what lies over the sea?'

Orm stood shoulder to shoulder with him. 'I do, for men have sailed there in my own lifetime. The West Land we call it, but it can't be reached by chasing the sun. The sea's too thick with ice. You have to follow the current north until you can't go any further, then cross a strait to the west. First you reach Slabland and Flatland, where the snow never melts in summer. Travelling south you pass Markland and the Wonder Strands before reaching Wineland, where even the winters are snowless and the nights of the Yule festival are as long as the days. It's so fertile that wheat ripens into loaves, and the dew is so sweet that cows only have to lick the grass to grow fat. In Wineland the trees reach halfway to heaven and the forests swarm with deer and sable and beavers. The seas are so thick with cod that a man can cross between islands by walking on the backs of them.'

Wayland smiled. 'Greenland's a harsh land. I'm surprised you don't leave it to make new homes in such a paradise.'

'They did. In my great-grandfather's day more than a hundred of them settled in Wineland. As a boy, I met the last survivor of the colony. Bjarni Sigurdason was his name and he never stopped talking about the wonders of the West Land.'

'Why did he come back?'

'Why did Adam and Eve leave Eden? Jealousy over the women. Sickness. Above all, strife with the skraelings.'

'Skraelings?'

'Screechers. Uglies. God in his wisdom has given the West Land to savages who don't even know his name. At first they were friendly and happy to trade. They were so unworldly that a settler could buy a bale

269

of pelts with a scrap of woolcloth no broader than a finger. Soon, though, they became a menace. They stole the settlers' livestock, not understanding that animals could be personal property, and they threatened hunters who went into the forests which they claimed as their own preserve. Blood was shed on both sides, but the skraelings were many and the settlers were few. After three winters the leader of the colonists decided that there would never be peace with the heathens and brought the survivors back.'

He lapsed into silence and Wayland assumed that he was thinking about the ill-fated colony. But when he spoke again, he pointed north.

'I've seen a skraeling in Greenland – at the furthest end of the northern hunting grounds. I'd been hunting seals out on the pack ice. I returned in the evening and found footprints around my camp. I took my bow and followed them. I climbed over a snow ridge and there he was. At first I thought he was a blind bear because he was dressed head to toe in fur and had white discs where his eyes should be. He saw me at the same time and drew back his spear. I had my arrow aimed at his heart but I didn't shoot. I don't know why. He held up his hand and I raised mine and then he began to back away. Nothing could have prepared me for what happened next.'

'What did he do?'

'He jumped on a sledge and eight white wolves bore him away.' Orm looked fiercely at Wayland. 'God's word. That was three years ago and ever since I've been wondering how he came to be in that place so far north, living with tame wolves where we Greenlanders can't survive for more than three months of the year.'

'Perhaps he came from the West Land.'

Orm stabbed his forefinger. 'You've got it, boy! That's what I tell my people, but they laugh and say how could skraelings who don't have ships, who know nothing about iron, who live in houses made of twigs and leaves – how could such savages cross the icy sea to Greenland? You'll see, I tell them. Where one has come, others will follow. Then where will we be?'

Glum gave an urgent cry on the other side of the ship. His father ran over and they both leaned over. 'Come quick,' Orm shouted.

The whole company gathered. Under the hull passed a school of fish or whales with pallid, mottled bodies and spiral lances sticking out of their heads.

'Corpse whales,' said Orm. 'Some call them sea unicorns. Forget falcons. Catch one of those and you'll be rich for life. I've heard that in Miklagard the value of a narwhal horn is measured by twice its weight in gold.'

'How do you catch them?'

'They swim into the fjords to calve and we harpoon them in their breeding bays.' Orm leaned out along the course taken by the narwhals. 'It's a good omen, lad. They're heading for the fjords where the falcons nest.' He pointed towards the coast. 'Red Cape. We're nearly at the hunting grounds.'

Wayland looked along the golden path laid by the midnight sun and saw that it ended at a colossal escarpment separating two ice-carved valleys.

On a dying wind the crew rowed towards the immense red prow. Hundreds of seals bobbed in the waves, watching them with limpid curiosity. Acres of eider drakes parted around the ship, only shifting when the bow was almost upon them. Giant auks as tall as geese with wings no bigger than a child's hands waddled to the edge of a skerry and flopped in. Underwater they flew as gracefully as swallows. 'God forgot to grant them wits the day he made those boobies,' Orm said. 'A man can stand in a flock of them and club them all day long.'

From the same islet ungainly leviathans with down-turned tusks and coarse moustaches humped forward on flippers and slid into the swell. 'Walruses,' said Orm, and stroked his own whiskers to make Syth laugh. From the cliffs above came a steady roar. Every ledge and gallery was packed with auks and gulls and God knows what other kinds of fowl. The cliffs loomed so high that the birds flocking around the upper heights looked no bigger than gnats.

'Falcons nest in both fjords,' Orm said. He indicated the precipices plunging into the southern sea-arm. 'One of the eyries is up there.'

Wayland's gaze panned up from the ice-littered channel to the summit crags, then back down again. The cliffs fell sheer to the sea or dropped to talus slopes pitched at sickening inclines. There was no coastal shelf, nowhere to put ashore.

Raul had a finger pressed thoughtfully to his lips. 'We ain't going to climb that.'

'Not from below,' Orm said. 'There's a path to the top on the other side of the cape. Glum will lead you up it. From the summit you can climb down to the nest. You won't be able to see it from above. I'll take the ship up the fjord to mark the spot. First we must make camp.'

They rowed on with the sun behind them, water falling like blood from their oarblades. Around the north side of the cape was a foreshore of tumbled boulders. The skeleton of a whale lay on the strand like the frame of a wrecked ship, each vertebra occupied by a cormorant holding out its tattered black wings in an unholy cross. Orm steered between bluffs enclosing an inlet and brought *Shearwater* to rest. Wayland jumped ashore into the stink of guano and the din of squabbling birds. A sea-eagle with wings the size of a table-top glided close to the tenements, chased by a mob of gulls. Beneath the rookeries, blue foxes sat waiting for the drizzle of eggs and nestlings that fell or were pushed from their nurseries.

Orm's base camp was a shieling built with granite slabs. The roof had collapsed under winter snow and the company's first task was to make it sound. Then they carried their equipment ashore and stowed it away. Orm proposed a meal and then rest, but Wayland knew that Greenland's summer smiles were fleeting and insisted on climbing to the falcon's nest straight away.

'Syth and the dog had better stay with me,' Orm told him. They sorted out the equipment. Glum slung two coiled ropes and an iron bar over his back. Raul carried another pair of ropes. Wayland strapped a wicker basket over his shoulders.

The sun had moved south and they climbed the boulder field in dusky blue shadow, jumping from one ankle-jarring stance to another. They laboured up a scree slope until they reached the foot of a diagonal rift in the escarpment. Between vertical crags fanged with icicles, an ice gully rose in a succession of steep chutes and steps.

Raul's jaw dropped. 'Orm said a path.'

'Use your ice axes,' Glum said. 'In the steep places I will cut steps for you. There are some difficult parts where you must use a rope.'

'Difficult parts,' Raul repeated.

Glum set off at an easy pace, chopping toeholds with his axe. Wayland stepped on to the ice and realised how tenuous his grip was. He hadn't climbed more than a few feet before he slipped. He would have fallen if he hadn't managed to claw the point of his axe into the ice.

Raul struggled up beside him. 'This is the stupidest thing I ever did in my life.'

Wayland looked up at Glum's foreshortened outline. 'Go back if you want.'

On he went, considering each step. Glum was approaching the top of the icestep by the time he reached its base. He surveyed the treacherous cascade. Looking down through his feet, he could see Raul's head and shoulders and the slick couloir falling away to the bottom of the cliff. If he slipped now, he would carry Raul away with him. Splinters of ice skipped past. Glum hauled himself out of sight over the step.

Use the steps I cut.

Wayland waited for Raul to reach him. The German's teeth were gritted in terror.

'You'd better lower the rope,' Wayland shouted.

Down it came. 'You trust him?' Raul gasped.

'More than I trust myself.'

Up he went, his feet skidding on the cobbled ice. At the top he found Glum wedged behind rocks at the edge of the gully. Wayland's gaze shot up past him, hoping to find that the ascent became easier. Instead, there was another cascade of ice even higher than the one he'd just scaled.

'You should have told us how dangerous it was.'

Glum regarded him calmly. 'If I had, would you have come?'

Wayland climbed most of the next pitch on the bare rocks at the side of the gully. One awkward manoeuvre involved shuffling around a pillar that had split away from the face and fractured into blocks. He was fully committed, gripping the stack with both hands, when he felt it begin to sway outwards. Somehow he got round without it toppling, but then he heard a scraping sound and saw as if in slow motion the cap of the pillar slide and fall. The rock was twice the size of a man's head and it shot down the gully towards Raul. Wayland jammed his fist into his mouth, and that's what saved the German. If he'd shouted a warning, Raul would have looked up and been struck full in the face. Instead, he was concentrating so hard on his next hold that he didn't hear the rock coming until it crashed in front of him and bounded over his body. It flew over the icestep and Wayland heard it shatter on the walls and go clattering away into the depths. Shocked rigid, he waited for Raul to join him.

The German groaned and collapsed against the crag with his head lolling back and his eyes closed.

'I won't hold it against you if you go back,' Wayland said.

'Too late. It would be as dangerous to go down as to go on.'

He was right. A grim fatalism overtook Wayland as he climbed the next icestep. If he fell, he fell – a swoop of terror as he lost his footing, a smashing impact, then oblivion.

Above the third step the gully widened and the going became easier. Wayland was able to climb without the use of his hands. A blue sky-light opened and he staggered on to the summit plateau. Raul thrashed up behind him and turned and pointed down the gully as if it were the throat into hell. 'I'm not going back down there. You hear?'

Glum was coiling the rope over his shoulder. 'Yes, you must. It is the only way.'

The climb had taken them most of the morning and the sky was beginning to skin over. From up here they could see the vast polar desert that covered Greenland's interior. A cold wind from the icecap stung their faces as they plugged over the plateau, the ground curving away on all sides so that they could see nothing but snow and sky and their footprints dwindling behind them. The slope began to descend and the snow cover grew patchy, exposing fields of frost-shattered rock. Wayland saw the ice-ribboned clifftops on the far side of the fjord, and then the edge of the plateau came into sight – broken columns and buttresses connected to the face by knife-edged ridges. Glum made his way out on to one of the projections. Very vulnerable he looked on that lofty promontory.

He made a slow overarm gesture towards his left and they trudged on into the wind.

'There!' Wayland shouted, pointing at a blocky silhouette perched on an outcrop along the escarpment.

'Yes, it is the falcon,' Glum said. 'The nest is close, I think.'

Wayland forgot the perils of the ascent and hurried forward. He'd got halfway to the outcrop when the falcon launched off and disappeared around its sentinel rock. It wasn't as large as he'd been expecting. 'That must be the male,' he said. 'The tiercel.'

'Wait here please,' Glum said, and walked nonchalantly on to another prow. He anchored himself with his pick and leaned over, then hissed and made a beckoning motion.

Wayland's heart beat fast as he picked his way forward. A ferocious updraught lifted him back on his heels. Eyes watering, he peered over the edge. The world spun. He drew back dizzy and afraid.

'Take my hand,' Glum said. 'See, my axe holds me very firmly.'

Wayland entrusted his life to the boy's grip and leaned over. The wind blew his hair back. The ship below was no bigger than a speck. He heard a creaking wail and out from an overhang to his left sailed the gyrfalcon. Wayland looked straight down on her, taking in her size and whiteness, her massive shoulders, the broad bases of her wings. She rode the updraught without effort and glided along the cliff face on slightly downheld wings, passing close enough for Wayland to see the highlights in her eyes.

He turned to Raul. 'Pure white! As big as an eagle!'

'The nest is below the overhang,' Glum said. 'It will not be possible to go straight to it. I will look from the other side to see if that way is easier.'

The falcon floated away, making height. Wayland's blood tingled at the thought of possessing her offspring before the day was out.

Glum came back shaking his head. 'This side is not so difficult, I think. Now we must find a place to fix the ropes.'

They explored the ground behind the eyrie. About fifteen feet back from the edge, Glum located a crack deep enough to sink the bar a foot deep.

Raul wiped his nose on his sleeve. 'Who's going down?'

Glum looked at Wayland. 'I think it must be me. It is not so easy for you.'

Wayland almost let him have his way. The prospect of descending the precipice made his heart quail and turned his legs to water. But when he looked into the void and saw the falcon patrolling her territory, he knew that his triumph wouldn't be complete unless he took the eyases himself.

'I'll go,' he said. 'Show me the route.'

Glum led him out on to the spur and pointed down the face. 'First you must descend to that ledge and follow it until you reach the rock shaped like a giant's nose.'

Wayland saw a neb of rock sticking out from the face on this side of the overhang. 'How do I get round it?'

'There is a place to put your foot. Do you see? Step on it with your left foot so that you can reach round the rock with your right hand. Once you are round, it is easy. You will see the nest above your head.'

Wayland nodded, too apprehensive to take it all in.

'I will stay here and guide you. First we must tie the ropes.'

They scrambled back and Raul took Wayland aside. 'Don't do it. Let the kid risk his own neck.'

Nerves made Wayland tetchy. 'You do your job and leave me to worry about mine.'

He stood like a child being dressed by its mother while Glum tied two ropes around his chest and slipped the basket over his shoulders. 'I won't be able to see you when you reach the nest, so you must signal by pulling with the rope. Tug two times if you want more rope. Tug three times to let me know you want to come up.'

'What does one tug mean?' Raul asked.

Glum's smile came and went. 'One tug means the rope has broken.' He took one of the lines in both hands and drew it taut. 'Do not hang all your weight on this. It is not so new.'

Raul studied Glum with one eye asquint. 'How old are you, son?'

'I am fourteen.'

Raul spat. 'You ain't going to make twenty.'

'Perhaps you are right. There are few old bones in my family. Every day my life is interesting.' Glum paid out the ropes, coiled them once around the bar, and handed the free ends to Raul. Then he escorted Wayland to the edge and placed a hand on his shoulder. 'Do not think about the height. If the cliff was only fifty feet high, you would not be so nervous, but if you fell you would still die.'

Wayland tried to smile. 'The difference is that I wouldn't have so long to think about it.'

Glum slapped Wayland's arm. 'Go now. The weather will not be good for long.'

Wayland lined up with Raul and backed to the edge of the drop. His gut felt hollow. He stirred at empty space with his right foot.

'Lean back,' Glum ordered. 'Further. Look at the sky.'

Wayland sucked in breath, tilted over and began to walk himself down the face. Grit and lichen dislodged by his feet flew up and scratched his eyes. Raul wasn't paying out the rope smoothly and the descent was a succession of jarring drops.

'Keep leaning back,' Glum shouted. 'You're nearly there.'

Wayland descended the last few feet to the ledge with all the elegance of a sack. He balanced and craned up. Only Glum's head and shoulders were visible. The boy raised a thumb. Craning the other way, Wayland saw the rock he had to negotiate about thirty feet away.

A furious *kack, kack, kack* drowned Glum's instructions. Wayland heard a rush of air as the falcon stooped past him. He turned to see her looking back at him as she completed her run-out. She swung round, stroked the air and closed up into a wedge. Her bunched yellow fists shot past two feet from his head. She banked and turned, rising like a ship riding a swell, and he saw her take deliberate aim and fold up before tearing past with all eight talons extended. Again and again she attacked, and though Wayland told himself she wouldn't strike, every pass made him flinch. She kept him pinned there until his legs begin to quiver with the strain.

He sidled along the ledge. His eyes and nose were streaming. The falcon had sheered off and his confidence began to grow. He came to the end of the ledge and spotted the foothold. Glum had told him to lead with his left foot, but the supplest contortionist couldn't have stretched that far. By fully extending his right foot, he could just paw the socket without getting proper purchase. He'd have to jump, but even if he footed himself, there were no handholds. Half a dozen times he rehearsed the move, as mindless as an insect. He turned his head towards Glum. The boy gestured with his left leg, his shouts whisked aloft.

Wayland felt his will and strength draining away. He had the awful sensation that the mountain was pushing him out and he pressed his clammy face to the wall and clung on. He glanced down into the great gulf and saw the slow, sickening crawl of the tide against the shore. Faint shouts reached him. Glum had descended to a perilous stance and was miming a skipping move that seemed to involve jumping on to the hold with his right foot and immediately following with his left foot while simultaneously slapping his right hand around the outcrop. Wayland tracked the ropes angling up the cliff. If the effort failed, at best he would crash more than thirty feet along the face. At worst the ropes would break and he would pulp himself with plenty of time to contemplate his end.

Or he could give up. His calves were fluttering and his fingers had lost sensation. He gathered one of the ropes in his hand and prepared to give the signal. He took a last look at the outcrop and paused. Glum's right, he thought. If that rock was only six feet above the ground, you wouldn't think twice about it – launch off with your right foot, into the pocket, balance, follow with the left, a brief moment of weightlessness before pushing hard and slapping your hand around the edge of the rib.

Glum had stopped shouting. Wayland wiped his nose, filled his lungs, gathered himself at the end of the ledge, bent his left knee and jumped. A quick two-step and then a lunge for the steep edge of the rock. He hung mainly by friction, and when he knew he wasn't going to fall, he brought his right leg round and groped for a foothold on the other side of the outcrop. Nothing at first, then he contacted a small projection. He didn't pause to think. He put all his weight on the hold and shimmied around the rock.

He was only a step away from a good footing. Above him, fissured blocks whitewashed with droppings led like a ladder to the nest shelf. He pulled himself up, crooked his elbows over the ledge and hauled himself into the eyrie.

Three hissing eyases flung themselves on their sides and thrust out their talons. They were ugly, toad-like infants with feathers budding through dirty grey down. Their mother was still patrolling, unable to mount an attack because of the overhang. A freshly killed gull lay in the eyrie, fragments of its dark red flesh stuck to the eyases' waxy ceres. The remains of other kills littered the eyrie and the ledges were plastered with feathers. Wayland sat on the midden as if it were a throne, enjoying his God's eye view. He found himself noticing the golden lichen on the rocks, the silvery veins in the granite, a small pink flower quaking in the wind.

He came out of his reverie to find that he was very cold. He thought he heard voices and sensed that they had been calling for some time. The eyases were still rolled on their sides, warding him off with their talons. He shivered. The sky had clouded over and the surface of the fjord had darkened to slate. Time to go. He took hold of the ropes and pulled three times.

This time he traversed the rocky nose without hesitation. Not a moment too soon. Cloud had rolled in from the sea and fingers of mist were groping up the cliffs. As soon as he gained the ledge, the falcon resumed her attacks. He ignored her and moved quickly until he reached what he thought was the line of ascent. He rested a moment then threw his head back to check the position of the ropes.

Something hit his forehead with stunning impact. He didn't even know he'd been knocked off the ledge until he found himself hanging with the ropes biting into his chest. The pain was excruciating, as though someone had taken a blunt saw to his skull. Through pulsing red waves he realised that he'd been twisted round and was dangling with his back to the cliff. Sticky warmth flooded down his face, half blinding him and filling his mouth with salt sweetness. He wiped the blood from his eyes and raised his hand to find out what damage the blow had done. His skull was still in one piece but a pair of lips seemed to have sprouted on his brow.

The pain subsided to a sickening ache. Blood wormed down his neck. He paddled at the rock, trying to spin himself around. Somehow the ropes had worked around his back, leaving him leaning out from the cliff, unable to exert any leverage. To make his position worse, the basket was holding him away from the face. He felt for the straps and found that one of them had snapped. He struggled out of the other and dropped the basket into space. Blood was still running into his eyes. He reached for the ropes and that's when he discovered that one of them had broken.

His blood-slicked hands couldn't get a grip on the remaining line. He wiped his palms on his thighs and was about to try again when the rope jerked around his ribs and he felt himself scrape a foot or so up the face. Raul was trying to drag him up. Another violent heave and he heard the rope sawing against rock.

'No!'

The movement stopped. He wiped his hands again and made another attempt to pull himself up. He had to reach behind him. The angle was all wrong. He tried a dozen times before giving up. He was weakening. His neck ached from the effort of trying to keep his head from slumping forward. Freezing fog streamed up past him. The cold had helped staunch his wound and his face was setting into a mask. The rope around his chest gripped so tight that he could breathe only in shallow gasps.

'Don't struggle. I'm coming down.'

It was Glum, not far above him.

'Wayland, I'm on the ledge. You're about ten feet below me. I'm going to drop another rope. Do you think you can hold onto it?'

Wayland half raised a hand.

'Here it comes.'

The rope fell hissing over his shoulder. He snagged it at the second attempt. His fingers were too numb to tie a secure knot. He made two coils around his right wrist.

'Put your weight on it. Then you will be able to turn and everything will be easier.'

Wayland gripped with both hands and strained. As his weight transferred from the rope pinned to his back, the pressure on his chest relaxed and air flooded into his lungs.

'Turn to face the cliff.'

Wayland gave himself more breathing space before kicking off with his feet. He spun and smacked chest first into the cliff. He blinked up through a bloody veil and glimpsed Glum peering down from the ledge.

'You are not strong enough to climb, I think. You must let Raul pull you up to me.'

Glum signalled by tugging on his own rope. Wayland felt himself borne upwards. Glum leaned down, gripped him by his tunic and hauled him onto the ledge.

'That was good. Rest now until you have the strength to reach the top.'

The formal phrasing from a boy who hadn't started shaving made Wayland laugh. It wasn't normal laughter. He balanced on the ledge until his breathing steadied and he looked up through the dank updraught.

'I'm ready.'

Raul dragged him up like he was a slab of meat. He crawled over the lip of the cliff and saw the German braced behind the anchor bar. As soon as Wayland stood on safe ground, Raul ran forward and caught him. He lowered him to the ground and took his face in both hands.

'What happened? Did a rock hit you?'

'It was the falcon. I don't think she meant to strike me. I leaned back at the wrong moment and . . . ' Nausea swept him.

Raul dropped to his knees and examined the wound.

'We have to get you back.'

'Is it bad?'

'Put it this way, you ain't going to be as pretty as you were.' Raul realised that Wayland didn't have his basket. 'The falcons. Did you lose them?'

Wayland swung his head.

'Don't tell me the nest was empty.'

Wayland stuck up three frozen fingers. 'Too young. Not ready.' His bones seemed to melt and he sagged into Raul's arms.

Glum was coiling up the ropes. He examined the one that had broken and frowned.

'You were right about that line being weak,' said Raul.

Glum clicked his tongue. 'No, it was the new one that broke.'

Syth burst into tears when they brought Wayland down. The Greenlanders placed him in a tent and crowded at the entrance. Syth shooed everyone away except Raul. She heated water and bathed Wayland's face. The wound began to bleed again.

'Bring me a mirror.'

Syth returned with a disc of polished bronze. Wayland held it up and examined his face. The falcon's hind talon had torn a gaping slash across the middle of his forehead. He felt for the bag that held his falconry furniture and fumbled out a bone needle and a thread he used to seel the eyes of newly caught hawks.

'You going to stitch it?' said Raul.

'It won't mend cleanly by itself.' Hands shaking, he tried to thread the needle. He gave up and passed the implements to Syth.

She passed the thread through the eye and gave it to him, then squatted back biting the tip of her forefinger. He tried to hand the needle back. 'You do it. It's not difficult. I stitched up the dog when he was young and got too close to a stag I'd wounded.'

'I can't.'

'You want me to have a go?' Raul said.

Wayland closed his eyes. He opened them and held out his hand. 'Give it to me. You hold the mirror.'

Wayland positioned himself and brought the point of the needle to one end of the gash. The flesh was swollen and discoloured and it was hard to manipulate the needle accurately. It took several attempts just to position the point. He pushed the needle through the lower lip of the wound. He flinched from the pain and ended up with a misaligned stitch. Blood ran into his eyes. Syth swabbed him with a cloth.

'It's no good. I can't see properly.' He held out the needle to Syth. 'Please,' he said. He lay back. 'Raul, hold my head.'

Syth's face leaned close and he shut his eyes. The first few stitches were excruciating, but then he seemed to float away from his body and though he could still feel each puncture, the pain seemed to be being inflicted on someone else.

He drifted back to find Syth gazing down on him. He brought up his hand and brushed at his brow. 'All done?'

'Yes. You were very brave.'

'Show me.'

She held the mirror. His forehead resembled a bulging thundercloud but the wound was stitched as neatly as a hem.

'I knew you'd do a good job.'

She was trying not to cry. 'You'd better have something to eat.'

He rolled his head. The thought of food made him want to throw up.

'Sleep then.' She began to withdraw.

He spoke without knowing what he was going to say. 'Syth, I love you.'

She stopped. 'Like a sister?'

'Like a woman.'

She slid down beside him and planted soft kisses on his cheeks.

He held her, his head cradled against her shoulder. 'What will we do?'

'Oh, Wayland, you say the silliest things. We'll do what all lovers do.' She laid a finger to his lips. 'When you're ready.'

XXIV

He was back on his feet next day and the following morning he resumed the search for occupied eyries. In the days that followed, he explored the fjords on either side of Red Cape and found another four nests. None of them presented such a formidable challenge as the first one. He climbed to two of them from below and let Glum rope himself down to the others. All the eyases were still too young to take. Wayland explained that falcons removed from the nest before they were fully fledged never grew out of their rude infantile habits. The best time to catch them up was when they were hard-penned and ready to make their first flight. Even then, some of them grew crabby and grasping, screaming for food all day long and mantling on the fist in a graceless fashion. That's why he preferred passage falcons trapped in their first autumn, when the winds of freedom had refined their immaturity. For sheer perfection of style, though, nothing could beat a haggard.

One of these paragons flew into his life as he was returning from the last eyrie. They were in the ship's boat, rowing down the fjord north of Red Cape. Ahead of them the westering sun hung in a flattened orb, casting long shadows across a glacial amphitheatre on the starboard shore. Hardly a ripple on the ice-littered water. The peace was broken by a covey of ptarmigan that sprayed past the boat, fleeing for the opposite shore. When Wayland sighted the gyrfalcon she was a hundred yards behind the grouse, driving forward with wingstrokes that seemed almost leisurely until she passed in a white flash and he saw that she'd already cut the ptarmigans' lead by half. She overtook them before they'd reached mid-fjord and plucked one of them out of the air. Her sails spread and she circled back with her prey tucked under her tail.

Wayland saw her take stand on a rocky tor on the seaward side of the glacier.

'Put me ashore.'

Raul groaned. 'Give it a miss. We've had a hard day and I'm hungry.'

'I won't be long.'

He landed and advanced until he had the falcon in clear view. She plucked and ate her kill and then she relaxed her feathers and dozed. He walked closer. She'd drawn one foot up and showed no fear at his approach. She'd probably never encountered a man before. He stopped when he could see the crisp outlines of her flight feathers. Her head and breast were immaculate and the few black markings on her wings only emphasised her whiteness. He moved closer and she lowered her foot and stood poised for flight with her wings held up like shields. Another step and she sprang off the rock and beat away across the snout of the glacier.

He climbed her lookout. Bones from many kills lay on the rock, together with castings. He picked up one of the falcon's moulted primaries. The heavy black markings on it told him that she was a year old, not yet grown so wild as to be irreclaimable. He looked across the fjord. Terns hovered above the milky green meltwater trailing from the glacier. Ducks in chevrons winged down the channel. The cairn was both a lookout and a feeding station.

He tramped back to his companions and produced the feather. 'I'm going to trap her.'

'This is not a good place,' said Glum. 'There is nowhere safe to camp. Now it is quiet, but sometimes storms rush down the glacier with a force you cannot imagine.'

Wayland looked about. On the inland side of the glacier a waterfall wreathed in rainbows dropped to a sunny shelf.

'It's more sheltered over there. Let's take a look.'

Raul grumbled at the diversion. He and Wayland had spent too long together and were beginning to grate on each other.

Syth and Glum followed Wayland onto the rocky beach. Warmth reflected back from the cliff. Fireweed, angelica and yellow poppies grew in the gravel, and the hollows between the boulders were thick with bilberry and dwarf willows. The waterfall dropped in drifting veils to a pool that spilled away in a bubbling stream. Under the cliff to one side of the cascade was a cave.

'I'll camp here.'

Glum voiced another objection. 'If you bait a net with a bird, the foxes will get it.'

A fox in its ragged summer coat was skulking not far away as he spoke. Wayland had brought a cage containing six pigeons that he'd intended to use for hawk food. His gaze roamed over the foreshore and settled on a moraine hard by the glacier. 'I'm not going to use a net.'

A short search revealed a natural hide formed by a slabby erratic that had come to rest across boulders, creating a den two feet high and long enough to accommodate him. He wriggled in feet first to check that he had a good view of the falcon's lookout.

'You'll freeze in there,' said Syth.

'Waste of time,' Raul complained. 'You've already found all the falcons we need.'

Wayland dragged himself out. 'None of the eyases will be ready to take for another week. We'll give it three days.'

They offloaded equipment and provisions, then they dragged the boat ashore and tied it down with ropes anchored to rocks. They pitched two tents in the cave and ate outside while the sun slid south of Red Cape and the cliffs darkened to maroon.

Wayland was too keyed up to sleep. Before the shadows had lifted from the falcon's lookout he shook Glum awake. Raul and Syth were still sleeping. The young Greenlander knuckled his eyes and stepped out of the shelter. Iron-grey clouds hid the top of the escarpment. A raw wind blowing straight down the glacier raised welts on the surface of the fjord.

'This is not a day to catch falcons.'

'Bad weather makes hawks keen,' Wayland said. 'She might come as soon as I show the bait.'

The wind buffeted them as they made their way to the hide. Wayland slithered into it cocooned in his sleeping bag and holding a live pigeon. He pulled a plaited willow screen across the entrance. 'Keep out of sight,' he told Glum. 'Come back for me when the sun reaches the west.'

'The sun will not show itself today. You will be stiff as stone by then.'

Glum was right. Wayland had hardly settled in the hide when the cold stored in the ground began to soak into his body. Sensation ebbed from the hand holding the pigeon. He pulled it inside and waited for the falcon to appear. The lookout remained empty and the sky darkened and the wind strengthened. By noon Wayland knew there was no chance of trapping the falcon. He was about to struggle out when a booming roar made his hair stand on end. A blast of freezing air came roaring down the glacier and surged past his hideout with a force strong enough to suck the breath out of his lungs. Sliding forwards, he saw that the surface of the fjord had been flattened into a mantle of flying spume. He grew alarmed. If waves couldn't stand up to such a tempest, no man could keep his feet in it. Then it began to snow and Wayland grew really frightened. The blizzard tore past in a white torrent. Trapped, cold to the bone, he waited. Surely a storm of such ferocity couldn't last long.

It lasted all day. He was sinking into the delusional sensation of warmth when the dog thrust its muzzle into his hide. Glum's muffled face appeared, his eyebrows caked with snow. 'You must come now!'

The pigeon had perished. Wayland was so stiff that Glum had to drag him out. The boy had roped himself to the dog and Wayland did the same. They crawled blind through the shrieking whiteout. Only the dog's instinct brought them safe to the cave. Raul dragged them inside. Syth ran forward.

'The dog knew you were in danger and began to howl.'

'She made me follow it,' Glum panted. 'If I hadn't, she would have gone herself.' A fire burned outside the tent. Glum held out his hands to it. 'Crazy,' he said. 'Crazy!'

Wayland's jaw juddered. He reached towards the embers. Syth grabbed his hands and her eyes widened in alarm.

'They're blocks of ice.'

She pulled him into the tent and lifted up her layers of woollens and placed his hands on her bare stomach and then pressed her back against him. He lay against her, the snow still streaking past his inner eye. Glum and Raul squeezed up on his other side and they huddled together like a litter of animals while the wind yowled with the fury of a monster cheated of its prey.

The storm blew itself out with a hushed roar. Wayland woke to an eerie silence. Under his right hand he felt something soft and comforting and he realised he was cupping Syth's breast. He shifted Glum's arm off his back, sat up and rubbed the sleep from his eyes. A warm light filtered through the weave of the tent. He went out into a golden midnight. More than a foot of snow blanketed the shore. Across the glacier the falcon sat on her pedestal like a carved image.

Glum crawled out and joined him. 'Now it is time to leave.'

'You and Raul go,' Wayland said. 'Return in three days. I'll have caught the falcon by then.'

Glum left with misgivings, but Raul was happy to be getting back to the rough and ready company of the Greenlanders. Wayland and Syth watched them row away through the bergs. She put her arm around his waist and smiled up at him. For the first time since they'd met, they were alone together. When he turned, the falcon was still footed on her perch and he realised that she might be sharp-set after her storm-imposed fast.

'Come to the hide with me,' he told Syth. 'If the falcon sees me enter alone, she'll know it's a trap.'

On the walk to the shelter Wayland spotted four or five foxes. They were a real pest.

He inserted himself into the chamber and looked up at Syth. 'Don't wander too far from the cave.' He cradled the dog's jaw. 'Keep good care of her.'

Syth retreated. The falcon sat with her head sunk into her shoulders. He agitated his left hand to make the pigeon flutter. The falcon paid no attention. A fox trotted past with a lemming in its jaws and stopped to stare at the pigeon. Wayland hissed and it bounded away. Despite the extra fleeces he'd brought, he grew torpid with cold. Sunlight glaring off the glacier made his forehead throb.

His attention wandered. He was daydreaming about Syth's breasts and her pliant waist when a spot floated across his vision. He blinked to dislodge it. The spot grew larger and he realised it was the falcon, gliding towards him on half-closed wings. Her velocity was deceptive. From fifty yards away he could hear the air whining through her pinions. Fifteen yards from the hide she feathered her wings, rowed back and landed on the snow. She was nervous. She kept staring at the pigeon and then glancing away. She'd never seen one before and couldn't understand why it didn't fly. At last she decided it was prey and ran towards it at a bandy-legged trot. She stopped again and now she was so close that Wayland could see the scales on her crocus yellow feet. He was easing the mitt off his right hand with his teeth when she bobbed her head at something behind the trap. She bobbed again and flung herself into the air with a harsh cry. Her wingtips whisked the snow and she was gone. Wayland groaned and sank his head on to his forearm. He was sure that the falcon hadn't seen him. A fox must have spooked her.

Rock clunked on rock. Wayland's neck prickled. Foxes were too light of foot to make a noise as loud as that. Syth must have grown worried and come to make sure he was all right. He forced back his irritation and waited for her to declare herself.

No call and no footfalls. Some instinct honed during his years living wild warned him not to make a sound. He waited. A sharp report made him jump. Only the glacier fracturing. The silence stretched. He lay listening with his mouth open and his eyes cocked upwards. The glacier groaned. The ice was always contracting and expanding, producing unsettling noises. The knocking sound he'd heard was probably just a stone released from the melting snow. But why had the falcon cried out in alarm? Lying in his cold pit, he remembered Orm's campfire tales of polar giants with bodies of stone and ice patched with the flayed skins of humans.

Something snorted. Wayland's scalp crawled. He listened unbreathing, his throat tight. The pigeon was terrified and lay splayed on the snow as if dead. He snatched it inside and felt inside his sleeping bag for his knife. His belt had twisted beneath him and he couldn't locate the sheath. He heaved himself up and ran his hand around his waist until his fingers contacted the knife. Before he could draw it, he heard snow creak. He choked back a gasp as a shadow fell across the entrance.

He brought the knife up. His bow lay beside him, useless. Another snuffle from outside – the sound of a predator homing in on prey. He knew what it was, had known almost from the start without daring to acknowledge it.

Two giant white legs dropped across the entrance, almost blocking out the light. The bear was on top of the hide. Two more legs appeared as it climbed down. The bear turned to face the hide. He could see only its huge shaggy legs clothed with yellowish fur that looked translucent against the sun. Its paws were as wide as trenchers and armed with black claws as long and thick as his thumbs.

Its head appeared, weaving from side to side. Shock made Wayland jerk back and crack his skull against the roof. The bear rammed its head into the entrance and blew a gust of foul fishy breath into his face. It snarled, exposing yellow fangs and black gums. He'd crammed himself back in his shelter and the bear's jaws were less than a foot from his face. It shoved forward, gaining another few inches. He gave a throat-lacerating scream and the bear grunted and pulled its head out.

He lay gasping. Moments later it was back, feeling with one paw. Claws scraped across rock and hooked into the top of his sleeping bag. It began to pull the bag out with him inside it. He braced against the walls. The bear increased its pressure and the bag ripped open. Eider down floated out into the sunlight. The bear reached in again.

'Here!' Wayland shouted, throwing the pigeon forward.

A pathetic flutter, a strike too fast to see, and the pigeon had gone. Wayland heard its bones being crunched like eggshells. He knew he had very little time before the bear resumed its attack and he used it to struggle out of his sleeping bag. He drew his knees up almost to his chin and struggled back into a foetal position. The paw reached in again. Cramped against the back of the hide, Wayland watched the armoured mitt feel this way and that. It took all of his strength to maintain his contorted posture and he knew that eventually he'd have to relax his limbs and then the bear would have him.

He raised his knife, waited for the paw to complete a sweep, and drove the blade into the meat of the paw. The bear squealed and pulled its paw away before Wayland could withdraw the knife. It spun out of his grasp and bounced into the snow beyond the entrance.

A long silence. Had the bear gone? The knife lay just out of reach. To retrieve it he'd have to expose his head and shoulders. He remembered how fast the bear had struck at the pigeon. Wait a little longer. His joints burned. Soon he wouldn't be able to move. He straightened out his legs with his hands and hissed with the pain of returning circulation. He flexed his knees. Still no sign of the bear. He'd given it a sore thrust. It must have gone. He eyed the blade lying on the snow. If the bear had turned tail, he didn't need the weapon, but unarmed he felt so defenceless.

The bear had gone. He was sure of it. Slowly he slid forward. He was about to extend his hand when he heard a crunching sound directly above. He shrank back and rolled on his side and looked up. The bear was on the roof scraping away the snow. Its claws gouged across rock and he knew that it was trying to dig him out. Impossible, he told himself. The roof was a one-foot-thick slab more than seven feet long, welded to its foundations by ice.

He remembered what Orm had said about bears flipping seals over their shoulders as if they were herrings. Something else Orm had told him. Sometimes a white bear would overturn a boulder the size of a hut just to get at a nest of mice. Wayland moaned with dread.

A paw groped down and hooked under the lip of the roof. It heaved up and with that single move the ice cracked along the foundations.

The bear strained again and the roof lifted and slid a few inches sideways before crashing back. Wayland could see part of the bear's flank through the gap. One more effort and he'd be exposed like some helpless larva. He grasped his bow and howled with cries such as men must have given before they'd discovered speech. The roof swung further askew and he felt a draught on his lower legs and knew they were exposed. The bear didn't have to pull him out. It would start eating him alive from his feet up. He didn't stop to think. Still screaming, he scurried out on his elbows.

He stumbled to his feet, lost his balance and skittered over the snow on knuckles and toes. He jumped up and spun, jabbing with his bow. The bear was only feet away, staring in the opposite direction, swinging its head in slow puzzlement. It was the dog. It came tearing over the broken ground giving tongue with a frantic two-tone baying. Wayland backed away and the bear turned and peered at him. He froze. For a long moment it studied him, then it swung its head back to face the dog. Wayland retreated and fumbled an arrow from his quiver. He dropped it.

The dog skidded to a stop in front of the bear. Still barking, it made furious rushes and retreats. The bear roared and galloped towards it. The dog danced off, playing the decoy. Wayland had drawn another arrow and was trying to string it when he saw Syth running towards him.

'Get back!'

She paid no attention.

The dog darted behind the bear and nipped one of its hams. The bear whirled and lashed out and the dog sprang to one side with a hair's-breadth to spare. The bear reared up on its hind legs and only when Wayland saw it towering over his giant dog did he appreciate its awesome size. The dog dodged and feinted and the bear dropped back on to all fours and loped towards Syth.

'Run!' Wayland shouted. He drew his bow and aimed, aware that the chances of killing the bear with a single arrow were remote.

The dog sprinted to cut off the bear and crouched with its head between its elbows. Syth stood only a few yards behind it. She reached down and scooped up a handful of snow and threw it. The pathetic missile didn't even carry as far as the dog.

Wayland sighted behind the bear's shoulder and released. In the same moment the bear veered off and the arrow skimmed its rump. The bear made for the fjord at a hump-backed lope, harassed all the way by the dog. It reached the shoreline and plunged in, cutting a V in the water. Wayland propped himself on his grounded bow and slid to his haunches. After a while he raised his eyes. Syth was still standing where he'd last seen her. He had to use his bow as a staff to climb to his feet. Very slowly he and Syth moved towards each other, as if each doubted the existence of the other.

'Thank God you came,' Wayland said. 'Another moment ...' He filled his lungs and stared blindly at the sky.

'It wasn't me. I was looking for firewood and the dog was with me, then its fur stood up and it rushed off.'

Wayland bent over, wheezing.

Syth put her arms around him. 'Don't cry. The bear's gone now.'

Wayland waved one arm and went on making strange mewing sounds. 'I'm not crying.'

Syth crouched so that she could see his face. 'What's so funny?'

'You,' he sobbed. 'Throwing snowballs at the bear.'

XXV

Wayland lay outside the cave watching the waterfall descending in slow veils.

'I'm going to give it one more try.'

Syth jumped up. 'You mustn't. The bear will come again.'

Wayland spread his hands. 'The falcon was this close.'

She grasped his wrists. 'So was the bear. What if it kills you?'

'It won't. I'll take an axe and spear.'

She released him and walked away, hands clutched across her shoulders. 'If you loved me, you wouldn't risk your life for a falcon.' She stamped her foot and whirled. 'You don't need to catch it. You've already found more falcons than you need.'

'This one is special.'

'More special than me?'

Wayland knew that logic wouldn't win this argument. He stood and took hold of Syth. 'The falcons aren't the most important thing. They're not even mine. When they're gone, I'll still have you. You'll still have me.'

Syth looked at him. 'For how long?'

Wayland experienced the hollow sensation he'd felt before climbing down to the first eyrie.

'For ever.'

She looked towards the hide and shivered. 'Wayland, if you don't catch the falcon today, will you promise to give it up?'

'I promise.'

They used levers to reconstruct the hide. Wayland hadn't seen the falcon since the bear put it to flight. He took a last look at the lookout rock and wriggled into the shelter.

'What if the bear comes back?' Syth said.

'It won't.'

Syth bobbed up and down. 'But what if it does?'

Wayland patted the axe.

'What about me? What if it creeps into the cave while I'm inside?'

'The dog will give you plenty of warning.' Wayland was more nervous than he sounded. 'Stay outside and keep watch. If I trap the falcon, I'll need your help.'

She looked down at him, her hands bunched at her throat, and then left him to settle into another cold watch. Axe and spear lay to hand and he kept touching them for reassurance. A pair of ravens alighted on the glacier, walked about with no apparent purpose and flew off again. A black-and-white bunting sang from a crevice a few feet from the trap. He looked at the empty sentinel post. The falcon probably had several vantage points and it might be days or weeks before she returned to this one. He poked fingertips into his eyes to keep from falling asleep.

He blinked. Between one moment and the next the falcon had taken stand on her lookout. She shifted position and Wayland's excitement died. He could see from her bulging crop that she'd already killed.

Now what? If he left the shelter she would see him and be suspicious of the place. He'd have to wait for the falcon to fly off or Syth to relieve him. The day stretched long and dreary before him until he realised that it didn't matter if he abandoned the hide now. He'd given

Syth his word that this would be his last attempt. That rankled. If she was frightened of the bear, she could go back to Red Cape with Glum. He was going to stay and catch the falcon no matter how long it took.

A fox placed its front legs on a boulder in front of the hide and stared at the pigeon. It began a wary stalk. Wayland hissed. The fox cocked its ears and resumed its approach. Wayland drew the pigeon into the hide. The fox was puzzled. It came on. Wayland reached for his spear. The fox broke into a stiff-legged trot. Wayland thrust out the spear and the fox flung itself into a reverse somersault and streaked away, looking back over its shoulder with such an aggrieved expression that Wayland laughed.

He stopped laughing and thrust the pigeon outside. The gyrfalcon was gliding towards him. Once again she alighted in the snow some yards from the bait and looked around before running towards it with the comical gait that reminded Wayland of Raul. A yard short she stopped again and made another survey. Her eyes fixed on the pigeon and she made another sally and stepped onto it with one foot. The situation was strange and her helpless victim didn't trigger her killer instinct. Wayland rolled his fist. Absent-mindedly the falcon bent and broke the pigeon's neck. She was still uneasy. Wayland saw her focus lift and lengthen and he tightened his grip on the pigeon just in time to prevent the falcon from carrying it off. She looked down in puzzlement, looked up, lowered her head again, looked up. Wayland had stopped breathing.

The falcon gave a flaccid rouse, tightened her grip on the pigeon and began plucking it. In her attempt to carry her prey, she'd dragged Wayland's left hand outside the shelter. If he tried to grab her with his free hand, she'd see it coming. He waited until she'd plumed the pigeon's breast and broken into the flesh, then he began to draw her towards him. She didn't seem to realise what strange forces were operating and went on eating. Wayland was worried about foxes. Even at this stage one of them could show up and frighten the falcon off. His right hand was poised at the entrance less than a foot from the falcon. He rolled his left hand, forcing her to adjust her stance so that she stood squarely on the pigeon.

Now!

He shot out his right hand and grasped her around both legs. She screamed and thrashed. Wayland held on and wormed out of his hideout. His main concern was to secure her before she injured herself. He hoisted the falcon over so that she lay spread-eagled and flapping on her back. A faint shout reached him from the direction of the cave.

The falcon stopped screaming and lay still and looked at him with wild black eyes. Her breast heaved at an alarming rate. He risked a glance over his shoulder and saw the dog with Syth following, jumping from boulder to boulder. The falcon convulsed and arched forward far enough to bite a wedge out of his knuckle.

The dog skidded into a prone position behind him. Before Syth reached him, the falcon took another bite of his hand.

'The stocking. In my belt.'

Syth threw herself down beside him and pulled out a woollen tube open at both ends. 'What should I do?'

'Pull it over her head.'

Syth eased the mouth of the stocking over the falcon's neck.

With his left hand, Wayland folded the falcon's right wing against her side. 'Do the same with the other wing. Gently.'

Between them they worked the stocking over her wing butts, and then it was easy. With Syth holding the falcon across its back, Wayland was able to pull the tube down her body, leaving only her head exposed. He tightened the drawstring around the top of the stocking and knotted it.

He rocked back from the trussed falcon and sucked his bleeding knuckles. Syth stretched out her arms and twirled. 'You caught her,' she shouted. 'You caught her.'

He carried the falcon back to the cave like a swaddled babe and laid her in the spare tent. He went through his bag of hawk's furniture and took out jesses, swivel and leash. He honed his knife on a whetstone. When he'd assembled the equipment, he lifted the falcon out of the tent and placed her upside down on a fleece.

'You'll have to hold her,' he told Syth. 'Watch her beak.'

Syth gripped the falcon around the shoulders. 'Are you going to stitch up her eyelids so that she can't see?'

'Not unless I have to.' It would be months before the falcons reached their destination and he was worried that prolonged blindness might harm them. Instead, he'd decided to transport them in wicker cages that could be blacked out with drapes.

He rolled up the stocking from the bottom to expose the falcon's legs. She shot out a foot and sank two talons into the ball of his thumb. He prised them out, licked the blood from his hand and examined the falcon's train. The webbing was ruffled and some of the shafts were bent, but he could straighten them by dipping them in hot water. He measured the thickness of the falcon's legs and cut slits in the jesses so that they would fit snugly. When he'd fitted them, he secured the free ends to a brass swivel and pulled a rawhide leash through the eye. He gloved his left hand and wrapped the leash around it.

'Ready?'

Syth loosened the drawstring and rolled the stocking over the falcon's head. It sprang up flapping and Wayland swung it onto his fist. The falcon sat hissing, her feathers puffed out, then bated. Wayland assisted her back onto his glove and carried her into her tent. He placed her on a stone block and tied the leash to a heavy granite spindle. She jumped off and plunged against her jesses. When she realised that she couldn't break free, she bounded back onto the block. For the first time Wayland had leisure to appreciate the marvel that was his to make or mar. She weighed twice as much as the largest peregrine he'd handled, and everything about her bespoke power. Face on, she was spotless, the thick down covering her chest and pannel as soft and white as drifted snow. Feathers like flags hung down each side of her pantalooned legs. Her large liquid eyes bored into his own as if to discern his intentions and it seemed to Wayland that fear was already giving way to curiosity. Like a courtier withdrawing from a royal presence, he backed out on his knees and closed the tent flaps.

He crawled off to bed after supper and was asleep the moment he laid his head down. When at last he surfaced, his body felt bruised and boneless. His first returning thought was of the falcon. From her tent came regular flicking sounds. She was preening. A good sign. He tiptoed towards the shelter, speaking softly so that his appearance wouldn't shock her too much, and cautiously opened the flaps. The falcon leaned back on her tail and hissed, but she didn't bate.

He closed the tent and went out into the warm day and stood blinking at the fjord. It was as calm as a millpond. Syth was washing clothes in the pool under the waterfall. She'd laid garments to dry over boulders. A fire made from a rare piece of driftwood smouldered close to the pool. In the centre of the ashes lay a clutch of large oval stones, and next to the fire stood a conical structure of woven willow covered with blankets. Wayland was still too dopey to take in these curiosities.

Sunshine lit Syth's smile. 'I thought you'd never wake up.'

Wayland knelt by the pool and dashed water into his face. 'We'd better pack up if we're to get back to the camp this evening.'

'It *is* evening.'

Wayland peered into the long rays of the sun. 'So it is. Glum should have returned by now.'

Syth dunked a pair of leggings into the pool. 'He came this morning with Raul. I sent them away again.' She turned to look at him. 'You were fast asleep and I didn't want to return to the camp just yet. Do you mind?'

He shook his head and sat down beside her. He, too, had no desire to return to the Greenlanders' camp. In the few weeks that they'd spent in the hunting grounds, the Greenlanders had turned their base into a butcher's shambles. They'd killed three walruses and taken from them only hides and tusks, leaving the carcasses to rot on the beach. Countless seals and foxes had been treated in the same prodigal fashion, and a fifteen-foot whale had been left drifting on the tide after its hunters had stripped its blubber and removed a few massive steaks for their larder. The only quarry they'd harvested whole were auks netted at their breeding ledges and preserved in barrels of fermented whey. The stink of putrefying flesh and the cloying smell from the cauldrons used to render blubber permeated the entire campsite.

Here the air was a tonic. 'I'm starving.'

Syth's face lit up. 'I caught a fish. Just you wait.'

Awareness of his own hunger made Wayland realise that the falcon might be keen. Two pigeons remained. He killed one, opened the falcon's quarters and sidled in. She shrank back, gaping defiance. Avoiding eye contact, he presented the pigeon. He didn't expect her to take it. When she didn't bate, he stole a look at her. She was still leaning back but she was sneaking glances at the pigeon. He began to count to ten. If she didn't accept the food by then, he'd leave it. On the count of seven she stretched out her head and grasped the pigeon in her beak. He hung onto it. She pulled at it and then, without hesitation, stepped onto his fist. She looked at him with that piercing falcon gaze. He stayed stock still and after a few moments she bent her head and clamped her beak around the pigeon's neck. He was so amazed that he glanced at her. She raised her head immediately, her eyes boring through his. As soon as he looked away, her attention returned to the food. She balanced on his fist as if it were a familiar perch and began plucking the pigeon.

Incredible. He'd once trained a falcon that had fed on the fist the same day it was captured and flown free after only eleven days, but even that prodigy hadn't possessed this haggard's composure. Amazement turned to concern. Perhaps her tameness was caused by starvation – a weakling hawk unable to provide for herself in the wild. She didn't look like an ailing falcon. Her crisp plumage, her bright and liquid eyes, her saffron yellow feet, the gracious way she ate – all a picture of health. Slowly he raised his hand. She flared up, the feathers on her nape standing out like a ruff. He felt her breast. Solid muscle, the keelbone hardly discernible. She nipped his finger as if to say, 'You're disturbing my meal.'

When she'd eaten most of the pigeon, he set her down on her block and left her to finish the carcass at leisure. He walked out shaking his head and grinning. If he hadn't trapped her in such a wild haunt, he would have sworn that she'd been manned before by a master falconer.

He went up the shore to relieve himself. On his way back he stopped. Syth was haloed by a rainbow near the pool, heaping embers against the rocks in the fire. He joined her.

'What are you doing?'

'You'll see.'

He frowned at the tent of withies. A lot of work had gone into it.

'It's a surprise,' Syth told him. 'Do you want to eat first?'

'You decide.'

'Eat after,' she said. She touched his face and examined his scar. 'How does it feel?'

He felt the wound with the back of his hand. 'Hot and itchy.'

'Part of it's swollen. I think the stitches should come out. Lend me your knife.'

She sat him down and snicked each suture in turn. Wayland tried not to flinch as she pulled them out.

She probed the infected part. 'This might hurt a bit. The flesh is so puffy that I can't see the stitches properly.'

She nicked his skin as she cut and pus squirted across her hand.

Wayland grimaced. 'Sorry.'

Syth was concentrating on her task. 'I had three brothers. The things I had to do for *them*. Stay still.' She wielded the knife a few more times and then rocked back. 'There. Do you want to have a look?'

Wayland examined his forehead in the mirror and made a rueful face. He was scarred for life, but without Syth's deft needlework the disfigurement would have been far worse.

'Come with me,' she said. 'Come on.'

She led him to the fire and pointed at the rock eggs. 'You have to carry them into there,' she said, indicating the wicker tent. 'Be careful. They're very hot.'

Being a man, he had to test for himself by placing his fingers on a stone. He snatched them away and blew on them. Syth rolled her eyes.

He wrapped his hands in a fleece and trotted the scorching stones into the shelter. Syth had constructed the frame around two flat boulders and she told him to pile the stones between them. To one side stood a pitcher of water.

When the rocks were in place, she pushed him out and pulled a blanket across the entrance. 'We mustn't let them grow cold.'

The dog looked on, cocking its head first to one side, then the other. Wayland returned its puzzled look and shrugged. 'Search me.'

Syth poked a hand out and dropped a tunic. Wayland darted a glance behind him. Out from the tent came a succession of garments, some of them discarded for the first time in weeks. Wayland ran a knuckle along his lips.

Syth stuck her flushed face out and blinked. 'Now you.'

'Now me what?'

Syth darted back inside. 'Take your clothes off.'

The dog seemed to grin at him. He stripped off his outermost tunic. 'All of them?'

'The lot.'

He dragged off his stinking clothes and stood with his hands crossed over his groin.

'What now?'

'Are you bare?'

Wayland looked around. 'Yes.'

298

'Then you can come in.'

He parted the drape and shuffled inside. The heat from the stones beat up at him. Syth sat naked on the boulder across the firestones.

'You sit there,' she said.

Wayland subsided on to the seat. He'd never seen a naked woman before – not completely naked. Unclothed, Syth's body was fuller than he'd imagined. Lust jostled with puzzlement. Syth's face was set in frowning concentration. He placed his hands across his lap.

She picked up the pitcher. 'I learned it from the women in Iceland,' she said. 'I hope it works.'

She poured water over the stones. They spluttered and hissed and Wayland snorted as a cloud of steam scalded his sinuses. Hot mist filled the enclosure. Sweat broke out on his body. Grubby runnels worked their way down his skin.

Her hand reached out of the fog holding a bone scraper. 'It's a way of cleaning. You clean me and I'll clean you. Like this.'

She ran the scraper down his arm and showed him the sludge that had collected on its edge. 'You're really dirty.'

He took the scraper from her and slid it across her shoulder. 'So are you.'

'I'll do you first.'

Slowly and thoroughly she removed the ingrained dirt that had accumulated on him during the journey. 'Stay still,' she ordered as she worked below his waist. 'You've got a nice body,' she said. 'Just right.'

He cleared his throat. 'So have you. You were such a skinny thing.'

She laughed merrily. 'Wayland, you certainly know how to make a woman swoon.'

He looked away, tongue-tied. 'I haven't ... I mean, you're the first ...'

She stopped laughing. 'I know.' She sat back. 'Finished.' She handed him the scraper and poured more water over the stones. 'Now me.'

She drifted into a smiling dream as he cleansed her. 'Turn round,' he said huskily.

His confidence grew and with it desire. He couldn't keep it down. She felt it and reached for him. 'Not yet. I've thought about this.' She gave him an appreciative squeeze and giggled. 'I know just the thing for that.'

She seized his hand and dragged him out of the tent. She ran laughing towards the pool. Wayland dug his heels in at the edge. She plunged in screaming, throwing up handfuls of icy water. Wayland thrashed in after her. The freezing water burned. He embraced her and they stood pressed together looking up through the falling spray.

'That's enough,' Syth said through chattering teeth. 'Back to the steam bath.'

The atmosphere inside the tent was soporific. Wayland and Syth studied each other without embarrassment. 'This might be the last time for ages that we'll see each other naked,' Syth said. 'I want to remember.'

Wayland reached for her. 'Syth.'

'Not yet. We have to jump into the water again.'

'Do we?'

'Yes.'

They plunged in and then they dried themselves and clothed themselves in clean garments. Only the sun's afterglow remained. Watching Syth comb out her hair, Wayland felt bewitched.

Her eyes widened. 'The fish!'

She'd caught a char weighing about three pounds. Wayland wrapped it in wild sorrel and buried it in the remains of the fire. They ate it sitting side by side, blankets over their shoulders, watching the slow pageant of icebergs. When the fish was gone, Syth produced a bowl containing perhaps twenty bilberries. 'That's all I could find. It's still too early in the season. You have them.'

'We'll share them.'

After they'd eaten, a gentle silence held them. Wayland had never felt so peaceful. He began to talk and Syth drew out of him all the poison of the past. She talked, too, telling him how her family had died one by one until only she remained to face the world. They pondered the trials that awaited them and pledged to face them together. Their conversation drifted to lighter topics, but everything they said was heartfelt and could never be unspoken.

Midnight came. Wayland drew Syth down beside him and they lay in each other's arms, each trying to guess the other's thoughts. Simultaneously they turned their heads and kissed. During their tender clinch a skein of geese flew overhead with the air singing through their wings, but Wayland never heard them. In her prison the falcon raised each leg in turn and bit at her tethers.

Syth drew away and looked at Wayland with cloudy eyes. 'What about the dog?'

He motioned with his head and the dog rose and shook itself and went away to the edge of the fjord. It lay down panting, briefly looked back at the camp and then raised its head to watch the returning sun.

XXVI

Midsummer passed and no report of *Shearwater* reached Iceland. Vallon kicked his heels and grew morose. Hero and Richard were glad when trade took them away from Ottarshall. Vallon was left with Garrick, who had the knack of knowing when to speak to the captain and when to keep out of his way. June gave way to July and Vallon's depression deepened. So long as he'd kept moving he'd been able to stay one step ahead of his demons. Now they came crowding in on him. Each day he rose late and spent hours staring across the blasted landscape. He grew careless of his appearance.

Rumours filtered in of a Norwegian ship wrecked on the Westman Isles. It wasn't until the second week of July that a ship arrived from Greenland carrying news of *Shearwater*'s safe passage and her departure for the northern hunting grounds. Vallon's spirits rose. Barring accidents or bad weather, the company should be back and ready to sail south by the beginning of August. With only two more weeks to get through, he shook himself out of his sloth. He resumed his English lessons and began a regime of exercise. It had been weeks since he'd practised his swordsmanship and his muscles had grown slack.

Garrick stuffed a sealskin with straw and hung it from a woolsack frame. Vallon shaped a wooden sword of the right weight and balance and by the end of a week he was attacking the dummy with four hundred strokes daily. Two hundred with each hand. Vallon's steel blade was lighter than most swords and he'd trained since childhood to be dextrous with either limb.

Children from a nearby farm sometimes came to watch. One morning when Vallon was thumping the target, the children squealed and ran off to await the passage of four riders trotting down the road towards Reykjavik. Their cries brought Gisla out. When she saw the party she exclaimed in delight and hobbled after the youngsters.

'What's all the excitement about?' Vallon asked Garrick.

'Not sure, sir. The old woman said something that sounded like "the princess".'

Vallon wiped his sweaty forehead on his sleeve and laughed. 'A princess? We mustn't miss this.'

He strolled over to the verge wearing only breeches and a shirt unlaced down his chest. The riders drew near. In front, stepping out smartly on a well-groomed grey, rode a statuesque woman in an embroidered white dress and a fur tippet. Her waist-length hair was the colour of garnets and framed a complexion as pale as chalk, as chilly as marble. A maid trotted behind her and in the rear rode two armed and well-turned-out chaperons.

The children fell silent and stood in a row with their eyes lowered while the procession clopped by. Gisla, thrilled to pieces, curtseyed for all she was worth.

Garrick dragged off his hat and bobbed. Enjoying the diversion, Vallon bent at the waist and swept one hand over the ground. The lady heading the procession turned smoky green eyes towards him and an expression bordering on revulsion crossed her face. She turned back to the front and flicked her reins. Her escorts pranced level. One of them had the same colouring as the lady and was clearly her brother. He didn't so much as glance at Vallon. The other sneered down his nose.

Vallon was amused by their arrogance. He raised his wooden sword. 'Good morning, gentlemen.'

Neither of them returned the courtesy. They rode on and Vallon heard a derisive laugh. The kids cheered and ran about. Gisla twined her fingers and raised her eyes as if she'd been vouchsafed a vision of the Heavenly Queen.

Garrick grinned at Vallon. 'Fine-looking woman.'

'Haughty,' said Vallon. He watched her tittuping away down the road. 'Ask the widow what makes them so high and mighty.'

Garrick made his report over supper. 'The lady's name is Caitlin Sigurdsdottir, but everybody calls her "the princess". On account of her beauty and pride. Caitlin's an Irish name. Her family were among the first to settle in Iceland. They trace their ancestry to a warrior called Aud who sailed in the first convoy from Norway.

'Anyway,' Garrick continued, 'it turned out that the Norwegians weren't the first Iceland settlers. A shipload of Irish monks and farmers had set up a colony a few years earlier. This man Aud fell in love with one of the Irish women, Caitlin, and she with him. He murdered her husband to make her his own but she died giving birth to their daughter. He called the girl Caitlin, and since then all the first-born daughters have carried that name.'

'What makes the family so grand?'

'Wealth and lineage. Being among the first settlers, they took the best land. They own one of the largest estates on the island.' Garrick pointed north-east. 'Their farm's about two days' ride from here. They've also earned a reputation for fierceness. They were party to a blood feud that ran for generations until Helgi – that's Caitlin's brother – killed the last surviving foeman.'

'A hundred sheep and a few murdered farmers doesn't make Caitlin a princess.'

Garrick smiled. 'You have to admit she carries it off. Every man of consequence has sought her hand and she's spurned them all. Now she's turned twenty-four and has run out of suitors, so she's contracted a marriage to a wealthy earl in Norway. The groom's a lot older than she is. She and her brother are visiting the coast to arrange their sea passage.'

'Tell me his name again.'

'Helgi. Called "the Fly" behind his back because he's so quick to bite. Quick to anger and slow to forget a slur. Very protective of his sister.' Garrick dropped his voice. 'It's rumoured that she rejects all suitors because he covets her himself.'

Vallon dismissed this slander. 'Do they know who we are?'

'Of course they do. You can't keep anything secret on Iceland.'

Vallon took to making solitary journeys into the hinterland. His excursions were a way of killing time, yet time was running out. August had arrived and the season was beginning to turn. If *Shearwater* hadn't returned by the end of the month, he would be faced with a hard decision: wait for the ship and risk missing the winds that would carry them south, or give up on *Shearwater* and arrange an alternative passage to Norway.

One of his journeys took him up the shore of a large lake and west past the site where the Icelanders held their annual parliament. Harvest time was here and families were at work in the home meadows, scything hay and hanging it on lines to dry. On a whim Vallon turned off the road onto a faint trail that climbed north to a saddle between ice-toothed mountains. From here he descended to a desert of black sand blistered with smoking cinder cones. All day he rode, borne along in a melancholy trance, not aiming for anywhere in particular. The desert gave way to moorland. In the gloaming he reached a river and made a fireless camp. After a meal of fish and bread he sat wrapped in blankets thinking of his wife dead and the children he'd never see again. It grew dark – the first truly dark night since he'd arrived in Iceland. He lay under a parchment moon with his saddle for a pillow, listening to the river, and towards midnight he slept.

When he awoke the sun was hidden behind clouds the colour of wet leather. His hobbled horse cropped the grass near by. He saddled up and forded the river. On the other side he gave the horse its head, knowing that eventually it would lead him to a farm. For mile after mile the country remained uninhabited. He was beginning to think he'd passed beyond the frontier of settlement when at last he climbed another watershed and sat looking across a wide green basin. The clouds parted and palings of sunlight illuminated a farmstead miles away on the other side. On he went, his route taking him towards a steaming caldera with slopes ribbed like a clam shell.

He tethered his horse at the base and climbed one of the lava gullies and looked over the rim.

He ducked back and lay with his fingers hooked into the ground. Imprinted on his eye was a vision of Caitlin, naked, wading into the lake on the other side of the crater. He couldn't shake the image loose. The heavy orbs of her breasts, the generous curves of her waist, the triangle beneath it. Tears of merriment squeezed into his eyes as he contrasted her luscious charms with the frigid figure who'd regarded him with such contempt.

Cautiously he raised his head again. The lake was a fantastic setting, paling from ultramarine at the centre to a delicate duck-egg blue in the shallows. Caitlin had waded in up to her breasts and stood with her arms outstretched, her dark red tresses floating all about her. A blue tattoo decorated one of her arms. Two young handmaidens, one blonde and one dark, stood behind her in demure attendance.

Watching the chaste scene, Vallon felt a flash of something like innocence, and then memory broke in and he tasted ashes. He slid down the slope and turned on his back with his eyes open to the sky.

He sat up, frowning. A faint vibration reached him through the ground. Horses. He grimaced as he realised the awkwardness of his situation. There was nowhere to hide. The riders were approaching from the other side of the crater and he could only stay put and pray that they didn't come round this side. The hoofbeats stopped. Voices carried. He heard a woman's laugh. There was a grinding sensation in his stomach. He knew that only Helgi would dare intrude on Caitlin at her bathing pond, and he could guess how the headstrong young Icelander would deal with anyone caught trespassing on his sister's privacy.

Vallon decided to sneak off while the bathers were engaged with their visitors. Feeling a complete fool, he crept over to his horse. He cast a furtive look over his shoulder. Still no one in sight. He was ashamed by how fast his heart was beating. He'd raised one foot into a stirrup when a shout told him that he'd been seen. A man stood pointing down from the rim of the crater.

Vallon leaned his forehead against his horse's neck. 'Damn!'

Around the crater galloped four men kicking up wedges of turf. They had their weapons drawn and Helgi rode standing in his stirrups. Vallon stood behind his own mount with his hand on his sword. The riders encircled him and he stepped away from his horse and spread his hands.

'Gentlemen, I rode without knowing my way and found myself in this lonely spot. Seeing the breath from the crater, I climbed up to satisfy my curiosity. I had no idea your sister and her companions were taking the waters. I offer my apologies.'

He used his limited English, trusting that his contrite smile and gestures would make his meaning clear.

Helgi spotted Vallon's tracks climbing to the rim. 'You've been spying on my sister.'

'I caught a glimpse of her by accident, but the water protected her modesty and I retreated immediately. No offence was committed either by eye or by thought.'

Helgi stared at the spot where Vallon had lain as if it would show evidence of his lust. 'Liar.'

His head turned as Caitlin and her companions ran towards them holding up their skirts. Caitlin saw Vallon and her mouth dropped. From shock to fury took only a moment. Hotspots blazed on her cheeks and she spat a stream of invective. Helgi said something that fanned her anger. She concluded her outburst by pulling a knife from her girdle and jabbing it at Vallon.

'Did you convey my apologies?' he asked.

Helgi rode forward and kicked him in the face. At least, that was his intention. Vallon swayed back and grabbed Helgi's ankle and pulled him off-balance so that his sword swung wide. Vallon sprang away and drew his own sword as the other Icelanders spurred in on him.

Helgi vaulted off his horse and threw out an arm. 'He's mine.'

Vallon backed away. 'It was an accident. I was lost. How could I have known that your sister was bathing?'

Caitlin launched into another harangue. Her wet hair hung in viperous coils. Venus transformed into a shrieking harpy.

Vallon addressed her for the first time. 'Why don't you shut up?'

For a moment she did. Vallon made one last attempt to negotiate. 'If my apology isn't sufficient, tell me how I can make amends.'

Helgi didn't understand and didn't want to understand. He jabbed with his sword. 'Fight!'

'Don't be a fool.'

'Fight! Or do you only play with wooden swords?'

Vallon squinted towards Caitlin. 'If you love your brother, I suggest you find another way to settle this squabble.'

She went into another ear-fraying rant. Vallon lost his temper.

'You stuck-up bitch! What makes you think I'd ride for two days across a wilderness on the off-chance that I'd snatch a glimpse of a woman with an arse as big as her pony's?'

'Fight!' Helgi shouted. His men took up the refrain, banging their shields. 'Fight! Fight!'

Vallon knew that he could kill Helgi with one hand tied behind his back. Whether he could kill all his followers was uncertain, but it didn't matter. He was an outlander in a country where men pursued feuds for generations and went to their deaths knowing that relatives would fight their cause beyond the grave. Somehow he had to appease Caitlin and repair Helgi's slighted honour.

'Listen—'

Helgi screamed and charged. Vallon parried with ease. Helgi's blade clashed against his sword and snapped off clean below the hilt. He goggled at the stub with such dismay that Vallon had to put all his mind to keeping a straight face. Bog iron worked by a smith more used to shoeing horses than forging weapons. He lowered his own weapon.

'You've made your point. My apology still stands. Now let it rest.'

Helgi stared at Caitlin and held up the remnant of his sword. She hiked her skirts to her knees and screamed at him. He glanced at Vallon and when he saw that his opponent wasn't about to kill him, he scampered towards one of his entourage and grabbed his sword.

Vallon pointed his own blade at Caitlin. 'So be it. Your brother's blood will be on your head.'

This time Helgi didn't charge in but skipped and feinted. Vallon tracked him, assessing his strengths and weaknesses. As a swordsman he was sorely wanting. For all his youth and agility, he wielded the weapon like it was a flail and signalled each stroke before he delivered it. Vallon played along, trading blow for blow, waiting for Helgi to tire and grow demoralised. When stalemate was reached, he'd deliver a few unnerving near misses and then offer to call it quits.

The problem was Caitlin. Every time her brother made another pointless lunge or wild sweep, she incited him to fiercer efforts. The fight would go all the way, Vallon realised, so why prolong it? He watched Helgi's eyes, the way his right knee bent, saw the haymaker coming, twisted away from it and then ran in and kicked Helgi's legs from under him. Before his companions had risen out of their saddles, Vallon had the point of his sword at his throat. He glanced at the Icelanders.

'Stay where you are.' He leaned down and plucked the sword from Helgi's grasp, tossed it away.

Helgi's eyes bulged. 'I'm not afraid to die.'

Vallon kicked him in the face and turned cold eyes towards Caitlin. Fists bunched to her mouth, she looked like a child who'd woken a monster. Vallon made his tone formal and pitched his voice as if addressing a much larger audience. 'I didn't seek this fight. By the terms laid down by your brother, I have to kill him. Only you can save him. Your brother issued his challenge on your behalf. Accept my apology and he'll have no more cause to take my life. Nor I his. We'll all stand even, and no word of what has passed will escape my lips.'

Caitlin's stare switched from one point to another.

Vallon swore under his breath. He drew back his sword with an exaggerated gesture. 'Accept my apology or your brother dies.'

One of Helgi's retainers said something. Caitlin brushed a hand across her breasts and panted. Surely the bitch wasn't going to sacrifice her brother to her wounded dignity.

Vallon had an inspiration. 'Princess.'

She stared at him.

He dropped to one knee and placed a hand over his heart. His face contorted with the effort of fabrication. 'My dear princess, I know how highly your reputation is esteemed and I apologise for the embarrassment I've caused.'

Helgi lay with one leg drawn up, his eyes swivelled towards his sister. Blood leaked from his nose. She had his life in her hands and he didn't want to die.

Vallon prodded Helgi's neck. 'Either she accepts my apology or you die. Last chance.'

Helgi spoke with his Adam's apple trembling against the sword. Caitlin looked at Vallon as if he were an evil wizard who'd defeated her brother by magic. She pointed at him, then at herself, and fluttered her hands in a far-off gesture.

'You're worried that I'll brag of having seen you naked. I swear I won't. Now, do you accept my apology? Yes or no?'

Her breast heaved. '*Ja*.'

Vallon saw relief flood into Helgi's eyes. He stood, made a curt bow, stepped back and sheathed his sword. In a silence brittle to breaking point, he walked towards his horse. Helgi's men blocked his way, ready with their swords.

'Kill him!'

Helgi had scuttled to his feet and was running to retrieve his own weapon. His men lunged forward. Vallon sprinted after Helgi, spitting with rage.

'Don't!'

The Icelanders stopped, weapons arrested at their highest point. Vallon heard Caitlin slither down the crater.

'Lower your swords. Let him go.'

'And have him boast how he bested me. Stand back.'

Caitlin seized Helgi's sword arm. 'No! I forbid it!'

He swung her aside. Vallon advanced on him. 'A coward and knave as well as a clumsy oaf. Do you really think that I couldn't kill you before your sheep-shagging friends reached me?'

Caitlin ran at him and pushed him away. 'Enough.'

Vallon had been roused to a pitch of violence that only blood could quell. He shoved past Caitlin, eyes fixed on Helgi. 'You want more? I'll give you more. You and your louts.' Helgi trotted backwards. Vallon's gaze swung back to Helgi's men. 'I'll take on the lot of you. What are you waiting for?'

A jarring collision as Caitlin threw herself against him. He seized her arm so tightly that she whimpered. He dragged her close. 'A bit late, isn't it?' he snarled. 'You could have stopped it before it started.'

She struggled in his grip. 'You're hurting me.'

The red rage of battle subsided. He released her.

'Please,' she sobbed. 'Just go.'

'And have your brother hound me across Iceland?'

'He won't. I promise.' Caitlin reached out and pressed a hand to Vallon's chest. 'Please.'

For a moment their gazes locked, pleading in Caitlin's eyes and some other expression that pierced Vallon to the quick. He removed her hand with care, swung on his heel, walked under the Icelanders' swords and mounted. He'd gone only a short distance when he stopped, looking back in a final fit of fury. 'As I said at the outset, I lost my path. I'd be grateful if you pointed me in the right direction.'

It was a long ride back and Vallon made it longer with several random diversions. Each time he reached a rise, he scouted for signs of pursuit. Of course it wasn't over. He'd humiliated Helgi in front of Caitlin and the memory would keep pricking at her brother's injured pride until his resentment boiled over. Vallon cursed the fluke that had led him to that particular wilderness lake. But as he jogged on, he had to acknowledge that his line of travel hadn't been entirely accidental. Garrick had told him where Caitlin lived and that's what must have steered his steps in that direction. What he didn't know was why. He felt no desire for

Caitlin. In fact, if she knew how cold his heart was towards women, her vanity would have been more aggrieved than her virtue.

Only a hint of light showed in the sky by the time he reached the hall. The house stood dark and empty. He waited in the yard trying to separate form from shadow. He didn't think Helgi would attack him on Ottar's property. For all his talk of family honour, the treacherous hothead would probably try to waylay him on a lonely backroad.

Vallon funnelled his hands. 'Garrick!'

No one at home. He rested his sword on his saddle and quieted his restive horse. Movement made his head swing. Someone coming across the meadow. He relaxed and dismounted. Only the old woman.

'Where's Garrick?'

It seemed that the Englishman had grown anxious over Vallon's long absence and gone to look for him. But it wasn't Garrick the woman wanted to talk about. Vallon caught the word 'Orkney'.

He took her frail arm. 'Speak more slowly.'

Piece by piece, Vallon assembled the news. A few survivors from the shipwreck on the Westman Isles had reached Reykjavik. Among them was a man who'd suffered at Vallon's hands and had voyaged to Iceland seeking retribution. The man had found lodgings at a farm near the coast.

Vallon clapped a hand to his forehead and groaned.

'Snorri!'

Vallon reined in hard, swung off his horse and marched towards the house. He kicked the door and banged on it with his sword.

'Open up! I know you're in there.'

He stepped back with his sword held ready.

'Who's there?'

'Vallon the Frank, from Ottarshall.'

A latch lifted and the door creaked inward. Beyond the threshold a farmer dressed in a nightshirt stood in a half crouch wielding an axe. Behind him children peered at Vallon like frightened mice.

'Where is he?'

The farmer's eyes rotated towards a byre on the far side of the yard.

Vallon strode towards it with his sword raised. He kicked open the door and followed the blade inside. A figure stooped on a bench lurched up with an agonised gasp and grabbed for the sword leaning against the wall. Vallon kicked it away and laid his blade against the man's neck.

'How fortune turns. Remember the night we met?'

Drogo clutched his ribs, trying not to double up. A blanket fell from his shoulders.

Vallon scooped Drogo's sword into the corner with his foot. 'I thought you'd gone warring against the Scots.'

Drogo straightened gingerly. 'They don't want to fight. It seems that they're prepared to make terms. King William gave me leave to hunt you.'

Sweat glazed his upper lip. All the spare flesh had wasted from his face. He wore borrowed clothes and his hair had grown long and hung greasy and uncombed.

Vallon withdrew his sword. 'I've committed no crimes. No!' he shouted as Drogo made to speak. 'Don't tell me about the Normans who lie dead by my hand. Corner a wolf and you'll get bitten. Every ill and injury was set in train by your hatred of Walter. That's what this is about. A feud born in the nursery.'

'You? Blameless?' Drogo's laugh collapsed into a tortured groan. 'I know the extent of your wickedness. You're a mercenary who slaughtered Christians in the service of infidels. A renegade who broke a treaty signed by his own lord. A cuckold and wife-murderer.'

Vallon nearly killed him there and then. He closed his eyes and breathed through his nose. 'Drogo, you didn't journey all this way to avenge the wrongs I might or might not have done to people you don't know who live in countries you've never even visited.'

'Everything I've learned about you confirms the justness of my quarrel.'

Vallon eyed him. He really was much reduced. 'You're in no state to quarrel with a cat.'

Feet pattered towards the byre. The farmer and two other men stopped outside the door, swaying from side to side and brandishing their weapons uncertainly.

'Go back to bed,' Vallon told them.

The farmer spoke to Drogo. The Norman made a helpless gesture and the Icelanders retreated muttering and shaking their heads. Vallon picked up a stool by one leg, set it down and seated himself.

'I heard about the shipwreck. Where are your men?'

311

A spasm ran along Drogo's jaw. He looked away. 'One of them drowned and the other two suffered broken limbs. They're too crippled to travel.'

Vallon leaned his hands on the pommel of his sword and regarded Drogo with a kind of wonderment. 'You're not the luckiest of men, are you?'

'When I've mended, we'll see who has the luck.'

'I should lop off your head right now and put an end to your pestering. There's no death penalty for manslaughter in Iceland. People rely on their kinsmen and followers to settle scores. You have neither. I still have my company.'

As Vallon said this, he realised that Helgi would soon find out about Drogo and his grudge. He could imagine how they'd stoke each other's enmity.

'How many of your gang are left?' Drogo muttered.

'All but the English youth killed in Northumberland.' Vallon frowned. 'You sailed from Orkney. Did you encounter Snorri, our shipmaster?'

'I thought he was here with you.'

Vallon clicked his tongue. 'Poor Snorri.' He was silent for a while. When he spoke again, his tone was almost conversational. 'Richard and Hero are away on trade. Wayland and Raul have sailed to Greenland in search of gyrfalcons. They've been gone two months and I begin to worry.'

'I'm surprised my weakling brother still lives.'

'Not such a weakling. He's grown in stature and confidence since escaping your tyranny. I've appointed him treasurer to the expedition and he's proved himself a shrewd handler of money.' Vallon leaned forward. 'Every man in my company is under my protection. I'll treat any attempt to harm them as an assault on my own person.'

Drogo shifted. 'You'll agree to a trial by combat once my ribs are mended.'

Vallon stood. He was dizzy from hunger and he still had the ride to his lodgings ahead of him. 'You won't be fit to fight by the time we leave. We're sailing as soon as *Shearwater* returns.'

'So you still intend to free Sir Walter.'

'Why not? The hard part's done.'

'What did Lady Margaret offer you in return?'

'Profits from trade.'

'There must have been more.'

Vallon set off towards the door. 'Whatever my reasons for completing the journey, they're more honourable than your reasons for stopping me.' He paused in the doorway. 'Do you need anything?'

Drogo winced. 'I'd die before accepting charity from you.'

'As you wish.'

XXVII

Hero and Richard finished their trade mission in Skalholt. There they bartered their remaining clay pots for half a dozen sacks of sulphur and bales of woollens. They dined that night with the bishop. Since it was a fast day they ate fermented shark and boiled seal, which counted for fish. The bishop asked his guests about their trading activities and told them that they could have struck much harder terms. Cooking vessels were in such short supply that even well-to-do households rented them, and the bishop had recently pronounced an anathema on a villain who'd used the baptismal font to make a stew.

The bishop was called Isleifur, son of Gissur the White, one of the first Icelandic chieftains to have been baptised. Isleifur confided that pagan practices hadn't been entirely eradicated in the remoter parts. In times of hunger parents still exposed infants to the elements and made blood sacrifices. Education was the dew that would help water the tender shoots of Christianity, he told Hero. To this end he'd founded a school where pupils were taught the Roman script. He himself had been educated in Germany and was deeply interested in Hero's medical studies and impressed by his facility in languages and knowledge of the classics.

They talked long into the night and next morning the bishop lent them two of his men to escort their pack train back to Reykjavik. Their journey took them through heathland ablaze with shades of russet and ochre. The pair hadn't covered many miles when they saw two horsemen riding towards them.

'It's Vallon and Garrick,' Richard said.

313

'The ship must have returned. What perfect timing.'

Richard's eyes were sharper than Hero's. 'No. It's bad news. I can see it from here.'

Vallon reined in. He didn't even greet them.

'*Shearwater?*' Hero said.

Vallon shook his head. 'Drogo's here.'

Hero almost fell off his horse. Richard's face drained.

Vallon's manner was distracted. 'He was on the ship that was wrecked in the south. He's not an immediate danger. He's broken his ribs and his surviving company are still on the Westman Isles.' Vallon nodded towards the armed escorts. 'Who are those men?'

'Servants of the bishop. He thought we should have protection on the road.'

'Why? Has anyone threatened you?'

Hero and Richard looked at each other. 'No, sir. Everyone has treated us with kindness. What's wrong?'

'I crossed swords with a chieftain's son.' Vallon looked back down the road. 'I was concerned for your safety.'

First thing most mornings, Hero and Richard rode to a headland over-looking the harbour and scanned the Atlantic for a ship sailing from the west. Days passed and the horizon remained empty. The nights grew longer and the air crisper, with frost at dawn. In the harbour three ships were being prepared for the voyage to Norway. One of them was the vessel that would carry Caitlin to her arranged marriage. Drogo had left the farm that had taken him in and that's all anyone knew. His appearance out of the blue had knocked the stuffing out of Richard.

Hero tried to reassure him. 'Drogo can't harm us once Helgi's left Iceland. It won't be long. The fleet is just waiting for a favourable wind.'

'Vallon's stupid if he believes Drogo isn't a threat. I don't under-stand why he didn't kill him when he had the chance.'

'Richard, you're talking about your own brother.'

'Do you think Drogo would spare me if he had me at his mercy? Or you? Any of us?'

'Your brother was helpless.'

'So was Vallon's wife.'

When they climbed to their lookout next morning they saw a fourth ship moored in the harbour. The convoy was complete and ready to sail. The morning following Hero woke to thick fog and a gale lashing from the north-east. For three days the storm howled around the house. When it eased the wind turned to the west, bottling up the convoy. Two days later a boy rode to the hall after dark with news that a Greenland ship had limped into harbour. Everyone threw on their clothes and rode pell-mell to the coast.

They found the skipper supervising the unloading of cargo from his battered vessel. Vallon pelted him with questions and received terse answers. They'd set sail from the Eastern Settlement more than two weeks ago. The storm had blown them far to the south-west. No, *Shearwater* hadn't returned to the settlement by the time they left. Yes, the ship could have started out since then. If it had, the storm would have carried it many leagues off course.

'They have a navigator.'

The captain regarded Vallon with eyes slitted by exhaustion. 'Your pilot's dead. He sickened during his stay at the settlement. One eye swelled up as though it would burst. He took to his bed and gave up his ghost inside a week. Without a pilot your men would find it hard to follow the correct course even in fair weather. If your men sailed through that storm, they don't stand a chance of reaching Iceland. You'd better look for them in Ireland.' He started towards one of the longshoremen. 'Hey. Careful with that.' He turned back to Vallon. 'I'm sorry about your ship, but I'm busy.'

It was a sober party that rode back to the farm for breakfast. Vallon ignored his food.

'What date is it?'

Richard kept the calendar.' By my reckoning, today's the twenty-second of August.'

'When did *Shearwater* leave for Greenland?'

'The last week of May.'

'Almost three months.' Vallon sucked in his cheeks and stared at the wall. 'We can't wait any longer. The sailing season will soon be over. Remember the ships stuck in harbour since last autumn.'

'We can't leave Iceland without Wayland and Raul,' Hero said.

'I gave them instructions to return no later than the first week of August.'

'The storm will have delayed them.'

'By a week at most. If they're not back by the end of the month, we have to assume that they're lost or dead.'

'What will we do?' Richard asked.

'How much money is left?'

'About fifty pounds.'

'More than enough to pay for our passage. We'll have to arrange it soon, though.'

'So that's it,' said Hero. 'Our quest is over.'

'Listen, I've ridden off to fight for kings who were dead or deposed before my orders reached me. I've fought in battles where neither side knew that their rulers had signed a peace treaty that same morning. If we can't keep track of the affairs of men, we can't expect to command the wind and weather.'

Vallon was wrong about finding a ship to take them to Norway. He and Garrick were gone for days, enquiring up and down the coast. When they returned, he sat in his place with such a grim expression that no one dared speak.

He ballooned his cheeks and slowly released the pressure. 'We're stuck. No one will take us. The only vessels sailing south are the four ships in harbour. And they'd have left days ago if this wind had relented.'

Hero felt his throat. 'The wind that thwarts them could be carrying our friends back.'

'They've had westerlies for a week. That sea captain was right. The storm either sank them or blew them so far south that they couldn't find their way to Iceland.'

Hero's head drooped.

Vallon drummed his fingers. 'I tried to purchase berths on the Norway convoy.'

Hero's head jerked up. 'With Helgi?'

'Not him. I sought out the other sailing masters. All of them peddled the same excuse. Every place taken. It's Helgi's doing. He intends to keep us here until he returns. He thinks his revenge will taste sweeter the longer it simmers.'

Vallon stood and leaned against the doorpost, looking out into a miserable rain. He drew his sword and made a lazy sweep.

'We still have a chance. Drogo has challenged me to combat.' Vallon turned his head. 'I forgot to tell you. Drogo's found shelter with Helgi.' He looked back into the rain. 'Helgi wants me dead, too. I'll oblige them both. I'll face them in combat – the two together if necessary.'

'You said that Drogo wasn't fit to fight.'

'He will be by the time we reach Norway. That's the challenge and that's the contract. We get a passage to Norway and in return I face Drogo in combat.'

Richard bolted up. 'Drogo won't honour it. Whatever terms he agrees, he'll break them.'

'Not if he's dead. Have more faith in me.'

'I have faith in Wayland and Raul,' said Hero. 'I know they'll come back.'

Vallon didn't seem to hear. His lips moved as if he were forming words in his mind. 'I'll couch my challenge tomorrow. In public so that neither dare refuse.' He gave an ugly laugh. 'Injured pride? Nobody has suffered more injury than I have. I'll teach them.' He slashed his sword into the doorpost. 'I'll teach them!'

'Wake up,' Hero whispered. 'It's getting light.'

Richard rolled away. 'What's the point?'

'We mustn't abandon hope.' Hero looked through the dim to where Vallon lay sleeping. 'I know what makes him despair. He lay entombed for months, resigned to a slow death. Although he escaped, the horror still preys on him. For Vallon, waiting is hell. But just because he's lost hope, that doesn't mean we have to do the same.'

'It's too late. Vallon will deliver his challenge today.'

'Then let's stand a last vigil.'

Richard buried his face in the pillow and rocked his head.

Hero stood looking down at him, then went out.

He was cinching his saddle when Richard stole into the stable. 'I'm sorry,' he mumbled. 'My hopes were crushed the day Drogo turned up.'

They rode towards the coast with their capes drawn across their faces. A following wind as fresh as this could have blown *Shearwater* back to Iceland in five days.

They reached their lookout and sat their horses, watching the rollers flooding in until their eyes watered. They retreated to the lee of a rock. Hero kept getting up to scan the sea.

317

'Vallon should never have let them go,' Richard said.

Hero slid down beside him. 'Do you think Drogo will accept his challenge?'

'I don't see how he can refuse. That's what scares me. The prospect of sailing to Norway with my brother.'

'We don't have to go. We could stay here. Vallon would understand. Without the falcons, the journey has lost its purpose.'

'What would we do?'

'The bishop will take us in. You heard him lament the shortage of Latinists. We could teach at his school.'

Richard blew into his hands. 'Spend the rest of our lives in Iceland?'

'Only until next summer. I don't want to leave until I've found out what's happened to Wayland and Raul.'

Richard fell quiet.

'What are you thinking about?' Hero asked.

'Staying here. Never tasting another apple or smelling another rose. Never being able to lie in the shade of a tree on a hot day. Dried fish morning, noon and night.'

Hero laughed. 'Our lives won't be that awful.' He stood and offered his hand. 'We'd better tell Vallon before he issues his challenge.'

Richard struggled up. 'Do you really think the bishop would take us in?'

'I know he will.'

They mounted and cast their eyes seaward one last time. Hero had already turned his horse when Richard stuck out a restraining arm.

'I saw something.'

Hero squinted into the wind.

'Something white,' said Richard.

Hero gave him a sharp look. Every part of the ocean was highlighted by white. Foam creaming on the waves. Fulmars gliding between the troughs. An island blanched by guano.

'It's gone,' Richard said. 'No, there it is again. It comes and goes.'

'Show me.'

Richard heeled his horse and leaned across. 'See the island? Look beyond its north shore. Almost at the horizon.'

Hero shielded one eye and squinted along the line indicated by Richard's hand. 'I don't see it.'

'There!'

Hero wiped his eyes with the hem of his cloak and peered again. It popped into focus. A shape as pale as a tooth. It vanished and then appeared again, rising and sinking in rhythm with the rollers.

'Are you sure it isn't waves breaking on a rock?'

'It wasn't there yesterday, or any other day we've stood here.'

Hero studied the speck and a tingling sensation crept over him. It was moving. 'You're right. It's a sail.'

'And heading from the right direction.'

Hero and Richard stared at each other as if they stood on the verge of a revelation.

Hero slapped Richard's horse. 'Fetch Vallon.'

'Wait until the ship reaches harbour. I don't want to miss them.'

'No. Quick. Before he makes his challenge.'

Richard wheeled his horse and galloped away. Hero clutched his cloak about him and watched the ship riding the combers. So small and frail. He looked behind him. He wanted Vallon to be here, not to shame him for his doubts, but to show him how hope could ride out the billows of fortune.

The ship was only about a mile from land when Hero heard a cry behind him. It was the rest of the company. 'We met on the road,' Richard shouted.

Vallon threw himself off his horse, strode to the edge of the cliff and leaned into the wind, his cloak flapping behind him. When he turned, his eyes were streaming. From the wind or emotion, Hero couldn't tell.

'It's *Shearwater*. Our friends have returned.'

Garrick and Richard crossed themselves. Vallon regarded Hero with a rueful expression. 'You were right,' he said. 'But so was I. I always discount miracles.'

Three riders appeared below them, spurring towards the harbour. *Shearwater* had drawn close enough for Hero to make out figures shortening sail for the final approach.

'Let's be there to welcome them,' Vallon said.

They rode down in a laughing and whooping chorus. They weren't the only ones heading for the harbour. It looked like half the county was converging on the haven. Vallon's company clattered onto the jetty. Their voices stilled as *Shearwater* entered harbour. The sail came down.

Richard jumped off the ground. 'There's Raul. How savage he looks.'

Hero waved. 'And Wayland. And Syth. She looks different. Oh, and the dog. They're all safe. Oh, thank God!'

Wayland lifted his hand in what looked like a salute. On it sat a large white bird.

Hero clutched Vallon. 'He's got the falcons.'

Syth hung smiling from Wayland's other arm.

Garrick chuckled. 'Manned the maid, too, by the look of it.'

Hero and Richard locked wrists and cavorted like lunatics. The Icelanders looked on with smiles, most happy, some poignant. Many of them had stood on this spot waiting for the return of loved ones, and some of them had returned to their homes alone.

Silence fell as *Shearwater* glided towards her mooring. Raul stood at the stem and hurled a line to Garrick. He leaped ashore and balanced for a moment as though to see which way the ground would move next. He looked very rough, his eyes blinking between raw lids.

'Ain't any of you going to greet us? You'd think we were ghosts.'

Vallon stepped forward. 'I'm not sure you are of this world. I'd given you up for dead. What the hell kept you?'

'Ha! There's a tale. But until there's time to tell it, all you need to know is that a gale blew us back to Greenland. Twice.'

'How's the ship? Is she sound?'

'Needs some attention. Nothing serious. Same goes for her crew.'

'We'll pamper you.'

The dog bounded off and rolled on the earth. Wayland handed Syth down and stepped after her. They looked altered. Hero felt almost shy in their presence.

Vallon hugged them. 'So there really are white falcons as big as eagles. How many did you capture?'

'I brought eight. I could have taken more.'

'That ain't all we're carrying,' said Raul. 'We got seal and walrus skins. Ivory and whale gristle. And something you ain't ever seen in your life.'

Last off the ship came the two monks, still shocked by their ordeal. 'Only our prayers brought us back safe,' Saxo confided. 'We haven't ceased praying since we left Greenland.'

'We're grateful to you,' Vallon said. 'You must conduct a service of thanksgiving. After that ... ' He swung round to face the Icelanders. 'A feast to celebrate the return of the wanderers. Everybody's welcome. Garrick, spread the word.'

Hero grinned at the crowd and then his grin froze. Bunched behind the gathering, Drogo and Helgi sat their horses with stone-cold expressions.

Hero felt for Vallon's arm. 'Is that wise? From what I've heard, in Iceland more people are killed at parties than die in war.'

Vallon smiled thinly at his enemies. 'You'd better invite the bishop.'

Raul fell into his pit and snored for as long as it took the sun to circle the earth. Wayland woke every few hours to feed the young falcons. Hero watched him at his task. He kept all except the white adult cooped in darkened wicker cages. The haggard perched bareheaded on a block by his bed and showed little fear of man or beast. On one occasion when the dog strayed too close, she raked its flanks with her talons and sent it scooting off like a scalded pup.

Vallon and Garrick had stayed at the harbour to guard *Shearwater*. They hired a gang of shipwrights to patch her for the next voyage. High pressure had moved in, bringing limpid blue skies. Now it was the lack of wind that delayed the convoy's departure.

The company held their homecoming feast in a field by the harbour. Hero and Richard had to keep revising the scale of the commissariat as it became clear that everyone who lived within two days' ride intended to join the festivities. The bishop accepted an invitation and sent a request that the company take the two German monks back with them to Norway. The first guests turned up in the afternoon and they were still dribbling in after sunset. Many of them had brought tents and a touching number pressed contributions on their hosts. Some brought their own wood for the cooking fire.

A dozen sheep were butchered and relays of volunteers turned the mutton over a driftwood hearth the length of a room. Another great pile of wood had been built solely to provide light and cheer. In the purpling dusk the bishop called for silence and delivered a short homily, followed by prayers for the travellers who would soon be braving the ocean's wrath. His words rang out over the bowed heads of the congregation. When he'd made the sign of the cross and sat

down, Raul lit a brand from the hearth and set the torch to the bonfire. A cheer went up and the feast commenced.

Platters of mutton were borne to the bishop and the other honoured
guests. The orderly ferrying of meat gave way to a free-for-all, men
hacking off portions ad-lib. People Hero had never seen before pressed
drinks on him. Signs of drunkenness became apparent. Somewhere on
the fringes of the feast a fight broke out. Hero looked anxiously at the
bishop, but his lordship turned a blind eye and ordered a second
helping.

Chains of sparks flew up from the bonfire. Hero looked up to
where the sparks expired and contentment welled up in him. He
looked around, wanting to share his happiness.

Syth was passing around a narwhal tusk. 'It's proof against poisons
and epilepsy and pestilence and, oh, every ill known to man.'

Wayland told a riddle of his own making.

I flew the skies, I sailed the sea,
I kept my master warm and dry.
One day he left me, went north by moonlight.
A fellow picked me up, took a knife to me and stripped me
    almost naked.
He plunged me into a black well.
Only when he took me out still weeping could I tell my story.

'I hope it's not obscene,' the bishop said.

Wayland smiled and shook his head.

Richard stared upwards in a seizure of concentration. 'I know the
answer. Don't say anything.' He clapped his hands. 'A goose quill!'

Hero watched Raul dancing with a buxom widow, romping around
her with the clumsy formality of a trained bear. Behind them a group
of horsemen wafted out of the dark. Six riders with faces bloodied by
the flames advanced stirrup to stirrup and halted on the far side of the
fire.

Vallon had already risen. 'They won't make strife in the bishop's
presence.'

Vallon had told Hero how enfeebled Drogo was, but he'd cropped
his hair and filled out and looked much as Hero remembered him.
Beside him was a handsome young man who could only be Helgi.

322

Vallon had brushed aside Hero's questions about the cause of the dispute, but Garrick had told him it must have involved Helgi's sister. Many of the other guests had noticed the arrival of the riders and were drawing in to see what it meant.

'The invitation stipulated no weapons,' said Vallon. 'I won't ask you to join us.'

The men remained in their saddles. 'We're sailing first thing tomorrow,' Drogo said. 'We'll be picking up my men before going on to Norway.'

'Looks like you've had a wasted journey.'

'There's a long way to go before it ends. I'll have you by the heels yet.'

Their stares bored into each other, then Drogo wrenched his horse around and the party retreated into the darkness. Vallon clapped his hands. 'On with the celebrations.'

Day was beginning to crack open when the convoy cast off and rowed out of harbour, the ships' wakes scribing the calm surface. A mile from shore the convoy caught a breeze and slowly bore south.

Vallon breathed out. 'That's the last we'll see of them.'

'Drogo will be waiting for us in Norway,' Hero said.

'Let him wait. We'll be stopping only long enough to drop off the monks.'

Hero watched the ships grow small.

Vallon clapped him on the shoulder. 'Forget him. We have work to do.'

Preparations for their voyage took three days. Wayland recruited a gang of children to trap birds for the falcons. The company would be taking the horses and they loaded enough fodder and water for a voyage that might take two weeks. They repaired the sail and rigging, recaulked the hull, fitted the rudder with new lashings of walrus hide.

It was after midnight when Raul told Vallon that everything was shipshape.

Vallon looked at the whorls of stars. 'In that case, let's be off. Hero, fetch the monks. Raul, get the horses on board.'

At the time of night when most people sleep deepest, *Shearwater* crept out of harbour. Only the harbourmaster was there to see them cross the bar. He held a burning torch. 'Come back soon,' he called.

'We will,' Hero shouted.

He knew that he'd never return to Iceland except in thought and memory, but memory went deep and thought cut across space. He watched the flame on the shore recede until it was no more than a mote, then he turned to face the starry universe with a flutter of excitement mingled with dread.

The White Sea and Rus

XXVIII

They rounded the Reykjanes peninsula next evening and set course south-east. During the night Hero took a sighting on the Pole Star to fix their latitude. Next morning dawned misty, the sun floating through layers of vapour like a dwarf red moon. Cloud-dappled skies by noon. Two days more saw the Westman Isles falling astern. The wind blew light from the south-west. If it held, it would carry them north of the Faroes.

Emerging into another tranquil dawn, Vallon was woken by Raul's shout.

'Icelandic ships ahead!'

Vallon made his way forward and studied the flotilla picked out against the rising sun.

'What do you make of it, Captain?'

'They're not waiting for us. They must have lost time picking up Drogo's men.'

'Do you want me to change course?'

'No need. We'll lose them sooner or later. Until then, we might as well tag along. Their navigators know the sea-road better than we do.'

Raul glanced at him. 'Hope it ain't out of order, Captain, but what did you do to rile Helgi?'

'Well, telling can't do any harm now. By chance I happened upon his sister while she was bathing in a hot spring.'

'Naked?'

'Not a stitch.'

Raul whistled. 'I ain't laid eyes on her. Is she as beautiful as they say.'

Vallon smiled. 'Lovely as Venus, but too hot-blooded for me.'

They shadowed the convoy for two days, settling into a relaxed shipboard routine. Vallon practised his English, went over the accounts with Richard, played chess. Hero monitored their position and held stilted conversations with the monks. Wayland and Syth fed the falcons each morning and removed the soiled moss from under their perches. Garrick tended the horses in the hold. In the long intervals of lying about doing nothing, the company listened to Raul and Wayland's account of Greenland and its wonders.

'Oh, I wish I'd come with you,' Richard kept saying.

They saw no sign of the Faroes and quit looking after the fifth day. Wisps of cirrus heralded a front moving up from the south. Around noon on the sixth day, the horizon disappeared behind a curtain of black cloud trailing a frayed and dingy hem. Raul and Garrick upturned the ship's boat across the stern thwarts and lashed it down. Wayland and Syth carried the falcons down to the stern half-deck. The monks also retreated below. Vallon remained on top with Raul.

The sky darkened. A few drops of rain pecked on the deck and the ship curtseyed before the first gust of wind. A slate-grey downpour advanced hissing across the sea and engulfed them. Vallon ran for the boat and squeezed under with the others. The rain fell in torrents, peening on the hull and bubbling over the deck. Vallon watched Raul steering through the deluge like some hairy Neptune. He grew chilled and stiff. He stuck it for as long as he could, then made his way to the helm.

'I'll take over.'

Shearwater dipped over the crests with ponderous grace, spray bursting over her bow. The rain pelted down, soaking Vallon to the skin. The four layers of thick woollens he wore didn't keep him warm, but they provided enough insulation to maintain his body in a just-about bearable equilibrium. At dusk Wayland relieved him and he crept to rest under the boat. He woke in pitch blackness to half a gale. Flurries of rain rattled against the sail. He crawled out and groped his way to the rudder. Wayland was still at the helm.

'How's she standing up to it?'

'We came through worse on our return voyage.'

Another burst of rain spattered against the sail. Bile rose in Vallon's gullet. He huddled on a thwart, blinking into the sluicing dark, sniffing up dewdrops on the end of his nose. The point came when he could no longer keep his stomach corked. He rose heaving and spewed over the side. Down he sank again until the next fit of vomiting, and so it continued all night.

At break of day he voided his gut one last time and stared apathetically at the dull sky. The rain had slackened to a scudding drizzle. The

convoy was nowhere within sight. Raul was back at the helm. Vallon
listed across the deck. 'Are we on the right course?'

'No. We're being blown north-east.'

Vallon sighted along the combers. Changing course would put
them beam on to the seas. Even if they weren't swamped by a big one,
the ship would take a hammering. 'This won't last for ever. Run with
it.'

Two days later the wind was still blowing and Vallon was beginning to
worry about running out of ocean. 'The Norway coast can't be far
ahead,' he told Raul. 'Organise a bow watch.'

Towards evening the wind tailed off and the sun flared briefly in the
west. A rent opened in the clouds and stars sparkled in the void.
Somewhere a phantom moon. It had grown much colder.

When Vallon took the next watch, the sea was beginning to settle
and the sky to the north was clear. He searched for the Pole Star and
found it high overhead. 'Hero.'

Hero peered out from under the boat.

'Work out our position if you can.'

Hero tried a dozen times to take a reading. 'It's no good. The ship's
pitching too much.'

'What's your best estimate?'

Hero studied Polaris. He checked the horizon. 'We're a long way
north of where we should be.'

'How far?'

'I don't know. Five hundred miles. Maybe more.'

'That's impossible.'

'Yes, sir. I'll try again when the sea's calmer.'

Hero returned to bed. Vallon raised his eyes to Polaris. The star
stood much higher than it had the night they left Iceland. The waves
rolled northwards in an endless herd. *Shearwater* had been running
before the wind for more than three days. They could easily have covered five hundred miles. He stared over the crests. So where was
Norway?

The night passed and a vague grey light rose in the east. The swell
was settling and only the occasional white crest broke on the waves.
Vallon examined his puffy and quilted fingers. He dabbed at the cracks
in the corners of his mouth, massaged his rheumy eyes. The rest of the

company emerged with blotched and haggard faces, their clothes covered with mildew, stinking of wet rot. Raul resembled an inmate from a pest house – his mouth black and scabby, eyes webbed with blood, a hideous carbuncle erupting from his forehead. Even Syth looked a fright. Last out were the monks, their chins and habits streaked with vomit.

The company tottered about. Raul stood in the bow chewing on a dry fish spread with butter. Suddenly he was taken by a choking fit. Vallon thumped him between the shoulders and he ejected a wad of pulverised cod.

'Ship,' he wheezed, pointing south.

The others hurried over. 'That's Helgi's vessel,' said Wayland.

Vallon drilled a finger into his ear. 'Are you sure?'

Wayland's voice dragged on phlegm. 'I recognise the patch on the sail.'

'Do you think they've seen us?' Hero asked.

'Must have.'

'He ain't stopping,' said Raul.

'Follow him.'

The day brightened, sunshine dazzling between clouds. Gulls mewed around the ship and Vallon spotted driftwood. Away to the south a range of pale cloud held station.

'That must be Norway.'

Raul cocked an inflamed eye at the sun. 'It's in the wrong place. Norway should be east of us.'

Vallon checked the position of the sun, looked at the land again. 'Hero, bring your magic fish.'

Hero placed the compass on a thwart and the company watched its needle spin and settle. The evidence was incontrovertible: the coastline lay due south of them. No one spoke. As well as being exhausted and hungry, they had no idea where they were.

At midday Syth served up gruel and coarse grey bread furred with green and black mould. Vallon pared away the rot and tried to take a bite. His jaws made no impression. He threw the bread to the gulls and sank onto a thwart. Wonky comets and asteroids floated across his vision.

'Sir?'

Garrick's face swam into focus. 'Sorry to disturb you. We've spotted two more ships from the convoy.'

Vallon pinched the bridge of his nose and thrust himself up. Garrick supported him by the elbow. He pulled loose. 'I'm not a cripple.'

He sighted on the ships. They were about a league off, drifting together with sails lowered. Helgi had set course towards them.

'What do you reckon?' said Raul.

'Take us closer.'

They drew within half a mile of the ships. Helgi's vessel had already run up on them.

'Looks like one of them's lost its rudder,' Raul said.

'Bring us within hailing distance.'

Raul manoeuvred *Shearwater* to within earshot of the convoy. Wayland and Garrick lowered the sail. *Shearwater* rocked on the groundswell. Vallon spotted Caitlin looking dishevelled and not at all regal. And there stood Drogo decidedly green about the gills, with another familiar Norman face beside him.

'I forget his name,' said Vallon.

Raul looked at him oddly. 'Fulk, Captain. You broke his wrist the night you arrived at the castle.'

'So I did. Find out where we are.'

Raul pointed at the distant coast. 'What land is that?'

Someone shouted an answer that made Raul whistle. 'We're more than a day's sail east of North Cape. The storm's driven us right round the top of Norway.'

Helgi and some of his men had rowed to the crippled ship and were in discussion with its master. Raul established a dialogue with the other Iceland skipper.

'They ain't got a spare rudder,' he reported. 'They're going to tow the ship to a haven.'

Vallon searched the vague coastline. 'Does the land have a name?'

'The captain called it Bjarmaland. Nothing there but wild men and beasts. I've heard of the place. It's north of Rus.'

Vallon eyed the sea behind them. 'It's going to be a long haul to the Baltic.'

Raul pulled at his beard. One of his eyes had grown a blain like a polyp. 'We'll have to land, too. Water's running low and Wayland's nearly out of food for the falcons.'

'What do you know about the route down the Norway coast?'

'It ain't easy. We have to follow a passage between a chain of sker-ries and the mainland, rip currents and whirlpools all the way. There's one place where the ocean pours into the vast pit of the abyss and sucks ships down to hell. The Maelstrom they call it.'

'Perhaps we can persuade one of the Icelanders to pilot us.'

'Another ship!' Syth cried.

The straggler was more than a league to the south, its sail just breaking the horizon. They watched it grow larger.

'She's damaged, too,' said Raul. 'She's crabbing. And see how low she sits.'

Wayland grabbed a shroud and sprang onto the gunwale. He pulled himself as high as he could and peered from beneath his hand.

Vallon saw him frown. 'Anything wrong?'

'It isn't an Iceland ship.'

'What is it then?'

Wayland looked down. 'It's a drakkar. A dragon ship.'

Raul slapped his thigh. 'Why didn't I spot it myself?' He faced Vallon's puzzled stare. 'A Viking longship, Captain. A warship. That's why her hull's so low. She's built long and lean for speed. There ain't nothing wrong with her steering. She's aiming to get leeside of us before attacking.'

No one on the Icelandic ships had recognised the danger. Helgi and the captain of the damaged ship were locked in argument. Helgi's ship had a spare rudder and he wasn't prepared to part with it.

'You'd better warn them,' said Vallon.

Raul's news prompted a moment's stillness, then the Icelanders scut-tled like panicked rats. A woman threw back her head in a despairing wail.

The longship had drawn close enough for Vallon to see the dragon head carved on its stempost. Figures swarmed and the ship's hull bristled.

'Taken to their oars,' Raul said. 'Must know we've recognised them.'

'How many men will she be carrying?'

'At least thirty. They're pirates or slavers and I say we don't wait around to find out which.'

'You said they're faster than us.'

332

'Faster under sail, faster under oar. The sooner we get going, the better our chances.'

Vallon gnawed on his lip. 'Bring us alongside.'

'Captain, I know longships and the kind of man that sails on them.'

'I won't ask a second time.'

Raul's mouth crimped. He marched off flinging out orders. Helgi's vessel had come alongside the rudderless ship and was sawing against its hull. The crew and passengers were abandoning the cripple. Men bundled its sail onto Helgi's ship and slashed the rigging. Others threw bales and other items of cargo across. Helgi oversaw the transfer of passengers. When Raul hailed him, he flapped his arm in a dismissive wave that made Vallon's blood seethe.

'Ask him what he plans to do.'

Raul bellowed across the gap. Two people on different ships called out together, jabbing in the direction of the longship.

'They're going to cut and run.'

Vallon watched the twinkling rhythm of the longship's oars. 'The Vikings won't be satisfied with an empty hulk. Tell him we can resist them if we stand together.'

Raul trumpeted the proposal and strained for the answer. He drew back, sniffed and spat. 'Anything you say, he'll do the opposite. We got to get going.'

Vallon saw light gleam on rusty mail. 'Drogo!'

The Norman turned and stared across the swell.

'Between us we can muster enough fighting men to repel them. You know how deadly Wayland and Raul are with their bows. We'll kill half a dozen Vikings before they can board. Tell Helgi.'

The Icelander was helping an elderly couple off the ship. Hands reached up to receive them. They were the last evacuees. Helgi sprang to his own ship, drew his sword and cut the crippled vessel loose. His crew hoisted sail and the ship gathered way.

Vallon spat with contempt. 'Picks fights with strangers, then flees from pirates who'd gang-rape his sister in front of him before cutting out his heart.' Vallon wiped his mouth. 'All right. Get us under way.'

The two Iceland ships were steering north-east, sailing close-hauled, Helgi's ship drawing ahead.

'Why aren't they sailing downwind?' Vallon asked.

'Makes sense,' said Raul. 'Longships have shallow draughts for raiding up rivers. Their keels don't bite as deep as ours and they make more leeway sailing across the wind. That's our only advantage.'

Vallon watched the abandoned knarr drifting in their wake. As the longship closed on it, all the oars rose to the vertical, then dipped and disappeared. The longship glided up to its prey.

'How many rowers?' Vallon asked Wayland.

'Sixteen each side.'

The Vikings swarmed aboard the knarr. Vallon hadn't given any thought to the time and he was surprised to see how late it was. The longship and its victim diminished in their wake. Dusk was beginning to encroach when the two outlines separated.

'They're coming after us,' said Raul.

'They won't catch us before dark.'

Raul eyed the weather vane. 'Wind's shifting to the north. The Vikings know we're making for the coast. They'll aim to get ahead of us and lie in wait.'

'Any ideas?'

'Wait until dark, let the Vikings sail past and then lie up on the weather side. By morning they could be twenty miles downwind of us. Too far to claw back. That'll give us plenty of sea room to find a safe haven.'

'They might have thought of that.'

'They might.'

'The sky's clearing and the moon's waxing full. We don't want the Vikings to find us drifting. Hold your course.'

'Aye, Captain.'

Vallon gave a yawn that threatened to dislocate his jaw. 'Wake me if . . .' He sketched a tired wave.

He tottered to his pallet, lay down and felt for his sword. His eyes fluttered and closed.

He woke batting away a hand. Someone was shaking him. He swung himself up into a sitting position and stretched his eyes wide.

'It's gone midnight,' Wayland said. 'Raul said to wake you if there was any change.'

Vallon blinked up. Everything had been transformed. The falcon on Wayland's fist seemed irradiated by white fire. The dog sat beside its master with its eyes burning pale and its hoary shape shadowed in deepest black on the deck. Vallon hoisted himself up. A full moon ringed by a halo cast a gaseous light over the ocean. Small clouds like puffs of smoke drifted low across the horizon, brightening as they crossed the moon's path. The sea had gelled into a huge plane of crumpled silver. Over to port a sail shone.

'Helgi's ship,' said Wayland.

Vallon spied another sail far away down their glittering wake.

'That's the other Iceland ship.'

Vallon probed every quarter. 'The Vikings?'

'No sign.'

A flight of meteorites glided overhead and disappeared one by one into the furthest reaches of space. The falcon swivelled her head and preened. She roused and ran her beak down her flight feathers. Vallon stroked her breast.

'How quickly you've tamed her.'

'Not my doing. She's naturally gentle.'

'How are the other falcons faring?'

'They're healthy enough so far. They don't suffer from seasickness as men do. My main worry is running out of food.'

'We'll land as soon as we've shaken off the Vikings.'

'What will we do if they attack us?'

'We'll make it go hard for them. How are you off for arrows?'

'I've got a full quiver.' Wayland paused. 'It's Syth I'm worried about – if I'm killed, I mean. I know what the Vikings will do to her.'

'Don't believe everything Raul tells you.'

'It's true, though. You know it is. Syth and I have talked about it. She has a knife, but I'm not sure she'll be able to use it if the time comes.'

'Nobody's going to harm her.'

'But if the worst happens . . .'

What could Vallon say? That there were grimmer fates for a young woman than being captured by sea pirates? That if Wayland was dead, it didn't matter to him what happened to Syth?

'If it's in my power, I'll make sure she doesn't fall into the Vikings' hands.'

'Thank you.'

*

335

Vallon stood watch until the moon grew wan and the stars that had guided them lay low in the east. The rest of the company rose and stood beating their arms across their chests and blowing into their hands. A cold breeze from the north-west had carried them back to within sight of land. Helgi's ship ploughed a furrow a couple of miles ahead. The other vessel had dropped further behind. No sign of the longship.

Garrick brought him a breakfast of bread and a bowl of purplish gloop. Vallon examined it at arm's length.

'It's dulse, sir.'

'Dulse.'

'Seaweed, sir. The Icelanders eat it in winter to keep scurvy at bay.'

Vallon spooned up a tiny portion, closed his eyes and tasted. His mouth puckered. He spat it out and slid the mess over the side.

'We've been at sea for less than two weeks. Don't tell me we've run out of proper food.'

'I can fetch you an egg, sir.'

Vallon brightened. 'A fresh egg?'

'Afraid not. They've been preserved in ash since last year.'

Vallon grimaced. He'd seen Icelanders sucking the green and watery contents of such eggs. 'Leave it. The bread will suffice.'

Garrick leaned his hands on the gunwale and surveyed the ocean. 'Looks like we've lost them.'

'I'm not so sure.'

Garrick nodded towards the laggard in their wake. 'If they do show up, they'll get that one first.'

The breeze carried them closer to the coast. Vallon watched it reveal itself. Undulating barrens tinged with the colours of autumn. No mountains or trees. Helgi was heading for the mouth of a large river. The sun reached its zenith. Both Iceland ships were still visible when one of Vallon's sweeps picked up something behind the laggard.

'Wayland.'

Wayland hurried up.

'Is that another sail?'

Wayland looked long and hard. 'Yes.'

Vallon glowered at Helgi's ship. Someone on board must have spotted the longship, but the knarr continued making for the rivermouth. 'Look at that. Thinks only of himself.'

'Can't blame him,' said Raul. 'He wouldn't be able to reach the knarr before the longship catches it.'

'They're his countrymen. He should have been escorting them. All he cares about is himself and his precious sister.' Vallon narrowed his eyes, estimating distances. 'If we take to the oars, we might be able to reach the Icelanders first.'

'No, we won't. The Vikings can row three times as fast as we can, and they've got the wind behind them. Captain, leaving the Icelanders don't sit comfortable with me neither, but we got no choice.'

Vallon cast another glance at Helgi's ship. 'Heave to. We'll give the Icelanders a chance to catch up.'

Raul gave a distraught hop. 'Captain—'

'Heave to.'

Shearwater lost way. The company waited.

It was a strange sort of day, the wind coming in gusts that blew alternately warm and cold. They must be at the confluence of currents. The Iceland ship slowly gained on them, but the longship was making the faster headway.

Garrick crossed himself. 'There are women and children on board. God help them.'

'Isn't there anything we can do?' Hero murmured.

'No, there ain't,' Raul snapped. 'We're putting ourselves in peril for nothing.'

Half a mile from their prey the Vikings took to their oars. The sea foamed at the blades and gnashed around the longship's bow. The monks fell to their knees, entreating God to intervene. Vallon checked the angle of the sun. He glanced at his ring, saw that the gem had darkened and dismissed its warning. There was hardly a cloud in the sky and it wasn't the first time that the jewel had predicted falsely. The breeze carried faint cries from the Icelandic ship.

Richard covered his face. 'I can't bear to watch.'

The longship surged up to the knarr and the Vikings leaped aboard. A brief melee and then across the sea drifted the blaring of a war horn.

'Permission to get underway, Captain.'

Two figures toppled from the knarr. Another followed. 'What's that about?'

'They're getting rid of the old and infirm – anyone who won't fetch a price in the slave mart.'

'Are they pagans?'

'Likely they are if they're from the north. Please, Captain …'

Vallon saw that Helgi's ship was almost out of sight. 'Make for the estuary.'

Raul clapped his hands. 'Jump to it.'

Up went the sail, round came the bow. They'd gone about two miles when the longship left its victim and set off in pursuit. A mile further and the wind failed. *Shearwater* glided to a stop. Her sail flapped once and then hung listless.

XXIX

Mist wafted from the surface in lazy coils. The air felt vacuous. Vallon consulted his ring and saw that the stone had turned as black as Cosmas's eye. The Vikings stroked towards them. They were tired from their exertions and knew that *Shearwater* couldn't escape. Vallon looked at the shore three or four miles away. Helgi's ship lay becalmed in a wide fairway that channelled inland between bare and rolling hills.

'You were right. I made a poor decision.'

Raul hefted his crossbow. 'We're in a pickle sure enough.'

'They'll have left a prize crew on the knarr. Reduces the odds.'

'Four or five at most. Not enough to make a difference.'

Vallon watched the oncoming longship. The sea had settled into an oily calm. A feather of cloud brushed the sun and the sky was dulling over.

'Do they have thunderstorms this far north?'

'One of the Greenlanders told me he ain't seen but one in all his life.'

The longship had closed to within a mile. The Vikings hadn't bothered to lower the sail and in the slack air it rippled back against the mast. The ship had no deck and the crew rowed in pairs sitting on thwarts with round shields slung over their backs. They'd herded the survivors from the captured knarr into the stern.

'What's the plan?' said Raul.

'Fight. What else?'

'To the last man?'

Vallon reviewed his force. Wayland had strung his bow and clad his dog in its spiked collar and a suit of armour tailored from walrus hide. Garrick, Hero and Richard had armed themselves with swords. That was all the defence they could muster. Vallon's gaze rested briefly on Syth.

'You make it sound as if we have a choice.'

'They think we're traders. If we sting them in their first attack, they might offer terms.'

'Such as?'

'Hand over our goods.'

'Including Syth?'

Raul fiddled with his crossbow and grinned a crooked grin. 'Ah, well, we all got to meet our doom sometime.'

'We'll take a few with us,' said Vallon. He waved Wayland forward.

'Shoot as straight and fast as you can. Make every arrow count.'

Wayland nodded, his features drawn. 'However many I kill, we won't be able to stop them boarding.'

'If that happens, do what you must do by Syth, and then face your own end bravely. If you're killed before then, I'll make sure you aren't separated by death.'

Vallon turned his attention back to the longship. It still had half a mile to cover, but the air was so still that he could hear the swish of its oars. He took another glance at the sun. The cloud had swelled into a baleful nebula.

'Lower the sail.'

Everyone looked at the lifeless panel. No one moved.

'Raul, Garrick, get the sail lowered. You, too, Wayland. Double quick!'

They stumbled into action. Vallon watched the longship approach. The Vikings had left a prize crew on the captured knarr, reducing their number to about two dozen. In the bow, rhythmically thumping the dragon-carved stem with the haft of his battle-axe, stood a yellow-haired giant wearing a chainmail vest.

'Kill that one first,' Vallon said.

Raul spat. 'He ain't going to be hard to hit.'

Vallon fell quiet. Raul was right. No man could foretell the time and place of his death and there was no point railing against this arbitrary assignment with fate.

The longship was only a furlong away when daylight drained away. The sea dimmed, as if a creature too vast to see had cast its shadow across the earth. From the Viking ship came the brazen blast of a war horn. A stroke of lightning flashed vertically down less than a mile away, followed by a dry crackle of thunder.

In a well-rehearsed move, every second Viking rower shipped his oar and ranged himself along the side. Several had bows. The others wielded swords, axes and spears. Two of them dangled grappling hooks. All of them carried circular wooden shields quartered in red and white.

Raul knelt beside Vallon and steadied his crossbow. Wayland took up position behind him.

'Shoot when you're sure of your targets.'

With movements that were ritualistic in their deliberation, the huge warrior at the stem donned a conical helmet fitted with a visor that ringed his eyes and transformed him into a figure of menacing power. He hefted an iron-bossed shield painted in the same colours displayed by the rest of his company. Only two other Vikings wore mail armour.

Water hissed around the longship's bow. Its dragon stem grew taller.

'They'll engage to starboard,' Vallon said.

Wayland lowered his bow. 'Out to sea. Something's happening.'

At first Vallon couldn't make sense of it. The horizon seemed to be fraying, lifting in a deckled edge. He'd seen the sea boiling where schools of whales were feeding and for a moment he thought that a herd of leviathans had driven a shoal of fish to the surface.

'Great God!'

It was a wave – a broken wall of water churning down on the longship. One of the Vikings shouted a warning, but they had no time to react. The wave hit the longship in a welter of spray and advanced tumbling on *Shearwater*.

'Hang on!' Vallon yelled, grabbing the stempost.

Wave and wind struck *Shearwater*, knocking her astern and

wrenching her round with a force that tore Vallon from his hold. He trotted backwards, the deck dropping away beneath his feet, and then he trod air before toppling over and whacking his head. He rolled helplessly, smacked into something solid and lay winded and dazed. When he tried to regain his feet, he couldn't. He was lying almost upside down against the gunwale, the sea foaming at the same level as his head and the deck rising almost vertically above him. The squall had knocked them onto their beam ends. They were on the point of capsizing. He made another attempt to rise, struggling like a man trying to extricate himself from a tub. He managed to get his feet onto the gunwale and balanced with his hands leaning against the deck. The wind shrieked overhead. He grabbed a flailing shroud and looked around. Wayland and Syth had wrapped themselves around a thwart. Hero and Richard were clinging to the yard. Another cluster by the rudder.

The wind stopped as quickly as it had blown up. The churning sea quietened. With a slow sigh and a heavy splash, *Shearwater* swung back and settled at a steep list. Cargo and ballast had shifted. Vallon felt the lump on the back of his skull. He shook his head and looked for the longship.

It wallowed off to port, barely a foot of freeboard showing. Its mast leaned perilously and its sail hung loose from the yard, rent from top to bottom. Several crew members had been washed into the sea and a boat was being launched to rescue them.

Vallon hurried aft. A horse screamed in the hold.

'Is everyone safe?'

'We lost Father Saxo,' Raul panted. 'Never even saw him go.'

Father Hilbert was running from side to side, calling out to his companion.

Vallon searched the sea. The squall was heading towards Helgi's ship.

Raul aimed his crossbow at the longship. 'Like shooting fish in a barrel.'

Vallon slapped his arm. 'Never mind that. Fix the ship. You and Wayland, repair the rigging. Garrick, do something about the horses. The rest of you, get us back on an even keel.' He checked on the longship. Most of the hands were bailing with buckets and anything else that would hold water. 'I don't see the other knarr.'

Raul scanned the sea. 'It must have sunk.'

Both crews laboured to make their vessels seaworthy, the men glancing up from their work to check on their enemies' progress. Garrick reported that one of the horses had broken a leg and Vallon ordered him to kill it. The sea had taken Father Saxo. Judging by the mournful shouts coming from the search party in the longship's circling boat, the Vikings had also lost some of their number. *Shearwater* had suffered only minor damage. By the time her company had trimmed the ship and replaced the broken shrouds, the Vikings were still emptying out the hull and trying to raise the mast.

Clean air from the north filled *Shearwater*'s sail. The Viking chieftain looked up from his work. Raul patted his crossbow and looked at Vallon. 'I won't get a better chance.'

'Make your aim true.'

The bolt shot through the air so fast that Vallon couldn't follow it, but the Viking leader must have seen it coming because when the blade thumped home, it was buried in his shield. He jabbed his axe into the air. Vallon turned away. The squall had dispersed back into its elements. He studied the coast.

'What's happened to Helgi's ship?'

'It's lost its mast,' said Wayland.

Raul spat. 'Now let's see how proud he is.'

Helgi's knarr lay low in the water, its rudder half-torn off, its mast shattered close to the deck and everything above gone by the board. A human chain was bailing out the hold and the rest of the able-bodied were cutting away the wrecked mast and waterlogged sail. Helgi stalked about exhorting everyone to greater efforts. Vallon saw Caitlin working as hard as anyone. Drogo straddled the broken mast, slashing away at the lines that fixed the yard.

Vallon hailed him. 'How badly are you damaged below?'

Drogo glanced at Helgi. 'Some of the planks have sprung. We've tried to plug the leak but we're still taking on water. As soon as we've cut away the mast, we'll row in.'

Vallon gauged the distance to land. About two miles. He checked on the longship. 'You don't have time. We'll tow you in.'

Drogo relayed the offer to Helgi. The Icelander gesticulated a furious negative. 'We'll manage without your help,' Drogo shouted.

'Let the fool sink,' said Raul.

In the stern of the knarr stood a group of the old and the young, including the elderly couple who'd already lost one ship. A young mother was trying to soothe her crying baby. Three horses occupied the rest of the deck.

Vallon glanced back at the longship. 'The Vikings took less punishment than you. They have more than twenty oars to your eight. They'll catch you before you get halfway to land.'

Drogo searched for Helgi, then looked back at Vallon. 'It's not my decision.'

'Are you going to let that fool dictate your fate?'

'He's in command.'

'In that case, they can take what's coming to them,' said Raul.

'No. Keep us hove to. They'll come to their senses.' He saw the expression on Raul's face and cut him off with a gesture before he could give voice to it.

Vallon paced the deck, flicking looks between the longship and the knarr. The sun was halfway down the sky when Wayland confirmed that the Vikings were on the move again.

'That's it,' Vallon said. 'Bring us alongside.'

Shearwater closed to within twenty feet. One brave Icelander had crawled out to the end of the half-submerged yard to cut the remaining rope-bands from the sail.

'This is your last chance,' Vallon cried. 'Accept a tow or we're leaving you.'

His words were foreign to the Icelanders, but his meaning was plain and they left off their labours and looked at each other with dismay. Helgi yelled at them to get back to work.

'You tell them,' Vallon ordered Raul.

'Captain, there are five men on that ship who want to see you dead.'

Vallon grabbed a fold of the German's tunic. 'I don't want to save Drogo and Helgi any more than you do. But there are two dozen innocent souls who'll be taken by the Vikings unless you can make that imbecile see sense.'

Raul went to the side and pointed at the longship. 'See that. That's death coming. Death for anyone too old or feeble to fetch a price in the slave market. For the rest of you, it's the end of everything you cherish. Wives snatched away, children lost. Sold to the highest bidder. Lord high and mighty there will never see his sister wed, but he'll see her maidenhead lost a dozen times.' Raul paused. 'Accept a tow or go to hell.'

A moan went up and a mob surrounded Helgi. Voices rose and a scuffle broke out. Drogo emerged from the scrum and spread his arms. 'We accept.'

Raul threw a line to the ship's master. He lashed it around the stem and it thrummed as *Shearwater* took the strain. The longship was little more than a mile off, bearing down under its torn sail.

Raul shook his head. 'It ain't working. We're towing a dead weight.'

'We'll pick up speed,' Vallon said.

'Not enough. Captain, this time you got to listen. We ain't going to outsail them. You got to act quick.'

Vallon looked at the longship. Even with only half a sail, it was catching up. The knarr was shipping water faster than the crew could bail it out.

'You left it too late,' Vallon shouted. 'You'll have to abandon ship.'

Helgi waved his fists. 'Never!'

'Stay and fight with us,' Drogo cried.

'You had your chance. If you remain on your ship, you'll face the Vikings alone.'

A hush descended. Vallon nodded at Raul. 'Cut the tow.'

Raul lifted his sword. 'I ain't pretending, Captain.'

'Cut it.'

Drogo waved his hands above his head. 'Let me speak to Helgi.'

'Make it quick.'

Drogo sprinted over to Helgi and swung him round to witness the threat sweeping up on them. Others joined him. He ran back to the bow. 'I've brought him round.'

'Send a boat-load of your strongest men and we'll haul you alongside.' Vallon turned to Raul. 'Tell the Icelanders to bring only life's essentials – food, clothing, bedding, weapons. No trade goods. Tell them not to leave the spare sail for the Vikings.'

Six Icelanders rowed up to *Shearwater*. With their aid the company dragged the knarr along *Shearwater*'s port beam. Before the ships had closed, baggage began to shower onto the deck. A young Icelander took a flying leap to safety. Raul slapped him in the chops. 'Weakest first, you selfish little shit.'

The knarr grated alongside. Its crew passed ropes through the oar ports to make it fast and the passengers began scrambling aboard. The Vikings still hadn't taken to their oars. They were saving their strength for a last spurt.

'Hey! Are you deaf?' Raul shouted at a man staggering onto the gunwale under two bales of woolcloth. 'No trade goods.'

'Let him be,' Vallon said. 'We're nearly done.'

Only Helgi and his entourage remained on the knarr. Drogo sprang on board, followed by Fulk. They skirted Vallon and his company like rival dogs. Caitlin balanced on the rail, her face begrimed and her hair a mess. Her eyes, wide with appeal, engaged Vallon's.

'For God's sake, what are you waiting for?'

Drogo assisted her to the deck. Her two handmaids followed, and then Helgi and two of the men who'd been with him at the lake came forward leading the three horses.

'What do you think you're doing with them?' Raul bellowed.

'We might need them,' said Vallon. 'For food if nothing else. God knows what's waiting for us on that shore.'

Helgi's men propped planks against the gunwale. Two of the horses were well-schooled and nimble. They negotiated the ramp and jumped down without putting a foot wrong. Helgi's mount balked. He whacked its rump and tried to push it onto the ramp. As he did so, the oars on the longship flashed.

'Leave your horse,' Vallon shouted. 'Get on board.'

Helgi grabbed the horse's bit and stood on the ramp and began hauling it up behind him. The longship was three hundred yards away and flying through the water. 'Cut us loose,' Vallon ordered. Raul and Wayland ran down the ship, slashing through the ropes. All except for the one by Vallon. He hesitated. Helgi had managed to drag the horse to the top of the ramp and his men were holding him while he urged the beast to take the last step.

Raul darted past Vallon and wielded his knife. 'I ain't dying for no horse.'

Helgi hung on to the horse and his men hung on to him. The horse tripped forward too late. The ships were drifting apart and the horse bellyflopped into the gap. Helgi would have followed if his men hadn't got such a tight hold of him. They dragged him onto the deck. He shook himself loose and reeled backwards in a half circle, reaching for his sword.

Raul ran at him and aimed his crossbow from a range of three feet. 'Draw and you're dead!'

Drogo flung himself at Helgi and dragged him away kicking and struggling.

Raul and Vallon ran to the stern. The doomed horse struggled in their wake, its head thrown back and its eyes rolling. Raul's crossbow twanged. The longship was only three or four ship's lengths behind them, coursing through the water. Raul cursed as he reloaded. The shields slung over the Vikings' backs made them difficult targets. Their chieftain held his position at the prow. Golden hair streamed from under his helmet. At a distance he'd looked like a god. This close, only his stature was god-like. The giant had a face like a horse – massive jutting jaw filled with splayed and discoloured teeth.

Shearwater had reached her maximum speed. Not fast enough. The longship was only sixty yards behind, her stem throwing up wings of foam. Raul had reloaded and Wayland was drawing his bow. The chieftain crouched, only his helmeted head showing above his shield. 'Aim for the helmsman,' Vallon ordered.

Wayland shot first and missed. Raul loosed his bolt and the helmsman sagged over the tiller. The longship veered to port and some of the rowers crabbed oars. One of the Vikings pulled the helmsman away from the rudder and strained to bring the longship back on course. Even now it looked as if the longship would catch them. They were towing the boat from Helgi's knarr and one of the Vikings in the bow swung a grappling hook to snag it. 'Cut it loose,' Vallon shouted.

Before Garrick could reach it, Wayland shot two more arrows, releasing the second while the first was still in flight. It flew in a hissing parabola and struck the new helmsman in the face. He reared up screaming, the shaft sticking from his eye like a ghastly wand. In almost the same moment, Raul's next bolt pierced one of the rowers through the chest and left him vomiting blood. Vallon roared defiance, his cries echoed by Drogo and Fulk and half a dozen sword-wielding Icelanders.

The Viking chief glanced back at the carnage. His men were committed to their oars, unable to defend themselves. He hadn't expected such lethal opposition. He shouted and his crew let their oars trail. The wave curling at the longship's bow died. Like a carnivorous water beetle that hunts in short dashes and never wastes energy, the longship slowed to an idle.

Jubilant cries rang out from the Icelanders. They thumped Wayland and Raul on the back. Vallon watched the longship fall astern, turn and row back towards the abandoned knarr. They'd left it too late. It was sinking. Before they reached it the gunwales sank beneath the waves and gouts of air erupted from its hull. It was gone.

Vallon turned to find every square foot of *Shearwater*'s deck crammed with refugees. Their grins thinned when they saw his expression.

'We haven't seen the last of the Vikings,' he told Raul. 'Separate the fighting men from the passengers. Everyone who can lift a sword to port, the rest to starboard.'

Helgi tried to interfere with the muster. Vallon ignored him. When the two groups had been separated, he took stock. Twelve men, most armed with swords, represented the Icelandic fighting force. The non-combatants numbered five – the old woman and her husband, and two younger women, one of them carrying a baby in arms. Helgi's party with Drogo and Fulk stood separate from both groups.

Vallon approached them in a tense silence. 'Don't you know which side you're on?'

'I won't take orders from you,' Helgi said. 'Nor will the Icelanders. They're my people. They'll do as I command.'

'In that case, choose a patch of shore where you and your followers would like to settle and I'll drop you on it.' Vallon eyed Drogo with scorn. 'I expected better from a professional soldier.'

'I have to take Helgi's side.'

'Then you can take your chances with him.'

Drogo's throat chugged. His hand drifted away from his sword and he glanced over his shoulder at the oncoming shore. 'This isn't the time to argue. We're nearly there.'

XXX

Shadows were lengthening along the coast when *Shearwater* entered the estuary. Their lead over the longship had stretched to more than a mile. A flood tide carried them up the river and the alien shores began to close in on them. A country much like parts of Iceland for the first few miles, rolling tundra flushed with autumn, studded with bald granite outcrops. What amazed the Icelanders was the bounty of dead trees tangled in the backwaters and unharvested by any living soul. Soon they came on stands of birch and solitary spruces standing on the banks like spiral obelisks. The river had narrowed to less than a mile when they rounded a bend and put the longship out of sight. Along this reach the trees merged into a sparse forest that straggled away to the furthest ridges. No trace of habitation. Not a sign that any human had set foot in those wastes.

Darkness was beginning to settle when they broached the forest. They navigated another bend. A tributary led away to their right. They passed a scrubby island and a huge hump-shouldered animal patched out of the gloom went splashing away through the shallows. Some of the Icelanders crossed themselves.

Raul stood at Vallon's side. 'We'd better find a place to land while there's enough light.'

'Keep an eye out for a quiet inlet. If the Vikings go past us, we can slip back to sea on the ebb tide.'

Shearwater held to the centre of the river. Soon it would be too dark to pick a landing site.

'What about in there?' Wayland said, pointing at a backwater between wooded bluffs on the left bank.

'We'll take a look.'

Shearwater nosed round, still under sail, running with the tide. Vallon glanced downriver. No sign of the longship. He heard the riffling of broken water.

'Shoal!'

Before Raul could steer away, the keel struck with a tearing squeal and heavy crash. The shock threw almost everyone down. Vallon picked himself up to find that *Shearwater* had run aground fifty yards from the bank.

He glared up at the heavens as if he knew where the agent of this fiasco were seated. Forget that. It was his own fault. He should have taken in sail and posted a leadsman. 'Raul, check the damage.'

He paced and fidgeted while Raul investigated. It didn't take long.

'We're holed and jammed. What makes it worse is that the tide's nearly full. We won't float her off tonight.'

Any moment the Vikings would come in sight. Think, Vallon told himself. Think.

'Launch our boat. Bring the other one alongside. Row the women and other non-combatants to shore, then take off the cargo. Wayland, I'm putting you in charge. Round up as many Icelanders as you need. Raul and Garrick, get the horses out of the hold.'

People were gathering up their possessions and staring fearfully downriver. Vallon wiped his lips.

'We must protect the ship at all costs,' said a voice beside him. 'Lose it and we're dead.'

Vallon glanced at Drogo's shadowed form. 'Ship or no ship, none of us will escape if we're constantly looking over our shoulders in fear of each other.'

'Agreed. A river of blood separates us, but I'll delay making that crossing until we've dealt with the Vikings.'

'You accept my command?'

Drogo hesitated. 'If I agree with your decisions, I'll back them.'

'Not Helgi, though. He'll try to thwart me at every turn.'

'Issue your orders through me.'

Vallon's eyes rested on Drogo before stealing downriver again. 'What would your strategy be?'

'Safeguard the ship but engage the Vikings on land. We have five horses where they have none. That's worth a dozen men.'

It had been a long time since Vallon had talked tactics with a fellow professional. 'We'll leave the swordsmen on board and post archers on the banks. I don't think the Vikings will press home an attack tonight. They're weary and must be feeling star-crossed after losing men and seeing two prizes sink.'

Wayland came rowing back. 'That's all the women and old folk landed.'

'Supplies next. When you've finished, muster the Icelandic bowmen and station yourselves at the edge of the forest.'

Raul and Garrick had rigged a derrick to hoist the horses out of the hold. Helgi and his men herded their own mounts over the side.

Vallon turned back to Drogo. 'Are your ribs mended?'

'I'll fight if called upon.'

'On the right side, I trust.'

Every man on board watched the bend downriver. Swirls of water welled up mysteriously and subsided back into blackness. The tide had ebbed, leaving *Shearwater* high and dry. Deep in the forest an owl gave a funereal hoot. Weapons chinked. Mosquitoes whined. Somewhere out in the river a big fish jumped.

'What's keeping them?' Fulk muttered.

'They'll struggle against this current,' said Drogo. 'They might have stopped for the night.'

'They won't call a halt until they find us,' said Vallon. 'They're searching every bolthole. Having forced us into a dead end, they'll make sure we don't escape.'

A mosquito bit his cheek. He raised his hand to swat it, then stopped, arrested by the eerie illumination unfolding in the northern sky. Down from the top of the heavens scrolled a gossamer curtain of pale green, its shifting drapes fringed with bands of purple. The folds undulated with a kind of beckoning motion, fading and returning.

'What in God's name is that?'

'The northern aurora,' said Hero. 'The Icelanders say it's the flames of Vulcan's forge reflected in the sky.'

In this unearthly glow the longship made its entrance, stealing around the bend with its sail reflecting the ghostly fire, pinpoints of light winking at its oars. It drew nearer and someone shouted as he caught sight of *Shearwater*. The Vikings rowed closer, then held station, feathering their oars. Laughter and jeers carried across the water when the Vikings realised that the knarr was stranded. The pirate chief stood at the dragon prow and bellowed a lengthy challenge or ultimatum that made the Icelanders gabble with dread.

'They know him by reputation,' said Raul. 'His name's Thorfinn Wolfbreath, a pagan feared for his cruelty all along the Norwegian coast. He eats the livers of his opponents. Eats them raw on the battlefield to feed his valour.'

The warlord shouted again.

'What's he saying?'

'Surrender the ship, our trade goods and our women, and he'll leave us to God's mercy. If we resist, he'll cut the blood eagle on every man he takes alive.'

'Blood eagle?'

'A cruel torture. I saw it performed on a thief in Gotland. They tied him face down, hacked away his ribs close to the spine, then reached into his chest and pulled his lungs out through the back. The Icelanders say he's a berserker, a warrior who can't be defeated by mortal means. Swords can't bite him and he can walk through fire without being burned. He can blunt a weapon just by looking at it.'

Vallon snorted.

'You and me know it's bollocks,' said Raul. 'But that's what the Icelanders believe. If Thorfinn attacks us now, half of them will jump over the side.'

'Remind him of your sting.' Vallon turned. 'Wayland, give them a volley.'

The bolt struck with a meaty thud. A flight of arrows whispered through the dark. Thorfinn laughed. Another volley of arrows swept overhead and a yelp of pain told Vallon that one of them had made a lucky hit. Thorfinn shouted. The longship began to fall back with the tide.

'Wayland, follow them and mark where they put in. Keep watch on them. Take someone to report back.'

Footsteps ran into the dark. The aurora was fading. Faint pulses of the elusive light showed the longship drifting downriver. Slowly it disappeared around the bend.

'They won't be back tonight,' said Drogo. 'We'd better establish a camp.'

'We'll divide what's left of the night into two watches, leaving six men on board for each shift. The rest might as well get some hot food into their bellies.'

Vallon posted pickets around the camp. He doubted that Thorfinn would mount a night assault across unfamiliar terrain. But then, he told Drogo, if he were in the Vikings' place, he would do what was least expected.

Drogo shook his head. 'They'll recruit themselves before attacking.'

They were sitting beside a crackling fire, devouring steaks cut from the horse Garrick had killed.

Vallon wiped his greasy fingers, placed his hands on his knees and levered himself up. 'I need to consult Hero.'

He found him helping to pitch shelters. 'Have you calculated our position?'

'I've taken a dozen sightings. Even the most optimistic puts us six hundred miles north of our starting point. That means a journey of a thousand miles before we reach the Baltic. We don't have enough food. Our own supplies won't last another week and the Icelanders have none to spare. One of the sailing masters told me that we won't be able to buy or barter fresh supplies within two weeks' sail.'

'There'll be game to hunt, fish to catch. The forest must be full of berries.'

Vallon became aware of Richard. He was sitting next to Hero with his knees drawn up to his chin.

Vallon dropped to a crouch. 'Don't worry about Drogo.'

Richard hugged his knees tighter.

Vallon took his arm. 'Would you have had me condemn the Icelanders to death? I couldn't take them and leave Drogo.'

'Why not? It's no more than he would have done to me.'

'Why would he want to harm you?'

It all came spilling out. 'He blames me for the death of our mother. And what warps his mind even more is the fact that Lady Margaret has no affection for him. She has no love for anyone apart from her precious Walter. As a child, I saw how she spurned Drogo when he tried to court her attention. I never even tried. I learned early on that cuffs and insults were all I'd receive from that lot. I thought I'd escaped them, found friends who cared for me. Yet though I've travelled to the end of the world, it seems that I can't shake Drogo off.'

'We do care for you. We're your family now. Hero and Wayland and all the other steadfast souls who've shared our voyage. I won't let Drogo harm you, I promise.'

Vallon rose and made his way to the fire, stepping around slumbering bodies. He stretched out, burdened with worries. No sooner had he laid his head down than Raul was shaking him awake.

'Syth's back.'

Vallon blundered up. The fire had died to coals and clouds fogged the moon. He'd slept for longer than he'd intended. Syth crouched panting by the fire. He hunkered down beside her. 'Did you find their lair?'

She accepted a piece of meat from Raul and sank her teeth into it. 'They're in a bay below the crook in the river. On this side, less than two miles from here.'

Vallon glanced towards the river. Mist lapped against the shore. He checked the position of the moon, then turned to Drogo. 'We'd better take a look before it grows light.'

Syth gave some of the meat to the dog. It stretched its jaws wide and closed its teeth on the offering with a grip that wouldn't have pricked a bubble, then it growled at the men and slunk off. 'You'll need the dog to find Wayland and avoid the Vikings. Four of them landed and hurried back this way. They're watching us.'

Helgi insisted on accompanying the patrol. Vallon took Garrick along to relieve Wayland. The dog led them into the forest by a roundabout route, baring its teeth at a rise over to their left to indicate where the Viking spies had posted themselves. Even with the clouded moon to light the way, the party found it tough going across fallen trees and rank heather and boggy hollows.

Helgi stumbled into a hole. 'The girl said two miles. We must have come twice that distance.'

'Not so loud,' Vallon whispered. 'The Vikings will have posted sentries. The dog's leading us around them.'

He sighted on the declining moon. A lifting of the dark showed east where he thought west should be. The dog was sitting down in front of him. It turned and looked at him, then rose and trotted on.

Vallon caught his first glimpse of the river since leaving camp. Then it had been to his left. Now it was below him to the right. The dog must be leading them back upriver. They hurried on and climbed a hill. Below was the river again and a bay swathed in mist. The dog had disappeared and so had the moon. Vallon smelled wood smoke. He turned in a circle.

'Over here.'

Wayland lay couched under a spruce tree, completely hidden by branches that draped across the ground like a skirt. Vallon and the others pushed in beside him. Garrick handed him food and a leather water bottle. Wayland gulped thirstily.

'Are they in the bay?'

Wayland nodded, still drinking. He put the bottle down and gasped. 'There are sentries on the next ridge. I thought it wise to hide downriver where they wouldn't think to look.' He lifted the bottle and drank again.

Now the lie of the land made sense to Vallon.

'How many of them are left?' Drogo demanded.

Vallon saw Wayland's eyes turn in his direction. 'You can answer,' he said. 'For the moment, we're allies.'

'It was too dark to count them,' said Wayland. He touched Vallon's sleeve. 'Sir, I'm anxious about the falcons. I didn't feed them yesterday and they'll go hungry again if I don't find food today. I know the peril we're in, but you mustn't lose sight of what brought us north. If we escape the pirates but the falcons starve, I won't count it a triumph.'

'There's plenty of fresh horseflesh.'

'I don't know if falcons can stomach such coarse fare.'

Dawn was stealing over the forest. Vallon wriggled closer. 'I can't spare you or your dog to go hunting. You're our eyes and ears. We have to float *Shearwater* and make her sound before the day is out. If the Vikings make a move and Garrick has to get news to us, it's vital that he doesn't blunder into one of their lookouts. Leave the dog with him and return with us. Use the day to tend your falcons and rest. I want you back here tonight.'

They waited. The sky brightened. Wayland fell asleep. His dog's forelegs twitched in a dream.

A thin stylus of smoke rose from the vapours hiding the bay. Vallon heard occasional voices and mechanical sounds. A weak yellow sun began to lift clear of the forest and the mist on the river dispersed, revealing the longship moored at the head of the bay. Inside, roped together at the stern, were the surviving Icelanders from the captured knarr – six men and two women. The Vikings had taken down the torn sail and eleven of them sat mending its edges, squatting like a convention of tailors. Two more were chopping firewood and another was stirring a cooking pot slung from a trivet. One of them sat on his own with a blood-stained bandage around his arm. Their chieftain went among them with a curious loping gait. He wore a wolfskin cape over a short-sleeved leather jerkin that exposed massive arms covered with tattoos from wrist to elbow. He was even bigger than Vallon remembered, standing a head above the next tallest man in his company.

Sixteen Vikings in the camp, four upriver, and probably as many again on guard around the camp. Vallon tallied with his fingers and came up with a total of twenty-four – five more than his own motley force.

The cook called out and the pirates laid down their work and wandered over to the fire.

'They're not in any hurry,' said Drogo.

'They'll repair their sail before coming after us,' said Vallon.

'They don't need it if they attack before evening. Thorfinn must know that we can't float *Shearwater* before the next high tide.'

'We'd see an assault from the river before they could press it home. I think they'll come by land and fall on us from several directions.'

'A night attack?'

Vallon tried to put himself in Thorfinn's place. 'My guess is that they'll hit us at first light tomorrow.'

'That gives us time to fortify the camp.'

A vague plan was beginning to take shape in Vallon's mind. 'We won't be waiting for them at the camp.'

On their way back the sky dissolved into smudgy grey clouds. A wandering drizzle fell. Raul greeted Vallon with a long face.

'Come and see for yourself.'

Shearwater rested bow up on the shoal, the rocks that had stranded her poking above the current. Vallon climbed aboard. They'd offloaded the cargo and a substantial amount of ballast. Raul had fixed a temporary patch of tarred sailcloth over the gash.

'I expected worse,' Vallon said.

'Look at the rib and crossbeam behind the hole.'

Vallon saw that the collision had jarred the heavy oak members out of position, ripping out the trenails that attached them to the strakes.

'We can't put to sea in that condition,' Raul said. 'We'd fold up in the first big wave.'

'How long to repair it?'

'Two, three days.'

Vallon surveyed the camp. It looked vulnerable by daylight, over-looked on both sides by tree-covered bluffs. The riverbanks were grey mud spiked with dead branches. The rain showed no sign of letting up and the Icelanders sat staring bleakly out from under rickety awnings piled with their chattels. Vallon remembered Hero's warning about the shortage of food. He pushed the worry aside. Deal with the Vikings first. That provoked a fresh concern. Under clear skies and a moon, the pirates probably wouldn't risk attacking from the river. But if this murk lasted into the night, they could creep right up to the bank with-out being spotted. They might attack by land and by ship. The camp would be empty, but *Shearwater* would be there for the taking.

'I want the ship moved to another mooring after dark. Can you patch her in time?'

'We'll try our hardest. We'll have to beach her to let in new planks. If the Vikings come while she's out of the water . . .'

'Garrick's watching them. He'll give us plenty of warning.'

'Captain, I don't know what you're planning, but I don't see how we can defeat them. There are too many. Even if we killed half of them, they'd still have their ship. All they have to do is wait downriver until we try to break out.'

'I know,' said Vallon. 'If only we could destroy the longship . . .' He broke off. 'Why not?'

Raul's head whipped round. 'You don't mean it.'

'They won't be expecting it.'

'Because they know it would be suicide.'

'Not if you attack while most of them are marching on our camp.'

'Me?'

'I'd do it myself if I wasn't needed elsewhere.' Vallon glanced at the cloud-heavy horizons. 'Everything depends on the weather. We'll hold a council after sunset.'

He ordered the Icelanders to throw up defensive positions that he had no intention of using. While they were chopping down trees and sharpening stakes, the tide reached full. With so much weight removed, Raul and his team floated *Shearwater* off the shoal without much effort. They harnessed four horses to the stem, dragged her onto the foreshore and set about repairing the hole. Vallon went in search of Wayland. The falconer lay sleeping on a bed of pine needles beside the caged hawks. Syth told Vallon through yawns that the falcons had eaten the horseflesh and showed no ill effects.

Next he sought out Hero. He found him talking to Father Hilbert. Vallon asked for a word and led Hero away a little distance.

'Do you know the secret of Greek Fire?'

Hero smiled as if he'd been expecting the question. 'Only the Byzantine rulers and a few senior engineers are trusted with the formula. I can guess some of the ingredients. Naphtha for one. Pitch. Sulphur. But as for the constituent that makes it light spontaneously and burn on water ... Does this have something to do with the Viking ship?'

'Yes, it does. A ship isn't as simple to fire as you might think. I need a substance that burns greedily and isn't easily quenched.'

Hero looked towards the stores. 'We have plenty of whale oil and sulphur, plus some turpentine. I could experiment with them.'

Vallon glanced at the surrounding heights. 'Be careful not to give away your intentions. The enemy is watching.'

Returning to check on progress at the ship, Vallon met Caitlin and her maids leading two horses laden with firewood. He nodded to her. She flinched and hurried on, throwing a quick look over her shoulder. Seeing him still watching her, she stamped one foot and went on at an even faster pace.

'Madam. One moment if you please.'

She stopped.

He strolled forward. 'You'd be captive or dead if I hadn't rescued you. A word of acknowledgement wouldn't go amiss.'

Slowly she turned. 'I cannot understand your language.'

'You understood me well enough to save me from your brother's cowardly treachery. I suppose I owe you thanks for that.'

Caitlin's eyes blazed. 'Helgi is not a coward and if I tell him you said so, he'll make you swallow your words in blood.'

'Tell him what you like, but be warned. If he plays false with me, I'll cut him down like a rabid cur.' He advanced another step. 'I command here. His life, your life, the lives of all you Icelanders – they're at my disposal and subject to my mercy.' Another step. 'Do you understand?'

Caitlin looked for rescue in all directions.

'I want an answer.'

'It's not easy to put a bridle on Helgi's temper.'

'Then take care not to inflame it.'

Caitlin stared at him, blood mounting in her cheeks. 'You are a wicked man.'

'Oh?'

'You killed your wife.'

'I did.'

Her eyes remained focused on his, fear and revulsion vying with some other emotion. She drew in breath and opened her mouth to speak, then changed her mind. She looked quickly around, perhaps worried that Helgi was watching, before glancing fiercely back at Vallon.

'Don't speak to me again.'

Watching her flit between the trees, Vallon felt oddly bucked up by the encounter.

The rain lasted all day. *Shearwater* lay on the mud and every moment Vallon expected Garrick to come running into camp with news that the Vikings were on the march or were mounting some action that Vallon hadn't anticipated. There were so many variables to consider. By the time twilight had deepened to dark, he had a splitting headache.

They lit fires. Around one of them he held his war council.

'Garrick hasn't returned,' he began. 'That's good. It means the Vikings are still in their camp.'

'They might have caught him,' Drogo said.

'If they had, the dog would have let us know.' Vallon turned to Raul. 'Is the ship ready?'

'We've fixed the hole. We still have to repair the crossbeam.'

'When Garrick returns, he'll move the ship across the river with the women and old folk. The Viking spies mustn't see what we're doing.'

'Why don't we use the dog to lead us to them? Kill them one by one.'

'I doubt we'd get them all. Besides, I *want* them to keep watching. Garrick will need a couple of oarsmen. Tell Helgi to select two of the weaker Icelanders.'

Helgi muttered grudging agreement.

Drogo mended the fire with a stick. 'The night's not so black that the Vikings won't work out that we've left the camp.'

'We'll leave a couple of men to walk up and down and show themselves in front of the fires.'

Drogo tossed the stick into the embers. 'This isn't my style. I fight battles. I don't stage shadow shows.'

'I'm not seeking a battle. I'd cut the Vikings' throats while they slept if the chance offered itself.'

An urgent pattering cut Drogo's answer off. He reached for his sword. 'Put it away,' said Wayland. 'It's the dog.'

It loped out of the dark and placed its head close to Wayland's. He stroked its ears. 'The Vikings are still in their camp.' The dog flopped down, its eyes red in the firelight. 'Here's Garrick.'

Vallon rose. 'What news?'

Garrick caught his breath. 'All day the Vikings did nothing but mend the sail and eat and ...'

'And what?'

'Sir, they abused the two women grievously.'

'What's he saying?' Helgi asked.

'They're raping the women,' Vallon said, his attention still fixed on Garrick. 'Did you form any idea of their intentions?'

Garrick slumped down. 'I think they planned to move against us at dusk. They took the prisoners off the ship and formed up at the river. I was sure they were about to embark, but then some sort of omen revealed itself. Two ravens flew across the river from different sides. When they met, they circled into the sky, talking together in croaks, then they separated and flew away to different quarters. Thorfinn seemed to interpret this as a bad sign because he made an angry gesture and walked back through his men, pushing them out of his way. Soon after that, it grew too dark to see and I thought it best to return.'

Vallon tapped Drogo's knee. 'We must set the ambush well before dawn.'

'They might come by a different route.'

'Wayland will let us know what path they take.'

'If it stays as dark as this, they won't come at all.'

'The sky could clear at any time. We have to be ready.'

'Why not use the dark to our advantage? Get Wayland and his dog to guide us to their camp. Ride on them as they lie sleeping.'

'Not a bad plan if we had the right men to put it into action. Instead, half our force have never used a sword in anger.' He looked up as two shadows approached. He shifted sideways. 'Come and join us.'

Hero and Richard settled in the space he'd made. 'We've been testing recipes for an incendiary,' Hero said. 'We achieved the best results with birchbark and dry pine needles soaked in turpentine, seal oil and sulphur.'

'What's he talking about?' said Drogo.

Vallon held up a hand. 'Can you demonstrate?'

Hero raised a mortar over the fire.

'Careful,' Vallon said. 'We don't want a display of pyrotechnics.'

Hero emptied the mixture onto the embers. It ignited with a soft *whoomph*, sending blue and yellow flames three feet into the air. Everyone recoiled. The flames sputtered and died down, leaving the stench of tar and brimstone hanging in the damp air.

'Once the fire has ignited,' said Hero, 'it can be flooded with more oil without the risk of extinguishing it.'

Drogo chased the fumes away with his hand. 'What's going on?'

'We're going to burn the longship. Hero, how much of that stuff do you have?'

'We filled two large sealskins and we have a keg of oil. Father Hilbert collected a bushel of kindling.'

'Burn the longship?' said Drogo. 'Why didn't you tell us?'

'Because I wasn't sure it would work. I'm still not sure, but I think the rewards justify the risk. Raul has volunteered to lead the firing party.'

The German gave a laugh from the crypt. 'It's so dark I ain't sure I'll be able to find the longship. I won't see where the sentries are hiding.'

'Wayland will make his way back to the Viking position after we've reached the ambush site. Arrange a system of signals with him.'

'What if the enemy's too strong?'

'I don't think they'll leave more than six guards.'

'Six! How many will be with me?'

Vallon looked at Drogo. 'I need three men to go with Raul.'

'Forget this folly. You said yourself that we needed every man for the ambush.'

'It isn't folly. However many we throw against the Vikings, we won't kill them all. And we won't come out of the encounter unscathed. Last night you said that *Shearwater* was our only means of deliverance. By the same measure, the dragon ship is our greatest threat. Destroy it and we render the Vikings impotent.'

Drogo crossed his arms. 'Fulk and I fight on horseback.'

'I'm not asking you to join the firing party.' Vallon turned to Raul. 'Explain my plan to Helgi. Tell him we need three Icelanders to make it work.'

Helgi gave his response before Raul had finished speaking. The German pulled a face at Vallon. 'He won't do it. He says that scattering our force will fatally weaken it.'

Vallon rocked back. 'Drogo, you tell him and make sure he knows I won't take no for an answer. '

'I can't force him to act against his will.'

Vallon leaned forwards and allowed a long pause before he spoke. 'We settled that I'm in command.'

'On this matter I agree with Helgi. We're already sending two men away with the ship. We should concentrate our strength against one target.'

Vallon struck the ground. 'I don't give a damn what you think!'

Drizzle hissed on the dying fire. The silence stretched so thin that someone had to break it.

'I'll go with Raul,' Hero said.

Eyes swung.

'And I'll go with you,' said Richard.

'That settles it,' said Drogo. 'Richard attacking the longship ... It's crackpot from first to last.'

Vallon looked up with ominous deliberation. 'I admit I've made some foolish decisions. I should have killed you when you landed on Iceland. I should have sailed away when Helgi spurned my advice to unite against the Vikings. I shouldn't have risked my company's lives rescuing you and those useless Icelanders.' His voice thickened. 'It's time you gave something in return.'

'Helgi was mistaken in not standing up to the pirates, I grant you that.' Drogo looked up. 'But you can't blame him for refusing to deal with you after your gross conduct towards his sister.'

'My gross conduct ...!' Vallon sprang up. 'I've heard enough. You and that puffed-up brat can fight your own campaign. From now on I'll look after the interests of my own company. Up you get, men. We're taking the ship across the river.'

Raul gripped his arm as he stormed away. 'About time, Captain.'

'*Give him the men.*'

Caitlin's voice. Vallon stopped in his tracks.

Figures scrambled up around the fire and a furious argument erupted, Helgi shouting and Caitlin giving back as good as she got.

Raul tugged at Vallon. 'Leave them to it.'

'Wait.'

'Captain, don't go back on your word. We ain't ever going to be trusting that lot.'

A crescendo from Caitlin, followed by the sound of someone storming off. Silence, and then Drogo's outline advancing against the flames.

'Vallon, are you still there?'

Raul gripped tighter. 'No, you ain't.'

'Three good fighting men and I won't settle for less.'

'You've got them.'

'Raul will choose them. Don't fob me off with cowards.'

'Very well.'

Vallon gave a sigh. 'Garrick?'

'Here, sir.'

'I want you to row the ship across the river without alerting the Viking spies. You'll be carrying the non-combatants.'

'Yes, sir.'

Vallon felt around in the dark. 'Hero, it was brave of you to offer your services, but there's no need for you and Richard to go with Raul.'

'Yes, there is. We talked about it and agreed that we didn't want to stay with the women. Besides, we know how to fire the incendiary.'

XXXI

The fires were faint red smudges in the blackness when Vallon accompanied the women and old folk down to the riverbank. Even standing at the water's edge, he couldn't see *Shearwater* moored only a few feet away.

'Garrick?'

'Here, sir.'

In darkness Vallon helped the evacuees climb aboard. His hand closed around a woman's arm, soft and resilient.

'Let go,' Caitlin said in a strangled whisper. 'I don't need your help.'

Vallon held on. 'But I'm grateful for yours.'

She must have turned. Her breath feathered his face and he smelled her perfumed sweat. Her hand cupped his neck, drew him closer.

'Vallon, bring Helgi back safe.'

She was gone from his grasp, only scent and sensation remaining. Garrick's murmur restored him to the moment.

'Everyone aboard, sir.'

Vallon stepped back. 'What's the state of the tide?'

'Still rising.'

'Make haste then.'

'How will we know if it's safe to return?'

'You'll know.'

Vallon listened for splashes that would betray their departure. He heard only a few muffled strokes soon lost in the random river noises.

'I don't like letting *Shearwater* out of our sight,' Raul murmured. 'If things don't go our way, Drogo and Helgi might try to seize her.'

'One threat at a time.'

Vallon returned to the camp and lit a torch and made a pretence of inspecting the defences. The rain was still falling when he went to take up a waiting position by one of the fires. Drogo and Helgi had crept away to muster the Icelanders and saddle the horses. Vallon stared into the embers, the pulsing coals shaping patterns that might have been a prefiguration of his destiny if he'd had the means to interpret them.

'Raul and his raiders are waiting by the river,' Wayland murmured.

Vallon riddled his eyes. 'I'm ashamed. You catch me napping while I run you ragged.' He shook his head and snorted. He couldn't see a thing. It was so dark that he almost lost his balance when he stood. 'Take my arm.'

Wayland led him to the bank. Only the muscular swirling of the current told Vallon that he was at the river.

'Everyone assembled?'

'Aye,' Raul answered. 'And everything loaded.'

'How will you fire the compound?'

'Each of us carries a shaded lamp and a firebrand.'

'The tide's in rhythm with our plans. You won't need to use your oars to approach the camp.'

'Fat lot of good if we can't see it.'

'Come here,' Vallon said.

One by one he embraced them and wished them good luck, the three Icelanders included. Then all six climbed into the invisible boat and pushed off into the invisible river.

Sightless as the blind, he returned to the camp. The fires were down to ash. He stoked them for the benefit of the watchers, then joined Drogo and the rest of the ambush party. In all they numbered fourteen – nine foot soldiers and five cavalrymen.

'Ready?'

'The night's as black as a chimney.'

'Not to Wayland. Let's go.'

They used the same method that had served them for their flight from Olbec's castle, each man holding on to a knotted rope with Wayland pathfinding. The dog went ahead to check that the route was clear and in the rear came the horses with their hooves muffled in sailcloth. It was a tetchy advance, the men tripping over branches and cursing the bogs and blood-sucking insects until Vallon grew so incensed with their racket that he felt his way down the line threatening to kill the next fool who railed against nature.

He and Drogo had decided on the ambush site with Wayland on their return from the Viking camp. It was on a broad ridge with a wind gap between the trees and it lay on the logical route between the rival positions. By day it offered a good view across to the next ridge and the river on their left. No river to be seen now, no trees, nothing. Vallon had only Wayland's word that they'd reached the right spot.

'See what the Vikings are up to. If they move, get back to us as soon as you can.'

The men dropped in their tracks and wrapped themselves against the rain and swarms of bloodsucking insects.

Drogo groped up to Vallon. 'They won't attack on a night as foul as this.'

'Then we'll have lost nothing more than a night's sleep.'

Vallon knew that wasn't true. He pictured the Vikings slumbering while his own force grew weary and demoralised. If the enemy didn't come tonight, he'd be hard put to impose his authority tomorrow.

Impossible to measure time in the blackout. The mosquitoes burrowed into his hair and brows. His face began to come up in bumps and weals. Men complained at the torment.

'I'll cut the tongue out of the next one who makes a sound.'

That didn't stop them cursing when the drizzle hardened into a drenching shower. Vallon stood with his back to it. He was ready to admit that their night's work had been wasted when the rain tailed off. There was no warning. The rain simply stopped and a cool draught stirred the trees.

Vallon turned to face the breeze. 'There's still time.'

The clouds peeled away layer by layer. The moon drifted out, bright enough to cast bars across the river and etch the trees in inky outline on the next ridge. Vallon gestured. 'Gather around, men.'

They shuffled up, shivering and rubbing their limbs. Vallon laughed and patted backs. 'A little exercise will set you all to rights. Nothing stirs the blood like shedding your enemy's.' He looked around. 'Drogo, position your horses in the trees on the left. Infantry, form up opposite.' He pointed at a spruce standing isolated in the wind gap, its branches spreading to the ground. 'I'll spring the trap from there. The moment I do, shoot a volley of arrows. Drogo, that's the signal for your force to hit them as hard as you can. Time it well and the Vikings won't know which way to turn.'

Some of the Icelanders didn't understand and shrugged at each other. Vallon repeated his orders, wishing he spoke better Norse.

Drogo sniffed. 'I'm surprised you choose to fight on foot.'

'Without an experienced soldier at their sides, the Icelanders won't press home their attack.'

Drogo left to make his dispositions. Most of the sky had cleared and stately white clouds drifted across the indigo gulf. Vallon stiffened at the sound of hurried footfalls.

'Wayland's coming.'

The sound grew louder. Vallon narrowed his eyes in concentration. Someone behind him hissed and his eyes bolted around. It couldn't be Wayland. The footfalls were approaching from the wrong direction. The Vikings must have seen that the camp was deserted and sent a runner to warn their chief.

Vallon ran for cover. 'Stay hidden. I'll deal with him.'

A man padded up onto the ridge, hurdled a toppled trunk and raced on. Vallon stepped out into his path at the last moment and the Viking ran himself through the heart with his own momentum. He dropped dead to his knees and Vallon braced one hand on his shoulder to withdraw his sword. As he did so, another figure crested the ridge. He saw Vallon, flailed to a halt and began to back away.

'After him!'

Half a dozen Icelanders sprang from their hiding places. The Viking flung himself to one side and hared off into the trees.

'Don't let him get away!'

Men plunged in pursuit. Vallon heard them tearing through the forest, the noises growing fainter until no sound was left except the wind sighing in the branches and his own thumping heart.

'We should have guarded our rear,' Drogo said.

Vallon swiped at the ground. 'The men should have been more alert.'

He crouched over his sword hilt as the searchers straggled back, blowing hard and shaking their heads. When the last of them returned to confirm that the Viking had escaped, Vallon rose with a long sigh and rubbed his itchy brow. Drogo idly kicked the ground. Vallon let his arms flop.

'We'd better return to camp,' said Drogo. 'The other two spies are probably plundering it.'

'You go. I'll wait for Wayland.'

The Icelanders were beginning to file away when Vallon spotted movement on the next ridge. 'Hold it.'

A shadow flickered through black palings. Vallon lost it, then picked it up again on the downslope. Two shadows moving in a soundless glide.

'It's Wayland and his dog.'

Vallon waited in the open. Wayland came flogging up the hill. He swallowed one breath straight after the other and glanced in bewilderment at the company. 'Why are you standing about? The Vikings aren't far behind me.'

Vallon rasped his hand along his jaw. 'The ambush has been discovered. The spies saw that we'd left the camp and sent two of their number to raise the alarm. We dealt with one, but the other got through.'

'No, he didn't.'

It took a moment to sink in. 'You killed him?'

'The dog caught him.' Wayland shoved Vallon away from the edge. 'Hide yourselves. They'll be here any moment.'

Vallon came to his wits. 'Quick! Back to your positions.' He dragged Wayland to the ground beside him. 'Did Raul make contact?'

'No. He hadn't reached the camp when I left.'

'Damn! How many are we facing?'

'Sixteen.'

Vallon looked for Drogo. He lay propped on his elbows a few yards away. 'Hear that?'

'Sixteen of them, fourteen of us. You might regret sending the raiders downriver.'

'The horses make it even.'

The dog whined. Wayland tensed. 'There they are. Crossing the ridge.'

Vallon made out a column filing through the trees, winding down from the ridge, disappearing into the dark sink at the bottom of the slope and then emerging again as they climbed towards the ambush. Moonlight glinted on axes and spearpoints.

Vallon gripped Drogo's arm. 'Direct your charge at Thorfinn. Take your timing from me. I won't attack until they're almost within touching distance. Be patient. Make sure the blood doesn't rush to Helgi's head.'

'I hear. Now let go. The enemy's almost on us.'

Vallon released his hold and Drogo hurried off.

'Where do you want me to stand?' Wayland asked.

'With the infantry. Aim for Thorfinn. Kill him and you could settle the encounter single-handed. Keep back from the fray and direct your arrows where they'll inflict the most harm. God spare you.'

Wayland nodded and ran off.

Vallon waited until the Vikings were committed to their path before worming back from the crest. Once he was out of sight he ran at a crouch towards the spruce. His eyes darted around, checking that everybody was concealed. He heard the slurred steps of the approaching Vikings and a muttered exchange. He pushed back into the branches and cleared a gap just wide enough to see through. He felt sick with excitement.

Up over the crest tramped the Viking leader, pale eyes roaming from side to side, breath misting. His axe rested over one shoulder and a sword hung from his hip and there was a shorter sword stuck in his belt. Lop off the serpent's head, an inner voice urged. Vallon resisted it. He waited with his sword held before his face. His breathing had steadied. Thorfinn Wolfbreath trudged past within twenty feet of him, his helmet dangling from his waist like the trophy head of some alien foe. Vallon counted off the men as they trooped by. '. . . eight, nine, ten . . .' He closed his eyes and kissed his sword.

'*Charge!*'

Helgi's cry, followed by thudding hooves, a dismayed shout from Drogo and the hiss of a single arrow.

Spitting with fury, Vallon pushed out round the back of the tree. Thorfinn stood unhurt, bellowing to his men. Helgi galloped towards the enemy line, spear levelled, Drogo and the other cavalrymen riding ragged behind him.

'I'll murder you,' Vallon mouthed, hurtling towards the nearest enemy and all his rage directed at Helgi.

The Viking swung round gaping and took Vallon's sword in his mouth, the impact sounding like a cleaver chopping through a rack of meat. Teeth and blood sprayed. The Viking dropped, clutching his face.

'At them, men!' Vallon shouted, his attention on the Viking in front of his first victim. The man swung. Vallon parried, disengaged, countered. His opponent blocked with his shield. Vallon feinted right, feinted left, left again, right, dragging the man off balance, saw the opening and slashed into it. The man dropped his sword and looked down at his arm dangling by a rope of muscle. Vallon leaped back, legs a-straddle, assessing the situation.

A mess. The Icelandic infantry still stumbling into action and Helgi prancing about with his liege men, looking for easy targets. Only Drogo and Fulk were fighting with discipline, riding against the enemy stirrup to stirrup, one hacking to the right the other to the left. Thorfinn stood swinging his axe in great arcs, roaring at his men to form up around him.

Vallon glanced round and saw an Icelander tottering away clutching the shaft of a spear that skewered him through the belly. The warrior who'd killed him avoided Vallon's blow and darted off to join the group around the chieftain. Vallon dragged away two Icelanders chopping at a fallen Viking.

'He's dead, you fools. All of you, form up on me.'

Only seven Icelanders joined him, leaving two of their number dead. He counted five dead Vikings, but the rest had thrown a shield wall around Thorfinn and were holding off the cavalry with their spears.

'Drogo, you have to break the wall! Back off and charge. This time do it right.'

Drogo cast a desperate look at him, seemed to shake his head, then wheeled away shouting at the others to follow. Twenty yards from the enemy they turned and bunched up. One of the horses was badly injured and slumped to its knees, spilling its rider. The Vikings knew that their position was almost impregnable and roared defiance.

Drogo whirled his sword above his head. 'Charge!'

Vallon grabbed the nearest Icelander. 'Follow me,' he shouted and plunged straight at the enemy.

The cavalry clashed before he reached them. Head and shoulders above his companions, Thorfinn leaned forwards and delivered a mighty blow. One of the horses galloped away with its rider lolling in the saddle.

Then Vallon was eye to eye with the foe. A spear lunged at him and he only just deflected it. He tried to follow up, but the shields closed again and he couldn't find a way past. Over to his right an Icelander maddened by battle tried to kick his way through. A Viking rammed his shield into his face, darted out and stabbed down, his victim dying with a bubbling scream. Almost in the same moment Thorfinn burst through the wall, his eyes burning with battlelust. His sword thrummed and an Icelander folded over like a cut sapling, his trunk almost severed.

Vallon knew that he'd lost all advantage and so did Drogo. He wrenched his horse away from the melee. 'It's no good,' he shouted. 'We'll try to cover your retreat.'

Vallon backed away. 'Withdraw in close order. Look out for each other.'

He'd retreated only a few yards when one of the Icelanders broke and ran, provoking a rout. Vallon found himself facing the Vikings alone.

'Flee!' Drogo shouted.

But Vallon stood his ground. His strategy had failed. This was his doom. He watched the Vikings, heard their exultant cries, saw them swell and surge towards him.

Drogo galloped across his line of sight, cutting down with savage precision. A gap opened in the Viking line. Through it ran another opponent.

Vallon adjusted his sword grip, his face an ugly snarl. 'Come and join me in hell.'

Six feet away his attacker stumbled and fell forward, an arrow wagging in his back. He struggled upright and twitched as another arrow thwocked into him.

'Run!' someone shouted, and Vallon glimpsed Wayland bending his bow for another shot.

Vallon fled after the Icelanders, the Vikings chasing in a screaming pack. Thorfinn's shout shivered the forest. His men stopped. Through the trees Vallon saw the warlord shake his axe above his head. His men left off their pursuit and ran to join him.

Vallon spotted Drogo. 'They're after our stores. Round up the Icelanders.'

Drogo spurred his maddened steed towards him. 'Impossible. The nearest is half a mile away and still running.'

'We would have routed them if you'd kept Helgi in check. Why didn't you follow my orders?'

'Don't blame me for your failure. It was lack of numbers that cost us victory.'

Vallon swore and staggered after the enemy. They were gone, the ridge empty. Vallon stood alone surveying his defeat when the distant blast of a horn rose up over the forest. It came again, drawn out and desperate. Vallon turned. For a moment everyone stood suspended, taking in the message signalled by the horn.

A roar from ahead and the chieftain came lumbering back. Vallon was standing in his path and didn't wait to contest it. He sprinted into the trees. The Vikings raced past and disappeared over the skyline.

Drogo spurred towards Vallon. 'Does that mean the German found the ship?'

Vallon folded over, fighting for breath. 'What else?'

The horn was still blaring. Vallon pulled himself upright and turned to survey the slaughter. Moonlight was giving way to grey dawn. Steam wafted from the wounds of the littered dead. Vallon found the Viking whose arm he'd all but severed writhing around the useless limb. Vallon reversed the grip on his sword and raised it above the man's chest. The man fell still and their eyes met, staring down opposite ends of a corridor that each must travel at the allotted time. Vallon brought the blade down and the Viking convulsed and then relaxed, stretching out one updrawn leg as if falling into slumber.

Drogo rode among the dead, taking stock.

'What's the count?' Vallon called.

Drogo looked over his shoulder. 'I make it six of them and five of us.'

'Don't forget the two scouts we killed.'

'There may be more dead on our side. Helgi's missing. He took a bad hit.'

Vallon remembered the rider swaying on the runaway horse. He pointed. 'His horse bolted in that direction.'

Fulk went in search. Drogo dismounted and wiped the blade of his sword with a handful of pine needles. He glanced at Vallon, shook his head and rammed his sword into its scabbard.

Vallon wandered away and faced the rising light. He filled his lungs with resin-scented air, astonished to be alive.

One of the Icelanders trotted out of the trees and called out.

'They've found Helgi.'

His horse had carried him a long way before he toppled out of the saddle. A circle of Icelanders surrounded him. He lay on his side with his back against the trunk of a fallen birch. His face was as white as clay, his eyes blank, blood dribbling from one corner of his greying mouth. Vallon began to crouch beside him, but Drogo pulled him back.

'Your face is the last thing he'd want to see.'

Drogo knelt and lifted Helgi's limp arm from his chest. Vallon grimaced. Thorfinn's axe had inflicted appalling damage. It had struck under his armpit and sliced diagonally through his torso, exposing the barely beating heart in its broken cage, cutting through entrails, releasing a fetid liquor from the torn bowels. Drogo took Helgi's hand.

Vallon looked at the Icelanders. 'Have you sent for his sister?'

'His spirit will have flown long before she gets here.'

Vallon sat down on the dead tree and mouthed along to Drogo's prayer. '*Gloria patri et filio et spiritu sancto . . .* '

When he looked again, proud and handsome Helgi was quit of this world. Vallon took no satisfaction in his death; he'd been a nuisance, not a foe. Vallon walked away and looked across the river. A fine day in the dawning, sunlight dappling the trees, splashes of gold among the conifers. A woodpecker jarred in the distance.

A shout went up. Someone else called out and by the time Vallon had dragged himself back to the ridge a chorus of excited cries rang through the forest. The sight that greeted him stopped his throat. From the direction of the Viking camp a column of sooty smoke rolled into the sky.

He shot a grin at Drogo. 'Not such a crackpot plan.'

Drogo gave the gusty laugh of a professional gambler beaten by the most improbable of flukes. 'One day your luck will run out and I'll be waiting.'

'Luck favours the bold.'

'Try telling that to Helgi's sister.'

Vallon sobered. 'You'd better break the news to her.'

Drogo nodded and mounted. Wayland was standing near them and when Drogo turned his horse, their eyes met. Drogo looked back at Vallon and gave an odd smile, then he rode away.

The Icelanders bore their fallen back to camp, leaving the slain Vikings stripped of their arms to be burned by their companions or abandoned to wolves and gore-crows. When the field was empty, Vallon and Wayland descended to the riverbank to await Raul's return. The falconer sat stroking his dog and staring across to the opposite bank. Watching him, Vallon thought that he'd be proud to have him for a son.

'You're a born warrior,' he said. 'Even though I was shaped for war from childhood, you've killed more men than I had at your age.'

'I don't take any pleasure in it.'

'I'm surprised. You told me that your grandfather was a Viking and would choose no other employment. You seemed proud of his exploits.'

'They were stories he told me while he was tending his vegetable plot.' Wayland gave Vallon a quick look. 'Do you take pleasure in killing?'

Vallon thought about it. 'I take satisfaction in the defeat of my ene-mies. The world's a dangerous place. Life's a vicious game. Your falcons know that.'

Wayland gave a scornful laugh. 'If you had lived among the beasts, you'd know that they kill out of necessity. Only men treat death as a sport.'

'I don't make war for sport.'

'Why then? Did you believe that the rulers whose armies you led waged war to make the world a better place?'

Vallon breathed in until his lungs pressed against his ribs. Two years ago, if a peasant had dared ask such a question, he would have had him flogged to death and forgotten his existence by next morning.

Wayland was watching him. 'You don't answer.'

Vallon's response rose in his throat but he couldn't give voice to it. *I made this journey to atone for a mortal sin and swore that I wouldn't take life except in defence of my own or my company. Six months later and I've lost count of the men who've died by my hand. And there'll be more.*

He smiled. 'I fight because that's all I'm good for.' He squeezed Wayland's arm. 'Off you go. Syth will be anxious for you.'

Wayland stood.

Vallon squinted up. 'Before Drogo left, you exchanged a look. As if you shared a secret.'

'What sort of secret would I share with Drogo?'

The oblique light left Wayland's face in shadow. Vallon nodded. 'I must have fancied it. Don't keep Syth waiting.'

When Wayland had gone, Vallon linked hands behind his head and stared at the sky. A line of geese flew upriver with their wings almost touching, the formation so precise. Soon they'd be going south, taking only a few days to make a passage that *Shearwater* wouldn't complete in a month. Winter would soon be on them. No food. The Icelandic skippers had told Raul that rounding the North Cape at this season might be impossible. So many things to worry about and yet his thoughts were so fickle that he found them turning towards Caitlin.

The boat appeared out of spangled reflections. Vallon stood and shaded his eyes. Six men had set off and only five were returning. He recognised Raul's squat form and prayed that the missing man wasn't

Hero or Richard. He walked to the tip of the bar and hailed the raiders. He gave thanks to God when he picked out Hero and Richard's features. A pang of remorse as he realised that the missing man was one of the Icelanders – a man whose name he'd forgotten and whose face he couldn't recall.

As the boat rowed closer, Vallon saw that Raul's beard had been burned to a frizzy mat and his eyebrows scorched to black speckles. Vallon helped him ashore.

'We saw the smoke. You saved the day.'

Raul stepped past him in a stink of burned hair. He threw himself down against a tree and plucked at his nitty brow with broiled hands. 'Didn't your ambush succeed?'

'We didn't hurt the enemy as much as I'd hoped. Tell me about your own action.'

Raul waved at Hero and shut his eyes.

Hero and Richard dumped themselves down beside Raul. They looked tired but surprisingly collected. The two surviving Icelanders joined them.

'The night didn't begin well,' said Hero. 'It was so dark that we lost all sense of place. The current kept pushing us into the bank. Eventually, from the sheer passage of time, we decided that we must have gone past the bend, but we couldn't locate the Viking camp. Insects were eating us alive. In despair we rowed for the shore with no more ambition than to make our way back as soon as we could see what we were doing.'

'We cursed you,' Richard said.

'You're not the only ones. On with your tale.'

'After a flurry of rain, the clouds parted and the moon showed itself. We worked out that we were below the camp.' Hero touched one of the Icelanders. Vallon recognised him as the youth who'd jumped aboard *Shearwater* ahead of the womenfolk. 'Rorik went up the bank in search of the Vikings. He wasn't gone long. Their camp was around the next point, no more than an arrow flight from our hiding place. Rorik arrived as the Vikings were filing out.'

'You waited for them to leave and then attacked the longship.'

They exchanged glances. Raul looked up from under his scorched brows. 'We were done in, wet to the bone and driven mad by the midges. Our kindling was damp, we had no idea how many Vikings

374

were guarding the camp or where they were laid up. Flog me or dock me, Captain, but my only thought was to save our skins.'

Vallon eased back. 'In those circumstances, I might have made the same decision.' He grinned. 'Something made you change your mind.'

Hero resumed his account. 'We rowed across the mouth of the bay, plying our oars as if they were feathers. The longship lay only fifty yards from us and there didn't seem to be anyone on board. We kept going and then Richard said, "We can't skulk away like this. What will we tell Vallon?"'

Richard smiled sheepishly. Vallon stared at him.

Raul spat. 'We all sort of looked at each other and then without a word we began pulling towards the ship. 'Course we hadn't gone more than a few yards when an almighty shout went up from the shore and two guards who'd been sleeping on board sprang up. Three Vikings came running down from their posts on the hills. I took aim on one of the ship-guards. Twenty yards range. Couldn't miss.' Raul spat again. 'Well, I did. The rain had made my bowstring limper than the pope's dick.'

Richard sniggered into his palm.

'We fought our way aboard,' said Raul. 'I dealt with one of the guards. Rorik and Bjarni finished off the other one. Skapti got killed in the scrap. He fell dead into the water, God keep him.'

Vallon nodded. He hadn't the faintest idea who Skapti was.

'By this time the shore sentries had nearly reached the bank. There was just time to cut the mooring and push off. Two of the Vikings ran into the water and we fended them off with oars. The other one stayed on shore blowing the alarm. While we were fighting off the two in the water, Hero and Richard set about raising a fire.'

'I thought it would never light,' said Hero. 'There was an inch of water in the hull and the timbers were soaked from the rain. Luckily for us, the Vikings had refitted the sail. We drenched it in oil, piled all the faggots around the mast, and poured our compound over them. Even then it took an age for the fire to take hold. When it did catch, the flames shot halfway up the mast. The Vikings had left their oars in the ship. We gathered them up along with anything else that would burn and threw them on to the blaze.'

Raul continued the tale. 'When the Vikings saw the fire, the one on shore launched their boat and the two in the water waded back to join him. Hero was shouting for us to get off, but the yard and sail had collapsed across the deck and there was a wall of fire between me and our boat. By now the three Vikings had nearly reached the ship. Captain, you know I'm no swimmer or I'd have jumped overboard. I held my breath, shut my eyes and ran through the flames. Tripped over a thwart. I thought I'd had it.'

'He was smoking when he came out,' Hero said.

'We jumped into the boat and rowed as hard as we could. The Vikings didn't chase us. They were too busy trying to save their ship.'

'Did they succeed?'

'Last I saw, it was burning like a torch.'

'So it's destroyed.'

'As good as,' Raul said. 'Mast gone, sail gone, oars gone, shrouds gone. The keel's probably no more than scorched, but the strakes amidships must be burned to cinders.'

'We didn't wait around,' said Richard. 'We knew the main Viking force would soon return and might pursue us in the ship's boat. The thought of what they'd do if they caught us kept us from flagging even when our strength was spent.' He gave a little laugh. 'And here we are.'

Vallon gazed at them in wonder. 'Here you are.'

Grief-stricken wails rose from the camp. Garrick had rowed *Shearwater* back to her mooring and the refugees ran down to the shore, clamouring for news. Vallon parted the crowd and walked towards the centre of the camp.

Caitlin knelt over Helgi's body, rocking back and forth. Her maids and her brother's followers stood behind her. Drogo frowned and waved Vallon back. He hesitated. Caitlin lifted her distraught face and caught sight of him. She ceased her lamentations and made a sound low in her throat. Seizing the sword lying on Helgi's corpse, she ran at Vallon mouthing gibberish. Drogo and her retainers raced after her, but she reached Vallon before they could catch her and drew back the sword with both hands. He shot out a hand and grasped her wrists. She struggled and then she went limp and dropped the sword. Her eyes gushed tears. She sagged against him and he had to gather her close to stop her falling. He hadn't held a woman for years and it was the strangest sensation to be holding to his chest a princess who wanted to kill him.

Her voice bubbled through tears. 'You promised to bring him back safe.'

'I'm sorry. Take comfort in the knowledge that your brother died bravely, engaging the enemy with no regard for his own life.'

She batted her hands against his chest. 'You threw his life away!'

Over her shoulder, Vallon saw Drogo striding up. 'What lies have you been spreading?' the Frank said.

'No lies,' said Drogo. 'You knew the charge was pointless.' He wrenched Caitlin from Vallon's grip. 'Get away from her.'

Caitlin's maids took her by the arms and led her away. Vallon stood chest to chest with Drogo. 'I should have known that you'd twist facts to your own end. Well, here's another tale for you to distort. The longship is ashes and two more Vikings have gone to their doom.'

Drogo's stubbled cheeks worked. He managed a stiff bow.

'Don't congratulate me,' said Vallon. 'It's your brother who deserves the credit.'

He swung on his heels.

'Vallon.'

Vallon wafted a blood-smeared hand. 'Enough.'

Drogo caught up with him. 'I grew close to Helgi. Last night, before we went into action, he asked me to act as Caitlin's guardian should he be killed. I told him that I'd be honoured to accept. I pledged to protect her with my life.'

Vallon kept walking. 'Very worthy and I'm sure you'll honour your pledge. But how does it concern me?'

Drogo's throat strained with emotions he couldn't express. He jabbed a finger. 'Just keep away from her. That's all.'

Vallon had retreated to a quiet stretch of the riverbank before he fathomed Drogo's meaning. Helgi must have dressed up the encounter at the lake to make it look like he – Vallon – was besotted with his sister. Drogo thought he was a rival for her affection. The Norman's stupidity angered him. He turned and glowered.

Garrick was approaching, carrying a bowl and bread. 'You haven't broken your fast, sir.'

Vallon ate in silence, looking across the river.

'What will we do now?'

377

'We'll set up camp on the far bank. It will take a couple of days to make the ship seaworthy. Wayland can use the time to gather food for the hawks. After that . . . ' Vallon checked himself. He'd almost said, 'We'll go home.' He smiled at Garrick. 'We'll continue our journey. Will you come with us to Constantinople?'

'What would I do there, sir?'

'Whatever you want. It's the greatest city on earth.'

'Cities don't agree with me. I went to Lincoln once. All those people in one place made my head spin.' He glanced shyly at Vallon. 'I dream of buying ten acres in the place where I grew up. Live my life out and go to rest in the soil I sprang from, the place where my parents lie buried, the plot where my children sleep. I know it's only a dream.' He laughed. 'That Daegmund wouldn't be happy to see *me* back. He'd make life hot, I can tell you.'

Vallon gripped his arm. 'You'll have your ten acres. If that's all I achieve by this endless wandering, I'll be content.'

Garrick's eyes found his, ducked away, face shadowing. 'I can't get quit of the sight of those women and what the Vikings did to them. They're mother and daughter – only a girl. Can't we save them, sir? I'd take up a weapon if you thought it would help.'

Vallon shook his head. 'I can't ask my company to make any more sacrifices. The season's growing late and we have a great distance to travel. We must press on.'

He'd risen to his feet. Garrick remained seated with an expression of gentle melancholy. Vallon touched his shoulder. 'I'm sorry. There's nothing we can do.'

XXXII

Wayland padded through the forest with Syth and the dog in ghostly attendance. To their right the horned moon laid a silver trackway across the river. From the Vikings' camp on the opposite bank came a ceaseless chopping and hammering. Day and night they laboured to repair their longship. When Wayland had spied on them the day after the battle, he would have sworn that the hulk was unsalvageable, its mid-section burned to the waterline. Returning the next day, he'd found that they'd already started replacing the strakes and yesterday they'd made good the starboard timbers.

He crept into a grove of willows and peered up through the tracery. Two plump silhouettes sprouted from a branch twenty feet above the ground. He turned to Syth, laid a finger to his lips and worked his way round until both roosting grouse were outlined against the moon. He dropped to one knee and raised the miniature crossbow Raul had made for him. The bow was drawn, an untipped arrow slotted in the track. He aimed low to compensate for the spring of the bolt at such close range. He loosed. A solid thump and one of the grouse fell flapping in its death spasms on the forest floor. Its mate uttered a cluck of alarm and shifted along the branch. Wayland reloaded and took fresh aim.

Missed. The bolt clattered away through the boughs. The grouse shuffled almost to the tip. Wayland loaded another bolt. The branch bobbed under the weight of the grouse. Wayland tried to adjust to the rhythm. No good. He shut his eyes, took a breath, raised the bow and loosed as soon as the grouse came into his sights.

Phut.

Wayland blinked. The branch was bare. The dog ran in to retrieve. He massaged the back of his neck. 'That's enough for tonight.'

'How many have we got?'

Wayland counted the bodies looped around his belt. 'That makes seven.'

Syth clapped her hands. 'Six for the falcons. One for us. I'll cook it right now.'

While she roasted the game, Wayland stared vacantly into the flames. He was worn out by his never-ending duties – tending the falcons, finding food for them, spying on the Vikings . . .

He ate his share of the grouse in silence. Across the fire, Syth watched him with eyes full of questions. He knew she was troubled by his moody silences, the fact that he hadn't taken her in his arms since leaving Iceland.

'This is half raw,' he said, tossing the remains to the dog.

'I know you're tired, so I cooked it as fast as I could.'

Wayland lay down and pulled up a blanket. Syth settled beside him, not quite touching. He could sense her unhappiness. He remembered the rows between his parents and his relief when they made up. He rolled over. 'It's not you that puts me out of heart. It's thinking of what we have to go through.'

'It's not only that,' she said. 'You're worried that you're stuck with me for ever and ever.' She snuggled close, her breath warm on his cheek. 'I might get sick of you first.'

Wayland bolted awake. Syth and the dog came tearing out of the sallows.

'Old Horny's in the river!'

Wayland grabbed his bow. 'Old Horny?'

'Black with horns and cloven feet, big as a house.'

Her eyes were huge and the dog seemed to have been seized by a fit, jaws gnashing, flanks trembling. Excitement not terror. He peered towards the river. Grey trees were beginning to gather out of the dawn. He heard water purling through a shoal.

'Stay here.'

He strung an arrow and worked towards the bank. Glancing back, he saw Syth creeping behind him with one hand clenched between her teeth. He gestured at her to go back.

She shook her head emphatically.

Wayland reached the edge of the thicket. Twenty yards from the bank stood a diabolical misshape backlit by the paling sky. He'd never seen such a monster. Several different creatures seemed to have gone into its making. Its dewlapped head had a trunk-like snout, jackass ears and a crown of antlers six feet across. A bull's humped shoulders sloped down to a puny crupper tipped with an apology of a tail. All supported on knobbly legs that looked too spindly to bear its weight. It looked up, masticating slowly. Water dribbled from its muzzle. It breathed a soft snort and lowered its head again. Wayland wormed back to Syth.

'It's not the devil,' he whispered.

'What is it then?'

'Some kind of deer.'

'Old Horny can take any form he chooses. Once when I was in the fen, I saw a flittermouse that—'

Wayland pressed a hand over her mouth and opened his eyes wide in warning.

380

She nodded and he took his hand away. He raised his bow. Syth clutched at him.

'You're not going to kill it.'

'We've nearly finished the horsemeat. A beast that big will feed us for a week. Stay here and don't make a sound.'

The beast hadn't moved. There was no wind to carry their scent and the current jostling down the shoal must have smothered their voices. The beast was standing almost head-on to him. Wayland waited for it to present its flank. He could make out the gleam of its eyes. It shifted its position and sighed. A melancholy misfit oppressed by its solitude. Wayland sighted behind the withers. Only a shot to the heart would bring down an animal that size.

He knew he'd hit his mark from the hollow sound the arrow made as it struck. The beast grunted and plunged forward, its hooves throwing up spray. The dog hurled itself into the water.

'Leave it, fool!'

Wayland drew another arrow and set off along the bank in pursuit. The beast was galloping towards a spit choked with willows and birches. It had almost reached it when it stumbled and sank down on its front knees. The dog whimpered and paddled faster. The beast groaned and regained its feet. It staggered forward and then stopped again, legs splayed, head drooping. Deaf to Wayland's commands, the dog surged up and sank its jaws into a hind leg, aiming for the hamstring. Spray exploded and the dog went sailing through the air to land fifteen feet away.

'I told you!'

The beast swung its head towards him. Gouts of blood poured from its mouth. It gave a sorrowing grunt and then it settled on its hindquarters and flopped over.

There was a ringing in Wayland's ears. The dog swam up to the carcass, apparently uninjured. He puffed out his cheeks and turned. Syth was standing a few feet away, staring in awe. He drew his knife.

'I'd better check that it's dead.'

It lay on its side, blood darkening the water around it. He looked into its eye and saw his reflection, growing duller with each passing moment.

The dog was watching him with a sheepish expression. He kicked out at it. 'You're lucky it didn't break your back.'

He dragged the beast into the shallows and tethered it by a line to a tree. Syth walked around it, studying it from all angles, but she wouldn't come within touching distance.

'Run back to camp and tell Raul to bring the boat.'

She turned and bounded away, her limbs whirling in the way that always made him smile.

'Better make that two boats.'

She ran on the spot and then darted off, the dog racing after her. Wayland looked again at the beast and his smile died. He ran a hand through his hair.

The new-risen sun lay like a chalice in a hollow on the horizon. He lay down with his hands behind his head. Above him, birch leaves winked like gold coins. He felt like a murderer.

The sun was shining in his eyes when he woke. He rose yawning and peered towards the Viking camp. The sounds of labour had stopped. The Vikings had dragged the longship out of the water to continue their repairs, and from here it was hidden by the curve of the bay.

He was about to turn away when a jerky movement caught his attention. Up over the trees fringing the bay rose a pale spar. Wayland grimaced. A mast swinging upright.

A creature in the forest gave a pained scream. The cry came again, from further off. He scanned the trees behind him. There were bears and wolves in the forest. He'd seen their spoor.

When he looked across the river again, the dragon ship was gliding out into the bay, its new timbers in bald contrast to the rest of the hull. Oars stroked and then rested. Even if it wasn't fit to take to the open sea, the Vikings could use it to block the company's escape. The oars dipped again and the longship reversed back into its lair. After a while the hammering and tapping started up again.

Wayland looked upriver and saw the two boats approaching. When Raul saw the beast he pushed his hat high up his scalded brow.

'How many arrows did it take?'

'One. Do you know what it is?'

'Elk. I've seen them on the Baltic coast. Good eating. Smoked, it will keep us fed until we reach Norway.' He noticed the grouse at the base of the tree. 'And you've got grub for the falcons.'

'It isn't enough.'

'Kill some more tonight.'

Wayland shook his head. 'The Vikings have repaired the longship. They've even made a new mast.'

Raul scanned the enemy shore. 'A mast ain't no use without a sail.'

'It doesn't matter. They still control the river.'

The company slept on *Shearwater* out in mid-river – a precaution against its capture by Drogo and Helgi's men. Come sunrise next morning, her crew brought her in close to the Icelanders' camp, dropping anchor in five feet of water. The refugees jostled on the bank with their provisions and the few trade goods they'd saved. Vallon lifted a hand.

'Before you board, some rules. First, all food goes into a common store.'

Voices rose in dissent and a few individuals clutched their bundles to their chests.

'It's up to you. Keep your own food, go your own way. Richard's in charge of the stores and will make sure everybody receives fair shares. You can appoint one of your own people to help him.'

The grumbles subsided.

'No Icelander is allowed to carry arms on the ship without my permission. Hand over your weapons as you board. They'll be kept ready for immediate use, but if any man takes up a sword without my say-so, I'll treat it as mutiny.' Ignoring the fresh wave of protests, Vallon turned to Garrick. 'Bring her in. Load the horses first.'

When they'd been lowered into the hold, the Icelanders began filing onto the ship. Raul and Garrick collected their weapons. Hero and Richard gathered in the provisions. As one man jumped to the deck, Raul seized him by the arm, reached into the man's tunic and pulled out a small sack. He opened it and sniffed the contents. 'Barley,' he said, and cuffed the smuggler across the deck.

The stern deck filled. Caitlin stood arguing at the foot of the gangplank with Tostig and Olaf, Helgi's men.

'We haven't got all day,' said Vallon.

Tostig looked up. 'We won't lay down our swords.'

'Then stay here. You'll be doing me a favour.'

Caitlin said something Vallon didn't catch. Tostig and Olaf climbed the plank in a fury, hurling down their swords so violently that Raul had to use both hands to wrench them from the deck.

Dressed in a plain wool shift, Caitlin mounted the plank with her maids. Hands helped her down and the Icelanders parted before her.

Only the two Normans remained on the bank. 'Fulk will hand over his sword,' said Drogo. 'You know I can't surrender mine.'

'I understand,' said Vallon. 'Garrick, raise the plank and leave Drogo with his honour unblemished.'

'You were glad enough of my sword the night we fought the Vikings. You'll probably need it again before this journey is over. I give you my word that I won't raise it against you until we reach a place of safety.'

Vallon glanced at his company, saw Raul shrug. He turned back to Drogo. 'I accept your promise. Now get aboard. We're wasting the tide.'

The Icelanders crammed the stern deck. Raul stood on a thwart to count them. 'Twenty-three. Captain, even if we could rescue the prisoners, there ain't no room for them.'

Vallon nodded, then called for silence. 'Most of you were sailing for Nidaros, but we don't have enough food and water for such a long voyage. We'll take you to the nearest haven. From there you'll have to make your own arrangements. In the meantime, here are some more rules. Some of you know that I campaigned against the Moors in Spain. I noticed that our Muslim enemies enjoyed better health than the Christian armies did. The Moors avoid fevers by washing their hands before handling food and after attending to the wants of nature.'

Raul was translating. 'Not sure they follow you, Captain.'

'Tell them to shit in the buckets provided at the stern and rinse their hands afterwards. No personal cooking fires. Meals to be taken in shifts.' Vallon lifted a hand. 'One last thing. The foredeck is reserved for my company. Nobody steps on it without my permission. That's it.'

Father Hilbert called for attention. 'Before we commit ourselves to the perils that await us, let us fall to our knees in earnest supplication of God's mercy and forgiveness for all the grievous wrongs—'

'Say your prayers on the move,' said Vallon. He nodded at Garrick. 'Hoist anchor.'

*

Shearwater rowed to within a mile of the Vikings' camp before their lookouts blew a warning.

'Keep to the left bank,' Vallon ordered. 'Raul, prepare to hand out the weapons.'

'They won't be able to launch their ship in time,' Wayland said. He'd returned from last night's prowling to report that the pirates had beached the longship for further repairs.

The tide bore them downstream at strolling pace. The bay came in sight.

'There they are!'

The Vikings streamed down to the shore, yelling and shaking their weapons. One group dragged behind them the roped and wretched prisoners. Their captors herded them to the water's edge, where they fell to their knees, raising arms in supplication, beating their chests, tearing their hair.

'We must save them!' one of the passengers shouted, and other Icelanders took up his cry. Many were relatives or neighbours of the captives.

'Keep going,' Vallon said.

'There's Thorfinn,' said Raul. 'Christ, he's a big bastard.'

Naked to the waist, the Viking chief ran into the river, pushing out the longship's boat. He jumped into it as *Shearwater* drifted below the lower edge of the bay. The boat soon appeared behind them, rowed by four men. Thorfinn crouched in the bow, shouting at the oarsmen to dig deeper and faster.

'What's he after?' said Raul.

'I believe he wants to negotiate.'

The rowers strained to catch up, keeping out of crossbow range. Four or five Vikings scrambled along the bank behind them. The boat drew level and Thorfinn cupped his hands around his mouth.

'Raul, tell the Icelanders to be quiet. Garrick, bring us within earshot.'

Shearwater steered to starboard.

'That's close enough.'

Thorfinn stood up. 'Hey, Frankish. Where are you going? You think you'll sail around the North Cape? No, you're too late. Hey, Frankish, listen to me. Even if you get round the cape, you'll starve before you reach the nearest settlement.'

'You understand what he's saying?' Raul asked.

'I get the drift.'

'Hey, Frankish, let's talk.'

'Raul, what do you think?'

'I say we keep going.'

'What about you, Hero?'

'I think we should find out what he has to say. We know the journey down the Norway seaboard is dangerous. The currents are treacherous and the mountains fall straight into the sea. Thorfinn knows those waters. We might get some useful information out of him.'

Vallon faced downstream, the forest sliding away on each side. At this rate, they would meet the sea before noon and then their fate would be determined by nothing more complicated than wind and weather.

'Heave to.'

'Captain, we ain't going to get nothing out of Thorfinn.'

'Anchor in the middle of the channel. Wayland, tell Thorfinn to approach.'

The Vikings stroked towards *Shearwater* and backed water about a hundred yards off.

'Come closer,' Vallon shouted. 'I can't hear you.'

Thorfinn mimed rowing motions. 'You come to me.'

Vallon looked for a way to end the impasse. Not far downstream the current divided around two smooth tongues of rock separated by a deep channel. After many false starts and cross-purposes, Vallon made it understood that he and one other would parley with Thorfinn and another Viking delegate, each pair to occupy a separate boulder.

Thorfinn waved agreement. 'You go first, Frankish.'

'Come with me,' Vallon told Wayland. 'Leave your bow.'

They climbed into the spare boat, rowed down to the boulders and climbed onto its polished surface. Wayland kept hold of the boat. Thorfinn put ashore to offload his men, then he and one of his lieutenants headed towards the rendezvous.

The Viking chief stood in the bow dangling his axe from one hand. Its crescent-shaped blade must have weighed fifteen pounds, yet he hefted it as casually as if it were an item of cutlery. In addition, he wore at his waist a plain broadsword and carried at the back of his belt a short stabbing blade or scramasax. He leaped on to the rock, appeared to trip and teetered at the edge of the channel. He recovered himself and looked up, his jaw split in a splayed ochre grin.

Vallon frowned. 'He's clowning.'

Thorfinn's grin died. He raised his axe one-handed and pointed it at each enemy in turn, sighting on them with eyes as cold as a gull's. He was built on a prodigious scale – close to seven feet tall, with thighs like wine tuns and a chest slabbed with muscle. Years of axe- and sword-play had made a hump of his right shoulder. Across his naked torso marched a fantasy in woad – winged eagles, writhing serpents, warriors on horseback. He let the axe head drop to the stone with a clang.

'You are in bad trouble, Frankish.'

'Not as bad as you. We have a sound vessel and plenty of fresh meat. You have neither.'

Thorfinn aimed his axe at the Viking camp. 'We've got a living larder.' He gnashed his teeth. 'Hungry wolves take big bites.'

'No sail or cordage, though. Without them, you're going nowhere.'

Thorfinn dropped to his hams and peered at Vallon over the haft of his axe. 'All right, Frankish, I'll trade you four prisoners for the sail from the Icelanders' ship.'

'I don't want your prisoners. I'm already carrying more Icelanders than I can cope with.'

Thorfinn said something to his lieutenant before turning back. 'What I say is true. You can't return around the North Cape. Ask the Icelandic captains.'

'I'd rather hear it from you.'

'The autumn winds will be against you. They'll crush you against the rocks. They'll drive you into the Maelstrom.'

'If that's the case, what are you doing so far east?'

Thorfinn wiped his nose. 'We didn't choose to land on this coast any more than you did. We were on an expedition to the Faroes when the storm blew us round the cape.'

'That shows how fickle the winds can be. Winter is still a few weeks off. All we need is two or three days of easterlies and we'll be back in the open ocean.'

Thorfinn stood up. 'Suppose you did round the cape. There are no settlements between here and Halogaland. That's my country. This year the harvest was poor. How do you think my people will treat you when you come ashore begging for food and shelter?' He clucked his tongue and drew the edge of his axe across his throat.

'I've no reason to believe anything you say.'

Thorfinn regarded him thoughtfully. 'The Icelanders say you're travelling to the Varangian Way.'

'The Road to the Greeks,' said Wayland.

'Suppose we are.'

'There's only one way to reach it.' Thorfinn felt in his belt purse and took out a stub of pigment. He wetted it in the river, knelt on the boulder and began tracing a shape on the stone. First he drew what looked like the outline of a thick thumb, and then from the base of the thumb, he added a squiggly V.

'What is that supposed to show?'

Thorfinn placed his index finger on the beginning of the line and jabbed it up and down.

'He's saying it marks the spot where we're standing,' said Wayland.

'*Ja, ja. Hit.*' Thorfinn pointed east, put his finger on the starting point and moved it in three arcs to the end of the thumb. 'After three days' sailing the land turns south into Danger Bay. The Rus call it the White Sea.' His finger described half a dozen more arcs before reaching the bottom of the V. 'Six days' sailing and you come to the head of Danger Bay. From there a river takes you south through the forest to Holmgard.'

'Holmgard's the Norse name for Novgorod,' Wayland said.

Vallon was intrigued. 'You've travelled this route.'

'Of course. For furs and slaves. The last time two summers ago.'

Vallon eyed the drawing, an unknown landscape dimly forming in his mind. 'Danger Bay, you called it.'

'Skraelings live on its shore. Lapps. Nomad fishermen and reindeer herders. On our last expedition they captured three of my men. I never even saw them taken. Their wizards can assume whatever shape is agreeable to them.'

'Is there food along the way?'

'At this season the shores swarm with wildfowl and the fish jam the rivers so tightly that there isn't room for them to swim upstream.'

'How far to Novgorod from Danger Bay?'

'From one new moon to the next.'

'A whole month?'

'Listen, Frankish, it would take you three months to sail to Novgorod through the Baltic.'

'He's probably right,' said Wayland. 'It took us three weeks just to reach the Orkneys.'

Vallon turned back to Thorfinn. 'Describe the journey overland.'

Thorfinn took up his chalk again. Working on a fresh area of rock, he drew a vertical line, followed by a small circle. 'You follow a river south until you reach a lake.' He drew another line and then a large circle. 'Another river and another lake called Onega, so big you can't see across it.' He slashed another vertical and followed up with a circle so large he ran out of space. 'One more river brings you to Lake Ladoga, even larger than the last. Follow the southern shore and you are in the land of the Rus.'

'What's to stop us from finding the route by ourselves?'

'A hundred rivers flow into Danger Bay. Only one of them takes you to Holmgard. All the others lead to the grave.' Thorfinn jabbed his chest. 'I know the right river.'

'Is that the route you're taking?'

'It's the only way left to us. Even if we had a sail, our keel's too weak to risk the ocean. Hey, Frankish, give me your spare sail and we'll voyage south together.'

Vallon stared upstream. 'Does this river have a name?'

Thorfinn shrugged. 'You can call it what you like.'

'It flows from the south. Wouldn't it bring us to the same place?'

Thorfinn shook his head. 'A day upriver it divides. One fork goes west, the other has rapids that can only be passed in small boats.'

'Will we be able to take our ship to Novgorod?'

Another shake of the head. 'Your knarr draws too much water.'

'We need to consider what you've said.'

Thorfinn gave an expansive wave. 'Take your time, Frankish.'

Vallon turned to Wayland. 'What do you make of that?'

'The route's probably more difficult than he makes out, but he wouldn't offer to guide us unless it was passable. What I don't understand is why.'

'Simple. First, unless we give him a sail, he and his men are dead. Second, he wants our passengers for slaves and our trade goods for booty. Since he can't seize our ship, he hopes to herd us like lambs to slaughter until we're close to market. That way, he doesn't even need to feed us on the journey.'

'A truce wouldn't last that long. One wrong word, one small setback ... Also, it would mean abandoning *Shearwater*. If the overland route proved to be impassable, there'd be no way back.'

'I know.' Vallon made a calliper with thumb and forefinger and clamped it across his forehead. He gazed at the ship upstream. All the passengers were watching, wondering what fate was being hammered out for them. 'It's difficult. What would your decision be?'

Wayland looked at the forest, looked at the sky. Vallon waited. He was struck by the incongruity of their situation – negotiating with a barbarian on a rock in the middle of a nameless wilderness river.

'It's the falcons,' Wayland said at last. 'If we go by the seaway, they'll die. All it would take is a few days without food. If the land described by Thorfinn is half as rich in game as he says ... I've come a long way for those falcons. If it was up to me, I'd risk the overland route.'

'So would I, for various reasons. One of them being that Drogo won't move against us while he's got the Vikings to worry about.'

Thorfinn was squatting on his islet, probing inside his mouth.

Vallon faced him. 'There are conditions.'

The Viking rose shaking his head. 'First you give me the sail and cordage. Then maybe we'll talk again.'

'I'll give you half a sail.'

'*Nei!*'

'Half a sail and enough cordage to rig it. In return you'll hand over the women prisoners and four of your men as hostages. We'll give you six men in exchange. Each set of hostages will guarantee the safety of the other. Once we reach the head of Danger Bay, we'll release them.'

Thorfinn's jaw hung loose. He leaned forward, eyes squinting for trickery. 'Why six of your people?'

'Because the Icelanders are a burden and the fewer I carry, the easier my life will be. I'll even supply rations for the six hostages.'

Thorfinn went into huddled council with his lieutenant. Finally he turned.

'I won't part with the women. Why do you want them? They're not your kin.'

'Unless you release them, I won't give you the sail.'

'Then we'll all perish.'

Vallon looked at Wayland. 'I can't jeopardise the lives of twenty for the sake of two. There'll be other opportunities to save them.' He faced Thorfinn. 'We'll settle the women's fate another day. The other terms aren't negotiable.'

Thorfinn smiled as if contemplating a sunny prospect behind Vallon's head. 'Give me six strong men who can ply oars.'

Raul hailed them.

'The tide's on the turn,' Wayland said.

'How soon can you make your ship ready?' Vallon asked Thorfinn.

'Tomorrow.'

'We'll make the exchange at the mouth of the river. If we're not there, it's because we've caught a wind from the east.'

A storm of outrage burst upon Vallon when he returned to the ship and announced his change of plan. The refugees surged forward. Raul pushed them back. Drogo shouldered his way to the front.

'You have no right to gamble with our lives.'

'Whatever course we take is a gamble.' Vallon waved his arms. 'Quiet! Hear what I have to say.'

The uproar diminished. 'You all know my story,' Vallon said. He pointed at Drogo. 'You know that this man pursued me to Iceland to exact revenge for a harm that exists only in his mind.' He pointed at Caitlin. 'You know that this lady's brother challenged me to combat for an imagined slight to her honour. Even so, I rescued Drogo and Helgi.'

The crowd was stone silent. 'You wonder why? Because abandoning them would have condemned all of you to death. God knows I'm no saint, but faced with the choice of saving my own company and leaving innocents to die, I chose the Christian course. That's still the course I follow. The alternative, the easier path, would be to hazard the voyage around North Cape and set you down at the first convenient haven. If I did that, most of you would starve or be cast into slavery. The path I've chosen will be dangerous. Some of us won't reach the end, but I believe that it offers the best hope.'

Vallon hadn't finished. 'You pleaded with me to rescue your neighbours and kinsmen. Now you can turn words into deeds. I need four men to travel with the Vikings as hostages. No harm will come to them.'

Words go only so far. *Shearwater* was nearly at the estuary before the Icelanders had badgered and browbeaten four of their number into standing surety.

Wayland frowned at Vallon. 'You promised Thorfinn six hostages.'

'The other two will come from my company. Garrick.'

The Englishman flinched.

'If you go as hostage, you might find a way of saving the women prisoners.'

'Yes, sir.'

The rest of the company stared in dismay. Vallon's gaze travelled over each in turn. 'I need someone to spy on the Vikings. Discover their strengths and weaknesses, learn their habits. After suffering so many setbacks, their morale won't be high. We might be able to bring a few of them over to our side.' His gaze passed over Raul and dwelt on Wayland before switching.

'Hero. I'm sending you.'

XXXIII

Squalls blew in on a cutting north-westerly. *Shearwater* lay under the lee of the estuary.

'Why me?' Hero said for the umpteenth time. 'Why any of us? It wasn't one of Thorfinn's conditions. Vallon threw me in like I was a token in a game.'

'It's not for long,' Richard said.

'Ten days with a gang of murdering savages!'

Someone cried out and the ship listed as the Icelanders ran to the side.

'Here they come,' Vallon called. 'Hoist sail. Get well to windward.'

The piebald hull of the longship bore down out of the rain.

'I'd go in your place if I could,' Richard said.

'I know you would.' Hero summoned a wan smile. 'The funny thing is that I'd do the same for you.' He stood, his blanket slipping to the deck, and kissed Richard on both cheeks. 'If you don't see me again, know that a piece of my heart will always be with you.'

Garrick retrieved the blanket and placed it around Hero's shoulders. 'I'll take good care of him.'

Shearwater heeled as she ran towards the eastern headland. Half a mile downwind of the longship, Vallon ordered Raul to strike the sail. The Vikings stopped rowing. Vallon watched them for a long time without speaking, and Hero thought that even at this last moment he might change his mind.

'The Vikings are readying their boat,' Raul said. 'Looks like they mean to go through with it.'

'Into the boat,' said Vallon.

Two rowers boarded, then the four Icelandic hostages climbed down. Father Hilbert told them they were suffering God's wrath for their sins, but that if they showed true repentance they might yet enter the glorious realm of heaven.

Vallon rounded on him. 'If you don't change your tune, you'll find yourself singing it to the Vikings.'

He spoke in private to Garrick before he descended and the Englishman grinned as he shook hands. Then Vallon turned to Hero.

'Don't hate me too much. I chose you because you have a quick mind and a persuasive tongue. You'll soon be back among your comrades.' He held Hero and laid his face to his cheek. 'You're as dear to me as my own son. There, it's said. Not a moment too soon.'

Dizzy from this declaration, Hero stepped into the boat. The half sail and rigging were passed down. Someone untied the boat's rope and then, to cries of pity and encouragement, the hostages were cast loose.

With the wind behind it, the Viking boat moved faster than the Icelanders could row. Hero's party had only travelled one-third of the way to the longship when the two sets of hostages crossed paths. Neither side could forbear to look at their counterparts. Two of the Vikings affected indifference. One hawked and spat. The fourth, a youth, looked as frightened as Hero felt. His face was pale, his jaw tight. Their eyes met and stayed locked until the boats had passed.

Hero wrenched his gaze to the front. A sharp chop flung spray into his face. In the troughs, he could see nothing of the longship except its mast. The gap closed and he began to shape out features on the men lining the ship's side. There were only eight left on board, Thorfinn towering above them all.

The boat came alongside. Hero noticed that the longship's new strakes were secured by crude wooden trenails, its hull braced by a framework of poles, the replaced thwarts of the crudest manufacture. The Vikings pulled the four Icelanders aboard and pushed them aft towards the prisoners. When Garrick made to follow, Thorfinn blocked his way.

'English?'

Garrick nodded.

'Did you burn my ship?'

'I'm a peasant. The Frank seized me as I was tilling my fields. I've never held a sword in my life.'

Thorfinn shoved him aside. Hero climbed into the longship and lost his footing on the sloping hull. Thorfinn caught him by the jaw and pulled him close.

'Frankish?'

'Greek,' Hero mumbled.

Thorfinn's teeth were scaled with plaque and his breath stank. 'Did you burn my ship?'

'No,' Hero croaked.

'One of the men who burned my ship had black hair. You have black hair.'

'Do I look like a warrior? I'm a scholar, a student of medicine.'

Thorfinn nudged his chin towards the Icelandic hostages. 'They know who burned my ship. They'll tell me.'

The Viking chieftain let him go. He staggered toward an empty thwart. One of the Vikings lashed him with a knout.

'Over by the English slave.'

Hero sat beside Garrick. Oars were thrust into their hands. Thorfinn began to beat on the stempost with his axe. 'Take your time from him,' Garrick said.

Hero studied the Icelandic prisoners as he rowed. The men looked furtive and ashamed, and the two women wouldn't meet his eye at all. They were mother and daughter, the girl no older than fifteen. Her father had tried to protect them with his bare hands and the Vikings had tossed him overboard.

He risked a glance over his shoulder and saw *Shearwater* drawing away.

Their course took them between a large tabletop island and a granite coast patched with perpetual snow. Not long after noon the Vikings finished rigging the sail, bringing a blessed respite from rowing. Even under half a sail, the drakkar fairly flew, her weakened hull twisting through the waves like a snake, the wind whipping spindrift off the crests and driving showers of hail that collected in drifts against the gunwale. *Shearwater* tore along ahead under reefed sail, sometimes vanishing into the squalls and then appearing again under a rainbow sky.

The two ships stayed in contact and that evening Thorfinn directed both vessels into a rivermouth where they dropped anchor off different shores half a mile apart. The Vikings ate elk meat provided by Vallon and gave the hostages stockfish so rank that Hero gagged at the first bite. One of the pirates studied him across the spitting driftwood fire. 'Is it true, Greek, that you voyaged from England?'

'Further than that. Vallon's journey began in Anatolia. Mine in Italy.'

The Viking grinned at his comrades and hunched forward. 'Tell us. Your tale doesn't have to be true, only entertaining.'

So Hero chronicled their journey, suitably amended, explaining that Vallon had set out to deliver a ransom for a brother-in-arms captured by the Turks at Manzikert.

Questions came tumbling. Who were the Seljuks? Where had Vallon campaigned? Had Hero visited Miklagard? Was it true that the pope ruled from a golden throne fifty feet high?

With darkness fallen and his voice grown hoarse, Hero said that he'd told enough of the story for one day. 'I'll go on with it tomorrow. Our journey's been so long and we've had so many adventures that it will keep you entertained until we reach the forest.'

He settled himself next to Garrick and closed his eyes. He hadn't been asleep for long when he heard men stirring and saw some of the Vikings walking away from the fire. He rolled over.

'Where are they going?'

'To the women. Stop your ears.'

From the darkness beyond the fire came a rhythmic panting and grunting. It stopped and one of the Vikings strolled back into the light and sank yawning onto his bedroll. The rutting sounds started again, broken by whimpers and the casual asides of the Vikings waiting their turn.

Hero stared into the fire as if the flames might burn away the pictures in his head. He sat like that until all the men had finished and had returned to their sleeping places. When he looked up, Thorfinn was regarding him with a homicidal stare. Every so often he blinked one eye and his tongue probed wincingly inside his right cheek.

Most days, wind and tide permitting, both ships set sail soon after sunrise and anchored around mid-afternoon. For the rest of the day, parties from both vessels went ashore to forage for berries and driftwood, striking out in different directions over the coastal barrens. The hostages' basic diet was unvarying – rock-hard bread and stinking wind-dried cod that retained the texture of boiled shoe leather no matter how long it was cooked. The atmosphere on board was saturated with the smell of the stuff. It was all the Vikings carried by way of rations, and after the burning of their ship, they'd had no leisure to hunt. One of them told Hero that when they had gone into the forest, they'd found sinister totems hung from trees, some of them left only yards from where their pickets had stood watch.

'That must have been Wayland,' said Hero. 'He was abandoned in the forest at birth and reared by his giant dog.'

The Vikings looked uneasily into the semi-darkness. They seemed much affected by nature's auguries.

Thorfinn slammed the flat of his axe down. 'Sow fright and you'll reap terror.' He glared at his company. 'The dog couldn't have raised the English youth. He's seventeen at least and a dog rarely lives half that long.'

No one spoke. If anything, the dog's agelessness made it more menacing.

On the third afternoon they put in at a stretch of coast sheltered by a chain of islands. The foraging party spread out and Hero found himself alone with Arne, a Viking whose mature years and easy-going manner sat at odds with his violent profession. They found patches of bilberries and crowberries and Hero fed his sugar craving until his lips were stained purple.

Arne crouched a few yards away, examining a flat rock. Hero went over. Etched into the surface were dozens of stick-figures of men hunting deer.

'Skraelings made it,' said Arne. 'They follow the reindeer to the coast in spring and return to the forests each autumn. We'll cross paths with them before our journey's over.'

The two men sat with their backs against the stone. 'Here,' Arne said, handing Hero a piece of smoked elk. 'Don't tell anyone.'

Both men chewed away. Arne gave up on his bread. 'What I'd give for a freshly baked loaf.'

'Or a dish of pancakes drenched in butter,' said Hero.

'And honey,' Arne added dreamily.

Hero laughed. 'Since fantasies come free, why not a syllabub? Tart cream poured over layers of fruit and almonds. All on a base of cake sweetened with the wine of Marsala.'

Arne threw his head back. 'Stop torturing me!' He sighed and looked at the toy ships, the dove-grey polar sea stretching away beyond men's reckoning. 'Your stories. They're not all true are they?'

'Every word.'

'The Frank is lucky, yes?'

'Crafty rather than lucky.'

Arne nodded. 'A warrior needs a strong body, but a body is no good without a head.'

Hero sensed an opening. 'Are you saying that Thorfinn is unlucky?'

'Be careful. The more Thorfinn is thwarted by fate, the harder he'll fight it. He'd pull the world down over our ears before admitting defeat.' Arne stripped a piece of heather. 'No, it's not luck that frowns on Thorfinn's ventures. The age of the sea-raiders is over. The heroes have gone to their funeral fires and the gates of Valhalla are closed. Perhaps Thorfinn will be the last warrior to enter.' Arne threw the stem away. 'Everywhere we go, the people live in citadels. When they see our dragon-head from their watchtowers, they bar their gates and stand on the battlements, jeering and baring their arses at us.'

'So why do you keep raiding?'

'Famine would make a pirate of any man. I have a wife and four children and a farm that supports only two cows and twenty sheep. My meadows are so steep that I have to tie myself to a rope to cut the hay. If this expedition doesn't show a profit, I'll be forced to sell my two eldest children into bondage.'

Across the tundra raced a puff of grey smoke. Arne drew his sword. 'It's Wayland's dog,' said Hero.

'I know. I've seen the brute watching us from the ridge above our camp.'

The dog stopped a hundred yards off and sat back on its haunches. Arne's mouth framed some kind of invocation. 'What does it want? Why does it sit there?'

'It might be carrying a message. Let me go to it. I won't try to escape.'

Arne looked round to see if any of his companions were in sight. 'Make it quick.'

Hero approached cautiously. 'Good dog,' he murmured. It looked straight ahead, its chest pumping. Tied to its spiked collar was a small roll of parchment. Hero removed it.

My dear friend.
I hope this letter finds you in good health and spirits. Vallon pampers our Viking guests to such an extent that I fear they will be reluctant to quit our company when the time comes. Until then, you and friend Garrick are ever in our thoughts and prayers. If the chance presents itself, let us know how you are faring.
Praying for your safe return, Richard

Hero had no means to respond. He gave the dog a tentative pat and it rose and galloped back the way it had come. Hero returned smiling with the letter.

'Show me,' Arne demanded.

'It's only a message from my friend Richard. He hopes that I'm in good heart and assures me that your companions are being well treated.'

Arne peered at the script, then crumpled the letter and pushed it into the peat. 'Thorfinn mustn't know about this. He believes that Christian rune-makers cast malicious spells.'

'Have you had any dealings with Christian missionaries?'

'Three years ago a priest came to Thorfinn's hall and showed him runes that he swore were the words of your god.'

'The Bible.'

'He said that this god ... I forget his name.'

'Jesus.'

'He said that this god sacrificed himself to redeem the wicked and sinful.'

'That's true. Jesus was sent by his father—'

Arne held up a hand. 'He said that the meek would triumph over the strong and that judgement and punishment belonged to god alone. Thorfinn asked what sort of god it was that gave up his life to save criminals and cowards. The priest would have been wise to shut up, but instead he continued preaching until Thorfinn asked him if he had the courage to follow his god's example.' Arne stopped. 'No, you don't want to know.'

'I can guess,' Hero said. He shivered slightly.

'Thorfinn told the priest about his violent deeds – how he ate the livers of his enemies and cut the blood eagle on them. Then he said that if this god was real, the priest must be prepared to sacrifice his life to save Thorfinn's soul. The priest was terrified and cried out to his god to save him. Thorfinn crucified him.'

Hero stared at the ground. 'Did he go to his death bravely?'

'Men die bravely only in battle.' Arne stood. 'We've been away too long. Thorfinn will be growing suspicious.'

Two days later they rounded the end of the peninsula and entered the White Sea, anchoring at twilight in an estuary overlooked by iron-grey cliffs capped with eaves of snow. In the calm of the anchorage, Hero used his compass to confirm their new course. His heart flew into his throat as a blurred iron arc splintered the thwart beside him.

Thorfinn bent and picked up the scattered parts. 'What's this?'

Hero scrabbled backwards. 'A direction finder. It can show the way when clouds hide the sun.'

Thorfinn loured over him, his right cheek puffed up, his eye closed in an obscene wink. 'You think I don't know how to find my way?' He flipped the compass overboard.

Hero's fear flashed into anger. 'You ignorant heathen,' he shouted in Greek. 'No wonder your expeditions end in failure.'

Arne pulled him away. 'Idiot! The tooth worm's driving him mad. The only way he can deal with pain is by inflicting worse suffering on those around him. You're lucky he didn't strike you dead.'

For the rest of the evening, Hero couldn't stop trembling.

When he boarded the longship next morning, two Vikings pushed him into Thorfinn's presence. His legs almost gave way at the thought that the chieftain had discovered his part in firing the longship. Thorfinn sat slumped on a thwart, his face swathed in a filthy bandage. He cocked his good eye. 'You claim to be a healer.'

Hero fingered his throat. 'I'm a physician, not a dentist. In my country we leave tooth-pulling to barbers.'

Thorfinn's pale eye twitched. 'I'm not in your country and I'm not asking for a shave.'

Arne nudged Hero. 'You'd better do it. I've seen men die from the tooth-worm, and if Thorfinn goes, he'll take you with him. Believe it.'

Hero linked his hands to stop them trembling. 'I'll need to examine you. Lie on your back.'

Pain and the hope of release from it can tame the most savage soul. Thorfinn reclined on a thwart and opened his mouth. Hero inspected the claggy teeth, tried not to breathe the fog of putrefaction. The seat of infection was a broken and rotted upper right molar. 'You've got a bad abscess.'

'Aargh.'

Hero considered lancing it with a fleam, but the relief might be temporary and the operation could make the infection worse. 'The tooth will have to come out. Any of your men will be able to pull it.'

Thorfinn grinned horribly. 'I don't want any of those ham-fisted butchers messing about with my jaw. I want *you*.'

Hero broke into a cold sweat. It would be like pulling a tooth from a bear. 'I don't have the proper instruments.'

One of the Vikings handed him a pair of blacksmith's tongs. 'These should do the job.'

'No, they won't. There isn't enough tooth left to provide a firm purchase. The tongs will crush what remains and he'll be in a worse state than before.'

Thorfinn patted his swollen cheek. 'Enough talking.'

Hero glanced up at the yardarm. An idea came to him. He dismissed

400

it as absurd, but he couldn't think of an alternative plan and he kept coming back to it. 'Show me the tooth again.' He studied the craggy stump, isolated in the infected gum. 'Who can make the neatest job of whipping a rope's end?'

The Vikings backed off. 'Arne's your man.'

Hero looked at him. 'I want you to whip a cord to the tooth, using fine gut thread. I'll supply the whipping.'

Arne inspected the tooth. He shook his head.

Thorfinn clubbed him. 'Do what the Greek tells you.'

Arne grimaced. 'The pain will make him lash out. I won't be able to tie the cord properly.'

Hero remembered the sleeping draught in his chest. He took out the bottle, unstoppered it and asked for a cup. He measured out half the contents of the bottle and passed the cup to Thorfinn. 'Drink it. It will dull the pain.'

Thorfinn smelled it and blinked. 'Are you trying to poison me?'

'Your tooth is poisoning you. Drink.'

Thorfinn tossed off the potion.

'We have to wait for it to take effect,' Hero said.

Presently Thorfinn's good eye began to wander and he broke into ragged song. The Vikings stared at each other. 'By Odin, I don't believe it. Our chief's drunk as a lord on a few spoonfuls.'

Hero nodded at Arne. 'You,' he said to one of the Vikings, 'hold Thorfinn's head steady.'

'Whoo-hoo,' crooned the chief. 'Iddy-biddy boo.'

Arne set about whipping the cord to the rotten tooth. He muttered as he worked and kept having to break off to clear the site of blood and saliva. At last he rocked back on his heels. 'That's as tight as I can make it.'

Hero looked up at the mast, calculating more like an engineer than a physician. 'Lay your chief on that thwart directly under the yard, head against the side. Tie the free end of the cord to a line long enough to run over the yardarm with about ten feet to spare. I need a heavy weight. A ballast stone will do. Also a sack for the weight and a short rope to hang it from the yard. Three feet should be enough.'

One of the men selected a large oval stone from the bed of ballast around the mast and held it up.

'My favourite little stone,' Thorfinn warbled. 'I picked it myself from the strand on Saltfjord.' He began to sing again, swinging one hand before his face like a pendulum.

'Place the stone in the sack,' Hero said. 'Tie the short rope to it and hang it from the yard.'

One of the Vikings climbed to the yard and pulled himself along it. Hero calculated angles and forces. 'Tie it there. Just outboard. That's the spot. Stay where you are and cut the rope when I give the word.' He looked round. 'Toss the line from the tooth over the yard. Good.' He estimated for a drop of ten feet and looked up at the man straddling the yard. 'Take in the line. That's enough. Cut it there and tie the end to the sack. Make it secure.'

With everything in place, Hero made a last inspection of the set-up. 'I want two men to hold Thorfinn so that his head doesn't move when the stone drops. Put his head as far back as you can. Someone had better hold his legs as well.'

The Viking on the yard held his knife ready. Someone sniggered. 'The Greek's going to drop it on our captain's head.'

'Cut!'

Down dropped the stone. Up flashed the line leading from Thorfinn's tooth. It twanged as it met the ballast stone's heft. Thorfinn convulsed, kicking off the assistant pinning his legs. The line whipped over the spar and the stone hit the sea in a spout and disappeared, dragging the line so fast that no one could see if was still connected to the tooth or had broken. Hero ran to Thorfinn. Black blood and pus poured from his mouth.

'Keep hold of him.'

Hero splashed water into the pirate chief's mouth. He mopped it with a rag and inserted a finger. Where the tooth had been was a gaping cavity.

He reeled back on his haunches. 'It's out. You can unloose him.'

Thorfinn groped to his feet like a drunken mariner waking in a storm. When he'd achieved a degree of equilibrium, he cracked open his maw and delved inside with a filthy finger. A crazy grin spread across his face. He pointed at Hero, took one step, crashed into a thwart and, after one last witless stare, fell full length, cracking his head a mighty blow on the gunwale. One hand closed and unclosed; one leg contracted and stretched. Then he fell still.

'You've killed him,' one of the Vikings marvelled.

Hero felt Thorfinn's pulse. 'He'll live. When he wakes up, tell him to rinse his mouth out with salty water. Keep food away from the cavity until it heals.'

Arne smiled at Hero and winked. The other Vikings slapped his back and guffawed. 'Hey, Hero,' one called, using his name for the first time. 'Give me a taste of your cordial. I'd pull out my own eye-teeth for a cup of that brew.'

They sailed south along the White Sea coast into the forest zone. Thorfinn hadn't exaggerated the bounty of wildlife. Salmon packed the estuaries, waiting for an autumn flood to carry them up to their spawning grounds. The Vikings speared them from the ship's boat, trapped them in wicker funnels, hooked them on gaffs as they threw themselves over the rapids like bars of silver.

Thorfinn's jaw healed. The swelling went down, and with it his boiling temper. In quiet moments some of the Vikings sidled up to Hero and sheepishly asked him to cure their ailments. He agreed to do what he could in exchange for better food. He told the Vikings that their comrades on *Shearwater* were dining like lords on the game killed by Wayland. It wasn't a lie. Once at a distance they saw Wayland, assisted by one of the hostages, catch a dozen grouse in a net drawn over the pointing dog and the sitting covey. At night the Vikings shifted to make space for Hero around the fire and sat rapt as children while he went on with his tale.

One fine morning Thorfinn shaped a course away from the coast until it sank below the horizon. In a glassy calm they approached at evening an archipelago of wooded islands a day's sail from the head of the gulf. The Vikings had used it as a waystation before and made for an islet set on the sea like a green crown, every tree and rock faithfully reflected in the water. Watching it draw close, Hero was reminded of the sacred groves where the ancients consulted the oracles.

He stepped ashore half expecting to see a rustic temple. What he saw confirmed his intuition and wiped the smile from his face. At the centre of the island rose a bubbling spring surrounded by pines and birches decked with votive offerings. Hero saw cast hammer amulets, the shrivelled wing of a raven, carved bone images of Freyr with his immense phallus. Scattered beneath the trees were many bones. Hero

403

recognised a horse's skull and a sheep's scapula, both green with moss. Hero spotted a more recent sacrifice and his blood ran cold. It was a human skeleton collapsed all of a heap, the bones still chalky white. His eye darted up. Directly above the skeleton the frayed end of a rope dangled from a branch.

He turned to see Arne studying a birch post carved with runes. 'Who did you hang here?'

'I don't know. A captive, a skraeling . . .'

'But why?'

'Punishment, sacrifice . . . Ask Thorfinn.'

'Sacrifice? You kill men to propitiate your gods? You're savages. Worse than animals.'

Arne showed anger. 'See that?' he demanded, pointing at the rune-post. 'It says "Thorolf made this for Skopti, died in the north." I knew Skopti. He had a brother, Harald, who lived up the valley from my own farm. Harald had a wife and two children, a boy and a girl under five. Six years ago we had a very bad winter, the worst anyone can remember. So bad that the snow rose above the eaves and trapped us in our homestead for months. When the thaw came, we went to see how Harald and his family had fared. We called greetings as we approached the house and when we received no reply, I went into the farmstead and found Harald and his wife dead. They'd starved. I didn't find their children, though. Only their bones. Their parents had eaten them.'

Hero began to walk away, but Arne grabbed his arm. 'What would you have done? You boast about your homeland with its fields of wheat stretching to the horizon, orchards laden with apples, pastures crowded with sheep and cattle. Land shapes men's lives. Don't stand in judgement over others until you've experienced their sufferings.'

Hero stood mute and sullen.

'We're here for one night,' Arne said. 'Tomorrow you'll go back to your friends. Shut your eyes and morning will soon come.'

That night the Vikings got drunk on birch ale and took the women into the grove and gang-raped them. Hero went to the other side of the island with Garrick and Arne and tried to blank out the sounds. The aurora danced in the north.

'The skraelings say it's the souls of the dead,' Arne said.

'Why don't you join the debauchery?' Hero asked.

404

Arne stared at the ghostly lights. 'I have a wife and daughters. I think, What if it were them?'

'Your companions have wives and daughters.'

Garrick put his hand on Hero's arm and frowned. The aurora faded. On a neighbouring island the flames of *Shearwater*'s company licked at the dark. Snatches of conversation drifted across the gulf. Hero recognised Raul's laughter. One of the women gave a smothered scream.

'You know this journey will end in blood,' Hero said.

'Yes,' said Arne. 'If Thorfinn doesn't take revenge, the men won't follow him again.'

'Change sides,' Hero said. 'Bring others with you.'

Arne rose heavily and went away into the night.

After silence had fallen, Hero and Garrick returned to the camp and settled down around the embers. Hero listened to the offerings clacking together in the sacrificial grove until he fell asleep. He dreamed of bones and woke in the dark to hear Garrick slipping back into his place, breathing in pained sighs. All around them the drunken Vikings snored and groaned. Garrick's breathing steadied and Hero's eyes closed again.

A commotion at daybreak snapped him awake to find men running in all directions. Arne hurried past with his sword drawn. 'The Icelandic women have escaped.'

Hero began to rise but Garrick restrained him. 'You don't want to see.'

A blast from a horn sent the Vikings racing towards the eastern side of the island. With a wondering glance at Garrick, Hero followed. He found the Vikings standing around the women. Mother and daughter sat side by side on the shore, slumped together as if they'd fallen asleep waiting for the sun to rise. Hero stepped in front of them. They would never see another dawn. They had cut their wrists and their life-blood had drained away, leaving their faces white as chalk and their laps drenched with blood. On the ground lay the bloodied stone they'd used to commit suicide. Arne tried to stop him from picking it up, but Hero swore and shook him off. The mother had sawn her daughter's wrists before hacking at her own. Hero's face lost shape. He hurled the stone into the sea.

'Curse you! Curse this place!'

Thorfinn laughed in Hero's face, then his eyes narrowed in baleful intensity and he strode back to the camp.

Arne caught Hero's arm. 'Listen to me. It was your English friend who gave the stone to the women. I heard him creep away in the night. When you go back, don't speak to him. Don't even look at him. If you think that Thorfinn can't read your thoughts, you're wrong. He sees into men very well, especially if they're hiding what he wants to see. Stay here until I fetch you.'

'Why? Are there more horrors to come?'

'Thorfinn is going to hang one of the prisoners. He thinks one of them gave the stone to the women.'

'Mother of God. You have to stop him!'

'I can't. He'll kill me.'

After Arne left, Hero found himself looking across the strait to where *Shearwater* lay anchored. A thin column of smoke rose from the island and then flattened out with the wind. Over there they would be blowing life into last night's embers, preparing breakfast, exchanging the everyday asides of travellers grown easy with each other's company. He was still wishing himself across the gulf when Arne returned.

'It's over.'

Hero followed him back to camp in a sick daze. Try as he might, he couldn't stop his eyes turning towards the hanged man. The poor wretch dangled with his head wrenched at a grotesque angle, eyes bulging from his mottled face.

'Hey, Greek.'

Hero's blurred gaze fell on what he'd imagined with horror but never really believed, and never for a moment thought he would see. It was true, though. Thorfinn sat on a log tearing with his huge teeth at the freshly plucked liver of his victim.

He waved the steaming offal at Hero like a man tucking in to a hearty breakfast. 'Put that down in your story.'

XXXIV

Hero watched the coast draw closer, the flat black contour forming into a forest wall breached by a muddy river. The treeline was beginning to slice into the setting sun and the tide rippled red where it lapped against the strand. Thorfinn ordered the sail to be lowered and the longship glided in and kissed the shore. The Vikings jumped down and then paused, half crouching, as if they were nervous of waking something. Hero followed and gave a shiver. It was so quiet. As if life here had still to be called into existence. The stillness amplified every stray sound. A leaf wafting down through branches clattered like broken earthenware. The shrilling of mosquitoes made him drill a finger into his ear.

He walked up the beach towards the forest. Many of the trees on the edge were blighted. Inside they clumped on islands surrounded by stagnant pools and bilious green bogs. Curtains of moss hung from branches like rotted mortuary shrouds. Clouds of mosquitoes danced in hazy spirals. The light was clotting in the thickets.

Along the beach stood some kind of effigy sited so that no one entering the river could miss it. Thorfinn studied it with his nostrils flared and then approached.

It was a tattie-bogle fashioned from ragged garments stretched across a wooden frame and crowned by a death's head. The skull must have been pickled in tannin because it still wore its leathery skin and hanks of ginger hair sprouted from its pate. Thorfinn made a sound deep in his throat.

'That's Olaf Sigurdarsson,' said one of the Vikings. 'I'd know his face anywhere.'

'And those are Leif Fairhair's breeches,' said another.

Arne leaned towards Hero. 'Two of the men Thorfinn lost on his last expedition.'

Hero's attention was riveted on a pair of stupendous double-curved tusks planted in the ground each side of the totem. 'Elephants don't live this far north.'

'They're the teeth of a giant rat that uses them to burrow through the ground,' Arne said. 'The rat dies if it comes into the air or is reached by sunlight.'

'Perhaps the skraelings left them as scat,' one of the Vikings said. 'Perhaps they hope that by offering tribute, we'll leave them in peace. That ivory will fetch a pretty penny in Nidaros.'

'Don't touch them,' said Thorfinn. He growled again, his eyes switching from side to side. A raven flew overhead and rolled right over. *Krok*, it said.

407

They turned to watch *Shearwater* dropping anchor off the beach. Vallon and company rowed ashore with the Viking hostages. Thorfinn's men fingered their weapons and looked to him for instruction, but the chieftain had his axe grounded and Vallon kept his sword sheathed. He stopped a few yards in front of Thorfinn. The hostages walked past him and rejoined their comrades with weak grins. 'We've spoiled them,' Vallon said. 'I hadn't realised how hungry you kept your men.'

Thorfinn motioned with his chin and his men shoved the four Icelanders forward.

'They're half-starved,' said Vallon. 'What happened to the rations we gave you?'

'Meat's too precious to waste on captives. If I didn't need the rest of the Icelanders for rowing and pulling at the portages, I'd let you take them off my hands.'

'Where are the women?'

Thorfinn didn't answer.

'They killed themselves last night,' Hero said.

Vallon shook his head. He put his arms around Hero and Garrick and led them away. 'Thank God you're back. Did you learn anything useful? See anything that we can turn to our advantage?'

Hero spluttered between laughter and tears. 'Where shall I start? The Icelandic women? The man hanging by his neck and Thorfinn eating his liver so freshly plucked that the steam was still rising from it. Is that useful intelligence?'

Vallon stared at him. 'We'll talk later. Go and join your friends.'

Vallon stood alone on the beach after the two sides had separated. His gaze probed this way and that. The sun sank below the trees and he hunched his shoulders against air grown cold as iron.

They were at work early by torchlight transferring cargo to the ships' boats. The craft were too small to hold all the people and horses. The Icelanders rejected Vallon's suggestion that they draw lots, with the losers to travel in the longship. After hearing how Thorfinn treated his prisoners, they said they'd rather walk to Novgorod.

'Good,' said Vallon. 'Because that's the only alternative.'

Wayland came over looking very subdued. Vallon frowned. 'Something wrong?'

'I won't find enough food in the forest to feed all the falcons. I'm going to release two of them.'

Vallon winced. 'All our hopes rest on bringing four white falcons to Anatolia. We can't afford to lose two of them this far from our goal.'

'I didn't reach the decision lightly. Better six healthy falcons than eight sickly ones.'

Vallon bowed to his judgement. Watching him prepare to turn the falcons loose, he thought of all the effort that had gone into their capture.

Wayland cast off the first eyas. It flapped away with clumsy strokes, tried to land in a tree, missed its footing and tumbled down through the branches. Syth cried out and ran after it. The second falcon headed out to sea, circled back and pitched on the beach.

'Will they survive?' Vallon asked.

'I've fed both of them a full crop. They won't feel the pinch of hunger for several days and by then they'll have learned to use their wings. Falcons are quick learners and ...' Wayland drew breath and shook his head. 'No. That's what I told Syth to avoid upsetting her. Almost certainly they'll die. They were the weakest of the eyases and haven't been taught to hunt.'

Vallon saw how much their loss pained Wayland. 'Don't reproach yourself. It's a tribute to your skilful handling that you've brought the falcons this far without loss. I confess I sometimes forget that they're the be-all and end-all of our enterprise. It frightens me to think how much our fortunes depend on them. If there's anything you need for their welfare, ask.'

'Fresh meat. A sixth of their body weight every day.'

'That much?'

Wayland nodded.

Vallon stared at the brooding forest. 'If necessary, we'll fast ourselves rather than let the falcons go hungry.'

The falcons weren't the only precious things they cast off. After six months' voyaging, *Shearwater*'s journey had run its course. She'd been their means of escape, their seaborne home and their vehicle of trade. For weeks on end she'd been their entire world, the cramped cockpit for their dramas and passions. To her crew she had come to seem like a creature in her own right – a bluff and willing workhorse, though not without moods and whims. They knew her down to her last creak and groan, and now they had to say goodbye to her.

Over breakfast they debated the most fitting send-off. Scuttling was out of the question. Like drowning your mother, Raul said. Burn her, he suggested, or leave her nodding at anchor until the next storm broke her into driftwood. The breeze decided her fate. It was blowing offshore and so a party went on board and raised anchor and hoisted sail one last time. As the panels filled and the water began to bubble under her stem, they climbed back into the boat and rowed ashore and watched her slant away to the north until she was just a tiny silhouette on a sea as bright as the back of a fresh-run salmon.

The longship had already begun the journey upriver. In a deathly hush the company climbed into the boats, fitted oars and began to row against the sluggish current. The shore party plodded along the right bank. When Hero looked back, the sea was already out of sight. It was like a door had shut behind them.

A short way upriver they caught up with the longship stuck in rapids. It was afternoon before they struggled into calm water. At dark the two parties pitched separate camps and set guards. Next morning when they set off, rain dimpled the surface and cloud hung in rags among the treetops. Mosquitoes and blackflies plagued them, whining inside their ears, infiltrating their clothes, crawling up their nostrils. The travellers wrapped their heads and smeared themselves with dung and oil. Nothing could keep the pests off. Worst affected were the oarsmen. Unable to slap away the bloodsuckers, they rowed as if afflicted by a palsy, hunching up their shoulders to rub their inflamed cheeks and brows. By the end of the day some of them had raw wounds on their wrists and their faces were so swollen they could hardly see.

The going wasn't any easier for the Icelanders trudging along the banks. They sank ankle deep in spongy moss that made each step an effort. They had to detour around sloughs of grey ooze and graveyards of fallen trees. Sometimes they were forced to stumble along in the river itself. Where the current was too deep and the forest impassable, the boatmen had to set down their passengers and return to ferry the pedestrians above the obstacle.

Wayland was right about the lack of game. He managed to kill enough grouse to keep the falcons on half rations, but most of the creatures he encountered were predators in a wilderness lacking prey. He saw a pair of sable streaking through the treetops like eels, and he surprised a pair of gluttons dragging out the entrails of a bear so grey and gaunt that it must have died of old age. These gluttons or wolverines were creatures new to him and he found their ferocity incredible. When the dog pranced up to them, they didn't give an inch, spitting and snarling with faces that haunted Wayland's dreams for nights afterwards. The dog rolled its eyes at him, asking for help. He called it off. All day it kept snarling round as if the gluttons were on their trail.

Four days upriver the boat carrying Vallon's company passed an old woman sitting on the bank beside the body of an old man. It was the woman Helgi had escorted from the abandoned Icelandic ship. The dead man was her husband.

One of the Icelanders called out. She raised cloudy eyes and said she didn't want any help.

'What's going on?' said Vallon. 'Why have the Icelanders left her behind?'

'It's her own choice,' Raul said. 'She doesn't want to go on. Her husband was all the kin she had.'

'Let me talk to her,' said Hero.

Vallon glanced upriver. 'Don't take too long. There's another rapid ahead.'

Hero and Richard stepped ashore. Raul tossed a spade after them. 'We'll be leaving them where they drop before the journey's over.'

Hero approached the old woman and cleared his throat. She peered at him.

'Goodness. You're one of the outlanders.'

He sank down beside her. 'How did your husband die?'

'Weariness. Despair. His heart stopped and those two men of Helgi's just slung him on to the bank. You'd think they didn't have fathers of their own.'

Hero put an arm around her thin shoulders. 'We'll bury him and when we've said a prayer we'll take you back to our boat.'

She looked up and Hero glimpsed in her features the ghost of

411

youthful beauty. 'Oh, no,' she said. 'Erik and I have been together sixty years. I'm not leaving him now.' She patted Hero's hand. 'You go on. I'm quite content.'

Richard leaned over. 'Don't you have any other family? Isn't that why you were sailing to Norway?'

Shadows flitted over the woman's face. 'All our children and grand-children are dead. Ah, it's a bitter fate to outlive your offspring. Our youngest died last spring. With him gone we were unable to work the farm. Erik decided to sell it and return to Norway. That's where he came from. We met when he sailed to Reykjavik on a merchant ship. Such a handsome man. Erik has family near Nidaros and he said we'd go and live out our days near his sister's farm. He never did take to the Icelanders. Too clannish, he said. Too busy looking after themselves to bother with the wants of others. We'd be happier among his own kind. I wasn't so sure. Better stay with what you know, that's what I told him.'

'I'm sure Erik's sister will welcome you.'

The old woman snorted. 'Imagine the fit she'll have if I turn up at her door. Seventy-eight years old, nearly blind and penniless.'

'You said you had money from the sale of your farm.'

'Helgi's men took it from Erik when we left our ship. That Caitlin said they'd look after it for me.' The old woman pulled Hero's head down. 'She's a bitch,' she whispered. She nodded emphatically. 'When you see her in a new dress and brooch, remember who paid for it.'

Hero glowered upriver before turning back to the woman. She paid no heed to the mosquitoes crawling in her thin white hair. 'Vallon will make sure they return the money. In any case, you don't need silver to come with us.'

'That's kind, but what then? I won't last long in this filthy forest. Even if I lived, I don't want to end my days as a pauper in a strange land. No, here I stay.'

'You'll perish of cold or hunger. Wolves and bears will devour you.'

She smiled and patted their hands. 'You're nice young men. You'd better be going. It will be dark soon. Your friends will be starting to worry about you.'

Raul came jogging through the trees. 'Vallon wants every man pulling.' His eyes were on the woman.

'She says she won't leave him. You try reasoning with her. I don't

412

know why, but sometimes your coarse logic works where finer reasoning fails.'

Raul formed his features into the benign goofiness of someone dealing with a half-wit. 'Now then, mother, you come along with us.'

Her face set. 'Go away.'

Raul laughed, gripped her under her shoulders and began to lift. She gave such a shriek that he set her back down. 'All right, mother. Have it your own way.' He scooped Hero and Richard out of the old woman's hearing. 'You're wasting your time. She's made up her mind. Now come away. We have to get clear of the rapids before dark.'

'We can't just leave her to die.'

Raul pulled off his cap and slapped it against his thigh. He stared into the sky. 'You're right. Talk to her again. Soothe her.'

Hero held the old woman's hands. He couldn't remember what he said and never finished saying it because Raul stepped behind the woman, raised his crossbow and shot a bolt into the back of her neck.

Another day's rowing and dragging brought them to the first of the three lakes sketched by Thorfinn. One glance at the empty horizon told Vallon that they could only cross it by boat. He ordered Raul to supervise the building of a raft large enough to carry the horses and most of their cargo. With the raft in tow, they headed away from land next morning, the boats loaded to the gunwales. They were on the lake for two and a half days and several times came close to foundering. All the time they were aware of how vulnerable they were to attack from the longship.

From the southern shore their route took them through waterways separated by raised bog which the shore party crossed like flies caught in honey.

It turned bitter cold. At night the wind moaned through the trees and wolves howled in the distance. Black ice webbed the ponds at dawn and at noon the dark sun bored down through corridors of fog. The monotony of the forest and the constant discomfort frayed their nerves. Tempers gave way under the strain. A clumsily wielded oar, the refusal of wood to burn, the upsetting of a dish – the slightest irritant was enough to bring men to blows.

Food ran short and the Vikings suffered most because the salmon they'd caught rotted for lack of salt. Smoked elk and salt fish, together with mushrooms and berries, kept Vallon's party going, while the Vikings and their prisoners were thrown back on stockfish so putrid that it turned their bowels to flux.

The Icelandic baby died and was buried on the riverbank with scant ceremony. Then one of the Vikings disappeared. He'd gone foraging and strayed from his companions. They searched until dark before giving up. The missing man had been one of the Viking hostages and Wayland agreed to track him. The falconer picked up his trail about a mile from the river and read the man's increasing desperation as he circled, backtracked and finally wandered off into a swamp. Wayland followed for as long as he dared and then made his way back to report that the Viking was dead.

A day later another Viking met with a fatal calamity. A gale was blowing from the north. The longship had reached a fork that Thorfinn swore hadn't been there on his last expedition. He sent men upriver to scout for the right channel. Wayland and Raul accompanied one of the parties, pushing through wind-lashed thickets of alder and willow. The trees thrashed with a violence that drowned all other sounds.

Emerging into a clearing, the dog stopped in mid-stride, one foot crooked to its chest, its tail sticking up.

Ahead of them one of the Vikings was parting a tangle of shrubs. 'Back!' Wayland shouted.

'What?' cried the Viking.

A blast of wind carried away Wayland's response. The Viking forced himself into the thicket and a huge dark ogre heaved up and flattened him with a blow too quick to see. The bear crashed away into the raging forest. When Wayland reached the stricken man, he saw that something was terribly wrong with his face, and then he realised that the man had no face at all.

His companions half-led, half-carried the victim back to the longship and set him down against a tree. He rocked back and forth, screaming and clawing at his bloody mask. Thorfinn paced with a face like thunder, then he ran at the man, kicked him over and brought his axe down into his chest.

Freezing rain fell all next day and it was well after dark before Vallon's company managed to get a fire going. They sat shivering around the hissing flames, replaying the trials of that day's journey, knowing they would have to do it all again.

Raul spat into the fire. 'Fuck it.'

Vallon looked up, his face all edges in the fireglow. 'Something you want to share with us?'

'It ain't just the shitty journey. Thorfinn's going to make his move soon. He ain't going to see his men starve while we go to bed with tight bellies.'

'He'll attack before we reach the next lake,' said Wayland. 'The one called Onega.'

'What makes you so sure?'

'Because once we cross it, we'll be in Rus.'

'The Vikings say it's as big as a sea,' Raul added. 'There ain't no way we'll get everyone across in our boats. Either we have to beg Thorfinn to take some of the Icelanders or we have to capture the longship.'

Vallon placed a log on the fire. 'Let me get this straight. Right now we've got what the Vikings covet – food, treasure and women. They've got what we need – a ship. And if we take it, we can find our own way to Rus.'

'That's it.'

Vallon patted the ground and stared off.

Raul shuffled towards him. 'How are you going to do it, Captain? You want me and Wayland to set an ambush?'

Vallon formed his words carefully. 'The Viking hostages didn't seem too happy with Thorfinn's leadership. Hero, you formed the same opinion.'

'Yes, sir, but if it came to a fight, they'd face us as one.'

All of them watched Vallon coming to a decision. He scooped up a handful of litter and tossed it into the fire. 'Light a torch. It's time to pay a call on Thorfinn.'

Wayland wrapped tow around a branch, doused it in seal oil and dipped it into the flame. By the light of the torch he led the company towards the Vikings' camp. Drogo and Fulk hurried up.

'Where are you going?'

'To challenge Thorfinn.'

The Vikings' fire appeared across a swathe of wind-toppled trees.

'Thorfinn!'

Shades darted across the firelight. 'Frankish!'

'The truce is over. It's time to settle our differences.'

'How?'

'By combat. You and me. Daylight tomorrow. Winner takes all.'

'Where?'

'Here.'

'I'll be there. Sweet dreams, Frankish.'

XXXV

Vallon took himself away from the camp and made up a bed under a spruce. He didn't think about the fight. A calm and empty spirit is the right frame of mind for combat. That's what his swordmaster had drummed into him all those years ago. He could remember his exact words. 'You're showing too much emotion. Don't let your mind influence your body or your body influence your mind. Got that?' Vallon smiled. His swordmaster had been one of the most peppery characters he'd ever known.

The rain stopped and a hard frost set in. Snug under layers of furs and fleeces, Vallon slept the night through. Raul and Hero crept up at dawn. 'Look at him,' Raul whispered. 'Usually he sleeps like hellhounds are on his trail, and then on the eve of combat he slumbers sound as a babe.'

Vallon was smiling at some pleasant memory that fled when Hero's hand touched his shoulder. He yawned and blinked around. The hoary shapes of the trees floated through freezing mist. The ground was stiff with frost. Steam rose from the basin that Hero offered him. He splashed water into his face.

'I'm glad you passed a restful night,' Hero said.

Vallon stretched his shoulders back like a rooster heralding daybreak. 'I would have slept sounder if the Vikings hadn't been making such a racket.'

'Arne told me that they always get drunk before going into battle.'

'Amateurs.'

'Can I bring you anything to eat?'

'God, no.'

Vallon saw a boiling cauldron slung from a trivet above the camp-fire.

'Hot water and clean cloths,' said Hero. 'In case you're wounded.'

Figures drifted from the camp. Drogo stepped forward bearing his armour and helmet on his shield. He held them out with his eyes averted. 'You'll need these.'

'I thank you,' said Vallon. 'I'll try to return them in the same condition.' He knew that the armour wouldn't offer much protection against Thorfinn's axe.

'Have you decided your tactics? The Viking must have a foot advantage in reach.'

Vallon scratched the back of his neck. 'I'm not going to slug it out with him. I'll keep moving and hope to wear him down until an opening presents itself.'

'Watch your footing on this surface. One slip and it could be all over.'

'Drogo, this isn't my first sword fight.'

'I wish you'd let me challenge him.'

'I've never doubted your courage. It's who you direct it at that I question.'

Vallon addressed his company. 'If I win, we'll try to persuade the Vikings to accept my command. It shouldn't be too difficult to bring them over, judging by what we've learned during our passage.'

'If the fight goes against you,' said Raul, 'I'm not serving under Thorfinn. Wayland says the same.'

'Of course not,' Vallon said. 'Have your crossbow ready and kill him before he can cry victory. Wayland should be able to spit a couple more before they can use their swords.'

'And Fulk and I stand ready with Helgi's men and the other Icelanders,' Drogo said.

'Good.'

Hero frowned. 'Then why fight Thorfinn? Let Raul kill him the moment he shows himself. That way you can direct the battle.'

Vallon smiled. 'I must observe the conventions even when dealing with a savage. There's another reason. If the day is mine, only one man needs to die. If we take on all the Vikings, some of us will be killed. Who knows? We might lose.'

'Who takes command if Thorfinn kills you?' Drogo asked.

'You do. Exercise it well.'

Caitlin ran forward and seized Vallon's wrists. Her eyes glittered. 'Avenge Helgi.'

Vallon inclined his head.

Father Hilbert stepped up. After blessing Vallon, he ordered him to kneel and make his peace with God. Vallon stayed on his feet and told Hilbert that he wasn't at war with his Maker.

Flanked by Wayland and Raul, Vallon made his way to the arena. Frost flowers bloomed in the puddles and thick rime furred the trees. The clearing was about fifty yards square, created by a storm that had ripped trees from the ground and left them strewn with their roots clutching plates of earth. Through the frigid haze Vallon saw the Vikings ranged on the far side of the clearing.

He stopped at the edge. 'Hero, help me dress. The rest of you leave us.'

He shrugged on the cold metal hauberk over the padded undercoat and cinched his sword belt to take up some of the weight of the armour. He decided not to wear the mail leggings. The fight might be a long one and he would have to stay nimble to avoid Thorfinn's attacks. When he was ready, he dismissed Hero, cloaked himself in a blanket and sat on one of the fallen trees. While he waited, he honed his sword with a whetstone, admiring the edges in the growing brightness.

Dawn had given way to leprous daylight when Thorfinn lurched belching from his tent. He undid his breeches and stood leaning one-handed against a tree while he took an interminable piss. When he'd finished he blinked sottishly around the clearing. Dead drunk, Vallon thought. Then he remembered Thorfinn's play-acting on the river.

'Over here.'

Thorfinn's smoking eyes found Vallon.

'Couldn't you sleep, Frankish? Have you been up all night?'

Vallon rose. 'Only a fool lies brooding over his problems. When morning comes he's tired out and his problems are the same as before.'

Thorfinn laughed. 'Spoken like a Viking. Well, your worries will soon be a thing of the past. Before the sun melts this mist, I'll chine you from neck to buttocks. Die bravely and you might earn a place in the hall of slain warriors.'

Vallon shrugged off his blanket, pulled the mail coif over his head and donned the helmet. He gripped his shield and hefted his sword. 'To the death.'

Vallon could tell if he faced a dangerous opponent just from the way the man stood and held his sword. Most men he'd met in battle fought like Helgi, wielding their swords like they were cudgels with sharp edges. They committed themselves to a position too soon, and because they were reluctant to leave their bodies open, they held their swords too close to their side, reducing the power of their blows and exposing their sword arm to attack.

Vallon suspected that Thorfinn had no finesse, but his sheer size and strength called for respect. By training and temperament, Vallon was an offensive fighter. The attacker has an inherent advantage in that he moves first, forcing his opponent to defend or counter. A skilled offensive fighter moves fluently, always ready to exploit his opponent's errors. The good offensive fighter creates mistakes; the defensive fighter can only react to them.

Against Thorfinn, though, Vallon suffered from several disadvantages. As Drogo had pointed out, the Viking outreached him. Vallon was tall, but Thorfinn was a giant. His axe was at least six inches longer than Vallon's sword and three or four times heavier. If Vallon parried that massive blade, it would shatter his sword to smithereens. The same applied to Vallon's shield. It was designed to block a sword-edge, not an axe delivered with the force of a sledgehammer. His best tactic would be to stay out of Thorfinn's reach until the Viking began to flag or dropped his guard. Vallon guessed that Thorfinn's contests rarely lasted long. Most of his fights would be won before they'd begun, by sheer bladder-voiding intimidation. A roar, a rush, a sweep of that massive blade, and in most cases it would be over before the terrified opponent offered a stroke.

Thorfinn walked towards him. His chain vest left his forearms bare and he carried his helmet under his left arm like a metal skull. He stopped twenty yards off and Vallon studied his face. Chalky blue eyes bathed in a bloody humour, sand-coloured teeth, stubble like copper filings. No trace of fear. He lifted up his helmet and in one movement transformed himself into a savage god.

Vallon raised his sword and angled it down behind his right

shoulder. He flexed his knees and balanced with his legs shoulder-width apart, right leg leading, weight centred. He gripped his shield by its lashings, partly supporting its weight against his left ribs, and held it edge-on towards Thorfinn.

Thorfinn roared and charged with his loping run. Vallon shifted his feet so that he could move in any direction. He watched Thorfinn wind up his arm and then floated left, cutting down at the Viking's exposed arm. Missed by a foot, whereas the axe came within a whisker of unseaming him with the same brutal cut that had killed Helgi. Vallon skipped and grimaced. He wasn't going to settle it quickly. Thorfinn's reach was so long that he couldn't penetrate the Viking's guard without opening himself up to even the crudest swipe.

'You smelled that, didn't you? Next time you'll taste it.'

Vallon evaded the next dozen attacks with barely a counter, all his attention concentrated on avoiding the axe. He used the fallen trees as cover, dodging between the trunks. Thorfinn's men roared their disgust. They'd gathered for a bloody clash between champions; instead, it was like watching a man with a cleaver trying to catch a chicken. Vallon's side hardly uttered a sound.

Thorfinn bared his teeth. 'You said you wanted to fight.' He leaned his axe on the ground and cupped his hand. 'Fight and die like a warrior or I'll cut your life away limb by limb. Come on, faggot. Fight!'

Vallon saved his breath. He feinted and retreated, dodged and side-stepped, his feet treading an eccentric black path in the frost. His breath grew short before he noticed that the weight of Thorfinn's axe was beginning to tell. The Viking grunted with the effort of lifting it and his recovery time was a bit slower after each swing. The axe was so heavy and carried so much stored energy that even a man as strong as Thorfinn couldn't alter its course quickly. It was an affectation, a boast of his strength, and it would be the death of him.

Thorfinn pulled his next attack, then followed up with a short chopping move that forced Vallon to parry with his shield. The axe struck the iron rim with a blow that almost dislocated his shoulder and numbed his arm from elbow to fingertips. He scampered back, working his hand to restore feeling.

Thorfinn followed up swinging. Too hasty. Too rash. Vallon drew himself in and swayed away from the whistling arc. Its momentum twisted the Viking's torso round. Vallon had anticipated his opening an instant before it presented itself and he thrust into the humped muscle of Thorfinn's shoulder. The tip of his sword penetrated the mail as if it were cheese and he felt steel jar against bone.

Next moment he was on his back, flattened by a reverse sweep that glanced off his helmet and scrambled his senses. He rolled away blind, sure that the next thing he would feel would be the axe cleaving the life from him. The blow never fell and he managed to stagger to his feet and get behind one of the fallen trees.

The Viking laughed breathily. 'You fight like a girl, Frankish.' And he mimed limp-wristed thrusts that roused anxious laughter from his men.

But Thorfinn was hurt. He ceased his rushes and began to stalk Vallon, his head lowered like a bull. Vallon let himself be herded, using the fallen trees as walls when pressed too hard. Blood from Thorfinn's shoulder ran down his arm. Drain him of strength, Vallon thought. He closed in, using his superior technique to threaten attacks that he didn't press home.

Blood dripped from Thorfinn's fighting hand, sliding down the haft of his axe, making it slippery. He hefted it to shorten his grip, reducing his advantage in reach and halving the power of his strokes.

'Decided to split kindling?'

The next time Thorfinn swung, Vallon had room to parry, slashing splinters out of the axe haft. Before the Viking could disengage, Vallon chopped another wedge out of the handle. Thorfinn clashed his shield against Vallon's and swung his axe to hook Vallon's ankle. Vallon reacted just in time, using the pressure of shield on shield to spring back. Thorfinn's scooping sweep threw him off-balance. Vallon darted forward, hooked his sword's cross-guard over the edge of Thorfinn's shield, pulled it down and then, in a continuation of the same movement, brought the sword down on Thorfinn's head.

The blade clanged off the helmet and Thorfinn recovered fast, swinging his axe like a scythe and nearly taking Vallon's legs off at the knees. Again Thorfinn left himself open and Vallon aimed another cut at his axe arm. The Viking was expecting it and jumped back, giving ground for the first time. Vallon followed up as he retreated down an alley created by two fallen trees. When Thorfinn reached the end he threw away his shield, gripped the axe in both hands and charged with a bellow.

Vallon realised his mistake. The trunks blocked him in, leaving hardly any space for manoeuvre. Thorfinn's rush was the do-or-die effort of a berserker. Vallon couldn't avoid the attack and his shield was too flimsy to ward it off. Thorfinn held his axe like a demented forester, making no attempt to guard himself. Vallon knew that he could run him through, but not before the Viking had cut him in half.

The axe swung and he darted back and to his right, the direction he'd calculated Thorfinn would least expect. He'd read him wrong. By a massive effort, Thorfinn checked his stroke, corrected for Vallon's dodge and brought his axe round in a flat crescent aimed at Vallon's midriff. Vallon's feet were grounded. All he could do was suck in his stomach and arch back like a cat.

He heard a faint snick. Nothing more, and then he felt a cold burning in his belly. Thorfinn's attack had pulled him through a semi-circle, but Vallon was too flat-footed to counter. He used the time it took Thorfinn to recover to retreat into open ground. He glanced down. He'd seen men in the heat of battle continue fighting with their entrails spilling down to their groin. What he saw was bad enough. Thorfinn had sliced through his hauberk, leaving the lower part of the gash hanging in a flap, the padded undercoat sucking up blood.

'I can see your guts, Frankish. I'll strangle you with them.'

Thorfinn's men whooped, urging him to finish the fight. Vallon pretended that the wound had drained his strength and courage. He moved clumsily, his uncoordinated efforts just enough to avoid the death blow. Thorfinn's face contused, first with triumph and then with frustration. Every time he thought he had his opponent at his mercy, a blundering move carried him away. Vallon lurched as if one leg had grown shorter than the other. His sword wavered. Thorfinn's eyes lit up. In his lust to kill, the Viking charged in too fast. He skidded slightly on the frozen ground, enough to make him drop his axe a few inches. Vallon danced forward and delivered a reverse sweep into the Viking's right hip.

'You're dead.'

Thorfinn loosed one hand on the axe and felt the wound. He tossed his head.

They circled each other, both of them wounded, aware that the contest was in its final phase. Thorfinn tried to bring it to a crushing conclusion by making another charge. Ten feet from Vallon he let fly with the axe. Vallon ducked and the blade whirled past his head, nearly decapitating one of the Vikings before skidding to rest somewhere outside the arena.

Before Vallon could take advantage, Thorfinn drew his sword and ran to recover his shield. Vallon walked toward him. He had no idea how long the contest had lasted. The sun was beginning to break through the mist and meltwater splattered from the trees.

Every sword fight has its own rhythm, yet there are only eight basic moves. The skill lies in stitching them together. First hypnotise your opponent without hypnotising yourself. When he's sure what your next move will be and has half-committed himself to countering it, change the line of attack. It's like scissors and stone played for lethal stakes and with many more variations.

Vallon was fully engaged now, trading blow for blow. The blades skidded and clattered, bit and battered, Thorfinn's sword striking in clanging contrast to the ringing chime of Vallon's blade. Back and forth, round and round, until the ground underfoot was trampled and greasy. Vallon had Thorfinn's measure and was using the technique called 'soaking in' – mirroring the Viking's moves.

He stepped back and switched his sword to his left hand, his shield to his right.

'Does your sword arm weaken?' Thorfinn panted.

'On the contrary. My left hand is my strongest.'

He attacked Thorfinn in all four quarters, aiming at his shoulders, his legs, his arms. The Viking could only defend, staggering back, holding out his shield and sword at arm's length. Vallon cut him across his shield arm, made a lazy pass that sliced his thigh. Vallon's eyes were the only fixed points in his body, while Thorfinn's stare had begun to dart like a hunted animal's.

The Viking rode the next stroke and brought his shield round in an attempt to punch Vallon in the face. His lunge ended in empty air. Vallon was a move ahead of him and delivered four strokes in less time than it takes to blink twice. With the last of them he cut all four fingers off Thorfinn's sword hand. The weapon dropped to the ground.

'Pick it up.'

The Viking threw his shield at Vallon and grabbed his sword in his left hand. He blundered like a beast, chest heaving, mouth dragging in snot. His supporters had fallen silent. Vallon heard Caitlin calling on him to kill, kill, kill!

He feinted to the head, making Thorfinn cock his sword. Feinted again, forcing the Viking onto the tips of his toes. And then as Thorfinn bellowed and charged to embrace him in a death clinch, he locked his right knee and rammed the point of his sword through mail and muscle and bone until the hilt was flat against Thorfinn's chest. The Viking's sword cartwheeled out of his hand. Vallon felt the weight of his opponent bear down on his sword. He braced one foot against Thorfinn's thigh and pulled out the blade.

Thorfinn dropped to his knees and slowly raised his head. A worm of blood crawled from his mouth. One hand groped behind him. Pink spittle popped between his lips. 'Finish it, Frankish.'

Vallon stepped in and raised his sword and in the same moment Thorfinn drew his scramasax and lunged up to find his enemy gone. He was still blinking around when Vallon at his back cut off his head. Thorfinn's body dropped into a kneeling position, two fountains of blood spouting from his neck. His hands groped at the ground as if he were trying to get up. Vallon shoved him on to his side. Thorfinn's heels drummed and then he stopped moving.

The Vikings and the company surged forward and then stopped. The two sides came into Vallon's focus.

Raul jabbed with his crossbow. 'I'll shoot any cunt who moves.'

Vallon began walking towards the Vikings. Blood squelched in his boots. He lifted his sword. 'Thorfinn died as he lived. Bravely. The Valkyries will welcome him into the shield hall to take his place with all the other heroes.' Vallon pointed his sword. 'He swore that you'd acknowledge me as leader if I defeated him. Break that oath and I'll send you down into the hellpit where the walls are woven from serpents.'

'If we join you, we want a share of your silver.'

The speaker was the lieutenant who'd shared the rock in the river with Thorfinn. His name was Wulfstan.

'You've done nothing to earn it. Food is the only thing I'll give you, and you won't get that until you've released the prisoners.'

'The slaves are all the treasure we have.'

'If you want to keep them, you'll have to kill me.'

Drogo tugged at his arm. 'You aren't in any condition to fight again. Leave it to me and Fulk.'

'I'm not going to fight,' Arne shouted. His companions rounded on him. 'What's Thorfinn brought us? Nothing but pain and hunger. We'd be better off serving the Frank. You've heard how he outwitted his enemies and gathered riches in the home of ice.'

Vallon was feeling sick and faint. He caught Hero's pleading look before turning back to the Vikings. 'You've got until sunset.'

Vallon retired from the field in a stumbling crouch, blood squirting through the seams of his boots. Hero and Richard attempted to support him, but he flapped them away. 'Can't let them see how weak I am.'

He reached the place where he'd spent the night and sank to the ground. 'It doesn't hurt much. Probably looks worse than it is.'

Hero took charge. 'Let's get your hauberk off.'

He and Richard dragged the mail over Vallon's head and stripped him of the blood-soaked gambeson. Then Hero pulled up Vallon's sopping red tunic. Thorfinn's axe had sliced through the iron mail and padding, severing the stomach wall for a distance of nine inches and exposing a bulge of intestine. Hero tested the depth of the wound. He grimaced.

'Bad?'

'It could be worse. No major blood vessels severed. The blade nicked your large intestine but didn't cut through. Half an inch deeper and we'd be preparing your burial shroud.'

'Let me look,' said Vallon. He sat up with Hero's assistance and examined the grey tube of gut with a lop-sided smile. 'It's a sobering thing to see your own innards.' He flopped back.

'I have to clean the wound. Richard, fetch the cauldron.'

Mosquitoes roused by the sun homed in on the reek of blood, speckling the wound as fast as Hero could clear it. He wiped his face on his shoulder.

'Light some smudge fires.'

'Just swab it and stitch it,' said Vallon.

Hero spat out a mosquito. 'There's a lot of foreign matter in the wound. Let me do it my own way.'

Vallon cuffed him and closed his eyes.

The company got two smudge fires going. Hero tweezered out fragments of metal and textile, bits of bark and pine needle. 'Richard, sprinkle some sulphur on the flames to purify the air.'

Vallon coughed on the rotten-egg atmosphere. 'Hero, your cure is worse than the cut.'

The brimstone fumes killed the mosquitoes in their thousands. Their bodies spiralled down and Hero had to keep removing them from the wound. He took a bottle from his chest.

'What's that?'

'Strong wine fortified with Venice turpentine and balsam. It fights corruption.'

Vallon recoiled from the volatile vapours.

'I'm not drinking that. It smells like embalming fluid.'

'It's for dressing the wound. It will sting.'

Hero decanted some of the antiseptic into a cup, dipped a squirrel-hair brush into it and dabbed at the wound. Vallon gasped as the mixture bit into his raw flesh. Hero swabbed the wound and the surrounding skin. 'That's as clean as I can make it. Now I have to close it. It will be painful. You'd better take some of the drowsy mixture.'

'Save it for someone worse hit than me. It's only a flesh wound.'

'Don't be such a hero.'

'This isn't the first time I've been wounded. Jam a stick in my jaws and get on with it.'

Raul knew what to do. He cut a branch of the right thickness and gave it to Vallon and gripped his arms. 'Wayland, you grab one leg. Drogo you take the other.'

Hero threaded a needle with gut. He clamped the edges of the wound with forceps. His hand trembled as he prepared to make the first suture. 'I've not done this before. Not on a live person.'

'Give it to me,' Wayland said.

Raul grinned at Vallon. 'You'll be all right with Wayland. I once saw him stitch up his dog's belly as dainty as you please.'

'That's a comforting thought.'

'Wash your hands,' Hero told Wayland. 'Scrub them clean.'

Wayland washed his mitts and Hero made him rinse them in the antiseptic. 'Sew each stitch about a finger's width apart. That way the wound can drain.'

Wayland looked at Vallon. 'Ready?'

Vallon clamped his teeth on the stick.

Wayland inserted the needle into the flap of muscle, pulled it through and threaded it through the opposite lip. Vallon's abdomen cramped up and the tendons in his neck stood out. Sweat beaded on his forehead. Wayland completed the first stitch and looked at him.

'Keep going,' said Raul.

Twenty-one sutures were needed to sew up the wound. Vallon sobbed, rocked his head and clawed at the ground, but he didn't call halt until the operation was finished.

'It's done,' Hero said.

Vallon spat out the stick, leaned to one side and retched. His eyes were streaming, his face almost black. Gasping like a woman in labour, he arched up, stared at his navel, gave a childlike cry and fell back.

Hero applied a poultice of sphagnum moss and bandaged it with strips of linen. 'You must avoid movement until the wound knits. No solid food until I say so.'

Vallon's laugh terminated in a wincing cry. 'Do I look as if I'm hungry or eager for strenuous activity?' The blood drained from his face and his eyes flickered. 'I think I'm going to pass out.'

Vallon woke at twilight to find Hero sitting beside him.

'How do you feel?'

'Sick. Sore. Like a horse had kicked me in the belly. Thirsty.'

Hero gave him some water. 'The Vikings have accepted your conditions.'

Vallon could hear a muffled roaring. He turned and saw the trees outlined by an apocalyptic glow.

'It's Thorfinn's funeral pyre,' said Hero.

Vallon lifted a hand.

'You mustn't move.'

'Prop me up.'

The Vikings had built a bonfire the size of a grave barrow and laid their leader on top of it. The blaze was at its height, the conflagration so fierce that the trees around it tossed in the updraught. Pillars of sparks whirled into the sky. Vallon shielded his eyes. Peering into the sizzling core of the pyre, he saw the shrivelled and carbonised corpse of Thorfinn Wolfbreath, last of the Vikings.

XXXVI

Vallon drifted up from fevered dreams. A soft cushion pressed against his cheek. After a while he worked out that it was a woman's bosom. His gaze tracked up across the swelling fabric and made out a creamy face framed by a copper-red aura. He unstuck his lips. 'Caitlin?'

'Don't talk,' she said, sponging his brow. 'Your body's burning.'

Vallon found that he was buried under a pile of furs and fleeces. He was wringing with sweat and his head thumped as if it would burst. His lips made another popping sound. 'Where's Hero?'

'Asleep. He was up with you all night. He's hardly slept a wink since the fight.'

'Which night? How many days have passed?'

'Three. The fever came on the second night. You've been delirious.' She rocked back into sharper focus.

'You've cut your hair.'

Her hand went to her head. 'It was impossible to keep clean and the weight made my head ache.'

'I'm thirsty.'

She cradled his shoulders and placed a cup to his lips. Some of the water chugged down his throat and the rest spilled down his chin. He gasped. 'More.'

When he'd drunk his fill, Caitlin kept hold of him, his cheek against her breast. At last she lowered him and he lay watching treetops drifting past.

'I'm as weak as water.'

'You've wasted to skin and bone.' Caitlin's forefinger traced the arc of his nose. 'Beak and talon. You look like a fierce ghost.'

'How's my wound?'

'It's healing. Hero's changed the dressing daily and he's pleased with progress.'

False reassurance, Vallon decided. 'Help me up.'

'You mustn't move.'

Vallon groped for the gunwale. 'I want to see where we are.'

Caitlin lifted him into a sitting position. 'The Vikings say we're nearly at the next lake.'

Hero lay curled up in the bow, so overwhelmed by exhaustion that it wrung Vallon's heart. Otherwise the boat was empty. Everyone was on the banks, straining against towropes. Up ahead was the Viking longship. Everything was drained of colour. Grey trees, grey river, grey sky. Vallon had the sensation of being borne down a corridor leading into the underworld.

He sank back. 'I don't see Wayland and Raul.'

'They're scouting ahead. Drogo's taken command until you're healed.'

Vallon closed his eyes. Caitlin was still there when he opened them. 'What a relief to let someone else bear the responsibility.' He sighed. 'People shouldn't be frightened of dying.'

Caitlin clapped a hand over his mouth. 'Don't talk like that.'

'I have to face the truth. Belly wounds don't heal.'

'Yes, they do. You're not going to die. I won't let you.'

Vallon's bleary gaze wandered over her face. 'You can't be the princess. The princess wants me dead.'

Caitlin swung her head away. 'I don't wish ill to the man who avenged my brother's death.'

Vallon thought about it. 'I wasn't avenging Helgi. I was fighting for my life.'

Caitlin turned her eyes back to him. 'Why do you hate women?'

Vallon had no answer. Had he blurted out some diatribe in his delirium? 'What makes you think that? I worshipped my mother, was devoted to my sister, and greeted my daughter's birth with joy.'

'You killed your wife.'

Vallon was forced to think about that on top of everything else. 'I loved her, too.'

Caitlin clasped herself. 'You hate me. I can't blame you. I have too much pride, too much passion.'

Even in his fuddled state, Vallon thought this was a bizarre gambit.

'I don't hate you,' he muttered. He wanted to sink back into his addled dreams.

'You said I had an arse as big as a pony's.'

A picture of Caitlin bathing in the volcanic pool flashed into Vallon's mind. Her white breasts above the chemical blue water, her dark red hair belled out on the surface. He laughed at the memory and then broke off clutching his stomach and spewed out the water he'd just drunk.

Caitlin mopped his face, ignoring the stains on her dress. 'I'm sorry. I shouldn't have raised the subject.'

Vallon retched again. 'I'm sorry, too. Can we save this conversation for another day?'

A couple of miles upriver, Raul was in a distracted frame of mind. 'I know Vallon's wound don't look too bad, but I've seen a dozen men get cut in the belly no worse than him and I can't mind but two that didn't die of it.'

'Give it a rest,' Wayland muttered. Earlier, Raul's chatter had spooked three black grouse the size of geese that racketed away through the treetops before Wayland could draw on them.

They went on, treading a silvery carpet of lichen. A large owl the same colour as the reindeer moss perched tight against the bole of a fir, one citron eye fixed in a conspiratorial wink. Wayland kept its secret and went on, combing the trees for prey. He hadn't killed game for two days and if he didn't find food today the falcons would go hungry for the first time since he'd captured them. His thoughts were drifting between Vallon's sickness and his own worries when he stopped as if a chasm had opened at his feet. Twice they'd cut the trails of reindeer herders, but those tracks had been old. This one was recent.

Wayland examined the moist droppings and the nibbled branches. 'Looks fresh,' Raul said.

Wayland rose from one knee. 'Two groups travelled this path. The first passed a few days ago. The second came through yesterday.'

He spied through the trees some kind of rudimentary architecture that turned out to be three conical tent frames made of spruce poles about twelve feet high. Inside each structure was a bed of ashes ringed by smoke-blackened stones. Wayland dug a hand into the embers. 'Still warm. They left early this morning.'

He criss-crossed the trail, peering like a diviner working out where to sink a well. At last he straightened up.

'How many do you make them?'

'At least thirty. Men and women. Old and young. They've got dogs with them.' Wayland looked both ways up the trail. It followed an esker raised above the bog. 'See that?' he said, pointing at piles of firewood stacked beside each shelter. 'They're expecting more to come through. Get off the trail and sit quiet. I'll warn the others.'

'Ah, hell. Let's rest here until they come up to us. They ain't far behind.'

But Wayland was already into his stride.

'Hey, Wayland.'

The falconer kept going, jogging backwards. Raul raised a fist and then lowered it. 'Never mind.'

Wayland waved. 'I won't be long.'

He intercepted the longship a mile downriver and was soon back at the spot where he'd left Raul. The German wasn't there and fresh tracks overlaid the Lapps' trail. Wayland cast about and soon found what he'd been dreading. He touched the ground and raised fingers spotted with blood. Everyone watched him. He set the dog on Raul's scent and a little way downriver it checked at a patch of churned-up ground. Here there was more blood. A lot of it, pooling in hollows gouged out by struggling feet. From this spot drag marks led to the river. Wayland went to the bank and saw that the trail continued into the forest on the other side. He looked round at the company. 'They've got Raul.'

'Is he alive?' Hero asked.

'He was when they took him across the river. They bound him. He killed a couple of them.' Wayland pointed to where he'd found the first blood. 'He shot one of them back there and then tried to flee. They caught him here and he killed another.'

Richard held a fist to his mouth. 'What are we going to do?'

Wayland stared across the river. 'I'll go after them. No sense anyone else coming. If we press them too hard, they'll kill Raul and scatter into the forest.'

'They've probably killed him already,' Drogo said. 'We should reach Lake Onega before nightfall. We'll wait for you there until tomorrow night. If you haven't returned by then, I'll assume you're dead.'

A voice spoke from behind. 'You're assuming rather a lot, aren't you?'

Vallon stood supported by Garrick. He looked like a corpse risen from the slab, his eyes flinty shards sunk in mauve sockets.

Drogo pulled himself straight. 'I was acting in the interests of the party.'

Wayland began cladding the dog in its leather armour.

Vallon's deathly gaze remained fixed on Drogo. 'Give him your mail.'

Drogo stepped back in amazement. 'Let a peasant wear my armour?'

Wayland shook his head. 'I don't want it. The lighter I travel, the faster I'll catch up.'

'You'll catch up with a horde of Lapps who think we're slavers.' Vallon turned back to Drogo. 'Lend him your armour.'

Face all knobbled, Drogo thrust the suit at Wayland. The falconer took only the hauberk with its gashed bodice crudely repaired.

'You'll need a sword,' Vallon said. 'Drogo, I won't ask you to part with yours.' His gaze drifted towards Tostig, one of Helgi's men. 'Give Wayland your sword.'

At the first peep of protest, Caitlin tore into Tostig with a fury that made him cock an elbow over his ear. He undid his sword belt and Wayland strapped it on.

'What's your plan?' Vallon asked.

'Trade for Raul's life.'

Vallon snapped his fingers. 'Arne, you've dealt with the Lapps. What do you think would be sufficient restitution?'

'Iron and colourful cloth are the goods they desire most. Iron above all. A knife, an axe and two yards of linen might be enough.'

A scurry of activity produced the reparation. Wayland packed the goods in his back-pack together with bread and fish. He held Syth by both hands, then he crossed the river and soon was lost among the trees.

A child could have followed the Lapps' trail. They were moving fast, a dozen men dragging Raul, pulling him this way and that as he struggled against his bonds. The clouded sky offered few clues as to time or direction. Wayland judged that twilight wasn't far off and that the Lapps were heading east. They kept to the winding ridge and he guessed he'd run about six miles when the dog stopped and tested the air. Wayland assumed that the Lapps would have posted men to watch for pursuit and he was hoping to initiate negotiations with this rearguard, rather than coming up on the main party. From the way the dog growled and cast fierce looks to each side, Wayland knew that they were watching him and that some of them had fallen in behind.

He went on. The light was beginning to fail when the forest opened out into a natural avenue. At the far end of the corridor, two spruce trees had been bent over and anchored by ropes to form an arch. From the apex hung a dark bundle. It was Raul, suspended twenty feet above the ground, tied between the trees by his arms and legs.

Wayland slung his bow and placed the iron goods and cloth in his outstretched hands. He advanced as if he meant to lay them under the dangling man. Lapps rose up on both sides. They wore hooded smocks of reindeer skin with the fur inside, the hoods trimmed with wolf or fox fur. They were a small race, the men not much more than five feet tall, but decently formed and nothing like the vicious dwarfs described by the Vikings. Most carried small bows or stone axes and some of them had horns made from birch bark. He didn't see anyone carrying Raul's crossbow. They probably didn't know how to work it or lacked the strength to span it.

Wayland stopped short of the arch. Raul hung with his arms upraised and his head drooping to his chest. His clothes had been ripped to tatters and were heavily stained. Much like the bleeding Christs Wayland had seen behind church altars. He'd never known Raul in any condition except bullish vigour and it was shocking to see him reduced to such a pitiful state.

'Raul, can you hear me? Raul?'

The German raised his head by degrees. 'Is that you, Wayland?' His voice was a husky croak. His face was bloody and bruised and one of his eyes had been gouged out. 'They caught me napping, Wayland. They were on me before I spotted them. They're stealthy devils.'

'How many did you kill?'

'Three, I reckon. One of them just a kid. I loosed at the first one I saw and took off running. They noosed me with ropes and then they all came down on me. They bust my ribs and God knows what else.' He coughed and dragged in a whistling breath. 'I'm hurt bad, Wayland.'

'Don't talk. I'll get you down.'

Raul's head rocked. 'There ain't no way you can save my bacon. I'm looking down on the heathens tending the ropes and they're ready to cut. The kindest thing you could do is put me out of my misery.'

'I'm going to make a trade. You just ... '

A cracked laugh. 'I ain't going nowhere.'

433

Wayland laid down his bow and placed the borrowed sword on top of it.

Raul sucked air and gave a racking cough. 'There ain't no use both of us dying.' His voice fell away. 'You know what they're going to do. They're going to tear me in two.' His body convulsed in a vague spasm. 'I never thought I'd go out like one of them martyrs.'

'You're not going to die,' said Wayland. He scanned the trees, searching for a leader. Some of the archers were women and striplings. He singled out an older man who looked like he might have a cool head and walked towards him with the trade goods laid across his hands. He'd gone five or six paces when one of the Lapps loosed a warning shot that darted into the ground a few feet ahead. He glanced back at his weapons. Another half dozen steps and he wouldn't be able to recover them if the Lapps attacked. His tongue stuck to his palate. He placed one hand on the dog's shoulder.

'Wayland,' Raul called in a voice from deep inside. 'I appreciate you coming after me. Appreciate it. You've done more than any comrade can ask for, so I'm begging you to save yourself. There ain't much time and I've got one last thing to ask.'

Wayland's face knotted to squeeze back the tears. 'Ask away.'

Raul dragged in a whistling breath. He couldn't expand his chest and was slowly drowning. 'You know how I bragged about going home with a swag of silver. You used to smile and swing your head like you knew I'd blow it away. Well, looks like I ain't going to get the chance to prove you wrong.' Raul fell silent for a moment and his head sagged. 'I ain't complaining. I got to tell you, Wayland, these last few months have been as good as I've known.' Raul strained against the ropes to relieve the pressure on his lungs. 'It ain't for my benefit, but if there's any silver coming my way, can you make sure it finds its way home? I know Vallon said we were on profits, but I don't think the captain will begrudge me a few coins. He ain't a mean man.'

Wayland couldn't speak. He shook his head.

'I know you can't take it yourself. But me and old Garrick were talking and he said that if he made it to Novgorod, he was planning on heading home. I told him to look in on my family and said that if he was thinking about going back to farming, there was some good land to be had. I told him about my sisters and said he might do worse than take one of them to warm his bed.'

Wayland swallowed the lump in his throat. 'I'll do that, dear friend, but it isn't over yet.' He wiped his hands on his thighs.

Raul gave a lacerated laugh. 'All the years I've known you and that's the first time you called me "friend". Pray for my soul, Wayland.'

Wayland took one more step. A horn blew and the Lapps shot a volley. At least three arrows struck Wayland, but the nomads' bows were light and their bone-tipped arrows splintered against his armour. He dashed back to his weapons, while the dog rushed forward in a series of terrifying bounds that made the Lapps tumble back. He glimpsed a shaft sticking out of its leather suit.

He scooped up his bow in his left hand, the sword in his right and ran yelling towards the Lapps guarding the ropes that tethered one side of the arch. Before he reached it there was a twang – another twang – and the two trees straightened up with a swishing sound. Wayland saw the ropes binding Raul spring taut.

'No!'

Black against the sky, Raul seemed to fly upwards, then he flung his limbs wide and there was a rending and a popping and the two halves of his body dragged apart and swung against the swaying trees. Blood and innards rained on Wayland. Something warm and wet choked off his scream. Loud ululations rose from the Lapps. They charged in and Wayland sprinted for the end of the avenue, knowing it would close before he reached it. Another arrow struck him in the ribs and its point pierced his mail. A youth sprang into his path, jabbing with a spear. Wayland took the point on his chest and hacked the pole away. The impact and his counter-thrust threw him off-balance. He staggered into the ground. Fighting for purchase, he saw a pair of feet plant themselves in front of him. He glanced up to see a man poised to strike with a stone axe. He rolled aside and swung his sword through a half-circle. It connected with his attacker's ankles and the axeman screamed and fell.

Wayland regained his feet and winnowed through his assailants. Most darted back, yelling as if assailed by a force not human. One man seemed mesmerised and Wayland clubbed him aside. He broke clear and the dog rushed up alongside him, two arrows in its leather trappings and its jaws all gory. It turned its eyes on him in a way that seemed to say, 'Now what?'

He flared away from movement ahead of him. A herd of reindeer.

435

Hundreds of them, plunging away in grey and brown streams. He accelerated to keep pace with the stampede. Half a mile further on the reindeer veered to the right. As the tailenders passed him, he ran left.

A backward glance showed no one in pursuit. The reindeer had obliterated his tracks. Raul's death might be enough revenge for the Lapps, and the injuries he'd inflicted must have taken the fight out of them. He slowed, nursing a stitch.

The dog whirled. Wayland turned and saw a pack of dogs bounding towards them, led by a pale wolf with blue eyes. The wolf-dog closed without hesitation and the dog met it head on and drove it to the ground in a whirl of fur and jaws. When the dog broke away, its attacker moved spastically. The pack streamed in, but instead of attacking Wayland, they fell upon their crippled leader.

Shapes flitted through the trees. A line of Lapps about a hundred yards wide. Wayland's dog rushed up to him, bloody slobber dangling from its jaws. The Lapps reached the pack and drove it apart with whips and boots.

Wayland hadn't taken flight. He planted the sword in front of him and readied his bow. The dog snarled. 'Enough killing,' he shouted. Tears of rage and frustration blurred his vision. 'Please. I'm sorry Raul killed some of your people, but we're not slavers. Nobody's hunting you.'

The Lapps looked along their line, taking courage from their numbers, and then they brandished their weapons and charged again. Wayland shot and didn't wait to see where the arrow went before haring off. He was running wild now, taking whatever course seemed most open. The sounds of pursuit faded. He ran on.

To get back to the river, he'd have to run in a great circle. He checked the sky. Not long until dark. He settled into a lope. The hauberk must have weighed thirty pounds, but he'd have been dead without it.

He thought he'd put himself in the clear when the sight of reindeer tracks brought him up sharp. Had he run in a circle? No. It was the trail of the group that had left camp that morning. They couldn't be far ahead. His eyes switched about. A horn blew from behind and then, closer and in front, an answering note sounded. Blocked. He struck out at a right angle.

He could manage no more than a weary jog and he was a long way from safety. The Lapps would track him and they would watch all the paths leading back to the river. He reached a bog that slowed progress to a cautious plod. Soon it would be dark. The dismal sky offered no clues to the direction of sunset. From the way the lichens grew on the trees, he guessed he was heading north.

Dusk deepened to dark, the night as black as night could be. Even with the dog's guidance, he couldn't plot a course through the ponds and bogs. After sinking to his knees for the third time, he knew he'd have to wait for the clouds to break or the sun to rise. He felt his way into a clump of alders and found a perch of dry ground. Somewhere in the forest a hand drum pattered. From a different quarter came an answering tattoo. The drums tapped out their messages and then fell silent.

'They're laying plans for tomorrow,' Wayland told the dog.

He shared out the food and resigned himself to sitting out the night. He was soaked to the waist and very cold. The chainmail sucked the warmth from his body and he took it off. He felt the arrow wound in his side. Only a puncture, but painful. The dog shoved its head into his chest. He laid his face on its craggy skull and stroked its ears, whispering a lullaby his mother used to sing.

He passed a hellish night and woke from a doze sick and shivering. Still pitch black. He forced himself to his feet and bent and stretched until he'd got his blood circulating. He watched the sky. When a crow cawed, he knew it was time to go. In the wildwood he'd learned that the first crow flight was the true herald of day. He put on the hauberk then, holding the dog with one hand, he groped across the bog. If he could travel a mile before the Lapps resumed their hunt, he might be out of the vicinity before they closed a circle around him.

Light when it came rose sourceless, like a grey mist. No hint of sun to give him bearings. Scattered trees loomed into being. Only the trees closest to him had solid form; the rest were dull phantoms.

Daylight found him still picking his way across the bog. Water squirted out under his feet and every step produced a sucking sound. He stopped often to survey his path, the ground wobbling beneath him. In one place it gave way and he plunged up to his groin. If the dog hadn't been there to lend its strength to his efforts, he might never have got out.

Eventually he learned that the trick was to skate across the surface, not resting his full weight on one spot. He went on at a faster rate and saw pine trees marking drier ground. As he made for it, a woodpecker's whistling cry rang through the still air. He paid no heed until another and more grating call sounded. He stopped and tried to locate the cries. The first bird called again, behind and to his left. The second bird answered, also from the rear and over to the right. Wayland had seen the birds that made these cries. They were twice the size of the woodpeckers he knew from home and their calls had become familiar. He'd never heard them delivered in duet. At the third exchange, he knew they weren't made by birds.

'They've found our trail.'

He hurried towards the firm ground, the calls passing back and forth behind him. He reached the ridge and examined the ground. He hadn't come this way yesterday and the earth carried no prints of men or reindeer. He patted the dog. 'Looks like we got out of bed earlier than them.'

He broke into an easy run. The signals behind grew faint and Wayland allowed himself the hope of striking the river without further drama.

Another birdcall from ahead stopped him as if he'd come up against an invisible barrier. He stalked forward, peering through the sketchy trees. The dog's hackles were up, a low rumble building in its throat.

Wayland nocked an arrow and drew his bow. 'I know you're there.'

Silence.

He scanned the treescape. 'You'd better get out of my way. You're not dealing with a lost Viking.'

The trees loomed in grey and spectral shapes. Behind him the maddening birdcalls drew closer. He slung his bow and took out the sword.

'I'm coming through and I'll kill anyone who tries to stop me.' He pulled the coif over his head and hoisted the sword. The dog watched him, tongue lolling.

'Go!'

He was at full sprint when a figure stepped from behind a tree and hurled a hissing rope so deftly that it seemed like an extension of his hand. Wayland dodged, glimpsed another coil snaking towards him from another direction. The third loop he didn't see at all. It dropped over his shoulders and yanked tight, converting forward motion into a violent reverse that whisked him off his feet and slammed the breath out of him. He sat up. Head awhirl, he saw two men pulling on the rope and then he saw them abandon it as the dog smashed into them.

Wayland's crash had deadened his left side from thigh to shoulder. He regained his feet only to be dragged back to earth by another lasso. A second loop fell over his sword arm and almost wrenched the weapon from his grip. He was bayed and trammelled and if the dog hadn't been with him he would have gone the same way as Raul. Trappings bristling with arrows, it charged each rope holder in turn, knocking them over, slashing with its jaws, panicking them into flight.

Wayland was still snared but he hadn't lost his wits or his sword and when the last rope dropped away he hurtled forward as if he meant to throw himself from this world into the next. The shouts of his ambushers faded. Without breaking stride, he pulled off the ropes and threw them aside. He knew where he was. He was on the path he'd followed from the river. He aimed a smack at the dog. 'We're through!'

The dog threw itself down, arched itself into a bow and gnawed at its belly.

Wayland ran back. 'What's wrong?' He took the dog's head in both hands and pulled it away from its midriff. 'Oh God!'

A broken arrow shaft jutted from the dog's abdomen. He couldn't tell how deep the head had penetrated. The dog lay on its side as though inviting him to deal with the wound. He reached for its head and the dog gave him a quick lick and stared away. He took hold of the shaft and gave a tentative pull. The dog uttered a low whine. 'Ssh,' he whispered. He pulled harder, feeling solid resistance, and the dog whimpered and clamped its jaws around his wrist. Gently he undid them. The arrow was barbed and had penetrated deep. The dog lay panting, its topaz eyes fixed on some faraway place. With swimming eyes Wayland looked about for some remedy or inspiration. There was none to be found – only the sight of Lapps running at him through the trees.

He pulled the dog to its feet. 'Come on. I'll deal with the arrow when we're back at the boat.'

The dog matched him stride by stride for about a hundred yards. Then it stopped again and gave a piteous whine such as Wayland hadn't heard it utter since it was a pup. It looked at him. The Lapps were getting closer. 'Come!' he ordered, clapping his hands. 'We're nearly at the river. Hero will have that arrow out in a trice. Come!'

The dog looked at him, its meaning so plain that Wayland groaned. There was no cure for the wound. The barbed arrow was buried so deep in its guts that no surgeon could have removed it.

The Lapps were only fifty yards away. Wayland stumbled back. 'Come! Please!'

The dog looked at him for the last time. It turned towards the Lapps, shook itself and hurled itself towards them. He saw it bowl over one of the attackers and then it disappeared, swallowed up in a crowd of axemen and spearmen. The frenzy of hacking and stabbing stopped and the Lapps squatted in a busy cluster, doing things with ropes and branches. When they rose, they carried the dog's carcass strung under a pole. It took four men to bear its weight. They shouldered their trophy and hurried away into the forest.

Wayland found the river and followed it upstream. The clouds shredded and the sun broke through. It was going down in a dim red ball when he caught up with the longship on the north shore of Lake Onega. His companions rose as he limped into camp. They opened their mouths to frame questions, then saw the answers plain on his face and held their tongues. Syth ran and threw her arms around him. He held her to his chest and stroked her hair.

Vallon limped over. 'The dog, too?'

Wayland nodded.

'I'm sorry. Are you hurt?'

'A prick from an arrow and some bruises. Nothing serious.'

'So you say. I want Hero to look you over. After that, food and sleep.'

Wayland shoved past. 'I can't sleep while the falcons starve.'

'I fed them,' Syth said. 'Vallon had one of the horses killed. There's enough meat to keep the falcons until we reach Rus.'

Vallon nodded in confirmation. 'I told you I wouldn't let them go hungry.'

*

440

Wayland woke in the longship, one shore a faint haze, the other invisible. It took four days to cross the lake, and the only thing he remembered of the passage was the geese passing overhead in ragged streamers, tens of thousands of voices raised in lamentation.

XXXVII

A broad river called the Svir flowed from Onega to Lake Ladoga and the land of Rus. Empty huts began to appear in clearings slashed into the forest. The dwellings were the summer quarters of hunter-gatherers. After weeks of sleeping rough, the travellers were grateful for the shelter offered by the simple lodgings. It was now early October and winter was treading at their heels. Each day the numbers of wildfowl passing overhead grew fewer. Each night the cold gripped tighter. Two more Icelanders had died, starved beyond recovery despite Vallon ordering the slaughter of the remaining horses.

His wound had knitted cleanly. He kissed Hero and told him that without the Sicilian's physicking he would have died a slow and suppurating death. Hero was trying to take satisfaction from that as he and Richard plodded one morning along the riverbank ahead of the longship. It was the only comfort he could dredge from their situation. Still days from Novgorod, the food almost gone, many of the travellers sick. Wayland was restored and spent most of the daylight hours hunting, but without the dog's help he couldn't kill enough to satisfy the falcons' appetites. All of them had lost so much muscle that their keels stuck out like knives, and one of them screamed for food from dawn to dark.

The Vikings and Icelanders couldn't understand why the falcons should receive any meat while they themselves were forced to boil moss for soup and chew on horse hide to dull their hunger pangs. The previous day, when Wayland and Syth returned from a hunting trip with a hare to show for their efforts, the Vikings and Icelanders had crowded round demanding that the carcass be handed over. Vallon had forced them to back off, but it had been close. If they didn't find food in the next day or two, a violent breakdown was inevitable.

After that, barbarism and worse. The weak left behind to die, cannibalism ...

Richard seemed to read his thoughts. 'Drogo takes care to stand back, but have no doubt, he's waiting for the moment when he can move against Vallon.'

Hero sighed and shook his head. The sky, heavy with clouds the colour of ploughshares, mirrored his mood.

They trudged on. Grey spots floated past Hero's eyes. He rubbed them and saw that snow was falling – big downy flakes already beginning to settle.

Richard stopped. 'We'd better go back.'

'There's a path,' said Hero, pointing to a winding depression highlighted by the snow. 'It probably leads to a cabin. We might not spot it from the ship.'

Soon the snow obliterated all trace of the path and only the sound of the river gave them their direction. Hero was about to step around a stunted bush when it jumped up and shouted. More shouts and vague figures darting through the snow. An arrow whizzed past his head.

'Peace! *Pax! Eirene!*'

The commotion stilled. Through the feathery whiteness he made out figures crouched behind dark bales. Three men with arrows trained on him stalked forward. They were dressed in pelts, their eyes narrowed in hostile squints. One of them jabbered in Russian.

'We're merchants. Travelling to Novgorod.'

The Russians understood 'Novgorod'. Their spokesman jabbed behind Hero, asking how many were with him.

He counted thirty on his fingers and the Russians yammered at each other.

The drakkar's dragon stem slid out of the snow with Vallon at the prow looking like death warmed up and Drogo beside him in his mail coat and iron helmet.

The Russians scattered. 'Varangians!'

'No! Wait. Not Varangians.'

Wulfstan shouted in Russian and vaulted off the longship. The woodsmen stopped at a distance. Wulfstan called again, making beckoning gestures. The woodsmen skulked back, bowing and begging the travellers' pardon. Wulfstan spoke a smattering of their language and established that they were frontiersmen who'd spent the summer trapping game and collecting honey and beeswax. They were on their way home by canoe to their village at the mouth of the Volkhov river, three days to the west.

Wayland emerged from the forest while the parties were negotiating. He took one look at the Russians and hurried up to a boy with a string of willow grouse slung around his neck. He flinched away when Wayland reached out for them. Wayland turned to Wulfstan. 'Tell him I want to buy them.'

The boy's father came over. He assessed Wayland's desperate gaze and said something that made the other Russians laugh.

Wayland lurched round. 'What did he say?'

'You can have them for five squirrels,' said Wulfstan.

'I don't have five squirrels. If I did, I wouldn't need the grouse.'

Wulfstan grinned. 'The backwoodsmen measure money in furs. Squirrels is their smallest unit of currency. Reckon a penny will buy all those grouse and a haunch of venison thrown in.'

For two silver pennies, Wayland purchased enough game to feed the falcons for three days.

Later, at the Russians' camp, Richard traded fox skins for a sack of rye flour and two dripping honeycombs. That night the wanderers squeezed hugger-mugger into a cabin and ate bread for the first time in a month. The cooked dough was of the crudest manufacture – charred and gritty bannocks consumed in a smoke-filled hut chinked up with moss – yet all sank their heads in reverential silence when Father Hilbert said grace.

Civilised Rus began at Staraja Ladoga, a fortified town a few miles up the Volkhov river. Here they stopped briefly to take on supplies. South of the town the forest thinned into sandy heath dotted with steely ponds and clumps of pines and birches. Then the voyagers came to farmland, rowing past sturdy log cabins set in meadows where geese hissed and flapped and cockerels crowed. Between the farms were fine stands of oak and maple that rang with the sound of axes. Farmers straightened up from their toil to watch the longship pass. Many of them crossed themselves, perhaps remembering their grandparents' tales of an olden time when the appearance of a dragon ship would have put the populace to flight. Their children had no such misgivings and chased the longship along the banks waving sticks. 'Varangians! Varangians!'

Four days after leaving the lake they reached Novgorod. North of the city the river branched around a large island with a tollbooth at its tip. Here an armed and mounted delegation directed them towards the shore. Their leader, a man with a face pitted by smallpox, was elegantly turned out in an ankle-length fur coat fastened with silver buttons. He addressed the stinking rabble as if they were exarchs on a mission from Byzantium.

'Welcome to Novgorod the Great,' he said in Norse. 'The hunters you met on the Svir sent news of your arrival. Allow me to introduce myself. My name is Andrei Ivanov, steward to Lord Vasili, a boyar of the city and master of its guild of merchants.' His eyes flickered about. 'Who speaks for you?'

Hands pointed at Vallon.

'The hunters said you travelled from the White Sea, but they didn't know where you began your voyage.'

Vallon looked for Wayland. 'You tell him.'

'We sailed from England this spring and journeyed here by way of Iceland and Greenland.'

Andrei guffawed. 'Listen, I've been in the shipping trade too long to be taken in by travellers' tales.'

'Believe what you like,' said Wayland. 'I'm English and so is that girl. Vallon our leader is a Frank. Those two are Normans. That lot are Icelanders. The rest are Vikings from Halogaland. If you doubt my word, ask the thin man with the tonsure. He's a monk from Germany. Until a few weeks ago, we had another German with us. He was killed by Lapps in the forest.'

Andrei traded wondering looks with his escort, then took off his hat. 'Forgive my scepticism. You're the first travellers to reach Novgorod by such a roundabout route. What goods are you carrying?'

'Walrus ivory, sea unicorn horns, eider down, sulphur, seal oil.'

'The hunters said you had gyrfalcons?'

'It's true. I trapped them myself in Greenland's northern hunting grounds.'

'Please, if you don't mind, I would like to see.'

Not without pride, Wayland uncovered the cage holding the white haggard.

Andrei crouched to inspect the falcon. When he spoke, his tone was matter of fact. 'My lord has a wealthy client who loves to follow the falcon's flight. He's a prince who pays handsomely for his pleasures. Even though this specimen looks like a feather duster, I'll give you a price far higher than you could obtain in the marketplace.'

'The falcons aren't for sale.'

Andrei frowned. 'Why bring them to Novgorod if not to sell them?'

'We're not stopping here. We're just passing through on our way to Anatolia.'

'Rum? You're going to Rum?'

'As soon as we've rested and purchased the necessities.'

Andrei laughed. 'Novgorod is as far as you'll get this year. Sell the falcons while they're still healthy.'

'I'm sorry. They're already spoken for.'

Andrei backed off. 'Do you have silver to pay for your stay in Novgorod?'

Wayland glanced at Richard. 'We can pay our way.'

Andrei bowed to Vallon. 'Then your comfort is assured. Our city has a quarter set aside for foreign merchants. You'll find Novgorod a welcoming place. It even has a Roman church.'

Vallon bowed in turn. 'Thank you. We'll need three separate establishments. The Icelanders and Vikings aren't here by my choosing.'

'Leave it to me,' said Andrei. His escorts assisted him into the saddle. 'You're only five versts from Novgorod. About three miles.' He spurred forward. 'I'll be waiting to welcome you.'

The longship rowed up the right-hand channel and soon the voyagers saw the city of Novgorod straddling both banks.

Richard whistled. 'I never expected anything half so grand.'

The metropolis was constructed entirely of wood except for a great stone citadel and a church crowned with five cupolas on the west bank. The company rowed under a covered bridge wide enough to let cart traffic pass in both directions. On the other side Andrei waved to them from a wharf on the east bank. A gang of labourers stood ready. The voyagers rowed to shore and tied up.

'Your lodgings are being prepared,' Andrei told them. 'My men will carry your cargo.' He clapped his hands and the porters jumped into the boats and began loading the cargo into handcarts.

'We don't want him to find out too much of our business,' Hero murmured to Vallon.

445

'I suspect that before we go to our beds tonight, he'll know our worth down to the last clipped penny.'

The steward led them up lanes paved with split logs and lined with stockaded houses. Most of the lots were about a hundred feet by fifty, but some were two or three times that size. Andrei stopped first at a gateway recessed in a paling fence. He opened the gate and pointed at a barn. 'This is for your Norwegians. No luxuries. Just straw to sleep on and clean well water. My men will make sure that they have enough to eat and don't disturb the peace.'

'I'll pay for your food and lodgings,' Vallon told the Vikings. 'Drink beer, but not to excess. If you get into trouble, don't look to me for help. As for whores, you'll have to make your own arrangements.'

Next they stopped at the Icelanders' lodgings. 'The house can sleep twelve if two share each bed,' Andrei said. 'The rest will have to sleep in the stables.'

Caitlin marched up to Vallon. 'I'm not sharing a bed and I'm not sleeping in a house with strange men. And I'm not bedding down in a byre. I insist on separate quarters. I'll pay from my own purse.'

Vallon shrugged at Andrei.

The steward gave an order and one of his men escorted Caitlin and her maids back down the road. 'I can see that one's used to having her own way,' Andrei said. His brows arched in enquiry. 'A lady of high birth?'

Vallon smiled. 'A princess. In her own estimation.'

Andrei watched her stride away with her maids hurrying alongside. 'Well, there are plenty of princes who'd be happy to make her their consort. I've never seen a woman so lusciously put together.'

When the Icelanders had disappeared into their compound, Drogo and Fulk stood outside looking at a loss. Vallon eyed them bleakly. 'I suppose you'd better lodge with us.'

Andrei's final stop was at a stockade enclosing a handsome house and outbuildings that included a bathhouse, stables and caretaker's cottage. Knotwork carvings decorated the gables. Calling out, Andrei ran up steps to a porch leading to a lobby. A raised door gave entry to a communal hall where a team of peasant women were whisking the plank floor under the supervision of the caretaker and his wife. All the domestics made servile bows at Andrei's entrance. He appeared not to notice them. Half a dozen sleeping benches lined the walls and a

446

domed clay stove belched smoke in a corner diagonally opposite the door. There was no chimney and the only ventilation was provided by a roof hatch and tiny slotted windows. Andrei spoke sharply to the caretaker. He in turn barked an order and one of the drudges knelt by the stove and tried to fan it into flame.

Andrei pushed open another door into a chamber furnished with a single cot, a table and a bench. An icon of the Virgin with Child hung in the right-hand corner. 'This is for you,' he told Vallon. 'It's small, but you might be grateful for the privacy.'

'To a man who's known only cold ground for bed and empty sky for a roof, it's a palace.'

'Lord Vasili reserves the property for his special guests. He requests that you do him the honour of feasting with him the day after tomorrow.' Andrei smiled. 'Bring the Icelandic princess and her attendants. A degree of formality is in order, but don't worry, I'll make sure you're presentable.'

Anyone walking through the compound next morning would have sworn that the house was untenanted. Inside, the voyagers sprawled like dead men, Drogo and Fulk curled up together on a shelf above the stove, both of them still dressed in their foul garments. Even Wayland didn't stir until after dark and he had to ask the caretaker what day it was before shuffling out to feed the falcons.

Next day the caretaker rounded up the male guests and shepherded them into the bania, while his wife took Syth off to Caitlin's lodgings. He made them strip off in the lobby, and as they shed their clothes a servant gathered them up and threw them outside to be burned.

'Hey,' Hero called. 'Those are the only garments we possess.'

The caretaker chivvied them into the steam room. They sat naked on low benches, sweat carving pale tracks down their filthy skin. When their bodies were passably clean, the caretaker handed out bundles of birch twigs and showed them how to scourge each other's backs. Then he drove them out into the courtyard where servants threw buckets of cold water over them before herding them back into the bania. After three sessions of the steam- and ice-water treatment, the company ran back into the lobby to find clean clothes waiting. Servants handed each man a plain linen shirt cut square at the collar,

447

a pair of loose-fitting trousers, and leather shoes that tied above the ankles. 'A gift from Lord Vasili,' said the caretaker.

'What does he want in return?' Hero whispered to Vallon.

Another surprise awaited them when they returned to the house. In their absence the hall had been converted to an emporium where half a dozen tailors and furriers had laid out woollen or silk caftans and pantaloons, robes and capes of marten, bear, wolf and squirrel, sable and beaver. There were jewellers, too, displaying wares of silver, enamel and cloisonné.

Vallon looked at the finery and then he looked at Hero. 'There's your answer. We can hardly refuse to buy and I'll wager Vasili takes a generous commission.'

But he blenched when the outfitters told them the prices of the garments. 'We can't afford that sort of money.'

'We can't insult Vasili by turning up in his hand-outs,' said Hero.

Richard rescued the situation. He took his treasurer's role seriously and kept himself informed on matters relating to currency and exchange. From the Vikings he'd learned that central Asia was the traditional source of their silver. In the last fifty years the Asian silver mines had become exhausted, leading to a debasement of the currency. Most of the coinage circulating in Rus had a silver content of only one part in ten.

'Our English pennies contain nine parts of silver,' Richard said. 'So the answer's simple. Offer one-eighth the tailors' asking price.'

It wasn't that easy, of course, but Richard held firm and the merchants eventually slashed their prices by more than half.

While Vallon was looking through the clothes, he saw Drogo standing awkward and aloof. 'You and Fulk had better choose something.'

'I told you I don't want your charity.'

'You've accepted enough of it already.'

'Then I won't take more.'

'Don't be so stiff-necked. Consider it payment for services rendered.'

Drogo gave a curt nod. 'What about Caitlin and the other women?'

Hero looked up. 'Let her pay for her clothes out of the money she stole from the old woman.'

Drogo's temper flared. 'Apologise for that slander.'

'It's true,' Richard said. 'I heard her make the accusation.'

'A malicious slur. Caitlin was keeping the money safe.'

'Shut up,' Vallon ordered. 'All of you. We've come through hell and you're squabbling about clothes.' He rubbed his brow. 'Wayland, get down to the women's house and tell them they can choose new clothes at my expense. Richard, you go with him to negotiate a fair price. Oh, Wayland, tell the princess to show some restraint.'

They ran down the lane to Caitlin's lodgings and found the women fresh from the bania, trying on costumes laid out by a bevy of seamstresses. One of Caitlin's maids screamed and nudged a breast back into hiding.

Wayland blushed. 'Oh, you've already started.'

Caitlin laughed. 'Don't worry. We're just playing at dressing up. Even the cheapest outfit is beyond our means.'

'Vallon said he'd pay.'

Caitlin's face lit up. 'Really?'

'With me doing the bargaining,' said Richard.

Syth put her hands around Wayland's waist. Her breasts stirred under a sleeveless linen dress. 'Do you mean it? Can I have a gown?'

'You look lovely as you are.'

She nudged him with her shoulder. 'Don't be a goose. This is what peasants wear.' She pulled his face down and spoke into his ear. 'Just for once I'd like to dress like a lady. It won't be long before I'm back in tunic and breeches.'

'We're making progress,' Richard called. 'A quarter off the prices already.'

'Go on then,' Wayland said.

One of the costumiers advanced on Syth displaying a misty blue gown with long sleeves edged with beaver.

'What do you think?' Syth asked.

'It's nice. It suits you.'

'Can't you do better than that?'

Wayland felt trapped. 'It goes with your eyes.'

The assistant moved him aside with her hip and held up another dress in a light turquoise silk. Syth draped it against herself. 'This one is tighter fitting. It will show my figure better.'

'Whatever you decide.'

'Wayland, you're not even looking.'

One of Caitlin's handmaids laughed.

'A third off and we haven't reached bottom,' Richard announced.

Syth decided on the turquoise gown. She took from the assistant a padlock-shaped pendant enamelled with a pair of lovebirds. 'This would set it off beautifully.'

'I don't know, Syth.'

'Don't you like it?'

'It's just that ... after Raul's death ... the dog ... it doesn't seem right somehow.'

Syth handed the pendant back and looked down, a tear trembling on her lashes.

Caitlin pulled Wayland aside. 'You really know how to make a maid happy, don't you? Let her be a lady for one night. Isn't she worth it?'

Wayland stared at her. He nodded and turned back to Syth. He took the pendant from the assistant. 'I'll pay for it myself.' He coughed. 'My first gift.'

Syth wiped her eyes, then leaned forward and gave him the lightest of kisses. 'Not the first.'

He was at the door when he remembered the rider to Vallon's message. Three dressers heaped with luxurious garments had homed in on Caitlin and others were waiting. 'Vallon said ... '

Caitlin gave him an imperious look. 'Yes?'

Richard swung round, fired up by haggling. 'We're down to bargain prices.'

'Don't go mad,' said Wayland, and fled to peals of laughter.

Watchmen were doing their rounds as Andrei escorted the guests in their finery to his master's city mansion. An avenue of torches lit the way to the entrance of the house, where Lord Vasili stood in welcome – a spruce dark man of about fifty with a gold incisor and a trim beard flecked with grey. His clothes bespoke understated wealth – a grey caftan of shot silk with gold brocade cuffs, over it a dark-blue robe with a belt of gold and enamel. He greeted his guests in Norse, but when Hero was presented, he switched to Greek and Arabic, lamenting his inability to turn an elegant phrase in either language. After each introduction, each solicitous enquiry, Vasili's steward directed the guest to his or her place at a banqueting table lit by a soft blaze of candles.

He seated Vallon and Hero at Vasili's right and left respectively, with the other male guests opposite and the ladies grouped at one end of the table. Two retainers circulated with drinks and appetisers and the guests found that they could choose from beer, kvas and four different brews of mead. A train of servants entered with the main meal and the diners gasped. There was a roast sucking pig, platters of game, pies and pastries, jellied pike and salmon, pots of caviar and sour cream, half a dozen kinds of bread, including wheaten loaves made with grain from the south and a special bake flavoured with honey and poppy seed.

While the guests made their selection, Vasili engaged those around him in conversation. Looking into each man's eyes by turn, he elicited their function and status while stating where their interests and experiences touched his own. He was a man of the world and therefore a friend of it. He'd built his fortune through trade with Kiev and Byzantium in the south; Germany, Poland and Sweden to the west; the Arab and Persian lands in the east. Twice he'd made the journey to Constantinople, and as a young man he'd traded with Arab caravans at Bolghar on the Volga bend.

While his guests ate, he listened to Hero's account of their own journey and plans.

'How many people will be travelling in your party?'

'If the Vikings join us, about a dozen.'

Vasili laid be-ringed fingers on Vallon's hand. 'Honoured guest, I hate to dash your intentions. Early summer, when the Dnieper is swollen with snowmelt, is the only time it's possible to travel the Road to the Greeks. At this season the rivers in the northern part are too low to navigate. Better wait until next year. Or, of course, you can sell your goods here.' He glanced at Wayland before turning his attention back to Vallon. 'I believe my steward mentioned that the falcons would find a ready sale with one of my Arab clients. He has a deep purse.'

Vallon watched Wayland chewing on a wodge of pork. Alone among the diners, he seemed immune to Vasili's charm.

'The falcons are the reason for the journey south. In a way, we're not taking them; they're leading us.'

'Hero said that the ransom demanded four falcons. You have six. Sell me two of them, including the white haggard.'

'No,' Wayland said, not even looking up.

451

Vallon glared at him before smiling at Vasili. 'We can't afford to part with any of the falcons. We lost two of them on the White Sea coast and came close to seeing them all perish in the forest. If we leave here with six, I'll count myself lucky if we reach Anatolia with four.'

Vasili withdrew his hand. 'Then I'll say no more on the subject.' He dabbed his mouth with a napkin.

Vallon sensed a straining of the mood and eased it by changing the subject. 'How do affairs stand in Rus?'

Vasili waved away a pastry offered to him by a retainer. He inclined his head towards Vallon and lowered his voice. 'Not well. It grieves me to tell you that you've arrived in my beloved motherland to find her fortunes at a low ebb. Under Grand Prince Jaroslav – God keep his soul – the federation was united from the Baltic to the Black Sea. Jaroslav was called "the Wise", but his wits must have fled him on his deathbed. Before he died he portioned out the realm among five sons. The three eldest formed a triumvirate – that most unstable of arrangements whether in love, war or affairs of state. Another poisonous element corrupted the realm. This was Prince Vseslav of Polotsk, an outsider from within, great-grandson of Vladimir the Saint. Vseslav is a sorcerer and werewolf. You smile, but I know the man and can vouch that he's an adept of the magic arts.'

Vasili sipped from his beaker. 'Five years ago the triumvirate imprisoned Vseslav in Kiev. Many people believe that his sorcery was responsible for our country's woes. The following year the nomads of the southern steppes took advantage of the rivalry among the Rus princes and attacked in force. When they defeated our army, the citizens of Kiev rioted, released Vseslav and proclaimed him their prince. He was dethroned a year later and fled back to Polotsk, where he sits weaving his spells and planning his next move. The reason I dwell on this character is that you'll have to pass through the wild country bordering his principality. A convoy as small as yours could disappear in the forests and no one would be any the wiser.'

Vasili sat up in concern. 'Honoured friend, my glum tidings are putting you off your food. Let me help you to a piroschki. Here, have some spiced mead. It's a great stimulus to the appetite.'

'It's not your warnings that blunt my appetite. Not many days ago a Viking laid my belly open. I still wear the stitches. My physician has ordered me to eat sparingly and avoid meat until I'm fully recovered.'

Vasili looked rather at a loss, as if he thought Vallon might be teasing him.

'Tell us more about the journey south,' said Vallon.

Vasili placed an amber spoon on the table. 'Novgorod.'

Picking up a silver salt, he placed it halfway across the table. 'Kiev.'

On the far side of the table he placed his gold beaker. 'Constantinople.'

Dipping a finger into his drink, he traced a line from Novgorod. 'From here you cross Lake Ilmen and travel up the Lovat. This part of the journey will cost you much effort. As I said, the river will be low and you can only navigate it in small boats. Even then, for every verst you sail or row, you'll have to tow for two versts.'

Vasili tapped the table between Novgorod and Kiev. 'Here you leave the river and make the great portage across the watershed. It takes about six days. The shortest route takes you to the Western Dvina and then to the upper reaches of the Dnieper below Smolensk. If I were you, I'd avoid that city. The merchants there are rogues.'

Vasili wetted his finger again and marked the course of the Dnieper to Kiev. 'At first the river is narrow and flows through a forest. Soon other rivers join it, swelling its course to two versts or more. From Kiev the journey is easy – seventy versts a day – until you reach here.' Vasili jabbed with his finger. 'Here the river funnels through a gorge and plunges over nine cataracts. Sometimes you will have to wade and guide your boats around the rocks by hand. Every year many ships and lives are lost. In your case, the loss is certain because you won't be able to find any pilots willing to guide you through the rapids.'

'Why not?'

Vasili stabbed a finger. 'Because even if the rapids spit you out alive, the greatest peril still lies ahead.'

'The Pechenegs,' said Hero.

Vasili smiled. 'So the reputation of the steppe nomads has travelled outside Rus. Well, I have news for you. The good news is that the Pechenegs were driven off the southern steppe about ten years ago. The bad news is that the warriors who scattered them are barbarians of the same stamp, but even fiercer and more insatiable. They are the same savages who threatened Kiev four years ago. Cumans, they call themselves. They lie in wait at the end of the gorge, but they move so unpredictably that you could encounter them anywhere beyond Kievan territory. Let me tell you something, my brother. The Cumans are so dangerous that no merchant dares travel through their territory except in the company of a fleet protected by soldiers. Merchants wouldn't spend money unless it was necessary. What chance do you think you have? None, I tell you. None at all.'

'The nomads won't be expecting us. If we run the gauntlet, will we be safe?'

Vasili shrugged. 'Yes, provided you stay on the river and camp on islands. At last you will come to the island of St Aitherios in the mouth of the river. And there, dear brother, you will find that all your efforts have been wasted.'

'How so?'

'Only small boats can negotiate the great portage; only a large ship can cross the Black Sea. At this time of the year, you won't find any merchant vessels at the mouth of the Dnieper. The estuary will be deserted.' Vasili leaned back. 'There. I've sketched your prospects. Are you still determined to risk it?'

'Hero once told me that a journey half-finished is like a story half-told. We'll go on to the end, wherever we find it.'

Vasili threw back his head and laughed. 'My friend, I hope that if you reach your goal, you find a bard worthy to immortalise your adventures.'

Vallon saw that the company had eaten themselves into a stupor, some of them yawning openly. 'Sir, forgive our lack of manners, but my companions are still weary and your splendid hospitality has overwhelmed them. If you would permit ...'

Vasili rose at once. 'Let them sleep. Yes, after food and drink, the balm of sleep.'

The company climbed to their feet and bowed while Vallon thanked their host again for his largesse.

Vasili wafted a hand. 'The pleasure is all mine. Perhaps you would favour me with a word in private.'

'Certainly. My Norse is poor. Can I bring someone who ...?'

'Of course.'

Vallon nodded at Wayland. Vasili ushered them into a chamber glazed with mica windows. He showed his guests to a bench padded with furs, spoke to his steward, then took up a seat opposite.

'Since I haven't curbed your wanderlust, I'd like to give you a favourable wind. First, I'll draft a letter of introduction that will open doors for you in Kiev. My steward will help you find suitable boats and I'll provide you with the guide I employ for my own expeditions. Oleg knows every inch of the portage and the river-men who'll take you across it. They're honest and willing toilers. If you wish, you can cross the portage humming songs and with your thumbs tucked into your belt.'

'I'm obliged. Naturally, we'll pay.'

Vasili waved away the offer. 'Oleg is my own man and I'll bear his expense. He'll make sure that the porters charge a fair price.' Vasili's cupbearer entered with an enamelled tray bearing a glass carafe and three silver beakers. 'Wine from the Greeks. I hope your physician will allow you the indulgence.'

Vallon sniffed the purple liquor appreciatively. Wayland wrinkled his nose. Vallon sipped and felt the spirit suffuse him with warmth. He sensed that Vasili had left something unsaid.

'If there's anything we can do in return . . .'

'Nothing. Trade is the lifeblood of Lord Novgorod the Great. Tell your merchant adventurers of the generous reception they can expect.' Vasili drank and then paused in afterthought. 'There is one small favour. I have some documents that I need to send to Kiev. With winter coming, I thought I'd have to wait until next year, but since you're determined to go, perhaps you wouldn't mind . . .'

'Not at all. Excuse me a moment.' Smiling, Vallon spoke to Wayland in French. 'Stop scowling.' Vallon transferred the smile to Vasili. 'He hasn't drunk wine before. I was telling him not to let it go to his head.'

Vasili's gaze dwelt briefly on Wayland before returning to Vallon. 'Honoured friend, I must make one last attempt to dissuade you from your course. I wouldn't be able to forgive myself if anything happened to you. Can't I persuade you to stay in Novgorod and put your affairs in my hands?'

'We'll leave as soon as we can find boats. As I said, the falcons aren't for sale, but if you're interested in purchasing some of our other goods . . .'

Vasili fluttered his fingers. 'I'm always willing to help a friend. If you want, I'll take the walrus ivory and sulphur off your hands. I'll

455

send my steward over tomorrow. Now, I won't keep you from your bed a moment longer.'

Rising from his chaise, Vasili escorted his two guests as far as the compound gate. 'Goodnight, dear friend. Think about what I've said.'

The gate shut behind them. They walked in drowsy silence through the empty streets. The cathedral bell rang out with chimes that sounded exotic to Vallon's ear.

'You displayed the manners of a churl,' he said.

'I don't trust him.'

Vallon stopped. 'If a man excites your suspicion, you keep your doubts hidden.' He resumed walking. 'Why don't you trust him?'

'I don't understand why he's buttering us up.'

'It's true that Novgorod lives by trade, and a sumptuous meal is a small price to pay for good will. Also, even with Richard's bargaining our new clothes didn't come cheap.'

'When we arrived at Novgorod, Vasili's steward wanted to buy the falcons. His lord expressed the same interest tonight. Earlier today I made some enquiries. In Rus a female slave sells for one nogata. That's about twenty pennies. Guess how much a gyrfalcon fetches.'

'Twice as much? Five times?'

'One gyrfalcon could buy twenty slaves. With the silver we'd earn by selling them, we could buy enough slaves to carry us piggyback to Byzantium.'

'Perhaps that says more about the cheapness of lives in Rus than the value of gyrfalcons. Anyway, it proves nothing. Vasili made it clear that he would give us a good price for the falcons.'

'I was watching him. I could see him calculating. He realised that we wouldn't sell them no matter how much he offered, but he's still determined to have them.'

'Meaning?'

'Ask yourself why Vasili should provide us with his own guide.'

'As a favour for us carrying his letters.'

'He tells us we'll never survive the journey and then entrusts letters to us. It doesn't make sense.'

'Perhaps they're not particularly important. Look, you're forgetting that he did everything to dissuade us from making the journey.'

'He knows we're committed. What made my ears prick up was when he said that beyond Novgorod territory we'd find ourselves in no-man's land where our disappearance wouldn't be noticed. And that story about the sorcerer prince ...'

'You're doing an excellent job of spoiling my evening.'

'I'm sorry. It's just that ... I don't know ... Something's not right.'

They'd reached the gate of their lodgings. Vallon jangled the bell and turned to Wayland. 'If you've got an itch, I'd be foolish to ignore it.' He couldn't keep from yawning. 'But right now, all I can think of is bed.'

The Road to the Greeks

XXXVIII

Vallon was finishing breakfast alone in his chamber when Hero poked his head around the door. 'There's a queue of people waiting to see you.'

'Who?'

'Just about everyone. Caitlin, Drogo, Garrick. Most of the Vikings.'

'I'll see Garrick first. Has Richard tallied up his wages?'

Hero placed two purses on the table. 'This one's Raul's. That one's for old Garrick.'

Vallon stood and weighed the bags, one of them the reckoning of a man's life. 'Poor Raul.' He put the purses down and rested his hands on them. 'Suppose I told you that I've decided to end our journey. Here. In Novgorod.'

'Give up now? What about the lost gospel?'

'More than a year has passed since Walter was taken captive. He might be dead by now. He could have negotiated his release. The Seljuks are nomads. The Emir might have moved Walter to Persia.'

'You could have used the same arguments six months ago.'

'The Emir insisted that the falcons be delivered by autumn. It's now October and the longest part of the journey still lies ahead. We probably won't reach the Emir's court until next year, travelling through the depths of winter.'

'Sir—'

'In the space of a week, I nearly died and we lost Raul and the dog. If we hadn't run into the hunters, we'd all have perished.' Vallon looked up. 'We're bound to fortune's wheel and I feel it turning.'

Hero's mouth worked. 'A year's toil and effort – and all for nothing?'

'I don't count our lives as nothing.'

Hero braced himself. 'What about the vow you swore in the chapel.' He looked at the floor. 'I heard you swear to complete the journey however long or dangerous.'

Vallon waved tiredly. 'I'm not interested in saving my soul if it means risking my company's lives.'

Hero was silent for a few moments. 'What will you do?'

'Stay here until spring and then resume my journey to Constantinople.'

'Where does that leave the rest of us?'

'With the money from our cargo, each of you would have enough to start afresh.'

'Start where? Wayland and Richard can't go back to England. I'm the only one with a place to call home.'

Vallon sat down. 'So you're determined to go on.'

'Yes, and Richard and Wayland share my resolve. But only if you lead us.'

Vallon smiled sadly. 'You've grown to manhood, Hero. Me, I've just grown old.'

'Nonsense. You're still weak from your wound. A week's rest will restore you to good health and spirits.'

'We don't have a week. If we're to continue, we must leave as soon as possible.'

'Whenever you say.'

'You're sure?'

'Certain.'

Vallon regarded him a moment longer, then sprang up. 'All right. Mustn't keep Garrick waiting.'

When the Englishman entered, Vallon clasped him by both hands. 'So we've reached the parting of the ways. I'll miss you, Garrick. You've been a staunch companion.'

'I'll miss you, sir, and all my other friends. If it wasn't for my promise to Raul, I don't think I could have borne the pain of parting.'

'If you hadn't made the decision, I'd have made it for you.' Vallon took one of the purses. 'That's for Raul's family.' He held out the other purse. 'And that's for you.'

Garrick stared at it. 'I can't accept all that. Even half would be too much.'

'I'll be the judge of your worth. Use it to buy that smallholding you were telling me about. It will give me pleasure to think of you working your own soil. So, not another word. Have you arranged a passage?'

'I'll travel with the Icelanders. There's a ship sailing for Sweden in a week.'

'We'll have left by then. Keep the money safe and secret.' Vallon led Garrick to the door. 'We'll say farewell properly when the time comes. Ask the lady Caitlin to come in.'

Vallon wasn't sure what stance to assume. Caitlin also seemed uncharacteristically awkward, entering with eyes downcast. 'Can I speak to you alone?'

At Vallon's nod, Hero left them and closed the door. Vallon cleared his throat. 'I understand you've booked a passage west.'

'I'm not going to Norway.'

Vallon frowned. 'But your marriage—'

'Will not take place. I left Iceland a lady of noble station.' Caitlin brushed at her hair as if she measured her reduction in status by the length of her tresses. 'I won't go to Norway as a refugee. Anyway, I was never enthusiastic about the match.'

'So you'll return to Iceland.'

'Not this year. Not with winter so close. Perhaps never. I couldn't bear the humiliation. I know how people will taunt me behind my back – left home to marry an earl because no one on Iceland was good enough for her. Now she's back and unless she takes one of her spurned suitors, she'll die an old maid.'

'Then what will you do?'

'I've decided to make a pilgrimage to Constantinople. I'll have a mass sung for Helgi's soul.'

'How will you travel?'

Caitlin didn't answer.

'You wish to come with us?'

'With you, yes.' She looked up. 'With you.'

Vallon felt a tingle of panic. 'Does Drogo know?'

'About me travelling to Constantinople or about my feelings for you?'

Vallon knuckled his brow. 'You're confiding more than I can take in. When did these feelings replace your urge to kill me?'

'I realised that the prophecy had come true the night I nursed you. When I held you in my arms and you spoke my name.'

'I spoke your name?' Vallon realised that he'd raised his voice. He glanced at the door.

'With tenderness. You called me your princess.' Her face coloured. 'Other things, too.'

'I was feverish. God knows what nonsense I spouted. I'm sorry if I said anything embarrassing.' Vallon's face went blank. 'What prophecy?'

'When I was a girl, a woman with second sight told me that a dark stranger from the outlands would steal my heart and carry me over the sea. The prophecy is one of the reasons why I never married an Icelander. I knew you were the one the moment I set eyes on you.'

'The day we met, you looked at me like I was something you'd trod in.'

'I had to keep my feelings hidden from Helgi. He knew about the prophecy and quizzed me about my thoughts concerning you. I had to pretend that I hated you.'

'You weren't pretending at the lake when you ordered Helgi to fight me.'

'What else could I do? You were spying on me while I bathed. He would have challenged you whatever I'd said. If I hadn't encouraged him, he would have suspected the true state of my emotions.'

There was a lot to pick over, including the nature of Caitlin's relationship with her brother. Now wasn't the time. Vallon shook himself. 'Drogo is infatuated with you. Drogo hates me. If he discovered that you ... that your affections ...'

'You must send him away. He still means to spill your blood. A boil that must be lanced is how he put it.'

'Let me get this clear. You don't reciprocate his sentiments.'

Caitlin tossed her chin. 'He wearies me. I can't care for a man who trails after me like a dog.'

Vallon wandered across the room. 'What about Tostig and Olaf?'

'They'll come with me to Constantinople. With Helgi dead, they plan to take service with the Emperor.'

'Anyone else?'

'Only my maids.'

'Only your maids,' Vallon repeated. He took a deep breath. 'You can take one of them – the young one. What's her name?'

'Asa.'

'We're not carrying passengers. You'll have to pull your weight.'

'I'm not afraid of hard work. You wait. You'll see that I'm as strong as you.'

Vallon's mouth twisted. 'A kitten could claim as much.'

Caitlin's eyes softened. 'How is your wound?'

'It's healed.'

'Let me see.'

'There's no need. Just take my word.'

Caitlin moved towards him with mesmerising slowness. 'I saw it when you were sick. I changed the dressing. I saw death sitting on your shoulder and frightened it away with my prayers.'

'I'm grateful. As you can see, your prayers have been answered.'

'Then show me.'

Vallon cast a desperate glance at the door. He yanked up his tunic and stood staring ahead as if on parade. 'There.'

She sank to her knees. 'You're so thin.'

He glanced down at the livid stripe, the bruise fading to yellow and green. To his astonishment he saw Caitlin move her face forward and plant a kiss on the ugly welt.

He yanked her upright. 'Madam!'

She hung in his arms, all womanly softness, her lips slightly parted. Looking into her green eyes was like staring into the ocean.

She smiled. 'Did you really find your way to the lake by chance?'

His voice came out husky. 'Complete chance.'

'You see. Guided by destiny.' Her eyes clouded. 'You're the first man who's ever seen me naked. Did the sight give you pleasure?'

'It was no hardship to my eyes.'

Her eyes closed with dreamy intent and her mouth floated towards his own. He didn't move. He couldn't move. Their lips met. He was kissing her. Not only that. He was caressing her, pressing against her. She moaned when she felt him. He broke away and stared blindly at the icon above his bed.

'A moment's weakness. It won't happen again.'

'It will. You can't stop it.'

'I won't let it!' He bunched his fists and glared at the icon. 'Do you hear?'

No answer came. He swung round in time to see the door latch shut. There was a long pause and then a peremptory rap. He turned back to the icon. He felt dizzy. 'Enter.' Footsteps halted behind him. 'Drogo.'

'Vallon. Caitlin looks flushed and agitated. What have you done to upset her?'

Vallon dug his nails into his palms. 'You're not here to talk about Caitlin. What do you want? No, don't tell me. You've grown so devoted to me that you can't bear to tear yourself away.'

'Caitlin still requires my protection.'

'She has Olaf and Tostig to look after her.'

'You forget my oath to her brother.'

Vallon turned with an unpleasant grin. 'Well, the thing is, I don't want you with us.'

'You were glad enough to have me and Fulk by your side the night we fought the Vikings.'

'Your sword's double-edged. It's time you returned to England.'

'I don't have the money.'

'I'll pay for your passage.'

'I can't accept.'

'Swim then.'

'Listen, Vallon, all I ask is that you let me accompany Caitlin to Constantinople. I have no intention of following you into Anatolia. What happens between you and Walter is no longer of any interest to me.'

'You're a liar. Request refused.'

'Then honour leaves me no choice but to challenge you.'

'Challenge refused. Ask the Vikings to step in when you leave.'

'Vallon, I can't leave Caitlin. It's not only my oath to Helgi that binds me. I mean to make her my wife.'

This was getting gruesome. 'I'm not a marriage broker.'

Drogo stepped up close. 'You need me and Fulk. With Raul dead, Wayland's the only fighting man you have left. What happens if you run into trouble?'

'I'd rather run into trouble than take it with me.'

'You're taking the Vikings. They'll outnumber you three to one. Suppose they turn against you?'

Vallon felt as if the strands of a web were being woven around him. 'Let me get this straight. You won't offer any violence to my company if we take you down the Dnieper.'

'Correct.'

'And when we reach the Black Sea, we'll travel our separate ways. You to Constantinople, me to Anatolia.'

'Yes.'

Vallon balanced the risks. 'Very well. I'll tolerate your presence on those terms.'

Drogo had something like a spring in his step as he marched to the door. Vallon checked him. 'I aim to be gone in four days. Find us three sound horses.'

Vallon eyed the space he'd left. Poor deluded Drogo, always on the wrong side of fortune. Deprived of his mother in infancy, starved of his stepmother's love, usurped in her affections by her natural son. The same son who Vallon, a complete stranger, had crossed half the world to save, humiliating Drogo in the process. No wonder the Norman longed to kill him. And how much more would he desire his slaughter if he discovered that the woman on whom he'd squandered his passions had been pressing herself against his enemy's cock moments before he made his entreaty.

The situation was so bizarre that Vallon had a crazed urge to laugh. He had to pull down his mouth to stop hooting with mirth. He was still standing in this attitude when Hero announced the Norsemen's entrance. Seven of them swaggered or shuffled in, some with their shoulders back, some cap in hand.

'Say what you have to say.'

Their spokesman was Wulfstan, a bruiser with moustaches like wings. 'Not much to say. Our ship's unseaworthy and we have no silver to pay for a passage home. The only road open to us is the Varangian Way.'

Vallon nodded. 'I'll provide your keep, but I'm not paying you. If things had gone differently, you'd be weighing my companions' lives in silver at the slave mart.'

Hero murmured in Vallon's ear. 'I'd rather you didn't take Arne. He has a wife and children. Only desperate poverty prevents him from returning home.'

'You told me that he took care of you and Garrick.'

'We owe our lives to him.'

Vallon turned back to the Vikings. 'I'm not sailing to Constantinople with a gang of heathens. You'll join me as Christians or not at all.'

Hero winced. 'Sir, they're not going to embrace the true faith overnight.'

'Just pack them off to Father Hilbert for baptism. Give the hypocrite seven converts to brag about when he gets home.'

They wheeled round and were filing through the door when Vallon spoke again. 'Arne, I'm not taking you. It would be a waste of time. You're too old to find a place in the Emperor's guard.'

Arne stopped dead while his companions trooped past him. With a horror-stricken glance, he made to follow, but Hero closed the door before he reached it. Arne payed the rim of his hat through his fingers. He glanced up, his eyes sparkling. 'It doesn't matter if I can't enlist with the guard. In Constantinople, I can find work of some kind.'

'I have a task for you closer to hand. Garrick is taking money to Raul's family. He's travelling alone. I'd feel happier if he had a companion. Keep an eye on him and you'll return home with something to show for your wanderings.'

Arne's mouth opened and shut.

'No need to thank me. Consider it a reward for the kindness you showed Hero and Garrick.'

When Hero shepherded Arne out, Vallon saw that the hall was empty. 'Is that the lot?'

'Yes, sir. Andrei's expecting us at the river.'

Vallon eyed the icon. 'In your opinion, Hero, would you say that Caitlin's mad?'

'I couldn't say, sir. Even though I have five sisters, I've never been able to fathom a woman's mind.'

'I want you to arrange a meeting between us. Nobody but we three must know about it. Understand?'

Hero hesitated. 'Not really, sir.'

They reached the riverside to find Andrei waiting with the guide. Oleg Ievlevich was a small, serious-looking man with slanting hazel eyes above high cheekbones. Nothing in his demeanour lent weight to Wayland's suspicions. With Andrei acting as middleman, they purchased three riverboats and a skiff. Each boat twenty-four feet long, clinker-built of larch strakes little more than half an inch thick. Although light enough to be towed or dragged, it took six men to lift them and a dozen would have been needed to carry them any distance. Each boat was fitted with eight oarlocks and was masted for a small sail. Behind the mast was a simple stall consisting of two posts and a sling to hold a horse. The skiff was for Wayland to go hunting in.

All the equipping and provisioning, plus the personal disbursements and other expenses, lightened their exchequer considerably. Selling the two ships' boats and some of their trade goods offset part of the cost, but by the time the expedition was ready, only thirty pounds of silver remained.

On the morning of their departure, Vallon and company left their lodgings before first light. It had rained heavily the day before and then frozen overnight. Vallon's face tingled in the cold and his feet made stars on the icy puddles as he walked to the riverbank. Caitlin's party and the Vikings had already gathered, their breath clouding in the still air. As they were loading, Garrick and Arne came down to see them off. A curtain of lilac-coloured sky was rising above the city walls when Andrei arrived with Oleg.

Fifteen men and three women would be making the voyage, travelling six to a boat. Oleg joined Vallon's company. The six Vikings took the second boat, while the third carried Drogo and Fulk, Caitlin and her maid Asa, and Tostig and Olaf. Vallon's boat would tow the skiff. Into it Wayland put the caged falcons, plus twenty live pigeons from Vasili's own dovecotes.

The sun was lifting clear of the city when the voyagers clasped their well-wishers and pushed off. Looking back from the first bend, they saw Garrick and Arne still standing on the jetty with their arms raised.

Hero pulled on his oar. 'I bet they wish they were going with us.'

Vallon's smile was noncommittal. Winter coming and more than a thousand miles of river and portage ahead of them before they reached the Black Sea.

Three or four miles upriver they rowed into Lake Ilmen and made twenty easy miles before entering the Lovat, the river flowing south from the great portage. As Vasili had warned them, it ran shallow with many hurrying shoals that forced them to disembark and tow the boats.

The weather was sublime. Nights of acrid frost that left the water margins skimmed with ice gave way to days of brilliant sunshine. Two days upriver Oleg halted the convoy at a farmstead in a forest of birch and pine. They'd passed many similar steadings. A log hut wreathed in blue smoke. A boat drawn up on the grassy shore, beside it a rack for drying fish. Two small haystacks raised on poles. A cow eating from a crib.

Oleg jumped to the bank and gave a loud hail. '*Dorogoy*, Ivanko!'

Out of the cabin stepped a man with rufous hair and beard. He flung up a hand in greeting. '*Dorogoy*, Oleg!'

Ivanko clumped down to the bank, his trousers flapping around his legs. An oddly proportioned fellow. Above the waist he was a big man, below it a small one, with stunted bandy legs shod in leather boots so large that it seemed that if he turned round, the boots would stay fixed to the spot. Behind him strode two hearty sons with the same peculiar physique. It was as if their waists had slipped to where their knees should have been.

'*Dorogoy*, Oleg,' they called. Each of them carried a hatchet tucked into his belt and wore crude bast shoes fashioned from birch bark. Perhaps Ivanko's seven-league boots were a badge of office, possibly inherited.

Vallon watched the guide and porters bantering together. There was nothing veiled in their manner. He glanced at Wayland and gave a little shrug.

Ivanko invited them into his house. A stove filled the interior with smoke. Hero coughed and rubbed his eyes. 'They've got it the wrong way round. The cold comes in through the chimney and the warmth goes out of the door.'

After a meal of porridge and kvas, Ivanko and his sons loaded equipment into a sturdy dugout canoe that they could convert into a sledge or cart by adding runners or wheels. They harnessed two horses and then, after a brief prayer, set off. They picked up more porters from farms along the way, and by the time they called a halt that evening there were twelve in their company, plus four more horses and two canoes. All the porters seemed delighted to be laying aside their everyday labours for the privilege of hauling three heavily laden boats through ninety miles of forest.

Next day they left the Lovat and began the portage. It wasn't as arduous as Vallon had feared. Oleg took advantage of every little stream and lake, and there was no shortage of either. Between watercourses, Ivanko's team fitted the boats' hulls with runners and dragged them with the horses, the men lending their weight and singing work songs. The route was well trodden, with timber causeways laid across some of the bogs. At night the caravan camped beside stone rings blackened by the fires of previous travellers. Twice on the portage they came across weathered wooden idols, the phallic pillars bearing a moustached face looking out to each quarter. When pressed, Oleg said that this was Perun, the thunder god. He affected not to notice the idols and seemed embarrassed when the porters bowed to them before crossing themselves. Vallon couldn't have cared less about their idolatry. They were cheerful and willing workers, adept at everything they turned their hands to, using their axes as knife, plane, saw or hammer as the task demanded.

Ever upwards they climbed, the slope never steeper than a gentle incline, until at last they emerged from the forest into a tract of turf swamps. Vallon had the sense of standing at the centre of the world. Whichever way he looked, he was surrounded by a gently rumpled continent of golden-brown forest that faded ridge by ridge until the last ridge was indistinguishable from the sky. Oleg pointed south. 'Dnieper,' he said. He swung his hand towards the north-east. 'Volga.' Then he nodded very seriously as if confirming a truth. That the arteries of Rus issued from this heartland.

'Hear that?' Vallon called. 'We've reached the watershed.'

'What a relief to be on the right side of gravity,' Richard said.

Hero laughed at Vallon's puzzlement. 'He means that from now on our journey leads downhill. All the way to the Black Sea.'

Around noon next day they floated off downstream into a forest untouched by man since the day of creation. Wayland lay back with Syth's head on his arm, watching the trees sliding across the sky. They were the old familiar trees of the wildwood grown to fantastic proportions. Many of the oaks and pines steepled up for eighty feet before branching, and some of the spruces must have stood a hundred and fifty feet tall. It was a place of rot and renewal, with live trees sprouting out of dead ones, trees of two different kinds fused in spiral clinches, mouldering giants melting back into the soil. This far south the leaves were still turning and the travellers drifted under a steady pattering of yellow, red and brown that covered the stream in mosaics.

A couple of short portages brought them to a broad, slow-moving river. 'Dvina,' said Oleg. 'Three days and we'll be at the Dnieper.'

Vallon had a quiet word with Wayland while the porters readied the boats. 'You're wrong about Vasili. I've been watching Oleg like a hawk and he's as honest as they come.'

471

'Too honest. Most guides leading travellers through foreign parts would take them for every penny.'

Vallon shook his head in exasperation. 'What was that phrase Raul used to use? "Your mind's as twisted as a pig's guts." You don't believe that the porters are part of Vasili's plot.'

'No. Which is why I think he'll strike after we've paid them off at the Dnieper. Sir, we have to reach the river at a different spot from the one Oleg chooses.'

'It's not my place to tell our guide which route to take.'

At that moment Oleg turned to say it was time to board.

Most of the company dozed at their oars as they floated down through the forest. Their rest was brief. Only a few miles downstream, Oleg ordered them to row towards a tributary emerging from the left shore.

'Where does that take us?' Vallon asked.

'Smolensk,' said Oleg. 'Two days.'

'Lord Vasili advised us to avoid Smolensk.'

'Yes, yes. We will reach the Dnieper below Smolensk. Tomorrow I will go ahead to hire more porters.'

That was the first fishy thing Oleg had said. Vallon kept his tone relaxed. 'I'd rather you stayed with us.'

'Ivanko knows the way as well as I do. Don't worry. Tomorrow, we'll eat supper together as usual.'

'It seems a pity to leave this fine river so soon.'

When Oleg smiled, his eyes almost disappeared above his cheekbones. 'Honoured sir, you can go down the Dvina all the way to the Baltic, but this is as close as it comes to the Dnieper.'

His manner was guileless. His behaviour had been exemplary. Wayland's instinct wasn't infallible. Two days and they would be at the Dnieper.

Oleg had turned away to oversee a rearrangement of the cargo. The porters were sharing a good-natured joke. Vallon could sense Wayland looking at him.

'Leave the goods where they are.'

Oleg looked up. 'Excuse me?'

'We're taking a different route.'

Oleg's face wrinkled in bafflement. 'But this is the route.'

'I don't like the look of it.'

Oleg assumed the manner of a man used to dealing with difficult clients. 'I know all the portages and this is the easiest, I promise.'

'It might be the easiest, but it isn't the one I want to take.'

Oleg hid his annoyance. 'There is another way, but it means rowing upriver and brings you out above Smolensk. You said you didn't want to travel through Smolensk.'

'I don't. I want you to reach the Dnieper from somewhere downriver.'

Oleg stepped from foot to foot and pointed at the tributary. 'But this is the path. There is no other.'

'Find one.'

Oleg tugged off his cap and wrung it in his hands. 'I don't understand why you're making this trouble.'

The porters and the rest of the voyagers looked on with incomprehension. 'Have you lost your mind?' Drogo demanded.

'Stay out of it,' Vallon said. He'd acted like a boor in the hope of dislodging Oleg's mask. He hadn't succeeded. The guide had behaved as any decent man would when confronted by a fool and an oaf. Well, it was too late to change direction.

'If you won't take us by another route, we'll find our own.'

Oleg shut his eyes. He muttered to himself and then he threw up his hands. 'Yes!' he shouted. 'Find your own way!' He called out in Russian and stormed over to the porters, cuffing them across their backs. Clueless as to what had provoked the turnaround, they began packing up their things.

'Leave the men,' Vallon ordered.

Oleg turned on him. 'They no longer work for you. There's no point in them dragging your boats on a path that doesn't exist.'

'I'm the one who's paying their wages.'

Oleg spat. 'Keep your silver. Vasili will pay them from his own purse.'

'Double wages for every man who stays,' Vallon called.

Only Ivanko met his eye, shaking his shaggy head at how badly things had turned out. His team couldn't get away fast enough. They paddled away upriver, Oleg punching the side of the canoe.

'What in hell was that about?' Drogo demanded.

'Wayland thinks that Oleg was planning to lead us into an ambush.'

'Oleg?'

473

'Acting on Lord Vasili's orders. He wants the falcons.'

'For heaven's sake, Vasili doesn't have to rob us to obtain falcons.'

'Yes, he does. We refused to sell them.'

'They're coming back,' Wayland said.

Vallon watched the canoes return. Oleg stepped ashore, his face crumpled. 'I can't leave you lost in the forest. Lord Vasili will hold me responsible if you come to harm.' He choked back a sob. 'Keep the porters and pay them for the unnecessary toil.' He thumped his chest. 'But I will not be coming with you. What use is a guide if his clients won't be guided?' Tears ran down his cheeks. 'Thank you very much. Lord Vasili entertains you like princes and you spit in his face. Thank you very much.'

He lurched away with Ivanko trying to soothe him. His anguish was so genuine that Vallon came close to running after him and begging his forgiveness.

'Marvellous,' Drogo snorted. 'Now we have the worst of all worlds. If Oleg did plan to betray us, he'll get to Smolensk long before we reach the Dnieper.'

Drogo was right. The only way to make sure was to murder the guide. The idea was so repugnant that Vallon put it out of mind immediately. The falconer had got it wrong, and that was that.

Not a word passed the porters' lips as they travelled down the Dvina. After about ten miles they rowed into another tributary. Vallon looked at the stream winding out of the forest. For all he knew, it would bring them to the same place Oleg had been making for. Well, the choice was made. He nodded at Ivanko. Mute as beasts, the porters led the passage through the forest.

It was a hellish struggle. Every few yards they found the stream blocked by beaver dams and fallen trees, forcing them to haul the boats onto the banks and manhandle them around the obstacles. The problem was that the banks themselves were choked with dead trees. In some spots, a tree in falling had dragged others down with it, four or five at a time, sometimes flattening them, in places leaving them suspended in a drunken huddle. At each hurdle, they had to unhitch the horses, empty the boats and then lift and slide them across the tree trunk. Only to repeat the process a few yards further on.

They were at this toil until darkness and Vallon guessed that they hadn't covered more than two miles. That night the porters ate around their own fire and refused the mead that Vallon sent them.

In the cold light of dawn they doddered to their feet and stood wincing and rolling the stiffness out of their joints. They plugged on. Unhitch, lift, push. Hitch, drag, unhitch, lift ... At this rate, Vallon calculated, it would take them a fortnight to reach the Dnieper.

Around noon the light turned ashen and the air grew frowzy. The whole forest seemed to take an enormous sighing breath and billows of leaves streamed from the trees. The porters were terrified of the oncoming storm and dragged their canoes onto land, entreating God's mercy and Perun's protection. Darkness veiled the sky. The storm when it broke burst overhead with a long sizzle of lightning that seemed to light up the inside of Vallon's skull. Thunder boomed and a mighty wind tore through the forest. Trees a hundred feet tall writhed as if they were saplings. From all around came the tearing groans of falling timber. A lightning bolt blasted a nearby pine, splitting it from crown to roots, hurling ten-foot splinters more than a hundred feet. Rain slashed down. Pagans and Christians alike crouched with their hands over their heads. Like apes.

The storm passed. The sun broke through. The voyagers took their hands off their heads and grinned weakly at each other. Every tree had been stripped of its leaves, each twig tipped with liquid crystal. Nobody had been injured. In fact the storm cleared the festering atmosphere and that night travellers and porters again ate around a communal fire. Vallon questioned Ivanko about the route and persuaded him to deviate from it so that they would strike the Dnieper at a spot never used on a regular portage. They clinched the arrangement with a handshake, silver transferring from palm to palm.

At sunrise the company found their way decked with cobwebs slung like silken canopies between the trees. The porters left their canoes behind and struck out overland, carrying the upturned boats on their shoulders. Their legs were caving in beneath them when they straggled at last out of the forest. Below them a wild meadow slanted down to a wide river curving away in a shining semi-circle. On the opposite shore unbroken forest sloped up from limestone bluffs.

Ivanko pointed like a prophet. 'Dnieper!'

Hero and Richard capered and even Vallon grinned and back-slapped his companions. But it was too soon to be certain that they were in the clear. Bends upriver and down restricted his view to no more than a couple of miles.

He pointed upstream. 'How far is Smolensk? How long would it take a boat to reach us?'

Ivanko pondered. 'One long day, maybe two.'

'And from the spot where Oleg wanted you to take us?'

'Half a day.'

Uncomfortably close. Vallon studied the terrain. A warm breeze blowing from the river tousled the grass. A brown bear and her two cubs browsed near the river. When Wayland clapped, she rose on her hind legs, peering myopically in their direction, then dropped to all fours and lumbered away like a giant furry inchworm with the cubs gambolling in her wake. On the other side of the river, a herd of deer popped into focus. They watched the intruders as though paralysed, then melted away into the trees.

'Nobody's been near this place in days,' Wayland said.

Vallon glanced behind him. 'It will take time to prepare the boats. Stay here and watch our backs until you hear the signal.'

'No one's following us.'

'And no one's waiting for us. You're the one who started this, so let's not relax our guard. You know the signals. One long blast of the horn means we're leaving. Three short blasts and we've run into trouble.'

XXXIX

A more tranquil spot would have been hard to imagine. Here in its upper reaches the Dnieper was less than two hundred yards wide, sliding down a long pool before spilling away in a series of sweet-sounding rills. Shoals of minnows darted in the shallows. Blue and yellow dragonflies hawked over the surface. At the tail of the pool was a ford, its banks churned up by cattle of extraordinary size. They'd crossed recently and if their spoor could be used as a yardstick, their herdsmen must have stood ten feet tall. Vallon could place his entire foot in one half of the cloven prints.

The porters slid the boats into the water, then Ivanko approached and said that their job was done. Richard handed out their wages, the men craning over each other's shoulders to keep a reckoning.

The voyagers lay in the grass enjoying the warmth. Some dozed with their palms shielding their eyes.

Vallon clapped his hands. 'Let's get the boats loaded.'

Hero opened his eyes. 'Can't we eat first?'

'No. I want to get away as soon as possible.'

Wulfstan walked up from the bank. 'Our boat's sprung a plank. It must have taken a knock in the forest. It'll need recaulking.'

'Damn,' said Vallon. The porters were kindling a cooking fire. If they'd had any hint of treachery, they would have cleared off as soon as they'd been paid. 'Repair the boat as quickly as you can. The rest of you may as well grab a bite. You two,' he called, addressing Tostig and Olaf. 'Take the skiff and keep watch on the other side of the river. Don't look so long-faced. We'll save some food for you.'

Hero joined Vallon with an ear-to-ear grin. 'At last we can dream of reaching journey's end.'

'There's a long way to go yet.'

Richard drifted up yawning. 'When I get on the river, I'm going to sleep for days. Wake me when we reach Kiev.'

The Vikings lit a fire to melt pitch. Over it the travellers hung a pot of broth. Vallon remained edgy, infected by Wayland's suspicions. Oleg must have reached the Dnieper two days ago. By now an ambush could have been set downstream.

The travellers were still eating when Wulfstan reported that his men had repaired the boat. 'Time we were going,' Vallon called. 'That bread will taste just as good on the river. Where's the man with the horn? Ah, there you are. Call Wayland and Syth.'

They knelt behind a windfall lime, watching the aurochs grazing in the clearing. Sixty or seventy yards away stood a solitary black bull with pale finching down its back. It stood taller than a man, longer than a wagon, its head armed with lyre-shaped horns. Behind it, at the far edge of the clearing, five young bulls grazed. A herd of reddish-brown

477

cows and calves came and went in the sun-dappled wood beyond. The beasts looked like they'd stepped out from a more ancient world, and what made the scene even more magical was the flush of brimstone butterflies swarming in the clearing. Hundreds of them fluttered around the old bull, attracted by the warmth radiating from its coat. The battle-scarred patriarch looked as if it were spotted with flowers.

'Don't you dare shoot him,' Syth whispered.

Wayland smiled and shook his head.

As the bull grazed, its pizzle slowly extended from its sheath.

'Golly,' said Syth.

Wayland coughed quietly into his fist.

'Wayland.'

'Ssh, you'll frighten them.'

Syth slid a glance at the aurochs, then compressed her lips and blew into Wayland's ear.

His jaw worked.

'Way-Land.'

'What?'

She lay back with a sigh, eyes closed, arms spread.

He looked down at her, then grinned and sprawled beside her. His hands reached under her tunic.

'Wayland, they're not puppies.'

'I love the feel of them.'

She draped a hand around his neck. 'I wish we'd had the chance to be together in Novgorod, when we had fine clothes and proper beds.'

Wayland nuzzled her ear. 'Adam and Eve didn't have clothes or a bed.'

'I bet Eve wished she had.'

'What? She fretted about not having fancy clothes to take off for Adam?'

'It's all right for you. You like living in the forest. Sharing a love nest with creepy-crawlies isn't my idea of bliss.'

Wayland leaned over her. 'You'll wear fine clothes, I promise. We'll live in a grand house. You'll see.'

She smiled, her skin luminous under its film of grime and her eyes reflecting the sky.

'Raul said you were a nixie. He said you could turn yourself into water.'

She reached for his belt. 'I can do more than that. I can turn *you* to water.'

When the horn blew, they were so absorbed in themselves and each other that they didn't hear it. Yet Wayland must have registered some vibration because he wrenched his lips from hers and braced up on his arms.

Syth opened dazed eyes. Her chest was flushed scarlet. 'Don't stop.' She wrapped her legs tighter. 'Don't. Stop.'

Vallon paced the bank, darting impatient glances up the meadow. A drawn-out cry floated across the river and the two Icelanders came sprinting down to the skiff. Vallon put his head in his hands and groaned. He looked up. 'Everybody into the boats. Look to your weapons.'

As Tostig and Olaf jumped into the skiff and pushed off, the disjointed shapes of horsemen appeared through the trees behind them. Down they ambled, attired as if they were out on a rustic jaunt. Their leader waved in greeting, not at all surprised to find a body of armed men in his path. He put his horse to the water.

'The porters are running away,' Richard called.

Ivanko and his men were hurrying up the meadow, casting frightened glances over their shoulders.

Drogo watched the horsemen file onto the bank. 'We can be away before they cross.'

'Not without Wayland and Syth. God knows what's keeping them. Blow the warning.'

He cursed their absence and he cursed the awful timing. The strangers were feeling their way across the ford, the water up to their horses' bellies. All were armed, most of them carrying bows. An ill-sorted pack of dogs paddled behind the horses.

'Perhaps it's only a hunting party,' Richard said.

Vallon kicked the ground. 'Who just happen to be crossing the river at the precise spot where we're embarking.'

By the time the Icelanders landed, the Russian column had reached mid-river. At its head rode a ruddy and compact man with a skull shaved bare except for a sidelock. He wore a sleeveless bearskin jacket over a linen smock and his feet were shod in green kidskin. He leaned back as his mount surged up the bank, then slackened reins and sat with his wrists crossed on his horse's neck, grinning down into the stony faces of the men and bowing lavishly to the ladies. From one ear hung a large pearl set between drops of filigreed silver. 'Greetings, brothers and sisters. What have we here? A convoy of merchants. I can't believe it. Why are you making the passage so late?'

'You speak Norse.'

'But of course. I often visit the Varangian trading station at Gnezdovo near Smolensk. I'm surprised you didn't travel that way. It's a lot easier than the route you've chosen. Did you get lost? Don't you have a guide?' He pressed one hand to his heart. 'My name is Gleb Malinin.'

'What are you doing here?'

'Hunting *tur*. How do you call them? The big aurochs.' He pointed at the spoor. 'They must have crossed the river last night. I've always wanted a drinking cup fashioned from an aurochs' horn.'

'We've been here a while and haven't seen any aurochs. You'll have to ride hard if you want to catch up with them.'

Gleb cast an appreciative eye over the meadow. 'You've chosen a good place. This is fine grass. We've been riding since dawn and deserve a rest.' He patted his soaking trousers. 'If you don't mind, we'll break our fast here.'

He put his horse forward and his party followed, sliding grins at the voyagers. They dismounted about a hundred yards up the meadow and tethered their horses and dogs to a tree washed inland by a flood. Some of them began breaking off dead branches for firewood. When Gleb had made his dispositions, he strolled back towards Vallon.

'Outnumbered two to one,' Drogo said. 'We'd better get in the first blow.'

'Hold your hand. He might even be telling the truth.'

Gleb smiled at Vallon. 'The food won't take long. Please share bread and salt with us.'

'Thank you, but we've already eaten. I want to be well downriver before the sun goes. You would have found this meadow empty if the rest of my party had returned. I sent ten of them into the forest to hunt game. You probably heard the horn calling them back.'

Gleb politely regarded the forest, then surveyed the modest convoy. 'Thirty men in those small craft. My friend, I worry for you. You'll never reach Kiev with boats so heavily laden.'

Vallon clenched his fists against his thighs. Where the hell were Wayland and Syth?

They lay half-asleep in each other's arms, Syth twining a lock of Wayland's hair around her fingers. Above them two squirrels chased each other through the crown of a pine tree. They proceeded by mad scampers and sudden standstills, as if they'd been magnetised to the underside of the branches.

'Wake up.'

Wayland backed up on his elbows and blinked over the trunk. 'The aurochs have gone.'

Syth shook with silent laughter. 'I wonder what scared them.'

Wayland sat against the trunk and laid Syth's head on his lap.

She sighed. 'Caitlin's lovely, don't you think?'

'Not half as lovely as you.'

Syth touched the tip of his nose. She sighed again. 'What I'd give to have her gorgeous curls.'

Wayland shifted. 'Why do you keep bringing her name into it? She's so devious. Surely you don't like her.'

'She's not so bad when you get to know her.'

'She's trouble. I don't understand why Vallon let her come with us.'

'She's in love with him.'

Wayland bucked. 'Vallon? But she tried to kill him.'

'Love and hate aren't as far apart as you might think.'

'Who told you that?'

'Nobody. Sometimes when you get moody or ignore me for the falcons, I get angry, and then I find that's when I desire you most.'

'Caitlin won't get anywhere with Vallon. After what happened with his wife, I don't think any woman could find a way into his heart.'

'Don't be so sure. He's not as grisly as I first thought, and love's a funny thing.'

Three urgent notes made them snap apart. 'That's the alarm!' Wayland sprang up and hopped around in search of a shoe. A thorn spiked his sole. 'Shit!' He grabbed Syth's hand and began towing her behind him. She hung back.

'We'll run into the aurochs.'

Wayland stared in the direction of the river. It was less than a mile away. His gaze darted, mapping out a path. 'We'll lose too much time

481

if we circle around them.' He seized Syth's hand and plunged straight ahead.

'Wayland!'

'We'll drive them ahead of us. I don't know what's happening at the river, but a distraction might be useful. Stand over to my right. Keep behind me. When you hear me shout, yell and keep yelling. Beat the trees with a stick. Make as much racket as you can.'

'What if they turn on us?'

'Climb a tree.'

As soon as Syth was in position, he hurried across the clearing and into the forest. The aurochs had left deep prints and piles of dung. The breeze blew towards him and he moved fast. The trail led into a dense nursery of saplings that cut visibility to less than thirty feet. He turned and waved at Syth, telling her to stay where she was. He went on more cautiously. Despite their size, the aurochs had moved neatly through the close-grown trees. He was in the middle of the thicket when the warning signal came again. This was serious.

He emerged into a storm wreck of toppled and listing trees. He crossed through and entered virgin forest drenched with shadow. He stopped to allow his eyes to adjust. Spears of gold-green light pierced the underwater gloom. He peered through dark bars and grids. Nothing. The horn had scared the aurochs and by now they were probably a mile away. He was in the act of stepping forward when a block of shade shifted. He blinked, blinked again and the giant bull reconstituted itself no more than forty yards away. It had sensed him and was facing his way, ears twitching, moist muzzle dilated. He'd lost sight of Syth. When he turned his gaze to the bull again, it had resumed grazing. Between them lay the carcass of a massive oak upholstered in moss and scalloped with fungi shaped like outsize human ears. He stalked towards it. Years of experience as a wildboy had taught him that the trick of creeping up on quarry was not to creep up on it. Become part of the air, part of the ground, but never be your conscious self. The moment you let thought intervene, the quarry sensed it.

Ten yards from the oak he stopped. The bull was still grazing. He sank down by degrees and bellied towards the oak's girth. He rolled onto his side, notched an arrow, and ever so slowly raised his head.

The bull was less than twenty yards in front of him, slatted with shadows, close enough for him to see the scars of old combats on its shoulders. He remained motionless. He was only a scrap of forest, his face a pale and unthreatening oval, no more significant than the fungi that clothed the tree. But the bull mapped its surroundings with every glance, and when it next lifted its head it registered that Wayland's face hadn't been there when it had last looked. It turned to face him and took a step forward. Wayland didn't move. It groaned deep in its chest and pawed the ground. In a moment it would charge.

Wayland flared up and screamed. The aurochs snorted and swung in its length and galloped away. Wayland vaulted the tree and screamed again. Ahead of him he heard thudding hooves and branches snapping. Behind him Syth loosed a shrill cry.

Without waiting for her to catch up, he darted after the aurochs. He could track their progress from the sound of tearing vegetation. They were well ahead of him, fleeing in an unstoppable panic, and he chased them with the guilty exhilaration of a man who's started an avalanche.

Gleb returned to the bank and this time six of his men accompanied him. The rest lounged around their fire, but Vallon could tell from their postures that they were waiting for the signal to attack. Gleb stopped about twenty yards away. 'Come. We're ready to eat. It's not much – a stew of pork. Kvas.'

'I told you. We already ate.'

Gleb's face flickered annoyance. 'It's the custom in my country for strangers who meet on the road to break bread together.'

'Just say the word,' Drogo said.

Vallon jerked his head. 'Keep your weapons hidden for now. Get everyone into the boats.'

Gleb cupped a hand to his ear. 'Hey, brother, didn't you hear me? Isn't the company of Russians good enough for you?'

Vallon played out the pretence. 'I'm worried that something's happened to my missing men.'

Gleb went along with the fiction. 'Ten of them, you said. Enough to protect each other. So forget them and share our meal. By the time we've finished, they might have returned. Who knows?'

'Now I think of it, there must have been a misunderstanding. They're probably waiting for us downriver.' A glance to the rear showed that everyone was in the boats. 'We'd better make haste to join them. I'm sorry to refuse your hospitality.'

Gleb stared at the ground and when he raised his face it had grown sad. 'But there is a problem. You've strayed onto Polotsk territory. Do you have permits to travel through Prince Vseslav's land?'

Vallon played for time. 'I carry a safe conduct from Lord Vasili of Novgorod.'

'Lord Vasili's letters don't entitle you to be in this place. I'm surprised he didn't provide you with a guide.' He said something in Russian that made his men snigger. He composed his own features into seriousness. 'The law is clear. A caravan that enters Vseslav's territory without authorisation is liable to arrest, its goods subject to seizure.'

'Let's cut the play-acting,' Vallon said. 'It was Vasili who sent you.'

Gleb grinned. 'And you don't have ten men hidden in the forest. By Oleg's count, there are only two, and one of them is a girl.' He shook his head in mock sorrow. 'You should have listened to Lord Vasili and sold him the falcons. I'm saving you a wasted journey. You'd never have got past the rapids and the nomads.'

He motioned with his hand and his men rose like a company released from a trance and drew their swords and strung their arrows and advanced.

Vallon drew his own sword and heard steel rasp behind him. 'I'll tell you one thing. You won't live to profit by your treachery.'

'Get in the boat!' Drogo shouted.

It was too late. The Russians were only thirty yards away and would catch the boats before they reached deep water.

'There's no need to fight,' said Gleb. 'Give me the falcons and I'll let you go on your way.'

Vallon backed to the water's edge. 'Hero, be ready to throw the falcons into the river.'

Gleb halted the advance. 'Don't be foolish. The falcons are the only thing that can save you.'

Vallon stepped into the river. 'Cast off.'

As Gleb raised his hand to launch the attack, the dogs began to yelp and tug against their leashes. A horse whickered and tossed its head. Gleb glanced over his shoulder, then looked back at Vallon.

'The falcons.'

'Do I look like a fool?'

A shout from one of the Russians cut off Gleb's answer. The horses had begun to whinny and tread, their ears pinned back and the whites of their eyes showing. The dogs howled and bit each other as they fought to break loose. A deep lowing came from the forest.

'What in the . . .?'

Out of the trees streamed a bawling herd of aurochs led by a giant black bull that seemed to fly over the ground. They poured down the meadow, hell-bent on reaching the ford. Gleb shared a last astounded look with Vallon, then shouted an order and sprinted towards the squealing horses.

'Get rowing!'

Vallon's boat was clear of the bank when he reached it. Richard and Hero dragged him aboard and he turned to see the aurochs halfway down the meadow and the Russians still struggling to free their terrified horses. Some of them realised that they wouldn't do it in time and began legging it to safety. Others managed to untie their plunging steeds but found it impossible to mount them. Two men subdued Gleb's horse long enough for him to climb into the saddle. By then the aurochs were nearly upon them. One Russian stood in their path waving his arms in a doomed attempt to turn the tide. They flattened him like a skittle. Gleb's horse spun and reared. He whacked it and sawed at the reins, one foot out of the stirrup. The black bull took horse and rider square on, one horn spearing Gleb's thigh to his mount. It hoisted them clear of the ground and tossed them aside as if they weighed no more than dolls. Vallon saw a man give up on his horse only to dash into the path of a cow that swept him aside and left him lying with his limbs the wrong way round. A half-grown bull stotted down the meadow in a crazy prance and stove in a man's face with a kick from its hind hooves. Bedlam. Aurochs bellowing, horses screaming, men yelling, dogs yelping.

The old bull hit the river at full gallop, parting the water in two great waves that fanned up like wings. Most of the herd followed his path, but some plunged perilously close to the boats, drenching their occupants with spray.

'Row for the opposite shore,' Vallon yelled.

'What about Wayland?'

'Don't you worry about him. He's the one who whipped up the storm.'

By the time the rowers had settled into a rhythm, some of the Russians had caught up their horses and were riding in pursuit, shooting arrows at a gallop. A few pounded ahead and dismounted at the end of the meadow so they could take surer aim as the boats passed. Every stroke carried the boats further across the river and by the time they drew level with the archers, the lofted arrows dropped short. From here the forest came down to the river and hindered pursuit. Gradually the yells grew faint with distance.

'Stop rowing,' Vallon ordered. 'Blow the horn.'

Three times the notes blared out before the voyagers saw two figures flitting down to the bank. Vallon brought the boat in close and Wayland and Syth waded out and boarded while it was still moving. Their clothes were muddy and torn, their skin scratched by briars and blistered by nettles. They sat side by side, fighting for breath.

'Where the hell have you been? Why didn't you come when we blew the first signal?'

'I didn't hear it,' Wayland panted.

'Didn't hear it? What were you up to?'

Syth choked off laughter with her fist. Vallon and Hero exchanged looks, only their eyes moving, then simultaneously they reached the same conclusion and stared off as if some distant event had seized their attention.

XL

Vallon scourged them on like galley slaves, the women as well as the men. They lay up overnight in a side-creek and were back at their oars before they'd properly woken. Only the Vikings could sustain the effort. Rowing was their life's work and their hands were as callused as a dog's paws.

For everyone else it was more than muscles and joints could stand. Something tore in Richard's back, forcing him to row one-handed. Hero jerked upright at Vallon's shout to find that he'd been rowing while asleep. They hobbled ashore that night with their hands crooked into claws and their backs as rigid as boards. Each boat's company cooked separately. An occasional snatch of conversation or laughter carried from the Vikings' hearth, but everyone else was silent. Wayland and Syth were keeping watch on the river. Hero and Vallon drooped by their fire.

Drogo barged out of the dark dragging Caitlin's maid, Asa. 'Show him.'

The girl held out her hands to Hero, whimpering with pain. He saw why when he unwrapped the bandages. The skin on her palms was peeling off like a glove. He held her wrists. 'Are your mistress's hands that bad?'

Asa nodded tearfully.

Vallon hadn't even looked up. He continued shoving food into his mouth. 'I warned her it wouldn't be a bed of roses.'

'There's no need to push us so hard,' said Drogo. 'They won't chase us, not with Gleb dead. They haven't even got boats.'

Vallon cocked a fire-reddened eye. 'They can find boats in Smolensk. We have three days' lead at most, and we're at least twelve days from Kiev.'

'I know that if you drive us at the same pace, by this time tomorrow you'll be left with nothing but cripples.'

Hero intervened. 'I'll treat your hands with salve,' he told Asa.

The girl couldn't have been older than twelve. He dressed her palms with an ointment of lanolin and seaweed. When she'd left, he looked at Vallon. 'Drogo's right. Richard can't sleep for pain.' He showed his own raw palms. 'I can hardly hold a cup, let alone an oar.'

Vallon stirred the fire. 'You think I'm not suffering?'

'That makes it worse. Your wound could open.'

'We have to press on. My nightmare is that the Russians will slip past us during the night. Imagine coming round a bend to find them waiting.'

'They won't. Not with Wayland watching the river. I'm serious, sir. Another day like today and we'll be fit for nothing.'

When Vallon didn't answer, Hero rose and stretched, bunching his fists into the small of his back. He hiked up his shoulders against the chill and set off into the dark.

'Will you treat Caitlin's hands?' Vallon said.

'I'm on my way now.'

'Thank you. You'll make a good physician if you live.'

Fog was streaming off the hills when they gathered at the river next morning. The light diffused through the forest, casting no shadows, softening all outlines. The water had a leaden sheen. A fish eagle's wild scream hung on the silence.

Most of the company were eyeing their boats with dull loathing when the Vikings jumped laughing and joshing into their own craft.

'Wulfstan,' Vallon called. 'Today we'll travel in two boats. Divide your men between them.'

Wulfstan eyed his men and gave an order. The Vikings trooped reluctantly from their boat and took up their berths.

They pushed off. Vallon told Richard to put down his oar and rest. He raised his eyebrows at Hero. 'Happier?'

Hero grinned. 'Much.'

The river ran slow, its current no faster than a geriatric walk. Even so, the boats must have covered fifty miles between dawn and dark. Their course led due south and after four days the river began to widen, in places stretching for two miles between shores, the surface like sheet metal under the great arc of sky. Hero drifted in a relaxed daze, only plying his oar to correct their course.

They meandered through a labyrinth of islands and sandbars and began to encounter fishermen and loggers poling rafts of timber. They paused in passing only long enough to find out how far they had to go before they reached Kiev. Villages began to appear every few miles. Sometimes they passed them in the dark, the only clues to their presence a bell tolling from a church, a rushlight shining through a door, a mother's voice calling her children to supper. The voyagers always camped in the woods, choosing islands for preference.

Now that he had more leisure, Wayland began manning the falcons. Each day he fed them on his fist, and since the task was time-consuming, he enlisted Syth's help, showing her how to balance the falcon with the jesses and food held between thumb and forefinger. Only Wayland handled the white haggard. His other favourite was a blocky tiercel with plumage that gleamed pewter and silver and steel all at once. Though tame, this bird wasn't as well-mannered as the haggard. She ate with the poise of a queen, always one eye on Wayland, her stare as quick and wild as the day he'd caught her.

Every second morning, weather permitting, he blocked them out by the river so that they could bathe. They rarely did, but spent the time bating against their jesses. The white haggard seemed to know she couldn't break her tethers and yet she yearned for freedom and would crouch, fanning half-furled wings before springing up into thwarted flight in a way that made Wayland wince.

He and Syth spent part of each day hunting game from the skiff and rarely returned empty-handed. At every bend and inlet waterfowl spluttered across the water or sprang quacking into flight. He made Syth a light bow from a bough of seasoned yew he'd bought in Novgorod, planing the wood with a spokeshave that had belonged to Raul. When finished, the bow was D-shaped in cross-section, pale sapwood at the front for tension, golden heartwood at the back to resist compression. Shaping it made him think of Raul – his cunning hand at work while he told improbable war stories and outlined even less plausible plans for the future. And Raul's death made him think of the dog and his gaze would wander over the forest as though its ghost still ran through these woods. Not even Syth knew how deeply he grieved for it. When she'd wept at the news of its death, he'd assumed an offhand manner. Only a dog he'd told her, until she drummed her fists against his chest and ran away to bawl her eyes out in private.

Only a dog. Its loss made him feel like a part of him had been torn out. Sometimes he spoke to it before realising with a clutch of his heart that it was gone. Once, a distant barking made him jump up in the delusion that somehow the dog had survived and had tracked hundreds of miles through the forest to find him.

One night a doleful howling woke him from sleep and he rose and followed the sound until he saw the silhouette of a wolf standing on a knoll above the river. It was howling at a full moon fretted with clouds. There were no clouds elsewhere in the sky and when he looked again he saw that the pattern was formed by wisps of geese crossing the moon like a mesh of black lace. He began to weep and he couldn't say for whom he shed his tears. For the dog and for Raul, but also for the solitary wolf and for the geese on their pilgrimage south and for some pain too deep to fathom.

In the morning he nocked the ends of the bow with horn and strung it with gut. He measured Syth's arm and shortened some of his arrows to fit her draw. He cut a target from cloth, pinned it to a tree and led Syth thirty yards away. He showed her how to stand with her weight balanced on both feet. 'That's good,' he said. 'Don't grip the bow with your fingers. Use hand pressure and keep your arm straight. You're too tense. Push with your whole arm as if you were reaching for the target. Cock your elbow sideways otherwise the bowstring will hit it. Grip the string with the first joint of your fingers. Draw and aim at the same time. See the target in your mind's eye rather than concentrating on it. Relax your arm and shoulder muscles. Let your back muscles do most of the work.'

Syth stamped her foot. 'I can't remember all that. Let me do it my own way.'

Wayland stepped back. 'We'll break it down later.'

Syth brought the bow up, drew and loosed. The arrow struck a foot above the target. She grinned at Wayland. Beginner's luck, he thought. 'You've got a sweet action,' he said, and handed her another arrow. This time she hit below the target, but not by much. Frowning, he passed her a third arrow. It lodged quivering almost in the middle of the target.

'You've used a bow before.'

'My brothers made me a little one and showed me how to draw it. Where are you going?'

'To feed the falcons. You're a natural. I'd only spoil your talent.'

Next morning they went hunting together at dawn. Mist rose in curls from the river and a rusty moon hung low over the far shore. Waterfowl cackled like maniacs in the reed beds. The hunters paddled softly, each stroke dimpling the surface. When they reached a headland they laid aside their paddles and knelt with their bows bent into arcs.

'Ready?'

Hundreds of geese clattered into flight. Wayland snapped a shot as they rose and when the flock had cleared the water, one of the birds lay bobbing on the surface with an arrow through its body. He paddled up and reached out to claim it. Then he saw the fletching on the arrow. 'It's yours,' he said.

'She's a Diana,' Hero said that evening, goose fat glistening on his chin. And when he'd explained that Diana was the goddess of moonlight and a huntress, Wayland looked at Syth with such pride that she widened her lunar eyes in enquiry.

'What?'

A wintry wind overtook them from the north, slashing the river into ribbons. With the sails up, the boats ran at a good clip, covering seventy miles for three days in a row. The forest thinned and river traffic increased. The left bank was flat, waterlogged and almost uninhabited. All the main settlements were built on the hilly right bank. It was on this side that late one morning they saw the gilded domes of St Sophia gleaming against a sky smogged with the smoke of ten thousand hearths.

They docked at a wharf beside Kiev's northern merchant quarter. A fussy customs officer wearing the badge of the port-reeve questioned them at length until Vallon mentioned Lord Vasili's name and produced his letters of introduction. For all Vallon knew, the birch bark documents instructed the official to arrest the travellers and seize their goods. He and Hero watched each other while the customs man shuffled through the papers. At last he looked up. Their eyes met. The officer drew himself up above his natural height, rocking on his toes and saluting. Lord Vasili was much respected in Kiev, he said. If there was anything he could do to make their stay a pleasant one. Accommodation for the voyagers and shelter for the horses and hawks? Of course. An airy click of his fingers brought a score of dockers running. The officer drove them up a street, wafting his hands before the voyagers as if to clear their passage. Under the city's inner wall he unlocked a gate leading into a compound occupied by a crumbling clay-and-wood tenement and a Norse hall-house roofed with sagging thatch. It had been built by Varangian merchants, the customs man explained, and hadn't been tenanted for years. If the travellers would prefer more luxurious quarters ...

'It will suit us fine,' said Vallon. 'We won't be staying long.'

He installed his company in the tenement and allocated the hall to the other travellers. The customs man promised to find them a cook and housekeeper and asked if he could be of further service. Richard slipped him silver and told him they needed a river pilot for the journey to the Black Sea. The man threw out his hand in a gesture that encompassed any number of pilots, and marched out.

'How long are we staying?' Richard asked Vallon.

'We'll leave the day after tomorrow.'

Richard showed disappointment. 'That doesn't give us much time to explore Kiev.'

'Make the most of it then. You've got the rest of the day.'

Vallon and Hero remained in the house waiting for the pilots and were still waiting when the sightseers returned after dark. They'd entered Kiev through a magnificent golden gate to find themselves in the most vibrant city any of them had ever seen. Forget Novgorod, said Richard. Forget London or Paris or even Rome. If art and commerce were the mirrors of civilisation, then Kiev must stand second to Constantinople. Wherever they looked, there were at least a dozen churches within eyeshot. Four hundred churches in all. They'd visited some of the city's eight markets and been entertained by jongleurs and fire-eaters and musicians who charmed snakes with pipes. In the city's squares and avenues they'd rubbed shoulders with Khazars and Greeks and Wends and Ossetians and Circassians and Armenians and people from places even Hero hadn't heard of. A month wouldn't be long enough to explore half of Kiev's attractions.

Vallon listened to this eulogy sitting on a bench with his back against a wall and his legs stretched out. He gave a crooked smile. 'Well, you might see a lot more of it before we're out of here.'

'Didn't you find a pilot?'

'None willing to take us to the Black Sea. Vasili spoke the truth, and that customs man was only after our silver. Nobody travels south at this time of year. Apart from the difficulty of negotiating the rapids, the pilots wouldn't be able to return to Kiev before next summer. In a month or so the Dnieper will freeze over and stay frozen until March.'

'What are we going to do?'

'Hero and I will try again tomorrow. If we draw another blank, we'll find our own way.' Vallon drew in his legs and grinned. 'We've sailed the icy oceans, trekked through the northern forests, navigated rivers with no names. Who needs a pilot?'

In the morning he and Hero worked their way along the docks, trying every hostel, tavern and eating-house. The response was always the same. A flat 'no' or a shake of the head. They spotted the customs officer at a distance but he scooted off before they could engage with him.

By noon they were back at the house, sharing bread and wine in the dusty silence. A shout from the Russian housekeeper below announced the arrival of visitors.

Their caller was a slave boy who told them in Greek that his master, Fyodor Antonovich, was waiting downstairs and wished to address them on a matter of business.

'Send him up,' Vallon said when Hero had translated. 'You do the talking.'

Soon they heard wheezing on the stairway and a short fat man oozing venality appeared. He gave the door a tentative tap even though it was open. His dark eyes and dangling flews gave him the look of an untrustworthy hound. His gaze wavered between them as if he were deciding which one to cheat.

'*Chairete, o philoi.*'

'*Kyrie, chaire,*' Hero replied. '*Empros.*'

Fyodor crept in. 'I understand that you carry letters of recommendation from my dear friend Lord Vasili of Novgorod.'

'It's true that we're travelling south with Lord Vasili's blessings.'

Fyodor took Hero's hands and kissed them. He did the same to Vallon, his jowls trembling. 'Any friends of my great friend Lord Vasili are *my* friends.'

Hero indicated the bench. 'Please.'

Fyodor insinuated himself on to the seat. 'I hear that you're bound for Constantinople and can't find a pilot.'

Hero shrugged. 'It's early days.'

Fyodor looked past him. Vallon stood at the window with his face in shadow. 'How many soldiers do you have?'

'A dozen.'

'Seasoned warriors?'

'Hardened killers to a man.'

Fyodor cast another glance at Vallon's angular figure.

Hero leaned forward. 'Perhaps you'd care to tell us where our interests coincide.'

'Yes, yes.' Fyodor dabbed at his brow. 'I have a cargo of choice slaves destined for Constantinople. The slaves were brought from Pechora, far to the north-east, and they didn't reach Kiev in time to sail with the summer convoy. They missed it by only three days.'

'How galling.'

493

Fyodor turned a tragic gaze on Hero. 'A disaster.'

'Oh?'

It transpired that the wheels had come off a trading venture. The slaves were to be sold to a business partner in Constantinople in exchange for silks and icons that Fyodor planned to sell to Kiev's nobility. He spread his hands. 'You see my problem? Until I sell the slaves, I can't buy the silks.'

'Why don't you sell the slaves in Kiev? They might not fetch such a high price as you'd get in Constantinople, but surely you'd make a profit.'

'It's complicated,' said Fyodor. 'Complicated.' His gaze rested for a moment on the pitcher of wine. He sighed. 'I purchased the slaves with money borrowed from my Byzantine partner. It was a short-term loan at high interest. I expected to pay it back within seven months, when the slaves reached Constantinople. With the profit from the Byzantine goods, I was certain to make a good return. But because of those three days, the seven months have stretched to twelve, and if I have to wait for next year's convoy, I won't see a penny for eighteen months. Imagine how much interest I'll end up paying. And of course I have to pay for the slaves' keep. Unless I can despatch them this month, I'm ruined.'

'You want us to escort your cargo to Constantinople.'

'It would be to our mutual benefit.'

'How many slaves are we talking about?'

'Thirty-one. Originally there were thirty-six. They keep dying. Every month that goes by, I'm losing money.'

'How many ships?'

'Two, each with a crew of eight.'

'A dozen extra soldiers won't count for much if we run into the nomads.'

'You won't. The Cumans will be in the steppes with their flocks. Since no convoys sail down the Dnieper in winter, there's no point in them waiting by the river. A fox doesn't sit by an empty burrow.'

'Then what's preventing you from sending your ships unescorted?'

'Ah, yes. It's the pilots. Without experienced pilots, I risk losing everything in the cataracts.'

'So even you can't hire pilots.'

'Oh, I can find pilots if I'm prepared to pay their price. And do you know what price that is?' He leaned close. 'Three silver grivna apiece.' He wriggled on his buttocks, one finger to his lips. 'Three silver grivna each.'

'How much are your slaves worth in Constantinople?'

'Ten grivna apiece, but that's not the point. There are my overheads to take into account, the interest to be deducted. Six grivna on top of those expenses will reduce my profit to less than nothing. But if you were to pay for the pilots ...'

Hero's brow furrowed. 'Excuse me. Did I hear you say that we should pay for the pilots?'

'You won't find one without my help.'

Hero leaned back. 'Fine. We'll do without.'

'Without an experienced man to guide you through the rapids, you'll lose lives and cargo. Don't take my word for it. Ask anyone who's made the passage. Anyone. Even with pilots, ships and men are lost in the cataracts every year.'

Hero traced meaningless patterns on the table. 'When you entered, I had the impression that you were asking for our help. Now it seems that you want us to pay for the privilege of escorting your ships. What's in it for us?'

'My ships. Your boats aren't big enough to cross the Black Sea and you won't find any ships to charter at the mouth of the Dnieper. They've all left and won't be back until spring.'

Exactly what Vasili had told them. Hero stroked his chin. 'So if we pay for the guides, your ships will carry us to Constantinople.'

Fyodor bared his teeth. 'Precisely.'

'I need to talk to the captain.'

Hero laid out the proposition before Vallon. 'I'm sure he's playing down the threat posed by the nomads,' he concluded. 'I suspect there are other things he's keeping to himself.'

'Do you think he's after our cargo?'

'No. He wants us to cover his costs and perhaps more than his costs. I'd lay odds the pilots won't see a quarter of what he claims they're demanding.'

'How much silver do we have left?'

'Little more than twenty pounds. Novgorod was expensive.'

Vallon drummed his fingers on the windowsill. 'We need a pilot and we need a sea-going ship. Fyodor can supply both. If we turn him

495

down, we'll probably end up being fleeced twice over in circumstances even less to our advantage. I don't want to stay in Kiev a day longer than we have to. Gleb's men could send word and have us detained on some pretext. The Vikings could slip their leashes and kill someone in a brawl. Every day that passes ... ' He broke off and stared over the rooftops at the Dnieper.

'Sir?

Vallon turned. 'It's not as if it's our own hard-earned money. Pay the rogue what he asks. Tell him I want to interview the pilots and that we must be back on the river without delay.'

Fyodor beamed when Hero announced their capitulation. He called out to his slave and the boy sprang away downstairs. 'They won't be long,' Fyodor said. 'I told them to be ready to present themselves.' He seated himself on the bench and twiddled his thumbs.

Hero picked up the flagon of wine. 'Perhaps you'd care to join us ... '

'Too kind,' Fyodor said. He raised his cup. 'To our mutual endeavours.'

Wayland and Syth stood under the central dome of St Sophia, holding hands like children and gazing up at a mosaic of Christ the Omnipotent surrounded by four archangels. They'd found their way into the cathedral after getting lost in Kiev's teeming streets and now Wayland was too nervous to leave. Every aspect of the cathedral was designed to remind him that he was under the scrutiny of his maker. The saints portrayed in mosaics and frescoes on every surface followed him with their eyes. When he moved, his footsteps were amplified by earthenware sounding-chambers embedded in the walls.

A choir began to sing, the lead chant echoed by a polyphonic response.

Syth squeezed Wayland's arm. 'This is what heaven must be like.'

'I'm not sure I want to spend eternity gazing at holy images and listening to a choir.'

'What would your heaven be like?'

'It wouldn't be very different from life on earth, except that nobody would go hungry or suffer misery and oppression.'

'Would Raul be there? Would Vallon? Would the dog?'

'I hope so.'

'But Raul was a sinner. Vallon murdered his wife. Dogs don't have souls.'

'I'd rather be with them wherever they end up than sit around with a bunch of saints.'

Syth pinched him. 'Ssh! God will hear you and then you'll go to hell.'

'I don't care.'

Syth thought about it. 'Suppose we died and I was allowed into heaven and you were sent to hell. That wouldn't make sense, because without you beside me it wouldn't be heaven.'

'That's what I mean. You'd have to join me in the fiery pit.'

'Don't talk like that. You're scaring me.' She moved closer. 'One of the priests is staring at us.'

He was a youngish man with a benign expression. When Wayland made eye contact, his smile widened and he moved towards them. Wayland took Syth's arm and began walking her towards the door. The priest called out and lengthened his stride. Wayland increased his own pace, saw the priest do likewise, and broke into a run. Feet flapping on the marbled floor, he and Syth raced towards one of the great arched doors and burst into the open, vanishing among the crowd while Syth's laughter was still echoing around the cathedral.

The pilots were brothers, sinewy men with faces as wrinkled as dried figs. One was called Igor, the other Kolzak. Igor had suffered some trauma that made his face when relaxed sag in chaotic folds, as if the strings holding it together had been cut. They stood before Vallon and Hero, their eyes straying towards Fyodor.

'How well do you know the river?' Hero asked.

'We've been navigating it every year since we were boys,' said Kolzak. 'Our father was a pilot before us, and his father before that. We know every rock and whirlpool, every ledge and chute.'

'How far do the rapids stretch?'

'Fifty, sixty versts,' said Kolzak, shrugging to indicate that distance wasn't the most important consideration.

About thirty miles, Hero calculated. 'So it shouldn't take more than a day or two to get clear of them.'

The pilots stared at him. Kolzak laughed. 'The convoys take a week.'

'A week!'

'Sometimes longer. There are nine rapids and we have to carry the ships over six of them. In some places we have to drag the ships along the bank. In others the men must get into the water and lift the ships over the rocks with ropes and poles. At the worst rapid – the Insatiable – the slaves have to make their way on foot for ten versts along the top of the gorge. That alone takes a whole day.'

Hero didn't have to confer with Vallon to know what his reaction would be. He addressed Fyodor. 'That's unacceptable.'

Fyodor laughed madly. 'The pilots are talking about the big ships of the summer convoy. With small boats, there's no need for all this lifting and carrying. Kolzak and Igor will run the rapids without you having to set foot on land once.' Another laugh. 'They know the river so well that they can run them in their sleep.' He thumped the pilots' backs. 'Isn't that true, men?'

They looked at their feet. 'Yes, master.'

Hero knew that they wouldn't tell him the truth while Fyodor was present. 'What about the nomads?'

'I told you. The Cumans have gone. They're like swallows that are seen only in summer.'

'Let the pilots answer.'

Kolzak shifted. 'It's true that the Cumans wander away from the river in winter. That doesn't mean they aren't a threat. They can turn up anywhere, at any time.'

'Are they as dangerous as people say?'

Igor answered with surprising eloquence. 'They devour the land as if it were food laid out for wolves. They sow our soil with arrows. They harvest our youth with their swords, winnow our fighting men with flails of iron and build haystacks with their skulls. They harry us like flies that can be beaten off but not destroyed.'

Fyodor laughed and gave Igor's arm a twist. 'Come, come. They're men not devils.'

'How soon can we leave?'

'As soon as you wish. My ships are waiting at Vitichev, a day downriver, where the summer convoy assembles.'

Hero turned to Vallon. 'He says we can go whenever you're ready.'

'I'm ready now.'

XLI

It was twilight when they reached the rendezvous at Vitichev. Vallon studied the place from mid-channel. Under the lacklustre sky the stockaded settlement presented a glum and shuttered air. Scores of ships crammed a dock, some of them half-submerged and others in the process of being cannibalised. A pair of small galleys that had seen better days lay moored along the quayside, each carrying three horses. Fyodor's slaves and soldiers were waiting on shore. In the dusk the slaves' faces looked as pale as winding sheets. Fyodor waved. The only other people in sight were four dim figures surrounding a horseman at the far end of the quay.

'Hero and I will go,' Vallon said.

They climbed a ladder to the quay. The slaves were of an uncannily pale race, with blanched complexions and hair as white as swans. All of them were children, the oldest barely pubescent and some as young as four or five. They squatted in huddles, hugging their shoulders, racked by croupy coughs, staring at the strangers with eyes that held neither curiosity nor hope. The soldiers were scarcely less apathetic. They gave the impression of slovenly and unwilling conscripts, their clothes shabby, their weapons second rate.

'Call those soldiers?' Vallon said in disgust. 'I thought it was supposed to be a valuable cargo.'

'Welcome, welcome,' Fyodor called. 'Welcome.'

'How did you come by the children?' Hero asked him.

'My agents purchased them from their parents.'

'Their parents sold them?'

Fyodor's mouth turned down. 'Last year's harvest was a poor one. They would have starved if I hadn't rescued them.'

'They look half-starved now.'

Fyodor flapped a hand. 'If I fed them any more, my expenditure wouldn't be commensurate with income.'

Hero lips curled in detestation. 'What will they be used for?'

'Angels.'

'Angels?'

'Isn't that what they look like? Most of the boys will serve as

499

eunuchs in the imperial court. The girls ... ' Fyodor widened his eyes and hunched his shoulders.

Vallon had been watching the figures in the gloom at the end of the quay. 'Who's the horseman?'

Fyodor pretended he hadn't been aware of the rider and his entourage. 'Ah, yes. That is a very important man in Kiev.'

'What's he doing here?'

Fyodor considered his response. 'He owns the ships.'

'The slaves too,' Vallon told Hero. 'We've been taken for a ride. Tell the fat fraud to start loading.'

Fyodor kicked one of the soldiers and they set about herding the slaves into the galleys. The merchant took Hero's hands and gazed at him with moist sympathy. 'I feel for you, dear brother. That captain of yours is a cruel man.'

They put the town behind them, navigating by the lines of tarnished silver that marked the shores. They slept in the boats and woke exhausted. Three days' rest wasn't enough to restore reserves of energy run down by three months' travelling. Three weeks wouldn't have been too much.

Before noon they passed the tributary leading east to Pereiaslav, the last city in Kievan Rus. Below the confluence there were no more towns, only isolated farms scratched out of the sandy soil and scattered pines. Then even these petered out and night after night passed when there was no sound to be heard anywhere along the river and their fires were the only pricks of light in the darkness.

The dingy yellow current carried them through the steppe. Weird rock formations where hermits had lodged flanked the west bank. On the flat eastern shore a wilderness of reeds fringed empty grassland and sand dunes. Rus didn't have a clearly defined southern frontier, the pilots said. It shifted according to the movements of the horse nomads.

Wayland had purchased a score of pigeons and chickens as a food reserve for the falcons. He had to start using it sooner than he'd expected because most of the wildfowl had gone, flown to the south. Now he counted himself lucky if he killed a brace of game a day.

Returning one morning empty-handed, he made his way over to the falcons' cages on the riverbank and stopped short, staring dumbfounded.

Vallon noticed. 'What's wrong?'

Wayland ran towards the cages. Two of them stood with doors ajar. He flung one open. Empty. He checked the other one. Empty. He knelt in stunned disbelief. 'They've gone.' He turned. 'Two of the falcons have gone.'

The other travellers hurried up. 'Are you sure you shut them securely?' Vallon said.

Wayland stared at him and it was Syth who answered. 'Of course we did. We always check each night.'

'And this morning? Did you check then?'

'It was still dark when we left to go hunting.'

Wayland rose. 'Someone released them during the night.' His gaze settled on Drogo and Fulk and his features contorted. 'It was you!' He ran at them. '*You* released them!'

Drogo drew his sword. 'Don't blame me for your sloppy husbandry.'

Sword or no sword, Wayland would have hurled himself against Drogo if Vallon hadn't pulled him away. 'We'll establish where the blame lies later. Which falcons have we lost?'

Wayland stood panting, casting desperate looks around. 'The white haggard and one of the eyases – the screamer.' He gave a despairing laugh. 'Drogo knew how much the haggard meant to me, and he was always complaining about the eyas's racket.'

'Is there anything to be done?'

Wayland stared across the river, trying to think straight. The reed beds on the other side harboured wildfowl. If the falcons were hungry, that would be the logical place for them to go hunting. But the chances of finding them in that maze of marsh and inlets were next to none. He turned to face the empty steppe. A dirty wind blew from the south-west, hazing the boundary of earth and sky. He fought for calm.

'Trained falcons often return to the spot where they were released. I'll wait close by with live lures. Send everybody you can spare into the steppe. If they spot a falcon, they must ride back as fast as they can.'

'We'll use all the horses and send parties on foot to search up and down the river.'

'If we haven't found her by midday, it means she's left the area.' By 'her' Wayland meant the haggard. The eyas had never known liberty

501

and was too weak to cope in the wild. She'd either been blown miles downwind or had pitched into the grass somewhere, an easy meal for wolf or jackal.

Wayland and Syth rode out into the steppe carrying a basket holding two live pigeons. They stopped about a mile from the river and watched the seven horsemen fanning into the distance. Soon they were alone, the riders gone into the immense sea of grass. Every time Wayland thought of the haggard, he felt her loss like a punch in the gut.

It was a long and miserable wait before the first of the Vikings returned. 'Didn't see a living thing,' he said.

The other riders rode back with equally dismal news.

Vallon cantered in last. 'I had one moment of hope when a large bird flew overhead. It was too dark to be one of your falcons. I think it was an eagle.'

Wayland gathered his reins. 'I'll search for her.'

'By now she could be a hundred miles away. You don't even know which side of the river she's on. If by some miracle you caught up with her, you won't be able to call her down. She hasn't been made to the lure.'

'I trapped her wild, didn't I? If I find her, I'll bring her to hand.'

Vallon looked back into the distance. 'The steppe goes on for ever, the horizon always retreating before you. Don't let it take you too far from the river. Nomads rode this way not long ago. I saw the trails left by their sheep and passed one of their campsites. Make sure you return by evening. We still have enough falcons to meet the Emir's demands.'

'This wouldn't have happened if you'd left Drogo in Novgorod.'

'Save the recriminations until you get back.'

'I'm coming with you,' said Syth.

He almost rejected her company. Searching for a lost hawk could be a long, tedious and soul-destroying undertaking.

'Take her,' Vallon said. 'Take a sword, too. It's a lonely world out there.'

They rode off, Wayland heading across the wind.

Syth galloped alongside. 'How will you know where to look?'

Wayland had only one tenuous hope. In England he'd searched for lost hawks many times and discovered something that flew in the face of the lore peddled by Olbec's keeper of falcons. This man, ageing and unimaginative, insisted that lost hawks always made their way downwind. That might be true of unfit birds, but Wayland had flown only confident and well-muscled hawks, and when he'd lost them, he'd usually found them upwind of the place where they'd disappeared. It was only logical. A fit falcon in hunting mode flies into the wind to gain height. Once she's reached a high pitch, she tends to circle across the wind, covering the sky with minimum effort.

As Wayland rode, he looked for the telltale signs that a falcon was in the vicinity. Back home rooks towering into the sky often betrayed a hawk's presence. Crows or magpies protesting in a tree sometimes marked where a hawk fed on a kill. Here on the steppe there were no signs to be seen, nothing but endless vistas of wind-bent grass, the occasional bush or stunted tree. Occasionally he put up a hare, and once they surprised a herd of gazelle that fled like a cloud shadow. Of birds he saw only a few and they had no tale to tell. A flock of cranes making a late passage south. A harrier quartering the grass. A raven that mocked them with its croaks.

His eyes processed hundreds of square miles of sky. The wind played tricks on his mind, drawing him on after the imagined sound of the falcon's bells. He rode an eccentric course, diverting to every rise where he stopped and swung a lure, shouting until his voice grew husky. The light began to go and the faint hope of finding the haggard sank into the sickening certainty that he would never see her again.

Syth rode up, pale with fatigue. 'It's growing dark. We'd better return.'

Wayland looked back and realised that he was lost. 'We won't reach the river before dark. We'll keep searching as long as there's light to see.'

The ground beneath their feet was almost invisible when he called a halt in a hollow that offered some shelter from the wind. He left Syth to scavenge brush for a fire, working his way up a ridge. He reached the crest. Far away but not far enough another wilderness traveller had lit a fire, its flames the only light in the universe. He put down his load of fuel and felt his way back to Syth.

'I couldn't find any wood.'

They ate biscuits and cold meat, then Wayland drew a blanket over them and clutched Syth close for warmth. She shivered in his arms.

'She's gone, isn't she?'

'Yes. Gone for good.'

'What will we do?'

Wayland trembled with anger. 'I'll kill Drogo.'

Syth gripped tight. 'Let Vallon deal with him.' She hesitated. 'I meant what will happen to us if we don't deliver four falcons.'

Wayland had never let himself imagine that prospect. 'I don't know.'

Syth began to weep. 'It's not fair. After all our hard work, all we've been through ... it's not fair.'

Wayland held her close. 'Hush.' He kissed her brow. 'We've still got each other.'

Long after Syth had fallen asleep, Wayland lay agonising over the haggard's loss, wondering where she was, worrying about whether she'd eaten. He imagined her flying back to the arctic, winging north above the clouds, steering by the stars.

In the night the wind dropped and the clouds slid away, uncovering a sky frigid with stars. Wayland rose while it was still dark and climbed the ridge. The fire still burned to the west. He made his way back to Syth and shook her. 'Wake up. We have to leave.'

She sat up in his arms, limber as a sleepy child. 'Why the hurry?'

'We're at least twenty miles from the river. If we don't start now, we won't reach it until gone midday.'

Wayland took his bearings from the stars. Greying sky ahead showed that he was travelling in roughly the right direction. The horizon bled and the sun rose on the frozen steppe, each grass stem glazed with ice crystals that collapsed into powder at a touch. Wayland searched the sky and every so often he glanced behind.

The sun was well up, the river not yet in sight, when a gamebird erupted under his horse's feet with a startled cry. He struggled to control his mount. The bird rose on rattling wings, its panicked take-off a signal for a hundred others to flush. They were larger than grouse, with longer wings that drove them through the air arrow fast, their pinions producing an extraordinary whistling sound. Wayland watched the flock stream away and lifted his gaze in slim hope. If the haggard was aloft, she would have seen the game rise from miles away and might fly over to investigate. He marked the path they took and saw them set their wings and glide to earth beyond a distant ridge.

Syth rode up. 'What were they?'

'Some kind of bustard.'

He waited. The sky remained empty. He shook his head and rode on.

He'd almost reached the ridge when high in the heavens he saw a point of light – gone at first blink. He kept his eye on the spot and had almost given up when it appeared again. A tiny flicker brighter than the glacial blue, at an eye-straining distance.

'What are you looking at?'

Wayland dismounted carefully and pointed. 'There's a bird up there, miles away and very high. It's circling and only shows at a certain point in its ...' He stopped, concentrating on the intermittent flicker.

'Can you see it yet? It's heading towards us.'

Syth stared blindly into the blue. 'Do you think it's her?'

'It's a bird of prey, but the chances of it being the haggard ...'

The bird was still circling, each circuit bringing it closer. Its path carried it close to the sun and Wayland blinked, lost sight of it and couldn't pick it up again.

'It's gone.' He thumped his thigh in frustration.

Syth pointed. 'There!'

The bird was sweeping towards them in a fast glide. Wayland took in the anchor profile, the silvery sheen. 'It's her! Fetch the pigeons. Hurry!'

Syth scrabbled to untie the basket. Wayland kept his eyes on the falcon. She came overhead at an immense height and he cried out and swung the lure. She didn't know what it was and didn't slow or alter her course. She skated past and was almost out of sight when she checked and swung around.

Wayland shot an impatient glance at Syth. 'What's taking you so long?'

'Here,' she panted, passing him one of the pigeons.

Wayland seized it without taking his eyes off the falcon. She was dawdling about half a mile to the west, probably two thousand feet high.

'Do you think she knows it's us?' Syth asked.

Wayland vented his tension with a laugh. 'Oh, yes. She knows.' With shaking fingers he felt in his hawking bag and took out a length of light cord with two loops at one end. 'Secure this to the other pigeon's legs.'

'What are you going to do?'

'I'll throw out one of the pigeons when she's still too far away to catch it. That should attract her attention and bring her over us. Then I'll toss out the tethered pigeon.'

The haggard held position, cutting lazy circles, occasionally hanging stationary in a breeze unfelt on the ground. Wayland called, held up the pigeon and let it flutter its wings. The falcon drew closer.

Wayland found it hard to measure how far off she was. He lowered his gaze to get a sense of scale, took deep breaths before looking skyward again.

Timing was critical. Release the pigeon too soon and the falcon would ignore it as uncatchable. Release too late and she might take it and carry it off.

She drew on, maintaining her pitch. She was about a quarter of a mile off when he flung the pigeon in the opposite direction. He glimpsed it flying away strong and true and saw the haggard shoot forward in a pumping stoop. Wayland thought he'd waited too long. Wings flashing, she passed overhead and he had to shield his eyes against the sun to keep her in sight. Half a mile away she set her wings and curved up into the sky, hanging like a daytime star.

Wayland groped out with his hand. 'Quick! Give me the other pigeon!'

'I'm trying. I can't get the loops ...' Syth broke off with a cry. Wayland heard a flutter and spun in horror to see the pigeon flying off untethered. A glance upwards revealed that the haggard hadn't even noticed the bait.

Syth turned to him, appalled. 'Don't be angry. My hands were cold and the pigeon struggled and ... Oh, Wayland, I'm sorry!'

Wayland was too stunned by the enormity of her blunder to be angry. Through dazed eyes he saw the haggard work her way back and hold station overhead, waiting to be served. The perfect position. Wayland's gaze darted towards the east.

'We still have a chance,' he shouted, and ran towards his horse.

'How?' Syth cried.

He leaped into the saddle. 'The bustards. Follow me.'

He galloped towards the ridge the bustards had crossed. The trouble was that in this wilderness of endless receding planes, no landmarks stood out with precision. Turn a few degrees either way and the spot you'd marked so carefully would have merged into the landscape when you turned back.

He rode with one eye on the haggard. She seemed to be following, but it was hard to be sure. When he reached the ridge, he jumped off his horse and handed the reins to Syth. 'Keep watch on the falcon. Don't lose sight of her. Let me know if she drifts away.'

He studied the terrain ahead and his heart sank. Flat steppe with knee-high grass for as far as the eye could encompass. He'd been right in the middle of the flock of bustards when they'd flushed and if his horse hadn't almost stepped on one he would have passed through with no idea they were there.

He waded through the grass. Last seen the bustards had set their wings to put in, but gamebirds usually landed further away than expected and then ran on to deceive any watching predator. He checked the sky. The haggard turned small and attentive circles overhead. Her menacing profile would keep the bustards clamped to the ground. He stalked through the grass, his eyes raking in all directions. If only he'd had the dog with him.

He broke into a run, quartering the area in the hope of flushing the bustards. At first he covered the ground methodically, but as time passed his movements grew random and desperate. Syth called out and he saw that the falcon had gained height and was beginning to drift out of position. Sobbing with frustration, he dropped to his knees and surveyed the grass at eye level. With every upward glance, the falcon was higher and further away, barely visible.

Something flicked into sight. Over to the left. He trained his gaze on the spot. There it showed again – a bustard craning up its head. He must be right in the middle of the flock.

He looked skyward and couldn't see the falcon. As hard as he tried, he couldn't make her out. He turned towards Syth, spread his arms, pointed into the sky. She spread her arms, too, signalling that the falcon had gone.

Wayland clutched his forehead in despair and lurched a foot to his left, almost treading on a bustard crouching invisible in the grass. It flushed and again the huge flock sprang up into noisy flight. He watched them grow small in the distance and groaned.

A faint disturbance in the air made his nape tingle. The sound grew, a long yearning sigh that gathered into a ripping tear so fierce it sounded like the canopy of the universe was being torn apart. Wayland's gaze shot up in time to see the white haggard stooping like an ice comet, descending at a speed that annihilated distance. She flattened out directly above him, adjusting her teardrop profile to correct her line of attack. One moment the bustards were quarter of a mile ahead of her, the next she was cutting through them, the tailenders spilling away from her path. She ignored them. She'd singled out her target the instant it rose and nothing could deflect her.

Wayland was too far away to hear the impact as she struck her quarry. It shot forward and tumbled to the ground trailing a coil of entrails. The falcon rebounded more than a hundred feet before winnowing down to her kill.

Wayland signalled at Syth to stay back. Even now the odds of recovering the falcon were against him. He guessed that her prey weighed no more than two pounds – light enough for her to carry with ease.

He ran in until he judged he was close to the kill site, then slowed to a cautious stalk, mouthing fatuous reassurances. In the long grass he didn't see the haggard until he was within fifteen yards of her. She looked up from plucking her prey and stopped him with a stare.

One clumsy move and she'd be off, and once spooked, she'd be almost unapproachable. He sank to his haunches and waited, pretending to look at anything but her. The longer she remained on her prey, the better his chances. He waited until the grass around her was strewn with her victim's feathers and then he lay on his side and dragged himself towards her. She continued pluming, casting the occasional dark glance at him. He was beginning to think the impossible was almost in his grasp when she left off plucking and fixed her gaze on something behind him. He turned and couldn't believe it. Syth was leading her horse towards him. 'Get back!' he mouthed.

She sank down and mouthed a warning of her own, stabbing one hand in the direction of the ridge. Wayland's blood ran cold. There was only one thing that could mean. Syth had spotted nomads, and if she'd seen them, they'd seen her.

No time now for caution. The haggard had finished plucking and was beginning to break into the bustard's breast. As smoothly as he could, he wriggled towards her. He was within arm's reach when she uttered a cry of alarm and leaned back. He grabbed the bustard. She struggled to carry it away, lost her grip and retreated a couple of feet. He waggled the prey. 'Come on,' he pleaded.

She eyed him with wild suspicion. Syth cried out, flapping her arms in terror.

Heart pounding, Wayland wriggled forward, pushing the bustard towards the haggard. She ignored it. Syth cried out in desperate appeal. Last chance. He moved the bustard closer to the haggard. Eyes fixed on his face, she shot out one foot and gripped her prey. One of her jesses had flicked within reach. Wayland closed fingers around the strap, grasped it and hoisted falcon and quarry off the ground.

She hung screaming and flapping from his fist. Syth had seen him secure her and was galloping towards him.

'Give me her cage!'

She pushed it at him and he bundled the haggard into her wicker prison. He flung himself on to his horse.

'How many?'

'Three.'

'Close?'

Syth nodded violently.

Wayland smacked her horse's rump and pointed. 'I'll catch you up.'

He slung the cage from his saddle. Wailing protests from within. After such rough treatment, she might never trust him again. He kicked his horse into a gallop, the wind stinging his face. He'd covered less than half a mile when the nomads rose up on the ridgeline behind him.

He whipped his mount to draw level with Syth. 'How far to the river?' she called.

'I don't know. Too far.' Even if they reached it ahead of the nomads, their course had been so erratic that they'd strike it miles from the camp. Each time he looked back, the nomads were closer. At this rate they'd overtake within a mile. They were better riders on faster horses and if half the stories about their bowmanship were true, there was no chance of fighting them off at full gallop.

'We have to make a stand.'

'Where?'

He saw over to their right a low mound, a tumulus crowned with patchy scrub. 'There.'

They reached the hummock with the cries of their hunters shrilling behind them. Wayland threw himself off his horse and hitched its reins to a bush. Syth did the same. He unshouldered his bow and pulled a fistful of arrows from his quiver. Syth fumbled with her own bow, the nomads little more than a furlong distant.

He pulled her down. 'Lie flat.'

The nomads spread out, one to the left, one to the right and the third charging head on. Two were young men, about the same age as Wayland or a little older. The third was only a lad. Their double-curved bows must have been two feet shorter than his own weapon, designed to be shot from horseback. He knelt to the rear of his horse, grabbing great breaths. The headlong attacker held his bow and reins in one hand, the arrow loosely fitted. Wayland ignored the other nomads and bent his bow. His target pounded closer and now he could see his eyes, his wind-glazed cheeks. He aimed for the midriff.

The nomad dropped his reins and snatched into a draw with his bow held above his head. He lowered it and released as his horse rose with all four hooves off the ground. Wayland loosed almost in the same instant. He heard an arrow fizz and strike and his horse screamed and bucked beside him. He thought he'd missed, then the nomad lurched left and clasped his bow arm. Another arrow lashed past Wayland's head and he saw the rider to his left already stringing another dart.

'I hit him,' he said. 'The arrow must have gone straight through his arm.'

The wounded nomad retired beyond range and his associates rode back to him and convened in a huddle.

'What will they do now?'

Wayland wiped his mouth. 'They've got us pinned down. They won't be so rash next time.'

The nomads separated, the wounded one cantering away to the west.

'He's going to fetch reinforcements,' Wayland said.

The two remaining nomads retired beyond range. The wounded horse had ceased thrashing and stood in a posture of abject misery, a barb buried in its hindquarters.

Wayland checked the sun. Past noon. The day would be well advanced before reinforcements showed up, but night wouldn't bring a reprieve. The steppe ahead stretched flat as a rule.

Their dire situation wasn't lost on Syth. 'We can't just lie here.'

'That's exactly what we have to do. Patience might be our best weapon.'

They lay in the bushes while the sun slid down the sky. He reasoned that while some nomads might be fabulous archers, able to bring down a goose in flight, he'd learned his skills in a far harder school than his two besiegers had known. They'd trained in sport and the occasional skirmish, while he'd depended on his bow for daily survival.

Inaction went contrary to the nomads' instincts. They faced two opponents, one of them a woman, and perhaps they anticipated the jeers of their companions when they rode up to finish the job. They began making sallies, shooting from long range and then retiring. The wounded horse was hit again and moaned and lay on its side. Wayland took cover behind it and lobbed a few arrows aimed well short of his attackers. Syth wormed up to him.

'What's wrong? I've seen you hit more difficult targets at longer range.'

'Unless I can be sure of a kill, I don't want them to know I'm a match for them. It would only drive them back. Let them grow in confidence and move closer. Until then, they can waste their arrows.'

The nomads kept their distance, riding in to a range of about two hundred yards before shooting. Wayland waited. The enemy didn't have swords and he didn't think they'd risk close quarters combat.

An arrow buried itself in the earth a few inches in front of Syth's face. 'Wayland, if we don't do something soon, we'll end up facing a pack of them.'

He checked the sun again. How quickly it sank at this season. He calculated that the nomads had half emptied their quivers. He still had eighteen arrows left and Syth had a full quiver. He studied the western horizon for riders. It wouldn't be long now.

He stood and held his bow above his head. The nomads stared in puzzlement. He mimed shooting an arrow, jabbed his chest and then pointed at his attackers.

Syth pulled at his leg. 'What are you doing?'

'Challenging them to an archery contest.'

'What if they kill you?'

'They won't. One's a boy who's yet to develop his bow arm. The other's an indifferent shot, but doesn't know it. He must think my bow's a crude weapon compared to his.'

He descended the mound and advanced towards the nomads, the sun throwing his shadow towards them. The youngster whooped and gathered his horse for a charge. His companion called him back. They watched as Wayland closed the gap. When he was about three hundred yards away, he stopped and spread his arms, inviting them to shoot.

The older of the nomads recognised the challenge and seemed to understand the rules from the start. He dismounted, handing his reins to his companion. He reduced the range by about fifty yards, drew and loosed without appearing to aim. His arrow flew in a flat trajectory and dived into the ground forty yards in front of Wayland. He reached for another arrow and would have shot again, but Wayland shook his hand and pointed at himself. My turn.

He guessed that the draw weight of his opponent's bow was less than fifty pounds, half that of his own weapon. He selected his lightest arrow for maximum range. In conditions as calm as these, he could shoot it more than three hundred yards. He had the sun directly behind him and he lofted his arrow high, saw the nomad throw back his head to follow its flight and jerk round as it pitched not far behind him. 'Beat that,' said Wayland. He advanced ten paces and spread his arms again.

Again the nomad's arrow fell short. Wayland maintained his distance and his answering shot lobbed down almost at his opponent's feet. The boy called on his companion to abandon the contest, pointing west to indicate that reinforcements would soon be here.

Wayland's opponent waved the boy away. He puffed out his cheeks and reached for his next arrow, committed to playing out the lethal game.

Twice more they exchanged shots, the range now down to less

than two hundred yards. As the nomad drew for the fifth time, Syth yelled.

'They're coming!'

Wayland looked behind and saw four dark nicks about two miles away. He stood his ground. His opponent shot again, his arrow almost parting Wayland's hair.

The boy shouted, jabbing towards the riders. His companion – brother, cousin – looked towards the advancing force, then turned back to face the last shot and spread his arms. Wayland nocked his heaviest arrow and gauged distance and windage – a good one hundred and eighty yards, the lightest of cross breezes. He rocked back and forth, concentrating his mind, before leaning away from the bow until he was almost in a sitting position, his arrow drawn back to his ear and pointing at space. He held it anchored for a moment before loosing. The moment he let slip, he knew he'd never made a truer shot. He watched the arrow race into the sky and curve into its descent. Blinded by the sun, the nomad peered up through splayed fingers. He never saw the arrow meet its mark. He dropped as if poleaxed, transfixed through the vitals from shoulder to waist. His companion wailed and rode towards him and Wayland sprinted to close the distance for another killing shot. If he could grab one of the horses, he and Syth might still reach the river before the nomads.

The boy realised his intention and veered away, dragging the dead man's horse behind him. Wayland ran back to Syth, untied their surviving horse, mounted and hauled Syth up behind him. The reinforcements were not much more than a mile in arrears, close enough for their wild ululations to carry across the steppe.

He kicked his horse into a gallop, but with so much weight to carry, it soon slowed to a labouring canter. The young nomad kept pace on their flank, well out of range. He had his hands full with the dead man's horse and contented himself with screamed imprecations that Wayland understood to be promises of the cruel death he would suffer when his kinsmen caught up.

As they surely would. They were gaining with every stride. Wayland slapped Syth's thigh. 'You take the horse and I'll try to hold them back.'

She pummelled his shoulder. 'You can't!'

She was right. 'In that case, give yourself up,' he said. 'They won't kill you.'

'Leave you?'

Wayland hauled the horse to a stop. 'Yes. Get down. Hold up your hands and they'll show mercy.'

'Never!' She whacked him around the head. 'If you die, we both die.'

No more time to argue. The nomads were so close that Wayland could hear their hoofbeats. He breasted a rise and the river sprang into view, a cordon of horsemen directly in front of them.

'More of them!' Syth shouted.

'No, it's Vallon!'

Seven riders cantered towards them in line abreast. Wayland screamed and lashed his foundering horse, his frantic efforts communicating to the approaching riders. They broke into a gallop and were as close to the fugitives as the nomads were when they poured over the ridge. Vallon drew his sword and his force bunched in a charge. Nine against five, one of them a stripling who'd seen two of his companions laid low by the foreign archer. The nomads scattered to a safe distance and the rescue party rode up.

Vallon halted, shaking his head. 'You two cut it fine. Losing the falcons is bad enough, but if we'd lost you ... '

'We caught the haggard,' Syth cried.

Wayland patted the wicker cage. 'It's true.'

Vallon stared. 'Tell us your story back at camp.' His raking glance took in the nomads. 'Do they pose any danger?'

'They're good archers,' Wayland said, 'but they're not soldiers. They don't carry swords. I think they're shepherds.'

Vallon nodded. 'Draw back in close order,' he called. 'Don't engage unless they attack.'

The nomads shadowed them all the way to the camp. The sun had set and the sky was acid blue marbled with smoky cloud bands. Vallon rode through the terrified Russian conscripts and cocked a finger. 'Drogo.'

The Norman affected nonchalance, approaching at a saunter, Fulk beside him with his hand on his sword.

Vallon looked down. 'Wayland says you released the falcons.'

'He's a liar. Do you value the word of a peasant above mine?'

'In Wayland's case, yes. You swore not to put our venture in jeopardy.'

'I haven't. Give me proof to the contrary.'

'Only you have a motive for releasing the falcons. Without them we won't be able to redeem your brother.' He jerked his head. 'Wayland, repeat your charge. Drogo, the judgement won't be mine. I'll let a jury decide.'

Drogo spat. 'Kept men.'

Vallon leaned down. 'And what are you?'

Drogo's mouth twisted in a snarl. 'If you're so sure of Wayland's accusation, test it in a trial by combat.'

'You released the falcons at night like a thief. I won't dignify such treachery with a trial of arms.'

'Because you know I'd defeat you.'

Vallon switched his gaze to Wayland. 'Repeat your charge.'

Drogo walked up to Wayland. 'Be careful before hurling baseless accusations. Consider your own interests before hurting mine.'

Vallon waved a hand. 'Wayland, speak up.'

Everyone had gathered to watch the trial. Wayland looked about with a hunted air. 'I can't be certain it was Drogo.'

Vallon wheeled in astonishment. 'You had no doubts when you discovered the loss.'

'My emotions were at a high pitch. I lashed out without any solid proof.'

Vallon dismounted. 'What are you saying? That the loss was due to your own negligence.'

'I was tired when I put the falcons to bed.'

Vallon's eyes narrowed to slivers. 'Wayland, I've seen you sick and exhausted, but no matter how feeble your state, I've never known you to neglect the falcons.'

'Perhaps Syth forgot to latch the cages.'

Her eyes bolted wide. 'Wayland!'

Vallon stepped up to him. 'So now you lay the blame on your faithful helpmate.' He jabbed Wayland in the chest hard enough to rock him on his heels. 'You should be ashamed.' He stepped back, jaw thrust out. 'Drogo, if another falcon goes missing or dies in suspicious circumstances, I won't wait for anyone else to lay the blame. I'll hold

515

you responsible and here's my sentence in advance. I'll deal with you as you treated the falcons, casting off you and Fulk to prey at fortune in the wilderness.'

With a savage glance at Wayland, he strode away.

Syth clutched Wayland's elbow. 'How could you? You know it wasn't me.'

'I'm sorry.'

'But why?' She pounded his chest. 'Why?'

Wayland moaned. 'I had to withdraw my charge. Drogo knows something that could put my own position in peril.'

'What is it?'

'I can't tell you.'

'But you promised to tell me everything.'

'And I did. All but one thing.' He started forward. 'Syth, come back. Please hear me.'

She'd gone and night had fallen. The white haggard's bells jingled in her cage and out on the steppe the nomads keened for their lost son.

XLII

On they went, the river flowing so wide and slow that it seemed as if they were motionless and it was the land that was moving. Two days after the skirmish, Kolzak pointed out a flock of vultures wheeling above a bluff on the eastern shore. Igor turned and relayed the warning.

'A Russian family farms up there,' Hero told Vallon. 'The pilots think something's happened to them.'

'Tell them to land.'

The pilots pulled in and the Rus soldiers disembarked with great trepidation and set off up a dirt track, stumbling along in bast sandals tied with coarse hemp cords. A raw breeze carried the smell of ashes and the taint of carrion. The house had been burned down to its mud walls. As they approached, a steppe fox careered off and three vultures trotted away from a half-eaten cow before getting airborne.

A family of five had lived here, said the pilots. Wayland found what remained of the man in a plot of buckwheat stubble. There was no trace of his wife and their three children.

'The Cumans haven't been gone long,' he said. 'Four days at most.'

Vallon looked at the steppe undulating in shallow folds towards the horizon. No other dwellings in sight. Not even a tree to give a sense of scale. The grasses tossed in the wind.

'Why did they settle in such a dangerous place?'

'The soil is rich black loam. The Cumans haven't been this far north for some years. They took a chance and lost.'

The emptiness gave the Russians the jitters. They fairly ran back to the ships, leaving the smallholder unburied. Vallon and Wayland remained a little longer, listening to the wind in the grass, watching cloud shadows sail across the steppe. They imagined the farmer looking up from some everyday task to see the mounted warriors mustering on the skyline.

Vallon hunched his shoulders. 'Let's go.'

The Dnieper flowed on with unbroken calm, then the left bank began to rise and the current quickened as the river narrowed between cliffs. Since leaving Kiev they had been heading south-east. Now the river swung due south and the voyagers saw that it disappeared through a cleft in a plateau about five miles downstream.

'*Porohi*,' Igor shouted, pointing at the gap. 'Rapids.'

The sun hadn't reached full height when the pilots cut short the day's journey at a grassy island below a tributary. No point going further today, Kolzak said. They were only a few miles above the first rapid. With the days now much shorter than the nights, it would take two days to get past all nine of them. If they started at first light tomorrow, they should be through the first five by sundown.

Vallon's company unloaded their horses and hobbled them before turning them out to graze. Wayland and Syth went off to hunt game for the falcons. Vallon and Hero strolled to the tail of the island and watched the clay-coloured current coiling towards the gap in the granite walls. The sky was a glazed blue dish brushed with fair-weather cloud.

Hero glanced at Vallon. 'Drogo will make another sabotage attempt. The closer we get to our goal, the more desperate he'll become.'

517

Vallon nodded. 'I'll set him and Fulk adrift once we've run the rapids and are clear of the Cumans.'

'They won't survive long in the steppe.'

'I'm not so pitiless that I'd condemn them to death. We'll give them the spare boat and enough food for the journey to the Black Sea. If they reach it ...' He broke off. 'Here come Wayland and Syth.'

They appeared from the other side of the island and jogged down to join them. Vallon smiled. 'No luck?'

'Horsemen on the west bank,' said Wayland. He took Vallon by the elbow and steered him round. 'They've dropped from sight, but they'll be watching. Better not let them know we've seen them.'

'Are they shepherds?'

'No, they carry shields and sidearms as well as bows. I counted four, but there may be more. We have to get off the island. The channel on the other side is shallow enough to ford.'

Vallon looked towards the camp. 'This requires delicate thinking. The Russians might turn back if they find out there are Cumans in their path.'

On the way to the camp they agreed a plan of action. They found Richard alone by their fire and told him about the horsemen. No one else. Hero went to the Russians' camp and invited the pilots to come over and discuss the journey through the gorge. Vallon greeted them cheerfully and Richard handed them cups of mead.

'So,' Hero said. 'Tell us more about the rapids.'

Igor answered, chanting his response like a litany. 'The first one is called Kaidac. It has four ledges.' He mimed rowing. 'Keep to the left. Next is the Severe One, called Sleepless by the Varangians. Very soon we are at the dangerous Wave-Waterfall, which has three ledges and many perilous rocks downstream. Then we come to the Echoer. As you pass it your heart quails at the terrible clamour of the Insatiable. Here the river pours down twelve ledges with the speed of a runaway horse. No time to think, no time to aim. Pray to God and put your life in his hands. A thousand souls and all their treasure lie at the bottom of the deep pools below. If you come through the Insatiable and the dangerous rocks downstream, your course turns west past a large island. For many versts the river flows gently. Don't relax. Don't cease your prayers. Ahead of you is the Place of Waves with billows that hold many hidden dangers.' Igor rocked from side to side, his eyes shut. 'Hardly have you given thanks to God for your deliverance than you are in the Awakener. Below that the river turns south again and descends the Lishni. It offers only slight dangers. Now only the Serpent awaits, winding and twisting through six ledges before spilling into the Wolf's Throat.'

Igor opened his eyes and quaffed his mead. Hero made a face at Vallon. 'He says we're in for a tempestuous ride.'

'Ask him where the Cumans set their ambushes.'

'Below the Serpent, at the Wolf's Throat,' Igor answered. 'There the river narrows to less than an arrow-flight and the horse-archers can shoot down into the boats. If you survive their barbs, you still have to face their main force at the ford between the end of the gorge and St Gregory's Island.'

Hero sipped his mead. 'Have you ever run the rapids at night?'

Igor snorted. 'Of course not.'

'Is it possible?'

'Only a madman would attempt such a thing.'

Hero smiled. 'Fyodor told us you could run the rapids in your sleep.'

Igor looked away. 'Yes, in the summer I could find the way with my eyes closed. But with the water so low everything will have changed. Some of the channels will be dry and others will be no wider than your boats. You can't thread a needle in the dark.' He drained his cup. 'Why do you ask?'

Hero poured them more mead. 'Because the Cumans know we're here.'

The pilots froze with their cups halfway to their mouths.

Hero pulled himself closer. 'Wayland spotted them on the west bank. By now some of them will be riding south to prepare an ambush. If we wait until tomorrow, there'll be an army waiting at the ford. We have to start as soon as possible and run all nine rapids tonight. We've still got some daylight and there'll be a moon to light the way after sunset.' He saw Kolzak glance at the Russians. 'Don't tell them until we're below the second rapid. Say that we're moving downriver to be sure of making an early start.'

Igor said something to Kolzak and they began to argue in Russian, working themselves into such a frenzy that the soldiers turned to watch. Igor made to jump up, but Kolzak pulled him back down. He clenched his arms around his chest, his face a furious wrinkled sack. 'Igor refuses to go,' Kolzak said. 'He'd rather suffer Fyodor's punishment than face certain death.'

Hero craned forward. 'Now listen. We haven't told the Vikings about the Cumans. When we do, do you imagine they'll let you scuttle back to Kiev leaving them to face the horse-nomads alone? And there's the silver we paid for your services. Vallon isn't the kind of man to overlook a broken contract.'

Igor sobbed into his hands. Kolzak spoke gently to him and helped him up. His arms flopped in resignation. 'God curse Fyodor Antonovich. A plague of ulcers on his soul.'

A palm's span separated the sun from the horizon when the convoy approached the gate in the plateau. The two galleys led the way, followed by Vallon's company towing the spare boat, Drogo and the Icelanders bringing up the rear. They entered the mouth of the gorge and the sun disappeared below the western wall. The cliffs on both sides rose three hundred feet, their walls fissured by gullies overgrown with trees. The river swung left and the voyagers heard the mutter of fast water. Wulfstan stood in the bow of the company's boat. 'Keep to the same line as the galleys. Right a bit. Don't look. That's my job. Here we go.'

Hero's stomach went light as the boat bucked. It bobbled down a ropy slither of broken water and glided out into slack.

Richard grinned. 'That wasn't too bad.'

'That was the easy one,' said Hero. He glanced over his shoulder and saw the gorge cutting south for miles. The sunlight had retreated up to the crests on the left bank, throwing the cliffs on the right into deep shadow.

Three miles on they reached the rapid called Sleepless. The water above it seemed to skin over and grow more solid, like a flexed muscle. The noise swelled. Wulfstan stood holding on to one of the mast's straining lines.

'Face the front for this one. Use your oars as paddles.'

They watched the galleys slide down the slant of water and pitch in a back-curling wave at the bottom. The boat followed, slapping into the current and scooting down before hitting the standing wave with a drenching splash. Then they were in the clear and only half a mile from the next rapid. Something was wrong, though. The pilots were waving them toward the middle of a ledge that ran almost right across the gorge, squeezing quarter of a mile of river into a brawling chute against the rocky right bank.

The voyagers came alongside the Russian galleys. Kolzak shouted, pointing at a fan of water slopping over the ledge behind his ship.

Hero strained to make out what he was saying. 'This is the line we're supposed to take, but the channel's disappeared. The river's five feet lower than it is in summer.'

'What are they going to do?'

'Drag the ships over. Lever them onto the ledge with poles, then some of us go into the water on the downstream side and pull on ropes, while the rest push from behind.'

Vallon jumped onto the ledge. To clear it they would have to haul the ships a hundred yards down a natural weir left high and dry by the falling river. The late-afternoon sun had already sunk behind the rim of the gorge. 'It would take all night just to get the galleys clear.'

'There's only one thing to do,' Drogo said. 'Our boats are light enough to carry down before dark. Take the pilots with us and leave everyone else.'

'Abandon the slaves?' said Richard.

'They're nothing to us.'

'Nor are you.'

'Vallon, you know it's our only chance.'

Before Vallon could reach a decision, he heard his name called and saw Wayland beckoning to him from the edge of the waterfall. It spilled down like a giant millrace before plunging into a pool and dashing against a crag jutting into the river forty yards further on. Swells crashed upon the wall, climbing and spreading and then falling away before humping up for fresh attacks. Fangs of rock and black-eyed eddies showed in the waves. The thought of being sucked down into one of those dark vortices brought Vallon out in a cold sweat.

He pulled Wayland closer. 'It would be suicide.'

'Wulfstan's got an idea.'

When Vallon heard it, he stared at the torrent and then he stared at Wulfstan. The Viking grinned. 'Makes your arse pucker, doesn't it?'

'A pound of silver if it works.'

*

521

After unloading the horses and falcons, the two boat crews rowed away from the ledge with the spare boat in tow, aiming for the shore above the head of the cataract. Wayland and Syth followed in the skiff. When the crews reached shore, they drifted down until they felt the current begin to tug and then they jumped out and made fast to the bank. They struggled to keep their footing on the slippery rocks.

They tied walrus hide cables to the spare boat's stern and stem. The men holding the stern rope wrapped their hands in cloths and sought secure stances among the boulders. Wulfstan gathered the bow cable and scrambled back to where Wayland and Syth waited in the skiff. Syth took the end of the rope and Wayland paddled away from shore. The slack cable payed out behind them in a dragging curve that threatened to pull them towards the chute. Wayland fought his way into calm water and made it back to the ledge. The pilots collected the rope and formed up the soldiers and slaves along the ledge at right angles to the rapid.

The sky had separated into lemon and burgundy stripes. Wayland raised a hand at the figures on the shore. The boat began to move, water creaming against its stern as the shore party braked its descent. It slid into the pool. A wave broke over its stern.

'Pull!'

The soldiers and slaves strained on the cable, yanking the boat round and dragging it into the slack water below the ledge.

'Now we'll try one of the galleys,' said Wayland.

Eight of the Russians rowed the galley to the bank. All of them tried to get out, but the Vikings pushed four of them back in. 'We can't take all of you in the boats,' Wulfstan shouted. They secured the galley as before and Wulfstan carried the bow line back to Wayland. 'The galley's ten times heavier than the boat,' he said. 'We won't be able to hold it once the current catches it. Start pulling before it hits the pool, otherwise it will smash into the cliff.'

Wayland and Syth paddled back to the ledge. The light was draining fast and the faces of the child slaves shone in the dusk like white flowers. From the ledge the figures on the bank were vague shadows. Wayland signalled and Wulfstan released the galley. It gathered momentum, the rope sizzling through the men's hands. 'Let go!' Wulfstan yelled.

The galley leaped forward and buried itself bow deep before rearing up and careering towards the cliff. The Russian crew clung to the thwarts, screaming in terror. It was only ten yards short of colliding when the gang straining on the ledge managed to bring its bow round. The galley listed, pinned by the current, then the towers slowly hauled it out of the cauldron. One of the Russians on the shore was yelling, clutching a hand burned to the bone by the rope.

Both parties had the feel of things by now and letting the second galley down should have been straightforward. Everything went well until Wulfstan shouted the order to give it slack. One of the Russians hung on a moment too long and the galley's surge yanked him into the water. If he'd kept hold of the rope he might have survived. Instead he let go and thrashed for the shore. He was almost within touching distance but the current caught him and carried him down and past the ship. The Russians on board didn't see him and even if they had there was nothing they could have done to save him. He whirled towards the cliff, beating at the water, and then he went into one of the whirlpools and disappeared as if something huge had dragged him down by the legs. Everyone stared at the water, expecting him to bob up again. He never did. The river had swallowed him entire.

There was no time to lament his loss. It was all but dark as Wayland and Syth made their next run. Vallon turned to Wulfstan. 'Whoever goes last won't have anyone to slow their descent.'

Wulfstan's teeth glinted. 'My Vikings will do it for another pound of silver.'

'Done.'

There were six in Vallon's boat, including three Russians. He took a two-handed grip on a thwart and they were off, the current hissing past the stern. The movement grew jerky and the line vibrated under the strain. Then the pit of his stomach emptied and they were rushing down the spillway. The Vikings had released too soon and the boat raced across the pool towards the climbing wave. A fluke of timing saved them. Just as Vallon thought that the swell would upend them, the bulge collapsed, pushing them back. He felt the bow line dragging them round. The boat heeled and shipped water. Then it rolled back on an even keel and they were in the lee of the ledge.

Wayland helped him out. 'Are you all right?'

'Fine,' he said. He passed a hand across his face. 'Fine.'

He remembered little of the Vikings' descent except that they sang as they went down into the torrent and that Wulfstan, stepping coolly onto the ledge, said, 'I'll take those two pounds of silver now if it ain't too much trouble.'

Between the rapids the river flowed as smoothly as watered silk. Stars stippled the sky and a pale aura showed over the eastern clifftops, where the moon would soon show itself.

Richard leaned into his stroke. 'I'm glad you rejected Drogo's cruel suggestion.'

'I would have left the slaves if Wulfstan hadn't come up with his plan. The Cumans wouldn't have killed them. They would have taken them for slaves. Better the nomads as masters than perverts in Constantinople.'

Richard looked over his shoulder at the pallid figures. 'Such a fragile cargo. It grieves me to think of what's in store for them.'

They rowed on through the dark, the current speaking in hollow gurgles. The moon appeared, close to its zenith. Its coppery light outlined the rims of the gorge, shadowing outcrops and crevices deep enough to conceal an army of ambushers.

Hero watched the heights. 'Do you think the Cumans are tracking us?'

'No,' said Wayland. 'They can't follow the crest because the edge is too broken. The only way they can keep track is to watch from headlands. They don't know that we saw them so they won't be too cautious. I've been keeping a lookout and I haven't seen any riders.'

Vallon nodded. 'If there were only four of them, at least two would have ridden south to raise a force. The pair left behind weren't expecting us to run the rapids tonight, so when they saw us leave, they would have had to warn the others.'

Wulfstan rose on tiptoe and scanned ahead. 'Approaching the next rapid.'

They lifted their oars and heard a faint seething. For a long time the noise didn't increase and sometimes it fell away to almost nothing. Strange and foreboding. Then without warning the hissing swelled to a sullen roar.

They turned to face it.

'There it is,' said Wulfstan.

Vallon made out a ragged streak in the dark. The river sucked and slurped. Ridges of water sped past the boat. The uproar deepened to a heavy rumble that boomed off the canyon walls.

'The Echoer,' said Hero.

'Back water,' Wulfstan ordered. 'Wait until both galleys are through.'

The first galley entered the rapid, showing its stern like a diving duck before yawing down the rip of foam. It came through safely. The second followed, also without mishap.

Wulfstan sniffed and spat. 'Piece of piss.'

Richard uttered an hysterical laugh.

They slid into the mouth and a snarling flood seized them. They jostled through tumbling crests, pitching in three planes at once. A wave slapped Vallon in the face.

'Rock ahead!' Wulfstan yelled.

'Which way do we steer?'

'Left! No! Right!'

Their efforts were puny compared to the power of the flood. Vallon saw waves gnashing at the boulder. They were going to hit it. He braced for the impact. The shock knocked him off the thwart, but the boat had struck only a glancing blow. Then the tail of the rapid was below them and they glided out into calm water.

The river slowed almost to a standstill. The moon hung halfway across the gorge. They rowed through a chain of islands towards the sound of thunder and when they passed the last one they saw spray misting the air in mid-channel.

'This is the big one,' Hero said. 'The Insatiable. It runs for half a mile.'

'We'll lose the line if we wait for the galleys to get through,' Wulfstan shouted. 'Give the second one a good lead before following.'

The rapid was so long and steep that the first galley had dropped from sight when they slid towards the funnel. Vallon saw Syth slip a hand into Wayland's. Hero took one hand off his oar and laid it on Richard's. Vallon had seen similar gestures performed many times before battle and he delivered his war-cry.

'Be strong of heart! Whatever happens, we'll still be together. If not here, in the hereafter.'

'Here or in the hereafter!' the company shouted, and paddled into the cataract.

The boat dipped with a heavy slop. Snarling white teeth leaped at them. They jounced over steps with a force that drove grunts from their bodies. Shock after shock hit them. Incredibly, Wulfstan kept his position standing in the bow, bellowing instructions they could hardly hear. Spray dashed over them. They dropped into a trough between ledges and an eddy seized them, holding them almost stationary and swinging them round. The boat they were towing overtook them and began to pull them clear stern first.

Wayland punched Vallon. 'The other boat's going to hit us!'

Vallon saw it pitching towards them. No room for it to pass. Wulfstan reacted in a flash, drawing a knife and slashing the towrope. The spare boat bounded away over the crests, carrying with it the skiff and one of the horses. Their own terrified horse flailed at the planks with its hooves. They were going backwards. They scrambled round to face the right way and as they did so the spare boat veered off from the main channel and cannoned down between rocks. It struck a boulder with the sharp crack of something terminally broken. A bursting wave hid it from sight and when the spray cleared it was gone. They could see the apex of the rapid now and the galleys in the pool beyond. The hull was half-awash, the second boat only yards behind them. More shocks and confusion, a squealing as they grazed a rock, and then with one last smack they popped out of the rapid like a cork shot from a bottle.

XLIII

They found the wreckage of the spare boat not far downriver. The horse was still tied in its stall, dead by drowning and massive concussions. Further on they recovered the skiff. Somehow it had broken free and its buoyancy had preserved it intact, allowing it to skim the waves like a leaf. They tied it to the stern and went on. The moon sank towards the western rim. After the turmoil of the rapids, the silent drift downriver worked on Vallon's mind. He couldn't shake off the sensation that they were being watched.

'What time is it?'

'Around midnight,' said Wayland.

'That early?'

The moon dropped below the cliffs, leaving only a scatter of stars to show the way. The boats bunched behind the galleys to keep them in sight. More islands ghosted past and the moon glided back, shining up the canyon like a cat's eye.

'We've turned west,' said Hero. 'This is the long calm reach.'

'How many more rapids?'

'Four.'

'Richard, do we have any mead left?'

'Half a barrel.'

'Break it out. A pint a man.'

The crews ran the next three rapids slightly drunk. The moon disappeared again and they took the third rapid almost blind. Only the Serpent lay ahead. They threaded a channel between islands in pitch dark. From ahead came a crash and frightened cries.

'What have you hit?' Hero shouted.

'A ledge,' Kolzac answered.

The company crept alongside the stricken galley. 'Are you holed?'

'By God's mercy, no. We're stuck, though. You'll have to pull us off.'

The slaves transferred to the other galley and the rowers hauled the stranded ship off stern first. The pilots proceeded down the channel with infinite caution, using poles to check for sunken rocks. The reverberations of the Serpent reached them and when they cleared the end of the island they could see its puckered lip in the darkness ahead.

Kolzak turned and shouted.

'He's not going to risk it at night,' said Hero.

'We have to do it in the dark,' Vallon insisted. 'If it's light enough to run the rapid, it's light enough for the Cumans to see us.'

'Dawn's some way off,' Hero said. 'Time enough to send a boat to look for a way through.'

'We don't even know there is an ambush,' Richard added.

Vallon calmed down and took stock. 'Ask the pilots how far to the ford.'

'Six versts,' Hero reported. 'A couple of miles.'

Vallon looked up at the walls. 'Tell the pilots to land at a spot hidden from any watchers above. Choose a place that offers a way up to the plateau.'

The pilots rowed for the right bank, landing in a deep bight over-hung by cliffs on both sides. Between them a gully climbed to the plateau.

Everyone except the slaves disembarked.

'Take one of the pilots and some men and investigate the rapid,' Vallon told Wulfstan. 'Hug the shore in case of lookouts.' He turned to Wayland. 'You know what I'm going to ask of you.'

'You want me to scout towards the ford.'

'It's less than a day since the Cumans spotted us. They might not have had time to round up enough warriors for an ambush. No point risking the rapid unnecessarily.'

Wayland was gone before Syth could object.

Wulfstan and Igor returned to report that the Serpent descended in a slithering ribbon of foam that twisted over six ledges, with only one safe line. Not impossible, but no one in his right mind would risk it at night unless a greater danger threatened.

Vallon was asleep with his arm around Syth when Wayland came stumbling out from the gully. He caught his breath. Syth threw herself at him. He held her to his chest and spoke over her head. 'They're gathered in force. A hundred at least and more riding in. They hold both sides of the river.'

'Christ! Does that mean they have boats?'

'Not proper boats. They're floating across on hide bladders.'

'What are our chances of getting through?'

'Not good.'

'Even if we catch them unawares?'

Wayland shook his head. 'We won't. They've posted three lookouts on the cliffs this side of the Wolf's Throat. Less than a mile from here. From where they're sitting they can see the Serpent. It's lucky we didn't try running it.'

'Any archers at the Wolf's Throat?'

'Not yet. It's too dark for accurate shooting.'

Vallon looked up at the stars. 'How long until dawn?'

'If we want to get past the ford in the dark, we'll have to leave soon.'

Vallon eyed the gully. 'Can we get horses up there?'

'Yes, with a struggle.'

Vallon brought his hands together and composed them against his lips. The rest of the company waited.

'Killing the lookouts would improve our chances,' Drogo said.

Vallon shook his head. 'By the time we've dragged the horses up and dealt with the lookouts and made our way back, it will be daylight.' He looked at Wayland. 'Describe the ambush site.'

'Where the gorge ends, the plateau slopes down to the river. The ford's at the bottom of the slope, on a bend. We won't see it from the river until we're nearly level with it.'

'Are the Cumans concentrated at the ford?'

'Yes.'

'No outlying forces?'

'Only the lookouts.'

'Is there anywhere below the ford where a boat could land?'

Wayland hesitated. 'The bank's so low that a boat could put in almost anywhere.'

Vallon walked to the edge of the river. When he turned, a dozen anxious faces confronted him. 'We don't have much time, so either you accept my plan or we get into the boats and start rowing.' He paused, his tactics still taking shape. 'Here it is. I'll take five riders. Drogo, Fulk, Tostig, Olaf and Wulfstan. We lead the horses up the gully. When we reach the top, the convoy starts out. We kill the lookouts and shadow the ships until they're almost at the ford. As they come through we attack the Cumans from the rear.'

Drogo laughed.

Vallon ignored him. 'In the dark they won't know what's hit them. We sow panic and confusion for as long as it takes the convoy to row past. Then we ride downriver and Wayland takes us off. We'll lose the horses, but that can't be helped.'

Drogo took a step towards him. 'You're not serious. Six against a hundred?'

'There'll be more than a hundred by the time we attack.'

Wayland had been translating for the Vikings and Icelanders. Wulfstan hitched up his belt and spat. 'I'd rather die wielding a sword than sit in a boat while a hundred archers use me for target practice.' He squinted at Vallon. 'Mind, it'll cost another pound of silver and a few cups of mead. Payable up front.'

Vallon laughed. 'It's a deal.'

Caitlin pushed Tostig and Olaf forward. 'They'll ride with you.' She planted herself in front of Drogo and harangued him in Norse.

He looked at Vallon. 'What's she saying?'

Vallon shrugged. 'You swore to protect her. She wants to know how you'll do that with a paddle in the middle of a river.'

Drogo's jaw worked. 'Me and Fulk want the pick of the horses. Most of them are fit only for the knacker's yard.'

Every able-bodied person helped push and drag the horses up to the crest. Vallon was sweating when they reached it. He sent everybody back down except Wayland. It was a relief to be out of the gorge, away from the rank river smell that reminded him of his dungeon. He breathed in the odour of dewy earth. A fleet of white clouds sailed down the sea of night. Everything below the horizon was black except for a fire burning out on the steppe. Impossible to tell if it was a mile off or half a day's ride away.

Wayland pointed to a headland leaning over the river like a wave poised to break. 'That's where the lookouts are, to the left of the highest point.'

Vallon marked the spot. 'Shoot an arrow when the boats leave. We won't be able to keep them in sight, so blow the horn just before you reach the ford. That will be the signal for us to attack, so time it well. If you don't find us waiting on the riverbank, keep going.'

Wayland grimaced. 'You don't mean—'

'Yes, I do. If we're not there, we're dead. Hero will decide whether to continue with the expedition. Follow his command as faithfully as you've followed mine.'

Wayland swallowed. 'Yes, sir.'

'Now make haste.'

Wayland disappeared down the gully. The raiders waited, watching the stars dip towards the horizon. The world slept in the unbroken sleep that comes before dawn.

Something fizzled past them. Vallon glimpsed or imagined he glimpsed an arrow towing a white ribbon. He peered into the gorge. The Serpent showed as a pale smear in the black gulf. The first galley nosed out of the inlet.

'They're on their way. Mount up.'

Vallon nudged his horse forward and led them away from the river.

It was like treading a black curtain. What light there was deluded rather than defined. 'What's that?' whispered Drogo, pointing at an expectant shape on a hummock. It looked like a horseman waiting to meet them, but when they crept close, they found they were aiming their weapons at a bush.

Vallon chortled. 'A useful lesson. If a shrub can scare the wits out of us, imagine the terror the Cumans will feel when armed phantoms appear in their camp.'

He led them in a half-circle and reined in about quarter of a mile behind the headland. 'No need to sneak up on them. They'll assume that we're fellow Cumans. Don't answer if they hail us. Don't draw your swords until we're within striking distance. Slaughter them without mercy. None must escape.'

Wordless nods. Vallon put his horse forward. They rode up towards the headland, its rim outlined by a gauzy film of stars.

'I see their horses,' Wulfstan hissed.

Vallon bent low, squinting along the skyline. 'Got them.' He felt for his sword.

They urged their mounts into a canter. The horse shapes became clearer.

Drogo leaned towards Vallon. 'Where are the riders?'

'They're close. Keep going.'

The horses had heard the raiders and turned their heads. One of them snorted. A pyramidal arrangement beside them shaped itself into three lances propped together.

'There they are,' said Fulk. 'On the top to the right of the horses.'

Vallon made out figures crouching along the crest. 'Mend the line. I'll take the one on the left.'

The Cumans had seen them. One of them stood and waved excitedly before turning back. When Vallon swung out of the saddle, they were still absorbed by whatever drama was playing out down on the river. The one Vallon had targeted chuckled and squeezed his neighbour's arm. Vallon cut off his chuckle along with his head. Drogo slew the second a heartbeat later. The third was beginning to turn when three simultaneous blows sheared away his life.

Vallon wasted no time on the slain men. He dropped to his haunches and scanned the black mirrored surface. It was empty. His gaze darted upstream.

Drogo laughed and barged against him. 'Well, they died happy.'

Vallon backhanded him across the chest. 'That's why.'

One of the galleys lay on its side two thirds of the way down the Serpent. The rest of the fleet were quartering below the rapid, searching for survivors.

Drogo clutched his head. 'Ah, no!'

Vallon broke the silence. 'Tostig, Olaf, ride downriver and warn us if any riders approach.'

The search didn't last long. Anyone on the galley who couldn't swim would have drowned. The vessels came together and then drew into line and began to move downriver. Vallon raised his head. The stars in the east were dimming, black thinning to grey.

'It's going to be close,' said Drogo.

Vallon picked up the head of the man he'd killed and studied its frozen countenance. Bold features framed by black plaits hanging behind the ears. The head wore a conical felt hat with a fur brim. Vallon removed it and put it on before tossing the head into the gorge. The man had been carrying a bow, quiver and round wicker shield. An iron-headed mace lay close to hand. Vallon removed the bow. It was of composite construction, the tips no more than four feet apart and curved forward for extra drawing power. He slung bow, quiver and shield over his back, then rolled the body after the head.

'Strip the others and wear their weapons. In the dark the Cumans won't look at us twice. Don't forget the lances.'

'My mount's lame,' said Wulfstan. 'Do you think I could ride one of the nomads' horses?'

'You can try. You'll find them more fiery than the nags you're used to riding.'

The convoy had drawn level with the headland. A figure waved from one of the boats. Vallon raised an arm. 'That's Wayland.'

Wulfstan swore. One of the nomads' horses galloped away. Vallon ran over. 'What the hell are you playing at?'

'Bastard bit me,' Wulfstan said, flexing his forearm. He was still holding on to the other two horses.

Even in the dark Vallon could see that they were superior to their own mounts. 'Take the other one,' he told Drogo. He handed him two lances. 'You and Fulk know how to use these.'

They portioned out the weapons and moved off, keeping well back from the gorge. It was still too dark for the riders to see with any certainty the furthermost of their own company. The steppe began to descend. They dropped into a swale and moments later a battery of hooves hammered past to their right.

'Control your horse,' Vallon hissed at Wulfstan.

The Viking turned circles on his grinning mount. 'Frisky, ain't he?'

The hoofbeats faded. Vallon waved the raiders on. They rode up out of the swale and halted again. Two blocks of campfires marked the position of the ford. Twenty or more fires on this side of the river, half a dozen on the opposite bank. Vallon could see figures moving like termites among the flames.

He levelled his sword. 'See that spit of land below the ford. That's where we'll rally after our charge. Let's draw closer.'

They rode to within quarter of a mile of the fires. The end of the gorge lay a furlong to their left. Grey light was beginning to steal over the steppe, leaving pockets of darkness in the hollows. Tostig's teeth rattled.

'You won't be scared when we get stuck into them,' Wulfstan said.

The Icelander bridled. 'I'm not frightened. I'm cold.'

Wulfstan laughed. 'Not for long.'

'Attack the archers on the bank,' Vallon said. 'Form a wedge behind me. Hit like a hammer, not a shower of hail. No drawn-out engagements. Strike and ride on.'

Another group of Cumans galloped into the camp to cries and countercries.

'Hear that?' said Vallon. 'As far as they're concerned, we're just another pack of wolves arriving for the feast.'

They waited. A sulphurous thread began to unravel along the eastern horizon.

Fulk kneed his horse alongside Vallon. 'What do we do if they don't come through until daylight?'

'We'll attack anyway. It might still save the convoy.'

Wulfstan spat. 'Ain't nothing else we can do. It ain't like there's anywhere to run. Nearest Russian garrison must be a week's ride off.'

Vallon smiled. 'You remind me of Raul.'

Wulfstan sniffed. 'Raul was all right. For a German.'

They fell silent, willing the convoy to appear.

Drogo slapped the flat of his sword across his thigh. 'Blow, damn you.'

As if in answer, the Viking horns brayed. Shouts rose from the ambushers and their own trumpets blared.

Vallon hoisted his lance. 'Advance.'

Semi-darkness still cloaked the steppe and to the nomads among their fires it must have seemed darker still. Vallon cantered into the attack. They reached the Cumans' lines. Everyone was hurrying towards the riverbank. Faces loomed out of the dawn. Someone shouted at them.

They were in the thick of the enemy. A nomad galloped past standing in his stirrups, reins hanging loose, left hand gripping his bow with an arrow loosely fitted and four more held in his fingers. Another two between his teeth. He moved as gracefully as a centaur.

'Here come the ships,' said Vallon.

The galley nosed around the bend and the first volley of arrows lofted up with the sound of tearing cloth. Vallon rowelled his horse into a gallop. The riverbank was ahead, dozens of archers spaced along the water's edge. More warriors kept riding up and throwing themselves off their horses, as agile as tumblers. He saw an officer directing the bowmen and levelled his lance. A rider cut in front, forcing him to raise the lance. As he aimed it again, the officer turned and saw him. He looked away, dismissing Vallon as just another Cuman galloping to join the action. When he next looked, the point of the lance was only feet from his chest. He was trying to raise his shield when the iron leaf struck, somersaulting him over the back of his horse. The shaft broke in Vallon's hand. He dropped it and drew his sword. He galloped down the line of archers, reaping death left and right. He must have killed or disabled six of the bowmen before reaching the end of the line.

He hauled in his mount. Four riders galloped up to him.

'Who's missing?'

'Tostig,' Drogo panted. 'I saw him go down.'

The convoy was halfway past the ford. The din of drums and trumpets blotted out the cries of alarm. It was still too dark to separate friend from foe and most of the Cumans had no idea that the enemy was among them. Along the riverbank the archers milled in confusion.

Vallon waved his sword. 'One more pass.'

He hacked his way back into the fray, striking whatever targets presented themselves. A horseman crossed his path and he chopped off his jaw. A man on foot raised a sword and he sliced through his skull. The trumpets sounded a shrill note and the Cumans raced to collect their horses. One rider already in the saddle engaged him head on. One, two, three parries and his opponent slumped dead off his mount. The Cumans had realised they'd been attacked from behind and were beginning to organise. From the corner of his eye Vallon saw half a dozen nomads dragging Olaf to the ground. An arrow struck the back of his shield an inch from his hand. Another archer aimed point blank at Drogo and then dropped his bow and felt for the arrow in his chest. He swayed back and forth, as if he weren't sure which way to fall.

Vallon fended off another attacker. The Cumans were closing around him. 'We can't do any more! Withdraw!'

As he dragged his horse round, Fulk grunted and pitched forward in his saddle.

Vallon galloped clear. The headland was empty and most of the convoy had passed it. The skiff was waiting about fifty yards from the bank and one of the boats hung in mid-channel behind it. Two men were kneeling in the skiff. What were they playing at? They were too far out to reach and the skiff was too small to carry all the raiders. He glanced back and saw Wulfstan whipping his horse. Behind him Drogo rode alongside Fulk, propping him in the saddle. A knot of screaming Cumans raced in pursuit.

Vallon drove his horse into the river. It stopped dead, throwing him over its neck. He found his feet and plunged towards the skiff. Wayland stood swinging an oar tied to a rope. He launched it.

'I daren't come any closer. The boat will pull us clear.'

Vallon ploughed through the water, grunting with effort. It was above his waist when Wulfstan surged past and grabbed him by the hair. Vallon beat at his arm. 'Save yourself. I'll wait for the Normans.'

He turned and saw Drogo leap off his horse and run into the river. Fulk remained mounted and at bay, fighting a rearguard action against half a dozen Cumans. Drogo stopped and looked back.

'Fulk, come on!'

'He's finished!' Vallon yelled.

He backed deeper into the river. Glancing over his shoulder, he saw Wulfstan swimming towards the skiff. Wayland shouted and pointed at the oar. It was only a few yards behind Vallon. He struggled towards it. The river was up to his neck when his hand made contact. An arrow struck the surface beside him.

He threw an arm over the oar and spat water. Drogo floundered towards him. Fulk still remained in the saddle, wafting his sword while the Cumans hacked him to pieces. A lancer speared him in the chest with enough force to punch the blade out through his back. Some of the Cumans drove their horses into the river and archers ran up and loosed arrows from hip level. One of the projectiles nicked Vallon's shoulder.

Wayland dragged on the rope.

'Not yet!' Vallon shouted.

The current was pulling him out of his depth. Drogo wore armour and if he didn't reach him soon, he was doomed. He lost his footing, went under and surfaced choking.

'Leave him!' Wayland shouted.

Vallon glanced behind. 'We didn't leave you!'

He faced Drogo and stretched out as far as he could. 'Take my hand.'

Drogo's face contorted with effort as he lunged forwards. Their hands made contact and they locked fingers like comrades sealing an oath.

'Pull!' Vallon shouted.

Wayland and the other man began to drag them towards the skiff. Arrows spat and popped in the water around them. Vallon reached the skiff and crooked an arm over the side. Wayland dropped flat, gripping him by the scruff. 'You'll sink us if you board. Hang on until the boat pulls us out of range.'

Yard by yard the crew drew them clear. Vallon was stupefied with cold when hands reached down and dragged him over the side. He flopped face down. Someone rubbed his limbs. He rolled over and saw several child slaves staring at him. Wayland's face loomed.

'You're wounded.'

Vallon felt the warm leakage of blood from his shoulder. 'A scratch. Help me up.'

He stood swaying, his underjaw twitching in a seizure cold. 'Syth safe?'

'She is, thank God.'

Valloon staggered round and almost tripped over the body of a slave girl lying with two arrows in her back. Hero sat in the stern, partly obscured by one of the Vikings. He seemed to be grinning but when Vallon lurched closer he saw from his expression that something awful had happened.

'Richard is hit,' he said. 'It's bad.'

XLIV

Hero held Richard slumped against him. Vallon barged the slaves aside to reach them. Richard breathed in shallow gasps, holding the left side of his chest. Hero gently moved him to show Vallon the arrow in his back. It had struck close to the spine and buried itself to within a few inches of its fletching. Vallon lifted Richard's hand away from his ribcage. The arrowhead hadn't come out the other side. Vallon cupped Richard's chin to examine his face. His pupils were dilated and bloody sputum leaked from his mouth.

Vallon kneaded his eyes with his fingers, then looked at Hero. Words weren't necessary. Both of them knew the wound was mortal.

'We have to land,' Hero said. 'The sooner I operate, the better his chances.'

Vallon glanced at the nomads galloping against the paling sky. 'We can't put ashore until we're clear of the Cumans.'

'I can't treat Richard on the boat. We'll be safe on St Gregory's Island. The nomads can't reach it without boats.'

Its rocky snout was in sight ahead of them, the galley working down the left channel. One of the slaves shrieked and pointed at the river. Two of their companions floated on the surface with their limbs spread like stars and their white hair trailing.

'Whose galley was wrecked?' Vallon said.

'Igor's. We didn't find his body. We saved these four and the other boat picked up two more and one of the Russians. Everyone else drowned.'

'Who else died at the ford?' Vallon asked, and then grimaced.

'Caitlin's maid and one of the Vikings on the other boat. I don't know how many died on the galley.' Hero noticed Vallon's bleeding shoulder. 'Let me look at that.'

'Later. Deal with Richard first.'

Wayland draped a blanket over Vallon's shoulders. 'You'd better get out of those wet clothes.'

The sun rose, stencilling the Cumans on a thin wash of vermilion. They were still following when the convoy approached the end of the island. Beyond it the Dnieper widened between steppeland stretching away without limits. Richard was breathing very fast, each shallow intake accompanied by a sob of pain.

Vallon returned in dry clothes.

'This is our last chance to land,' Hero said.

'If we stop, the galley will go on without us,' Drogo said.

'Richard's your brother!'

'And Fulk was my closest comrade. I couldn't save him and you can't save Richard.'

Hero made a last appeal to Vallon. 'Please. I'm begging you.'

Vallon stood shivering, supporting himself on the empty horse stall. Wulfstan and the other Vikings watched him from the other boat, their oars resting.

'Row for the island,' he said. 'Tell Kolzak to wait while we treat a wounded man.'

They propped Richard against a giant oak that had given shade to the first Vikings to travel the Road to the Greeks. Deals had been struck under it, treaties signed and broken, sacrifices offered. From here one of the early Rus rulers had launched a thousand ships against Constantinople. Here Grand Prince Sviatoslav had stayed one winter before the Pechenegs killed him and mounted his skull with gold and drank fermented mare's milk from his brain pan.

The Vikings stood around, shaking their heads in grim finality as Hero cut away Richard's tunic. The arrow had struck at a shallow angle, entering between the third and fourth ribs and penetrating the left lung. It would have flown right through him if the head hadn't struck the ribs on the other side, below the left armpit. A contusion showed where the arrowhead was buried. Hero led Vallon out of Richard's earshot.

'The point's below the ribs. I think I can get it out.'

'How? The arrow's barbed.'

'I have an instrument designed for removing barbs, but in this case the arrow's too deep to draw without inflicting mortal damage.'

'There's only one method of dealing with a wound like that. Saw off the arrow close to the entry point and hammer the head through the ribs. Brutal, but I've seen it work.'

'The shaft will break. Either that or the head will sever a major blood vessel. No, I have to cut it out.'

'Hero, Richard's almost certain to die whatever you do. Let's direct our efforts at making his last hours as painless as possible.'

Kolzak yelled and pointed at the Cumans. They were separating, one group riding back to the ford, the other heading south, red dust trailing in their wake. 'It's too dangerous to remain here.'

'Wait until I've treated Richard,' Hero shouted.

'You're not the only ones with wounded men. We have to leave before the nomads set another ambush.'

Ignoring Hero's pleas, the galley began to draw away, Kolzak shouting and pointing downriver.

'What's he saying?' Vallon demanded.

'If we don't catch them up, they'll wait for us at the estuary.'

'No, they won't,' Drogo said. 'Kolzak's already lost his brother and half the slaves.'

Vallon spun towards the Vikings. 'Wulfstan, stop them. Use force if necessary.'

Wulfstan's gaze latched onto his, and Vallon knew what would happen next and could do nothing to prevent it. Wulfstan ran towards his boat. 'Follow me, lads. There's our booty getting away.'

The Vikings sprinted to the riverbank and shoved the boat out. Everything unravelled. Drogo grabbed Caitlin and dragged her after the Vikings. 'Wait for me!'

The Vikings hesitated. Drogo reached the river and plunged in, towing Caitlin behind him. She broke free and Drogo lunged for her. He managed to seize one arm. With the other she whacked him across the face, knocking him backwards. She thrashed back to shore and Vallon caught her and held her while he aimed his sword at Drogo.

'Go with the Vikings.'

Drogo turned, but it was too late. The Vikings were rowing after the galley like maniacs, and from the way the Russians redoubled their own efforts, it was clear they knew what fate awaited them if the pirates caught up. Vallon watched the Vikings overhaul the galley and storm aboard, hacking aside the feeble opposition. One of the conscripts toppled into the river and the Viking warhorn blew.

Wulfstan ran to the stern and cupped his hands to his mouth.

Vallon strained to hear him. 'What's that?'

Wayland stood beside him, his bow trained on Drogo. 'He says it's nothing personal.'

Vallon watched the galley draw away downriver. Drogo watched it, too, and then shook his head and began trudging to shore.

Wayland glanced at Vallon, waiting for the command to shoot. But right now, Drogo was the least of their worries. Without a sea-going ship, they were done for even if they reached the estuary.

Drogo stopped and managed a sick grin. 'Don't look at me like that, Vallon. You'd have done the same.'

'Kill him,' Caitlin whispered.

Vallon reached for Wayland's bow and moved it aside. 'I've seen enough death for one day. Now it's time to look out for the living.'

Richard was breathing as if he'd run a mile, each intake accompanied by a mew of pain. He was still propped against the oak. In any other position, he couldn't breathe at all and his heart went into alarming palpitations.

Hero stroked his face. 'Can you hear me?'

Richard opened glazed eyes. 'I feel like I'm drowning. And it hurts. God, it hurts.'

'The arrowhead's behind your ribs. Just here. Will you let me remove it?'

'Will it make any difference?'

'Yes.'

'And you'll give me some of your drowsy potion.'

'Enough to dull the pain. Your heart is stressed and your lung is full of blood. If I send you to sleep, you might not wake up.'

Richard whimpered.

'To reach the arrowhead I'll have to make a cut about an inch deep.'

Richard's face contorted. 'Do what you have to. It can't hurt any worse.'

Hero laid out his instruments. Caitlin heated water on a fire. When everything was ready, Hero gave Richard a spoonful of the drowsy mixture. He coughed it up together with a cupful of blood. Drogo stood watching in a baleful trance. 'Lend a hand.'

Hero selected a scalpel and knelt at Richard's side. Vallon gripped Richard's shoulders. Syth lifted his left arm as if it were a broken wing. Drogo held his brother's legs.

Hero didn't know in which plane the arrowhead was lying. His hand trembled as he laid the blade against the skin. He had to be decisive. His hand steadied. He cut down hard and made an oblique incision centred on the middle of the bruise. He felt the blade nick bone. Blood sprang. Richard's body bucked.

Hero held out a hand. 'Water.'

Caitlin passed him a cloth soaked in cold river water. He applied it repeatedly, but the blood kept welling.

'Another.'

At last the bleeding almost stopped. Hero pulled apart the lips of the incision, sponged it and saw the gleam of a rib before blood covered it again. He did this several times and then looked up.

'There's a fracture in the rib. The arrowhead must be directly behind it.'

'Can you see the head?'

'No. I'll have to probe for it.'

He inserted the tip of the scalpel between the ribs to the left of the fracture and drew the blade to the right. He hadn't cut deep enough and he had to make a second attempt. Blood covered his hands. This time he felt resistance.

'I think I've found it.'

He made another probe, this time from right to left until the blade stopped. He felt a leap of hope.

'The head's jammed between the ribs.'

'How will you reach it?'

'I'll have to prise the ribs apart.'

Vallon winced. 'The pain will be unbearable. Let me try working it through from the other end.'

'Be careful. The shaft is in the lung. It will snap if you push too hard.'

Vallon gripped the arrow close to the entry wound and pushed, gently at first, then with increasing force. Richard cried out like a beast under torture.

'It's not moving.'

Hero washed away the blood. 'Try twisting slightly.'

Richard uttered another pitiful cry.

'I think it's coming,' said Hero. 'Keep twisting. The edges of the arrowhead are probably bent over.'

Vallon sat back. 'Damn!'

'What's wrong?'

'The shaft's come loose of the head. I can turn it freely.'

'Don't move it any more,' said Hero. He drenched the incision and saw a tongue of iron protruding between the ribs. 'Part of it's through. Enough to get purchase on. I'll have to make another cut.'

He made the second incision parallel to the ribs. He wiped sweat from his eyes and selected a pair of forceps. He cleaned the cuts again, clamped the hooks on the point and pulled. The pincers slipped off. He tried half a dozen times but couldn't get a proper grip. With each tug, Richard screamed.

'I can't get a firm purchase.'

Vallon held out his hand. 'Let me try.'

Hero held apart the wound to reveal the iron point. He sluiced blood away to let Vallon align the forceps.

'I've got it,' said Vallon. His jaw trembled with effort. He pulled and Richard shrieked. He pulled so hard that he tumbled backwards when the forceps slipped. 'I felt it shift.'

When Hero inspected the wound, half the arrowhead was clear of the ribs.

'Oh God!' Richard cried. 'Let me die!'

Hero mopped Richard's brow. 'It's nearly out. One more effort.'

Vallon clamped the forceps again and this time he tore the arrow-head out, ripping through muscle and blood vessels. Arterial blood spurted and it seemed like Richard's life essence would drain completely before the cold-water dressings staunched the flow. He'd fallen unconscious and his heart fluttered like a bird's. Vallon withdrew the shaft from his back and another spout of blood gushed and ebbed. Hero turned the buckled arrowhead in his hands.

'You're a braver man than me,' Vallon said. 'And so is Richard.'

*

They were back on the river when Richard recovered consciousness. He breathed a little easier and could drink water one sip at a time. They camped that night on another island and took it in turns to support him in the position that caused him the least severe pain. In the morning the Cumans had gone. Hero changed the dressing on Richard's wound. He'd left it open so that it could drain. In the dull light, Richard had the pallor of a corpse two days dead, his dark eyes sunk in his skull.

They drifted through empty steppe. The next day Richard was able to take a cup of broth. The surgical wound hurt him less than the internal pain. At each breath, it felt like a stitch was being pulled tight inside his lung. Cupping the wound afforded some relief, allowing him snatches of sleep. After three days Hero dared to hope of recovery. Morning, evening and night he changed the dressing. There was some suppuration, but that was to be expected, and the lips of the wound were beginning to granulate.

Hero's fragile hopes were crushed on the fourth day, when the cupping treatment produced a copious effusion of foul-smelling pus. By evening Richard had a high fever and was delirious. The next morning gas was bubbling from the wound, enveloping the boat in stinking purulence.

On the sixth day they reached the mouth of the Dnieper and landed on the island of St Aitherios, more than a mile from either shore. It was about half a mile long, flat and featureless except for a few grave-barrows. The travellers knew it was deserted even before they went ashore and found the remains of recent campfires and a freshly dug grave. No trees grew on the island and they propped Richard against a Viking runestone erected to commemorate another traveller who'd perished on the Road to the Greeks. They ate supper in a morbid silence while Hero sat with Richard, waiting for him to die.

In the middle watch Richard recovered consciousness. 'Hero?'

'I'm right here.'

'It doesn't hurt any more.'

'That's a good sign.'

'I won't live to see tomorrow. Don't weep. Remember the happy times we've shared. Think of what I would have missed if I'd stayed at home. I've lived a lifetime in the last eight months. I've seen so much, learned so much and learned how much more there is to know. I'm still a fool, but I'm a fool who can ask questions that ten wise men can't answer.'

In the starlight his eyes were dark pools of shadow.

'I wish I'd reached the sea.'

Hero held him. 'We *have* reached it. Look at the clouds. See how the light from the sea reflects against them.'

'I don't want to be buried here. It's full of ghosts. They talk to me. I don't want to be with them. Cast my body into the river.'

Those were Richard's last words. His breathing grew increasingly feeble. Drogo came over and laid a hand on Hero's shoulder.

'I want to speak to him.'

'He can't hear you.'

'It's what I have to say that matters.'

Hero went to the shore and squeezed his skull between his hands. Waves sighed on the bar. He could hear Drogo murmuring, his monologue broken by many pauses, as though he had to dredge the words from deep inside. At last he stopped. Hero stood and watched him approach.

'He's gone.'

'I should have been there when his soul departed.'

'I wanted to make peace with him.' Drogo's mouth quivered. 'He was a better man than I gave him credit for, but when you grow up in a family like mine . . . ' He swung round, his body shaking.

'It's not too late to make your peace with Vallon.'

Drogo whirled. 'Richard never did me any harm. But Vallon . . . ' Drogo shot out a hand. 'That man has taken everything I have.'

In the morning they wrapped Richard in a shroud and laid him in the skiff and consigned him to the sea. A cold wind raised whitecaps and a flock of pelicans stood on the shore facing a window of light in the grey sky. After the others had left, Hero remained, watching the boat drifting away.

He was deep in mournful reverie when Wayland said his name. He turned, smiling. 'I was miles away. Has Vallon called a council? Am I holding things up?'

'It's Syth. She's sick.'

'Oh, no! Why didn't you say?'

'She didn't want to bother you. She only told me this morning. She's been sick for three days.'

'In what way sick?'

'Throwing up. Three of the falcons are showing signs of sickness, too.'

'I'll tend to her straight away.'

Syth watched him with a very guarded expression when he approached. She didn't look her usual bright self. There were bruises under her eyes and her hair was brittle and lifeless. He took her pulse, listened to her breathing, felt her brow. Nothing untoward there.

'Describe your symptoms.'

She made a gargoyle face and uttered a retching sound.

'Vomiting?' said Hero. 'After eating?'

'At the thought of eating. Sometimes a smell makes me throw up.'

'You don't have a fever. Perhaps it's something you ate.'

Caitlin walked over. 'What's wrong with the maid?'

'She's ill. Vomiting.'

Caitlin put her arms around Syth. 'What time of day does the sickness come?'

'It's worst in the morning.'

Caitlin looked up at the men. 'Leave us alone.'

Hero watched Wayland pacing and rubbing his mouth. 'She'll be fine. All she needs is rest.'

'Where's Syth going to find rest? Ahead of us is the Black Sea and behind us there are two hundred miles of steppe infested by Cumans.'

'Blockheads.'

Hero turned. Caitlin stood with her hands on her hips, smiling.

'I can understand why Wayland didn't recognise Syth's condition, but as for you ...'

Hero reddened. 'I admit my medical knowledge isn't perfect.'

'You don't have to be a physician to know what's troubling Syth. The girl isn't ill. She's pregnant.'

Vallon held counsel over their midday meal. 'I didn't want to discuss our predicament while Richard was alive. We're in a mess. The question is, how do we get out of it?'

'We have to follow the galley,' said Drogo. 'Head west, keeping to the coast. The Russians don't sail directly to Constantinople. They stop at trading posts along the way.'

'Is that your advice?' Vallon asked Hero.

'I'm not sure. The nearest haven is at the mouth of the Danube. It might take a week to reach it and we'd have to land each night. The nomads occupy the coast and sooner or later we'll run into them. It might be safer to go east. Igor told me there's a Greek colony on the Krym peninsula.'

'How far?'

'I don't know.'

'How much food do we have?'

'Enough for four or five days.'

'Wayland? Any thoughts?'

The falconer looked at Syth before answering. 'Have we given up our plan to reach Anatolia?'

'Forget Anatolia. Our survival is the only thing that matters.'

Wayland looked at Syth again. 'I don't know what direction to take.'

Vallon stroked his lips.

'East or West,' said Drogo. 'Which is it to be?'

'Neither.' Vallon pointed out to sea, at the boat carrying Richard's corpse. 'We'll follow the course set by your brother.'

'What! We won't cross the sea in our little boat.'

'The Greeks have colonies throughout the Black Sea. That means maritime traffic. We'll sail south until we reach a shipping lane and wait for a vessel to pick us up.' Vallon looked around. 'Anyone got a better idea?' He slapped his knees. 'That's settled then.'

XLV

On the eve of departure, the three sick falcons had taken a turn for the worse. Two of them wouldn't eat. The other took a small crop and cast up its meal undigested, standing flat-footed with its plumage loose and its eyes narrowed to ovals. When Wayland checked in the morning, the falcons lay stiff in their cages with their feet clenched and lice scurrying on their feathers.

They left under a cold and overcast sky. Where the colour of the water changed from muddy yellow to grey they came upon Richard's funeral boat. Four vultures perched on the gunwales and gulls and kites hovered above the shrouded corpse. The travellers crossed themselves and raised the sail and headed into the open sea.

By nightfall they were out of sight of land and hadn't seen a single ship. In the dark the wind strengthened and waves broke over the boat, making it necessary to bail. A sleepless night gave way to another cold grey day. They sailed on, not sure what course they were following. Towards evening Wayland thought he saw a sail miles to starboard. No one else could see it and soon darkness fell.

Morning on the third day broke clear and sunny, the sea still choppy, still empty. The wind was carrying them west and they looked at each other with bloodshot eyes, aware that they were too far from land to turn back.

Before noon Wayland spotted a sail approaching from the east. They mended their course to intercept it. Hero recognised the ship as a Venetian merchantman. It passed close enough for the frantically waving company to see its crew pointing at them. It sailed on without altering direction, carrying the curses of the castaways.

Not long after it sank from sight another ship appeared, also westward bound. This vessel was much larger, running under two lateen sales.

'It's a *dromon*,' said Hero. 'A Byzantine war galley. Look at the two banks of oar ports. She must be carrying three hundred men.'

Vallon studied it. 'Lower the sail. Don't signal.'

Drogo sprang from his seat. 'Are you out of your mind?'

'Calm yourself. There's only one reason why they'd pick us up. I've no wish to work out my days as a galley slave.'

They watched the galley glide past. 'Don't be downhearted,' said Vallon. 'We've seen two ships already. We're in the right place.'

No more ships appeared that day or the next morning. In the afternoon Wayland opened the cages to feed the two surviving falcons. The white haggard still had a healthy appetite and alert eyes. The eyas tiercel crouched in the corner of its cage. When Wayland placed it on his fist, it stood unsteadily and paid no attention to the food. He put it back.

He didn't tell the company about its imminent death. They sat slumped in their own private miseries, their hair stiff with brine, faces masked by salt, crusts of dried vomit at the corners of their mouths.

The sun was dipping into the sea when Wayland's last sweep of the horizons registered another sail. A tiny silhouette on the reddening sky. Everyone watched it in silence, not daring to put hopes into words. It grew larger.

'Heading our way,' said Wayland.

'East,' said Drogo. 'The wrong direction.'

'There isn't a wrong direction,' Vallon said.

The ship was hugging the wind, making slow progress. The evening star was shining when its hull cleared the horizon.

Drogo stopped waving. 'It's too dark. They can't see us.'

'Light a torch,' said Vallon.

The ship was lost in darkness by the time they kindled the damp tow into flame. Wayland held it above his head.

'They won't stop for a torch,' Drogo said.

'Shout,' Vallon said.

They waved the torch and called into the darkness until their voices grew hoarse.

Hero pointed. 'Over there!'

A spark shone somewhere to port. The light grew and another joined it. Then a third. The torches drew closer until at last Hero could see by their light the faces of the men who held them. He could make out the ship's profile. An oddly shaped vessel with a very high stem, broad in the beam and broadest aft. One of the torch-bearers stood on the foredeck and when the wind fanned his flame, Hero glimpsed an eye painted on the bow and a name in Greek. *Planetes* – '*The Wanderer*'.

'Who are you?' a voice called. 'What happened?'

'Shipwrecked merchants,' Hero shouted. 'We were on our way from Kiev to Constantinople when our ship sank. We've been adrift for five days and our food and water are almost gone. There are women with us. For love of the Queen of Heaven, save us.'

The torches clumped together. From the mariners' gestures, it was clear that some of them were for leaving the castaways adrift.

'Let's take a closer look at you,' the voice called.

Four rough-looking men and a boy peered down from the deck as they came alongside. 'Who are those two?' the captain demanded, pointing at Vallon and Drogo.

'Soldiers on their way to join the Varangian Guard.'

'I'm not taking armed men on my ship. Hand over their weapons. You don't look like pirates, but you don't look like honest merchants either.'

When they surrendered their arms, the mariners pulled them aboard and led them forward past a hold containing a score of horses tethered in stalls. The ship was a battered tramp stinking of bilge-water and old cargoes of oil and fish. Her skipper was as ugly as sin, with an enormous hooked nose and hair like a bunch of dead serpents dangling from his bald pate. Bardas, he was called. He didn't know what to make of his passengers, but the sight of Caitlin holding Syth and stroking her hair seemed to stir in him some spirit of gruff compassion.

'Don't move from the bow. I'll bring you food as soon as I can.'

The crew retired to a sunken and roofed galley in the stern. In a little while the captain and two of his men returned with water and a stew of beans and some bread. Hero asked him where he was bound. They were five days out of Varna, Bardas said, carrying horses to the Greek garrison at Cherson on the Krym peninsula, a day's sail to the east.

'Will we find a ship to take us to Constantinople?'

Bardas shook his head. 'Not this side of Christmas. A few days before we sailed, a freighter from Trebizond arrived at the capital with its crew dying of plague. The authorities are placing all vessels from the east in a month's isolation at the mouth of the Bosporus. Nobody's voyaging to Constantinople unless they have to.'

Vallon laughed when Hero relayed the news. 'So the Russians did us a favour by deserting. Let's see if we can turn it to further advantage.' He stared towards the firelit galley. 'You said we had about twenty pounds of silver left.'

'More like fifteen.'

'Drogo, the horses you bought in Novgorod cost about two pounds each.'

'I was cheated. They weren't worth half that.'

Vallon stroked his mouth. 'You know what? We might reach our destination after all.'

549

'You mean, go on into Anatolia?' Hero said. 'There's no longer any point. The ransom hawks are dead.'

'It's not about the ransom. If we sail to Cherson, we could be stuck there for months. You've seen how the natives fleece us. By the time we reach Constantinople, we'll be lucky if we still have shirts on our backs. On the other hand ...' Vallon paused. 'We could reach the Emir Suleyman's camp within a fortnight if we persuaded Bardas to land us on the Anatolian coast.' Vallon looked around. 'I won't force anyone to join me against their will. Anyone who wants to go to Cherson, say so.'

Nobody spoke for some time. They were all weak and demoralised. At last Hero put up a hand. 'I'll come with you. I know it won't achieve anything except the satisfaction of reaching our goal. I'll do it for Richard's sake.'

Wayland looked at Syth. 'It will be a hard journey. We have to consider the child.'

'Wayland, I'm not going to give birth in the next month. If you want to go, just say so.'

'Are you sure?'

Syth rolled her eyes at Vallon. 'We're coming.'

'So am I,' said Caitlin.

Drogo's face set. 'Do I have a say?'

'No, you stay on the ship. I'll leave you with enough silver to keep body and soul together.'

With the die cast, Hero grew animated. 'How are we going to persuade Bardas to take us to Anatolia?'

'Wait for an opportunity to catch him on his own. Tell him I want to discuss a business proposition in private.'

Wayland looked dubious. 'They have our weapons. Once they know we're sitting on a pot of silver, what's to stop them cutting our throats?'

It must have been close to midnight when Hero got a chance to take the captain aside. The only other crewman on deck was the helmsman. Bardas eyed Hero suspiciously. 'I told you not to go wandering over my ship.'

'Can I have a word?' Hero gestured towards the helmsman. 'Not here.'

He led the way amidships, leaned on the gunwale and looked across the sea.

Bardas kept his distance. 'Well?'

'Come closer. I have something for you – a token of Lord Vallon's gratitude.'

Bardas approached. Hero slipped him a purse. 'It's English silver.'

Bardas palmed the purse under his tunic without looking at it. 'What's he want?'

'A business matter. He'll tell you himself.'

'What sort of business?'

Hero put a finger to his lips.

One of the crewmen had poked his head out. 'Hey, Captain. We're ready to eat.'

'Later,' said Bardas. He kept his eyes on Hero. 'I'll talk to him tomorrow.'

'It has to be tonight. Our situation is urgent. Help us and Vallon will reward you well.'

Bardas breathed heavily. 'I'm not walking into some hole-in-the-corner trickery. If your master wants to talk business, I'll bring my crew with me. I don't hide anything from them. They're all kin.'

'By all means invite them along. The problem is, that would mean letting them know how much money is involved.'

Bardas glanced towards the galley. 'Fetch the Frank here.'

'He'd rather discuss matters in the bow. Where the money is kept.'

Bardas whipped a knife out from somewhere and held it against Hero's throat. With his other hand he gripped Hero's arm and pushed him towards the bow. 'This had better be genuine.'

Vallon pretended not to see the knife. He rose to greet the captain and invited him to sit. Bardas shoved Hero forward and remained standing. 'What's this about?'

'Ask him about the horses,' said Vallon.

Hero nodded towards the hold. 'The horses. Are they broken?'

'That's what it says on the bill of lading.'

'Do you have saddles and tack for them?'

'What's it to you?'

'You'll find out. Let's keep it businesslike.'

'We've got saddles for about half of them.'

'Good. We want to buy six horses and trappings for five.'

'They're not mine to sell. I'm only the carrier. If you want them, bid for them in the market at Cherson.'

'We're not going to Cherson. That's why we must reach an agreement tonight.'

Bardas retreated a step. 'I knew you weren't merchants.'

'Who we are doesn't matter. How much would it take to persuade you to sell us six horses and land us on the coast of Anatolia?'

Bardas's eyes bolted towards the south. 'I'm not taking you to Anatolia. That's more than two hundred miles out of my way.'

'Show him,' Vallon said.

Wayland uncovered a cloth to reveal a hoard of slithering coins.

'It's yours,' said Hero, 'in return for six horses and a landing on the Anatolian coast. Drop us off and we'll never trouble you again. Easier than killing us, and it will sit lighter on your conscience.'

A crewman pulled himself out of the galley and began making his way forward. 'What's keeping you, skipper?'

'Cover it,' Bardas muttered before turning to the seaman. 'I'll be with you in a moment.'

The sailor tossed a hand and returned to the galley. Bardas stared at the pile of silver. 'How do I explain the loss of six horses? How do I explain why a six-day voyage has taken two weeks?'

'Horses die on every voyage. The sea imposes its own timetable. Your ship's old and leaky. Nobody would be surprised if you were delayed.'

'I'll still be held to account.'

'How much are you being paid for this voyage?'

Bardas didn't answer.

Hero spoke for him. 'Even if you have to pay for the horses, you'll make a good profit.'

'What do I tell my crew?'

'Whatever suits you.' Hero stirred the coins with his hand. 'Take half now. We'll hand over the rest when we reach Anatolia.'

'Which part of the coast are you making for?'

'Somewhere uninhabited. We're heading for Konya.'

'Konya's fallen to the Seljuks.'

'We know that.'

'Then why do you want to go there?'

'We're delivering a ransom for a Norman knight captured at

Manzikert.' Hero divided the silver into two roughly equal piles and covered one of them. 'Take it. Go on, take it.'

Bardas trembled. 'Keep a lookout.' He began scooping the pile into a bag held open by Wayland. When he'd finished, he was panting. 'I'll have to speak to my men.'

'Of course.'

Bardas returned to the galley and the company heard voices raised in debate.

'You've signed our death warrants,' said Drogo. 'That's what you've done.'

'We'll see,' said Vallon.

The argument went on for a long time before the crew emerged, armed with the castaways' weapons. The company rose to their feet.

'I told you,' said Drogo.

'Bardas,' Hero called. 'There's no need for swords.'

Vallon took Hero's arm, advanced towards the mariners and stopped in front of the skipper. 'You're a good man, Bardas. Not many captains would have stopped at night to rescue strangers.'

'He's been shipwrecked himself,' Hero said. 'He couldn't sail by and leave us to die.'

'Do we have a deal?

Bardas pulled a crucifix from the neck of his tunic and kissed it.

'He swears it on the cross.'

Bardas held out the crucifix. Vallon reached out and touched it. 'On the cross.'

At an order from Bardas, the crew began hauling on the shrouds and the helmsman strained at the rudder. The constellations overhead rotated until the bow was pointing at the Pleiades clustered to the south.

Anatolia

XLVI

They approached the shores of Anatolia in falling darkness. A range of forested hills smothered in cloud rose from the narrow coastal strip. Nearly fifty miles to the east a navigation beacon twinkled on the cape above Sinop. No other lights.

'You're sure this is the right place?' Vallon said.

Hero nodded. 'Bardas has put in here several times to pick up timber. He says this is where Jason and his Argonauts landed in their quest for the Golden Fleece. Xenophon passed through it on his march with the Ten Thousand. We're treading in the footsteps of gods and heroes.'

Vallon smiled. 'Let's keep it down to earth. How do we get through the mountains?'

'A track used by loggers leads up through the hills. We'll pass a few hamlets. If we ride all night, we should reach uninhabited country by dawn. We cross the range through a pass between two high peaks. After that we keep heading south.'

Vallon heard the slow surge and wash of waves breaking along the shore. He looked over his shoulder. 'Are the horses ready?'

'Saddling the last one,' Wayland answered from the hold.

Vallon saw Drogo's brooding figure standing amidships. 'Settle our account with Bardas,' he told Hero.

When he returned, the coast was close enough for Vallon to see surf foaming around headlands.

'All done,' Hero said. 'That's us almost cleared out.'

'I don't think silver will be much use to us where we're going.'

They entered a bay between two wooded promontories. Bardas waited until the last moment before striking the sail. *The Wanderer* slid on to the beach and Wayland and Syth ran up it to check that the coast was clear. The crew fitted a ramp from the hold to the foredeck. They coaxed the six horses up it, then the crew laid the ramp against the gunwale and Vallon and Hero led each horse down to the beach.

Syth ran back. 'Nobody's about. Wayland's found the track.'

Bardas bade them farewell, shaking each man's hand and blessing them. When he came to Syth, he took off his crucifix and placed it around her neck. 'It was my mother's,' he told her. 'I would have passed it on to my daughter if I'd been blessed with a girl child.' She kissed the ugly old seadog on his cheek and he touched the spot as if she'd bestowed a benison.

The crew pushed out the ship and climbed aboard.

'Mount up,' Vallon said.

The Wanderer was pulling away into the dark when they heard a heavy splash.

Hero turned and groaned. 'You know what that is, don't you?'

Vallon cursed and drew his sword. He dismounted and ran to the sea's edge, peering into the night.

'We can't let him come with us,' said Hero. 'He'll ruin whatever chance we have of freeing Walter.'

Drogo waded out of the sea and halted in front of them. Vallon raised his sword. 'I gave you a chance when you'd have granted none. Now you leave me no choice.'

Drogo stood with empty hands outstretched. 'Go on then. Kill me. What purpose will it serve? You don't have the ransom. Your efforts have been nothing but vanity and I want to be there to witness your humiliation.'

'Why should I give you that satisfaction?'

Drogo advanced within striking distance. 'I can't do you harm now, and you forget the good I did you. Without me and Fulk at your side, you wouldn't have reached Novgorod. If Fulk hadn't held off the Cumans, you'd have perished at the ford.'

Caitlin clutched Vallon's sleeve. 'Don't listen to him.'

Vallon unhanded her and gripped Drogo by his tunic. 'Let me tell you something. I undertook this expedition in a spirit of penitence. Don't sneer. I swore not to take life except when I and my company stood in dire danger. That's the only reason I didn't kill you back in Iceland.'

'Then I won't give you any reason to break your oath.'

Vallon shoved him away. 'Take the spare horse. Stay out of my sight.'

Vallon remounted and turned his back on the sea for the last time. Hero rode beside him. 'What will Walter think when we arrive at the Emir's camp with his hated step-brother?'

'I don't care what Walter thinks. I don't even know the man. Drogo's right. This venture has been nothing but vanity and delusion.'

'Even if it's for nothing, I'll still feel proud the day you lead us into Suleyman's court. Nobody has made such an epic journey as us.'

'It cost Richard and Raul their lives.'

'Richard never regretted his decision to join you. Nor do I.'

They had entered the forest. Vallon reached out and squeezed Hero's arm. 'That gives me some comfort.'

Hero leaned closer. 'And Drogo doesn't know about the lost gospel. Perhaps fortune still has a trick or two to play.'

Wayland led the way up through the trees. The horses' hooves jarred on the stony track and they hadn't gone far when a dog began to bark and a voice challenged them. Twice more they woke households. At one of them two watchdogs ran snarling out of the darkness and frightened the horses before Wayland drove them off. All night they climbed through evergreen oaks and sweet chestnuts. When dawn broke they could see no settlements and halted beside a stream in a limestone gorge.

After eating, they slept until noon and then continued upwards through pines softened by mist. The vapours thickened, swirling cold and grey from the summit. Pockets of snow appeared and the horses panted in the thinning air.

They emerged from the mist and saw the two peaks dazzling in a rift of clouds. They climbed towards the pass, the snow up to the horses' hocks. At the top of the snowfield a raptor with the silhouette of a giant falcon glided low and slow across their path, one wing almost brushing the snow. Its head shone gold in the sun and it looked at them with blood-red eyes set in a black and bearded mask, gazing with such intensity that each traveller felt as if he or she had been singled out for judgement.

They slogged over the pass, their shadows stretching long and thin in the shallow light. Beyond the watershed the range fell in thinly wooded spurs that ran out onto an arid upland plateau, a world of horizontals receding in a rosy bloom. Even as they watched, the sun's glow faded and the land chilled to a sullen grey. They led their horses down through cold shadows and were still above the snowline when it grew too dark to see. Wayland found a shelter under a ledge pitted with old hearths and strewn with ancient bones. The flames from their fire played on the walls, animating paintings of animals and hunters dead ten thousand years.

Next morning they completed their descent and set off across the plateau. They rode all day, always the same drab vista unfolding before them. Towards evening they came to the top of a scarp and spied the bat's-wing shapes of nomad tents scattered across the basin below. Dozens of them under a drift of smoke. They made a lengthy detour and bivouacked in a badlands gully. The company ate their rations and stared into the red core of the fire wherein the thoughts of wilderness travellers are forged.

'How much food have we got left?' Vallon asked Hero.

'Enough to scrape by for another day or two.'

'I've run out of food for the haggard,' Wayland said.

Vallon stirred the fire with a branch. 'We won't avoid the nomads for much longer. We'll give ourselves up at the next camp and ask them to send a messenger to the Emir.'

'They might kill us,' said Drogo.

'The Emir gave Cosmas some sort of safe conduct,' Vallon said to Hero. 'Do you still have it?'

'It's in my chest.'

'Keep it to hand.'

'Nomads can't read,' said Drogo.

'They'll recognise the Emir's seal.'

'What if they belong to a rival clan?'

Vallon pitched the branch into the fire. 'Drogo, why don't you shut up?'

Noon next day found them slouching up a glissade of shale towards a col, the horses making slow going on the loose rock. A vile wind blew grit into their faces so that they rode with eyes asquint and didn't see the mounted Seljuks rise up silent as cats until they were right beneath them. There were six – no, twice that number. And as the vagrants cast about, more of them appeared until a crescent of twenty horse soldiers blocked the path. They sat their horses with casual aplomb, lances held vertical, the pennants below the iron heads buzzing in the wind. All of them carried double-curved bows slung from their belts or laid across their saddles. For sidearms they wore swords or maces, and each man bore a circular wooden shield on his back.

'Nobody move.'

Hero scrabbled in his tunic while trying to keep his eye on the Seljuks. He found the safe conduct and held it up. 'From the Emir Suleyman,' he called in Arabic. 'Look, his *tughra*.'

Like oil separating on water, the Seljuk formation formed into two columns. They descended on their neat-stepping horses and closed in. Broad, hairless faces patinated with soot and lanolin. Quick agate eyes. They wore quilted wrapover topcoats divided below the waist, felt breeches tucked into high boots, conical hats with fur brims. Some were mantled in sheepskins against the cold.

One of them plucked the document from Hero's hand and passed it to an officer wearing a surcoat of patterned silk. He was barely out of his teens, his face as shiny as an apple. He studied the seal and held it out for his men to inspect.

They agreed that it was Suleyman's *tughra* and his name passed from lip to lip.

The young Seljuk captain addressed Hero in his guttural tongue.

'I don't understand your language,' Hero said. 'Do any of your men speak Arabic?'

The captain summoned a rider with features darker and sharper than those of his comrades. The man rode up to Hero. 'What do you want with his Excellency?'

Hero gave thanks for that 'Excellency'. It suggested that these Seljuks were in the Emir's service. 'We're travelling to his Excellency's headquarters to deliver a ransom for a soldier captured at Manzikert.'

That was a word they recognised. They grinned and nudged each other while the Arabic speaker translated for his captain. Then he turned back to Hero. 'What ransom have you brought?'

Wayland was holding the caged haggard on his saddle. Hero pointed at it. '*Shaheen*,' he said. 'Noble hawk.' He didn't know the Arabic for gyrfalcon.

The Seljuk captain drew his sword and lifted the drape off the cage with the point. The startled falcon thrashed and the captain recoiled. His men laughed. The captain laughed too before making a closer inspection. '*Sonqur*,' he told his men. '*Chagan sonqur*.'

He appraised the travellers anew, skating over the two women and finally settling on Vallon. His gaze took in the jewelled pommel of Vallon's sword and he raised his eyes and gave the merest tilt of his chin. Vallon nodded back. At a terse command the Seljuks formed up around the prisoners. Another command and they were off, two of the horse warriors galloping away over the col to carry the news of their capture ahead.

The Seljuks rode without rest and they were still riding long past dark, their prisoners reeling in the saddle. Snow began to fall. Vallon was beginning to wonder if they intended to ride blind through the night when from somewhere ahead a dog began to bark and a man's voice hailed them. Somehow the Seljuks had found a nomad camp. The captain ordered the company to dismount. While his men led their horses away, he ushered them into a wool tent. Groggy with cold and exhaustion, they took off their footwear and collapsed around the hearth.

In the background, three generations of nomads hurried about, preparing food. Most of the company were asleep where they sat when the tentholder attended by his family carried in a stew of chickpeas swimming in mutton fat. At Wayland's bidding, Hero told the Seljuk captain that the falcon hadn't eaten for two days. One of his men went out and returned carrying a live cockerel by its legs. Wayland wrung its neck and quartered it and took the haggard out of its cage and fed it. The Seljuks paid scrupulous attention, exchanging admiring comments. The mood grew relaxed. The captain told them that his name was Chinua, meaning 'Wolf', and that he'd fought at Manzikert and killed many Greeks. He asked his prisoners how they'd reached Anatolia and Hero managed to tell something of their tale, the Seljuks listening with great interest, embellishing the fragments they understood as if it were a story they'd heard at their grandparents' knee.

Some of the nomads were already astir when Vallon woke and went out into the night. The snow had ceased and a million stars swarmed in the blue-black sky. The air cut like a knife and his feet creaked on the frozen crust. He was halfway through a luxurious piss when a clutch of icy hummocks in front of him buckled like monster hatchlings and three camels lurched to their feet with plates of snow sliding off their flanks. Snow thatched their eyelashes and small icicles hung from their muzzles.

They were on their way again before dawn, riding up a wide river valley occupied by overwintering nomads. Two more days of this and they breasted a stony rim and saw vanishing over the horizon a milky blue lake rimmed with mineral flats of the purest white. *Tuz Gölü*, Chinua told them. The great Salt Lake. They camped on its eastern shore by an ancient tower and continued south next morning along the remains of a paved road built by the Romans. The lake had no outlet and the rivers that fed it seeped in from the south through a wild tract of reed beds and swamp. They rode on over a flat plain that ended in a sea of shadows beneath a mountain capped with two icy cones. The sun was throwing the slopes into relief when they turned west on a broad highway. They passed other travellers heading in both directions and as the last flush of pink faded on the twin peaks behind them, they clattered through the brick portal of a caravanserai on the Silk Road east of Konya.

They slept in a dormitory with other travellers and were back on the Konya road before dawn. Ten miles further on they left the highway, turning north on the plain along a river lined with poplars. They passed black hair tents and rode through flocks of fat-tailed sheep and shaggy goats guarded by dogs. The crystalline flats of Salt Lake were back in sight when Chinua rose in his saddle and pointed towards a tented city rising from the plain.

'Suleyman.'

Hero grinned at Vallon. 'Well, we made it.'

Watching the complex of pavilions and kiosks draw closer, Vallon had the sense of an impending collision. He'd been travelling so long that he'd forgotten that even the longest journey must end.

XLVII

Riders galloped out of the compound and exchanged a flurry of words with Chinua. The captain gave an order and before Wayland realised what was happening, four riders boxed him in. One took his horse's reins and steered it at a trot down a roadway between the tents. Looking back, he saw that the other Seljuks had separated Syth and

Caitlin from the men. His escort led him to a central arena occupied by half a dozen marquees, some of them linked by tented walkways to a huge golden-yellow pavilion. They passed it and crossed a training ground where a group of horsemen tilting at a dummy broke off to watch him pass. On the other side Wayland's escort pulled up outside a large felt tent and ordered him to get down.

He dismounted with the caged falcon. One of the soldiers pulled aside the entrance to the yurt and motioned at him to enter. Three men stood at the far end and he saw that the tent was a mews and workshop. The men watched without expression as he approached. The central figure had a wispy moustache and calm, hooded eyes. He could have been any age from fifty to seventy. The other two were much younger. Along one wall was a series of booths, each occupied by a pale falcon on a padded block. Wayland studied them in passing. They weren't much smaller than the gyr, but they were more rakish in build, softer of feather, with shorter toes.

The hawkmaster noticed his interest. '*Saqr*,' he said.

'Saker,' said Wayland. He'd heard falconers speak of them.

At the hawkmaster's bidding he placed the cage on a table cluttered with hawking paraphernalia. He removed the drape and pulled on his glove.

The two assistants frowned. '*Tch!*'

He glanced up. 'What's wrong?'

The hawkmaster motioned him to get on with it. The falcon stepped on to his fist as soon as he reached into the cage. He lifted her out and the assistants sucked in their breath. The hawkmaster narrowed his eyes. Then he said something. One of his assistants went to a shelf lined with what looked to Wayland like upside-down leather purses embroidered with gold. The assistant selected two of these objects and offered them to the hawkmaster. Wayland saw that they had drawstrings around the opening and tassels on top. The hawkmaster made his choice and approached the falcon. Holding the purse with the mouth uppermost, he raised it towards the falcon's head. Her feathers tightened, but before she could bate, the hawkmaster popped it over her head in one smooth movement. Another deft move and he'd tightened the brace. Only then did Wayland realise that the purse was a hood. He'd never seen one before or even heard of such a thing. Noticing his surprise, the hawkmaster looked at him enquiringly.

Wayland shook his head and mimed the act of stitching the falcon's eyelids. The Seljuks shrugged at the infidel's ignorance.

With the falcon hooded and leashed, the hawkmaster slipped a leather cuff over his right wrist. To Wayland that seemed awkward, but it explained the Seljuks' disapproval when he'd picked up the falcon with his left hand. The hawkmaster brought his cuffed hand up behind the gyrfalcon's legs. She stepped back onto it and only a slight tension in her stance showed that she was aware of a different handler. The hawkmaster palped her flight muscles, assessed the amount of flesh on her keel, pinched her thighs. He passed the falcon to each assistant in turn so that they could make their own assessment. The youngest handled her last and when he felt her weight he gave an exaggerated gasp and dropped his fist as though he could hardly support her.

Wayland grinned. 'She's a powerful bird, isn't she?'

The hawkmaster flapped a limp hand and buried his fist in a silk cushion, indicating that the falcon's muscles were soft and flabby.

He said something and one of his assistants came up behind the falcon holding a silk cloth in both hands. He seized the falcon around her shoulders, lifted her off the fist and held her belly down on the cushion. She struggled for a moment, wailing pathetically, and then she lay still. The hawkmaster fanned out each wing in turn. Wayland winced. All her primaries were broken and jagged, the webbing limed with droppings that had set as hard as mortar. Her train was in the same sorry state. Wayland tried to explain that on such a long journey, with the falcon cooped up in a cage, it had been impossible to keep her in good feather. The hawkmaster responded at some length, mentioning the Emir more than once. From the way he shook his head, Wayland understood that he couldn't present the falcon to Suleyman in her present deplorable condition.

The assistant lifted her clear of the cushion. The hawkmaster gripped her legs and examined her feet for signs of bumblefoot. The undersides were clear of lesions or inflammation, the dimpled and pleated soles curiously reminiscent of a baby's palm. Then he opened her beak to check that her mouth was free of frounce or other infections.

One of his assistants had placed a small bronze mortar over a charcoal brazier. While it was heating, he went through pots containing moulted flight feathers, choosing the palest. He brought his selection to the table and laid out about two score wooden needles of triangular section. Wayland knew that the Seljuks were going to imp the falcon's broken feathers.

At a word from the hawkmaster, his assistant spread out the falcon's left wing on a board. The hawkmaster picked up a knife, honed the blade on a leather strop and cut the innermost primary well below the broken shaft. He sorted through the moulted feathers, selected one, compared it with the broken one, rejected it, picked another and did another match. When he was satisfied he cut it to length. The other assistant had melted resin in the mortar. The hawkmaster took an imping needle, dipped one end in the resin, inserted it into the replacement feather, dipped the other end and pushed it into the hollow shaft of the primary. He waited a few seconds, then pulled. The grafted section held. The repaired feather corresponded to the primary's original length and was so carefully matched and aligned that only close examination would have revealed the join.

Feather by feather, the hawkmaster restored the falcon's left wing. Although she submitted calmly enough, Wayland was worried that such a lengthy operation might overtax her. He himself felt faint and queasy from the heated atmosphere. The hawkmaster noticed him wiping his brow and ordered one of his men to bring him a drink.

The ice-cold liquor was sweet and sour, soothing and refreshing. Wayland handed back the bowl with thanks. The hawkmaster, pausing in his work, mimed the fact that Wayland was tired.

'Very tired.'

The hawkmaster made it clear that the job would take a long time and that Wayland should get some rest. He wouldn't take no for an answer and one of his assistants led Wayland to a couch covered with a kilim and gently pushed him down. He sat watching the Seljuks working quietly at the table.

'Ibrahim,' said the hawkmaster.

Wayland looked up.

The hawkmaster pointed at himself. 'Ibrahim.'

'Wayland.'

'Wellund.'

Black fog began to cloud his vision. The figures at the table seemed to recede down a tunnel. The next thing he knew, someone was tugging him out of sleep.

It was almost dark in the tent and for a moment he didn't know where he was. One of the assistants was offering him a hot drink. He remembered the falcon and saw that the table was empty. The hawkmaster emerged from the shadows and pointed towards one of the hawk pens. The falcon sat hooded on a block, illuminated by a single lamp. Wayland tottered to his feet and went over. The Seljuks had repaired every single flight feather and coped her talons and beak so that she looked almost as perfect as the day he'd first set eyes on her. As Wayland began to thank the falconers, a wave of emotion swamped him and he wept.

The Seljuks turned away to hide their embarrassment and when he'd regained control the hawkmaster encouraged him to drink. The cup contained a spicy infusion that cleared his head and warmed his stomach. He realised that night had fallen and that he must have slept since noon. One of the assistants brought him a basin and a ewer of hot water. The clothes he'd bought for Lord Vasili's feast lay clean on his bed and the hawkmaster indicated that he must change into them for his audience with the Emir. They left him to his toilet. The clothes he discarded were so stiff with filth that they stood up on their own. He washed his hands and face and combed his tangled hair. While he was dressing, a Seljuk put his head through the entrance and announced that the Emir had summoned them. The hawkmaster waved him away.

He studied Wayland and decided that he'd pass muster. Then he walked over to the hooded falcon and bent to pick her up. He untied her leash and was reaching out for her when he had a change of mind. Slipping off his glove, he slid it onto Wayland's hand.

'Thank you,' said Wayland. 'We've come a long way together.'

Hero stood with Vallon and Drogo in the Emir's throne room, a spacious and richly carpeted chamber at the centre of the golden pavilion. A line of guards faced them. More guards stood behind them. A dozen braziers and a hundred oil lamps fogged the atmosphere. Timpani rolled and a trumpet blew. The guards pulled themselves to attention. Out from one of the chamber's two entrances strode an officer followed by half a dozen officials wearing high pointed hats and silk gowns with dangling sleeves. They took up positions behind the throne. The roll of drums drew nearer.

'Prostrate yourselves,' said one of the officials in Arabic.

With his forehead on the carpeted floor, Hero caught a glimpse of the Emir's entrance. A small spare man with the bandy legs of someone who'd spent most of his life in the saddle. Almond eyes and a thin moustache. Like a lynx.

Suleyman seated himself cross-legged on a cushioned dais under a silk canopy.

'You may stand,' said the official.

Hero's joints creaked as he climbed upright. A retainer held out a tray to the Emir. Suleyman took from it a bulb of raw garlic and began eating it, peeling each clove and dropping the skins into a dish held by another retainer. One of his officials spoke into his ear. He smiled – or seemed to smile. Hero couldn't fathom what was going on behind those feline eyes.

The silk canopy rippled in a draught. The Seljuks leaned, looking at something behind Hero. He risked a glance and saw an elderly man guiding Wayland forward, whispering instructions. The falconer carried the haggard on his right hand and seemed apprehensive. When he saw Hero he mouthed a question: 'Is Syth all right?'

'She's fine,' Hero whispered from behind his hand. 'She's in the women's quarters with Caitlin. Kneel and bow before the Emir, touching your forehead to the ground.'

When Wayland had made his awkward obeisance, the Arabic-speaking official stepped forward. He was a fleshy individual attired in sumptuous silks, adorned with expensive jewellery and wearing an air of massive self-importance.

'I am Faruq al-Hasan-al-Baghdadi, Chief Secretary to his Excellency.' He pointed a hand winking with jewels in Hero's direction. 'Step forward.'

Oddly enough, Hero felt less nervous than he had when delivering the ransom terms to Count Olbec. He bowed to the Emir. 'Peace to you, Lord. Your Excellency's health is good by the grace of God?'

Faruq translated Suleyman's languid wave. 'His Eminence is strong in body and keen of mind, thanks be to almighty God. Be so good as to address your answers to me. Now then, state your purpose in coming here.'

Suleyman already knew. Hero decided that this audience served only to satisfy the Emir's curiosity or reveal the character of his guests. He chose his words with care. 'His Excellency will remember his generous dealings with Cosmas, the Greek traveller who undertook to raise a ransom for Sir Walter, one of his Excellency's prisoners captured during the Seljuks' great victory at Manzikert. Alas, Cosmas died soon after reaching Italy, charging me with his last breath to continue the mission. I was too young and weak to complete the task, but providence led me to this man here, Vallon, who agreed to help me reach our goal. Under his brave leadership, we travelled to the wildest corners of the world to obtain the white falcons desired by his Excellency.'

The Emir pulled Faruq's sleeve and spoke into his ear. Faruq nodded and turned towards Hero. 'Are the Frank and the Norman prisoner former comrades in arms?'

Hero hesitated. 'No. They've never met.'

'Then why did he embark on this undertaking?'

Vallon had learned enough Arabic in Spain to be able to follow the exchanges. 'Tell him I did it for money. Keep it simple or we'll be here all night.'

The Emir mulled over this reply and Faruq voiced his concerns. 'His Excellency is puzzled that your expedition was commanded not by the prisoner's brother, but by a mercenary who has never laid eyes on Walter. Furthermore, his Excellency cannot help observing that while the Frankish captain's bearing suggests a man at ease with himself, Walter's brother seems to have drunk from the cup of bitter sorrow.'

'The two captains are men of different temperaments. Drogo's melancholy is caused by deep concern over his brother's fate. He's—'

Vallon cut him off. 'Don't lie. They'll find you out and it will count against us.'

Hero nodded. He was sweating. He took a breath and gave a neutral response. 'We've been travelling for more than a year. During that time we've received no news from civilised lands. Cosmas assured me his Excellency treated Sir Walter generously. Can I assume that under the Emir's protection, he still lives?'

'No harm has come to him.'

'Has he been told of our arrival?'

'No.'

'When will we be allowed to see him?'

'That's for his Excellency to decide. It's disrespectful to ask so many questions. The details of your journey can wait. Tell the young man with the yellow hair to show his Excellency the falcon.'

Hero sat down with relief. Wayland's escort led him forward and turned him this way and that so that the Emir could study the gyrfalcon from every angle. He ordered the hawkmaster to unhood her. She gripped the glove and fanned her wings, creating a draught that extinguished a dozen lamps and made the silk hangings billow. The hawkmaster slipped her hood back on and transferred her to the Emir. Suleyman held her up with a grin and spoke with animation to his entourage. At last he passed the falcon back and his features settled into immobility. Faruq straightened.

'Where are the other falcons?'

'Alas, they died. We left the northlands with eight. It was a long and dreadful journey and one by one they sickened.'

'The ransom stipulated two casts.'

'And that's what we intended to deliver. It's a matter of deep regret that we were unable to satisfy the terms to the letter. Perhaps his Excellency will view the deficiency less harshly when he learns that the falcon has been brought at the cost of men's lives. Of the original company who set out on the quest, three are dead, including my dearest friend, Sir Walter's youngest brother. We have faced great perils. Many times we considered giving up. Instead, we stayed true to our task, confident that his Excellency would reward our efforts with magnanimity.'

Ash rustled in a brazier. Suleyman picked his teeth. He held out his cupped hands. One of his attendants filled them with water from a bronze aquamanile cast in the form of a lion. The Emir rinsed his hands and the attendant towelled them dry.

'His Excellency will consider what you have said and deliver his judgement tomorrow.'

XLVIII

Permission to call on Sir Walter arrived next afternoon. Vallon left with Hero and Wayland. He'd insisted on Drogo being housed in separate accommodation and had no intention of allowing him to confront his brother at this stage.

ABOUT THE AUTHOR

Robert Lyndon has been a falconer since boyhood. A keen student of history, he was intrigued by accounts of hawks being used as ransoms during the Middle Ages. Some of the scenes in *Hawk Quest* were inspired by Lyndon's own experiences as a falconer, climber and traveller in remote places.

ACKNOWLEDGEMENTS

My agent Anthony Goff encouraged and guided me from start to finish. My thanks to him and the foreign rights team at David Higham Associates.

I should also like to thank my editor, Daniel Mallory, my copy-editor Iain Hunt, and all the other team members at Little, Brown who steered *Hawk Quest* to publication.

Fellow-falconer Neil Johnstone and good friend Mike Newth kindly read the book in typescript and picked up some silly blunders. All remaining errors are my own.

Consultant haematologist Dan Thompson checked my descriptions of medieval surgery. He pointed out that Hero seems to have anticipated Germ Theory by eight centuries. It's true that the germ theory of disease was scientifically proved only in the nineteenth century, but the Roman writer Marcus Terentius Varro warned of disease-carrying 'minute creatures, invisible to the eye' as early as 36 BC.

I'm grateful to Bill Massey for more than I can say. Writing this book brought back happy memories of autumn days hawking with Bill and Neil on Scottish grouse moors.

My wife Deborah supplied the Latin and Greek and much else besides. *Hawk Quest* is dedicated to her and to our daughter Lily, with love.

Two Seljuk escorts led the way. 'When are you going to tell Walter about Drogo?' Hero asked.

'I'll pick my moment.'

'He's bound to suspect a double-cross.'

'I know. I should have killed Drogo the night we landed, but without him and Fulk we wouldn't be here. It's hard to slay in cold blood a man who's fought at your side and lost a close companion.'

The escorts marched ahead to a small pavilion on the other side of the encampment. One of them shouted through the door flap in Turkic. A voice answered in the same language. The Seljuks called again and the entrance opened and a slender young man wearing eye shadow hurried out covering his face. '*Tch!*' the escorts said. One of them smacked the youth across the head and gave him a tongue-lashing as he hurried off. Vallon stared ahead with his mouth slightly pursed.

The escorts pushed the callers into the tent. Vallon entered the carpeted interior first, Wayland lagging behind Hero. Walter lolled on a divan, dressed in a loose Persian gown, a flask of wine and two empty cups beside him on a large brass tray. His puzzled expression showed that he had no idea who they were. He rose, looking from one to the other. He appeared much as Vallon had envisaged – tall and broad of shoulder with wavy yellow hair and a square jaw deeply cleft. Perhaps a suggestion of jowliness, a slight bagginess beneath the eyes. His smile revealed perfect white teeth.

'You have the advantage of me. Are you diplomats? Have you arrived on a mission from Constantinople?'

'I'm Vallon, a Frankish soldier of fortune. This is Hero, a Greek scholar. You already know—'

But Walter had recognised the figure standing inside the entrance. 'Wayland? My God, I don't believe it.' He strode forward and placed his hands on Wayland's shoulders. 'It really is you. How tall you've grown. How serious you look.' He turned to Vallon. 'My head's spinning. Does this have anything to do with the ransom?'

'Yes. It would take a day to tell the whole story.'

'Master Cosmas?'

'Dead. He tried to raise your ransom in Constantinople. When that failed, he set off for England with Hero. I met them in the Alps as Cosmas lay dying and I agreed to continue the journey. We reached your home in February. Your mother pawned her lands in Normandy to raise funds for your release. We've been making our way here ever since.'

Walter opened his mouth, but too many thoughts and conjectures got in the way of speech. 'I'm neglecting your comfort. Please sit. Let me order you some wine.' He went to the entrance and shouted. As he returned, he ran a hand over Wayland's back and his smile flashed. 'Dear Wayland. All this way for love of your master.'

Vallon and Hero perched on the edge of the divan. 'Before you ask,' said Vallon, 'I travelled here with the intention of claiming the reward you promised to Cosmas.'

'The Gospel of Thomas and the letter from Prester John,' Hero said.

Walter glanced towards the entrance. 'Where's that servant?'

Vallon slid one of the cups on the tray. 'We interrupted at a delicate moment. He probably didn't want to disturb you while you were entertaining company.'

Walter's smile froze. 'I'll serve you myself.'

He fetched clean cups. His hand shook as he poured.

'The gospel and letter,' Hero repeated. 'Do you still have them?'

'They're safe,' Walter said, handing them their wine. 'Not here.' He raised his cup. 'So my mother raised the ransom money?'

'Part of it.'

Walter drained most of his cup in one draught. 'I wouldn't have thought that my mother's estate would raise a quarter of the sum Suleyman demanded.'

'We're not redeeming you in gold. The Emir specified an alternative. Two casts of white gyrfalcons. We've spent the best part of a year on that chase.'

'And you have them?'

'We have one – one falcon that is.'

'Only one?'

'The rest died.'

'What does Suleyman say?'

'He'll announce his decision this evening.'

Walter set down his cup and grimaced. 'This is awkward. Worse than awkward. If the ransom specified four falcons, he won't settle for less.'

'I'm sorry to hear that. Wayland tended the falcons with the utmost diligence.'

Walter kept his smile, just. 'You know, Vallon, it might have been better for me if you'd never come.'

Vallon regarded him with bleak intensity.

Walter looked away. 'A mercenary, you said. Perhaps you'd care to tell me more about what set you on this course.'

'The gospel and the letter. We can discuss my motives at length another time. For now, it's more important that you tell us what sort of man Suleyman is.'

Walter picked up the flask and held it out. Vallon covered his cup. Walter refilled his own and settled back into the cushions. 'He's the son of Kutalmish, a cousin of Alp Arslan and a former contender for the Seljuk empire. When Kutalmish died, Suleyman and his three brothers were branded traitors and forced to flee for their lives into the Taurus mountains. Alp Arslan sent expeditions against them and succeeded in killing all the brothers except Suleyman. When he left the mountains, it was as commander of all the Turkmen in southern Anatolia.' Walter took a draught. 'That tells you all you need to know about Suleyman's character.'

'Why did the Sultan reward him with the title of Emir?'

'He had little choice. Suleyman's army is too powerful for Alp Arslan to crush. Besides, it suits the Sultan to have a strong Seljuk force in western Anatolia. Suleyman's territories are a buffer against the Byzantines, and the Sultan knows that the Emir won't attack him in Persia because that would mean leaving his own lands exposed.'

'So Suleyman covets the Seljuk throne.'

'He's more interested in consolidating his position in Anatolia. Since Manzikert, he's been exploiting the power struggle in Constantinople, allying himself first with this faction, then with that one. Don't be fooled by his coarse manners. Suleyman's as shrewd as they come.'

'You don't sound too concerned about your own situation.'

'As you can see, it isn't an uncomfortable one. I'm a valued member of the Emir's war council. He's convinced that Christendom will wage a crusade against Islam, striking first at the pilgrim routes now controlled by Suleyman. He looks to me for advice on military strategy, particularly the use of heavy cavalry. I'm also active in his negotiations with the Byzantines.'

'So you've changed sides.'

That touched a nerve. Walter thrust forward, spilling his wine. 'The Byzantines are on no one's side, not even their own. The Emperor Romanus lost Manzikert because of treachery within his own ranks. The Sultan released him with full honours in exchange for a peace treaty and a marriage alliance. And what did the Byzantines do? They dug out his eyes and drove him into the wilderness with his head full of rot. When the Sultan heard of his murder, he declared the treaty void.'

Vallon hadn't touched his wine. 'Have you petitioned the Emir for your freedom?'

'No.'

'And if you did?'

Walter considered. 'I think he'd grant my request.'

'Why haven't you asked to be released?'

Walter turned the cup in his hands. 'The truth is, I find the life to my liking. I drink wine instead of sour ale, eat grapes and peaches in winter, wear silks and brocades. I earn a handsome commission from my dealings with the Byzantines. I've no burning desire to return to that cold castle in the north and spend the rest of my life skirmishing against savages. When I inherit on my father's death will be soon enough.'

'Have you been in touch with your family?'

'I sent letters this spring. I haven't received a reply yet. The only news I've heard from England is that my half-brother Drogo was killed campaigning in Scotland.'

Vallon put down his cup. 'Your parents are much as you left them. Your half-brother Richard is dead. He joined us on the expedition and died of an arrow wound at the mouth of the Dnieper.'

'Richard? Richard was in your company?'

'A much-loved and much-mourned companion.'

'I'm distressed to hear that. Poor Richard. I always suspected that he would never reach manhood. Whatever possessed you to take such a weakling with you?'

'He volunteered. He was desperate to get away from your family.' Vallon stood, ignoring Hero's signals to remain.

Walter rose. 'Leaving so soon?'

'We'll meet again tonight before the Emir.'

Walter stepped forward. 'Wayland. Don't you go.'

Everybody stopped.

Walter threw his arm around Wayland's shoulder. 'Remember the hunts we enjoyed together? They were nothing compared to the sport we'll share in Anatolia. Bears, lions, leopards – creatures you've never even seen.'

Vallon noticed how strained Wayland looked. 'Do you want to stay?'

Wayland shook his head.

Vallon took his elbow. 'Come on then.'

Walter gripped Wayland's other arm. 'You don't have any say in the matter.' He was still smiling. 'Wayland's my personal property, affirmed by legal process. You probably heard how I found him starving in the forest and took him into my household.'

'Norman law carries no weight in these parts. If Wayland wants to rejoin your service, I won't stand in his way. He can answer in his own words.'

'Is that a joke? The boy's dumb.'

'I'm not your slave,' Wayland said. 'I serve Vallon as a free man.'

'That seems clear enough,' said Vallon.

He led the way out. Walter caught up with them. 'Not so fast, Vallon. How much did my mother raise on her estate?'

Vallon kept walking. 'A hundred and twenty pounds.'

'It must be worth at least twice that.'

'It was all the moneylender was prepared to advance. I've got the papers.'

'How much is left?'

'Nothing. It's all gone.'

'You've spent more than a hundred pounds of my mother's money and all you have to show for it is one gyrfalcon?'

'The price was much higher than that.'

'How much have you kept for yourself?'

Vallon halted. 'Not a penny.'

Walter only just stopped himself from poking Vallon in the chest. 'Coming from a mercenary, I find that hard to believe. I expect a full accounting.'

Vallon looked at Walter's outstretched finger. 'One thing I have to add. You were misinformed about your brother's death. He's here, lodged in the Emir's camp.'

Walter's face went blank. 'You told me that Richard died on the Dnieper.'

'I'm talking about Drogo.'

The blood drained from Walter's cheeks. 'Drogo was killed in Scotland.'

'He travelled north, that much is true. But only in pursuit of us and with the aim of wrecking our attempt to win your freedom. I know it casts a bleak light on our enterprise, but when I explain the circumstances that led to—'

'Say no more.' Walter backed away, pointing. 'You swagger into my quarters claiming that you've come to redeem me, and in the next breath you casually admit that you've brought Drogo.'

'Sir Walter, let me explain.'

'There's only one explanation. The moment I looked into your cold eyes, I knew I faced an enemy.'

Hero forced himself in front of Vallon. 'Let me speak. Sir Walter, the very fact that Drogo is here argues our good intentions. If we meant you harm, do you think we would have willingly brought along your worst enemy? Give me leave to explain how we were saddled with his company.'

But the old sibling rivalry had tapped into a part of Walter's brain immune to reason. A strangled sound escaped from his throat. 'I don't know what plot you and Drogo have hatched, but I warn you not to trifle with me. The Emir holds me dear. When I tell him you came here with murder in your hearts, you'll find his reaction cruelly disappointing.'

On the walk back to their lodgings, Vallon saw Hero darting glances of reproach.

'You think I handled the encounter badly.'

'Dismally. Why couldn't you have been more diplomatic?'

'It wouldn't have made any difference.' Vallon looked back, shaking his head. 'The ingrate didn't even thank us for our efforts.' He stalked on through the camp. 'God help me, I almost prefer Drogo.'

Hero hurried to keep pace. 'We'll never see the lost gospel now.'

'We lost our chance when the ransom hawks died. One thing Walter said was true, and I didn't need him to confirm it. I saw it at last night's audience. The Emir isn't a man who'll soften his terms.'

They entered their quarters and Vallon fell onto his bed, covering his eyes with his forearm. Hero wandered about in a pall of misery.

The entrance flap parted and Drogo looked in, wearing a smile from the gallows. 'Well, how did you find him?'

Vallon breathed deep. 'Less charming than his reputation had me believe. To think that Richard and Raul sacrificed their lives for that vain wretch. And here's what makes the pill even harder to swallow. It seems that Walter's free to leave whenever he pleases. Or he was. Our arrival without the full ransom only complicates the situation and makes him resentful rather than grateful.'

Drogo laughed. 'How did he react to the news of my presence?'

'With fear, rage, blind hatred. He's not without influence in the Emir's court. If I were you, I wouldn't walk alone at night and I'd employ someone to taste my food before eating it.'

Drogo looked down on Vallon with something close to pity. 'You should have listened to me. You wouldn't have grasped the challenge so eagerly if you'd known what kind of man my brother was.'

Vallon uncovered his eyes. 'If we knew the outcome of our actions before we committed to them, we wouldn't get up in the morning.'

Prayers mingled with smoke as the company made their way to the Emir's pavilion. Stars streamed across the plateau in a misty arch and a splinter of moon hung between the icy cones to the south. The throne room was packed. The Emir must have decided to make the occasion a public demonstration of his judicial wisdom. He carried a ceremonial mace and sat aloof, picking his nose, while the infidels abased themselves. Faruq ordered them to stand.

'Certain new facts have reached his Excellency. He's asked me to examine them.'

Vallon could guess who'd brought them to the Emir's attention. Walter stood to one side of Suleyman's counsellors watching Drogo with a stare you could have strung beads on.

'I'll deal with this,' Vallon told Hero. He bowed to Suleyman before addressing Faruq. 'Excuse my poor Arabic. What little I have I picked up while I was a prisoner of the Moors in Spain.'

Murmurs rippled through the crowd and those at the back stood on tiptoe to get a better view.

Faruq hushed the chamber. He didn't speak until the loudest sound was the guttering of the oil lamps. 'Here is the first difficulty. You say that you came here to rescue Walter.'

'There was no other motive.'

'Yet you brought with you his step-brother, a man who nurses hatred for Walter.'

'Drogo's presence wasn't part of my plans. The very opposite. He tried to thwart our efforts at every turn. When we escaped from England he was so determined to stop us that he followed us to Iceland.'

'Where you had him at your mercy.' Faruq pointed at Drogo. 'Yet look. Here he is.'

'He's a hard man to get rid of.'

'You could have killed him.'

'I could, but if I had, we wouldn't have completed our journey.'

The interpreter cupped his chin. 'Oh, yes?'

'Drogo fought bravely with me against the Vikings and Cumans. After standing shoulder to shoulder with a man in battle, it's hard to dispose of him.' Vallon glanced at Suleyman. 'It is for me, anyway.'

Faruq began to pace, enjoying his role of prosecutor. 'So, you allowed Drogo to live.' He smiled at the audience and they responded with sceptical shakes of the head. He whirled and shot out an accusatory hand. 'Do you deny that you used the moneys entrusted to you by Walter's mother to line your own pocket?'

'Every penny was spent on the enterprise. We kept accounts. Examine them if you wish.'

'But you're a mercenary who undertook the enterprise for personal gain.'

'I hoped we would profit from trade. Unfortunately, our expenses exceeded our costs. It's all in our accounts.'

'Accounts you kept yourself. How much is Drogo paying you?'

'Drogo doesn't have any money. He's only here by my charity.'

'I don't believe you. Walter doesn't believe you.'

Vallon felt as if he were sinking in a mire. 'Believe what you like. It's the Emir's decision that counts, and I'll bow to his judgement.'

Faruq glanced at Suleyman before striking another judicial pose.

'This is what I think. You travelled here with Drogo for the purpose of releasing Walter only so that you could kill him. With Walter dead, Drogo would inherit his father's title and estate. In return he would reward you with gold.'

Vallon's answer came out as a snarl. 'If I wanted to get my hands on Walter, I wouldn't have arrived with only one quarter of the ransom.'

'Stay calm,' Hero whispered.

Vallon nodded and faced Faruq. 'Examine the bare facts rather than dig for ulterior motives. Interrogate us separately if you wish. We travelled here from the grim north and in the course of that journey we lost many men and all the falcons but one. His Excellency has inspected the haggard and I know that with all the powers and forces at his command, he couldn't obtain one half so beautiful. Does it satisfy the conditions or not?'

Faruq and Suleyman engaged in close debate, the audience straining to interpret the outcome. At last the Emir waved Faruq aside and began deliberating. He expounded for a long time, swaying on his throne and using both hands to indicate how painstakingly he'd weighed the merits or otherwise of their case. The audience nodded as he made each point. Finally the Emir lowered his mace and Faruq stepped forward to deliver judgement.

'His Excellency has heard with interest the story of your labours. He commends you on your perseverance, offers his condolences for the deaths of your companions. The falcon you have brought him is a bird of rare beauty and promise. Nevertheless, it doesn't satisfy the terms of the contract. The problem is this. His Excellency asked you to bring him four falcons. You have delivered only one.' Faruq pressed a finger to his lips. 'Now, in all his dealings his Excellency is a man of his word. If he undertakes to grant one of his captains two horses, two horses is what he will give the man. Likewise, if a captain pledges ten archers for a campaign, ten archers is what his Excellency expects to receive. There can be no exceptions. How could it be otherwise? If today his Excellency were to ignore the deficit in your ransom, tomorrow his followers would expect him to demonstrate the same leniency towards themselves. They would say, look at the forbearance with which our lord treated those infidels. How much more generously will he overlook the shortcomings of his own people.'

579

'Sir Walter told me that his Excellency would have given him his freedom, ransom or no ransom.'

Suleyman darted a poisonous look at the Norman.

'Sir Walter presumes too much,' said Faruq. 'What is in his Excellency's power to give is also in his power to withhold.'

'If he's decided to keep Sir Walter a prisoner, I have nothing more to say. My task is finished and my interest in these proceedings is exhausted.'

'The proceedings are finished when the Emir says so.'

Vallon shrugged.

Faruq approached him with an expression of contrived friendliness. 'His Excellency is intrigued to learn that you were a prisoner of the Moors. Presumably you bought your release with a ransom. Yes?'

'No. A ransom was promised but never delivered. After eighteen months of degrading captivity, I killed my guard and escaped.' Vallon looked at the Emir. 'It was because I'd been a prisoner myself that I felt a degree of empathy with Sir Walter.'

Suleyman ignored Walter's attempt to attract his attention. He stroked his moustache and studied Vallon and then summoned Faruq and murmured into his ear. When the interpreter addressed Vallon again his tone was as soft as balm.

'There is a way to resolve the difficulty to everyone's satisfaction.'

Vallon saw Walter grin and nudge one of his companions. Whatever cat-and-mouse game the Emir was playing, Walter was part of it. Possibly the instigator.

Faruq walked away. 'You brought with you two things that exceed even the falcon in beauty. I refer to the women.'

Vallon's cheeks grew hot. 'The women aren't chattels.'

Faruq pretended he hadn't heard. 'The captain who escorted you here wishes to take for his wife the girl with the sun in her hair and the moon in her eyes.'

'Syth is betrothed to Wayland and is carrying his child.'

Wayland stiffened. 'You mentioned Syth's name.'

Vallon shook his head. 'Later.'

The Emir gave an airy wave when he heard of Syth's condition. 'Very well,' said Faruq. 'His Excellency will not separate a man from his wife. He'll say no more on the subject.'

'It's all right,' Vallon told Wayland.

'What's all right? What's going on?'

Vallon hushed him as Faruq began speaking again.

'His Excellency understands that there is no such claim on the Varangian woman called Caitlin. The Greek youth who speaks such good Arabic told us that her family is dead and that she's alone in the world. His Excellency takes pity on her and pledges to place her under his personal protection. Agree to this and the Emir will discharge all other claims. He will release Walter, if that's what he wants, and you'll be free to continue on your way. Separate ways.'

It occurred to Vallon that the Emir had wanted Caitlin from the start and that all the posturing was directed to that end.

Drogo tugged his elbow. 'What's he saying about Caitlin?'

Vallon took one pace forward. The audience craned.

'Hero is misinformed about my relationship with the Icelandic woman. The truth is, I sealed a union with Caitlin in Novgorod.'

'You're betrothed?'

'We're lovers.'

Hero gasped. A moan rose from the audience. Their Emir had been humiliated in public. Suleyman's face set in a scowl. He said something to Walter that made the Norman wince.

'Once again we have two stories,' Faruq said. 'One from the Greek and one from you. Where lies the truth? Be warned. His Excellency will find it.'

Suleyman shielded his mouth and held muttered discussions with his counsellors. Vallon's company all spoke at once, Drogo demanding to know why Suleyman had mentioned Caitlin and Hero apologising for creating the awful misunderstanding. Out of the clamour it was Wayland who made himself heard.

'Ask him why he needs two casts of gyrfalcons.'

'Because that's what he demanded. Forget it. This is no longer about the falcons.'

'No, I mean what practical purpose do four falcons serve? Ask him. Go on.'

Vallon put the question wearily and passed on Faruq's blunt reply. 'He says that one falcon can't catch a crane.'

'Not one of his sakers, perhaps. The gyrfalcon can kill almost anything that flies.'

'You don't know that.'

'You've only seen the falcon in a cage. I watched her hunting and she's deadly. On the night we first met, Hero said that the Emir was planning to hold a contest with a neighbour to see who had the best falcon. I'll back my gyrfalcon against any cast of sakers. Tell him.'

'She's not your falcon. If you're convinced of her qualities, describe them to the Emir and let him test them for himself.'

'She won't fly at her best for anyone but me.'

Hero broke in. 'Do as Wayland says. The Emir's about to announce a decision, and you can be sure it won't go in our favour. If Suleyman agrees to the contest, it will give us time to straighten out the lies and confusion.'

Vallon saw the wisdom of Hero's suggestion. 'You tell him. Dress it up in such flowery language that the Emir won't be able to refuse. Get the audience on our side.'

Hero began to speak just as Faruq turned away from Suleyman. He spoke again of the perils of their journey into the realms of ice and fire. He described Wayland's ordeal with the white bear, the battle with the Vikings, the four-month journey to the south. He extolled the gyrfalcon's virtues, pointing out that she alone had survived the ordeal and that the Emir must surely take this as a sign of God's will.

Suleyman chewed one of his moustaches while the audience waited for his decision. He summoned his hawkmaster and the two men spoke at length, breaking off to point or stare at Wayland. Faruq hovered in an attentive stoop until the Emir raised his mace, and then he straightened up.

'This is not a trifling matter. Is the English falconer certain that the falcon can kill a crane unaided?'

Vallon glanced at Wayland. 'I've never heard him make an empty boast.'

'On no account must the falcon disgrace his Excellency. She must win the contest.'

'Even if she doesn't,' said Wayland, 'she won't shame him.'

'You don't understand,' Vallon said. 'She has to win.'

'She will.'

'You don't even know the rules of the contest.'

'There's time to learn them.'

Vallon put aside his misgivings. He looked at the Emir and gave a stiff nod. 'The falcon won't disappoint.'

Faruq glanced at Suleyman. 'His Excellency agrees.'

The audience buzzed. Faruq raised his voice to outline various practical matters.

Vallon turned to Wayland. 'How long do you need to prepare the falcon?'

'Three weeks.'

'You have twelve days. If that isn't enough, say so.'

'She's a haggard. She's been killing almost daily for more than a year. All I need to do is get her fit.'

Vallon faced the interpreter. 'The falcon will be ready.'

'His Excellency will issue a challenge tomorrow. If the white falcon outflies his neighbour's sakers, he will release the Norman and send you away with gifts.'

'And if it doesn't?'

'His Excellency is even-handed in his dealings. You have declared before his court that the falcon won't fail.' Faruq let the claim linger. 'If it does, his Excellency will be put to scorn by his rival. You can't accept the rewards of success while refusing to pay the cost of failure.'

Too late, Vallon saw the pit he'd dug.

Faruq continued. 'If the falcon doesn't triumph, his Excellency will give the English youth to Walter as his slave.' Faruq stayed Vallon with an upraised palm. 'And you as champion of the falconer must also pay a forfeit.' Faruq allowed a space so that there could be no misunderstanding. 'In your case, the Varangian woman.'

Wayland grinned. 'What was that last bit?'

Vallon knew there was no way back. Before an audience of a hundred, he'd promised Suleyman a victory. It took all his self control to give a calm response. Behind Wayland he could see Hero's appalled gaze and Walter's smirk. He smiled and patted Wayland's arm. 'Nothing important. From now on, concentrate all your attention on preparing the falcon.'

XLIX

Wayland began planning his campaign the moment he hurried away from the Emir's pavilion. First he had to sharpen the haggard's hunting urge by cleansing her of the internal fat she'd accumulated during her months of inactivity. Washed meat and stones was the remedy. He calculated that two days after purging her she would be ready to fly free, giving him nine or ten days to harden her muscles. Her flight at the bustards had demonstrated her innate fitness. The cold would act as a tonic. In his mind's eye she was already raking through the sky, climbing into the clouds, stooping with destructive splendour.

Ibrahim the hawkmaster brought him back to earth. He was waiting beside the gyrfalcon's enclosure at the far end of the tent. He shook his head and was still shaking it when Wayland reached him.

'You wait and see,' Wayland told him. He rummaged in his bag of hawking furniture and brought out a dozen pebbles, each about the size of a horsebean. He showed them to the hawkmaster. 'Rangle,' he said. He set a pot of water on the brazier and dropped the pebbles into it. When the water was scalding, he drained the pebbles and spread them on a cloth. He mimed eating them and rubbed his stomach to show that they would stir up the grease and mucus in the falcon's crop. In the morning she would cast them up covered with glut. A four- or five-day course of stones would make her as keen as if she'd gone without food for a week.

He prepared to unhood the falcon. Ibrahim stopped his hand. He waggled a finger and went off to his store of nostrums and potions. He muttered to himself and returned with a spatula heaped with fine white crystals.

'What's that?'

Ibrahim didn't say. He told Wayland to cast the falcon. With the falcon firmly gripped, Ibrahim cut a piece of pigeon breast about the size of a grape and coated it with the crystals. He opened the falcon's beak and shoved the meat so far back in her throat that she was forced to swallow it.

He indicated that Wayland should place her on her block and give the purgative time to work. Then he retired yawning into his sleeping quarters. Wayland stayed up, watching the falcon. Only one lamp had been left burning and it was very quiet in the mews. After a while the falcon stretched her neck up and gaped. Wayland looked towards the hawkmaster's quarters. He tried to relax. His thoughts turned to Syth. He hadn't seen her since they'd arrived. Hero had told him she was well looked after, but why had the Emir mentioned her name? Vallon hadn't explained. There didn't appear to be any Seljuk women in the camp.

The falcon staggered on her perch. Wayland jumped up. She hunched over, making gagging sounds. He hurried into the sleeping chamber and shook the hawkmaster.

'Something's wrong with the falcon.'

Ibrahim grumbled and rolled over, pulling his blanket over his head.

When Wayland returned to the mews, he found the falcon on the ground, snaking her head back and forth. She cocked her tail and excreted a copious and foully discoloured mute. He unhooded her and moaned in panic. She'd been poisoned. He carried her up and down the mews until his arm drooped with exhaustion, then he placed her back on the block and sat watching in a stupor of despair. Her mouth leaked a greasy drool. Sinister clicking sounds came from her innards. His head sagged into his hands. The lamp burned out and his eyes closed.

Faint bars of sunlight criss-crossed the interior. Wayland blinked and saw Ibrahim's assistants opening the mews' ventilation flaps. The gyrfalcon's perch was empty.

He lurched to his feet as Ibrahim emerged from the chamber where newly caught hawks were kept isolated. 'Where is she? Is she dead?'

Ibrahim crooked a finger and Wayland followed him into the chamber. The falcon sat bareheaded on a block and the moment he entered she bated at him, bright-eyed and ravenous. The hawkmaster held out a small square of cloth. On it lay a slimy leaf of grease and fat that the falcon had disgorged while Wayland slept.

Now she was ready for her first session of exercise, said Ibrahim.

The chamber was furnished with a stool placed about ten feet from the block. Ibrahim handed Wayland a strip of meat and made him stand on the stool. Then he unhooded the falcon. 'Call her.' The Seljuk and the Englishman had no more than a dozen words between them, but their common interest was a shared language.

Wayland held out his fist. The falcon winnowed furiously and rowed up in strenuous flight to claim the titbit.

'Set her down again,' said Ibrahim. He gave Wayland another mouthful.

'Call her.'

585

After three steep flights to the fist, the falcon was panting. Three more and Wayland could see that she was wondering if the reward was worth the effort. When he held out his hand for the eighth time, she refused to come.

'Enough,' said Ibrahim. He counted off on his fingers to show how the sessions would proceed. Tomorrow the falcon would make ten jumps, the day after fifteen. When she could jump twenty-five times without distress she would be fit enough to fly free.

Wayland had worked out his own plan, and making the falcon flog up to his fist wasn't part of it. It was demeaning. He'd always fed the haggard her daily ration in one go. She was a wild hawk after all, used to satisfying her hunger unstintingly. Food was the only thing that bound her to him. Break that bond and she'd come to hate him.

'Your method will take too long. I'll fly her free tomorrow.'

'No!'

'Yes. Only flying will make her properly fit. I have to get her used to being carried on a horse. She has to grow accustomed to crowds. She needs to learn the terrain.'

The hawkmaster asked him if he'd flown the falcon loose.

'Yes, and she killed a bustard at her first flight.'

He wouldn't back down and eventually the hawkmaster agreed that he could fly the falcon free if she proved her obedience by coming immediately to the lure while tied to a creance.

They waited until late afternoon. On leaving the mews, Wayland was taken aback to find a squad of mounted Seljuks waiting to accompany them. To chase after the falcon if she flew off, Ibrahim said.

They rode out of the encampment and headed west until they came to a bald stretch of plain. The escorts sat their horses at a distance while Wayland dismounted and removed the falcon's leash and swivel. The hawkmaster tied a line to the slits in her jesses and carried her away about thirty yards. Wayland produced a leather lure garnished with pigeon. The hawkmaster unhooded the falcon. She bobbed her head and launched off, flexing her sails half a dozen times before gliding in to the lure. Wayland knelt beside her while she ate, picked her up as she swallowed the last mouthful, and replaced her hood. He untied the line and held her out to Ibrahim.

'Now we'll let her take the air.'

The hawkmaster was reluctant. He'd noticed how the falcon had tried to fly off with the lure. Putting her on the wing would be too risky. He fluttered his finger in the direction of the horizon. He pulled a doleful face, pointed towards the camp and drew a finger across his throat.

'You're saying the Emir will have me killed if I lose the falcon.'

There was nothing in the hawkmaster's response to suggest otherwise.

Wayland looked across the bleak plain, the sparse and withered grass. His features set. He held out his fist. 'Take her, before it grows too dark to fly.'

This time the hawkmaster retreated a hundred yards before unhooding her. Wayland could see that her behaviour was different. After registering his presence, she began scanning around. The sky was empty, the plain lifeless, yet her gaze settled on something only she could see and she took off and beat away.

At a shout from the hawkmaster the Seljuks spurred their horses and galloped in pursuit.

It was all but dark when Wayland caught up with them. A horse warrior cantered out of the gloom and pointed behind him at a ridge. Wayland handed him the reins of his horse and made in on foot, speaking so that his approach wouldn't alarm the falcon. She'd taken stand on a rock no more than waist high and was staring off to the north. When she turned towards him, it was as if she'd never seen him before.

Foot by foot he moved closer. She seemed lost in a dream, only noticing the food when he placed it against her feet. She looked down, looked away again. Her shoulders bunched up and Wayland grabbed her jesses an instant before she took flight. His hands shook as he fitted her leash. He knew he'd been lucky. Without the Seljuks he wouldn't have found her before nightfall. Roosting on the rock, she would have made easy prey for wolves or jackals. Even if she'd survived until dawn, she would have woken a lot wilder than when she'd gone to rest.

He returned chastened to face the hawkmaster's censure. But Ibrahim only told him to reduce the falcon's rations, pointing out that when a wild bird feels the wind under its sails again, it forgets its hunger. Don't feed or fly the falcon tomorrow, he ordered.

587

'I can't afford to miss a day,' Wayland said. 'The riders unsettled her. Tomorrow I'll take her out on my own.'

Next morning he went to find Syth. She and Caitlin were accommodated in a harem tent linked to the Emir's pavilion. A stout woman covered from head to toe came to the entrance and studied him through the slit in her veil. He asked if he could see Syth. She went away and then another woman appeared dressed in a flowing silk gown that clung to her breasts and hips, emphasising her slim and shapely figure. A scarf covered her hair and she held one end of the scarf over the lower half of her face so that all Wayland could see were her eyes outlined with black.

He felt awkward in the presence of this exotic maiden. 'I wanted to see Syth,' he muttered.

'Don't tell me you've forgotten what I look like so soon.'

'Syth! I didn't recognise you. What's that black stuff around your eyes?'

'It's called kohl. Don't you like it? Where have you been?'

'Preparing the falcon for the contest. That's why I'm here. I need your help.'

'Is that the only reason you came?'

'Of course not. I've missed you.'

'I've missed *you*. Why didn't you come earlier?'

'I'm sorry. The first two nights I hardly slept, and the days have been taken up with the falcon.'

She glanced behind her. 'I'll have to ask.'

During her absence the stout, veiled matron guarded the entrance and watched him with a dark stare. A commotion behind her made her turn. Syth came flying out, face and hair still covered, dressed in leggings and a quilted wrapover coat. The woman shrieked and tried to grab her, but Syth dodged. Wayland tried to take her hand. She slapped it away.

'No touching in the camp.'

They rode out with the falcon, making for the empty stretch of plain where he'd flown the day before. Wayland kept glancing at Syth. Three days' absence had made her a stranger. She seemed more grown up. More grown up than him.

'Can I touch you yet?'

She laughed and uncovered her face. She'd washed the kohl off and her skin had regained its bloom. She brought her horse alongside and allowed herself to be kissed. She smelled of musk and roses.

She stroked his cheek. 'I was worried about you. I didn't know you were safe until Vallon told me when he visited Caitlin.'

'How is she?'

Syth laughed. 'She loves being pampered. You should see her in her new clothes and jewellery. She's ravishing.' Syth noticed Wayland's lip curl. 'Don't sneer. I like Caitlin. She talks a lot of sense about men. Don't worry. She approves of you.'

Wayland wasn't sure he liked Caitlin discussing him with Syth. 'And Vallon?'

Syth's smile grew mysterious. 'Wait and see.'

The day's flying was a failure. Wayland had more ambitious goals than making the falcon flap to the lure. He wanted her to spend a good time on the wing. She would have to mount high and fast to stand any chance of catching a crane. Ibrahim had explained how the flight was managed. The falcon would be thrown off at a crane located upwind, either feeding on the ground or passaging between feeding grounds and roost. Either way it was likely that a ringing flight would result, hunter and quarry spiralling up into the sky. Sometimes they disappeared into the clouds and the flight ended three or more miles from where it started.

Ibrahim had also described the nature of the quarry. With a wingspan of more than seven feet, cranes were powerful in level flight and as buoyant as gulls even in a flat calm. Wayland had seen them migrating through Rus, always flying above the geese, flying so high that only their faint trumpeting betrayed their wispy formations. Even if a falcon beat one in flight, killing it wasn't easy. They weighed as much as a farmyard goose and when brought to earth they used their long bills to lethal effect.

And then there was the opposition. The sakers weighed about a third less than the gyrfalcon and their softer plumage put them at a disadvantage in rain or strong winds. By way of compensation, their sails were almost as broad as the gyrfalcon's, giving them the ability to gain height very quickly. More important, the rival emir's sakers were made birds, having flown as a cast for two seasons. Between them they'd accounted for more than twenty cranes. A dozen times Suleyman had matched his falcons against those of his rival, and only twice had his birds carried the day. That's why he'd demanded two casts of gyrfalcons. That's why Wayland mustn't fail.

All this was going through his mind when he turned his horse into the wind and unhooded the gyr. She pulled at his glove, looking for food.

'You have to earn it,' he said. He rolled his fist, forcing her to take off. She flew about a hundred yards and settled on a rock. Wayland rode upwind, dismounted and showed her the lure. She came straight away. Before she reached him he hid the lure, expecting her to fly past and circle. Instead she pitched on the ground.

He picked her up and rode to another spot and she did the same, landing beside him as soon as she lost sight of the lure.

'Perhaps she's too hungry,' Syth said. 'Or not hungry enough.'

Wayland didn't answer. A depressing truth was beginning to emerge. Gyrfalcons used their powers of flight only when they had to. In Greenland he'd noticed that they usually launched their hunts from a standing start, the falcon waiting on a perch until quarry came within range and then flying it down in a tail chase. The flight at the bustards had been an exception. Unlike peregrines, gyrs rarely sought their prey from a great height or killed from a lofty pitch.

Next day's efforts were just as dispiriting. Hero had come out with them and Wayland vented his frustration on the Sicilian.

'Only a week to go and she hasn't gone above forty feet. I'd stand a better chance with a peregrine picked up in the local bazaar.'

He lapsed into fuming silence.

Hero cleared his throat and pointed across the plateau. 'Do you think she might fly up to one of those if you baited it with food?'

Half a mile away two shepherd boys were flying kites. At first Wayland had no idea what Hero was talking about. 'Why would she fly to a kite? It's not natural.'

'Nor is a leather pad with a pair of moth-eaten wings tied to it.'

Wayland locked his hands around his knees and scowled.

'You're right,' Hero said. 'What do I know about falconry?'

He'd planted the seed, though. Wayland could hear the wind droning past the kites' taut lines. Almost against his will he looked up and studied the diamond-shaped sails.

'Do you really think it might work?'

'You won't lose anything by trying. Let's talk to them.'

They rode over and greeted the boys. Two identical packages in thick, square-cut coats. They didn't look like Seljuks. Their features were finer and they had shocks of black hair and hazel eyes flecked with green.

'They're from Afghanistan,' Hero said after speaking to them. 'Their father's a Seljuk auxiliary.'

He asked if he could hold a kite. One of the lads passed the line to him in an agony of shyness. Hero's eyes widened in surprise and when he handed over, Wayland understood why. Only a gentle breeze blew, yet the kite had so much lift that he had to tense to keep his balance. He asked the boys to bring the kites down and they ran them into the wind until they fluttered to the ground. They were about three feet across, made of cotton stretched over a willow frame. Wayland held one of them in his hands and then looked at the sky.

'Try it,' Hero said.

'What, now?'

'To see if the falcon will take food from it.'

Wayland tied the lure to the kite's bridle and handed it to Hero. 'Hold it up with the lure about chest height.' He crouched and unhooded the falcon. She bated away from the strange contraption. He recovered her and she bated again. 'Lower the lure.'

Hero brought it to within a foot of the falcon. This time she recognised it and hopped up to grab it. Wayland let her eat the garnish before hooding her. 'One more go. Stand on that rise and hold the kite as high as you can.'

The falcon was a quick learner. She flew straight to the lure and dangled from it, dragging the kite out of Hero's hands and trampling it underfoot. The Afghan boys looked on in bewilderment as Wayland disentangled the falcon from the wreckage.

'We'll need a much bigger kite,' Hero said. 'And it would help if we could attach the lure to some kind of release mechanism. I'll work on it.'

He asked the boys who had made the kites. They pointed to a cluster of distant tents and told him that the kites were the handiwork of their grandfather.

'Would he make one for us? A large one.'

591

The older boy gave a solemn nod.

'Tell your *buyukbaba* that we'll visit him early tomorrow. We'll bring all the materials.'

'The falcon's ruined their kite,' Wayland said. 'Is there something we can give them?'

Hero grinned. 'I have the very thing.' He fished in his purse and produced one of the Afghan coins that Cosmas had left him.

He presented it to the boys and they ran off over the plain.

'They must think we're crazy,' said Hero.

Wayland laughed and slapped him on the back. 'You're a genius. I would never have thought of that in a hundred years.'

'And in a hundred years I could never learn to shoot an arrow straight or track game.'

Wayland smiled at him. 'We make a good team, don't we?'

Hero nodded. 'I only wish Richard was here.'

'And Raul. If he'd lived, I don't think he'd have left us at Novgorod.'

'Nor do I.'

They left for the nomad camp at sunrise, cantering through rivers of bleating sheep and strings of groaning camels. By the time they arrived, the peaks to the south were awash with blue and gold. The two Afghan boys came racing out of their tent at a curving run, their cries bringing the rest of the family to the entrance. The stooping patriarch wearing an immense black turban must be the kite-maker. There was no sign of the boys' father. Their mother cradled a babe-in-arms and her three daughters stood beside her spinning wool on drop-spindles.

But it was the dog tethered by a stone kennel that made Wayland and Syth exchange stares. Huge, shaggy and menacing, it reared on its back legs, straining against its collar and uttering cavernous barks. It was a nursing bitch. Behind it five woolly pups wrestled with a scrap of hide.

The visitors dismounted. The boys led the horses away. Their grandfather came forward and pointed with pride at the bust on the coin Hero had given his grandsons.

'I think he's saying that he fought with Mahmud, Emperor of Ghazni.'

The old man led them into the tent and seated them at the hearth. The three girls withdrew to a corner, poking each other with their elbows. Syth smiled at them and they collapsed in giggles.

Hero handed the kite-maker a bolt of cotton. Wayland had obtained it through Ibrahim without trying to explain what he needed it for. He'd also acquired a bundle of canes for the frame and a couple of hundred yards of braided silk line. The kite-maker unrolled the fabric and felt it between thumb and finger, passing remarks on its quality to the woman. Hero told him that the kite would have to be as tall as a man and asked if he could construct it today.

The old man took the materials to the door where the light was better and set to work with knife, needle and thread. The woman fed her guests flatbread and curds and then they all waited in a mellow silence. The girls had gone back to their spinning and the boys were outside practising with slingshots. Through the weft of the tent Wayland could make out the distant mountains. One of the pups wandered into the tent. Before the woman could chase it out, Syth hoisted it onto her lap and smiled over her scarf at Wayland.

It was past noon when the kite-maker had finished. He would go out with them, he said, and test fly the kite and make any necessary modifications.

They set out, the kite-master carrying his youngest grandson on his saddle, the older boy riding his own horse. They halted on the plain and the grandfather laid the kite down and ran out line from a spool in a wooden frame.

'I've made a release mechanism,' said Hero. He showed Wayland a short line with a button at one end. 'This hangs from the bottom of the bridle.' He produced another line about ten feet long with a spring-loaded peg at one end. 'You tie the free end to the lure and clip the peg over the button. When she grabs the food, she'll pull the peg off. At least, that's the idea.'

Wayland tested the mechanism, clipping the peg over the button and then pulling to see how much force was required to spring it loose. A firm tug was enough. He nodded. 'It's going to work.'

He attached the lure. Grandfather gave an order and the older boy ran upwind with the kite and released it. Its maker sawed at the line like an angler playing a fish and the kite shot up into the sky. The old man laughed and began to pay out line.

593

'Too high,' said Wayland. 'Reel it in. Lower. Lower still. That's it. Keep it there.'

The kite rode the wind sixty feet above him. He walked downwind and unhooded the falcon. She snaked a look at the kite, half spread her wings, scissored them shut, unfurled once more. Wayland let her choose her moment. His fist rebounded as she left it and beat up towards the lure.

She slashed at it and the kite jerked. The falcon had plucked the lure off. With nothing to restrain her, she just kept going.

The two boys leaped onto their horse and galloped after her. Wayland watched the falcon dwindle to a dot.

Hero winced. 'I should have thought of that.'

'She won't go far. The boys will find her.'

She'd carried the lure more than half a mile and was trying to pull it to pieces when they caught up with her. Wayland picked her up and thanked the boys.

'Have you got a spare swivel?' Hero asked on the ride back. 'If you have, I can add a fitting that will prevent the falcon from carrying the lure.'

'Do you think we should have another try? I don't want to push her too hard.'

'Only seven days left.'

'You're right.'

Hero fitted an anti-carry line, tying one end to the lure, the other to a swivel. He threaded the kite line through one of the swivel rings so that when the falcon took the lure, she would be forced to descend, the ring running freely around the main line.

The sun was squatting on the horizon when the boys released the kite again. Now that they understood the game, they threw themselves into it, urging their grandfather to fly higher and higher. The old man's toothless grin showed that he was as enthusiastic as the children.

Hero smiled at Wayland. 'The old man says he built this kite to climb into heaven.'

'It's too high. Tell him to bring it down.'

Wayland rode downwind and unhooded the falcon. This time she didn't make straight for the target. Fifty feet up she began to circle, using the wind for lift. She was as high above the kite as it was above the ground when she set her wings in a shallow stoop. She took the

594

lure and tried to fly off with it, only to be checked by the anti-carry line. From that point, things went wrong. The kite line was stretched at too shallow an angle for the anti-carry line to run down it. The falcon hung upside down from the lure like a furious bat, fighting the upward pull of the kite. It looked awful.

'Cut the line!' Wayland shouted.

Hero threw out a hand. 'Wait.'

The falcon stopped flapping and tried to fly downwind. The anti-carry line thwarted her, forcing her round in a circle. Relieved of her weight, the line began to slide. By the time she'd descended halfway, she'd worked out that it was easier to reach the ground by gyrating around the main line.

Wayland expected to find her exhausted and furious. Instead she seemed rather pleased to have wrestled the strange prey into submission.

Wayland returned to the nomads' tent with a sense of fulfilment. The kite-maker agreed to come out with them every day until the contest. Before they parted, Syth whispered something to Hero and he tried to press another coin on the old man. The kite-maker clutched himself and turned away.

'The leftover cloth is sufficient payment,' Wayland said.

'It's not for the kite,' said Syth. 'I asked if I could buy one of the pups.'

The old man wouldn't accept payment and told her to take any pup she wanted. She chose the one that had strayed into the tent and they rode off with it sitting upright on the bow of Syth's saddle, alternately pricking its ears at the night sounds and squirming round to lick Syth's face.

'I've thought of a name for him,' she said.

Word of the infidels' bizarre training methods spread among the Seljuks and next day about twenty of them rode out to watch. That day the falcon flew to about three hundred feet and descended without drama. On her next outing the kite-maker ran out the full length of the line and she climbed to five hundred feet witnessed by a crowd of spectators.

There was more encouraging news waiting back at the Emir's encampment. Suleyman's rival had requested a four-day postponement in order to sort out a clan dispute. Suleyman was within his rights to cancel the contest and would do so if the falcon's training had shown her unequal to the task.

Wayland didn't even have to think. 'Tell him to agree to the new date.'

Each day's kite exercise honed the falcon's powers until she was climbing a thousand feet. Seljuks came out with picnics to marvel at her prowess. With three days to go, Wayland returned home – he'd begun to think of the encampment as 'home' – to be met by the hawkmaster. Ibrahim took him into an annexe used for storage. In it stood a large wicker cage and inside the cage stood a crane with brailed wings. The hawkmaster told Wayland that every day since the contest had been agreed, he'd sent trappers out to snare a bird. Great efforts had been expended, for cranes were hard to catch, being vigilant and unapproachable. By day they fed out on the plateau and at night they roosted in the marshes around Salt Lake. This bird had been trapped in a mist net rigged on a field of cut millet. Tomorrow Wayland would fly the falcon at the crane in circumstances that would guarantee the falcon's success.

Wayland observed the captive's panicked eyes. 'Let it go,' he said. 'The falcon doesn't need easy game.'

Ibrahim showed dismay. Free the crane? Ridiculous. Yes, the falcon was a good flyer. What did that prove? Catching a lure tethered in the sky wasn't the same as tackling an equally strong flier that could climb and shift and fight back. The falcon hadn't hunted a crane before, hadn't even seen one. What if she turned tail at the challenge? Most falcons did. Hardly one in ten would close with such a formidable opponent even when supported by another hawk.

Ibrahim wouldn't yield. He'd appeal to the Emir if necessary.

Wayland gave way. 'One condition,' he said. 'No spectators.'

Only the hawkmaster and his assistants rode out with Wayland next afternoon. They didn't halt until the plain lay empty to the horizon in every quarter. The underfalconers placed the crane on the ground and prepared to remove its straitjacket. Earlier they'd sewn some of its primaries together to hamper its flight. If Wayland hadn't intervened, they would have seeled its eyes. Blinded, it would have flown straight up towards the sun.

'I'm not flying the falcon at a blind bird,' Wayland told Ibrahim. 'You told me how difficult it was to catch a crane. Let's make this trial as close to the real thing as possible.'

He and Ibrahim waited about an arrow-flight downwind. The day was overcast with a light breeze from the north. Good flying conditions. The falcon was keen. If anything, she was too keen, jumping against her jesses in anticipation of a flight.

The assistants removed the crane's bindings. One of them held its bill. He raised a hand to signal that they were ready to release. Wayland nodded at the hawkmaster. The assistants stepped away from the crane and it staggered into flight. Ibrahim shouted and waved to scare it upwind. It found its rhythm and began to climb. Ibrahim rested a hand on Wayland's arm and tightened his grip.

'Now!'

'Not yet.'

Wayland waited until the crane had climbed about fifty feet before attempting to unhood. The falcon was so excited that she clawed at his hand and twisted her head. He couldn't slacken the braces. By the time he'd struck her hood the crane had gained another hundred feet.

Wayland had often wondered how a falcon emerging from total darkness could react with the speed of thought. She flung herself off his fist and flew low and fast over the plain before beginning to climb. The crane saw her and rose more steeply. At her superior height the breeze blew more strongly than at ground level, increasing lift. Wayland chewed on a knuckle. He'd slipped too late. The falcon was pumping up on her tail, climbing twice as fast as the crane and taking a slightly different course. But she still hadn't gained enough height to command her quarry. Any moment the crane would use its advantage to turn downwind over the falcon.

There! The crane turned and set off downwind, the falcon still a hundred feet below it. Ibrahim wailed as the crane stroked overhead, long legs trailing. He berated Wayland for not releasing soon enough. Wayland kept his gaze on the falcon. She was still working into the wind, gaining height, and he wondered if she'd even recognised the crane as quarry. Perhaps she was looking for the kite.

The crane had a huge lead when the falcon flipped round and launched her attack. She raced back over their heads with deep strokes of her wings, still climbing at a shallow angle and still climbing when Wayland could no longer pick her out against the sky.

Ibrahim was close to tears as they set off in search. Quarry lost, falcon lost. If only Wayland had listened to him. If only the infidel hadn't provoked fate by thinking he could master it. On and on he went until the passage of miles of empty plain crushed him into silence.

They found the gyrfalcon feeding up on the crane a league from where Wayland had slipped her. She'd already taken a good crop and she mantled as he made in to secure her. He hooded her, handed her to Ibrahim and examined her prey to work out how she'd killed it. One wing flopped loose at the elbow where she'd struck it in full flight, sending the crane spinning to the ground. Wayland checked the crane's neck, assuming that she'd delivered the coup de grâce with her beak. But the neck was uninjured. He ruffled the feathers on the crane's body and showed Ibrahim what he'd found. The hawkmaster exclaimed in astonishment and waved his assistants over. The falcon had broken most of the ribs on the crane's right side, extinguishing life with one slashing blow from a hind talon.

'*Yildirim*,' said Ibrahim. He pointed at the sky and described a zig-zag stroke of lightning, concluding with an explosive puff of breath. '*Yildirim*.'

'Thunderbolt,' said Wayland, and nodded. The bird of Thor, war god of the frozen north, wielder of the lethal hammer. 'It's a good name.'

On the ride back the Seljuks raised their faces to the sky and sang songs in praise of the falcon. Wayland didn't join in. Night fell, and when he saw the fires of the encampment pricking the dark, he reined in and leaned over his horse's neck with a sigh.

Ibrahim noticed his sombre mood. 'Why the gloomy face?'

'It's nothing to do with the falcon.'

Each of them had only the haziest idea of what the other was saying. Ibrahim searched Wayland's face. 'You're a strange youth. Always making things more difficult than they need be. Fate will strew your path with enough problems and heartache without you creating your own.' He wagged a finger. 'Don't tempt fate by flying tomorrow. Feed the falcon a light meal without castings. Let her have victory fresh in her mind when she spreads her wings for the duel.'

L

The walls of the tent stirred in a light breeze. Wayland went out through the flap. A dusting of snow had settled in the night, but now the sky was clear and stars burned in the dark vault, casting a glacial light on the peaks to the south. Ibrahim knelt facing the mountains, prostrating himself in prayer. The breeze that sucked at the walls of the tented city was so faint that Wayland could hardly feel it.

Ibrahim rolled up his prayer mat and made his way back. He called down God's blessing and Wayland repeated the formula. He squinted at the sky.

'Ideal conditions for the sakers.'

Ibrahim flicked his hand. 'Pah! How is the Thunderbolt?'

'I haven't seen her yet. I thought I'd let her sleep for as long as possible.'

'What about you? Did you rest well?'

Wayland smiled. 'I spent most of the night fighting the contest in my head.'

They checked on the haggard. She recognised his step at a distance and gave a *chup* of welcome. When he approached she fanned her wings in pleasurable anticipation before jumping to his fist. She wasn't upset that it didn't hold food. Wayland let her nibble his finger.

'Will the Emir fly her himself?'

'No. You carry her and slip at his Excellency's command. If she triumphs, he will receive the credit. If she fails, you will take the blame.'

Wayland stroked the falcon's head. 'Well, she's as ready as she'll ever be.'

'Not quite. I have a special tonic that will put fire in her blood.'

'She doesn't need dosing. I'll offer her a bath. It would be a disaster if she raked away in search of water.'

The underfalconers appeared yawning and began preparing lures and carrying the saker falcons out into the weathering area. The Emir would fly them in the morning. The contest between the crane hawks would be the last event of the day.

Wayland took the gyrfalcon out to weather in the first flush of dawn. Once the sun had risen she bathed with gusto, dipping her head under the water, squatting down in it and shaking herself like a dog.

Afterwards she jumped to her block and hung out her wings before preening herself.

Wayland dressed with care in the costume provided for him. Ibrahim stood back, inspecting him. He nodded approval and placed a fur-trimmed hat on his head before leaving. Wayland sat on his bed, trying to steady his nerves. He kept coughing as if a hair were caught in his throat. He jumped up in relief when a trumpet blast announced that the day's sport was about to begin. He hooded the falcon, mounted his horse and rode with Ibrahim and the underfalconers to the arena at the centre of the camp. Emerging into the open space, he pulled back, astonished to find a thousand armed and armoured horsemen milling across the ground. It looked more like a military muster than a hunting party.

Vallon rode smiling out of the crowd. 'Welcome, stranger. We heard about your achievement. Not many falconers kill a crane at their first attempt.'

'It wasn't a sporting flight. It was bagged quarry.'

Vallon took him to one side. 'I know the contest means a lot to you. So it should after all the work you've put in. But there's more to it than that. I didn't tell you earlier because nothing I said could have made Suleyman call off the challenge.'

'I don't want the contest to be called off.'

'The night Suleyman agreed to the contest, he set conditions. Win and we ride away with a reward. Lose and you forfeit your freedom.'

'I don't understand.'

'Lose and you'll become Walter's slave.'

'I won't be anyone's slave. I won't bow to any man. Why didn't you tell me?'

'I didn't want the threat preying on your mind while you trained the haggard. I'm telling you now because I can make the Emir grant you your freedom if your falcon doesn't claim the prize.'

'What if he doesn't? What will happen to Syth?'

'You won't be parted. Trust me. Put up your best performance, but don't worry too much about losing. Do exactly what the Emir tells you and don't attempt anything too ambitious.'

'I won't.'

Wayland was still dazed when Hero greeted him. 'Don't worry. Whatever the outcome, Vallon won't hand you over to Walter.'

'How can you be so sure?'

'The night before last we had another meeting with Suleyman. It went well. He nurses more ambitious plans than beating his rival in a duel of falcons. He wants to create a sultanate in Anatolia. If you lose, Vallon will offer his services in that cause.'

'But what about his plans to join the Varangians?'

'His first loyalty is to his company. Now put it out of your mind and concentrate on the contest.' Hero pointed to a knot of riders wearing uniforms emblazoned with an eagle motif. 'See the man in the golden coat? That's who you're up against. His name's Temur. It means "Iron".'

Wayland studied the plump figure in the centre of the group. His face was as round as a dish and wreathed in a smile. 'He looks like he's made of butter.'

'Appearances deceive. You recall that he asked for a postponement so that he could settle a dispute. Something to do with the theft of camels. He condemned the guilty party to be sewn into a wet hide and then left in the sun so that the hide would crush the life out of him as it shrank.'

Wayland looked around the arena and spotted Walter suited in mail with a group of Seljuk friends.

'Why is everyone wearing armour?'

'It's a military exercise as well as a sporting event.'

'Is Syth here?'

Hero shook his head. 'Women aren't allowed.'

The crush parted in front of them. Suleyman rode up at the head of his entourage, clad in a leopard's skin cape over a coat of scale armour. He quizzed the hawkmaster and then he turned his cat's gaze on Wayland and spoke to Faruq.

'He wants to know how the falcon will perform,' Hero said.

'Tell the Emir that, due to his Excellency's generosity and the skills of his hawkmaster, the falcon is at the peak of her powers and is equal to whatever challenge presents itself. God willing.'

Suleyman felt under the falcon's wings, assessing muscle tone. He said something to Ibrahim and the hawkmaster bowed. One last searching look at Wayland and the Emir wheeled his stallion. Trumpets blared and the horsemen began to flow out of the arena.

Hero grinned at Wayland. 'How far you've come. When we first

601

met, you couldn't speak. Now you're exchanging diplomatic niceties with a Seljuk emir.'

The army fanned out under an ice-blue sky and commenced to kill every wild animal in its path. It was some time before Wayland realised that the slaughter was methodical, an exercise for war. Spotters carrying flags had been sent out to locate quarry. One of them signalled from the skyline ahead and a trumpet blast brought the field to a stop. Another note and the wings of the army detached themselves with precision and advanced at a canter. They disappeared over the horizon, leaving the plain in front empty. The two emirs waited at the centre of the line with their retinues.

Distant bugles sounded. A puff of dust rose on the horizon and the first horsemen of the returning advance party appeared, streaming over the skyline in two lines a mile apart. A herd of gazelles raced into view between them. Behind the gazelles, rising from the earth, rode the rest of the Seljuks in crescent formation, driving the quarry between the horns. Suleyman pointed right and left with his mace and two more squadrons peeled off, galloping forward to prevent the game from breaking around the flanks. Every fifty yards one of the Seljuks dropped out, until by the time the foremost riders had linked up with the tips of the horns, they'd thrown a cordon around the quarry. They began to tighten it, waving flags, forcing the gazelles towards a funnel between the two emirs.

Thirty gazelles entered the corridor and so sure was the aim of the waiting archers that not a single animal broke through to the rear.

Walter rode over to Vallon. 'Now you know what we faced at Manzikert.'

They moved on and Wayland's recollection of events became disjointed. The Seljuks staged impromptu horse races and archery matches. They flushed a jackal in a dry riverbed and thirty riders lashed their horses in pursuit, Suleyman's men on one bank, Temur's on the other. One of Suleyman's men drew ahead of the quarry. Twisting right round in his saddle he shot straight back over his horse's tail and hit the jackal square in the chest. Suleyman showered silver on the marksman.

The two emirs selected saker falcons and cast them off at hares and bustards put up by the advancing army. Wayland thought it poor sport. The falcons coursed the hares, buffeting them until their wits were so scattered that they didn't know which way to turn. The flights at bustards were tail chases that rarely rose above fifty feet. If the quarry put in to cover, the Seljuks kicked it up and flew it again, repeating the process until the bustard was brought down or escaped.

'It's a rat hunt,' Wayland told Vallon. 'I'm not going to fly my falcon like that.'

'Careful. First, it's not your falcon. Second, the Emir hunts in any way he pleases.'

A trumpeter signalled the end of the morning's entertainment. Servants erected a kiosk and the two emirs dined on skewered lamb and rice, figs, melons and pomegranates, walnuts in syrup, sherbets cooled with ice brought from the twin peaks.

Wayland picked at his own meal and then withdrew from the bustle, worried that the commotion would unsettle the falcon. A figure slipped down beside him.

'Don't look. I'm not supposed to be here.'

'Syth!'

'I would have joined you earlier if the puppy hadn't pissed on my leggings. I had to change and then wait for a chance to sneak out.'

Their hands slid towards each other.

The breeze had strengthened from the north-west and the servants striking camp struggled with the flapping tent panels. The army resumed its advance, skirting the southern shore of Salt Lake. The sun was in steep decline and the serious business was about to begin.

Two scouts breasted a ridge and the army halted. One of the scouts stayed put, while the other galloped towards the emirs to make his report. Ibrahim listened in and told Wayland that outriders had spotted a large gathering of cranes feeding on the other side of the ridge.

They advanced. Wayland heard the cranes' clarion calls long before he saw them, flocked in their thousands along both sides of a river flowing into Salt Lake.

It was too risky to slip at such a huge number, Ibrahim said. The falcon would be intimidated. Even if flown in a cast, the birds would lose sight of each other in the storm of wings.

'Who takes the first flight?'

'Temur, at his own request. The wind will soon be too strong for his sakers.'

Wayland was relieved. If the emir's falcons failed to kill, the pressure would be off the gyrfalcon.

Half the field advanced in two files and rode a wide circle around the cranes. As the horsemen tightened the circle, some of the cranes stopped feeding and stretched their necks up. Another circuit and the flocks closest to the riders took off with clanging cries. Their alarm communicated itself to other groups. One after the other they flew off. Only about thirty cranes remained when the horsemen halted their encirclement. Ibrahim pointed at the smallest group, indicating that it was the target.

Falcon on fist, Temur cantered upwind towards the quarry. At his side rode another falconer carrying the second saker. They closed to within a furlong before the cranes rose, springing into the air as if their wings were operated by strings and levers. As the last of them cleared the ground, Temur whooped and threw off his falcon.

It flew with speed and purpose, making height to block the cranes' escape downwind. The five birds in the group scattered, the saker staying true to the quarry she'd singled out. Sensing that they weren't the target, the other cranes slipped downwind to safety. Only then did the emir's falconer release the second saker.

Wayland watched fascinated as the two falcons shepherded their quarry into the wind. Temur's bird strove to pressure the crane, while her partner flew her own course, intent on gaining height. Realising that it couldn't get past them, the crane sought escape in the sky. It began to ring up, turning in small spirals, the sakers cutting larger circles beneath it. They rose like carousel figures, the wind drifting them south-east. Wayland urged his horse into a canter to keep up. There wasn't a cloud in the sky and the difference in the size of the birds made it difficult to judge which one had the ascendancy.

The sakers were no bigger than swallows when one of them put in a jabbing stoop that made the crane sideslip. The stoop was a feint. The falcon threw up, sunlight flaring from her undersides as she rolled over for a second attack. Her partner continued to ring higher. Another sharp dive and the crane rolled and kicked out its legs. It had just recovered when the second falcon delivered a long stoop from a different direction. The tempo quickened, both falcons rising and falling like hammers, never quite making contact. Each feint drove the crane lower. Wayland no longer knew which falcon was which. One of them put in a stoop that connected, drawing a cheer from Temur's supporters and leaving a puff of feathers drifting in the wind.

The crane decided it was beaten and plummeted with upstretched wings. Wayland had lost sight of one of the falcons. The saker that had feathered the crane poised herself above her quarry, taking aim before hurling down. This time Wayland heard the impact and saw the crane stagger. While he was still watching the saker throw up for the next attack, her partner swept down and bound to the crane's back. Hunter and hunted fell in a wild whirligig. The second saker tore into the crane and all three birds dropped like wreckage. The horizon tilted back into Wayland's view. Crane and falcons were spinning to earth at a speed that threatened destruction for all three. Less than fifty feet from the ground the falcons released their quarry. The crane landed with a thump and turned to face its foes with stabbing bill and flailing wings. One of the sakers grabbed it from behind, bowling it over. It lashed out with its feet and then Wayland lost sight of it as a dozen Seljuks galloped up. One of them vaulted off his horse. It was Temur himself. Squeezing through the scrum, Wayland arrived to find the crane dead and the emir with knife in hand encouraging his sakers to feed on its exposed heart. Buglers celebrated the kill. Temur looked round with a manic grin.

Wayland turned and found Vallon. He gave a rueful smile. 'That's going to take some beating.'

Some of the Seljuks had ridden after the main flock of cranes and marked down a dozen birds in a small marsh close to Salt Lake. Wayland waited at the southern edge while a hundred mounted beaters combed the reed beds. The wind was blowing hard enough to raise licks of snow from the ground. Ibrahim kept repeating instructions that Wayland couldn't understand. All he could gather was that he mustn't make any move without the Emir's command. Suleyman and his senior officers had stationed themselves about forty yards away. The Emir pointed his mace at Wayland, reinforcing Ibrahim's warning.

The gyrfalcon's keenness made her difficult to manage. Every movement on Wayland's part she interpreted as the prelude to flight, making her lunge and paddle at the air. He'd removed the swivel and looped the leash through the slits in her jesses. Remembering the difficulty he'd experienced when casting her off at the disabled crane, he slackened her hood so that he could whip it off at a moment's notice.

He concentrated on the Seljuks working their way through the marsh. It was a good set-up. Salt Lake lay more than a mile upwind, its swamps the obvious sanctuary for any crane flushed ahead of him. None had showed itself yet, and the beaters had already combed half the marsh. Fear of committing the falcon to flight began to give way to anxiety that he wouldn't get a flight at all.

Four ducks sprang quacking from the marsh and cut upwind. At the furthest point of their outrun, they seemed to tread air and then hurtled back as though pulled by cords. The falcon heard them arrow past and bated blind at them. Wayland's horse shied. He tried to gather it, while struggling to swing the falcon back onto his fist. She'd tangled her leash around the jesses and in her struggles she dislodged the hood. It was the stuff of nightmare – a skittish horse and an unruly falcon, the possibility of game rising at any moment. One of the underfalconers grabbed the horse's bridle. Wayland slid off and looked for the hood. The horse had trampled it. Ibrahim shoved a spare into his hand and he crammed it on.

Someone shouted and pointed south. Three hundred feet above the plateau and half a mile downwind, a solitary crane was making a leisurely passage towards Salt Lake. Wayland finished unravelling the falcon's leash. She was panting, but the crane had a lot of air to cover and the haggard would have regained her composure by the time the quarry got upwind.

Ibrahim's shout jarred him out of his calculations. Wayland looked to see the Emir lashing down with his mace, giving the order to release the falcon.

Wayland couldn't believe it. 'That's crazy! The crane will turn tail before the falcon gets anywhere near it.'

'Do what you're told,' Vallon yelled.

Wayland rode up to Ibrahim. 'Tell the Emir to wait until the crane passes over our heads.'

Suleyman was riding towards him. Ibrahim headed him off. They shouted at each other, the hawkmaster pointing first at the crane and then at the lake, Suleyman staring at Wayland with an expression that would have made most men fall to their knees and beg mercy. The Emir swept out a hand in fury. With one last glare at Wayland, he pulled his horse round and rode off fifty yards.

Wayland tried to put it out of mind. The crane drew on, gaining height. She must have been at more than five hundred feet when she passed overhead. Wayland drew the leash from the jesses. He watched the Emir, waiting for the order to slip. Suleyman glowered ahead as if he'd lost interest in the proceedings. The crane had worked two hundred yards into the wind. Wayland waited, throwing increasingly anxious glances at the Emir. The crane was now four hundred yards upwind and the Emir hadn't glanced up.

'What's keeping him?' he asked Ibrahim. 'If he waits any longer, the crane will have too big a lead.'

Suleyman turned and flicked his mace.

Wayland reached for the falcon's hood.

Ibrahim lunged for his hand. 'No!'

'I don't understand.'

Faruq shouted something. 'The Emir's ordering you not to fly,' Hero called. 'He says the crane's too high.'

Wayland exploded with frustration. 'He knows nothing. No wonder Temur always beats him.'

Vallon galloped over. 'Don't make matters any worse for yourself.'

Wayland glared at Suleyman, then he looked at the crane and with no further thought he struck the falcon's hood and cast her into the wind.

Vallon was too appalled to speak. Hero clutched his face. 'What's got into you?'

'What's got into me? I brought the falcon two thousand miles for the Emir to fly at cranes. First he orders me to take on an impossible slip then, when I'm in the ideal situation, he forbids me to slip at all.'

Suleyman might have struck him down on the spot if his attendants hadn't drawn his attention to the gyrfalcon. She was climbing up on her tail, making height at a tremendous rate. She'd closed the gap by half before the crane noticed the threat and quickened its pace. The falcon kept going, levelling off in order to power ahead of her quarry and cut it off from cover. Wayland spurred his horse after them. The falcon made its point and eased off, waiting for the crane's next move. Although the quarry still had several hundred feet advantage, the falcon had gained enough height to command the airspace below, whether the crane flew upwind or down. It took the only route left open and began to ring up like a feather trapped in a thermal. The falcon followed, buffering up in steps, sometimes taking the opposite direction from its quarry. Already they were so high that Wayland had to tilt his head back to keep them in view. Up and up, the falcon scintillating in the golden light. Wayland's neck ached from the effort of keeping them in sight. The crane was no bigger than a bee pestered by a fly. Wayland blinked to clear his vision because soon a blink would be long enough to lose them. The bee shrank to the size of a fly; the fly became a gnat. The gnat disappeared, leaving only one tiny speck in the sky. Then nothing. Wayland's eyes were so sharp that he could spot a pigeon a mile away, yet the two birds had simply vanished into space.

The spectators waited, rubbing their necks. Most flights ended downwind of the slip, but nobody moved. Dusk began to hood the earth and pleats of violet shadow ran up the mountains.

Vallon rode over. 'Do you think she took it?'

'I don't know.'

'Pray God she does. A kill is your only chance of escaping punishment. I'll plead for leniency, but I doubt if my words will carry much weight. What possessed you to defy the Emir?'

Wayland couldn't answer. Turning away he saw Syth's frightened face.

'The Emir's going to punish you, isn't he?'

'Not if the falcon takes the crane.'

'If she doesn't, he might kill you.'

'Syth—'

'Didn't you stop to think what will happen to me – to our child?'

A Seljuk shouted. Wayland's gaze whipped up, bright with hope. He saw the falcon falling ... falling ... falling. Stooping so fast that she seemed to descend in a series of flickers. Five hundred feet above the plateau her teardrop shape threw up in a tearing arc. She swung into the wind and rested on the rushing air. Suleyman's men groaned and Wayland covered his face. It was over. The crane had outflown the falcon and he would suffer the consequences.

Ibrahim galloped up, grabbed Wayland's reins and dragged him away. 'Call her down.'

Wayland swung his lure. The falcon ignored it. She rode the wind, her wings curved back in a bow. She was still full of flying, waiting for fresh quarry to be flushed.

Ibrahim threw out a live pigeon on a line. At the second throw, the falcon flicked over. Wayland blinked. She was heading in the wrong direction, driving towards the setting sun.

'She's after something.'

For a moment he thought she'd spotted the crane. Only for a moment. She was chasing a pigeon. It had such a huge lead that if he'd been flying any other falcon, he would have groaned in dismay at her vain pursuit. But she wasn't any other falcon and he concentrated on keeping her in sight. The pigeon flew towards the setting sun. Wayland shielded his eyes and saw it graze the fiery disc. The falcon flew straight into it. The glare burned the back of his eyeballs. He dashed tears away. When he picked the falcon up again, she was only a short distance behind the pigeon, reeling it in as if it were tethered. The pigeon went into a dive. The falcon lifted before powering after it. The two specks merged into one and then the sky emptied. Wayland marked the spot where they'd disappeared. Over the marshes fringing Salt Lake.

He turned to Ibrahim. 'She took it.'

Riders were lashing towards them. 'Find her,' Ibrahim ordered. 'No, wait.'

The nearest riders were only yards away when Wayland spurred his horse towards the lake. Ibrahim was trying to win him a reprieve. If he recovered the falcon, he was to wait until well after dark before returning to the encampment. Ibrahim would use the time to speak on his behalf. He'd tell Suleyman that Wayland had misunderstood the Emir's commands. He'd explain that the falcon was so fired up that she'd broken loose.

The flight had ended more than a mile away and Wayland knew there was little chance of recovering the falcon before dark. The sun smouldered on the horizon and the falcon could have landed anywhere in the briny wastes. She might have carried her prey right across the lake.

Hooves clattered behind him and two riders drew level. One of them was Syth, the other Walter. He swiped a hand into Wayland's face.

609

'Base wretch! You've made Suleyman a laughing stock. There's no saving you now. I've a good mind to cut off your head myself. I'll plead with him for the privilege.'

Wayland rode on pell-mell. He reached the marsh stretching into the lake and pulled up. The sun was already halfway below the horizon and the wind cut like a knife. He studied the landscape. Over to his right and about quarter of a mile into the marsh, an eagle quartered the reeds, sometimes rowing back in a clumsy hover. It must have seen the falcon land with her prey and was searching for her. He cantered towards the spot. His mare splashed across a salt pan and stumbled as she broke through the crust. He slowed to a walk, his attention fixed on the area where he'd seen the eagle. Thousands of islets dotted the pools and creeks. He dismounted and led his horse, listening for the sound of bells above the swishing of the reeds. A hundred yards further on the water rose above his mare's knees. She dapped a foot at the surface and refused to go any further.

'You'll never find her in there,' said Walter.

Wayland handed the reins to Syth. 'I'll go on by foot.' He took a few steps then hesitated. He looked back at Walter. 'The falcon isn't far away. Help me search for her.'

Walter flushed in anger. 'Who do you think you're speaking to? I'm not going into the marsh.'

'I'll come,' Syth said. 'I'm light of foot and I grew up in the fens.'

Wayland kept his gaze fixed on Walter. 'I have something important to tell you.'

Walter frowned. 'Concerning Drogo and Vallon?'

'Concerning murder.'

Walter looked back, one side of his face burnished by the last rays of the sun. Suleyman and an escort of about thirty men were galloping towards them. Alongside rode Vallon and Drogo.

'I knew it. Tell me how they intend to do the deed.'

'Not here. Suleyman will reach us before I can explain.'

'What's this talk of murder?' Syth said. 'Why are you acting so strange?'

Wayland touched her wrist. 'Wait until I return.'

The Seljuks were close. The last segment of sun had sunk, leaving a flaming band on the horizon and dimming fire on the twin peaks. Wisps of charcoal cloud floated high in a sky of purple and saffron.

Wayland entered the marsh, wading through brine, pushing through reeds. Walter followed, labouring in his armour.

'Out with it then,' he panted. 'If I can turn the knowledge to my advantage, I'll intercede for you with Suleyman.'

'Let's recover the falcon first.'

Walter gripped his arm. 'If I save you, you'll be my loyal slave.'

Wayland hurried on. The reeds grew so tall that only the light draining in the west told him what direction he was taking. Every few yards he stopped, listening for the sound of the falcon's bells. It was hopeless. Suleyman's entire army could search all day for the falcon and never find her. She would have dragged the pigeon into cover when she saw the eagle. Even if he passed within five yards, he'd probably miss her. Falcons froze on their kill if anyone approached.

He came to what looked like a shallow pool furred with weeds. Something warned him off crossing it. He skirted it, only to run into another. And another. His course was so erratic that he no longer knew where the eagle had been hunting. He was trying to find a way between bogs and he'd have only the stars to show him the way back.

Walter took a false step and sank to his knees. The surface quivered around him. Wayland helped him onto firm ground.

'That's far enough. My armour makes it too dangerous.'

'There's still enough light to find her.'

'We're already in too far. Take me back.'

'You return if you want.'

'I don't know the way.'

'Then stay with me. I won't be long.'

Walter drew his sword. 'Tell me what Drogo's planning.'

'We're wasting time better spent on searching. Come on.'

Walter dragged him back and raised his sword. 'You're wasting *my* time.'

Wayland looked into Walter's eyes.

'Well?'

Wayland's gaze darted. 'I heard her bell.'

Walter yanked his arm. 'Liar. The wind's loud enough to drown a church peal.'

'No,' Wayland said, disengaging from Walter's grip. He walked away, his eyes tracking right and left before stopping. He pointed. 'It came from over there.'

Walter stumbled along beside him. Every few steps Wayland called out. The bell didn't sound again. He slowed his pace, scared of treading on the falcon. He peered through the reeds, trying to sieve her form out of the darkness. 'Where are you?'

The faintest of tinkles. Wayland placed a hand on Walter's arm. 'She's close. Don't move.'

He dropped on to hands and knees and crawled forward, mouthing sweet nothings. The rasp of the bell came again. He advanced a few feet and the haggard uttered an anxious *kack* from behind him. He turned and lay flat on his belly in an icy puddle, scanning around at ground level. Too dark to make anything out, but his gaze kept returning to a blur within the base of a thick stand of reeds. It didn't move and it was the wrong shape. 'Is that you?'

He pulled himself towards it. He was only a yard away when the blur shaped itself into the haggard, lying prone with her wings outspread. She was frightened by the darkness and wind, the threat from the eagle. His arrival reassured her and she stood and mantled over her prey. Her bell shivered.

Wayland stretched out his right hand. She hadn't even started plucking the pigeon. If the eagle hadn't menaced her, she would have gorged by now and flown off to roost.

His cold fingers fumbled before getting a grip on her jesses. No time to fit the swivel. Teeth chattering, he threaded the leash through the slits. When he'd looped the leash around his glove, his pent up breath burst out.

'Where are you?' Walter called. He'd been calling for some time.

Wayland lifted the falcon and her prey onto his glove and rocked back on his knees. 'I've got her.'

The wind blew Walter's response away.

Wayland slipped the hood on and made his way back.

Walter seized his arm. 'Now tell me how Drogo and the Frank intend to murder me.'

'Wait until we're clear of the bogs. Stay close. Tread where I tread.'

He took his bearings by the twin peaks and set off. The wind had strengthened to a gale and the reeds lashed over his head like swords.

'Slow down, damn you. I can hardly see you.'

Wayland increased his pace and reached one of the quagmires. He stepped onto it and felt the surface give. He looked behind him.

Walter was out of sight, thrashing through the reeds. 'Wait for me.'

Wayland took a breath and crossed the bog at a gliding run. On the other side he stopped with a hand held over his thumping heart. He heard a splash and a shocked cry.

'Blood of Christ! Another foot and I'd have been lost. Where are you, damn you?'

'Here.'

Walter's dim outline appeared on the far edge of the bog. 'Why do you go so fast? What path do I take?'

'Straight across.'

'This isn't the way we came. It's a bog.'

'It's the path I've just taken. There are my footprints.'

'You aren't wearing sixty pounds of armour.'

'The surface will bear your weight.'

Walter took one cautious step. 'It trembles. I'm going to find a way round it.'

'It's too late to find another way. Walk towards me. Don't linger on one spot.'

Walter shuffled forward, knees bent, hands outstretched. Wayland watched with detachment. If he reaches me, he thought, I'll let him live. Step after step he came closer, muttering to himself. The surface around him wallowed in slow undulations. He looked up, face white with fear in the starlight. 'It won't hold.'

'Keep moving.'

Walter took three more steps and was halfway across when the surface gave way and he plunged into the bog like a man falling through the hangman's trap. He floundered waist-deep. 'I can't move,' he gibbered. 'The swamp holds me fast. I'm sinking. Oh my God! Help me!'

Wayland watched him.

'Save me! Why do you stand there? Why don't you speak?'

Wayland's tongue stuck to the roof of his mouth.

Walter stopped struggling. 'Is this why you brought me? I understand now. It's Drogo's doing. You're the instrument of his hatred.' His voice fell away in a moan of despair.

Wayland recovered his voice. 'It's nothing to do with Drogo or Vallon!'

Only the stars for witness. Walter's teeth chattered.

'Why do you want to harm me? I rescued you from the wilderness. I gave you house space, made you my falconer. Why do you want to harm me?'

Wayland bent forward, his face ugly. 'Because you cut off a man's head.'

'I've killed many men in battle. What are you talking about?'

Wayland dropped to a crouch. 'It was my father's head.'

'I don't know your father. I can't remember every English warrior who fell by my sword.'

'He wasn't a warrior and you didn't kill him in battle. He was a farmer and you rode into his farmstead one evening four years ago as he was splitting firewood. Your men held him down over the chopping block and you hacked off his head and you laughed. When he was dead, you took my mother and my older sister into the cottage and raped them. Then you cut their throats and set fire to the house with my grandfather inside.'

'That wasn't me. It must have been Drogo.'

'It was you and Drax and Roussel and others. I was there. I was watching.'

Walter began to pant. 'I did no more than any other Norman would have done. Your father was poaching my deer. The penalty for poaching is death.'

'My mother and sisters weren't poachers.'

Walter groaned. 'Wayland, I could have killed you when I found you in the forest. Show me the same mercy I granted you. Drogo wouldn't have spared your life.'

Wayland straightened. 'Confess your crime and repent.'

'Confess? To an English peasant?'

'Repent or die.'

'I repent nothing. My only regret is that I didn't kill you.'

Wayland's voice fell to a mumble. 'All you have to do is repent. Beg forgiveness and I'll save you.'

'Never.'

Wayland clawed at his face. All his dreams and hopes had turned rotten. Before the night was much older, he too would be dead, leaving Syth and their unborn child alone in an alien land.

Walter breathed in juddering spasms. 'This is your own revenge, isn't it? Vallon doesn't know.'

'I've told no one.'

Walter's voice rose to a screech. 'You fool. If I die, the secret of the gospel dies with me.'

Wayland stared in incomprehension. 'What secret? What gospel?'

'The Gospel of Thomas and a letter from Prester John. Treasures beyond price. Why do you think Vallon risked his life to save me? Why do you think Cosmas negotiated my ransom?'

'Where are they?'

'Where no one can find them but me. Now pull me out of this foul mire.'

Walter had sunk to his chest. Cries floated down the wind. A smear of flame appeared through the reeds.

'Help!' Walter shouted. 'Help!'

The cries came closer. Torches flickered.

'Oh thank God,' Walter gasped. He stopped struggling. 'Now you'll pay for your treachery. What I did to your family is nothing compared to the punishment I'll deal out to you.'

Four figures shoved out of the reeds.

'Wayland?' Vallon called.

'He led me into the bog,' Walter cried. 'He tried to murder me. For the love of God, help me!'

Vallon edged towards Wayland, Hero following. The other two men were Seljuks, carrying poles and rope. They took in the situation and unlooped the rope.

'Don't struggle,' Vallon told Walter. 'We'll pull you out.'

'Oh, thank God!'

Hero pushed forward. 'Where's the gospel?'

Vallon slapped him. 'The man's in peril of death.'

'He won't tell us otherwise. Once he's safe, he'll turn against us. Walter, tell us where you've hidden the documents.'

'You swear to save me?'

'You're wasting precious time,' said Vallon. 'Of course we'll save you.'

'They're in a Roman bastillion on the eastern shore of Salt Lake. Hurry!'

'We camped near the fort. Where will we find the gospel?'

'The top of the staircase. Behind a stone carved with a lion. Hurry before it's too late.'

Vallon ordered the Seljuk to throw the rope. 'Reach for it carefully. Don't move more than you have to.'

Walter clung to it. Vallon and Hero and the two Seljuks heaved. Vallon turned to Wayland. 'Help us.'

They strained and grunted until sweat broke on their brows. Each heave raised Walter half a foot, but all their efforts couldn't break the bog's grip.

'Take your hauberk off,' Vallon called. 'You won't sink if you rid yourself of your armour.'

Walter clawed at the slippery mail with icy, mud-coated hands. 'I can't. Every movement pulls me deeper.'

'Send one of the Seljuks for more men,' Hero said.

Vallon wiped his forehead. 'It's no use. It would take a team of horses to drag him loose, and the strain would tear him in two.' He raised his head. 'Walter, you have to break the suction. Paddle with your legs.'

Walter had sunk to his shoulders. 'I can't feel them,' he whimpered.

Vallon seized the rope again. 'Another effort.'

They hauled first in one direction, then another. Something popped and the rope sprang loose, sending them tumbling backwards.

'My shoulder!' Walter screamed.

Vallon picked himself up. He cast the rope towards Walter. 'Take hold of it. At least we can keep you from going under.' He turned to Hero. 'Send one of the Seljuks to fetch a team carrying ladders.'

'He'll freeze to death before they get here.'

Walter's left hand groped for the rope. His fingers closed on it. When Vallon drew it taut, it pulled straight out.

'I can't hold it. All feeling has gone.'

The bog was above his shoulders. Vallon doubled over, hands on knees. 'Walter, there's nothing more we can do. Make peace with your maker.'

The surface was up to Walter's chin. 'Oh mother of God, save me in my hour of need. Oh merciful mother of God . . . ' He broke off with a sob.

They watched in horror as Walter sank deeper.

'What a terrible way to die,' he said, his tone remote. He called out in Turkic to the Seljuks. 'I've told them what happened here. The Emir will make you pay for your crimes.' His voice rose to a shriek. 'I curse

Wayland! And I curse you for bringing him here and I curse Drogo! I'll be waiting for you in hell!'

Water closed over his mouth and he delivered his final curse as a gargling scream. Wayland's flesh crept, but he remembered his family massacred in their home and didn't regret his crime. Bubbles erupted from Walter's mouth. He heaved up as the water rose above his nose. He sank again and more bubbles burst. His eyes still showed, rolling with terror, and then they went still and glazed over. They sank from sight. Slowly his head disappeared. The surface quaked one last time and went still.

Vallon was down on one knee. He turned his head. 'Is it true? Did you lead him to his death?'

'He slaughtered my family. Father, mother, brother and sister, grandfather . . . He raped the women and cut their throats.'

Vallon looked at him for a long time. 'That's why you joined us. I set out to rescue Walter, and you were planning to kill him.'

'Only at first. Once I met Syth, once I saw how gallantly you led us, I swore to bury my hatred. I haven't even told Syth what Walter did. But then he threatened to kill me. He gloated about it. I know the Emir will probably execute me for disobeying his orders. I know I won't see the child Syth's carrying. Walter followed me into the marsh and revenge was all I had left. Even then I gave him a chance. I would have tried to save him if only he'd confessed his crimes and repented.'

Vallon heaved an exhausted sigh and stood. 'The Seljuks don't know what happened. We'll tell the Emir it was an accident. At least you recovered the falcon. That might go some way to assuaging his wrath.'

Wayland broke down. It wasn't fear of Suleyman's punishment that overwhelmed him. It was the stress that had built up in him from the moment chance presented him with the opportunity to kill Walter. It was despair at the thought of what would happen to Syth.

Hero put his arm around him. 'Come on. Let's leave this awful place.'

They picked their way out of the marsh. About twenty men remained with the Emir, rags of flame whisking from their torches. Suleyman rode forward, hunched and malevolent. Vallon and Hero stepped in front of Wayland and pleaded for mercy. Half a dozen Seljuks dragged them out of the way at swordpoint. The Emir stopped in front of Wayland and gave an order. Ibrahim approached. From the pitiful expression on his face, Wayland knew that the Emir wouldn't show mercy. Ibrahim took the falcon. He held up a hand, showing Suleyman the pigeon. The Emir dashed it to the ground.

Wayland raised his eyes. 'Let me see Syth one last time.'

Drogo spoke out of the dark. 'They took her back to the camp.'

'I'll take care of her,' Vallon said. 'I promise she won't come to harm.'

The Emir raised his mace. Wayland stared at the twin peaks. The torches guttered.

One of the underfalconers threw himself down and scooped up the pigeon. He thrust his hand up. The Emir's stallion flared its nostrils and side-stepped.

Ibrahim grabbed the pigeon and called for light. Two torchbearers ran up to him. He held the pigeon towards the flames and Wayland glimpsed something gleaming on its leg. Suleyman looked down at it and waved his hand. Faruq dismounted and hurried up. Ibrahim cut the object off the pigeon's leg and handed it to him. He held it between thumb and forefinger.

A tiny cylinder. Wayland had no idea what it meant.

'A messenger pigeon,' he heard Hero say.

'I know,' said Vallon. 'The Moors used them in Spain. Wayland, stay where you are and don't say a word.'

Nobody was paying any attention to him. Everyone was leaning into the cluster of torches, intent on what Faruq was doing. He prised a cap off the tube and extracted its contents. He called for the torches to be brought closer and unrolled a tiny piece of fabric. From the way his lips worked, it must have contained writing. He gasped, collected himself with conscious effort and beckoned the Emir closer. Suleyman leaned down until Faruq was able to speak into his ear. What he said made the Emir sit bolt upright. His gaze roamed through the night. When it returned it settled on Wayland. He squeezed his horse's flanks, rode forward and ruffled Wayland's hair. He threw back his head and laughed.

The other Seljuks were as baffled as Wayland. They spread their hands at each other, hitched their shoulders.

'What's going on?' said Drogo.

'A miracle, that's what,' Vallon answered.

Suleyman unslung his quiver and passed its contents out among his company, pointing in a different direction as he handed over each arrow. One after the other the Seljuks galloped into the night, heading to all points of the compass. When the last of them had gone, the Emir grinned at Wayland, shook his head in fond amazement and turned his stallion. The remaining riders formed up around him and they raced off, their horses spraying gravel.

LI

Hero watched the torches dwindle into the dark. 'What's the meaning of the arrows?'

'Suleyman's summoning his army,' said Vallon. 'He must be mobilising for war.'

'He doesn't seem dismayed by the prospect. In fact he was so excited by the message that he didn't even notice Walter's missing.'

'What's happened to him?' Drogo demanded. 'Where is he?'

'You two go on,' Vallon said. He waited until Hero and Wayland had left. 'Walter's dead. He lost his path and fell into a bog. We couldn't pull him out and the weight of his armour dragged him under.'

Drogo looked back at the marsh. When he turned his head, he was smiling. 'Wayland.'

Vallon's eyes narrowed. 'You knew, didn't you?'

'I found out the day you fled from the castle. He led my men into the wood and killed Drax and Roussel. They'd taken part in the killings.'

'Think yourself lucky that you weren't party to the crime.'

'Slaying the family wasn't a crime. I would have killed them, too, just as I would have killed Wayland if it had been me who'd found him in the forest.'

'Your answer to everything.'

Vallon set his horse into the crosswind, masking his face with his cape. Bits of dry scrub skipped and tumbled across his path. The whole plateau seemed to be on the move. Overhead the stars clumped in swirls and blotches of phosphorescence.

Drogo caught up. 'Droll, isn't it? Walter kills Wayland's family and then adopts him as a pet. He was genuinely fond of him. I wish I'd been there when Wayland told him who he was. I'd have given anything to see his face.'

Vallon quickened his pace.

Drogo laughed. 'All this way to save a man who didn't need saving, and then it turns out that Wayland only joined you for the chance of murdering Walter.'

Vallon whipped out his sword and laid the blade against Drogo's throat. 'It was an accident. Say different and I'll kill you.'

'Don't excite yourself. Accident or murder, Walter's dead and I've got what I want.'

'Have you?'

'Nothing stands between me and my inheritance. My father's sick. I don't expect to find him alive by the time I return to England.'

'A lot can happen between now and then.'

They jogged on. The Emir's encampment appeared as a faint red pulse on the plain.

'What about you?' Drogo said. 'The money's gone and you've got nothing to show for it.'

'Don't be so sure.'

'You mean Caitlin.'

'I'll escort her to the capital if that's what she wants.'

'You'll find her affections have cooled now that you're penniless. If you enlist with the Varangians, you'll probably be posted to some backwater in Greece or Bulgaria. Caitlin's too fond of her comforts to enjoy life as the wife of a field captain.'

'I never said I intended marrying her.'

Drogo seized Vallon's bridle. 'Then let me have her.'

'It's not me who stands between you and Caitlin.'

'Who are you speaking of?'

'If you understood Arabic, you'd have heard the Emir asking to take her for his wife.'

'Caitlin wouldn't make a match with that bandy-legged dwarf.'

'Why not? You're the one who says she covets luxury and status. Suleyman rules a fief larger than England. He probably possesses more wealth than your King William. Did you see how much silver he threw at the archer who killed the jackal?'

Walter was silent for a while. 'What did you tell him?'

'I told him that Caitlin was my woman. That we were lovers.'

Drogo flinched. 'That's not true. I've been watching her close. You haven't had any opportunities.'

'Drogo, if a man and a woman want to satisfy their lust, they'll always find a way to avoid prying eyes.'

Drogo's hand fell on his sword.

'Go ahead,' said Vallon. 'You'll never possess Caitlin. She despises you. In Constantinople she can take her pick of rich and noble suitors. A woman as beautiful as Caitlin could snare an emperor in the making.'

'By God, Vallon, if I thought that you and Caitlin had lain together ...'

Vallon ignored him and rose in his stirrups. 'Whatever message the pigeon was carrying, it's caused a mighty stir. The encampment looks like a wasps' nest that someone's poked with a stick.'

Seljuks raced hither and yon. They were striking camp. Pack animals jammed the lanes. A group of nomads loaded baggage onto a train of camels. A dismantled tent dragged away downwind, towing a dozen men behind it. Vallon reached his quarters and turned to Drogo.

'This is where we part for good. From now on, you make your own way.'

'Vallon—'

He jumped off his horse and pushed through the entrance. Only Hero was inside.

'Where's Wayland?'

'He went to see Syth.'

'Have you discovered the cause of the upheaval?'

'Not yet. All I know is that all non-combatants are returning to Konya. Faruq told me we can expect a summons before midnight.'

'That will be interesting. Is there any food? I'm famished.'

'Even the servants have gone. By tomorrow the camp will be deserted.'

Vallon pulled off his boots. He found some bread and a conserve of apricots and ate sitting on the edge of his pallet. 'A strange day. From the heights to the depths, and now we're suspended somewhere in between.'

621

'Were you shocked by what Wayland did?'

'Shocked but not surprised. I always wondered about his reasons for killing Drax and Roussel. Then more than once I saw him and Drogo exchange odd looks. I quizzed him about it and he denied hiding any secrets. I should have realised the truth when he didn't press charges after Drogo released the falcons, but I always thought that Wayland was incapable of deceit. It just shows the wisdom of taking no one at face value.'

'Are you angry with him?'

Vallon paused in his chewing. 'Part of me deplores a peasant killing a knight, but Wayland had every reason.'

'And he's rescued our hopes. If he hadn't led Walter into the swamp, the wretch would never have told us where he'd hidden the gospel.'

'We still have to get our hands on it. If Suleyman sends everyone to Konya, we might not get a chance to return to the tower.'

'I think fortune will find us a way.'

Vallon laughed. 'It scares me how much we've been sucking from that teat. It can't be long before it runs dry.'

Wind gusted into the tent. Chinua marched in with Faruq and six soldiers. 'His Excellency commands your presence.' Faruq clapped his hands. 'At once.'

Vallon put down his bread, wiped his hands and pulled on his boots. He and Hero walked to the entrance and went out into the turbulent night.

Suleyman paced up and down the throne room in his armour, his commanders trotting behind, a scribe taking notes. The Emir stopped when Vallon entered and waved his entourage aside. Wayland was already in attendance, standing pale and subdued beside Ibrahim, the gyrfalcon sitting on the hawkmaster's fist. Vallon squeezed Wayland's arm. 'I think it's going to be all right.'

The Emir hopped up on to his throne. Faruq exchanged a few words with him before facing the company. 'There is no time for formalities. The pigeon was carrying a message from Persia. The Sultan Alp Arslan is dead – may his glorious deeds be rewarded in Paradise. He died two weeks ago while his army was putting down a rebellion on the Oxus river. A prisoner drew a knife and delivered a mortal wound. That's all we know.'

Suleyman rocked on his throne, thumping his mace in glee. Faruq forced a smile.

'The pigeon belonged to the Emir Temur.'

Vallon squeezed Wayland's arm. 'You're safe.'

'I don't understand what's—'

'Nor do I. Listen.'

Faruq was speaking again. 'Alp Arslan's empire stretches from the Hindu Kush to the Mediterranean. His son and heir is only thirteen. The succession isn't settled. While the rival factions in Persia plot and connive, his Excellency means to establish his own sultanate in Rum.' Faruq raised a hand. 'All blessings proceed from God, exalted be his name, and since his Excellency perceives the hand of God in today's events, he has decided to reward the agents of his good fortune.'

Suleyman clicked his fingers. A guard at one of the entrances called down the passage. A servant hurried in carrying a pair of balance scales with one end adapted to some purpose Vallon couldn't work out. The menial placed the scales on a table. Next to it sat Suleyman's war helmet, sporting a panache of osprey plumes.

The Emir clicked his fingers again and Ibrahim stepped forward with the gyrfalcon. He set it down on the scales and Vallon realised that one side was a perch.

Suleyman descended from his throne and held out his hand. Another servant passed him a leather pouch. The Emir scooped out a handful of silver coins and dropped them on the empty pan. Two or three bounced out and rolled away. Officers hurried to retrieve them. The wind moaned outside and the walls of the throne room bellied in and out. The Emir grabbed another fistful of silver and grinned.

'How heavy is the gyrfalcon?' Vallon said from the corner of his mouth.

'About five pounds,' said Wayland.

'Well, we won't leave empty-handed.'

Suleyman heaped handfuls of silver on the pan. With a flourish he upended the bag and sprinkled the remaining coins. The beam tilted. The pan containing the silver settled, then rose again. The Emir frowned. He pressed down the scales in favour of the silver and let go, but it was wanting in the balance and settled in favour of the falcon.

Vallon began to rise. 'His Excellency is more than generous. Please tell him—'

Suleyman waved him back. He looked around with furious intent and his eyes settled on Faruq. He grabbed the official's hand and removed from it a ring set with a ruby. He held it above the heap of silver.

'This had better tilt the scales,' Vallon muttered.

Suleyman dropped the ring on to the pile of silver. The pan wavered and sank. The falcon rose. The spectators applauded and Faruq managed a feeble smile. The Emir held out the bag to Vallon.

'The silver is yours,' said Faruq.

Vallon nudged Wayland. 'You won it. You take it.'

Wayland advanced awkwardly. He picked up a coin, dropped it in the bag and looked back.

'It's not a trick,' said Hero.

Wayland filled the bag until about a handful of silver remained on the pan. He hesitated, gathered up the remainder and presented it to Ibrahim. The hawkmaster embraced him. The audience applauded once more.

Suleyman had resumed his throne. Faruq listened to him, stroking the finger where his ring had been. He faced the company. 'His Excellency has more blessings to bestow.'

Here comes the catch, thought Vallon.

Faruq walked up to him. 'His Excellency offers you a position as captain of a hundred in his personal guard. With the title comes land and a property in Konya. A band of trumpeters will proclaim your rank outside your gate each sunset.'

Hero sidled closer. 'Accept the position if that's what you want. Don't worry about me.'

'What about the gospel?' Vallon bowed to the Emir. 'His Excellency does me more honour than I deserve. Convey my humble gratitude and tell him that I've pledged my services to Byzantium.'

The Seljuks murmured and shook their heads. The Emir pinched his nostrils. He tugged at his moustache. Faruq approached Hero.

'His Excellency esteems all branches of learning. He invites you to choose a position in his household as scribe, translator or physician. He intends to establish a hospital in Konya and would like you to work in it.'

Hero glanced at Vallon in panic. 'How am I supposed to answer?'

'Truthfully. If you want the position, say so.'

Hero plucked at his throat. 'His Excellency has formed an inflated impression of my medical expertise. I'm only a student, with years of study ahead before I qualify. When I do, I look forward to returning to Rum and sharing what skills I've mastered with his Excellency's physicians.'

More disapproving whispers from the Seljuks. The Emir settled in a malign slouch. He said something and Faruq addressed himself to Wayland.

'The Emir's offering you a position as assistant keeper of his falcons,' Hero said.

'I don't know. I need time to think. I have to talk with Syth.'

Hero glanced at Suleyman. 'In his world, men make the decisions. He expects an answer now.'

Vallon smiled at Faruq. 'Allow us a few moments to consider.' He turned Wayland aside. 'Do you have any plans for when we reach Constantinople?'

'No. I don't want to live in the city.'

'Quarter of the silver is yours. Enough to set yourself up as a farmer.'

'I don't want to work the soil.'

'You could return to England.'

'I can't travel while Syth's pregnant.'

'Then I suggest that you consider the Emir's offer seriously. You know what sort of establishment he runs. You've seen how cruel he can be when crossed; but having come so close to death at his hands, I don't think you'll make that mistake again.'

Wayland looked at Ibrahim. The hawkmaster smiled encouragingly.

'I wouldn't accept if it meant leaving Syth.'

'It won't.'

'Will I have to convert to Islam?'

'The Emir won't insist on it. He employs Jews and Christians in his entourage.'

Wayland took a breath, looked at the gently smiling Ibrahim. 'Tell him I accept.'

The Seljuks gave a smattering of applause. Vallon patted Wayland's arm. 'I think you've made the right decision.'

Suleyman slipped off his throne. Chinua began escorting the company out.

'Vallon.'

He turned and saw that it was the Emir who'd spoken. 'I'll catch you up,' he told the others.

'I'm disappointed that you turned down the offer to serve in my army,' Suleyman said in serviceable Arabic. 'I'll be here until dawn in case you change your mind. If you don't, you and the Greek will leave for Konya tomorrow. From there an escort will take you to the frontier with a safe conduct.'

The opposite direction from the tower where the gospel was hidden. Vallon's skin prickled at the risk he was about to take. 'An escort isn't necessary. We'll make our own way. We'd planned to take the northerly route, riding back up Salt Lake.'

Suleyman shook his head. 'I won't allow my guests to travel without protection.' He shrugged. 'As for the route, choose your own.'

Vallon hid his relief. Almost there.

'Will Walter's brother be travelling with you?'

'No. I've suffered his presence long enough.'

'What do you want me to do with him?'

Vallon knew that if he said 'Kill him', the Emir would attend to the matter as casually as if he'd asked for a drink of water. 'Let him travel to Constantinople on his own. I'll provide funds for the journey.'

Without turning, Suleyman gave an order. Two of his men went out.

'Is that all?' Vallon said. 'I don't want to intrude on your time more than necessary.'

Suleyman looked up at Vallon from under drooping eyelids. 'The Icelandic woman.'

Vallon forced a smile. Here it comes. If he tells me that he won't let her go, there's not a thing I can do to stop him. 'Caitlin? What about her?'

'She'll be travelling with you to Constantinople?'

'If that's what she wants.'

'Isn't she sure?'

'We haven't discussed it.'

'You haven't discussed your plans with your lover?'

'We aren't lovers. That was a lie to protect her.'

'I know. Her maids report everything she says.' Suleyman stepped close. His head came up to Vallon's shoulders. He pointed at the scales. 'Leave her with me and I'll give you as much again.'

Vallon shook his head.

'In gold.'

A fortune. Vallon swallowed. 'I won't force her to do anything against her will. If she wants to stay, I won't try to dissuade her. It will be her choice and I won't accept any payment. If she wants to leave, I'll take her with me.'

Suleyman studied him, nodding. 'Very well. Let's leave it in God's hands.'

Vallon bowed and began to back away. Suleyman reached out to detain him. 'Before we part, tell me what brought you here. The real reason. It wasn't money and it wasn't for love of Walter. So what?'

Vallon looked at the carpet. Its maker had woven a design of carnations and scorpions. 'All journeys have secret destinations.'

'And what is yours?'

'I'm not sure I understand.'

'When Cosmas negotiated Sir Walter's ransom, I was curious why a senior Greek diplomat should bother himself with a Norman mercenary.'

'I don't know. I only met Cosmas on the night he died. We hardly spoke.'

'I set a high price for Walter's release, never expecting Cosmas to raise it. Then more than a year later, you arrived, having voyaged from the end of the world to save a man you've never met. Why all this interest in rescuing a Norman of modest rank?'

'In the beginning ...' Vallon looked up. 'It was penance for a crime I committed.'

'Penance?'

'Expiation. I killed my wife and her lover.'

Suleyman's eyes crinkled. 'That's not a crime.'

'I have no regrets about killing the man. He betrayed me in other ways. But my wife ... Killing her has left my three children orphans. I'll never see them again.'

Suleyman tapped him on the chest with his mace. 'A good commander never regrets his actions. If I think someone means me harm, I kill him first and leave God to do the judging.'

'That's why you're an Emir and I'm only a captain.'

Suleyman pressed his mace against Vallon's chest. 'Did the falconer kill Walter?'

'Why would he do that? Walter saved Wayland from the forest.'

627

'If you save a wolf, it doesn't mean it loves you. Walter told the Seljuks that the falconer led him into the bog.'

'How would they know? They weren't there when Walter lost his way.'

The pressure of the mace increased. 'Walter swore it was murder.'

'Men often rave when they come face to face with death. I'm sorry Walter died. We tried our hardest to save him.'

Suleyman relaxed the pressure on the mace. 'It's as well that he's dead. His behaviour was becoming a scandal and I suspect that he was playing a double game with the Byzantines. I would have had to deal with him myself if . . . ' Suleyman raised his eyes ' . . . he hadn't fallen into the bog.'

He swung on his heel and joined his officers. 'My offer still stands. You have until dawn.'

'Can I ask you something, your Excellency?'

Suleyman looked back over his shoulder.

'How many wives do you have?'

Suleyman's eyes went vague. 'Nine, I think. My chief secretary will give you the precise number.'

'Eleven,' said Faruq and pointed to the exit.

Hero jumped up, agog for news when Vallon returned to their quarters. 'Are we free to return to the bastillion?'

'Yes. Under escort.'

'That could make things difficult.'

'Suleyman's suspicious. He can't understand why Cosmas and me were so desperate to win Walter's freedom.'

'Do you think he has any idea of the gospel?'

'No. I told him I'd made the journey to atone for killing my wife. It seems strange now, but it's the truth.'

Vallon divided the silver into four equal parts, keeping two parts for himself and leaving the rest to be shared between Hero and Wayland. He washed and changed before heading back out into the night. The Seljuks had cleared most of the camp and scores of men were dismantling the Emir's pavilion, wrestling with billows of flapping felt. Vallon stooped against the wind, making for the women's quarters.

A eunuch led him down a corridor with chambers leading off it. The roar of the wind fell away to a distant sigh. The eunuch stopped outside an entrance and called out. A woman's voice answered. He nodded and Vallon went in.

It was like entering a silken womb. Caitlin sat at a dressing table attended by two maids. She rose, her eyes outlined with kohl, her hair dressed in a complicated oriental style. She wore a costume of many gauzy layers, each layer semi-transparent. Jewellery sparkled at her neck and on her wrists.

Vallon smiled. 'You look like a queen.'

She hurried towards him. 'Is it true that the Emir's going to war?'

'I need to talk privately.'

Caitlin gestured and the maids went out. She sat on a divan. Vallon remained standing.

'Yes, the Emir's mobilising his army. Alp Arslan is dead. Suleyman intends to take control of Rum while the Sultan's rivals squabble over the succession.'

Caitlin patted the divan. 'Sit beside me. Would you like something to drink? Are you hungry? You look tired.'

Bowls of fruit and vases of flowers stood on a table. Finely knotted silk carpets covered the floor.

Vallon sat and picked a grape from a bunch. He could smell Caitlin's heady perfume.

'I've heard so many rumours. One of my maids told me that the Emir had offered you a senior position in his army.'

Vallon popped the grape into his mouth. 'It's true. Captain of a hundred, with a grant of land and a house in Konya where trumpeters will serenade me each sunset.'

She eyed him uncertainly. 'That's wonderful. I've heard that Konya is a beautiful city, full of palaces.'

'I turned it down.'

Her smoky green eyes widened. 'Why?'

'Suleyman's a Turk; I'm a Christian. Sooner or later the two faiths will clash and I don't want to find myself fighting men who wear the cross.'

Caitlin let go of his hand. 'So you still mean to join the Emperor's guard?'

Vallon was sick of being asked what he would do. He'd spent the last year *doing*. What he wanted was time and space to think. He picked up an orange, turned it in his hands, put it back.

629

'I didn't come here to talk about my plans.'

'*Our* plans. Wherever you go, I'll follow.'

'I'll probably be posted overseas. I might not see you for years.'

'I can wait.'

Vallon reached for her hand. 'You told me a witch prophesied that a foreign prince would steal your heart. I'm not a prince. Suleyman is. The jewels you're wearing come from him, not me.'

Caitlin pressed his hand to her lips. 'I don't want Suleyman. I want you.'

'Come with me and you face years of lonely uncertainty. Stay here and become Suleyman's wife—'

Caitlin slapped his face and jumped up. 'Is he paying you to act as a pander?'

'Caitlin—'

She rained blows on his head. He managed to grasp her hands. She toppled on to him and the next moment they were kissing.

Caitlin pulled her lips away. 'I love you. How much more proof do you need?'

'Hear me out. If you become Suleyman's wife—'

'One of twelve.'

'And the most beautiful. Your son might be Emir one day, perhaps even Sultan.'

Caitlin shivered. 'I'm not a brood mare. I want a husband who'll cherish me as much as I cherish him. I know you're that man.'

'Suleyman offered me five pounds of gold if I left you here.'

Caitlin's face turned white. 'Five pounds of gold?'

'Enough to buy a broad and fertile estate. I refused the offer. The choice must be yours.'

'I've already made it.'

Vallon looked into her eyes. 'Tomorrow, Hero and I are leaving alone. No, listen to me. We have one last piece of business to conclude. If we're successful, it could make us richer than if I'd taken Suleyman's gold.'

'What business? Tell me.'

'I can't. If we find what we're looking for, I'll return for you the day after tomorrow. I promise.'

'By then I'll be in Konya.'

'Then I'll look for you in Konya.'

'Once you've left, the Emir might hide me away. Let me come with you.'

'No. It's too risky.' He rose.

'What if you don't find what you're looking for?'

He was already walking towards the entrance. 'While I'm gone, consider what's best for your future.'

She rose in a rustle of silk. 'Don't go.'

'I think it would be better if I did.'

An orange flew past his head. 'Is that another of the Emir's orders?'

Vallon stopped. 'At our first audience, I told him we were lovers. I did it to protect you. He knows it's a lie. Your maids spy on you.'

'Then stay and make it true.'

He turned. A tear sparkled on Caitlin's lashes. 'Did you reject his gold because you set my value at nought? Do you hate me? Am I so repugnant? Are you so bound to chastity?'

'No to all your questions.'

'Then what do I have to do to persuade you?'

He took one step towards her.

Caitlin removed a layer of silk and let it fall. It floated down as light as a cobweb. 'Is that enough or must I do more?'

Vallon's throat pulsed.

Caitlin removed the second gossamer layer. 'Still not enough?'

Vallon massaged his throat. 'I'll tell you when.'

She gave him a sharp look. 'I've not done this for any other man.'

'I imagine that in Iceland you tear off your homespun and dive under the fleeces before the frost can nip your tender parts.'

She laughed and discarded another veil. Beneath it she wore a gown so flimsy that he could see every curve and cranny against the lamp-light. She slipped it from her shoulders and it slithered to the floor with a sigh and pooled around her feet. All she wore was a gold girdle with a jade pendant hanging below her navel. A gift from the Emir. Her hand felt for the clasp.

He took her in his arms. 'Keep it on,' he said, voice congested.

She lolled against him, 'What was it you said about seeing me naked? "It was no hardship on the eyes."'

Vallon buried his mouth in the hollow of her shoulder. 'Forgive a rough and ready soldier. You're the most beautiful woman I've ever seen.'

She led him into her bedchamber through curtains embroidered with birds amid fruiting vines. Lamps flickered around her bed. She slipped under the cover and spread her arms and gave a long expiring sigh.

Vallon undressed and slid in beside her. He put his arm around her and she rested her face against his. Her eyelashes fluttered against his cheek. He breathed in her fragrance and closed his eyes. It was like returning to a blissful place he thought he'd never visit again.

He murmured into the soft curve of her jaw. 'I haven't lain with a woman for three years.'

She sat up, her breasts jiggling. 'Is there something wrong with you?'

Vallon closed his lips around her nipple. 'The Moors don't provide prisoners with women.'

'Who was the last woman you made love to?'

'My wife.'

She subsided on top of him. 'Were you faithful to her?'

'Why do women ask so many questions?'

'Because we're interested in the answers. So ... were you faithful?'

'I was.'

She wriggled up so she could see his face. 'I don't believe you. All those years campaigning and you never gave in to temptation?'

'I must be a bloodless soul.'

She settled back and her hand crept down his belly, pausing on the scar, moving lower. 'I wouldn't say that.'

He rolled her onto her back, raised himself up and looked down into her eyes. She looped her arms around his neck. 'You'll always be my prince,' she said, and then gasped and arched her neck back as he entered.

LII

He woke to utter stillness. The lamps around the bed burned without the slightest tremor and the drapes hung motionless. Wincing with the effort imposed by stealth, he extricated his arm from under Caitlin's neck. She moaned and nuzzled her forearm. He dressed and stood looking down at her. He extended a hand towards her face, drew it back without touching. She sighed and slid an arm into the space he'd left. Was that sleep?

632

He nipped out the lamps by the bed, parted the curtain and crossed to her dressing table. Reaching into his tunic, he removed one of the bags of silver and placed it next to her shrine of powders and scents. He heard her turn over and he held his breath, wondering what he'd do if she called out. She gave a purring snore and he relaxed his lungs. He took a last look, then he left, stealing down the empty corridor and out into the hushed night. He stood for a moment, his face tilted to the firmament.

The Seljuks had all but cleared the site. A column of riders trotted away in a silent line to the east. Teams of menials were still working on the Emir's pavilion, pulling down the antechambers. This time tomorrow it would stand proud in the centre of Konya.

The throne room was the last piece of the web still standing. Vallon asked one of the guards if he could speak to Suleyman and after a while Chinua appeared to escort him inside. Only half a dozen officers and advisors remained with the Emir. He waved them away when he saw Vallon.

'You've changed your mind. Good.'

'I've just come from Caitlin.'

Suleyman took his elbow and walked him out of earshot of his men. 'From her bed.' It wasn't a question.

'Yes.'

Suleyman's face tightened in a snarl. 'You interrupt me fresh from your rut. I can smell her on you. I can smell you both. If you came here to rub my nose in it—'

'I want Caitlin more than anything, but I know that love isn't enough. I can't provide for her in the way that you can, the way I know she wants. I've told her what advantages will fall her way if she stays and set them against my own poor prospects. I came here to confirm that I'll keep my side of the bargain and to implore you to honour yours. I'll be gone before she wakes, leaving her to reach a decision. I intend to return to hear what she's decided the day after tomorrow. If she's chosen you, so be it. If she wants to come with me, will you allow her to leave?'

Suleyman cast about as if he'd been accosted by a madman. 'If you desire her, why don't you just take her?'

'I need to be sure it's what she wants.'

'If I didn't know that you'd travelled through the wilderness of the world, I'd call you a coward. Serve in my army and within two year you'll have acquired enough wealth to keep four wives in luxury. Suleyman examined Vallon's face. 'I can't make up my mind whether you're a trickster or a fool.' He flicked a hand against Vallon's chest. 'I'm too busy to waste any more time on the matter.' He made a quick gesture to his guards. 'If the woman wants to go, she can go. Now leave before you exhaust my patience.'

Hands fell on Vallon's shoulders and propelled him out of the pavilion. Faruq's voice followed him into the night. 'Don't impose on his Excellency again if you have any regard for your life.'

Vallon wandered through the camp in a daze of elation and apprehension. Suleyman's elite troops sat in firelit circles, some holding the reins of their saddled horses. A few raised a hand as he passed. He paused outside his quarters. The sky to the east held the first grey light of day. He went in and felt his way to his bed.

'No need to tread softly,' Hero said. 'I was too anxious to sleep.'

'Don't be. It's nearly dawn. We'll be off soon.'

Hero rose, placed kindling on the brazier and blew life into it. Vallon joined him close to the glow, firelight and shadows playing across their faces.

Hero broke the silence. 'I've been thinking. If we don't recover the gospel today, we won't get another chance. Perhaps we could ask Wayland to collect it and bring it to us in Konya.'

'I won't do anything that might put him in harm's way. He's Suleyman's man now.'

'Did you spend the night with Caitlin?'

'Yes.'

'Did you tell her about the gospel? Is she coming with us?'

'No. I told her that we were looking for something and that I'd come back tomorrow if we found it.'

'Won't Suleyman think it strange – you travelling to the tower and then returning?'

'He won't be here. He'll have left on campaign.'

Wayland and Syth arrived with bread, cheese and olives as the first light of dawn showed through the weave. Watching Syth bustle about, Vallon remembered the night he'd ordered Wayland to put her ashore.

If the falconer had obeyed, how would things have turned out? At any stage, their course might have taken a different turn.

'Sir?'

Syth bent towards him, holding out food, bobbing her head in her inimitable way. He reached up and caressed her cheek. 'Ah, Syth, I'll miss you.' He smiled at Wayland. 'Our last meal together. It's good of you to rise so early.'

'We didn't want to miss your departure.'

'We wouldn't have left without saying goodbye.'

Syth frowned. 'Does Caitlin know you're leaving?'

'Yes. We've made an arrangement. I hope to return for her in a day's time.'

'Why can't you take her with you today?'

Wayland shook his head at her in warning.

A coarse-featured Seljuk entered and announced that it was time to leave. They went out, the mountains rising blue against a sky of steel and violet. A troop of Seljuks galloped past, headed by Suleyman. He reined in hard, his stallion pawing the air, and waved his mace. Then he and his followers rode off in a dust cloud of their own making.

Four unfamiliar and shabbily outfitted Seljuks had been detailed to escort them to the border. Boke, their commander, could hardly speak a word of Arabic and seemed dull-witted. Their poor turn-out was encouraging, suggesting that Suleyman had lost interest in his guests.

Vallon collected his horse and walked it towards Wayland and Syth. 'For now this is where we take our leave.' He clasped Syth close.

Her wide eyes gazed up at him. 'You will return for Caitlin, won't you? She loves you. I know she does.'

'And I love her.'

Vallon kissed her and separated himself with delicacy. He laid a hand on Wayland's shoulder. 'Who would have thought when we set out that you'd end up in the service of an Emir?'

'I'd rather circumstances meant I remained in your service.'

'You'll be a father by next summer. You have no place with a vagrant soldier.'

'All the same, it saddens me to think that we won't meet again.'

'We will.'

'I don't mean when you come back for Caitlin.'

635

'Nor do I.'

'Where then? When?'

Vallon swung up into the saddle. 'Here or in the hereafter.'

Seams of sunlight were spreading across the plateau. Vallon consulted the weather-wise ring as he did before each day's journeying. As part of the same routine, he twisted it on his finger. He frowned. 'Here's sorcery,' he said, holding out the ring between thumb and forefinger. 'It's consented to loosen its grip now that our journey's over.'

Hero laughed. 'We still have a few days' ride ahead of us. What does it say about our prospects?'

Vallon studied the gemstone. 'Bright, I'd say.'

A stir behind the escorts drew his idle attention. A string of camels plodded past, heading for the Konya road.

'Vallon!' Caitlin screamed. 'Vallon!'

He jerked his reins. The Seljuks spun their horses. Through them he saw Drogo standing outside the women's quarters, holding Caitlin with his sword across her throat, both of them stained with blood. The Seljuks were already unslinging bows and levelling lances. Boke kicked his mount into a charge.

'Stop!' Vallon shouted. 'Tell him to stop!'

Wayland called out in Turkic. Boke was only twenty yards from his target when he veered away.

Vallon's heart raced. He flung out a hand left and right at the Seljuks. 'Nobody move. Wayland, make them understand.'

He reached out and took a lance from one of the Seljuks. He rode forward at a walk.

'Let her go, Drogo.'

The Norman's face contorted in a frenzy of effort as he tried to control Caitlin. She kicked and struggled and managed to sink her teeth into his forearm. He jabbed his sword hilt into her face and she sagged down.

Vallon halted. 'You said you'd got what you want. Walter dead, the inheritance assured.'

'I changed my mind. My honour's more important.' Drogo's speech was slurred, his eyes bloodshot.

'You call holding a woman hostage honourable?'

'The whore's my way to revenge.'

'Let her go and I'll let you live. I've given Suleyman money to send

636

ou back to Byzantium. In dignity, not on hands and knees.'

Drogo laughed and pointed his sword at him. 'That's what twists my guts. Your charity. I've suffered enough humiliation from you.'

Vallon rode a few yards closer. 'You won't regain your pride by killing Caitlin. Before she falls to the ground, you'll be skewered by arrows and I'll still be alive to kick your corpse. Or perhaps I'll order the Seljuks to let you live so that they can devise the cruellest and slowest way to end your life.'

'I'll release Caitlin only if you agree to fight me man to man.'

'You're drunk. Even sober you're no match for me.'

'Then you have nothing to fear.'

'If you were lucky enough to strike a mortal blow, you wouldn't have a moment to savour your victory before the Seljuks killed you.'

'Then I've got nothing to lose.' Drogo pulled Caitlin's head back and pressed his sword against her neck. 'I swear to God ...'

'I'll fight you.' Vallon looked for Wayland. 'Tell Boke and his men not to interfere. Tell him this is a feud that can only be settled by single combat.' He turned back to Drogo. 'Now release Caitlin.'

Drogo flung her aside. She stumbled away, clutching her face. Syth ran forward, gathered her in her arms and led her back.

'Don't hazard your life!' Hero cried. 'Leave it to the Seljuks.'

Vallon raised a hand. 'My word means something or it means nothing.'

Stillness descended on the arena. Overhead in the silence a kite whistled. The sun was lifting clear of the horizon. At the margins of Vallon's vision, Seljuk labourers spectated in scattered groups. Drogo stood about forty yards away, the ground completely open. Vallon shifted his grip on the lance and nudged his horse forward.

'Get down off your horse,' Drogo said.

'We'll engage the way we did that snowy night when we first met, you on horseback telling your men to take me downriver and cut my throat. I bested you then. Are you scared that you can't match my skill?'

Drogo drew his sword back. 'Any way you want.'

Vallon heeled his horse into a trot. Twenty yards from Drogo, he broke into a canter and levelled his lance. Drogo shuffled from side to side. Vallon had seen enough of him in action to know that he was a good swordsman, his skills honed in many battles. Unafraid and with a suicide's disregard for his life. Vallon maintained his easy pace, the point of his lance aimed at Drogo's chest. He was sure that his target would spring aside the instant before contact and then make an immediate counter.

Closer and closer. Drogo was going to jump to his right. Vallon corrected, lifted in his saddle and drove the lance forward.

Into empty space.

Drogo had dropped to a squat and as the lance passed harmlessly over his head he sprang up and swung his sword back-handed. Vallon dropped the lance and tried to fling himself off, drawing his sword at the same time. Drogo's blade sliced into the horse's haunch. It screamed and spun like a snake-bitten cat, throwing Vallon completely off balance. His left foot was still trapped in the stirrup. He could feel the horse toppling over and he couldn't jump clear. From the corner of his eye he saw Drogo jumping about on the blind side, trying to get in a killing blow, then the ground rushed up to meet him.

He landed left hand first and heard the crack as his wrist broke. He still held his sword in his right and was trying to propel himself clear when the horse crashed on to his left leg. Something tore in his ankle, the pain so intense that he screamed. He dragged himself free and saw Drogo running towards him. Using his sword as a crutch, he clambered upright, left arm and foot useless, a standing target. He managed to ward off the first stroke by blind instinct.

Drogo laughed. 'No left-handed trickery today. No fancy footwork.'

Vallon stood flatfooted, sick with pain and Drogo attacked with all his strength. Only Vallon's superior sword-play kept him at bay. At the fifth stroke Vallon saw an opening, dropped and opened up Drogo's left arm with a counter the Norman didn't even see. Drogo skipped back, looked at the wound and grinned. 'You're good. The best I've crossed swords with. But not as good as me.' He walked in a tight fast circle around Vallon, flicking his sword contemptuously. 'Let's see you hop.'

Vallon had no choice. He tried putting his weight on his left foot and almost collapsed.

'Hop!'

Vallon lost his balance and had to use his sword to stay on his feet. Drogo gripped his sword two-handed, stepped round Vallon's right ide and swung at his midriff. Vallon reverse blocked and skipped back. His right foot collided with a forgotten tent peg and he sprawled full length on his back. He tried to scramble away, but Drogo was already looming above him, sword poised to strike.

'I told you you'd feel my foot on your neck.'

Vallon gathered himself and coiled forward with all the force he could muster, at the same time driving his sword upwards. It deflected Drogo's descending blade, entered the pit of his stomach and came out through his back. Almost simultaneously, three Seljuk arrows punched into his torso. He flopped on top of Vallon, striving with his dying breaths to raise his sword.

Hooves pounded and Drogo jerked sideways, his brains dashed out by a blow from a Seljuk's mace. Vallon clawed hot jelly from his face and pulled himself away. People were running towards him, calling. Hero flung himself down beside him. 'I told you not to risk your life.'

Vallon tried to sit up. 'That's my job.'

Hero pushed him back down. 'Lie still.'

Caitlin dashed up and dropped to her knees, her cheeks flooded with blood- and kohl-streaked tears. He reached for her. 'Did he hurt you? You're covered in blood.'

'My maids. He burst in while I was dressing.'

'Give me room,' Hero said. Caitlin pillowed Vallon's head on her lap while Hero examined him. He gasped when Hero palped his wrist. 'It's a clean break, thank God.'

Wayland cut off Vallon's boot and Hero manipulated his ankle. 'I don't think it's broken. You must have torn a tendon.' He winced. 'Painful.'

Vallon closed his eyes and sucked in a breath. 'I hurt more than I've ever hurt before. I'll need some doctoring before we leave.'

'You're in no condition to travel. Your ankle won't heal for weeks.'

'I'm not walking to Byzantium. Strap it up and let's get going. If we don't leave soon, we won't reach the tower today.'

Hero splinted Vallon's broken wrist and strapped his ankle. Wayland made a pair of crutches. The best part of the morning was over by the time he'd finished. 'It's a full day's ride to the tower,' Hero said. 'Night will fall long before we reach it. Stay here tonight and rest. We'll leave before dawn to make the journey as easy as possible.'

Vallon looked around. The last tent had been struck and the plateau lay empty on all sides. A cohort of mounted Seljuks ringed a group of women. Drogo's body still lay where he had fallen, curled up like a sleeping child, a burgundy stain on the bare ground around his head. 'There's nowhere to stay. We have enough time to reach the caravanserai before dark.'

Hero and Wayland assisted him to his feet. Boke led a replacement mount up and Hero and Wayland lifted him into the saddle.

Caitlin clung to his leg. 'Take me with you.'

'I told you, if I find what I'm looking for I'll return.'

'What is it that's more important than me?'

'Did you find the silver?'

'The final insult. The price of a night with a harlot.'

'I left it so that if you choose to travel to Constantinople on your own, you would have the means. Suleyman won't stop you.'

Caitlin stepped back and passed a hand over her eyes. 'Why are you treating me like baggage? Didn't last night mean anything?'

'It meant everything.'

Boke had witnessed enough. An attempted homicide on a man he'd been charged to protect. Now this unseemly argument with a half-dressed woman stained with blood. He shouted an order and his men hazed the foreigners' horses away.

Vallon looked back over his shoulder at Wayland and Syth. 'Take care of each other,' he called. 'Remember us in your prayers and don't grow too proud.'

Caitlin ran after him. 'Don't leave me!' She stooped and threw a slipper. 'Come back, you bastard!'

LIII

Vallon's injuries forced him to ride no faster than a plodding walk and it was well after dark when they reached the caravanserai. A pain-racked night and they were on their way again before dawn. They reached Salt Lake as the sun rose like a blood-filled blister on the far shore and jogged north. Vallon rode one-handed, his left foot

irrupless, unable to find any position that didn't cause spasms of
ain. The Seljuks marked time, disgusted at being put in charge of
ich troublesome passengers. Vallon told Boke that they could find
heir own way, but the man had his orders and wasn't going to break
hem.

The journey along the lake was far longer than they remembered
nd the light was already leaching from the sky when the bastillion
ame in sight. Boke detoured past it. Hero caught up and told him that
allon couldn't travel any further. They had to make camp now. With
l grace, the Seljuks agreed to call a halt, pointing out a stream half a
ile beyond the tower.

'We'll stop here,' Hero called. Boke said they could camp with the
evil for all he cared, and led his men away.

'They probably think the tower's haunted,' said Hero.

'It probably is.'

They studied the bastillion. A round tower about sixty feet high,
pering to its crenellated turret, surrounded by the crumbling walls of
derelict barracks.

'What was it for?' Hero asked.

Vallon looked both ways along the lonely road. 'It must have been
relay station and signal tower.'

'The light's going. We don't have much time.'

The Seljuks had hobbled their horses and were beginning to pitch a
nt. 'They'll be suspicious if we go into the tower before making
amp,' Vallon said. 'Collect the makings of a fire.'

e remained mounted while Hero foraged for wood. The sun was
ouching the horizon when Hero returned and led him to the tower.
ero helped him out of the saddle and he flopped to the ground, his
ace hollow with pain. Hero felt his forehead and reached to take his
ulse. 'I knew the exertion would be too much for you.'

'Never mind me. Get the gospel.'

Hero peered in through the arched doorway. Pigeons flapped
rough the broken roof on clapping wings. The atmosphere was
usty with their droppings. Something scurried away over the heaps
f masonry covering the floor. Much of the debris had fallen from the
taircase spiralling up the ancient walls.

Vallon dragged himself in, holding on to the wall with his right

hand. His gaze probed up through the gloom. 'It's too dim to see prop
erly. Wait until morning.'

... until morning, said a weak echo.

'This is our only opportunity,' Hero said. 'The Seljuks will leav
before dawn.'

He lit an oil lamp and picked his way over the spoil towards th
staircase.

'I can't help you,' said Vallon. 'Are you sure you can manage?'

Hero turned a wan smile. 'Stay here and warn me if the Seljuk
come.'

Vallon glanced at the campfire burning in the gathering dusk. 'The
think it's a tomb. Wild horses couldn't drag them in here.'

Hero raised the lamp and followed its shadow up the stairway, step
ping with many mutters and hesitations across the gaps. Some of th
paving rocked under his weight and he dropped to a crawl. He cam
to a section where a dozen treads had collapsed, leaving a steep glaci
of rubble. He took a shuddering breath and stepped onto the lip of th
slope with his back to the drop. He shuffled up it, sliding his hand
along the wall. He'd almost reached the next step when the surfac
rolled under his feet. He threw himself at the step and clung on. Stone
cascaded onto the floor. His lamp had gone out.

'Are you all right? Where are you?'

Hero pulled himself to safety. 'I'm about halfway up. Part of th
stairs gave way.'

'If you break your neck, I'll never forgive you.'

Hero laughed. 'Wait until I light my lamp.' He struck another flam
and saw that he'd spilled most of the oil. He peered up. 'That was th
worst bit. The stairs above don't look too bad.'

Clammy with fear, he made his way upwards. A flicker of move
ment made him flinch. Only a bat cutting erratic paths through hi
light. He reached the top of the staircase and found himself on th
remains of a gallery. The first bright stars of evening winked throug
the holes overhead. He shuffled around the gallery, moving his lam
up and down the wall. A stone carved with a lion, Drogo had said
The flame was too puny to illuminate any detail beyond a radius o
two feet. He came to a gap in the gallery and held out the lamp as fa
as he dared. A stone bounded away into the dark.

'Hero?'

'I can't see it. The light's terrible.'

'In the morning I'll tell Boke I'm too sick to travel. That will give you enough time to search by daylight.'

'I'm not sure I can summon the courage to make another attempt.'

Hero worked his way back to the head of the stairway without finding the carving. He sat on the topmost step, placed the lamp beside him and hissed through his teeth. The gospel must be here, probably within touching distance. Walter had been in no state to invent the details about the bastillion and the carved stone.

The lamp spluttered and the flame dwindled. Hero watched it, darkness closing in. Very carefully he tilted the lamp, holding his breath until the flame waxed bright again. He looked up with a sigh of relief and in the same moment some belated impression registered. Frowning, he slid down to the next step and ran his hand over a stone inset into the wall at knee level. He angled the lamp to pick out the chiselled relief of a lion-headed figure standing on a stone ball entwined with snakes – Mithras, the Persian sun god adopted by the Romans.

Vallon struck a flint. Light pooled in the well below.

'I've found the stone.'

'Good. Grab the documents and let's get out of here. This place gives me the willies.'

The stone wasn't part of the original construction. Walter had pushed it into the wall without mortar, leaving gaps wide enough for Hero to insert his fingers. It slid out easily, revealing a deep cavity. He reached in and contacted something smooth and cold that made him gasp and pull back his hand as if it had been burned.

'What's the matter?'

'Something in the hole ... I have a nasty feeling ... '

He pushed the lamp up to the aperture and laid his head to the paving so that he could look in. Dull black eyes stared back at him.

'Hero, what's going on?'

'There's a snake inside.'

'Christ!'

'It's curled up on a package.'

'What kind of snake?'

'A rock viper. Venomous. I think it's asleep.'

'Kill it and get yourself down here. Now.'

Hero studied the viper. Its head rested on its coiled body, slitted eyes regarding him with a cold and lidless stare. He drew his knife and extended it. The snake didn't move. Hero didn't trust himself to kill it. He touched it with the blade and it gave a torpid stir. Placing the point behind it, he drew the snake towards him. Its tongue flickered and the coils began to unwind. He flicked it out of the hole and it hissed. With an indrawn cry, he scooped it off the step with his foot. It hit the floor with a flaccid smack.

'I've dealt with it.'

'The damn thing nearly landed on me.'

Hero was reaching into the aperture when it occurred to him that where one snake had gone to hibernate, others might be nesting. His lamp made faint popping sounds and the flame drew down the wick. Before it went out, he grabbed the packet, held it to his chest and clamped his eyes shut.

'Hero?'

'I've got it.'

'Thank God. Careful how you descend.'

Hero tucked the package inside his tunic. Not trusting his feet in the dark, he eased down the staircase on his rump, step by step – like a baby. Vallon held up his own lamp, his shadow enormous on the walls. Hero reached the top edge of the collapsed section and pawed at the rubble. Infill spilled away.

'You'll have to take it at a run,' Vallon said.

Hero launched himself down the slope, felt his feet skid from under him and toppled into space. A long moment of weightlessness before a jarring collision that filled his head with starbursts of disconnected memory.

'Hero, are you hurt?'

He sat up groaning and gingerly flexed his limbs. 'I don't think so. The fall's scattered my wits. I can recall something that happened to me when I was about three as if it were yesterday. Two of my sisters rolled me down the stairs.'

'If you have any wits left, use them to get out.'

Hero felt the package. He picked himself up and stumbled towards the doorway. Vallon grasped his wrist and yanked him out. 'Have you still got it?'

Hero's head cleared. The shores of the lake lay blanched by moon-

644

ight. Sparks whirled up from the Seljuks' fire. He patted his chest and nodded.

They staggered towards their campsite, Vallon peg-legging on his crutch. He sank down with a groan and Hero muffled him in a blanket before lighting a fire. Flames crackled through the scrub. They pulled themselves close to the heat and Hero placed a pot of rice on the flames. Vallon blew through puckered lips and hunched his shoulders. 'God, it's cold.'

Hero kept feeling the package under his tunic.

Vallon gestured. 'Aren't you going to look at it?'

'Don't you think we should wait until we're out of Seljuk territory?'

Vallon glanced towards their escorts' camp. 'Boke can't read or write. It won't mean a thing to him. Let's see what we've got.'

Hero took out the package and undid the wrapping. Inside were two documents, one a letter, the other a book in codex form. He took out the letter first. 'It's the same writing material as Prester John's letter, the same script.'

'What does it say?'

Hero squinted. 'Here's a description of a desert that travellers must cross before they reach his realm. *There is a waterless sea and its billows are of sand that surge in waves and never rest. In this desert dwell many imps and demons. Three days' journey from the sea of sand you must ascend a waterless river of stones . . .*'

'What about the gospel? That's what interests me.'

Hero hid the letter in the casket's secret compartment and opened the book. 'It's written in old Greek on papyrus.'

'Read it.'

'The ink's faded. I need more light.'

Vallon heaped the fire with what remained of the scrub. Flames flared four feet high. Hero held the pages towards them. 'The beginning is just as Cosmas transcribed it, and then it says: *These are the secret words which the living Jesus spoke, and Judas Thomas called Didymus wrote them and said, "Whoever finds the interpretations of these words shall not taste death".*'

He turned the page, tracing the text with his fingers. 'This is interesting. It's a section describing Jesus's boyhood and education. None of the other gospels does that.'

'A rare prize indeed.'

The fire was already beginning to die down. Hero held the book closer to the light and selected a page at random. He peered at the script, his lips moving.

Vallon shuffled closer. 'Don't keep it to yourself.'

Hero spoke softly, almost tentatively. *'Jesus said to his disciples. "Compare me to someone and tell me whom I am like."*

'Simon Peter answered, "You are like a righteous angel."

'Matthew replied, "You are like a wise philosopher."

'Thomas was troubled and said, "Master, my mouth is incapable of saying whom you are like."

'Then Jesus took Thomas aside and told him three things. When Thomas returned to his companions, they asked him, "What did Jesus say to you?" Thomas replied, "If I told you even one of the things which he told me, you will gather stones and throw them at me. A fire will come out of the stones and burn you up."'

Vallon leaned forward, intent. 'What was it that Jesus told him?'

Hero had been moving the book closer and closer to the waning light. 'It's no good. I can't see.'

'I'll light a lamp,' said Vallon. He pulled a glowing stub from the fire and got a lamp burning. He handed it to Hero. 'Go on from where you stopped. What secrets did Jesus tell Thomas?'

Hero illuminated the page and peered at it. His eyes rose wide with wonder and his mouth opened.

Vallon laughed. 'What? Are the secrets so profound that you can't share them with a hell-bound sinner?'

But Hero wasn't looking at Vallon. His hand rose trembling. 'Sir.'

Vallon whirled. Black against the stars a dozen mounted figures advanced. 'Holy God!'

Faruq rode up at the centre of the Seljuk line. 'Did you really think you could outwit his Excellency?' He clicked his fingers. 'Give it to me.'

'It's only an old book that Hero reads to me at night to pass the time.'

'Give it to me.'

Hero handed it over. Faruq flicked through the pages. 'What is it?'

'I told you – a book of stories that help while away the hours of darkness.'

Chinua assisted Faruq off his horse. The Chief Secretary held the gospel over the embers. 'Then you won't lose anything more than idle entertainment if I burn it.'

Hero and Vallon didn't speak.

Faruq dropped the gospel onto the embers. Hero flung himself forward, grabbed the book and brushed away the sparks. Chinua aimed his sword at his throat and tore the gospel from his grasp.

'Stories,' said Faruq. 'His Excellency knew that you hadn't told him the whole story.' He slapped the book against his hand. 'I ask you for the last time – what is it? Why is it so important?'

Vallon met Hero's eyes, conceding surrender. 'It's a lost gospel. The Gospel of Thomas, one of Jesus's disciples. Walter came by it in Armenia and agreed to give it to Cosmas if he raised the ransom.'

Faruq held the book up to the stars. 'You came into his Excellency's realm to steal a Christian book.' He shook his head. 'That is a very serious crime. Very serious.'

Hero lunged to his feet. 'Vallon knew nothing about the gospel when he set out on this mission. Cosmas told me about it but I didn't share the secret until well into our journey. If anyone should suffer, let it be me.'

Faruq regarded them. 'What else did you take from the tower?'

Vallon sat with his back to him, staring into the embers. 'Nothing.'

Faruq nodded at Chinua. 'Search them.'

Chinua took Hero's chest and passed it to Faruq. He explored its contents, stroked its carved lid, tapped the sides. Hero watched with bated breath, certain that a man of Faruq's sophistication would suspect it contained a secret compartment. Faruq looked at him. 'You took nothing else?'

'Only the gospel.'

Faruq laid down the chest. His men hoisted him back into the saddle. He raised a finger. 'His Excellency will be disappointed that you lied to him.'

Hero and Vallon waited for the pronouncement of punishment. The moon stood high above the centre of the lake, its mottled face mirrored on the still waters.

Vallon shrugged. 'His Excellency will be delighted to be proved right.'

Faruq smiled. 'It would be too much trouble to take you to the Emir to stand trial.' He tucked the gospel under one arm. 'I will keep this and you can go on to Constantinople.' He began turning his horse, pulled it back. 'I almost forgot. My ruby ring. It was a gift from the Emir. It means a lot to me.'

Vallon dug it out and held it up without speaking. Faruq slipped it on and gave an order. The Seljuks swung round and rode towards Boke's camp.

Vallon huddled over their own miserable fire, right hand trying to tug the blanket over his left shoulder. An owl shrieked from the top of the tower and jackals yipped out on the plain.

Hero rose and arranged the blanket. Vallon lifted his eyes and saw his devastated hopes mirrored in Hero's blasted stare. He cupped his hands over his face and shook his head. 'Don't say anything. Let's just sit in silence.'

LIV

In the morning they woke to find themselves alone, the Seljuk camp deserted and the road empty in both directions. They ate breakfast in a continuation of last night's despondent silence, then Vallon went through the laborious business of getting into the saddle.

Hero mounted his own horse. 'Which way?'

Vallon turned his horse north.

'What about Caitlin? She'll be waiting for you.'

Vallon kept going. 'Waiting for what? Look at me. A helpless cripple. Even my plans to join the Varangians lie in tatters. No one would employ a soldier in my condition.'

Hero caught up. 'She knows what condition you're in. She still wants to be with you. I heard her declaration of devotion.'

'A declaration made in the heat of passion. By now she'll have had time to reflect and her head will rule that she can make a far better match.'

Hero pranced ahead so that he could look into Vallon's eyes. 'You don't know that for sure. At least give her the chance to make her wishes known.'

Vallon's dull stare remained fixed straight ahead. 'We made an greement. If we found the gospel, I would return. We haven't got it and so I go on.'

'She might not want to remain in Suleyman's court.'

'She has enough silver to reach Constantinople in comfort.' Vallon waved his good hand. 'Forget Caitlin.'

Hero dropped back alongside Vallon. Another fine day, a cloudless porcelain sky over the blinding white salt flats. Flamingos flocked across Salt Lake in lines of bright crimson script. Vallon plodded on, aware that Hero kept glancing at him. 'I told you I don't want to hear another word.'

'It's not Caitlin I'm thinking about.'

'What then?'

'I've been thinking about the gospel.'

Vallon uttered a hollow laugh. 'So have I.'

'Not like that.' Hero hesitated. 'I'm not sure you'll want to hear my thoughts.'

'You can't make its loss any more painful.'

Hero drew breath, held it, then released it all at once. 'I don't think we would have been able to sell it. That is, nobody in the Church would buy it.'

Vallon stared at him. 'You told me that it's one of the most important books ever written.'

'Important for the wrong reason. If someone did buy it, they would do so only to suppress it. Destroy it.'

'Suppress the testament of one of the apostles? Destroy a piece of the Bible?'

'The Bible is the word of God, but the Church decides what words it wants the world to hear. After reflecting on the sections of the Thomas gospel I was able to read, I've concluded that the ecclesiastical authorities wouldn't want to share them with their flock.'

'Explain.'

'First, all four canonical gospels state that Jesus was the son of a humble carpenter and Luke says he practised the trade himself. None of them discuss his boyhood or upbringing. They must have had some knowledge of his early life, yet they chose to draw a veil over it. Not Thomas, though. He says that Jesus was the son of a *tekton*, a master mason or architect who was also a teacher of the Torah, and that Jesus was educated in Jewish law, becoming an eminent rabbi.'

649

Vallon winced as his left foot jarred against his horse's flank. 'Are you saying that Thomas was a liar and his gospel a fake?'

'No. In fact, I think his version is more convincing than the others. Remember Luke's story of how, when Jesus was twelve, his parents lost him in Jerusalem? After five days they discovered him in the Temple, astonishing the scholars with his knowledge of religious matters. The elders would have recruited such a prodigy into their schools, singling him out as a future leader. Elsewhere in the gospels, he's frequently described as "Rabbi" or "Doctor of Law". Respected Jewish scholars come to hear him preach. They wouldn't do that with a carpenter.'

'I don't see why the Church would reject the gospel because Thomas claims that Jesus was a great scholar and teacher. The opposite, I would have thought.'

'That's not the only way in which it differs from the Biblical accounts. Thomas calls Jesus "the Son of Man" rather than the "Son of God". That's an important distinction, one that challenges the belief that Jesus was truly divine. Another thing. Thomas refers to Jesus as *chrêstos*, spelled with an *ê*, rather than *christos*, with an *i*. The two words are pronounced the same but mean different things. *Christos* with an *i* means the "anointed one" – the Messiah sent by God to proclaim the Second Coming. *Chrêstos* with an *ê* simply means "good".'

'How do you know all this?'

'One of my uncles is a priest. For a time I was destined for the Church.'

'Well, I'm no book scholar, but it seems to me that you're splitting hairs.'

'That's what theologians do. They've been doing it for a thousand years and the result is the faith as practised today, down to the last liturgical detail. Anything that doesn't fit the official version has no place in the canon. The schism between Rome and Constantinople is a good example. Do you know what caused it?'

Vallon thought. 'I have no idea.'

'The main doctrinal issue concerns a single word, *filioque*, which the Roman Church added to the Nicene Creed. It means "and the son" and appears in the affirmation "And I believe in the Holy Spirit, the Lord, giver of life, who proceedeth from the Father and the Son." What it does is emphasise that Jesus, the Son, is of equal divinity with

God, the Father. The Eastern Church won't accept the addition, concentrating on the supremacy of God the Father. For five hundred years they've been arguing about that word.'

'So the Church only hears what it wants to hear.'

'Precisely. It would take an enormous weight of evidence for the authorities to alter the accepted gospel story by so much as a jot. One book discovered by adventurers in Anatolia wouldn't be enough.'

'Not for Rome perhaps. The Greek Church might be more receptive.'

Hero shook his head. 'Whatever their other differences, both Churches would treat any book that emphasised Christ's human nature as a loathsome heresy.'

'So if we still had the gospel and tried to sell it, we might be burned as heretics.'

'I don't think they'd go that far. They'd probably burn the gospel, though.'

Vallon plodded on in silence for a while. 'Hero, if that was meant to console me, it hasn't worked.'

'I thought you'd want to know.'

'You only read a few passages. Cosmas had the opportunity to study the entire book. He was a learned man. He must have noticed the same problems as you, yet it didn't quench his desire to get his hands on it.'

'He sought the truth above all things. Perhaps he found in Thomas some revelation that would shake Christendom to its foundations.'

'Such as the secrets that Thomas said would strike fire from the rocks.'

'Possibly. Or it might have been something else, some revelation concerning Jesus's death and resurrection.'

'Like what?'

'I'm not sure I dare speak it aloud. It's blasphemous.'

'Don't worry about the fate of my soul. Come on, spit it out.'

'Very well.' Hero composed his thoughts. 'Several sources say that Thomas evangelised in India and made many converts on the coast. Cosmas met some of the communities and he visited Thomas's shrine near a city called Madras. These Christians call themselves "the Christians of St Thomas", but Cosmas told me that they belong to the Nestorian sect.'

'I know little about them except that the Latin Church denounces them as heretics.'

651

'Of the most damnable kind. Nestorius lived four centuries later than Thomas, and like him had doubts about Jesus's divinity. Even though he was the Patriarch of Constantinople, he preached that Christ had two distinct natures, one divine, one human, and that mankind would find redemption not in Christ's divinity, but in Jesus's human life of temptation and suffering. The Orthodox Church found Nestorius's humanisation of Jesus scandalous and at a council called by the pope they stripped him of his office. His teachings spread, though, east into Persia and on into India. I think the Christian communities there embraced them so readily because they were very similar to the doctrine taught in the Gospel of Thomas.'

Vallon turned it over in his mind. 'But that wouldn't shake Christendom. Where's the revelation?'

'I really don't think I should speculate any further.'

'Oh, for God's sake!'

'What could it have been that made Thomas doubt Jesus's divinity?'

'Don't ask me. I know my creed and paternoster and that's the limit of my learning.'

'There's a clue in the Bible, in the Gospel of St John, where he describes how the resurrected Christ showed himself to all the disciples except Thomas. Remember?'

'Of course! Doubting Thomas. He refused to believe that Christ had risen from the dead until he saw Him in the flesh and felt his wounds with his hands.' Vallon gave Hero a sharp look. 'He doubted, and then Jesus banished his doubts. We're no further forward.'

Hero didn't answer.

Vallon glanced at the sky as though he suspected a heavenly eavesdropper. He leaned slightly towards Hero and dropped his voice. 'Are you saying that Thomas didn't see the risen Christ?'

'I'm saying that if he witnessed the resurrection, he could have had no reason to doubt Jesus's divinity.'

Vallon dropped his voice further still. 'You mean Thomas says that Jesus didn't rise from the dead? That he was mortal like any man?'

'It's speculation, nothing more.'

Vallon leaned back and crossed himself. 'Dark waters. Well, we'll never have a chance to go deeper. By now the gospel will be ashes.'

'I'm not so sure. I think the Seljuks will hide it away in a library. A thousand years have passed since it was written. Who knows? A thousand years from now, it might surface again.'

The end of the lake came in sight. Vallon heard Hero sigh, saw him shake his head.

'What's troubling you now?'

Hero grimaced. 'I loved Richard, feared and hated Drogo and for Walter felt nothing but contempt. But I can't help being distressed at the thought of their parents waiting in Northumberland for the return of their sons, not knowing that none of them will come home again. As much as I hate the prospect, I feel it's my duty to write and bring their futile waiting to a close.'

Vallon had nothing to add on the matter. 'I was recalling Aaron's prediction that our enterprise was doomed to failure. He was right.' Vallon frowned. 'Nearly right. We're no worse off than when we started out.'

Hero snapped out of his musings. 'We're better off by far. We have enough silver to take us to Constantinople, and we still have Prester John's letter.'

Vallon's own spirits lifted. 'Do you really believe that he dines at a gold and amethyst table and sleeps in a sapphire bed and rides into battle perched on a golden castle borne by an elephant?'

Hero laughed. 'I suspect that his royal sublimity has stretched the truth a little.'

'The priest-king's a weaver of fantasies, peddling dreams to feed our craving for the unknown. He probably dwells in a mud fort and eats porridge off bare boards.'

'There's only one way to find out.'

Vallon eyed him asquint. 'I would have thought that you'd done enough travelling. Haven't you followed enough wilderness rivers and crossed enough deserts?'

'If only a tenth of Prester John's claims are true, it would be a journey worth making.'

'You look as if you're already planning it.'

Hero shook his head. 'One day, perhaps.'

'Don't ask me to join you. This expedition has cured any lingering wanderlust I might have had.'

Hero smiled. 'The day we met, you said that a journey is just a tiresome passage between one place and another.'

'I wasn't wrong, was I? You can't deny that the last year has been the most uncomfortable, the most painful, the most unprofitable of your life.'

'Also the most instructive and exciting. Admit it, sir. There's satisfaction in having completed a journey no other man has made.'

Vallon nodded reluctantly. 'There is that. We both have a stock of tales to last us until we turn old and grey.'

They rode on, Vallon scanning the empty ridgelines with a soldier's caution. 'Not all rivers end in the sea.'

Hero had been miles away. He blinked. Vallon was pointing at the lake.

'We talked one night in England of how men's lives follow a course like a river, finally ending weak and tired in the sea.'

'I remember.'

'This lake has no outlet. The rivers that enter it will never reach the sea.'

Hero saw Richard's shrouded corpse drifting out of the Dnieper estuary. 'Richard's journey ended in the sea. He was only seventeen. His journey had hardly begun.'

'Every journey, no matter how short or long, has a beginning and an end. Some travellers stride out on a journey and die happy, having failed to reach their destination. Others spend years striving to attain some blissful goal only to realise when they've reached it that it wasn't the place they were looking for.'

Hero's eyes flooded. 'I wish they were all here. I wish the journey wasn't over.'

Vallon took his arm gently. 'Come on. You and I still have a long way to go.'

They reached the northern shore of Salt Lake and turned west over a fly-specked plateau, following their shadows across the empty highland. Looking back, Vallon saw the summits of the twin peaks shining with the soft lustre of a fire opal, the same colours as his gem. Far back down their trail a column of dust had appeared. He reined in, his mouth dry with hope and dread.

Miles before it reached them, the dust cloud turned north, gradually dispersing. Unknown travellers following their own path.

Vallon turned back to the west.

Hero remained where he was. 'You hoped it was her.'

'It wasn't. Let's go.'

'You still have time to return. Tomorrow will be too late for anything but regrets.'

Vallon's face twitched. 'What do you know about affairs of the heart?'

Hero's features set. 'I know about love.'

Vallon lifted a hand in apology. 'Forgive me. Of course you do.'

'Sir, you mustn't wait on her to follow you. It's not gallant. If you love her, go back.'

'The day we met you said I was suffering from lovesickness.'

'I wasn't wrong then. I'm not wrong now. If you don't find her, you'll never be happy.'

Vallon sat his horse, tortured with indecision. 'I can't leave you to travel to Constantinople on your own.'

'I'm not the one who needs care. You can't even mount or dismount without my help.'

Vallon looked up. 'You don't mind retracing our steps all that weary way?'

Hero rolled his eyes. 'I've been trying to persuade you to do nothing else.'

Vallon eyed the sun, excitement rising. 'If we press hard, we should be back at the tower before dark. With luck, we'll reach Konya in three days.'

They were back in sight of Salt Lake's north shore when Vallon spotted a smudge of dust approaching from the south. He watched it draw closer. 'Two riders moving fast.'

Hero screwed up his eyes. 'Is it Caitlin?'

'Too far to tell.'

Vallon watched the riders approach, his heart beating with painful thuds. The riders took on shape, then form resolved into features. He covered his eyes, overcome by faintness. 'It's her,' he said. 'Caitlin and Wayland.'

Hero whooped. 'Aren't you glad you turned back? Now you can meet her with your honour intact.'

'She'll probably take one look at me and ride on with her nose in the air, just as she did the day I first saw her.' Vallon glared at Hero. 'What's so funny?'

'Two days ago you fought a contest with a broken arm and a torn tendon. Yet watching your beloved approach, you quake like a timorous youth.'

'Fighting's easy. Giving your heart to another isn't – not for someone with my bloody history.'

Hero sobered. They waited. Wayland and Caitlin galloped up in a breathless hurry, faces pale with dust. Caitlin wore plain garments and no jewellery. No one spoke at first.

Hero broke the silence. 'We're sorry you had to travel so far to catch up.'

Caitlin guided her horse alongside Vallon and stared hard into his face. 'Wayland told me that whatever you were looking for was hidden in the tower we passed half a day since. You were riding away, weren't you? You weren't going to come back for me.'

Vallon contemplated the ground. 'I was sure you'd reject me.' He looked up. 'But in the end I had to hear it from your own lips.'

Caitlin's features rippled in exasperation. 'I gave you my decision. How many times more do I have to tell you?' She looked around. 'I take it you didn't find what you were looking for.'

Vallon shrugged. 'Found it, lost it.'

'What was it?'

'A book. Even if we'd kept it, it turns out to be less valuable than we'd hoped. All our wealth is contained in the silver Wayland won with his hawk.'

'That's more silver than most folk see in a lifetime.'

'What happened to the jewels Suleyman lavished on you?'

'The eunuch who rules his harem took them back.' Caitlin gave an enigmatic smile and laid a hand on Vallon's wrist. 'All except the gold and jade girdle,' she whispered. 'I wasn't letting *that* go.'

Wayland extended a hand containing a purse. 'Syth and I agreed that this belongs to you. You were too generous.'

Vallon waved it away. 'Keep it. You have a family to consider.'

Caitlin ran a finger down his sunken cheek. 'It's time you considered yourself.' She rounded on Hero. 'Whatever were you thinking of letting him chase after books hidden in castles? He can't continue to Constantinople in that state. We'll stop at the next town and find lodgings until he's fit enough to travel.'

Hero made a gesture halfway between a cringe and a bow.

Vallon tried to protest. 'I've outstayed my welcome in Suleyman's territory. The sooner we reach Byzantium, the safer we will be.'

Caitlin swept his opposition aside. 'You're not in any danger from the Seljuks. We passed Faruq early this morning and he told me to take care of you.'

'Faruq?'

She smiled. 'You underestimate the respect the Seljuks hold you in. Their soldiers are already composing tales about you as if you were a hero of old.'

Wayland looked on, feeling curiously cut off from his friends as they prepared to vanish from his life. Vallon rode up. 'Thank you for bringing Caitlin.'

'She brought herself, and if I hadn't gone, Syth would have escorted her herself.'

Vallon looked south. 'Dear Syth. Just the thought of her brings a smile, and that smile will be with me for as long as I live.' He slapped Wayland's knee. 'She'll be missing you. Return as quick as you can.'

Wayland conned the landscape, postponing the final separation. 'If you don't mind, I'll ride with you a little way further.'

They rode to the west and at evening time breasted a ridge to see the plateau folding away in soft greys and mauves, the sun pulsating halfway below the horizon, the peach- and lavender-coloured sky brushed with a few streaks of fiery cloud. Vallon halted and looked hard at Wayland. 'Now it really is the last farewell.'

They said their goodbyes with no great outpouring of emotion except from Caitlin, who planted a kiss on Wayland's lips and enjoined him to treasure Syth all his days.

Hero dabbed a speck of dust from his eye and spoke in a voice pitched higher than normal. 'Well, the weather's set fair.'

Vallon raised his hand to check and stared at the empty finger with dull incomprehension. 'The ring's gone.' He glanced back. 'It must have slipped off.'

Everyone turned and stared back down the tracts of barren space.

'Do you have any idea where you lost it?' Hero said.

Vallon shook his head. 'I last saw it when we set off this morning. It could be anywhere.' He shook himself and drew a deep breath. 'It's gone. No point looking for it.'

'Are you sure? The ring's valuable. It has magical properties.'

'And that's why I lost it. I bet the damn thing's gone back to Cosmas.'

A last nod at Wayland, a last penetrating look and a touch of the hand and then Vallon led his party away. Hero and Caitlin kept turning to wave, but Vallon didn't look back, nor did Wayland expect him to.

He watched them for miles, their shadows lengthening behind them, merging into one and dissolving in the creeping dusk.

A movement in the air made him look up. Caught on the cusp of remaining light, a falcon on passage skated in smooth ellipses, intent on the ground far beneath. Its wings flickered and it slid forward, bunching up into a missile that fell in a steepening curve until it was plunging earthwards as true as a plumbline. The tide of shadow engulfed it, and though Wayland waited, it didn't appear again. When he looked west again, Vallon, Hero and Caitlin were gone.

He waited a little while longer. A single cloud with its edges burnished by the last rays of the invisible sun glowed like a scrap of charring parchment. When the flame died he turned his horse back. The twin peaks lay sunk beneath the earth and the ridges rolled away soft as lampblack.

On his solitary journey homewards he passed within yards of Cosmas's ring, lying buried in the winter grasses at the edge of the track. The gemstone recorded his fleeting passage, his image elongating as he approached and then contracting to a dot. Gone in a trice leaving a dark blank eye highlit by the gleam of stars.

Wayland rode on, wishing he was at home with Syth, regretting that the quest was over. He looked back only once, to record the moment to draw the line, to seal the memories. He raised one arm in salute before turning away.

Here or in the hereafter.